MW01092132

BOOK TWO OF
THE *HOOK & JILL* SAGA

ANDREA JONES

REGINETTA
PRESS

The Reginetta Press
www.reginettapress.com

www.HookandJill.com

Interior design by Gary M. Burton
Book jacket designed by Erik Hollander
www.HollanderDesignLab.com

LCCN: 2012900559
ISBN: 0-9823714-0-3
ISBN-13: 978-0-9823714-0-4

Printed in the USA

The *Hook & Jill* Saga
by Andrea Jones:

Book One

Hook & Jill

Book Two

Other Oceans

For pirate lasses…
part heaven, part heathen.

For Nancy —
Sail on,
to Other
Oceans

Andrea
Jones

Contents

A Disappointment

After all his worries to the contrary, she was easy to find.

She was burning.

The smoke wrapped around the ship like a shroud, visible for miles. The stench of it crept across the waves. To LeCorbeau's beaky nose it stank worse than death. It reeked of missed opportunity.

He cursed. Some pirate had gotten to her first!

"Raise the colors! Our own French flag! We will come to her, eh… aid." He dropped his voice. "Maybe there is *something* left." He cursed again, and paced in his small, quick steps, his hands locked together behind him. He eyed the smoke furling and unfurling like sails in the rigging. His own agile ship, the privateer *L'Ormonde*, glided closer.

"Renaud, the spyglass!"

Renaud, a model of his captain's taste, more slim than tall, hastened to his master's side to hand the instrument over. LeCorbeau yanked the spyglass from his mate, jerked it to its full length, and raised it to a beady eye. He made out men rushing about topside. The ship was burning, but only above. The deck and hull were untouched. Not a wisp of smoke bellied up from below decks.

She was still seaworthy. LeCorbeau searched for the name to be sure. It was painted on the bulky bow: *Julianne.* She bobbed on the brine, her hold obviously empty. Slowly, he lowered the spyglass. Squinting now, Captain LeCorbeau formed a suspicion in his mind. It wasn't difficult; he was a suspicious man.

He spoke under his breath. "Who would attack her, and take such care to leave her floating?" Which scavenger of the sea would ensure that her crew lived to tell his story? "There is only one so arrogant." LeCorbeau was too familiar with his methods. Only one captain was so self-assured. One pirate! LeCorbeau's lip curled.

"Hook!"

He spat. Renaud hunched over and grasped the spyglass as it slammed into his skinny belly. His cocky captain stamped his foot while the first mate refilled his lungs and lifted the glass to scan the horizon. Renaud had an ache in his gut, and it wasn't from the impact of the spyglass.

"*Monsieur*, can your friend have survived this attack?" But he fell silent as he surveyed the *Julianne* and he, too, recognized the wreckage left by the legendary pirate. Knowing the tantrum that was building, Renaud backed to a prudent distance, but he didn't dare desert the deck. LeCorbeau rounded on him.

"We shall soon see if he is alive! Tell the men to stow their weapons. She's an English merchantman, but we will approach as friends."

"*Oui, Commandant!*" Renaud hustled off, glad to escape. He adjusted his uniform and set about making the ship and her crew look respectable. If anything was left to salvage aboard the *Julianne*, they'd have to get it by guile. Hook's pirates would have taken everything in plain sight.

As the ship neared its wounded sister, the stink of burning canvas thickened, assaulting the nostrils of her crew. Cries of alarm reached their ears, and panic pounded the merchant's deck. *L'Ormonde's* sailors assembled along her elegant rail, grimacing. Fire was one enemy they were loathe to face. It could eat the boards out from under their feet and leave the sailors alive to be eaten themselves, by fish or by flame. But they had faith in their captain. He was like a rooster, strutting and pecking, but he knew the sea, and he knew his job. It was rare that his temper or his taste got in the way of business.

Their faith was well placed. The distress of the English ship made little impression on Captain LeCorbeau. With a wave of his hand, he slowed *L'Ormonde's* progress until he was sure no sparks would jump from the flaming sails to his own. He watched the *Julianne's* crew chopping the masts like trees, then shoving them overboard to hiss and steam in the sea. Her captain shouted orders and her sailors let down buckets to dip in the water. They hauled them up, thumping against the hull, and sloshed seawater over the deck, dousing renegade embers.

Only when the mopping up began did the French privateer allow his vessel to drift close. Then he cupped his shapely hands and shouted in English through a heavy accent and his most heroic tone, "Ahoy! *Mes amis!* We have come to assist you! Let us board, and we will see to your needs."

The English captain lifted his weary gray head, and shrugged. He'd lost his hat. His hair was thin, but wrinkles lay thick on his brow. His uniform was tattered and smudged with ash. He called back, his voice slumping like his shoulders. "We have nothing left to lose. You are welcome to board, Sir, if your intention is to help us." He signaled, and as *L'Ormonde's* deck hands grappled the *Julianne*, his men brought out planking to bridge the ships. Dispirited, they stood back and watched as the French captain in his well-cut coat promenaded across with a party of officers. The group of privateers carried few visible weapons, but after losing masts and sails, cargo and personnel, the crew of the crippled vessel didn't care either way. They were dead in the water. It would be a long row to the nearest land.

The *Julianne's* commander welcomed this set of boarders very differently from the first. Swords and pistols not stolen were set aside now. The watchdog cannons sat silent, unable to bark without ammunition. Looking as empty as his ship, the old man extended his hand, and his voice was hoarse and tired. "I am Captain Whyte. You are well met, Sir."

"DéDé LeCorbeau, Captain of *L'Ormonde.*" Seeping solicitude, LeCorbeau kept Captain Whyte's hand in his own. "What do you require?"

"We'll need water, of course. A few of the lads lost their heads when the pumps failed, and our supply has gone in fighting the blaze. And have you a surgeon aboard? Some of my men are wounded."

LeCorbeau dropped Whyte's hand, taken aback. "Eh— yes...water, of course, naturally...but— surely you have a surgeon of your own?"

"We *had* a surgeon."

The French captain tensed. "You mean to say he was murdered?"

Whyte released a heavy sigh. "I'm sorry to report that he was taken by the pirates who left us burning. Very fortunate for us that the fire was limited to the rigging!"

The privateer's face twisted. "Very fortunate. But your doctor?"

"Dragged away. Most irregular! I expect to lose cargo to such scum, but not my officers."

LeCorbeau pivoted toward his mate. "Renaud!" He shouted orders to disguise his shock. His face was ashen, but his anger soon erupted. "Don't just stand there, idiot! You heard the gentleman! Send for water for our friends, and also…" Closing his eyes, LeCorbeau paused to force his features under control. He turned to Whyte and bowed, the image of courtesy. "You shall have better than that. We will also provide you with a cask or two of wine. We must revive the sagging spirits of your crew." Restraining Renaud, he waved his second officer away instead. "Go, Guillaume! Quickly! And bring medical supplies as well."

"Really, you are most kind. Yes, we could use some cheer just now. We're all rather parched. Please, come to my quarters, Sir, while your officers and mine inspect the damage and do what they can."

LeCorbeau had mastered his emotion. He was already adjusting his original scheme to straighten this nasty turn. As he flourished his hands in gestures of sympathy, the lace cuffs flounced at his wrists. "*Oui*, by all means! You must tell me about this most terrible experience with these pirates." He shot more orders to his men, quick but emphatic. "Search the ship for wounded. No one must be left suffering! Check every deck, every hiding place."

His officers understood. Fixed on their purpose, they stepped along the wet, salty deck toward the hatch while the disordered crew of the *Julianne* made way. Under the guise of rescuers, *L'Ormonde's* men would be thorough while the captains were closeted together. Nothing of value would be left behind on this ship. The privateers smirked as their esteem for their quirky captain rose again. Hook and his pirates would steal the blame along with the booty!

"And Renaud—"

Renaud halted to stand at attention.

"You will personally visit the doctor's quarters. Look there for anything the injured might need." LeCorbeau leveled a stare at his mate. "You know what we are looking for."

Renaud bobbed his head, a glint in his eye. *"Oui, Commandant!"* He hurried below, his boots tapping on the stairs.

LeCorbeau supported Captain Whyte as the man turned his dragging steps toward his cabin. The privateer clucked and fussed over him. "Allow me to help you, Sir. Such a horrid state of affairs!"

Dazed and puzzled, the Englishman pondered the problem. "I can't think why they'd take my surgeon. He seems a man of good character, a modest man. He'd no wealth to sue for ransom. None, at least, of which I am aware."

"Eh, who can understand these buccaneers? It is the mission of my government to wipe them out."

"Now that I think of it, I really don't know much about our doctor, after all. Very close-mouthed. Foreigner. He seems to have no family, except for his daughter. I do hope she is safe. I must send a man to her quarters to see about her." He shook his head. "Poor girl!"

LeCorbeau spoke through gritted teeth. "It is to be hoped she is not now an orphan, *Monsieur.*"

"Perish the thought!"

"Yes, yes, but something tells me it is not yet this man's time to die. I am afraid that in circumstances like these, your surgeon will suffer much before death." There would be no doubt of it, if LeCorbeau had any say in the matter; he was a suspicious man. He managed to keep the vitriol out of his voice. "But these vile, eh…kidnappers— they cannot have left you long ago?"

Whyte leaned more heavily on the captain's sympathetic arm and squinted to check the position of the sun. "No, only an hour or so. It seems longer!" The hard-earned calm dissolved in a woman's scream. Whyte blanched as fresh alarm etched his face. He wheeled toward the hatch. "What is it? What's happened now?"

One of LeCorbeau's men hauled the woman up the steps. She quivered in her dressing gown, weeping and clutching his uniform. Locks of graying hair tumbled from her nightcap as she shook her head, still shrieking. The French officer tugged her toward his captain, raising his voice to be heard above the cacophony.

"I found her hiding in a bunk below, *Commandant*. She is hysterical!"

Captain Whyte corrected his sagging posture, and his frailty left him. He held out his arm, every inch a gentleman now that a lady was in distress. "My dear, hush! You are quite safe now."

Released, she staggered toward him and turned to point at her former captor. "Pirates! Oh, Captain, help me!"

Whyte placed his arm around her shoulders and patted her elbow. "No, no, the pirates have gone. These men are our saviors! Calm yourself, Madam. The attack is over."

But the woman cried, "Gone? Oh, no! No, they can't have gone!"

Unable to follow her reasoning, the captain of the *Julianne* said, "You are beside yourself. Come, come, you must sit down. Something to drink, perhaps."

LeCorbeau eyed the middle-aged spinster with distaste. "This is surely not the doctor's daughter, Captain?"

"No, indeed. She is her nurse."

The nurse's cries burst forth anew. She clamped her hands over her mouth, and Whyte was hard-pressed to comfort her. Long in the habit of discipline, he appealed to her sense of duty. "Please, you must collect yourself for your young charge. She mustn't see you so upset."

And with a look of horror, the woman uncovered her mouth to speak the dreadful words. "Captain! That's just it! Those horrible men— I couldn't stop them! I couldn't do a thing! They took all her belongings, and—"

"Yes, yes, it's all very disturbing. But belongings can be replaced—"

"Captain." LeCorbeau put up a hand. His shrewd black eyes narrowed as he scrutinized the nurse. "Excuse me, *Monsieur*, I think the lady has a more serious concern?" He pressed his lips together.

She took a deep breath.

"They took all her things, and…and…they took Miss Hanover, too!" She wailed, *"She's gone!"*

Whyte reeled. Letting go of the woman's shoulders, he stumbled against LeCorbeau. "No. Oh, no…"

LeCorbeau caught the old man, and his face contorted. "*Mon Dieu!* It is worse even than I believed!" Livid now, he steered his charge none too gently toward the cabin, abandoning the female to the officer.

"Here is my handkerchief, Sir— no, no, I insist!" They mounted the stairs in measured steps. "Guillaume! Bring that wine!…There is no end to the infamy of these sea rats! At least, *Monsieur*, the father and daughter are together. There may be some hope they will be ransomed, after all."

Whyte was shaking now. "But what those brutes will do to her! A young, innocent girl. And she was under *my* protection. The poor girl will be ruined— if she lives!"

The French privateer didn't care a fig for the girl's virginity. More precious valuables lay at stake. "You cannot be blamed, Sir. Here, lean on me." Compelled by the bantam captain's energy, the two men paced the companionway.

LeCorbeau talked. He soothed. He commiserated until he wore the older man's shock away. And when he judged the moment to be ripe, he smiled most ingratiatingly; he could do so when the need arose.

"But tell me, Captain Whyte. Did you happen to notice— so difficult in alarming conditions, I understand— but you are a seasoned seaman, it would be natural for you to observe. These pirates, when they left you…"

LeCorbeau halted to fix the merchant captain with his greedy, glittering eyes.

"Which way did they sail?"

Captain's Treasure

Hook's Jill was his own share of plunder from the *Roger*'s recent foray to the Neverland. Captain's treasure. Once she was Peter Pan's Wendy, and Hook had pursued her as an enemy to be hunted down. But the moment he beheld her face he changed course, determining instead to take her. She was his Beauty, his dream come alive. Since that day, her valor had been tested many times.

So far, she hadn't disappointed him.

Yesterday at dawn, the pirate crew of the *Jolly Roger* sighted a merchant vessel and took its first prize since sailing out of Neverbay. By noon the captain was dividing the booty according to the terms of the ship's articles, and after stowing it they spent the rest of the day and night carousing, celebrating their victory and quaffing the newly won wine. The captured ship had been a bountiful one, a good omen at the start of their adventures, and the mood was high. Buoyed up all around the feast was music, and song, and the men had called for the storyteller to spin them a tale, but in the midst of the revelry, the captain dampened the company's cheer by dragging his Jill away.

Only the bo'sun, Mr. Smee, had entered the master's cabin since, and then briefly, to inform the captain of the ship's disposition.

Smee had seen it, then. The captain's coffer, opened, and spilling its lustrous contents in the lanternlight, all around the rug. The beard on Smee's rugged face had spread in a smile. He'd attended the mistress the first time she sampled the captain's bounty. His own big hands had fastened the necklace about her throat, and he'd looked down at her reflection in the captain's mirror. He'd caught the lust in her honest eyes. Treasure-lust. It must be shining a hundredfold by today!

But neither Smee nor anyone else had seen her this morning. Jill had been detained, forcibly, in the captain's quarters.

James Hook was a ruthless man. Disregarding the appeal in her dark blue eyes, he had taken pleasure in denying her requests, and he prevented her flight. Those eyes of hers matched his own, and he possessed the power to read her heart. He had long since found and claimed her hidden kisses. Now he knew what she was thinking. She was watching the two brass keys that unlocked his door and his coffer. They hung against his chest as he advanced upon her, smirking.

Morning sun cascaded through the portside windows, illuminating her countenance and glistening in her fair hair. She lay on his bed, and, like the jewel she was, he had her displayed there, arranged in a setting of diamonds. And chains.

His voice was silky, low. Threatening.

"If you move, my love, you will lose everything."

But looking at him— the arrogant, damaged man through whose darkness she had traveled— Jill felt compelled to move. Her breathing came quick, and her breast rose and fell with it. She was fast weakening. "Captain…" The chains had struck chill against her flesh as he laid them on. Now they radiated her own heat.

"Come now, Jill. We've done this before. You learned the value of obedience." He sat on the foot of the bed, lightly, so that he wouldn't jar her, and inspected the links across her ankles. Running a finger under them, he smiled, half-way. "Not too tight, I hope?"

"Just tight enough for your intention! Get it over with—" Remembering the precariousness of her position, she checked her passion. "Sir."

Hook laughed. "Watch yourself, Madam. I will brook no insubordination. I've taken many things from women over the years, but orders, only once." He mounted the bunk, lowering himself astride her. He moved slowly, just touching her, sending shivers through her thighs. As she fought to control her body, he sensed her efforts. Her trembling delighted him, but he continued, stern now.

"You'll remember that occasion. But you mustn't imagine I'll allow it again." His keys swung from his sun-gilded flesh, away and back, hypnotically…like the strings of jewels he'd hung at his windows, and on his bedposts…on his curtains…his walls. They glittered all around Hook and his Jill, seductive little stars, kissed by the sun, and swaying with the roll of a swelling sea.

His black waves of hair almost blotted the gleam of an earring, but his tattoo was visible; a mermaid wrapped her tail around his empty wrist. A deadly iron claw usually hid her inky image, but now his hook impended within reach, hanging from a hook of its own, and tapping at the wall.

In his one good hand a necklace twined, loosely draped. Jill's captain held it over her heart and dangled it for her to see. "Rubies, love. To match your hand." He inched them lower, and dragged them across her flesh. The jewels in his fingers scintillated with his movements, compounding her distress. He pulled the rubied chain around the peaks of her breasts, down her torso and into her strategic point, then trailed it tingling back again, up her neck to her chin.

She beheld the baubles, and her eyes followed as he suspended them from his fingers, rich with rings. Almost imperceptibly, her lip twitched. Hook saw it. His eyes narrowed. "Do these gems stir your passion— as much as your lover?"

Her breathing ran away with her again, no matter how she tried to curb it. "Hook. Show mercy! You know you're the only—"

"Yes, I see that they do. I shall avail myself of the opportunity they afford me." He laid the necklace across her throat, neglecting to fasten it. "I do apologize, but you understand…" With an ironic smile, he held up the grisly stump at the end of his arm.

Jill didn't wince. She knew better than to invite discussion of his maiming. It wouldn't distract him one whit from his purpose— quite the opposite. She had woven his story. She knew he blamed her. Averting her eyes from the ruin of his wound, she concentrated on the ruby necklace.

Its blood-red drops lay just above the scar she earned in her first real struggle, emblazoning it. The sight of that mark still sent victory, like fire, surging through the captain's veins. He had settled that score. He had taken her. She was so completely his now, he'd already forgotten just where he left off and she began. The rubies pulsed against her throat, and the ends of their chain tangled with the locks of her hair.

His jewels afflicted her. Fountains of opulence flowed all around her, waterfalls of plunder that never quite poured into her. "Captain, have done with your torture." Sometimes he called her a vixen, and for good reason. Even now she was crafty, calling one of her ready smiles to her service. "Please, Sir. Just give me what I want. I promise you, you'll not regret setting me free."

"You can set yourself free, Jill. In one way only." Looming over her, he lowered his body, preparing to join with her. Knowing pleas would be futile, she set herself to withstand him. She would simply obey him this time, submit to his will. She understood the consequences, otherwise. She wouldn't dare move her limbs until he was finished with her.

But it was difficult to remain still. The keys suspended from his neck kept dancing. He was so close. His eyes already possessed her. Now he was touching her. Her forehead creased; why was he so cruel? She had done her best to satisfy him! The motion of the keys was interrupted as they lay down to recline between her breasts. They were warm. With an effort, she closed her eyes and held her breath.

It wasn't any use.

Hook smiled. His voice and his jewels had done their work. He slid into place, slowly, in order not to disturb her unclasped necklace. He heard her exhale. Then, moving within her, he watched the torment on her face as she strove, under orders, to remain still. In command, he stirred nothing but her desire as, with his weapon of choice, he killed her with his kindness.

Above her head, she clenched the pale fingers of her left hand and the reddened ones of her right into fists, and pressed against the bed linen, trying not to lose control, this time. Her nails dug into her palms as she willed her hips not to rise to meet him. But he was Captain James Hook, every bit as wily and handsome as her storytelling had created him, and one of the few things he cared enough to hold in his one-handed grasp was his lust for victory. Jill never really had a chance. Not then, as his cunning had won her, and not now, when he triumphed again.

For he was relentless. The heat kindled between them, the musk of rapture rose with their warmth. His skin, taut over muscle, glided along her own. Her breaths grew deeper, her wits dizzy. Bit by costly bit, Jill's hold on her senses slackened. Hook laid siege to sensation, with a steady application of force. At last, his rhythm drove her to recklessness, and she clenched her teeth and sacrificed the golden chain on her right ankle. It slithered off her skin and thumped on the bedclothes as, surrendering the first spoils, she wrapped one leg around him. He laughed, and the thrill of it through her abdomen provoked a sigh, and her other ankle betrayed her. In a flash of gold, the second shackle fell away as her legs curled about him.

He smiled. But he didn't stop.

Now only two silver chains and the ruby necklace restrained her. Surely she could endure his torture for the sake of these prizes? His keys nestled between their bosoms. She shut her eyes to the surrounding splendor, believing in herself. But he had begun to kiss her now, all around the rubies, and soon the rough of his whiskers and the firm of his lips robbed her of that treasure, too. She arched her neck to luxuriate in his kisses, crying out as the slippery settings deserted her throat.

"No!"

"Jill. You are profligate! Haven't I taught you not to squander your takings?" As he rose above her, his keys dangled again. She saw their imprint in the triangle between his ribs.

"But I can be a generous master. I shall compensate you for your losses." His silken voice was growing harsh. "I will give you another gift…while I take yours." And he delivered again, and then again, until she screamed her frustration, throwing off the silver chains at her wrists. Naked now, her arms encircled him at last, turning the tables. It was the captor who was constrained this time, in the priceless bonds of his prisoner's embrace. Free at last, she gave herself back to him, abandoning herself completely, forgetting just where she left off and he began, kissing him with a passion that would melt gold— and they both seized the precious prize, once Jill had lost her jewelry.

When at length these pirates were sated, they rolled back, breathless, to lie in sunshine on bedclothes that shimmered with swag.

Hook's most treasured gem clutched two brass keys in her scarlet fist. She separated them, and, with a gracious air, granted him the key to his coffer. But the key to his door?

He read her heart. "Give me what I want, love. I promise you, you'll not regret setting me free."

Her voice was low, and threatening. "Come now, Hook. We've done this before." She smiled, half-way.

His men knew that Captain James Hook was a difficult master to satisfy. Red-Handed Jill was his mistress.

And she had mastered him.

Signs of Weakness

Mr. Smee had been thorough with the cat-o'-nine-tails. Faithful, as always, to the captain's commands. Mr. Cecco hadn't worn a shirt in ten days, since Hook's ship sailed out of Neverbay and got back to work. Cecco's last painless labor was the flaying of the crocodile, but that job was part of his punishment and proved tricky, due to the leather scourge dangling from Smee's waiting fist. Cecco bore its stripes on his back, but he bore no grudge, for two very good reasons: he had forgotten his duty, placing the captain's life at risk; and the image still burning behind his eyelids— the image of that woman— was worth every knot on every lash.

Cecco had been on watch in the crow's nest that day. Had he not been distracted, staring at the woman, he'd have given the warning. The captain dispatched the deadly crocodile, but it was the red-handed lady who saved the situation, plucking her pistol from her sash and blinding the beast first. *That* part of the scene Mr. Cecco watched avidly. She was a crack shot.

He smiled as he stood on the forecastle, leaning with the wind, gripping the rail and tasting the salty spray on his lips. His broad back was marked, but he didn't cover it. Not because of pain, although the sting was strong yet, but because of pride. It gratified him to show off the wounds he'd won for the lady's sake, the ugliness her beauty had inflicted. Besides, didn't she have a weakness for damaged men? After all, the captain bore his own disfigurement, more gruesome than his sailor's. But under the scars, Cecco's flesh was healing. He'd earned a fair share of the spoils yesterday, and more trinkets to bedeck his half-clad body. Golden bracelets bound his biceps, but his oath to his captain bound his hands.

He couldn't touch her.

Any woman who would sign on to sail with a ship full of pirates was a rare prize, and this one was living loveliness, the woman who inspired the *Roger's* figurehead. Cecco leaned over the rail to feed his hunger for her again. The Beauty, with her looping mermaid's tail, her flowing tresses draping her breast. She gripped a sickle to match the captain's hook in one hand, and the other she held open, beckoning, irresistible, like her smile. A wooden wonder. But the real woman was more. She was a queen.

Hook had recognized her, too, as his own pirate queen. He had claimed her and he awakened her. Only Hook had the right to touch her, and then, what a shame— Cecco shook his head, commiserating— with just one hand! A regrettable twist of fate. That difficulty was why Hook allowed the bo'sun, Mr. Smee, to wait on her.

A rare shadow crossed Cecco's dusky face, betraying his envy. To Smee belonged the pleasure to stand near her, to handle her belongings, to listen to the music of her skirts, watch the face reflected in her mirror. To finger her silken hair as he fastened this and that. For the captain could heap jewels upon his mistress— but he couldn't secure them. Cecco's gypsy heart took this circumstance to be favorable, a sign portending some future opportunity. But, for now, for her, the man was Hook.

And Smee. The tall, brawny bo'sun was discreet. He held silence about the mistress, but Cecco imagined the scene many times, and read the Irishman's smiling face after he'd been closeted with her, in the master's quarters.

Like Mr. Smee, the lady was clearly aware of her position. She didn't invite the men's attention, yet to one as observant as Cecco, her demeanor revealed her consciousness of commanding it. She was young, but to Cecco's eyes she behaved as if she knew her effect on each of them, lowering her guard only for her sons. They had a right to be near her, of course, the two new sailors, Tom Tootles and Nibs the Knife. The three of them had been part of that Island boy's band. She was free now, though. She made her own choices. For the time being, she made an exhibition of choosing the captain. She flaunted it. Although she was careful to afford the captain full respect, she loved to demonstrate to the men just who belonged to whom. Her manner appealed to Cecco's showy nature.

And she had a temper to match Hook's own. Cold and sudden. Cecco had made the mistake of asking her to intervene for him, but it was she who insisted he be whipped, even requesting the captain's permission to do the job herself! Just remembering the icy fire of her regard caused Cecco's smoldering eyes to ignite. She was his ideal woman! To catch that flame in his arms, to melt the ice in her heart—

He jerked himself out of his reverie. Mr. Smee was shouting, ordering the change of shift.

Cecco heard boots and bare feet slapping the deck behind him, and men's voices rousing and responding. He pulled his hands from the rail and his thoughts from the fire. Flexing his shoulders, he felt the tug of tight skin as he stretched his scabby back. He turned to climb down the stairs and strut over the deck, nodding to his mates and taking up his station behind the wheel, to steer his captain's vessel. He wouldn't shirk his duty again.

But his dreams were bound wherever this ship was headed. With his captain's 'vessel.'

As tempted as he was, the only time even the daring and dashing Mr. Cecco might touch Red-Handed Jill would be when she encouraged him to do so. He smiled, and his teeth shone white in the setting of his complexion, darkened from the Italian sun of his birthplace. She'd have to reach that red hand out to him.

All he had to do was find a way to make that happen.

The girl in the brig wept there, in silence. Of the many noises she heard, none were familiar to her ear.

The old sounds were dead. Yesterday, in the space of an hour, the world she had known since childhood ceased to exist, leaving not so much as an echo to prove her home aboard ship had ever sailed. Even in her inexperience, she sensed that the course of her life had changed again, forever.

Not ready to keep that thought, she shut down her hearing, and her soft gray eyes searched the dark corners one more time for something much smaller to think about. But in her heart, she believed she would never touch the beloved little thing again. She twisted her naked fingers. The ring was gone. Even more than the loss of her universe, she mourned her ring. The ship had been her home. The ring— she had to think it, quietly— the ring had been her mother. It might have gone away with the ship. Most likely it was stolen, ripped away by one of those—

Her slight frame shuddered. She didn't want even her thoughts to give voice to those men. She wanted to forget them, forget the hands that had seized her from her bunk and tore her from her nurse's arms. Two of the outlandish creatures ransacked her cabin, and the hands tossed her over their bright-colored shoulder and bundled her up and out while she pushed away from them, hearing the screams of her nurse fading to blend with the sounds of gunfire and shouting and clashing swords, and flames chewing in the rigging. She had smelled the smoke, smelled the sweat on the shoulders, and she'd tasted her own fear under her tongue.

And then she'd reversed tack completely and clung to her abductor, her hands slipping on his too-moist skin and its tattoos as she saw the sea roiling beneath her. But he peeled her grip away and the wind whipped her nightdress as she flew across the chasm between ships, the rude men laughing at her, and the arms with jingling bracelets catching her, only to drag her into darkness below decks and end her voyage here, in this dank cell. He kissed her fingers and clanged the door shut and rasped the key in the lock, and after he left, all she could do was grip the cold, flat, iron bars and listen as her ship and her life drifted away, becoming inaudible.

Pirates.

And ghosts. She thought she'd seen her, just for an instant, standing on the deck, erect— regal amid the chaos. She'd worn a red dress that wrapped itself lovingly around her, and jewels flashed at her throat. Her long hair billowed in the breeze, like the spirit of a ship, a phantom sail open to whatever wind would take it and breathe it into life.

But the wind had already taken that memory, and as superstitious as life on the sea made this girl, she knew that lady was not her mother, not even her mother's ghost.

But she was magnificent. It was better to think about the red lady than to remember.

The familiar sounds were dead, but new ones had tempted her ears. First came a lot of shouting and laughing. The slap of water always assailed the hull. Sometimes a sharp order rose above the stomping and the rolling of barrels and the scuff of heavy objects being placed in storage. She knew what caused that noise, the goods from her vessel. The booty. And then the celebration. The odd music, the whistle pipes, the singing. And every now and then, a woman's voice. She hadn't heard that sound since last evening. The ruckus went on all night, but it hadn't kept the girl awake. She had curled up on the bench with her brown hair loose over her face, allowing her exhaustion to stifle all sound. Her eyes refused to open until sunlight stabbed its way in through the shaft from the upper world.

Now, suddenly, the girl heard her own heart again. Just over its hammering she heard boots on the steps, keys jingling, and the tip of a sword scraping down the stairs. Brown breeches came into view, too tight, enclosing a burly young man.

Pirate.

The girl shrank back into the cell and covered her ears, watching, but too afraid to hear any more.

"Thus, we have killed two birds with one stone."

Red-Handed Jill smiled as her lover spoke. She had given up everything to him, including the key, and having returned the favor, he was dressing to go out. Hook donned her favorite suit, black velvet with his silver sword belt— the long coat, waistcoat and breeches he wore the first time she'd ever seen him. She'd been frightened the day this notorious captain cornered her, but she had appreciated his appearance all the same. In fact, her apprehension had heightened the effect. She admired him again, but she attended his words, and answered him.

"I caught a glimpse of the girl, Hook. She looked at me so strangely."

"You are a pirate now, my love. You will have to accustom yourself to that."

"Aye, Captain. I'm becoming accustomed to a lot of things. But not yet to you." With a sly look, she freed his hook from his coat sleeve. She worked her fingers delicately, for the inside curve of his claw was razor-sharp. Mock concern creased her brow. "Whatever would we do if I became used to you?"

"I shall ensure that you don't. Beginning with the rubies— wear them today. They suit you." He placed the point of his hook under her chin. "I will remove them from your care when it suits *me*."

Her eyes were radiant yet. "Thank you! But lending me the rubies is the least you can do, Hook, after stowing away the rest of our morning's treasure."

"And I had thought it such a grand gesture. I shall know better next time." He slung the sword belt over his shoulder. "To business, Madam. I will interview the father, then the girl will be brought to you. You may decide her fate."

Jill settled the sword belt and buckled it. "I want you to send me Mr. Smee first, to fasten the rubies. Perhaps just this last time."

He flourished his hook. "You mustn't imagine I regret the loss of my hand any longer. My weakness, ironically, has made me all the stronger. And if I had not had a score to settle with you, I'd not have sought you out."

"Nor should you believe that I regret the settling of that score. On the contrary, it is an honor to bear the mark of our unity. A bloodstained hand is a far lighter punishment than I deserved."

He hooked her tangled hair, and pulled her toward him. "You have more than compensated me for your carelessness, Storyteller."

She laid scarlet fingers on the edge of his iron hand, the back side of the curve, and closed her eyes to feel its potency. A thrill ran through her. "I regret nothing."

His deep blue eyes beheld her, then he bent to claim a kiss. She kept him just longer than was necessary, and ended by presenting his rapier to him. In the next moment, she slid easily into consideration of the matter at hand. In her many adventures in the Neverland, she'd grown adept at changing roles at a moment's notice, turning pirate, princess, or prisoner on demand. And quite unexpectedly, the ruthless leadership of the boy, Pan, had prepared her for a pirate's life. His games, too, were full of danger and intrigue. The difference in her previous and current situations was not that she no longer enjoyed make-believe— this morning's play held plenty of that— but that her longing had become reality. She was a woman, and her captain was her lover. And now, as always when discussing business, she addressed him with the respect due his rank.

"Have you any instructions, Sir, before I speak to the girl?"

"Yes. Remember what I have taught you. Identify the weapon…" He raised his sword and sent her a pointed look.

She recited his rule: "Identify the weapon, and use it first."

Nodding his approval, Hook fitted the tip to its scabbard. Jill paused to listen to the exquisite rasp as he shot the sword home. It sent a chill down her spine, followed by a wave of warmth that lingered as she returned to the subject.

"You have tutored me by your example. I've seen you at work, first hand—" she glanced at the hook, "So to speak. I shall also seek her weakness." Remembering, she thought how cleverly Hook had disarmed the boy's Wendy with these tactics.

Hook was pleased, but his face grew stern. "And understand. However young and vulnerable, she is not your family. She is your captive. Bear that fact in mind at all times."

Jill acknowledged his concern and allayed it. "Aye, Captain. I will."

"I must insist that your sons be clear on this point, also. Mr. Starkey will speak to them. It is difficult, yet necessary, for sailors of any age to maintain the proper perspective where females are concerned. That is why untried girls are considered bad luck aboard ship. A superstition to which I am certain the crew of the *Julianne* will attest. If you decide to keep her, you must weigh her value in the balance."

"Aye, Sir. I do understand." She cocked her head. "Wendy would have mothered her. A difficult habit to break." His lady pirate smiled, darkly. "How fortunate that I am Jill now."

Her smile hit its mark. "I shall leave you before I myself lose perspective and allow you to tempt me away from my duties. Again." He swept to the wardrobe to collect his hat. "I advise you to make use of Smee. He thinks himself irresistible to children. In reality, they find him most intimidating."

Jill laughed. "I wonder what his Lily would say to that? But I think the girl in the brig is not exactly a child."

"All the better. Intimidation grows with age."

"How well I remember!"

He smiled warmly.

She opened the door for him, concealing her state of dishabille behind it. She had been careless with her blue brocaded dressing gown. Though the captain was formal in matters of dress, Jill often flouted convention in Hook's quarters, inducing him to show his appreciation of her form. This morning was no exception, but the key had ultimately been reinstated to its position in the lock. She gazed upon her lover's fine features, and fingered the trim whiskers of his beard. "It would be too easy, wouldn't it, to have another key made?"

Hook donned the hat, producing a smug smile. "And unnecessary, my love." He slid his good hand into his coat pocket. "I keep its twin on my person." He held up a ring of keys for her inspection, then replaced it. "You see, I, too, am your captive." He raised his boot, kicked the door out of her hand so it slammed with a bang and he lifted her off her feet, sweeping her into his embrace. He kissed her with a violent passion, until her heart hammered in her ears and her lungs begged for breath. Then he set her down to bow to her, and after wrenching the door open, he strode off onto the companionway, to take the steps like hostages and stare down the gazes of his always curious crewmen.

Behind him, Captain James Hook left a woman clinging to his doorway, on fire. She would be difficult to satisfy by tonight.

Red-Handed Jill was his mistress, and he had mastered her.

Identify the weapon. Discover the weakness. Rules, literally, to live by. Tactics that assured him victory in many a conflict, whether of physical strength, or of wits. Hook knew from long experience the value of these lessons. He had used them to his advantage countless times, not excepting in his battle to win Jill from Pan, and from herself as the girl Wendy. But now at last he possessed her, and a new dilemma had arisen. Jill herself was both his weapon and his weakness. *She* could be used against him.

She matched him in every respect, not least of which in fearlessness. A fearless woman was, ironically, more difficult to defend than a coward. More worth defending, as well. Hook cared about few things, but on those things he cherished, he lavished the full intensity of his personality.

Hook cared about Jill, deeply. Although they were united only a short time, their history was a long one. A story of magic. Even as Wendy, she was no ordinary female. While telling her tales to a pack of boys, she was unaware of their impact. Yet word by word and feature by feature, she had crafted her captain until he loomed before her, a solitary man with a hook for a hand, lusting for revenge. His design had been to dispense with the child, but she was changing— maturing— and as he discovered her powers, he found himself wanting the woman. Moved to mercy, Hook offered an exchange. Death to the girl, deliverance for the lady. She proved as valiant as he imagined her to be, accepting her culpability for his maiming and joining him as his consort. No, more than that. His partner.

Hook led Jill into a life of danger, and although she relished it, he was obliged to see to her safety. And his own, for she lived under his protection now. Courageous as she was, if he abandoned her for any reason, her situation would be tenuous. She was safe enough aboard the *Roger* in current circumstances. His men he held under tight control, but his enemies…

Hook's eyes narrowed as he observed the horizon. His enemies must not be allowed the chance to use her. They must believe her to be his paramour, his light-of-love. A vessel in which to pour his pride. Nothing more. They must never guess the truth.

Hook's reflections occupied him as he waited for his prisoner to join him on the forecastle. The day was bright, the sea air spicy and invigorating, snapping in and out of the sailcloth above him. No doubt the captive was in need of a stroll about the deck after a dank night in the hold. And Hook had ordered him isolated. The gentleman was as yet ignorant that the girl was here as well. His daughter, and presumably, his weakness. Doubly useful, she was locked in the brig, as unaware as her father that they had both been captured, and ripening for her first meeting with her mistress.

Jill. The thought of her sank into his soul, an anchor settling to rest in saturated sand. Beneath Hook's sometimes turbulent surface, Jill was a constant and profound satisfaction. He was grateful for her.

The sound of boots approached, and the clank and drag of ankles in iron: Mr. Smee, guiding the prisoner up the steps. Hook's ship was powerful, resplendent with ornamentation, the perfect setting to complement his person. The captive's first impression of his captor was sure to be dramatic. Hook's velvet coat cuffs graced the gilt of the railing as he extended his arms and waited until the men stood stationary and expectant behind him. Timing was a tool, for Hook.

"The gentleman, Captain. Mister Hanover, Captain James Hook."

Hook raised his head in his magnificent hat with its glittering gems, its plumes flowing in the wind, and turned slowly to lower his imperious gaze upon the prisoner. He looked on the man for only a moment, then addressed his bo'sun.

"Thank you, Mr. Smee. Release him, and see to the business in my quarters." He turned away, and his hook resumed its place on the rail, where it shone sharp in the sun.

"Aye, Sir." Smee pulled a set of keys from his belt, and his vigorous frame hunkered down, working the iron fastenings. When the prisoner's ankles were free and his soft-leather shoes set adrift, Smee released the man's hands. Gathering up the jingling chains, Smee excused himself. But before leaving the captain's presence, he waited his opportunity, then, peering over his spectacles, he tapped an imaginary ring on his finger and made a slashing motion across his throat. Message sent, he turned away to stow the irons and head for the captain's cabin.

Armed with Smee's information, Hook addressed the gentleman. The cursory glance had informed him. This was a man in good circumstances, dressed modestly but tastefully in a gray velvet suit adorned only by a gold pocket watch, a wedding ring, and a signet.

He was of average height, with an athletic build. Nearing middle age. Fair. He exhibited all the usual traits of a man one night into captivity— unshaven and unsettled. Unremarkable, to Hook, in every respect but one. That mark told Hook all he needed to know.

"Tell me, Doctor. Have you kept up your fencing skills?"

The man, who had opened his mouth to protest his abduction, left it hanging open. He raised his fingers to the old saber scar on his cheek, and blinked at this pirate captain, so cool and arrogant. And informed.

Hook said, "Don't trouble yourself; I shall answer your questions. Once you have answered mine." He watched the man expectantly. "Well?"

The prisoner blinked again. "I'm sorry. Well, what?" His voice was crisp, retaining a trace of his Austrian heritage.

"You'll not improve your situation by playing the fool with me."

The doctor shifted uncomfortably, as if his ankles were still clad in iron. This was not his first voyage, nor his only encounter with buccaneers. It was, however, his first experience of a criminal so obviously a product of the aristocracy. Why on earth would a gentleman like this Hook turn to piracy? And that barbarous claw, so stark in its contrast to the elegant costume! The surgeon clutched his pocket watch as he answered.

"Yes. I have kept in practice, as your men discovered yesterday morning before they outnumbered me! But of course my rapier is gone with my ship." He allowed a touch of anger to coat his words.

"Nothing of importance has gone with your ship. We have secured everything you value." Hook observed the man's charcoal eyes as a spark of apprehension ignited in them. The prisoner's thumb rubbed his watch.

"Do you mean that you have also taken my— belongings? The instruments?" Doctor Hanover peered intently at the pirate. "The medicine bag?"

"You would be of little use to us without the trappings of your profession."

The doctor seemed relieved, then assumed an air of professional concern. "Use? Is someone aboard in need of a physician?"

"Certainly. And since your wife is no longer living, perhaps you'll enjoy a change of venue. The post of ship's surgeon is vacant. I cordially invite you to join us."

Taken aback, Hanover dropped his watch and let it dangle on its chain. The long scar reddened from cheekbone to chin as he allowed his outrage to dominate his response.

"What! Preposterous! You can hardly imagine that I would throw in my lot with the pirates who have abducted me and dragged me away from my— my employment." He looked away from the captain.

"Of course, Doctor, I understand. You need further encouragement, some incentive, to persuade you. I assure you, the material rewards will be plentiful."

"You yourself are evidence of that. Every seaman has heard of the nefarious Captain Hook, and of the bounty he commands. I see now that the stories are true! Yet I insist you put me ashore at the first opportunity."

"The men of my crew are as entitled to medical attention as any others. And you have taken an oath, have you not, to preserve life?"

"Not at the expense of others' lives, Sir!"

"Very well. I perceive the nature of your inclination. We shall speak further when you are more in temper to consider the offer."

"You will wait a long time for that."

Among Hook's men, his courtesy was known as a warning sign. "Doctor. I admire your courage. I choose to attribute your attitude to *that* quality, rather than to foolishness. Courage is a necessity aboard the *Jolly Roger*." The captain stepped close to the surgeon, to tower over him, his smile calculated to put the man on guard. "Take the air while you may. You will be shown to your— berth— again shortly. And you will dine in my quarters this evening."

"Thank you, but I should rather not."

"I shall overlook your insolence, this once. Mr. Smee will call for you at the appropriate time. Your belongings will be returned to you." Hook's glance swept over his captive. "See that you shave." He turned away and strode down the deck.

The surgeon sputtered, indignant, but as the captain moved away, he hastened to follow, the skin under his unaccustomed stubble suffused with a flush. "Captain! If you please, one question."

Hook paused at the top of the steps. He turned an impassive stare upon his prisoner while the breeze buffeted his hair and fingered the plumes of his hat.

"I couldn't help but notice as your men…" This time the doctor applied prudence, resorting to civility, "escorted me…to your ship. A young woman, dressed in scarlet. She stood on the deck. Another captive?"

Hook raised an eyebrow. "And what would be your interest in her? You display disdain for everything else aboard the *Roger*."

"Well, she is lovely, and rather young. I would seek her release, if I might bring that about in some way, before…"

The captain lifted his chin with an amused expression. "Before what?"

"Sir, I believe you understand me perfectly well. Before anything untoward happens to her."

"And so you offer me a bargaining chip for your cooperation. An interesting concept, Doctor. I see you are a gentleman of the old school. We shall discuss it at supper. I assure you, nothing *'untoward'* will happen to her— before then." Hook turned again, but halted at the tone of the surgeon's next question. His face relaxed, but he concealed his satisfaction.

"But who is she?"

Not bothering to face the man, Hook spoke over his shoulder. "When you have agreed to join us, Doctor, she'll be a female under your care." Then he smiled, leaving the man with the dueling scar and the modest suit floundering in his wake and reassessing his attitude toward the pirate's proposition.

Another weakness laid bare.

The young man approached, keys jingling, to survey the girl between the bars of her cage. The captive peered from under her elbows; she wouldn't unclasp her ears for him. Through the iron strips, the light from the stairway cast crisscross shadows on his face, and on the yellow shirt beneath, with its loose sleeves and tight shoulders.

Another garment hung limp over his arm.

"Good morning, Miss. We haven't forgotten you. We all had a night of it, and we roused a bit late today!" He smiled. His easy countenance showed no markings or tattoos as yet. He was youthful, just turned a man. But a sturdy man, all the same.

The girl had no use for him. He was a pirate.

"Ah, Miss. We thought you'd be ready for some conversation."

In spite of her indifferent posture, her eyes asked. They were gray and curious.

" 'We' is me and my brother, Nibs. You'll know him by the orange kerchief on his head. I'm Tom. Tom Tootles. We've just joined up. Yours was the first ship we've taken." He looked off into a corner of the brig, reliving the memory and sighing. "It was glorious, wasn't it?"

With renewed disdain, the girl yanked her elbows down and uncovered her ears.

"Sorry, Miss! Got carried away. Can I get you some breakfast before you meet the mistress?" He recognized the look in her eyes, then, the hunger to understand the lady. Tom smiled. "Aye, she has that effect on everyone aboard." Jill had always commanded authority in some form, even when she'd been only the girl mother of a handful of Lost Boys. "Her name's Red-Handed Jill, and she's the queen of this vessel."

The girl inched a half step forward. Her bare feet prickled in the straw.

"She'll be sending for you soon, so you'd best eat while you can. Will you?"

She shook her head. She backed away.

Tom shrugged. "Your decision. Let's just clean you up a bit. You're in no condition to wait upon a queen." He held up the circle of keys so that they slid together, selected one, and turned the lock with a grinding. The door protested as Tom swung it open, and then he stepped in. The captive cringed and covered her ears again.

"What's the matter with your ears? Covering them's not going to stop anything. You'd better be listening. We mean no harm to you. If we did, believe me, it would already be done!" Laughing, he seized her wrist to pull her toward him. He shook the garment off his arm and tossed it over her shoulder. "Here's your dress. Put it on like a good girl, and I'll be back when the mistress is ready for you." He pulled a brush from his back pocket, handed it to her, and turned to go.

As he moved away, she relaxed enough to allow her other hand to fall from her ear. She shrugged the dress off her shoulder and looked at it. Like the brush, it was her own, one plundered with her other belongings. In her surprise, she dropped her guard too soon.

Tom turned on his heel, strode two steps, and took the girl's face between his hands. "You'll tell me if you need anything, won't you? Hairpins or whatnot. I don't know much about girls' things." He flashed a smile. "I know a bit about ladies, though!" And he kissed her, right on the lips. Not just a peck, as her father might once have extended to her, but a real kiss, the kind that bound up her lips and sucked them in. His mouth was firm, and tasted like strong spirits.

He let her go. "Remember, it's Tom."

The object of his sudden affection was so stunned she didn't react at all. She stood in the straw, blinking in the dim light of the brig for what felt like hours, listening to the key in the lock and his boots stomping up the steps.

The girl drew the back of her hand across her mouth.

Tom.

Her lip curled. For some reason she didn't understand, she wished he hadn't kissed her. She couldn't hear a kiss.

She wished he'd hit her instead.

Mr. Smee headed for the master's quarters, watched by the eyes of his shipmates. Eyes of men who had once been relieved not to walk in his boots. Envious eyes now, begrudging his proximity to the volatile captain, or rather, to the captain's lady. One pair of eyes, dusky brown, followed his progress more intently than the rest.

"Another service for your mistress, Mr. Smee?" Cecco's armbands glinted as he hailed the bo'sun from behind the wheel at the helm. His English had improved over the years abroad. He now owned a fine command of the language, and he enjoyed the double meaning of his words.

"Aye, Mr. Cecco. And I'm just the man for the job. Whatever it is!" Smee's lilting voice was as melodious as the tune he whistled on his way up the steps of the companionway. As he climbed, he made sure his striped shirt was tucked, showing his taut torso to best advantage. She must need something done for her, some little thing. Something necessary, but beneath the captain's dignity. Lucky thing for Smee— he had no dignity to be worrying about. He'd do anything for James Hook. Anything at all.…Absentmindedly, Smee knocked on the door. Aye. He'd do anything for her.

Jill opened the door and backed up to make room as he entered. She had to gaze up to welcome him; Smee stood fully as tall as the captain. "Good morning, Mr. Smee."

Looking out on the morning's activities, she found her eye caught by Mr. Cecco's. Not quite condescending, she inclined her head to acknowledge the warmth of his greeting. Cecco had always been cordial, in spite of the beating he'd taken at her urging, and Jill was satisfied he didn't hold the incident against her. He held his raw back erect, like a trophy adorning his body along with his earrings and his necklaces. Jill well remembered the Italian sailor smiling and kissing his fingertips in salute that night when, still a girl, she descended nervous and excited to the deck of the *Jolly Roger*. Whatever might pass between them in the future, Mr. Cecco held the distinction of having been the first of Hook's men to welcome her here.

Mr. Smee noted the direction of her gaze. His eyes tightened as they shifted to his shipmate. He cleared his throat. When the door was safely closed, Jill didn't forget about Cecco, but she tended to necessity, presenting her back so charmingly to Smee that he ceased to care where her attention was anchored a moment ago.

"Would you be so kind?"

Smee grinned again. He had become adept at lacing her dresses, but found that, for some reason, it always took him every bit as long to perform the service as the first time. She'd worn forget-me-not blue that morning, to match her eyes. And the captain's. Smee resettled his spectacles and began by gathering Jill's hair and laying it over her shoulder. That task alone demanded a degree of concentration, and Smee was a man who never dodged his duty, however pleasant.

Taking his time, he held off speaking as long as possible. He liked giving her this little pleasure. "The scarlet again today, Ma'am? Two days in a row!" Mr. Smee's sinews belied his interest in domestic affairs.

She opened her eyes and smiled over her shoulder. Once again, she had succumbed to the sensation of Smee's hands in her hair. "Aye! The captain has granted me the rubies today. He says they match my hand."

Smee's roughened face showed his surprise. "You're never telling me you won them from him?"

"Only for a day. He's a shrewd one, but I'll have his treasure yet." She moved to the looking glass hanging inside the wardrobe door. He followed close behind, and, with reverence, she lowered the precious necklace to his palm.

Smee's big fist closed on it. "If I didn't know better, Ma'am—" If he didn't know better, he'd believe her words. He'd believe that, maybe, her lust for pirate gold exceeded her lust for her pirate captain. It was a mark of her confidence that she could speak so openly to Smee. But he kept himself on guard. A body never knew when she'd go all royal. She could be cold as these jewels when she chose.

He held the rubies up to the light of the windows bordering the captain's quarters. The stones weren't cold now. Each one glowed with red fire. Smee was reminded of a bonfire, and the last time he'd been ashore.

Jill had turned to study him. "You can't fool me, Mr. Smee. You're thinking of your own treasure."

He laughed. "Leave it to a woman to know when a man's mind's a-straying! Aye. I was remembering the golden bracelets I brought her. The captain's gift for the Indian ladies' help in winning you. Lily fair turned up her nose, but she accepted them right quick enough." His smile broadened. And she'd given as good as she got. Better.

Jill turned her back to him again. "You're missing her while we're away, aren't you?"

Watching Jill's reflection, Smee spoke over her shoulder. "It's always worst at the outset. But she'll not be lonely without me. And to be honest, when we get to port I'll not pine away, either. Going from her makes us that much happier when I return."

"And your baby girl? Do you long for her?"

"She's just a wee thing now. Ask me when she's older."

Jill understood. He was a pirate. Her own Hook had no tender tendencies toward children but, rather, an aversion to them. Hook had no use for children. And, until Wendy brought her influence to bear on the Lost Boys of the Neverland, they had proved his point. But she had raised those boys. That was enough.

She smiled now at Mr. Smee's indifference. In spite of their dissimilarities, Smee and Lily were a match. There were no strings between them except a warm, mutual regard. Lily was a graceful native woman on the island of the Neverland who enjoyed children and whose outlook on love was exceedingly inclusive. Smee's daughter didn't lack for fatherly attention in his absence. Upon leaving Pan's band, Wendy's Twins finished growing up in Lily's care. The Twins still lived, in every sense of the word, with Lily and two other Indian women in what used to be Wendy's house. It was Hook who ordained it, acting on his wish that Wendy should join him. Hook's arrangement suited Mr. Smee's inclinations, too.

Stroking the gems at her throat, Jill brought her thoughts around to Hook's more current wishes. "With regard to the girl's father, Smee. What more have you learned?" She checked that the clasp of the necklace was fastened tightly, assuring that, whatever passion might grip her, these rubies wouldn't slide from her throat again. Her eyes still reflected their fire.

Smee's hands could find no more excuses to touch her, so he removed them from her shoulders and drew himself up to his full and generous height, turning his mind to business. "He's a widower, Ma'am. Name of Hanover. A gentleman. Lost his wife a few years ago. Illness, as near as I can figure it. He'd not talk much— Austrian. Not like my own countrymen! A cup of wine was all he'd take, and not much good it was to loosen his tongue."

"I don't blame him. He's lost his liberty. But we'll make him come round, won't we? Bring me the girl now. And Mr. Smee, the captain requests you stay with us while we discuss her situation. He trusts your way with children."

"Aye, Madam. I enjoy the captain's trust. I've never known him to be wrong in where he places it." He lifted his hand to discipline a stray wisp of her hair. It was a reason to stand next to her for another second or two. Sometimes, when near to her like this, inhaling her perfume, Smee wished the captain wasn't such a good judge of men. But, conscious of his duty, he released her shining tendril and nodded his respects. Then he went about her errand, content to have a reason to return.

The door to the captain's quarters clicked shut, and Smee's heavy footfalls faded. Jill freed the strand of hair again.

Even if she could, she wouldn't hide the fact from Hook that one of the pleasures she'd discovered in her short life as a pirate was the warm regard of so many men. And she wasn't a girl anymore. She saw right through Mr. Smee. She knew what he wanted.

Smee was Hook's man, and, as such, he had become her own. But Jill prized honesty, and she readily admitted the conflict she perceived within the bo'sun. As much as he respected her, he didn't quite trust her. Smee's loyalty to the captain was his most fundamental characteristic, lodged right next to the instinct to protect him. Hook knew it, too, and that loyalty was the reason Smee alone among his men was trusted behind the door of the master's quarters. As Smee attested, Hook had never yet erred in placing his confidence.

Jill, too, held a loyalty to the captain she was sure would pass the test of time. Smee's devotion to Hook, even his doubts concerning Jill herself on the captain's behalf, endeared him the more to her heart. The man played a role far beyond his office of bo'sun. Smee acted as Hook's attendant and squire, first mate, and liaison to the crew. He had served the captain longer than any of the other men. And Mr. Smee, true to his reputation, was as strong and as sweet as rum. Jill made that claim many times in her stories, and now that she'd tasted that spirit, she affirmed her assertion, and appreciated him.

Smee radiated a sense of security that lured many a woman to the shelter of his powerful arms. For Jill to pretend she wasn't drawn to him would be untruthful. She looked forward to Smee's touches every morning— courted his attentions, in fact. Certain intimacies could be allowed, even enjoyed. But much as the lady and the bo'sun valued one another, neither would make the move that would betray their captain.

Thinking back on the morning, Jill also appreciated Mr. Cecco, and the intensity of his greeting. She hadn't missed his golden armbands, the white teeth within his smile. He wore his thick hair bound back in a leather lace, and never a shirt since his flaying. His attentiveness, and Smee's, gave Jill a sense of power she'd never known as mother of the Lost Boys. Hook told her once that she would find men easier to govern than boys, and of course he was correct. Her boys had vaguely wanted both nothing and everything from her. The men aboard the *Roger* knew exactly what they wanted, even if they couldn't get it, and the bo'sun and the Italian were only the most obvious about their desires. Like Cecco, Smee was always ready to offer his attention, his service, or his arm, to escort her on the steps or along the rail. Like Smee, Cecco was a strong man. Smee was red and rugged; Cecco was dark, and strikingly handsome.

Perhaps it was because, in her storytelling, she had a mysterious hand in choosing Hook's crew that Jill found something appealing in each of his men, such as shy Mr. Noodler, with his gold teeth and his hands on backward, and Bill Jukes, whose stem-to-stern tattoos intrigued her. She intuited their individual stories to a greater or lesser extent. The men often asked to hear her tell their histories. Each man held interest for her, and, apparently, she for them.

And all of them were pirates. Buccaneers, brigands. Hook's band of ruffians was held in check by an oath to the captain, and by the advantage of membership in this ship's company.

Jill turned to the captain's mirror and observed her regal smile changing as it became tempered with the truth— the power she felt came in good part from her union with the master of this vessel. Captain Hook was teaching her, but she hadn't yet learned enough about sailing to seize command herself, should the need arise. As independent as she was, she acknowledged that until she gained more experience, without Hook's ironfisted authority, Red-Handed Jill could well become the property of the next strongest among his crew.

And just how might that man be determined? A cold stream poured through her veins as she contemplated her position. Jill would survive, always. Her instincts and intelligence would carry her. But her spirit might not live through that kind of subjugation. It was in her best interests to see to the captain's safety, to support him in every endeavor, to remain completely loyal— and to maintain cordial ties to the heartiest men aboard. Quickly, her thoughts ranged among the crew, then settled again on Mr. Smee, Hook's chosen right-hand man, and she was comforted.

Jill had every confidence in her lover, but the pirate's life into which Hook had drawn her was not a stable one. Her heart began to pound as she thought again of the decision she had made. Not many would judge she'd chosen wisely. The alternatives might seem, if not more attractive, then certainly more secure. She might have escaped, although not unscathed, to the safety of London. She might have remained on the Island, a frightened child. Instead, against all convention, she had chosen to throw herself, so young and so inexperienced, on the mercy of a potent enemy. With no guarantees, she placed her future in Hook's one remaining hand. The pirate and the girl had formed their liaison without the structure of those familiar words, 'for better or for worse,' yet she had wounded him and bled for it, and— for better or for worse— now she was his partner. Until death.

But, like Hook, Jill was no coward. She had chosen a challenge. And duties to perform. She took a deep breath and straightened, inspecting with a sharp eye the richness of the quarters Hook, in his generosity, shared with her. Then she shook out her crimson skirts, preparing to interview her first prisoner.

Captain James Hook had made Red-Handed Jill his queen. And although she was new to piracy and a life at sea, Hook and Jill were one. Whatever twists the course of their story took, she believed nothing could cause her to regret beginning it.

Certainly not a little captive.

A knock thumped the door. Jill processed to the satin-covered couch and enthroned herself. She lifted her head, placed her hands on her lap, and waited for just the right moment. Hook had tutored her; timing was a tool. She allowed it to work for her.

"…Come!

Captivation

Mr. Cecco manned the helm, the sun his companion, throwing its rays through the clapping canvas above. Its warmth soaked into his skin, both the smooth and the tattered, and he appreciated the feel of the weathered wheel in his grip and the bands of gold around his muscular arms. Smiling, he cast his gaze toward the captain's cabin. His strong, striped back was the first thing anyone, any woman, opening that door would see. The leather laces with which he tied his hair dangled over the markings, another scourge, but a pleasant one.

"And what are you grinning about now, Cecco?" It was Yulunga, his huge black frame blocking the breeze. The colorful strings of beads around his throat threatened to burst as his neck swelled to speak. He had a deep, fluid voice. "You are up to something, friend."

Cecco showed his even teeth and replied in his pleasing accent, "Ah, you know me too well, mate!"

Yulunga was everybody's 'mate.' Cecco was one of the few who had formed a friendship with the fearsome African, but no one except the captain dared to call Yulunga by name. The sound of it still struck terror in the souls of his native land, who feared that speaking the name might call him back across the water to wreak his vengeance. Hook alone had curbed some of Yulunga's murderousness, and now the man posed in his usual stance, a boarding ax in his belt, and his arms hanging from his bulging shoulders at an angle, too thick to lie at his sides.

"So tell me." Yulunga said. "I will try to keep you away from trouble, as always."

Cecco thrust his hand into his pocket. The trinket was still there. The ring. He pulled it out and fiddled it in his fingers, sending Yulunga a self-satisfied look. "I have found a 'key' to the captain's quarters."

Yulunga reached for it, exhibiting marks of manacles on his wrist. He appraised the tiny object and snorted. "How will two pink pearls get you through the master's door, my ambitious friend? I think even our Mr. Cecco's gypsy magic cannot work such a charm." His dark face broke into a smile as he tossed the ring back. "Although I am certain you will attempt it."

Uneven footsteps approached, and both men turned to watch as a small procession passed, Tom Tootles and Mr. Smee, escorting the sullen captive— persuading her, really— toward the stairs to see the mistress. The girl balked as they neared the companionway.

Tom cajoled her, "Come along, Miss. The lady's waiting to meet you. Don't let her see you're afraid."

The girl scowled at Tom, but when her eyes rolled toward Cecco and Yulunga, she shuffled closer to him.

Smee pushed Tom aside. "Let me show you, Mr. Tootles, the way to do with reluctant prisoners." He gave the girl's backside one boost of his hand, and she opened her eyes and lifted her wrinkled brown skirt to scurry up the steps like a squirrel in a tree. Smee turned to Cecco and Yulunga, grinning. "And you two tell me I've no way with the ladies!"

Tom, who had witnessed Smee's winning way with the opposite sex, chortled and ran up the steps behind the indignant captive, to knock at his mother's door.

Yulunga slapped Smee on the back, and the beads at his neck nearly popped again as he laughed. "I know better, Mr. Smee. It's Cecco here who doubts the skills of every man but himself."

"Aye, and on his back we can all plainly see the reward those skills have earned him."

Cecco smiled. "Others' rewards are not so easily seen, Mr. Smee." But once Smee bounded after the girl, Cecco corrected his friend, and his smile stiffened. "No. Mr. Smee seems to enjoy much success these days. And there is one other I do not doubt, mate." He shot an envious glance up the steps. "Our captain."

"So that is the problem! The mistress."

"I do not think of her as a problem. And it won't be long now before my good luck begins."

"Sooner or later you share everything with me, so that must mean good luck for myself, as well!" But Yulunga's broad face creased a bit. "What's the scheme, friend?"

Mr. Cecco turned back to the helm and stared ahead at the sea as he anticipated the way it would happen. "The little girl will have realized by now that I have stolen her ring. She will ask for it back. And if she's humble about it, the kind mistress will be generous enough to return it."

Yulunga raised his eyebrows. "Only…?"

"Only the lady will have to request it from her devoted sailor, Mr. Cecco, first. And compensate him for it."

"Cecco, you are always thinking."

"Always. And I seize my opportunity. I kissed that little girl's fingers, and plucked her ring like a peach from an orchard." But this one was just bait, to catch a more exotic fruit. Mr. Cecco rubbed the lustrous surface of the pearls between his fingers and imagined they were the tender parts of a lady. *The* lady, pink and ripe.

"Well, 'devoted sailor,' I look forward to the trouble you will cause. Hook keeps things too quiet on this ship. But you'd best be careful, mate." Yulunga bore his own marks, carved into his hide by the master's iron hook. "It may be a long time before the captain lets her loose."

Cecco pocketed the ring. "I have much time, my friend. Until then, I am not going anywhere."

"The gypsy, settling down at last?"

"I will always be a wanderer, but my reckless days are over." The dashing Italian gave his attention to the horizon then, cultivating his new habit of discipline, and concentrating on the compass. He had a goal to pursue.

Yulunga observed Cecco's determination. "You are changing since our last visit to the Island, and since your whipping. But I always enjoy stirring things up. Let me know if I can help you, if only to save your scarry skin!" He strolled away, shaking his head.

Cecco attended his duty at the wheel, keeping the ship on course, and all the while another course mapped itself out in his mind. The most direct route to the master's quarters, and it wasn't as simple as the path he liked to imagine— up the steep steps of the companionway, through the door with its engraved brass plate, and into the cabin. All lit with candles and her beautiful face, and in the warm light, her red hand reaching out to him, to accept his pearls.

The pirate queen sat enthroned upon her couch, the crimson curtain that usually shielded it drawn aside to admit the girl to her presence. Rubies glowed on her throat, and both the matching scar above them and the glint in her eye hinted of the lady's willingness to engage in the fray. These signs were not lost upon the girl, who, upon entering, was sufficiently moved to extend the courtesy of a curtsy.

"Madam." Tom Tootles, who had recommended that curtsy, nodded to the mistress and backed out.

The girl knew he was gone by the click of the door behind her, and by the sinking feeling that accompanied it. The little prisoner had disdained Tom's companionship, but now acknowledged to herself that she missed it. Telling herself she didn't care, she had nevertheless made an effort to gather her composure for this interview, smoothing the brown dress and pinning up her hair. She needn't have bothered. Nothing would have steadied her. She stood squeezing her hands together, listening to the heavy tread on the carpet that told her that Smee, the big redheaded sailor, loomed behind her.

The lady observed, waiting for the bo'sun to take his place before she spoke. She kept her hands laid flat on her taffeta lap. Her seat was a reclining couch, a divan, and the wooden swan carved on its back seemed to bow to her, frozen in the act of opening its wings.

"I am Red-Handed Jill. What is your name, girl?" Her voice was clear and cool.

The captive heard the question, but her eyes couldn't say the word.

"Very well. I shall call you Liza, after another servant girl I once knew."

The girl's eyes widened with surprise. The lady guessed her name!

Jill smiled, complacent. "You will find I know something of the story behind everyone who boards the *Jolly Roger*. So that is your name, after all?"

Liza's vehement nod confirmed it. Peering over her shoulder, she looked up to witness the smug smile on Mr. Smee's face. But the lady commanded, "Pay attention, please," and Liza's head snapped back to face her.

"I should regret to send you back to the brig. I've arranged for a nice, comfortable cabin to be ready for you…if you agree to my terms. Will you listen?"

Liza's curtsy consented, but her gaze now wandered the quarters, taking in the velvet and carving, the swords, crystal, and shining woodwork. Through the open windows, she heard the swish of water as the hull passed through on its way— where? Beyond the scent of the sea hung a trace of tobacco, interwoven with lavender. Behind Mr. Smee, the girl had glimpsed a glassed-in bookcase, and left of the mistress' couch, starboard within the ship, stood an ornate wardrobe. Next, a sideboard and dining table in the corner; beyond that, and all along the stern, a cushioned recess basked under the windows. A harpsichord, a polished desk covered with maps and navigational instruments, and on the right, portside, an escritoire. Next to the escritoire posed the grandest piece in the place, the bunk, resplendent with silken coverlet, sculpted bedposts and tapestried curtains.

The room was littered with Oriental carpets and illuminated by the sun, which blazed through mullioned windows to display the tasteful trappings. The light bounced off the sea onto the ceiling, and jumped around in playful pools above. Liza's attention was drawn to the bunk again, and as her gaze lit on the treasure chest at its foot, all her preconceptions about pirates converged to settle at that point.

Jill allowed the inspection, intuiting the effect a grounding of awe could have on a young servant. "By all means, acquaint yourself with my quarters, Liza. You will need to know your way around when you begin your duties."

Here Liza collected herself and studied the woman. This lady pirate would appear equally at home in a forest. Like some sylvan nymph from a fairy tale, she wore her hair long and loose, with strands of shorter hair overhanging her forehead. Her eyes were the deep, passionate blue of forget-me-nots. And she was impressive for one so petite, so slender. Her bearing, as Liza witnessed on deck during the mayhem yesterday, was regal. Yet her smile, icy when it was useful to be so, was enticing, as if it longed to give and receive kisses. Liza squinted, trying to remember her mother's smile, but the face in front of her interfered with her memory.

For jewels, this woman wore only the ruby necklace and two golden rings of filigree piercing her ears. Upon examination, the lady's unadorned arms seemed too free, as if they wished to bear the burden of bracelets. Now she waited, but before Liza's curiosity was satisfied, Jill spoke again.

"My proposal is this. I'm wanting an attendant, to look after my clothing and person. In exchange, you will be amply paid and provided room and board. And the protection of the captain."

The girl froze.

Smee nudged her elbow. "Miss, do you heed?"

Liza flinched at his touch, but nodded.

"Apparently, Mr. Smee, our little captive hears, but refuses to speak. We will humor her. There is no need for her to speak in order to serve me. I may even prefer it that way." Jill scrutinized Liza. "You look to be…" She chose to flatter the girl. "Going on fifteen?"

Another nod, and Liza felt an unexpected twinge of pleasure. She was going on fourteen.

"I believe that, like me, you have been brought up in a genteel manner. You know how to behave yourself. If you do so, and if you follow my instructions, you'll not regret your time here. I don't expect to keep you forever. When the proper time comes, you will be released. And then, if we agree, you may decide whether you wish to stay on. So you see, I'm not looking for a companion. Nor for a slave."

Liza indicated understanding. She wondered if she would be given a choice.

The lady's blue eyes were penetrating. "I also believe you are missing your deceased mother."

Liza blinked, then looked down and unclasped her empty fingers, spreading them.

"So I am correct in assuming you haven't a home to which you may return, other than the ship from which we plucked you?"

A lethargy overtook the girl. She shook her head. The lady lifted her eyes to Mr. Smee and regarded him for a few moments. Liza heard the man's breathing quicken. He cleared his throat. The woman's gaze dropped once again to Liza.

"The alternative to this service, or the penalty for disobedience, is to be put ashore. We aren't particular where. I should hope that if you cause such circumstances to arise, you won't be particular, either." She spoke casually, as if she had issued such threats a hundred times.

"My men have collected your things from the *Julianne* and you may keep them, whatever you decide." The lady raised her left hand to study her nails, then spoke again, seemingly in afterthought. "Oh, yes, we've taken your father aboard as well." She raised her eyes.

Liza startled.

"It is our hope, the captain's and mine, that Doctor Hanover will sign on as ship's surgeon, in which case you will share quarters with him."

Liza's face had become eager, relieved at the mention of her father, and in the space of a moment, it grew guarded, and the girl seemed to shrink.

"I see the thought does not comfort you. A pity. What is your decision, Liza?"

The girl in brown cast her eyes about the cabin, lifted her shoulders, and drew her eyebrows together.

"You are afraid. Of the captain?"

Plainly wondering how the woman guessed, Liza nodded, then aimed another look over her shoulder.

Jill noted the direction of the girl's glance, affirming Hook's evaluation of Smee's effect on children. She used it. "Mr. Smee. Kindly tell the girl what the captain expects of those who serve him."

"Aye, Madam. The captain demands that all hands follow orders, and that smartly. It's smooth sailing for anyone who does his job and makes no noise about it." He had a musical voice, the hypnotic lilt of an Irishman. Placing his heavy hand on the girl's shoulder, he regarded her over his spectacles. She swallowed.

"And stay below when there's action. You'd best keep out of the way when we're at work."

Liza's face soured. She remembered the work these pirates had done aboard the *Julianne*.

The lady collected her skirts and rose from the couch. "So there is nothing to fear if you do your duty. If you don't, there is always another island to call your home." She smiled. "What say you, girl? Shall you try the pirates' life?"

After only a moment's hesitation, Liza held up her hands and twisted an imaginary ring on one finger. Her eyes questioned.

The woman understood again, and raised a shapely eyebrow. "A ring was taken, by my men? Who?"

Liza thought, then reached over her shoulder to pat her back. Holding up her fingers, she shaped them into claws that scraped the air.

With a warm, indulgent smile, the lady nodded. "Mr. Cecco! Of course it was he. I might be inclined to see if he can be persuaded to give it up. Are you with me?"

Liza smiled as nicely as she was capable of doing. She hadn't had much practice.

"Very well, Liza." Her mistress extended her right hand. For the first time, the girl beheld the blood-red stain, palm to fingertips. Gasping, she drew back.

The gaudy hand remained extended.

"Liza."

Under the steely gaze of eyes that lost all likeness to flowers, the lady's hand turned, palm downward. Clearly, the opportunity to shake it in a friendly fashion was past.

Even Liza knew that only one course could be followed now. She took it. She reached her own hand out, touched the underside of the crimson fingers, and sank into a curtsy. As she looked down, she spied a slender foot peeping from beneath the lady's skirts. Except for a silver ring round her middle toe, her foot was bare. This queen wore no slippers! Startled, Liza dropped her fingers.

Her new mistress condescended to smile. "Very good. You have been warned. Serve me properly— and above all, keep out of the captain's way. Then all will be well with you. Tom Tootles will show you to your quarters now. Settle in, and Mr. Smee will instruct him to escort you to me before dinner. Your father will be dining with us, and we must prepare for a formal occasion." Jill turned away. "You may go."

Liza stood staring as the woman glided to the escritoire, seated herself, and picked up a quill, then the girl yielded to the pressure of Mr. Smee's hand.

"Come along now, Miss Liza." She preceded him from the room. Smee turned at the door and tipped his head to the lady. "Madam." Liza heard a smile in his voice.

As she picked her way down the steps, Liza was happy in a way. She'd get her ring back, her link to her mother. But at what price? Liza looked around her at the sailors on the deck, so big and rough and wild. Servitude, among all these strange people and their raucous voices, their demands. *Her* demands. The pirate queen.

And Liza had yet to meet the king. She shuddered to think of him. He must be horrible! Probably scarred and leering, bellowing orders, maybe missing an eye or a leg. Liza still couldn't remember her mother's smile, but she knew the mistress was like her, and yet not like her. She felt Mr. Smee's hand steering her shoulder. Soon it would be her father's again, the manicured hand for which she had longed while imprisoned, and yet from which she felt oddly free for a time, there in her cage.

The mistress was like her mother. Could the master be worse than her father?

"I can't figure her out, Nibs. She's nothing like Jill or the Indian ladies." Tom reclined on his hammock, just under his brother's, at the end of a long line of hammocks and sea chests below decks. Dusty daylight filtered through a porthole behind him. Having swabbed the deck beneath them, the newest sailors aboard the *Jolly Roger* kept their voices low to avoid disturbing the others at rest, those who guided the ship through the night.

"Well, that's it, isn't it? They're ladies. She's just a girl." Nibs the Knife had chosen the upper bunk, as his wiry frame was most at home high up in a tree, or nowadays, in the rigging. But Tom preferred to plant his ample feet on the ground— with one unusual exception. These young men were new to professional piracy, yet they commanded a talent most people, pirates included, would envy. The men of the *Roger* knew their secret, but the captain had instructed the ship's company to keep it quiet.

These youths could fly. Just a pleasant thought and a twist of the shoulders, and up they'd go, thanks to the magic of fairy dust and a childhood spent on the island of the Neverland with the wonderful boy as their chief. Ironically, it was that boy— Hook's enemy— whose training made them fit for piracy in the first place. By the time Hook got his claw into Nibs and Tom, they were eager to sign on. The more so upon discovering his ship's figurehead to be carved in the likeness of their mother, Wendy, now called by her pirate name, Red-Handed Jill. And only her captain and her sons knew for certain that she still took to the air as well. Hook was a wily man. They all trusted his judgment in the matter, and kept mum.

Tom locked his fingers together behind his head and listened to the creaking of the ship as she flew over the water. He liked her constant chatter. He was beginning to understand it. The ship and her men had a natural connection, but getting to know the girl would be more challenging. "Maybe I don't need to understand her. Maybe I just want to kiss her again."

Nibs sat up and goggled between his dangling feet. "Again? You never! Already?"

Tom smiled up crookedly, pleased with himself. "Well, I did."

"She's a *proper* girl! And just kidnapped by pirates." He smiled. "She slap you?" Nibs tightened the knot of the orange kerchief round his head, always his habit when concentrating. His swarthy countenance lit up as he beamed on his brother.

"Funny thing, she didn't! I fully expected her to."

Nibs leaned precariously farther, or it would have been precarious, had he not used his secret talent to balance on his perch. "Well?"

"She just stood there. I got the feeling she expected worse."

"Sure, but Jill's got her pegged for service. Better keep hands off until Jill says go." Nibs' smile contorted itself and his real objection bared its chest. "Dammit, Tom, you beat me to her!"

Tom sent a sly grin up to his brother. "I know. Next time we celebrate a prize, you'll let *me* finish the bottle!" But these boys had grown up together, at the very same moment. "You're welcome to her, Nibs, if you can get her. But after talking to her once, I think we'll both have to wait for port call."

"Aye, but Mr. Starkey warned me he'll keep a sharp eye on us, first time ashore."

"That's just because he's eager to get ashore, too. I'm not sure I'm ready for another of his lessons this afternoon."

"Knife-fighting this time. Fancy the poor boys he used to teach at that school! No wonder he's so scarred about the face." Nibs nursed his swollen knuckles. " 'Gentleman' Starkey sure packs a wallop with that ruler."

"Better Mr. Starkey's ruler than the captain's cat-o'-nine-tails. What he teaches us is for our own good. I don't want to fail my duty and find my back in shreds, like Mr. Cecco's."

"And all because of a woman! You realize, Tom, we've started down a slippery slope. It goes to show that better men than us have met their dooms over females like Jill."

Tom looked up at his brother. They both smiled broadly. "Aye!"

Nibs rearranged his nether regions, and lay down again. Tom wondered idly, "Do you suppose she's seen a knife-fight before?"

"She doesn't look like she's even seen a sailor before."

"I get the feeling she's seen plenty. She's just not talking." Tom sat up then, pulled the oiled rag from his pocket, and picked up his knife and whetstone. "Pass yours down, Nibs. I've got to get this energy worked off."

The men of the *Roger* would often remark after this day that the newest crewmen had the sharpest and the brightest weapons aboard. Even if they didn't use them very much yet.

Liza's tongue slipped between her lips as she tugged the lacing tighter. She wasn't accustomed to waiting on a lady. She was used to being waited upon, if only by her nurse. She was too old for a nurse now, but her father had insisted the woman remain so that Liza should be properly chaperoned, the sailors on the *Julianne* being, in his estimation, exactly like sailors aboard any other vessel. Liza wasn't very pretty yet, but what her sharp ears had overheard those sailors say was complimentary, if not polite. And her own lacings were feeling tighter every day.

Still, Liza didn't fool herself. She owned too much of her father's distaste for the ordinary to appeal to average men. It showed in her face as it did in his, something about the mouth that turned down instead of up, in spite of the generous lips. That same something about Jill's mouth turned up, always, Liza noticed as she stole glances at Jill's reflection in the glass. Even when the lady was displeased, as she was now, that something was alluring.

It made Liza want to please her, and she fought it.

"Don't be distracted, Liza. It's nearly time." Liza's fingers weren't as nimble as Mr. Smee's, but Jill observed that even so, the girl finished the lacing more quickly than he. Jill smiled to herself, but continued in a strict tone. "Next time don't discard my gown. It will wrinkle. You are to hang it in the wardrobe. Now fetch me the brush, please, and look after the dress."

Liza followed her orders, fingering the rich red taffeta as she worked, and wondering how to ask about her father. His situation puzzled her. Was he to be courted, or forced? Earlier, the mistress had directed Liza to the sideboard, and they set the dinner table together. Amid cheery clinks and pings, they laid out silver, creamy china, and crystal. Liza thought she heard the table service laughing in anticipation of the evening to come. As she crumbled lavender into the fingerbowls, the aroma reminded her of a starched, formal dining room left behind in England, with stiff brocade curtains, and doors opening onto an immaculate garden. But the mistress, unlike Liza's mother, was lighthearted, as if unafraid to seek pleasure rather than perfection. Liza's father would surely not approve of this lady— but he would find her interesting.

Liza had moved on to polish the harpsichord, startled at first by its frank tones, then lingering over them, and then she had brushed the plush fabric of its stool. It seemed there was to be music as well, and the lady slid on a pair of black satin slippers stitched with silver, slippers that simply demanded to dance. Liza had helped her mistress into a black silk dress with puffed sleeves, a low, square neckline and a full flowing skirt. She loved the sighing sound of it as next, the mistress moved about the room, setting out candelabra into which Liza pushed smooth, waxy tapers. But Liza didn't understand; the scene was set for a party, as if Liza's frowning father were a colleague, rather than a captive like his daughter.

While decanting the wine, Liza spilled a crimson splash on the sideboard. She expected a reprimand, but Jill handed her a cloth to wipe it up and, astonishingly, that smile appeared, and the woman dipped her finger into the pool of wine and touched a drop to Liza's lips. Liza's tongue got it before her hands thought to use the cloth. It tasted warm and mellow, like burning apple wood. And Liza remembered flaming sails over the water, and only then did she recall that she stood on a pirate ship, and that the finger that had touched her mouth was scarlet, and she grimaced and spit into the cloth. But it was too late. The taste of redness lingered, like blood.

Yet Liza wondered as she looked and listened, touched, smelled, and tasted. In all her life, she had never enjoyed such casual luxury. A very young woman, one who had been carefully watched in gentility, she couldn't help but envy her mistress the sense of freedom she exuded, and the pleasure of these surroundings. It was as if the stain on the lady's hand granted her not shame, but satisfaction. Was *that* the color Liza tasted?

There had to be a drawback. No doubt it took the form of the master. Liza was old enough to understand that one paid for one's pleasure. Her mother had paid, although Liza was never quite sure to which of her parents the pleasure had belonged. But she had no doubt that this lady earned every priceless day— earned them by the nights she must spend with the pirate. Liza shuddered. They would be long nights! The captain must be demanding indeed to repay her with all this grandeur. The man who granted such extravagance to his mistress must be rich, rough, and imposing. A man to be avoided. As the dinner hour approached, Liza found herself listening apprehensively for clues beyond the door, the first warning sounds of the two men who would rule her new life. Her father, and his captor.

The mistress, while seeming merely to supervise the girl's work, watched her closely, reading the emotions that played across her features. In spite of the gratification Liza displayed as she handled Jill's belongings, she had a dissatisfied face. Jill had marked her restlessness at the very first, in Liza's entrance alongside Tom. The girl was unhappy before she ever met a pirate. Beyond the basic discontent, Jill now detected Liza's apprehension, and drew her own conclusions.

She was well aware of the workings of a young woman's mind. While Jill tended her appearance before the mirror, she doled out information as it suited her purpose.

"You've no cause to be nervous, Liza. You'll not be serving us dinner. We will apprise your father of your presence then, and you will be reunited later. If he complies with the captain's terms."

Liza looked doubtful. In her memory, her father had never complied with anyone's terms but his own.

"The doctor is an intelligent man. He will be persuaded to look after his own interests, and yours." Jill adjusted her necklace. "You needn't come to me early tomorrow. We'll be up late, and you may use the morning to speak with your father." Her cool voice warmed. "Are you comfortable in your quarters?"

Astonished at the new, solicitous tone, the girl only blinked.

"All of this is new to you, I know, and perhaps frightening." Jill gestured her closer, then drew her toward the couch. "Sit down with me." She sat facing Liza, and laid a gentle hand on Liza's jaw to turn her face. She pulled the pins from the girl's hair and watched it fall untidily around her shoulders. Jill tucked the pins into Liza's pocket and gave the brown locks several strokes of the hairbrush, pushing them away from the girl's forehead before setting the brush aside. "That's better, isn't it?"

Liza shrugged, but moved her head to feel the swish of her hair. She liked the loose feel of it.

Jill smiled, pleased with the change, and bestowed an understanding look on the girl. "Liza, not long ago, I was new to this ship as well."

In spite of herself, Liza's face betrayed interest.

"But you're reacting to more than that, I think. It isn't only the ship and your new situation, is it?"

Curiosity crossed the young features.

"It is the excitement. The adventure." Jill watched, gauging her audience. "And there is much adventure to be found in our way of life. It is most exhilarating, if you are open to it." The storyteller had begun to spin her magic web. "You're beginning a new chapter of your life, Liza. Your tale can be far different than you imagined it might be. You may discover it to be a fascinating experience, after all."

The discontent was dissolving.

"What happens next is up to you. You can become a new person. A young woman."

Liza's face had cleared, like a blank page eager for writing. Plainly, she wanted to hear more. As promised to her captain, Jill had studied the girl. Her weapon had found the weakness.

"Growing up is a wonderful adventure. If you are brave enough to face it, change can be welcome. So many opportunities lie ahead of you, now that you're free of the old ways. New places, new people. New sights and sounds."

She had her now. "But it is somewhat overwhelming, is it not…" Jill tilted her head, "to be among so many men?" She waited for Liza's eyes to confirm it. Continuing more casually, she aimed her dart. "Presumably you will benefit from the guidance of your father. I'm sure he will counsel you wisely." Jill pitched her voice and thrust it, ever so softly, and right on target.

"But listen to your dreams, as well."

Liza was listening.

"You don't speak, but I know you listen, perhaps with more perception than others acknowledge. Hear your heart, also."

New words, words such as Liza had never heard spoken before. Spoken by that mouth Liza wanted to please. The girl moistened her own lips as she watched Jill's. What would they tell her next?

Next, for Jill— first, last, and always— came the welfare of the ship. Picking up the thread of Hook's warning, she wove it in.

"You are young, but not too young to think of male companionship. Keep an open mind. You may find my men colorful, interesting." She smiled. Liza hadn't yet realized what her eyes had seen among the sights on this ship. She realized it now. A consummate storyteller, Jill paused, allowing time to advance her purpose once again.

"If, after some time has passed, one or more of the men suit your fancy, you may consult me and I will be pleased to advise you. I only caution you to go slowly. Keep your distance from all of them, even my sons, in the meantime."

Liza gathered the implication. Jill would be watching.

Jill's enchanting smile softened the message. "I wouldn't be much of a mistress if I didn't look after you."

Liza wanted to keep that smile. She tried one of her own.

The mistress acknowledged it with a nod. "I want you to learn and to grow, as a young woman should do. But where the men are concerned, remember. What cannot be acquired easily is valued longer." She laughed as the question grew in Liza's expression. "Yes. I might tell you my tale one day. Even the captain had to struggle to acquire me. I believe he thoroughly enjoyed it."

Liza came to herself, blushing at the lady's forthright words. They roused the memory of Tom's kiss, her first kiss from a boy. There were no rigid restraints here. The crew aboard this ship, even the mistress, knew what they wanted and lost no time going after it. Liza wasn't used to people expressing their desires so honestly. She had been taught to keep herself in check. Her father was a model of self-control, at least in public. He had always controlled Liza strictly. And her mother.

And now this lady with her entrancing smile was showing kindness. The woman who had stolen Liza's freedom was offering liberty of a kind she'd never—

Liza's ready ears caught the cadence of steps on the stairs. She looked to the lady, who stood at once and turned toward the sound. The lovely face tensed with anticipation. Was it dread, or elation? Was the lady herself treated kindly? Was *she* free? And then Liza whipped around to watch the monster stalk into his den. She pushed herself up from the couch and shrank back, and her eyes opened as never before, preparing to take him in.

The door was thrust open…and the most magnificent man Liza had ever seen launched himself through it in a storm of black velvet, and entered into her awed imagination. Jill smiled on him, and in the instant became a radiant goddess. She held out her slender arms, and in two strides of his fine, shining boots, he had entered her embrace and engulfed her. His jewels glistened, and the flash of metal that was his right hand buried itself in the black folds of her skirt as the man kissed his mistress, mercilessly.

Forgotten, the girl stood staring, and felt herself disappear. In her mind, coming alive for the first time in years, Liza understood that she didn't matter for this space of time. She was no one, and she was listening to— was it love?

What else could it be? A man like that didn't waste time on sentimentality. Liza knew from her father's example. He had used to love her mother like that; he had loved to use her mother like that. Watching this pair was all the more painful to Liza because she also knew her father had stopped loving her mother, just before she died. Liza dragged her gaze from the pirate to her mistress, and wondered. As willing as she seemed, how long could such a fragile creature endure that kind of love?

But, careless of anything else, Liza's regard reverted to the man. So *this* was the pirate king! In one instant, he had far exceeded her expectations. She blinked and caught up her breath, and listened, watched, and even smelled him. The lady had been right. Right about everything. 'Overwhelming' was the exact word to describe this experience. And Liza now determined she would follow Jill's advice. She would keep an open mind.

And then the man turned to Liza. Unbelievably, his blue eyes took hold of her, and the silkiest voice she had ever attended spoke to her ears alone.

"You are dismissed."

She wanted to die. His was the voice she had waited all her life to hear, the perfect sound. His voice tore her heart apart, and in stopping, tortured her ears. And the moment he turned away from her, Liza did die. She ceased to exist. She had never existed— she closed her eyes and stopped breathing— because for this man, she had no purpose.

Not yet.

Still numb, Liza turned to the entrance and slipped away, out the door and down the steps of the companionway. She glided along, straight to her quarters, to shut the door without a sound and fling herself on the bunk and listen to her imagination as that pirate captain burst in and undressed her and bound her wrists together and kissed her, and ravished her with his lush voice. His hair felt like silk against her skin, and he smelled of leather; his mouth was firm and he tasted like strong spirits. She lay twisting and naked on her bed, breathing unsteadily and feeling the waves swell under the ship. Her heart pounded in her ears like the water against the wood.

Yes, Liza would keep an open mind. And an open body.

She didn't have to hear her father say it. She knew he would already be hating that man. And wanting that woman.

The woman with the smile Liza no longer wanted to please.

He would fall under the spell of that woman, exactly as Liza had fallen under the man's.

Liza rolled on her bunk and stuffed the pillow into her teeth, as she had watched her mother do, gagging herself so that her screams would be muffled as he had his way with her, over and over again, and not a soul would come to her rescue.

Reluctantly, the surgeon allowed the uncouth Irishman to usher him across the deck toward the upper aft cabin, under the quarterdeck. At least, like he, the sailor had made the effort to shave and don a clean shirt. In his morning pacing, the doctor had not encountered one man who came close to matching the social standing of the captain. Hanover wondered again what on earth motivated this Hook to take up piracy and embrace its necessarily low standards.

He was not looking forward to the ordeal of dining with a pirate of any class, but Mr. Smee gestured toward the steps, and the doctor applied himself to climbing them, deliberately slowing his movements. When he faced the door, he found himself confronted with a bold brass plate. In elegant lettering, it proclaimed the name of 'Capt. Jas. Hook.' As if the man took pride in his profession! Hanover just stood there, and the Irishman was obliged to push past him and do the knocking himself.

"You'd best get over it, Doctor. The captain will have his way, and you and I have nothing to say about it." The doctor disagreed, but his only reply was a twist of distaste along his lips. When the bo'sun's knock was not answered, Hanover turned his gray eyes to question Smee. Smee only grinned. "So you're in a hurry, then?"

The doctor was spared the burden of retorting by a female voice, surprising to his ear. The sound of it was all the more unexpected because it was such a calm female voice.

"You may enter, Doctor Hanover."

He stared at the door for a moment, intrigued, then decided to open it himself, if only to deny Smee the pleasure of responding to the lady.

He stepped into the cabin and entered another dimension. Nowhere had he experienced a more elegant and comfortable room, on land or sea. Compelled to regard the woman in the soft pool of candlelight, the doctor didn't see, but rather absorbed her environment. He stood collecting its comforts, taking in the sight of her. Smee had followed him in, and now prodded him to the center of the cabin. Making no sound, Hanover's soft shoes traversed the Oriental carpets toward the loveliest of visions. He was glad, now, that he had used his razor.

She stood by the dining table, the flaming taper in her hand reflected in the many bevels of the window behind her. "Thank you, Mr. Smee. Please join us at the table, Mister Hanover." She was smiling, dressed in black silk that contrasted favorably with the color of her hair. The doctor didn't approve of unbound hair, but in this case, he had to admit that its flowing fairness complemented the severe cut of her dark gown. She looked away to finish lighting the candelabra that gleamed on the table service. The skin of her arms, her throat, and the tops of her rounded breasts glowed in the aura of the candles. She set the taper in its holder and lifted the crystal decanter.

"Will you have some wine before dinner, Doctor?…Or would you prefer stale bread and water?" Her smile turned sly. Blood-red stones studded her throat, and a ruby line, clearly a recent cut, showed above them. The surgeon wondered; what had these barbarians put this young woman through?

"Mister Hanover?"

He blinked. Then he bowed. "Miss, I am at a disadvantage. I do not know your name, although you seem to be acquainted with mine."

"Yes. Will you take some wine?"

"Of course. Thank you, Miss…?" He raised his eyebrows.

Again, she ignored his question. "Mr. Smee?"

"Aye, Madam, just a drop." Smee stepped to her side and took over the serving. His movements were oddly gentle for a pirate, and a big pirate at that. He removed the decanter from her care as if it were too much of a burden for the lady's hands.

It was then the doctor saw her mark. He recoiled from the sight. What could be the meaning of this bloodstained hand? It was not an injury. His practiced eye determined that she used it easily and painlessly as she raised two shining goblets.

The doctor watched, and his lips compressed as Smee covered the beauty's fingers with his own, and poured the wine. Her left hand was unmarked. She offered one cup, the one in the crimson hand, to Smee, waiting until he had set down the decanter and grasped the glass before granting the other to the surgeon. Hanover accepted it, dropping his watch and allowing it to swing from its chain. She took none for herself.

"Doctor Hanover. Won't you be seated?"

Mr. Smee pulled out a chair, looking meaningfully over his spectacles. Awakening with a start, Hanover realized that Smee's goblet had disappeared. When he found the presence of mind to look for it, he noted an empty glass on the sideboard. Sitting down at last, the surgeon wondered how long he had been staring at the young woman, who had obviously been staring back at him.

The flush crept up his face again. Over the course of this afternoon's confinement he convinced himself he had been foolish; this young woman could not be as he imagined her during the stress of yesterday's events. Now he knew he was correct in this assessment, but in the opposite direction. She was even more captivating than he at first believed.

And bold. She stood unashamed in front of him, openly admiring his physical attributes, entertaining two men in a private room, and serving wine at a pirate captain's table— as if it were all quite proper! Unheard of, in the surgeon's experience.

"Who *are* you?"

She laughed. "So much for manners! Do I remind you of her so strongly, then?"

Hanover stammered through his astonishment. "I'm sorry. Yes, you do— And yet you don't."

"It's a fine excuse for a gentleman to stare, anyway, comparing a pretty woman to a loved one."

He shook his head. "I would not call you pretty, Miss."

The woman affected to be offended, and her smile disappeared. "Oh, really? How blunt you are. You can't be much of a favorite among the ladies."

Hanover shot a glance at Smee and became uncomfortable at the keenness of his regard. Standing with his arms crossed, the sailor exuded a protective, almost possessive attitude toward this female that caused Hanover to wonder again about her situation. He pressed a napkin to his lips to stifle a question, and then he lowered it. He had to ask. "You bait me, but you already know you are exquisite. Please, tell me about yourself."

She smiled in satisfaction. "Much better. And I regret to say that the captain neglected to inform me just how handsome and distinguished our ship's surgeon is." She looked him over once again, approvingly, then glanced over her shoulder into the shadows.

Hanover winced. Ignoring Smee's chortle, he recovered. "I thank you, Miss, for the compliment. I am not accustomed to young ladies who state their opinions so readily."

"How odd, Doctor, when you have stated yours without hesitation. But I pray you, don't change for my sake!"

Hanover inclined his head to her. "Very well, then, I take you at your word. You are incomparable! But how shall I address you? You are…?"

"It is my turn to thank you. And as comparisons go, I happen to have met someone recently who resembles you rather strongly—"

"Let us not bore our guest with petty social conventions, Jill." The low, smooth voice emerged from the darkness of the far window seat.

Startled, Hanover swiveled to locate the speaker.

"The man is positively panting to know who you are. Shall you have mercy, *ma belle dame*, or must I apologize for *your* lack of manners, and send you away in disgrace?"

The doctor threw down his napkin and surged from his chair. "No! Do not send the young woman away on my account. It is I who took an improper liberty. I shall be most grieved if the lady is punished for my sins."

"How gallant."

"Surely we must all dine together?"

With a languid grace, Hook rose from the cushioned recess. "I am pleased you have dropped your idle protestations about dining with pirates, Hanover. Allow me to pour you another glass. A fine vintage…from your former ship."

Abruptly, the doctor clapped his cup on the table. The fruity taste of the wine on his tongue turned sour. "No. No more. I won't partake of your ill-gotten bounty. Captain."

Jill removed his cup. "I see you are a man of principle." Warmly, she smiled upon him. "But you've already…'partaken.' " And she poured again. She lowered the decanter and lifted his glass. Automatically, his hand raised itself as she placed the goblet within his grasp, and he receded into his chair. She nodded once, and he drank.

Having digested this exchange, Hook strode to the table. Smee hastened to hold his chair, but Jill held up her red hand. She herself drew out the captain's chair.

"Jill." Hook touched her cheek and his eyes appraised her. "Do you not find the fairer sex captivating, Doctor? And so seductive, compelling even the strongest of us to do her bidding." Hook dallied a few moments, admiring her, then sat down to lean on the table, leaving one long leg extended outward. His lethal hook loomed over the glossy finish. As he gazed again at Jill, his face displayed the satisfaction her presence brought him. "One feels one would do anything to win the favor of such a creature." Smiling at her, he held out his hand. She placed hers within it and he kissed it, and then he turned to the surgeon, abandoning her hand as casually as if it had never honored his own.

Doctor Hanover frowned and searched the woman's face for enlightenment. "Jill?"

Hook waved his claw. "A common enough name. Now I believe you have some scheme or other to propose to me regarding the lady?"

The doctor forced his intelligent gaze from the fair face to Hook's. Business must be attended. "Yes." Sitting up, Hanover felt for his watch. "I offer you my services as ship's surgeon, for a specified amount of time, upon the release of this young woman. I ask that you return her to her home, wherever that may be."

"An interesting notion, Hanover." Still watching the doctor, Hook spoke over his shoulder. "Do you wish to go home, Jill? Here, it would seem, is your very last chance."

With an unreadable expression, Jill served Hook a goblet of wine. "You do enjoy tormenting me, Sir, don't you?" She raised her eyes. "As it happens, Mister Hanover, I come from London. The memory of my life there is like a pleasant old storybook that one doesn't pick up and dust off very often."

"But surely you have not been away from home for very long? You are so young."

"I really don't know how long I've been away. Time has lost track of me."

"Poor girl! And are your parents living, do they have any idea where you are?"

In a guarded movement, she ventured a glance at her master before replying. "I weary of the subject, Doctor. Tell me of your own history."

"Yes, Hanover. Do tell us how you acquired your mark of distinction, your dueling scar?" Hook gave a knowing smile. "Over a woman, no doubt?" His claw reflected the candlelight as, delicately, he tapped it on his cup.

The surgeon stiffened. "A point of honor demanded to be settled. I would be less than a gentleman were I to discuss it. Let us say no more." Drawn back to Jill, he said, "But, to answer your question, Miss, I come from Austria and attended an illustrious university in Germany. It is there I learned my profession, and also my fencing skills."

"And met your wife?" Her lovely eyes engaged his.

Hanover drew a breath. "No. I met her in England. Bristol, in fact. She graced my life for only a handful of years, and then she died. It was then I took up my duties as ship's surgeon aboard the merchant vessel that was so— tragically attacked yesterday." Hanover shifted his gaze away and repositioned himself in the plush chair. Providentially, his possessions were restored to him. He had been relieved in the extreme to find the valuable contents of his medicine bag intact. But these people knew too much already; he didn't want to inquire what they knew about Liza. Was she here, was she dead, or was she still aboard the ill-fated vessel he had called home?

"And why did you have to leave England, Doctor?" Hook's expression was mild. Jill knew better than to believe in it.

Hanover paused before replying. "Why did you?"

"*Touché*, Doctor!" Hook's laugh was generous. "I see you fence with words as well! That story is one for another evening, perhaps, when we know each other better." Hook pulled Jill toward him. He draped her arm over his shoulder and idly stroked it. Hanover noticed that her fingers spread over the man's chest, but whether in affection or resistance he couldn't tell. Hook directed the conversation back to business.

"So you offer me your service in exchange for my Jill. I wonder. Just what amount of your time do you think a woman is worth to me?"

"Of course I cannot know that, but I am willing to serve you for, say, a year, if you will grant her freedom and see her safely to port. I will be more than happy to arrange for her safe passage home, and to provide the necessary papers."

"Do have some more wine, Doctor." Hook signaled to Jill to replenish the glasses. Mr. Smee had turned his back to the company and was decanting another bottle. Hanover examined his goblet. He hadn't realized he had drained it. When Jill brought the decanter to its lip, he placed his open hand over it. Hook appropriated the flask and filled another goblet, which he handed to Jill, and the indispensable Smee stepped forward to hold a chair for her. Sweeping her skirts aside, she joined the company at the table.

Hanover observed Smee's hands resting just below Jill's shoulders, and, as his fingers lingered, she turned her head to acknowledge Smee. The sailor's embrace tightened on her arms before he returned to the sideboard. The surgeon's tone became urgent.

"I mean of course, that the young lady should return home *unharmed*."

Hook's smile was ironic. "On my honor as a gentleman, Hanover. I have never harmed her." He turned to Jill. "You have heard the doctor's offer, my love. I do have need of his services. What would you have me do with you?"

Hanover was fascinated by the cavalier manner with which the man tossed his hook in the air to accompany his words. He noted Jill's eyes following it, too, and that her breathing accelerated.

"Oh, Sir. You know my heart. But if you are truly giving me the choice, I would consider carefully before accepting any offer of return. I'm afraid what is called 'civilized society' might not welcome one such as I so readily back into it."

"So. It is as I feared then?" The doctor bowed his head. "You have already been compromised by your captivity." He lifted his face again to catch her expression.

Hook raised an eyebrow. Jill stared at the man sitting so very upright, with his gray suit and his gold watch. Her eyes narrowed. "I never compromise, Mister Hanover. But in the interest of harmony, I shall try to overlook your presumption."

Hook's face had hardened. "Yes, Hanover. Be warned. I should hate to have to call you out and carve you another scar."

As the doctor looked uneasily from Hook to Jill, he noticed the uncanny likeness between them. A similarity between their mouths. And their eyes— so perfectly matched. For the first time, it occurred to him that there might be more here than pirate and prisoner. He studied Jill more closely.

"I apologize for my misapprehension, Miss." His voice took on an unpleasant edge. "Or is it Madam? I simply seek to be of service to you."

Hook smirked. "There is no shortage of service to 'Madam' aboard the *Roger*. Is there, Mr. Smee?"

"Oh, no, Captain. And I'll be just as happy to go on doing the stitching that needs done if you decide to cast the gentleman adrift, Sir." Smee turned a cold smile on the doctor and Hanover recognized that, of the two of them, it was the educated and conscientious surgeon who was expendable.

"Thank you, Mr. Smee. It will be up to the gentleman himself to chart the next leg of his voyage." Hook directed a subtle nod to Jill.

She sensed it, although her gaze remained fixed on Hanover. "What of your own girl's service, Doctor? Exactly when do you intend to ask about Liza?"

Hanover became cognizant of three sets of eyes watching him with intensity, and, at last, his confidence was shaken. Now he knew. They had her. "I was hoping you knew nothing about her. But I see that you really did take everything of value to me. And of course, I *am* asking. Where is she?"

Leisurely, Hook sipped his wine. He set down his goblet, then toyed with it. He sent it sliding along the tabletop to clink as his hook met the stem. Never taking his eyes from his prisoner, he slid it and caught it again. "She has been persuaded to join up with pirates, Hanover. Your own daughter, compromised....But then, you can limit the damage to her, can't you, by staying on as well?" Hook set his goblet aside. "What do you say to a trial arrangement?"

Hanover turned pale with fury. "What *can* I say, but yes? Of course there is no question of leaving her here! But, what exactly do you mean when you say she has joined you?"

Jill's voice cut through his confusion. "Liza has agreed to stay on as my personal attendant. She will be compensated, protected, and not overworked. As I told her this morning, I intend to keep her for a limited time, unless the arrangement works to our mutual satisfaction and she chooses to stay longer. She knows you are aboard. She waits even now in your quarters." Jill watched closely, but the man's face had displayed no surge of tenderness at the mention of his daughter. Only a grim assumption of responsibility. Now he turned on Jill.

"So you have sold yourself to piracy? You, the captive, now have a captive of your own to give you some sense of power in your helplessness? And to think I sought to save you! I see now it is much too late for that. You are already tainted by—" he shot a look at Hook, "experience. And I am to be rewarded for my good intentions by seeing my daughter pressed into service along with me."

Hook drew himself up to an imposing height. "Do not presume to chastise my mistress, Hanover. Any insult to Jill is insulting to me. The *lady* is in no position to satisfy your urges, whether you desire to perform good works or to follow your baser instincts. There was never any question of putting her ashore, with or without you, and well she knows it. I see we do not agree, personally or professionally, but I will allow you time to adjust to your situation. There is no choice in any case, as we'll not be putting into port soon. And if your daughter is too good to wait upon my lady, then you are too good to attend to my men, and you can both enjoy the hospitality of my brig. Mr. Smee, kindly do the honors."

The doctor sat back in his chair and watched while Smee strode to the door and opened it, and a parade of willing servers entered the cabin with silver salvers to wait upon the diners. A sumptuous feast was laid before him. His goblet was refilled time and again. The lady, making the best of her circumstances, was charming and gay, and the captain warmed to regale his company in recounting the more colorful of his many voyages. After dessert and liqueur offered in exquisite crystal, cigars were passed with the lady's kind permission and the music began at the harpsichord and ended in song. And the lady consented to dance with all the gentlemen present, while the candles burned lower and the ship plowed on through unknown waters and the moon trailed her slippery silver strings in its wake, visible through the grand, velvet-lined windows of the very comfortable quarters of the quixotic, enigmatic, and apparently, even romantic, brass-plated Capt. Jas. Hook.

Doctor Hanover shook his head and doubted as he sat ensconced in a velvet chair, overwhelmed and fingering his watch, if he would ever manage to disentangle himself and his impressionable young daughter from this finely woven web of luxury, corruption, and delightful deceit. He watched the woman, this Jill, whose name was common enough, and wondered if she, herself, might be persuaded to be common, and if she already had been. And until he could lower himself to partake of her mysteries, did he really care enough for himself and for Liza to escape these barbarous pirates after all?

After a pleasant struggle, the rubies had been locked away, and the brace with its iron claw hung from its hook by the bed, swinging with the motion of the sea. Jill reclined in the master's arms, listening to the beams croon as the ship settled into the night, and considering the evening's events.

Hook was solicitous of his mistress. "A successful evening, but tiring for you. I suggest you rest, my love."

"And you, Hook."

"You must be aware by now that I am incapable of rest until *you* sleep."

"And you never knew what kept you awake, did you, until you found me?"

"My storyteller must be dreaming before I can close my eyes. And then she dreams more life into me."

Jill smiled to think of the power she held. "I will be kind, always, and ensure that you sleep. When it suits me." She stroked the neat whiskers of his beard. "But sometimes *I* like to be kept awake."

He laughed. "As I well know!" He trapped her fingers and kissed them. "And how did you enjoy our little dinner party?"

"You are a magnificent host, Hook! I believe our surgeon has already begun to recognize the benefits of employment in your service."

"And your service. You have the man at your feet. Rigid as he seems, you bent his will tonight, more than once."

"The doctor's attitude is certainly ambivalent. He seems both attracted and repulsed by me."

"I might point out your similar reaction to the doctor." As her eyes slid toward him, he half-smiled at her. "And I might not."

She matched him. "You must do as you see fit, of course." Unruffled, she went on. "He never once touched my right hand, even as we danced."

"I cannot fault him for that. It is much more pleasant for a man to slip an arm around your waist."

"It is much more pleasant for me as well....Did you notice how he keeps his affection for his daughter at bay? I believe he regards her more as a possession than family."

"Yes. I had assumed the girl's situation would grant us a secure hold on him. But I have now more accurately identified his weakness."

Jill pondered Hook's meaning, wanting to be sure she understood him. She remembered how possessively the surgeon's arms had held her, the strength of his grip belying his reserve. She recalled the intensity behind his gray eyes from the moment he first addressed her. Clearly, Jill had tapped a vein of passion under the man's controlled façade.

Now she smiled. "Hook. You mean me."

"I mean you."

"And your new plan is to use me to bind him?"

"I have already done so."

Jill's smile faded as she considered Hook, alarmed at first, and then her expression grew shrewd. As was her habit when discussing business, she addressed the captain formally. "Sir. Exactly how far do you wish me to take this game?"

"You must not engage in it at all— unless you play to win."

"A challenge, then?"

His eyes gleamed. "A gamble, with fabulous stakes."

"You know how such stakes tempt me."

"I am well aware, Madam, of your weakness. And your strength. I'd like to have observed the doctor's reunion with the very unusual contents of his medicine bag. My guess is it was much more tender than the reunion with his daughter."

"Different men value different treasure. And we'll have it from him."

"We have it now, but patience, Jill, will yield us more. If he can be persuaded to join us, all to the good. If not, we can at least discover the source of his mysterious cache. You will find a way."

"A way to win the game. But I don't accept him or his medicine at face value. Proper as he appears, my instinct tells me he is not entirely a gentleman."

"All the more reason to play."

Jill hesitated. "And…if he isn't a gentleman?"

"All the more reason to prevail."

She studied him, her head at an angle. "You are a fascinating man."

Hook raised an eyebrow. "Are you playing with *me*, now?"

"Mr. Smee thinks so. He doesn't quite trust you to me. Perhaps I'm only wanting your treasure, after all."

"But I trust you implicitly. I know for a fact you are after my treasure." He laced his fingers through her own. "I know you. You are my soul. But you understand, do you not, why I feign to esteem you so lightly before strangers?"

"Yes, Hook. You are protecting me— protecting us. Our adversaries mustn't discover that you and I are two sides of the same coin."

"No. Never expose our vulnerabilities. But we cannot be torn apart. And so, whatever game you play, you will do what you must, and always come back to me."

"And you will come back to me."

"No matter where I go."

"But there is *nowhere* I wouldn't follow you."

Immediately, Jill knew she had said the wrong thing. Hook glared at her, then sat up abruptly. He pulled her along with him, roughly, and seized her face between his hand and his broken wrist. Her eyelids fluttered in surprise. He controlled his emotion, but his voice conveyed his urgency.

"Listen to me."

She stared, unaccustomed to this rude handling. His piercing eyes transfixed her.

"When I go into danger, you must not follow." He shook his head. "As your lover I deplore it. As your captain, I forbid it!" His gaze raked her face, and fell to the scar at her throat. "You needn't prove your courage again." Savagely, he kissed the crimson line.

Jill tilted back her head. "Hook…" The ferocity of his embrace overwhelmed her. She plunged her fingers into his hair and drew him closer. "Captain." Caught up in his fervor, she felt the grip of a sudden dread, and she had to know. "What, then, would you have me do?"

Hook pulled back and shook his hair from her grasp. He was her commander now, at his most imposing. "You must do as I would do. Your duty is to preserve yourself, and preserve our ship, at all costs. If any undertaking calls me from you, the *Roger* is in your charge. While I am alive, you will feel it, and know that I will find a way to return to you here."

"But what of the men? Would they follow me?"

"You are my queen. As long as you conduct yourself as such, they will respect you. And you may always rely on Smee. He may not completely trust you, but he knows my orders. He will obey."

Jill was stabbed with cold. The ship pitched in the darkness, and the hook tapped sharply against the wood of the wall. Yet Jill's grip on his arms remained firm. "Hook. I don't want to be a queen without a king."

Unyielding, he said, "You will do what you must. With or without me." And then, more gently, "As you always have done. That is my order."

She closed her eyes, relieved to feel the burden of responsibility lifted by the captain's command. She couldn't guess how it might affect her, but the decision was made. "Aye, Sir."

Softening, he gathered her into his arms again, and, slowly, the cold receded from her heart. She opened her palm and gazed at it; he covered it with his own. Neither of them had forgotten who she was. Red-Handed Jill.

Her voice was steady. "What must I do now?"

Hook smiled, although she didn't see it. But she felt his body changing. Rest, apparently, would have to wait.

"You must do your duty. To your captain."

"Sir…"

"Madam. First answer the question I put to you before the doctor. What would you have me do with you?"

Her answer rushed out, passionate, "Take me home, of course!"

"I have already done so."

She looked down. Impatient now, she asked, "And have you any further unnecessary questions this evening?"

"Only one. You have won my love. But to what lengths will you go to secure my treasure?"

"Hook—"

"Jill." He pressed a finger to her lips. Once again, he made his orders clear. "Don't answer. Simply demonstrate."

She bit his finger first.

5
A Company of Gentlemen

Disregarding Jill's order to delay, Liza rapped early on the captain's door. She waited a moment, then Jill's voice answered, clear as morning bells.

"Come, Liza."

The girl entered, closing the door behind her without a sound. She kept her eyes lowered only until she dropped a curtsy, then raised an eager gaze to the bed.

The cabin was lit with morning sun where one bedside curtain hung open. The fabric stirred, as the sea with its invisible hand rocked the room. The aft and starboard draperies were drawn, and Liza in her brown dress stood like a shadow in semi-darkness.

Her gamble was rewarded. Jill didn't appear angry to be awakened. Better yet, Liza filled her eyes with the sight of her captain, just leaning on his elbows to force himself up against the pillows. She liked what she could see of him. What she could see of him was naked.

His blue eyes rolled toward her for only a moment, then, uninterested, his gaze shifted toward the sea. Jill reached for her dressing gown. As she wrapped herself within it, Liza had time to stare at the man, unobserved. His face and neck were darkened with the night's growth of beard. His hair cascaded over powerful shoulders, and his black-fringed chest swelled as he breathed in a draft of morning air. Liza was both relieved and disappointed that his right forearm remained under the bed linen. She had spent a good deal of the night wondering what his hook might hide during the day.

When Jill glanced again at the girl, she was staring, fascinated, at the wall beyond the bunk. Jill followed her gaze to the hook and its leather harness. "Liza, you needn't—"

A firm knock struck the door. Jill smiled at Hook. "We can't fault our crew for laziness, can we? Enter, Mr. Smee!"

Smee stepped in and halted when he saw Liza. He blinked over his spectacles. "Good morning, Madam, Sir. I see now why my knock at young miss' door went unanswered! I didn't open though, Miss Liza. Captain's orders that the surgeon and his daughter should be keeping their privacy."

Interested now, Hook looked keenly at his bo'sun. "Where is the surgeon?"

"In the galley, Sir, hunting up a mug of tea to settle his stomach." Smee grinned. "A fine dinner it was, Ma'am, but it seems the wine was a bit too plentiful."

Jill arched her eyebrows. "I found it to be perfect."

"It served its purpose." Hook leaned forward and rolled his shoulders. Liza watched as the bed linen fell to his waist. "What is our disposition?" With his only hand, he unhooked his harness from the wall.

Smee strode forward and took it from him. "On course and all clear at the moment, Sir. Mason sighted that ship again, early, but it seems to have sheered off to the north. Couldn't get a good look at it."

"Come Liza, help me dress." Jill crossed to starboard, threw open a curtain for light, and moved to the wardrobe. "Slide the drape closed, please."

Liza followed and, with reluctance, drew the velvet cloth that hung in front of the couch. It closeted her and her mistress in a tidy space that included the couch and the wardrobe. The girl's ears could still hear the captain moving, but her eyes were denied. His voice hadn't gifted her with a word yet this morning. Her ears were disappointed.

Jill pulled the brass handle of the wardrobe. As it opened, daylight from the portside window flashed within its mirror, until the door settled wide. "The brush, please, Liza. Thank you. Take down the gold taffeta for today."

As Liza ran her fingers over the gowns, she eyed the captain's coats. She glanced over her shoulder, and then she stroked them, each of them, black, red, tawny-brown, blue. The velvet felt soft and supple between her fingers. Warm. She seized the sleeve of the black coat and, stealing another glance at Jill first, buried her face in it. She breathed deeply, then dropped the sleeve and took down the golden gown. She had just laid it out on the couch when her mistress' next words startled her.

"Take out the captain's suit, Liza. The golden brown one." Jill smiled in that way Liza had found so enchanting, yesterday. "Captain Hook and I are a perfectly matched set."

Liza pretended to return the smile, and obeyed. With the clothing over her arm, she raised her hand to open the curtain.

"No, Liza. Give it to me." Jill held out her arms to take it. "Mr. Smee, I think this will do for today." She moved around the curtain, out of Liza's sight. The girl listened, and, to her delight, it wasn't Smee's voice that responded.

"Thank you, my love."

Smee's weighty footsteps retreated toward the foot of the bunk, and Liza heard a click and little stirrings as the shaving cabinet over the chest of drawers opened and its contents were removed. Then a silence.

Liza cast around to find a way to look and not be seen. She caught sight of the mirror on the wardrobe door. Her eyes widened.

In the quiet beyond the curtain, she saw Hook and Jill kissing. Jill's back was turned to Liza. Her face tilted all the way up, and Hook bent down to meet her. His hand was buried in her hair, supporting her head. His leather-strapped arm wrapped around Jill's shoulders, and from that arm, his hook hung harmless. Liza clearly saw the lady's sky-blue dressing gown, and on either side of it— Liza sucked in her breath. On each side of Jill stood a naked, firmly muscled leg, foot to thigh, braced against the movement of the ship.

Liza's jaw fell. Her breath became shallow, and very quick. The silence vanished, driven off by the heavy sound of her heart beating. As she listened to her heart, and stared, Liza could feel it as well, pulsing warmth throughout her body. Her face felt flushed and hot, and she beheld her mistress and her master until their kiss broke apart.

He still held her. With a twitch of his lip, the captain smiled at his lady, and he spoke over his shoulder.

"You came to us too early, Mr. Smee. But I assure you…I have roused now."

Jill gave a conspiratorial laugh, and Mr. Smee chuckled. At the sound of Smee's merriment, a thought occurred to Liza: a looking-glass reflected the couple from the shaving cabinet— from Mr. Smee's standpoint— as well.

Jill turned toward the curtain again, and Liza dragged her gaze from the mirror. With shaking hands, the girl dressed her mistress and hung up her robe. She fetched a diamond and opal necklace from its drawer and brushed Jill's shining hair, and when she'd finished these tasks, she was commanded to open every curtain in the cabin. She was surprised to find herself alone with the lady. Dazed by a vision of raw masculinity, Liza had tended the feminine chores without engaging her senses, unable to hear another word nor catch another movement from the opposite side of the velvet. Now, Smee and the master were gone. Overcome by what her eyes had seen, Liza's ears had failed her. She hungered to hear more, to see more.

Jill, looking lovely in the golden gown, commandeered the brush and smoothed Liza's locks again. "Your hair is most becoming down like this. It softens your features. But I see that you're anxious this morning, Liza. In time, you'll feel more accustomed to your situation."

The girl managed a nod.

"I'll speak to Mr. Cecco about your ring today."

Liza was surprised. Jill had remembered her treasure.

Liza had forgotten all about it.

"Starting tomorrow, please bring a tea tray each morning. Two cups. Cook knows how to prepare it for me. Now fetch my cloak. I want you to tidy the room and make the bed. That's all for this morning. I have some business to attend on deck, and then I'll spend the rest of the morning writing." She gestured toward the bookcase by the door. "You may borrow a book if you wish. There is nothing like a good story."

But Liza looked blank, and shook her head.

For the first time, her mistress seemed disconcerted. "You don't mean to tell me you can't read?"

Liza nodded.

Jill didn't hesitate. "We will begin tomorrow, first thing."

Liza shook her head vigorously, then pretended to take a watch from her pocket and finger it.

"As I told you yesterday, Liza, your father is an intelligent man. But he is only a man. You must not fear him. We will do what is best for you." But remembering the captain's warning, Jill stopped herself short. "No." This girl wasn't her family. "I will not teach you personally; I'll find another way. I must go now."

After Liza lowered a fur-trimmed cloak over Jill's shoulders, the mistress left her alone. The girl stood by the door and shut her eyes, breathing a sigh of relief. Idly, she lifted a cover of the bookshelf and stroked the textured bindings. The golden titles winked in the sunlight, but she found she'd never really cared if she could read or not. She still didn't. Like so many things, like Liza herself, reading had lost all importance after her mother's death. She had forgotten the few letters she knew then. But the leathery scent of the volumes reminded her of something else, and as she loitered by the case, she indulged in the one thing she did care about now. Closing her eyes to the books, she filled her mind with him, instead.

Then, like a good servant, she followed orders.

Liza was attentive to her work. After setting the dining area to rights, she approached the captain's sleeping area willingly, even eagerly. She plucked the shaving towel from the floor by the chest of drawers. Short black hairs resided in its soapy folds. After examining them, she leaned out a window and shook them into the sea. When the towel was neatened and replaced near the shaving stool, she tugged the bedclothes all the way down to the foot. Bending over the bed, she straightened the sheet in a manner to rival the most conscientious of chambermaids'. Her palms ran over the linen weave, and Liza caressed every wrinkle smooth, until the skin of her hands tingled and burned. Dutifully, she plumped his feather pillow as she hugged it, then held it to her face in case it might need airing. After scrupulous consideration, she determined it didn't. It smelled just right.

She shouldn't have been surprised to find his jeweled dagger underneath. She dropped the pillow to stroke it. The gems glowed in the sun, and the blade felt like solid silk under her finger. She replaced his pillow over the dagger and patted the other pillows into place, interrupting her tasks only to gaze out the window to see what his eyes had seen, and to touch the cold metal of the hook from which his leather brace hung each night— every night, while he eased his passions in this bed. She felt her pulse pounding again.

At last she drew up the top sheet, then the comforter. She folded it neatly beneath the pillows. Stroking its silkiness, she arranged it over both sides of the bunk. The side in which he had lain, and the side she coveted.

And then she balanced on the edge of the bed and looked up. She looked across the cabin. Her eyes observed the crimson curtain before the couch, open now, bunched and gathered at the end of its rail. She saw the curtain's velvet hem brushing the expensive carpet, no gap between them. The red drape swayed with the ship's motion, as if someone were already moving behind it.

Her eyes fixed on the mirror in the wardrobe. She imagined a slim girl reflected in the glass, concealed within the curtain and hidden in the shadow of nighttime, watching. Her hair was tucked behind her ears so that she could listen. She wore a brown dress, so that she would blend into the darkness. She never spoke. She was quiet, unobtrusive. The kind of girl to whom no one but hungry sailors paid any attention. She was barely breathing. Only her pulse pounded in secret as she stood stock-still, in her hiding place.

Yes, Liza saw it perfectly. That girl would never be noticed by the lovers moving together on the bed. She would see it all perfectly.

She would see it tonight.

Jill stepped from her quarters and pulled the cloak tighter against the mild morning chill. A quick survey of the ship showed that the scene was set and ready to begin. Yulunga stood behind the wheel, Mason perched in the crow's nest, and far less hands than usual manned the deck and rigging. A knot of sailors consisting of Starkey, Noodler, Cookson, Jukes, and Tom huddled by the forward capstan, while Nibs perched on top of it. All their heads turned toward Jill, watching as a distinguished gentleman in beige walked her way. The lady made her entrance, directing her steps toward the stairs.

Doctor Hanover had tucked a walking stick under his arm, and he carried a tray containing a single cup covered by a saucer. His sandy hair was combed neatly back and his watch pocketed in his waistcoat. Above his otherwise orderly appearance, the dashing slash on his cheekbone seemed out of place, hinting of a less orderly past. At the foot of the steps he halted to look up at Jill. With a curt nod, he smiled in his stiff manner.

"Good morning, Madam. I have brought you a cup of tea. And also, an entreaty."

She descended, one hand on the rail and the other on the clasp of her cloak. "If I accept one, must I accept the other?"

"To appreciate either one, you must accept my sincerity."

She stopped one step above him. "Mister Hanover. I am compelled to accept your logic, if nothing else." The morning was chill, but warming.

"Will you take the tea, then? I have put sugar in it, supposing that you like it sweet, and strong."

Jill smiled, raising the temperature by several degrees. "How clever of you to guess. Thank you." She accepted it, noting once again that his fingers didn't touch hers, and that the surgeon averted his gaze from her red hand. The stick under his arm, she observed, was carved into a ram's head, its ivory horns curling down like the handle of a sword. He set the saucer and tray on a stair, leaned his well-formed frame on his cane, and waited for her first sip before he spoke again.

"As for my entreaty.…Please accept my apology for the insults with which I afflicted you last evening. I very much regret that I behaved in a manner so unbefitting a gentleman."

The tea was hot. Jill didn't have to pretend to appreciate it. Cupping her hands around it, she drank. She lowered the teacup to study him over the rim. Then, glancing about, she lowered her voice and her eyes too. "You must not press me to play lady to your gentleman, Sir."

The surgeon also looked around. Yulunga's gaze bore steadily ahead, the men in the rigging rode high aloft, and, toward the bow, the other sailors oiled weapons and talked among themselves, chuckling every now and then. Hanover appropriated Jill's cup and set it on the tray. He offered his arm. "Will you walk with me?"

"Thank you." Skirting the cannons, the couple began a slow promenade along the starboard rail.

Hanover said, "Please, explain what you mean."

"I'm not sure I can explain to your satisfaction. Doctor Hanover, due to peculiar circumstances which I admit I cannot regret, I now exist in a most unusual situation. I have had to invent new standards as to what comprises a lady, and what makes a gentleman. My own rules, if you will."

Hanover believed he succeeded in hiding his distaste. "I suppose that is precisely what is to be expected on such a ship, full of those who prey on decent society and disregard its laws."

Jill's gaze engaged his. The tea left a sugary aftertaste at the back of her throat. "I cannot worry about what reputation society would lay on me. I am concerned only that the men aboard this ship respect me."

"Both your conduct after my rude behavior last night and your generous forgiveness this morning inform me that you are a lady. Why is it important to be respected by such men?"

"Such men make up my world, Sir. The *Jolly Roger* is now my home. And yours."

"I tried to change that for you. Quite unsuccessfully, I am afraid."

"You mustn't blame yourself, Doctor. Captain Hook is a powerful man, a master of manipulation. But, as strange as it seems, in time you may come, as I have done, to admire him."

"It is not likely. I won't be mastered."

"You won't think you are mastered. You don't know him yet, and by the time you do, it will be too late. You will have willingly given him all your secrets."

"Fortunately, I have no secrets."

"Everyone has secrets. But now you challenge me." Her smile was intriguing. "Now I must know what you hide."

Hanover laughed, a short, forced gust.

"Ah, there is one secret revealed. You *do* laugh. I had begun to wonder."

"Madam, tell no one. I have a reputation to protect!" But his smile fell away, and he bowed his head. "I am sorry. I was insensitive to make such a remark when we have just been discussing your own reputation."

"No, Doctor Hanover. I think you quite remarkable. I will find it most interesting to watch you preserve your integrity aboard our ship. And your secrets."

"You think me remarkable? I am flattered. It is…more than I had hoped."

"You set your sights very low, then."

"It seems that I set them too high last evening. I confess I was disappointed."

"I know better, Doctor. A man as accomplished as you will not give up after one disappointment."

The surgeon halted and turned to look on her. His eyes were interested, curious. "Again, Madam, your candor gives me pause. I am not good at games. Are you encouraging me?"

She smiled, half-way. "I am very good at games. I don't give my strategies away."

"How can I know, then, what is play and what is real?"

The lady dropped her levity. "When you know me better, Mister Hanover, you will know that I always tell the truth."

She tried to walk on, but his sudden pressure on her arm restrained her.

"Then you will answer me truthfully. *Are* you encouraging me?"

She looked down at his hand, then up to his face. He relaxed his grip.

They continued their walk, in silence.

As they neared the cluster of sailors, Jill acknowledged them. "Gentlemen."

The men inspected the surgeon, but greeted the pair with bows to the lady and cheery good-mornings.

"Are you all acquainted?" she asked.

"Aye, Ma'am, Mr. Smee saw to it earlier."

"Good. Where is the captain?"

"In the galley, Ma'am."

"I see. Mr. Tootles, is it fencing today?"

"Aye, Lady. Mr. Starkey's orders."

"Quite right. I may join you tomorrow. Mr. Nibs, please send Mr. Cecco to me at the change of shift."

"Aye, aye, Madam!"

The pair walked on toward the armory under the forecastle and crossed to port, the gentleman's stick tapping slowly, every other step.

He commented, "This morning I was given to understand that those two young men are your sons."

"Yes. I am very proud of them. You might say I adopted them, when I was quite young."

"Most unusual. And they consider you to be their mother, yet, I observe, they address you formally."

"Ship's discipline, Doctor," she replied. "I'm sure you understand the concept very well. Neither Captain Hook nor I will tolerate favoritism. It breeds no end of trouble."

The surgeon stole a glance at her face. "Yes, certainly. But Captain Hook allows you personal involvement with some of his men? Your Mr. Smee, for instance?"

"Mr. Smee is the exception to every rule." She watched his eyes. Was that a flash of jealousy?

"Is this not a form of favoritism?" His clipped tone conveyed only a hint of irritation.

Not disguising the warmth of her affection for the bo'sun, she smiled. "Perhaps it is. As I say, Smee is the exception."

"The man appears to me to take liberties with the captain's trust."

"You begin to sound as if you care— about the welfare of our company."

He attempted to make it a simple observation: "He touches you."

"You, Sir, are touching me now."

Looking down at her hand on his arm, Hanover registered the truth of her statement. He bent his elbow further to secure her grip, but otherwise allowed the comment to pass.

"This Mr. Cecco for whom you send. Isn't he the Italian, with— I'm sorry. The subject is most unpleasant. Never mind."

"Yes. He is the man with lash-marks on his back."

"Barbaric!"

"I would appreciate it if you would examine him to see that his cuts are healing properly. Tell him it is my wish."

"I will do so, of course, but it is too late. The man will be hideously scarred for the rest of his life."

Jill dropped the doctor's arm to lean on the portside rail. Her voice when she spoke was quiet, but firm. "Sir. You and I both know that one can live with scars. We can even take pride in them."

"It is one thing to have a mark accidentally or honorably inflicted. It is quite another to suffer from intentional cruelty."

"And another to commit dereliction of duty."

He paused. "And Hook ordered this done to him?"

Jill lowered the temperature once more, turning a stony look upon him. "I will tell you the truth, Doctor. I was the reason for Mr. Cecco's punishment. I might have stopped it. Instead, I insisted on it."

Hanover's face contorted with incredulity. "But how— how could you cause such torture to be inflicted?"

Clearly, Jill's confession had dealt a blow to the surgeon. Now she looked out to sea, allowing time to deepen his wound. Eventually she answered.

"I don't expect you to understand. You cannot see the need, but believe me, Doctor, in such matters, the manner in which I am regarded by this crew is my only interest. My survival depends upon it."

He, too, rested an arm on the rail, and as he stood, his posture stiffened. "No, I admit that I cannot see the need to impress these buccaneers. Please enlighten me."

"Doctor Hanover, you are a strong man. You were taken aboard this ship as a prisoner, yet now you stroll among her crew unafraid. You are skilled, you are able to defend yourself." She turned to face him. "How if you were a woman? What then?"

His eyes lit with understanding. "Madam, I begin to comprehend."

"It is no longer as simple as right and wrong, as what is proper and what is not. Is it?"

"Yes, yes....I see. You are caught indeed, in a delicate situation."

Jill restrained a smile. She could see the particulars of that 'delicate situation' taking shape behind his eyes. He wanted to believe the best of her. How else could he justify his attraction?

She said, "Last night I disappointed you. I am not a maiden in what you perceive to be distress."

"Perhaps, nonetheless, you require the services of a white knight."

"I prefer dragons. A woman knows just what to expect from them."

He studied her face. "My Lady. You have done what you had to do."

She waited a moment, and then she deliberately laid her crimson hand, the one she knew revolted him, upon his arm. "You understand, then?"

He stared at her hand. "I see now. You are not to be censured. Quite the opposite; you are to be commended for upholding your standards, and for gaining the cooperation of these— well, what else can I call them? Pirates."

"Pirates. Yes. We are *all* pirates." Her regard grew keen. "We all have hidden treasure to protect."

The scar on Hanover's face twitched. He changed the subject.

"I have wondered from the first." With his cane, he gestured behind him. "Excepting your sons, of course, these sailors are obviously common men. But how does a man born into gentility turn to such a life? Surely Captain Hook has always commanded the best that polite society can offer?"

"I cannot tell you his story. Only mine."

"And *will* you tell it? Will you tell me how you came to be marked in such ways? Your hand," he hooked the ram-horned stick on the rail, and brought himself, at last, to lay his hand over hers. His eyes rose to her scar, "Your throat?"

Jill slid her fingers from the heat of his hand and grasped her cloak. "I'm sorry. I find after all that I prefer you not to touch me. I am touched by so many here. But you are different. I believe you understand the meaning of your touch, and you will, therefore, honor my request."

Immediately, Hanover bowed. "Of course. I will respect you, and in the true sense of the word."

Jill's gaze filled with gratitude. "It is most satisfactory, Sir, to be in the company of a gentleman. I find your attentiveness very agreeable. Even—" She looked down.

With mounting hope, he studied her. "Yes?"

"No. That will be *my* secret." She allowed a smile to cross her lips, then turned toward the sea and touched her throat, lightly. "But to answer your question, the wound you can see was not inflicted by pirates, Doctor. I innocently placed my trust in one who was not deserving, and one day found a knife at my throat. Hook delivered me from that innocence. It was he who saved my life. I owe him a great deal, and I learned from that experience." She smiled. "It is part of my pirate treasure."

"And— forgive me for asking— your hand?"

Straightening, she faced him. "Among my men, I am called Red-Handed Jill."

"He named you this?"

"No. I chose the name. And I chose the mark."

"It would appear to be—"

"Blood. Yes. It is Captain Hook's. And someone else's."

"But, ah…what is the nature…Whose—?"

"It is the blood of a girl. She no longer lives."

The meaning of her words struck him, and he recoiled. "So! The captain saved you from a knife at your throat, only to take your life himself, in an even crueler way! And in some heathen blood ritual?"

Her temper flared. She seized his hand and forced his wedding ring to the level of his face.

"Have you never murdered a girl, Doctor, in just such a way— in the ritual of the wedding night?"

He stood frozen, speechless.

"I think you are no more innocent than the rest of us!"

The dueling scar became an angry line on his cheekbone. "Madam!"

She almost laughed, but her eyes blazed as she dealt the final blow. "Welcome, Sir, to the order of gentlemen— aboard the *Jolly Roger!*" Then she turned on her heel and left him, flinging her cloak over her shoulder and moving in light, quick steps toward the helm.

The surgeon watched her go, staring in an ungentlemanly fashion. The lady exchanged a word with Yulunga, who bent to hear her as he stood behind the wheel, his huge shadow falling over her brightness, and then she lifted her skirts and continued up the steps of the companionway, passing Liza coming down. She nodded to the girl and glided on to enter the captain's quarters. Liza turned to watch her. The door closed, and Doctor Hanover heard, all the way across the deck, the click of the brass bolt as bloodstained fingers shot it home.

Behind his back, the huddle of sailors had fallen silent, grinning and exchanging glances. Mr. Starkey jerked his head at Nibs, who slid off the capstan and silently headed for the galley.

Hanover blinked, and his fingers felt for the neglected watch. She couldn't know…There was no way for her to know!

But the lady had shocked the gentleman in beige, utterly and completely. She had shaken him right down to the soles of his soft-leather shoes.

Why, then, in heaven's name, was he smiling?

Liza collected the tea tray and turned to study her father. It had been long since she'd seen him that way. He was smiling.

She knew why.

Just as Liza had foreseen, he'd fallen under the enchantment of the pirate queen. The storyteller. She'd overheard the men call the mistress by that name in the morning as she'd loitered outside the galley, listening. The storyteller had woven him into her web, just as she'd done to Liza yesterday.

Liza couldn't read, but she knew herself to be smart. She had broken free of the lady's silken strands, but for all his manners and book-learning, the reality was exactly as Jill had told her— her father was only a man. He wouldn't break free of the lady's tangle, even if he did feel the strangling threads at his throat. He would let her suck him dry.

No, he would *make* Jill do it. And Liza knew how. Her father would apply his very special skills, and then he and the mistress would feed on each other until there was nothing left. Except the captain.

One good thing about life aboard this pirate ship, Liza thought as she made her way forward. She was learning how to smile again.

Lowering his gaze, her father noticed her. The softness in his charcoal eyes hardened, and he snatched his cane from the rail. Waiting for her to come to him, he appeared to Liza, once again, like what he was. A gentleman, with a stick and a scar.

He pitched his voice discreetly so that none of the men might hear him. "Liza! Take that tray to the galley and get to our quarters. We have matters to discuss. And for God's sake, girl, pin up your hair! You look like a strumpet." He thumped the tip of his cane on the deck for emphasis and strode toward the hatch without its assistance. For all his temper, he moved with grace, swiftly descending below.

Liza didn't know she hadn't moved until Tom was there in his yellow shirt, taking the tray from her hands and bending his head to look into her eyes.

"You go on, Miss. I'll take care of this tray for you." Tom stole a glance at Mr. Starkey, who stood glowering with a cutlass in his hand and a sturdy schoolroom ruler protruding from his pocket.

Tom turned back to the girl. "Here, then." Balancing the tray in one hand, he pulled out his polishing cloth. His dagger gleamed, sharp and secure in the grip of his belt. He snapped the rag loose. Dabbing at the tear swelling in each of her eyes, he was careful to keep his distance.

"Just to touch you would fetch any of us a beating— the captain's especial order— so I'm not allowed to kiss you again. However much you want me to." He smiled at her indignation. "Ah, Miss, I can see you're disappointed!"

He had guessed correctly; his banter was just what the girl needed.

Shoving his hand and his rag away, she glared at him, then stalked off toward the hatch, her brown skirts swishing, wiping her nose with the back of her hand. No sailor lad would pity Liza Hanover! She was a queen's lady. When she chose to be.

Tom nodded at her angry backside and stowed the rag. Tucking a thumb in his belt, he swaggered over to his mates, who eyed him with raised eyebrows and new respect.

"Well," said Mr. Starkey, his head at an angle. "Aren't we the gentleman, now! You're learning Mr. Smee's way with the ladies, aren't you— *Sir?"* His scarry face soured. "I won't warn you again. Now pick up your sword and show me what else you've learned, you randy billy goat!"

Tom just had time to seize his weapon. The tea tray smashed on the boards as yet another fencing lesson began, accompanied by the howls and laughter of Red-Handed Jill's lusty gentlemen.

At the change of shift, Mr. Cecco knocked just below the polished brass plate bearing his captain's name. Like all shining metals, it drew his eye. He wondered if he heard or if he imagined the song of his lady's skirts, and then the door opened.

Jill inclined her head. He bowed, taking in her beauty as he did so. He didn't have to speak his appreciation. His dusky eyes said it for him.

"Madam. You wished to see me." His smile flashed like his bracelets.

She stepped onto the companionway. "Yes, Mr. Cecco. Concerning a ring belonging to the girl."

"Ah, yes! The pink pearls."

"Liza has asked for its return, and as a gesture of good faith at the beginning of her service…"

"Of course. I have no attachment to it. Like the girl, it is only a trinket compared to the magnificence of her mistress."

Jill smiled, but made light of the compliment. "Then why did you take it?"

"Madam, like you, I am much attracted to beautiful things. Nor do I have to look far to find them." He stopped smiling and stared directly into her eyes. "When something lovely becomes available to me, I take it."

Jill felt herself pulled, like metal to a magnet. But, regaining her poise, she laughed, and put him in his place. "Right off the finger of a girl!"

Cecco shrugged. "A girl today. Perhaps tomorrow, a woman."

The lady was not unmoved, but she was shrewd. She returned to business. "What will you require in exchange for this 'trinket,' Mr. Cecco? I wish to be fair."

"I wish only for you to think well of me, Lady. Or simply to think of me. That is all. A fair price, yes?"

"It is no price at all, yet I will honor it."

"The next time your little girl comes to you, she will receive her pearls. May they make her as happy as they have made me." Cecco slid his hand into his pocket and pulled out the ring. He held it up between the supple finger and thumb of his right hand and, cordially, he offered it to the lady.

"Thank you."

He had anticipated this moment, imagined it many times. It played out just as he had hoped. Cecco watched avidly, savoring it.

Jill raised her forearm. Her hand turned upward. Her scarlet fingers banded together to accept the little object. She reached out to him…and he touched her.

He placed the fingers of his left hand under hers. He bent his head to her hand, and he kissed her ruby palm. Startled, Jill pulled back, her smile frozen. His lips pressed warm upon her skin, and then he removed his fingers from hers.

She didn't want to obey the urge to look at his face. She looked at her hand. The smile slipped from her lips, and she stared as she comprehended what she held. A little golden ring with two pink pearls, nestling in her palm. His right hand, which seemed not to have moved, was empty.

Cecco, her devoted sailor, smiled a secret smile, all the way from his lips to his eyes. His voice entered her ear, intimate. "I thank you… *Bellezza*."

Jill didn't see him stride down the steps to take the helm. She didn't see Yulunga turning back to the wheel, grinning. She was gazing into her palm, trying to understand what had happened.

Yulunga could have told her.

It was gypsy magic. And not the last of it.

Old Acquaintance

It was late afternoon and the captain was at the wheel when the call came from the crow's nest. Jill stood before him, learning the feel of it, the pulse of his ship. The first things she'd noticed were the scars on the wheel, wherever her right hand settled. His hook had left its signature in sharp, dry cuts within the spokes and on the handles. Now, standing with her arms just below his, Jill was learning the names of the sails, and the manners of the winds, and how best the two should meet. She was still new to sailing, and Hook was teaching her with words, to begin. The rest she'd have to learn from the sea's lessons, on the voyages that lay ahead.

Jill looked up at the surging canvas, rising in layers of elegant tiers. She sensed Hook following her gaze. If this ship could fly, these sails would be her wings. She was a bird of prey, stretching out white and borne on the wind, but she flew in her own way, skimming over the sea. Jill had seen her from above, a master-crafted gem set in the ocean, her decks and her crew worth more to Hook, perhaps, than all his other treasure combined.

Hook read her thoughts. He leaned close to her ear so that his whiskers brushed her. She closed her eyes to feel him speak to her.

"Perhaps tonight, if all is quiet—"

"Sail ho! To portside, Sir!" Jukes' voice sang out from above. The deck hands rushed to the rail, and Hook turned sharply to port. Jill could see a speck on the water some leagues away.

"Take the helm." He left her, snatching up a spyglass and striding to the side. He supported the glass in the crook of his hook, and watched in silence. The sailors surrounding him caught his tension. They were suddenly alert, excitement coursing through their veins, and more men soon assembled though the bell on the quarterdeck had not yet summoned them. Smee materialized at his captain's right.

"Sir? The lads are ready."

"Thank you, Mr. Smee." The breeze buffeted the feathers on the broad hat brim, but otherwise the captain was still. Nibs, standing with the rest, quickly tired of waiting and shoved away from the gunwale to leap up the ratlines to the crow's nest. He swung his lanky limbs over its rail and hopped down next to Jukes.

"Have a look, Mr. Nibs, and see if you can spot her flag before the captain does. Look sharp!"

Nibs grasped the glass and focused. The speck, magnified, became a ship, and the ship inched nearer, rounding to bear straight for the *Roger.* "She's—"

"She's French! We know her."

Nibs lowered the glass and shrugged at Jukes. Jukes' tattoos contracted as he winked, taking the instrument back.

Hook handed his spyglass to Smee and squinted at the horizon while Jukes confirmed the captain's words.

"It's *L'Ormonde*, Sir! Still flying the French colors!"

"No need to hide ours, then. Run up the Roger!" As soon as the black flag unfurled to grin in sunshine, a puff of white smoke erupted from the starboard side of the oncoming ship. Several seconds later the shot was heard, a peal of distant thunder. Hook exchanged a significant glance with his bo'sun.

"She has business with us."

Smee snorted. "What business would that little rooster be having with us, I'm wondering?"

"Something important to him, otherwise he'd never cross my path."

"Shall we finish it once and for all, Sir?"

"I think not, Mr. Smee. He amuses me. More importantly, his ship rides high in the water."

Smee spied through the glass. "Aye, nothing there to be bothering with."

"Furl sails, and fire an answering shot."

"Aye, Sir." The bo'sun turned to the men. "Away aloft! Furl sails!" The deck gang swarmed up the ratlines and manned the yardarms to clip the *Roger*'s wings. Smee picked out Starkey in the crowd. "Fire one shot off the bow!"

Starkey bobbed his head. "Aye, aye! Mr. Nibs, Mr. Tootles! You heard the order." Tom looked up at Nibs, who swung easily down from the crow's nest, and under the direction of their tutor and the master gunner, the new sailors applied themselves to the forwardmost cannon.

Smee turned back to his captain. "We'll make him welcome, then, and see what he's about?"

"Yes, a cask in the galley. I'll allow a small party to board. But set some men on watch. These privateers have light fingers." The *Roger*'s gun exploded with a boom that lodged in the chests of all aboard. Erupting from a shroud of smoke, the iron ball arced, whistling far across the waves, and, having served its purpose, plunked into the sea. The gun backed off like a stubborn mule, bouncing against its breechings. Smiling, Tom dusted his hands on his britches and Nibs whipped his orange kerchief off his head to beat it against his thigh. He waved it at Jill before tying it on again, and she saluted them from behind the wheel.

Always on guard for the mistress, Smee saw her. He asked the captain, "And Sir," he cocked an eye toward the helm, "What about the lady?"

Hook raised his chin. "Nothing to fear there, Mr. Smee. Captain LeCorbeau is impervious to feminine charm. But I'll attend to her; you watch the ship. Assign someone to the helm. My lady and I must lay our plans. You may report to me in our quarters."

Smee nodded and tramped up the deck, calling and gesturing. "Mullins! Cecco! And you, mate…" He spotted Yulunga and jerked his head to avoid speaking the ill-omened name. "You're to keep strict watch on these Frenchmen. Cap'n's wanting to show them his hospitality, but not too much of it."

Hook returned to Jill at the wheel. "My love, it seems we must prepare for visitors. An old acquaintance. Will you join us in the galley?"

"Of course. But who is it?"

"DéDé LeCorbeau. A privateer. More accurately, a pirate, with papers to prove it."

"I see. A rival?"

"He flatters himself so."

"French?"

"With all the name implies."

"I'll see that Liza hides away, then."

"No need. More to the point, keep an eye on your sons. The man is like a magpie. He'll steal anything that catches his fancy."

Jill raised one eyebrow. "Indeed? I have been warned."

"I will join you in our quarters shortly, Madam. We shall map out the evening's events."

"Aye, Captain." She turned away, leaving the helm to Hook and nearly colliding with the surgeon.

"My apologies, Madam." Hanover steadied her, then, catching her eye, grew conscious of his touch. He let go of her. "What is the commotion about? And the cannon fire?"

Looking past him, Jill saw Liza standing, watching, by the hatch. The girl had pinned her hair up and changed into a more attractive dress, blue trimmed with white lace that suggested a lower neckline. The bodice laced tight in front and the skirt rippled in the wind. Liza stood in an awkward pose, leaning her weight on one leg.

"Doctor. Those were hailing shots. A ship has been sighted, a French privateer with which the captain is familiar. We will welcome her *commandant* and a few of her sailors aboard. You may join us if you wish."

Immediately, Doctor Hanover's attention shifted to the approaching vessel. "Excuse me." He marched to the rail and stared at the approaching ship. Jill noted the rigid line of his back, and his face paling beneath his scar. He stood for some moments as if rooted to the deck, then his posture relaxed and he took a long breath. He reached for his watch, and, abruptly, he called to his daughter.

"Liza!"

She looked to her mistress, who consented, and then she hastened to her father's side. Jill thought the girl lurched a little. She didn't seem as steady on her feet as she had been that morning.

"Fetch me my cane, and then you are to stay well away from these brigands, do you hear?" Having dismissed his daughter, Hanover turned away to study the progress of the privateer.

Again, Liza glanced at the lady, then slid silently away.

As Jill watched the doctor, she felt her attention drawn toward Hook. He was standing tall behind the wheel, his earring gleaming in the slanting sunlight, regarding her with a question in his eyes. He, too, had caught the surgeon's reaction to the sight of *L'Ormonde*. The three figures stood motionless beneath the activity in the rigging.

And then, amid the shouts and the shufflings of canvas, the doctor surprised them.

"So," he remarked as he addressed Hook and Jill in his most cordial tone. Unnecessarily, he tugged his irreproachable waistcoat into place. "It is to be another party tonight, with privateers! I wonder. Are we raising our standards, Madam, or lowering them?" He regarded Jill quizzically, and she saw the smile break through his generous lips, and then the doctor loosed his quick gust of a laugh.

Jill looked sly. "It is as I told you, Sir. We are reinventing them."

Hook smiled shrewdly. "An interesting question. I will leave the final assessment up to you, Hanover. You are a man of science. Like the rest of us, you should enjoy the experiment."

On board the *Jolly Roger* at last, Captain LeCorbeau cut a jerky bow, smiling. "*Alors, mon ami!* It has been long since we have shared the pleasure of a meeting." His hair was tied back with black ribbon, the shorter hairs in front spilling over his forehead. He was dressed in his splendid best, an embroidered coat of auburn and brown, iridescent like a cock's tail, with shining brass buttons. Supervised by Mr. Starkey, Nibs and Tom were stowing the planking. Mason had joined Jukes in the crow's nest to keep an eye on *L'Ormonde*, which floated to a safe distance to await her captain's return. She had watchers of her own on guard; her sailors lined the rail, weapons discreetly but handily near. Both ships had furled their sails and now lay bobbing at anchor, at the whim of the sea.

Flanked by the musculature of Cecco and Mullins, Hook stepped toward his three guests. Beneath his gem-studded hat, his sleek black hair fell like a lion's mane. "LeCorbeau. I was thinking the very same thing. To what twist of fate do we owe today's fortune?"

LeCorbeau pulled his attention from the two young men working by the gunwale, his lace cuffs fluttering as he answered. "Eh, merely a happy accident. So kind of you to invite us aboard for a taste of Hook's famous hospitality." He stole another quick glance along the deck, then, "Sir, may I present my first officer, *Monsieur* Renaud. My second, *Monsieur* Guillaume. *Mes hommes*, the legendary Captain Hook!"

Renaud and Guillaume, dressed in uniforms of red and blue and brushed to perfection, bowed formally, but remained silent. They were under strict orders.

Hook inspected the two dapper officers with an indulgent smile. Any one of his men could snap these gentlemen in two. As he gestured, his hook flashed in the late sunlight. "May I present my bo'sun, Mr. Smee, whom you already know, LeCorbeau. You are also familiar with Mr. Cecco and Mr. Mullins…and I would have you know my ship's surgeon, Doctor Hanover.…*Monsieur le Commandant*."

The surgeon's gray eyes met the French captain's beady ones, and he bowed, a model of courtesy. "Sir."

Pleasantly, LeCorbeau smiled. "Why, Captain! A new addition to your officers? I have often thought of hiring on a surgeon, myself." His voice took on the least bit of an edge. "But it seems not likely at this point." The little captain bestowed a brief nod in Hanover's direction. "Sir."

Jill's bare feet moved silently over the boards. It was the tread of Yulunga walking behind her that caught the notice of the two captains and their men. The black man's enormous frame accentuated her elegance. Liza followed them, almost invisible even in her pretty blue dress. Captain Hook acknowledged Yulunga, but his gaze swept past the girl, whose eyes fixed hungrily on his handsome face. As Jill approached, he reached out to her, his rings sparkling. "Madam, you have arrived." In gold taffeta and tawny brown velvet, they presented a well-matched pair to the company.

"Allow me to introduce our guests. Captain DéDé LeCorbeau;

first and second officers Renaud and Guillaume of *L'Ormonde*…my lady, Jill Red-Hand."

LeCorbeau registered the bulk and height of the African sailor and the slight little girl in his wake with her mistress' cape draped over her arm, but during Hook's introduction his eyebrows rose to disappear under his hair. It wasn't the presence of a fancy-woman that surprised him. It was her demeanor. He managed to look the lady up and down without offending etiquette, then took three quick steps toward her, his deportment gracious.

"*Madame!* A welcome novelty. Just as I begin to believe I know this pirate king, he defies prediction and takes a queen! I had no idea your captain had acquired such a treasure." He held out his hand to her.

Jill condescended to smile. "And I had no idea my captain had such a compatriot. I can see that you, Sir, are a novelty yourself." She raised her left hand to accept his, and as he bowed over it, his large nose inhaled an expensive scent. Hook kept her right hand within his own.

Hook smiled half-way. "Yes, LeCorbeau, I have taken a… companion. Like you, I have ensured that my voyage will be not only profitable, but pleasurable."

"And the lady? She is also profiting from the pleasure…of the voyage?"

Hook eyed him. The surgeon watched, too, and the hand on his cane went rigid.

The lady spoke for herself. "Certainly. Captain Hook is a most generous man. He allows me to win at cards. But whether that is chivalry or the result of one-handed dealing, I cannot say."

"Heh! heh! Eh, *bien, Madame!* I see why Hook has chosen you to brighten up this hulk of a ship!"

Jill indicated the privateer where she floated, trim and polished. "You may call her a hulk, Sir, but to my eyes the *Roger* and *L'Ormonde* are well matched." She aimed a look at Hook under her eyelashes. "Perhaps perfectly matched."

"Like your captain, you have an eye for quality, *Madame*." LeCorbeau addressed his host, "Sir, you seem to have increased your company significantly and most delightfully since last we met." His glittering gaze darted once again to the youngest crewmen, who, with

Gentleman Starkey, had taken up stations under the mizzenmast to guard the ship while her guests remained aboard. Tom stared openly at Liza's blue dress while Nibs watched the guests with curiosity. The Frenchman's focus sharpened upon Nibs.

Hook noted LeCorbeau's interest. "Indeed, I have increased my company. And I am not thinking of parting with any of them, LeCorbeau. Shall we adjourn to the galley? I perceive that you are… thirsty. Mr. Smee, if you would."

"Aye, Sir. This way, gentlemen, Lady." Smee took the lead, and the party wended its way down and forward through the gun deck to the ship's galley, already prepared with plentiful lanterns, mugs, and a corked cask. The room's walls were lined with square, open gunports and barrels of all sizes, and it was furnished with benches. Its tables hung suspended upon ropes from the ceiling, to remain level as the sea swelled, and to be hauled up and out of the way when the deck must be cleared for action.

Mr. Smee guided the visiting officers to a scrubbed and sanded table where he, Cecco, and Mullins hunkered down to join them. Renaud and Guillaume peered high up over their shoulders at Yulunga, who took up a position behind them, manning the cask and dispensing the ale into jugs.

Hook hung his hat on a peg by the door and escorted Jill to a decorative table, obviously his own, in the center of the room, with comfortable, carved chairs. Here he seated Jill on his left and opposite the French captain. Hanover took a place not too close to LeCorbeau's side, where he could observe them all. Hook had given permission for the *Roger's* company to partake in moderation, and gradually the galley grew crowded with off-duty sailors sitting on benches, cannons and casks, even standing against the walls. Swinging yellow lanternlight replaced the sun as it faded from the gunports. The lady's deep blue eyes glowed in it.

Liza hung her mistress' cloak on a peg. Peering around first, she spread her hand over the velvet of her master's hat brim. Her fingers bumped over its gems, and then she held her fingertips to her lips before pressing forward to wade through the stream of voices. Her ears buzzed with the noise. The sailors turned their heads to watch as she stopped at the cask and reached out to Yulunga with expectant arms. He topped off the pitcher he was filling, and his smile swelled to intimidation as he looked down at her, murmuring, "You are getting bolder, little girl. Like your mistress. It is a pretty dress, too. Have you decided, as Lady did, that we are maybe not so bad after all?"

Despite her fright, she tossed him a haughty look which she proved unable to sustain. He spoke again before letting her tug the pitcher from his hands. Only his eyes had ceased to smile.

"Keep closer watch on your pearls, Miss. You don't want to go tempting pirates again."

He smirked at her discomfort as, conscious of both her neckline and her ring, Liza blushed but won the jug. Unsteadily, she lugged the vessel to the captain's table. Standing between Hook and Jill, she waited for the only man in the galley who *didn't* seem to see her to hold out his cup for her offering. Hook ignored her, but Jill was quick to accept the pitcher.

"Thank you, Liza." Jill set the jug on the table. Under the watchful eyes of the Frenchman, Hook picked it up and poured for his guests. He raised his glass, and Liza backed away, the corners of her mouth turning down again as she listened for one entrancing voice.

"Shall we drink to old acquaintance, LeCorbeau?"

"As good a reason as any, Sir! Old acquaintance, and recent acquisition." He lifted his glass to Jill and smiled. The look he sent next, toward the doctor, was not as warm. They drank. LeCorbeau lowered his mug and with some delicacy settled it on the board, then laced and unlaced his fingers around it. "But you must tell me, my old friend, where did you happen upon such a jewel as this, eh, lady?"

"On an island of intrigue, my dear 'compatriot.' Do not ask me to disclose its location. If you should beach a coracle there, you would find it Paradise, and never wish to leave it again. You would become a prisoner of your own device. Only my deep regard for you compels me to keep the secret."

"A port of Paradise? Intriguing indeed! And, eh, did you also discover your excellent doctor in this Paradise?" LeCorbeau fixed his gaze on the surgeon, squinting over his beak-like nose. "Or somewhere else, perhaps, not quite so mysterious?"

With an air of negligence, Hook waved his claw. "The surgeon's arrival was not mysterious at all. I discovered Mister Hanover aboard a prize. The doctor was persuaded to join me, and here he is."

Hanover searched for his watch. Suddenly animated, he took up the conversation. "Yes. I have found Captain Hook to be a most persuasive man, Sir."

The Frenchman leered. "*Oui,* the captain *and* his lady, I imagine! Who could resist jumping ship for the sake of such a vision— a veritable sea siren? Certainly not a man such as yourself, eh, doctor?"

"I found I had very little choice in the matter, Sir. But of course, you are quite correct to pay the lady such a compliment. In any case, my career has taken a turn I did not expect, nor could have predicted a few days ago."

"A few days…Then you are new to the *Jolly Roger!* And are you new to the sea, also?"

Hanover stirred uncomfortably, and took a bitter sip of ale.

"Until I found him," Hook answered, "Hanover was ship's surgeon aboard a merchantman. An excellent vessel. I hope to meet up with her again one day."

LeCorbeau said, "Ah, as usual, you spared her. It is a daring game you play, *mon ami.*"

"A profitable game, Captain. I take no risks without the prospect of proper compensation."

"Of course. But perhaps I know this ship. Did you leave her burning, a few days west of here? English?" He took another swallow and, seeming to enjoy it thoroughly, licked his lips.

Hook raised an eyebrow, his instincts alert. "Yes. The *Julianne.* You saw her, then?"

"But yes! She was in distress, so naturally I came to her aid—"

"And were much put out to find her hold already relieved of cargo."

Coy, LeCorbeau smiled and looked down. "Well, yes, of course. But, eh, I was able to salvage a few items of value."

Hanover blinked. "But what could you have possibly found? Captain Hook and his crew, I believe, were quite thorough."

"I, too, take the risks only for proper compensation. I held a very interesting conversation with her captain, Doctor! He told me some most marvelous stories regarding the pirate scum— eh, *pardon*, his words, not mine— who relieved him of his goods."

Jill's laugh sparkled over the men's. In his velvety voice, Hook, too, conveyed amusement. "All right, LeCorbeau, I'll indulge you. What did the man say?"

"Such stories…" He shrugged. "One can hardly believe them, but then, the man was distraught. He is not to be credited! These pirates, he said, seemed to sail out of nowhere, on a ship born of the morning mist. But even stranger— one minute they were tossing their grappling hooks, another, descending from his own rigging! Almost, he said, as if they had flown from one ship to the other, across the sea! Even the black devil of a captain himself! Heh, heh! Devils flying like angels, no?" Apparently much amused, LeCorbeau wheezed a laugh and pulled a lace handkerchief from his waistcoat. He dabbed his lips. "As I say, the man was beside himself. He was quite concerned about the situation of a young woman he feared you had kidnapped."

Hanover stopped rubbing his watch, to grip it tightly. Deliberately, he kept his gaze averted from Liza, hoping the Frenchman would not make the connection between father and daughter. He watched LeCorbeau intently as the little captain's regard bored into him, and finally, LeCorbeau turned an ingratiating smile on Jill.

"I see now that the gentleman must have meant you, *Madame*. And I also see he need not have worried. I am confident your captain defends *your* virtue. Such a relief to a man of conscience!"

Hook rejoined, "Which excludes all present company, LeCorbeau! What an interesting story. I see my legend has grown, even sprouted wings! How very gratifying. And all I sought was the plunder." Captain Hook leaned back and laughed. His sailors joined in, hoisting their glasses to toast him. The crowded galley swelled to full capacity with the merriment of the *Roger*'s men.

Taking advantage of the sailors' distraction, Liza slid her hands from her ears, pulled the pins from her hair and tucked them in her pocket. Smoothing her hair, she crept forward once more. She lifted the jug from the captain's table and moved to LeCorbeau's side. Pouring for the stranger, she avoided her father and his disapproving eyes, and worked her way toward her master, topping off Jill's glass and stepping around the couple to offer her service to Captain Hook. As if oblivious, he turned his back to her and wound his arm around his mistress. Liza jumped as he struck his hook into the surface of the table in front of her. She looked down to discover she had spilled on herself. Her bodice clung to her ribs in a damp patch.

"Jill, my love, do you have a tale to match LeCorbeau's?"

The men raised their voices in a cheer. "Aye, Madam, spin us a yarn!"

"A tale from Red-Handed Jill!"

The Frenchman flourished his handkerchief. "But *Madame*, do you tell the stories?"

"Yes, *Monsieur*, it is a habit of mine." She regarded Hook, considering her repertoire. "But I cannot top the story you just told about my captain. I think I must settle for another sailor's story."

It was what the men had hoped to hear. Alert and listening, they set their tankards on the tables and leaned forward on their elbows. Hanover stared at them, astonished at the respectful silence that reigned. LeCorbeau shot him a glance, then looked past the doctor to the neglected daughter. With a benign expression, he replaced his handkerchief in its pocket, and he, too, regarded the lady. His men, who had relaxed during the preceding banter, watched their captain and emulated him.

Quietly, Liza set the jug down at Hook's elbow, hesitating as his gaze scraped over her, then, barely able to breathe, retired to stand leaning on one foot against the doorjamb, her hands clasped together over the clammy stain on her bodice. Only after her heart calmed could she listen as attentively as the men.

Jill's clear voice broke into the hush. "But I will leave it up to our guest to choose. *Commandant*, of which of our sailors shall I speak?"

LeCorbeau cast his gaze about the galley, moving in little jerks. His attention fastened on Yulunga, whose head bent to graze the beams of the ceiling. "Surely, *Madame*, the tallest tale would be the one of the tallest man! Why not speak to us of your fierce African warrior? Eh," he addressed Yulunga, "What is your name, *Monsieur?*"

No one spoke. In the silence, only the moans of the *Roger* sounded warning. Under the hostile stare of the black man, LeCorbeau looked about himself, his eyebrows rising. Jill sat up straighter.

"Almost no one speaks the name, *Commandant*. And with good reason." She turned inquiringly to Hook. "With your permission, Sir?" He assented, then she looked to Yulunga, still looming by the cask. She drew a breath. "My friend, may I tell your story tonight?"

Yulunga's face creased into an ominous smile, and in his low, liquid voice he said, "I have no objection. But I won't be responsible if you frighten anyone, Lady!" He and Cecco, who sat before him with the two polished Frenchmen, exchanged a look of amusement, and then Yulunga's colorful beads bounced on his throat as he laughed, malevolent.

But Jill gestured her thanks to him, and her face grew serious as she sat back and concentrated on a far-away place.

The story came to her, like water from a well.

"There is a place, in the heart of Africa. A long, deep river set into a valley lush with green growth and piping birds. The air is heavy there, so heavy it presses against the spirit, beating on it like a drum. Only the strongest of peoples live along this water, tribes with stature, and the endurance of trees. Few travel this river, for these tribes are known for their ferocity. With moaning songs and rattlings, the dusky people warn strangers away. Only newcomers, greedy and overconfident, journey between this river's banks, looking to feed off their fellow man, seeking treasure in dark human form.

"The son of a powerful chieftain was born by the river. His mother worked deep magic, exchanging her own life for his, so that the boy inherited all the strength of his ancestors, and stature beyond even that of his forefathers. But with no woman to guide him and too strong for his age, the son used his body to assert his supremacy long before it was time to take his father's power. As the boy formed into a young man, the people grew to fear him, and begged his father to send him away from their valley so that he might grow in wisdom before he should return to become their chief.

"But having sacrificed his woman in the bearing of his son, the father was unwilling to part with him. Proud of the boy, he kept him near, and turned a deaf ear to the pleas of the people. And at every turn of the moon, the boy grew in strength and in selfishness. Soon, there was not a man living along the riverbank whose bones were not crushed or broken. There was not a girl who dared to refuse him. The younger children ran from his sight, to bury their faces in the bright-colored cloth of their mothers' laps, and the mothers trembled, too, for they knew that one day the old chieftain would pass on, abandoning the river and his people, and this giant would become their tyrant.

"Weary of living in fear, the elders of the village banded together and approached their leader. Their painted faces showed also the markings of despair. 'You have been wise and just,' they said, 'but your son does not follow you. You must send him away, or bone by bone he will destroy our people.'

"Still, the father refused. 'Go,' he told them, 'tend to your families and I will tend to mine.' But the same markings of despair lined the father's face, and proud as he was of his boy, he, also, had come to fear him. The truth was that he did not know how to harness the young man's strength, and failing that, how to be rid of him. A sad day, for not-knowing is the sign that a chieftain must step aside in favor of a son.

"But not this son.

"The old men of the village understood. They met together in the secret light of torches, and all agreed. Another sacrifice must be made. And instead of chasing the strangers away with wailing and jangling, this time they hailed the newcomers who next paddled a boat between the fertile banks of their river. The people wanted no part of the struggle, but told the strangers where and when to find the old chieftain's son. They accepted the silver that the strangers poured into their hands, and they sent an offering, a young woman, to the giant, to make sure of the place he would be. And there he was when the newcomers came upon him. He lay naked and, she saw to it, unarmed.

"Even with the snare around his neck, it was a task to seal the chains on his wrists and on his ankles. It took many pale men, and none of them unharmed. The young woman ran away and crouched watching in the green brush at the edge of the river. She bit her lip so deeply that her blood flowed to drip upon the riverbank. Here, it is said, her red blood marks the place of sacrifice. And it was to this spot the girl returned months later, bearing and burdened by bracelets made of beaten silver money, to deliver the grandson of the chieftain, who one day, it was to be hoped, would rule the tribe, justly and wisely.

"The slave ship bore the strongest man away from his people and his place. In darkness and in bondage he traveled far over the water. No one speaks the name anymore, in fear of calling him back to his rightful position. In his absence, the name itself carries forth his terror, for even as they bound him, he swore his revenge upon his people. His curses echo along the riverbank still, in the heavy air pressing against the spirit, beating like a drum and laden further now— with silver, and with betrayal.

"Only the strongest of peoples live along this river, tribes with stature, and the endurance of trees.

"Amid the lush green growth along this water, where the piping birds nest, the question hangs forever, like strangling vines among the branches: who is betrayer, and who, betrayed? And the answer is unspeakable, a name the bravest dare not pronounce…

"Yulunga."

He stood in the silence, staring, as did everyone else, at the storyteller, his powerful arms dangling at their unrestful angle.

The lady had spoken his name.

She was looking at him, too, as if seeing him for the first time. Only Hook's face bore the trace of a smile as he attended his Jill. Once again, she had proven her valor. She had never disappointed him.

Jill continued. "Yulunga, who passed through a time of darkness and enslavement. The matchless man owned by many, and mastered by none. He couldn't be kept. He broke free of his slavery, but before turning homeward to wreak his vengeance, a new captain commandeered the ship on which the chieftain's son sailed— not as cargo in the hold, but as a buccaneer. That captain, alone among men, stood unafraid, and Yulunga felt his rage dissolve. Released from other men's fear, there was one now who held him, without chains. This captain captured the strong man's loyalty. It is the only bond that holds him."

In the stillness of many men, Yulunga breathed deeply. He nodded. The darkness of his face opened into a smile, and his fellow sailors grinned with relief, shuffling their feet and leaning back.

Cecco stood to clasp Yulunga's arm. The gypsy regarded Jill with heat in his eyes, and then his white teeth flashed as he looked up at his friend. "Yulunga! Mate…" The tension was broken.

Jill looked content, but she was breathing rapidly. Surveying her closely, Hook supported her with his arm. "Madam?"

"I'm all right. Just fatigued, perhaps, from last night's festivities."

The doctor leaned toward her over the table. "Madam, you have exerted yourself. Please, you must rest."

Turning a jaundiced eye on the surgeon, LeCorbeau remarked, "A party last night, too? But Hook, what a ship of pleasure you now command!"

"We welcomed our surgeon in proper fashion, DéDé, as we have done for you." Turning his gaze upon his mistress again, he raised the slender hand that rested below his hook, and touched his lips to her fingers. His speech was brusque. "It is my own fault, Madam. In my selfishness I overtaxed you, but you must retire early this evening…and regain your strength."

"But Captain, I assure you, I am quite enjoying myself."

The Frenchman played the game of chivalry. "As much as I would like to hear another story, *Madame*, I should only relish it if I was certain you were well."

"Oh, but have you another subject in mind?" Her breaths came shallow.

LeCorbeau smiled slyly. "Well, eh…perhaps a poetic history of your handsome doctor?"

Hanover sat stiff. "Do not tire yourself, Madam. I am quite sure my history is of little interest to anyone."

"We cannot judge that until we hear it, eh, *Monsieur?* Or perhaps, like your shipmate, you have an unsavory chapter you may not wish to reveal?"

Jill smiled warmly on the doctor. "I am certain our physician is ashamed of nothing." She fluttered a look to Hook for her cue, then gasped and pressed her hand to her breast. "But— I'm sorry! I believe

I am a bit too fatigued to continue after all."

Immediately, the surgeon leapt from his seat and hurried to her side. "Madam, your wrist, if you please. You are pallid." Remembering his promise not to touch her, he waited as she took her arm from Hook's to present it to him, and then he encircled her wrist with his fingers.

He shook his head. "The pulse is too rapid. I insist upon escorting you to your quarters."

"The doctor will attend you, Madam. You must give our guest your regrets."

"Of course, Captain. As you will it." Jill gathered her skirts, and Hook assisted her to stand. She said, "*Commandant*, good evening. It was a pleasure."

LeCorbeau rose to bow with ostentatious elegance. "*Madame*. We shall meet again! I hope your rest will restore you."

"As do I, my love." Hook smiled wryly.

Hanover scowled, then called a crisp command. "Liza! The lady's cloak."

The girl plucked it from its peg and moved toward Jill. Her father snatched the wrap from her fingers and flung it open, then gently but firmly draped it over the lady's shoulders, where his hands lingered for only a moment. The Frenchman was watching.

Hook kissed Jill's palm and laid it on the surgeon's arm. "I shall come to bid you good night, Madam." His voice sharpened. "Hanover, see to her." The sailors stepped aside, and Jill leaned on the doctor, accepting his support as he issued his order.

"Liza, bring my walking stick and fetch my bag."

Doctor and patient made their way out the door. Liza, her eyes darting between the captain and his mistress, collected the cane and reluctantly followed.

As the silence of concern broke apart, the sailors, too, finished their drinks and began to leave the galley. Flipping his coat out of the way, LeCorbeau sat down again to sip his ale. He clapped the cup on the table, tidied his mouth, and addressed his host. "You are lucky to have happened upon your Hanover. I observe that he is very attentive— eh, to your mistress. But she is a lovely creature! It is no wonder you have abused her."

Unperturbed, Hook gave his guest a sardonic smile. "I endeavor to control myself, DéDé."

"As you do so very well in relation to the little girl…her attendant?"

"Water to wine, LeCorbeau. The one cannot be compared to the other."

"Indeed? Your men seem to have no such difficulty! They are, I think, appreciating all that is served."

Hook studied the young French officers, still seated with Smee, Mullins, and Cecco, smiling and draining their glasses, their postures finally at ease. "I would say the same for yours, *Monsieur*, now that their captain isn't watching."

LeCorbeau shrugged. "Eh, it is good for these young men to broaden their horizons. And speaking of this gives me the idea. My friend, you must now accept my own hospitality! I insist that, once we are assured of the woman's welfare, you come aboard *L'Ormonde* and take supper with me. And your newest crewmen must also gain the experience of another ship, you must bring them. They have been on duty all this while and have missed the party! Yes, and your Mr. Smee also, and any others you wish. In this way we can continue our festivity without disturbing your so-delicate mistress."

As if it hadn't been his own idea, Hook beamed with delight. "An admirable plan, DéDé. I accept. Do you still employ that fat little chef?"

"*Mais oui*, his cuisine is the finest France can produce!"

"Mr. Smee, we are invited to partake of my compatriot's excellent fare! Relieve our young men of duty. It will be edifying for them to inspect another vessel. And we'll bring Mr. Starkey, too, of course, to further their instruction."

"Aye, Captain!" Smee shoved away from the table and turned to the lingering sailors. "Finish up, lads, back to work." He left the galley to spring up the steps, smiling, and take his post outside the master's quarters. Starkey and his pupils already knew what to do. The doctor bore watching.

Mullins cast an inquiring look toward his captain. Hook made a light nod in the direction of the door, and Mullins got up, indicating to Cecco and the French officers that they should return to the deck.

Benches scraped and boots scuffled. LeCorbeau excused his men, and rose to follow as the galley emptied. But Hook remained seated, amused by the growing discomfort of his guest as Mullins closed the door behind the sailors and crossed his thickset arms, leaning respectfully but firmly against it. The two captains were left, one sitting, one standing, in the swinging lanternlight.

"DéDé. Do sit down."

LeCorbeau did so, in quick, stiff movements. He seemed undecided what to do with his hands.

Hook leaned forward to rest his claw on the table. It appeared stark and menacing against the mellow wood. "If you have anything to tell me, now is the perfect opportunity."

The little Frenchman drew back, his hands stationary at last, having wrapped themselves around his cup. "Hook, *mon ami*, you surprise me! What could I possibly have to tell you?"

"You could start with the reason you spent the last three days following my ship. Yes," he nodded as LeCorbeau's eyes widened with innocence, "we have spied you on the horizon, slipping in and out of sight. Exactly what do I have aboard the *Roger* that you believe belongs on *L'Ormonde?*"

"I assure you, Hook, this evening I seek only the pleasure of your company! Our meeting is entirely happenstance. You may have seen *L'Ormonde*, yes, I admit, but eh, we are in something of the same business, no? And as we have come together, I being somewhat competitive, you are naturally skeptical as to my motives, thinking perhaps I am desiring to reach the next prize ahead of you."

"That idea, among others, had entered my mind."

"But since you press me, I will be frank with you. This is not the case."

"Enlighten me, LeCorbeau. Just what *is* the case?"

"Well, eh, it is my intention— with your agreement, of course— to sail closely behind the *Roger* for some time....As I have found with the wreckage of the *Julianne*, staying within close proximity may prove most profitable for me."

"Profitable? To scavenge off my leavings?"

LeCorbeau could afford only the barest hint of annoyance. "If it pleases you to put it in that way. But eh, being a man of some pride, I should prefer a more complimentary description."

"Very well. We shall say you are gleaning a harvested field. But how does this profit you?"

"Ah, it is a most excellent role to play, that of savior! This is the word the poor captain of the *Julianne* used, and I very much enjoyed to hear it! Imagine, I was able to board his ship with no bloodshed, not a shot fired! The man welcomed me, and toasted my health, all the while my officers assisted his, conveniently locating anything of value left behind by your pirate scourge— eh, *je m'excuse*...Heh! heh! I make a friend, my ship develops a noble reputation. Perhaps I select a new crewman, help myself to the items you are in too much of a hurry to locate, and *voilà!* The job is done at no cost to myself. Hook's pirates have committed the raid, and my hands are full, but lily-white...yes, even kissed!"

Hook's eyes narrowed. "LeCorbeau." He raised his claw, and aimed its lethal point at the Frenchman's heart. "I will now be frank with you, also." Hook's blue eyes threatened the man as effectively as his hook. "Not only are you a privateer, pretending to be above piracy but respecting only those laws that protect you. You are also a despicable little Frenchman. No, *mon vieux*, I have never had any use for you."

LeCorbeau sat frozen.

Hook smiled. "Until tonight!" And then he threw back his head and laughed. Eventually, his rival joined in, all the while tidying his very damp throat with his handkerchief.

"You will excuse me now— shall I call you once again, 'compatriot?'" Hook shoved the jug across the table. "I shall send for you when I am ready to board *L'Ormonde*. Have another cup of ale while I say goodnight to my 'so-delicate' mistress, making an effort not to 'abuse' her too much, and then we'll adjourn to your own fine vessel where we will come to terms regarding the handsome percentage you will pay me for allowing my men to take all the risk and all the blame. Then we will drink to our new understanding!" He rose quickly, Mullins stood aside, and Hook swept from the galley, grabbing up his hat and calling for his man to follow. He still didn't know what that little rooster wanted, but Hook was, *eh, so much enjoying himself!*

His new partner, meanwhile, the amusing and despicable little Frenchman, sat in the galley, spitting the taste of the foul English ale from his mouth.

Honorable Intentions

Jill reclined on the silk of the daybed, her hair spread like satin over the pillows. The ship's surgeon perched at her side, still dignified, and every bit as attentive as Hook had been the first time she'd lain there. But on that occasion, she had been truly in pain.

"I have no reason to feel faint. I am usually quite strong."

"Hush, Madam, let me take your pulse again."

She held out her hand to him. It was the scarlet one, and she smiled. Hanover regarded it stoically, then took her wrist between his thumb and third finger.

"Better, now, but let me look at you." He peered into each of her eyes. He removed his stethoscope from the black bag at his feet. She watched as he raised its cold metal cone to her breast, then she allowed herself to shiver. He looked up at her face. A vein on his temple gave evidence of his own pulse's misbehavior, but he tucked the cone under the edge of her neckline, scrupulous in avoiding contact between his fingers and her flesh. He leaned forward and listened.

Raising his head, he observed her amused expression. He managed to ignore it.

"Your color is good. Have you ever experienced such a spell before?"

"Oh, no, Doctor."

"Have you any pain, discomfort?"

She shook her head.

"None at all? You must tell me truthfully."

She lowered her eyes. "Well, perhaps…"

Sudden concern creased his face. "What is it?"

"I may have allowed my…undergarment…to be laced too tightly."

The doctor straightened. "I see. That might explain the shallowness of breath."

"Yes." She said it breathlessly.

"Have you any other symptoms? Do you have difficulty sleeping?"

Several different expressions crossed her face before she shrugged. "I can't decide how to answer that question." She observed the dueling scar running from his cheekbone to his jaw. It grew darker.

"Lady. Under the circumstances, I have to ask. Are there any signs—"

"No, Doctor."

"You are certain of this?"

"Quite."

"And…in the past?"

"No. Never."

Visibly relieved, he put the instrument away, then he lifted his hands to her throat. "May I?"

She inclined her head, then raised it. Touching the sides of her neck with his fingertips, the doctor pressed up to her jaw line, and then down, frowning. "Does he mistreat you in any way, strike you?" He heard a quick intake of breath and once more became aware of his daughter standing behind him.

He didn't look at her. "Liza. You will help the lady prepare to retire. I want you to stay with her until she falls asleep. You will alert me if she experiences further distress. Of *any* kind."

For a moment, Liza stared at the red velvet curtain draped near the couch, then she dropped her gaze and nodded.

"Now wait outside."

The girl's eyes asked her mistress. The lady acquiesced. "Leave the door half open, Liza. You may go change your dress." She had seen the blotch of ale.

Grateful that her father was too obsessed with the woman to notice the stain or to comment on her unconfined hair, Liza tiptoed from the room to hurry to her quarters. She knew now he wouldn't bother with her again. Not until he needed her.

"You must listen to me, Madam. I forbid you to exert yourself in the next few days. You will remain quiet."

"I had intended to practice fencing tomorrow, but it can wait."

"Fencing, Madam. You surprise me again."

"The captain insists I be ready for anything."

"I see that I must be the same. As you know, swordplay is also an interest of my own."

"Perhaps you will show me one or two of your strategies. But not tomorrow. I will obey your orders. I hope you will allow me to walk, though? Fresh air always does me good, and I did promise myself to inspect your daughter's living arrangements. I have neglected it."

"It is kind of you to concern yourself for her. Fencing is out of the question until I have examined you again, but yes, you may take the air if you wish. Otherwise, rest. To make sure you do not overdo, I shall personally escort you to— our quarters." The doctor's handsome face flushed as he realized the implication of his words, and he made a business of neatening his medicine bag.

"You see, Doctor Hanover, you are already falling in with our unconventional manners! A gentleman showing a woman to his quarters? What next?"

"Of course Liza will accompany us. But perhaps you are right, Madam. You have a strange effect on me. I find I am not as strict in my thinking as I once was."

"I am trying to think now. What can have made my heart race in such a way this evening? We were only discussing—"

Hanover looked at her sharply.

"Or rather, we were about to discuss your history. Weren't we, Doctor?"

"The inquisitive Frenchman seemed eager to use your talents to pry into my past."

"I admit, I should like an excuse to learn your history."

"Until I came aboard your ship, Madam, I had no history." Hanover leaned closer. His crisp tone softened. "And as far as I am concerned, you had none either."

She tilted her head. "Doctor? Whatever do you mean?"

He snapped his bag closed and set it aside. The surgeon's duty was at an end, and he became a man like any other. "I hardly know, myself! But as of this evening, I have new hope. Perhaps this elusive weakness you are experiencing is a fortunate thing after all. It gives us a chance to speak together. Privately."

Jill cast a look at the door. The ship's motion had nudged it, or was it her bo'sun? But it remained slightly ajar. "Are you implying that I deliberately feigned illness?"

"I am implying that I hope you have done so."

"But that would mean I have lied to you. And to my captain."

"I hope you have lied to me. Lied *for* me."

Her eyes remained clear. "I have no need to lie. Quite the opposite; I find candor to be protective. Truth, itself, is a weapon."

"Then do not wound me with it!"

"So once again you hope for falsehood? You are indeed compromising your principles, as I predicted."

"Like you, Madam, I find myself inventing my own standard of conduct."

"And what do you hope to gain by it? However we have come by our moment of privacy, what should we have to say to one another within it?"

Hanover glanced over his shoulder at the door. He spoke quietly. "What I have to say is quite simple. I am an experienced and intelligent man. I am able to weigh evidence and make decisions quickly. It is a necessity in my profession. I have come to understand that you are exactly the woman I need."

"Need?"

"It sounds cold to put it thus." He blinked. "The woman I want."

"Still, you sound cold. Do you mean desire? Or love?"

"…Yes."

She pushed herself back to sit up higher. "You will excuse me if I fail to swoon. I am becoming accustomed to such declarations."

"Do not mock me!"

"No, once again, I only tell you the truth." She laid her hand on his arm, becoming aware yet again that his was a swordsman's arm, firm beneath the velvet. "It is also true that I appreciate your frankness, Doctor. I have done so from the first, even though you don't yet appreciate mine.

I must say, you are most attractive when most uncomfortable— for instance, when you are speaking of things you would much rather hide."

Urgently, he hiked himself closer to her. "Please, Madam, we haven't the time to spend in flirtatious pretense, nor am I skilled in it. Perhaps you yourself aren't aware of it, but this morning you gave me to understand— that is, I have begun to believe…"

"No. I gave you nothing but a clear picture of our situations."

"Yes, exactly. I am now attempting to do the same. Ah, perhaps I should approach the subject from another direction. Tell me, honestly. I know— I am not an innocent— what you give to Hook. You have made me understand that particular situation perfectly."

"If I shocked you—"

"I find there is no time for shock, Madam. What I want to know is, what do you really feel for this man?"

"You have heard the tales. You know his legend. He is rich, he is strong. Hook has everything—"

"He has you."

She regarded him steadily. She paused briefly. "Yes."

"Lady. Has he your heart?"

"Any woman could give him what I give. If he didn't believe he held my heart, how would I be preferable? I am uniquely placed, Doctor. I cannot go back, and I cannot move on." She shot him a bold look. "Yes. I give him my heart."

"Why then, if Hook values you so highly, does he not marry you? Despite his casual use of you, he has demonstrated even to me that he is willing to fight for your honor. Marriage is the least he could give in return for your affections."

"Doctor Hanover, don't you see? That kind of marriage is simply an act of law. What use has any pirate for any law?"

"Of course. And you emulate him, operating within your own set of rules. But I have always thought of marriage as a sacred institution, one I have found worthy to uphold."

"It is pointless to conjecture; I am satisfied with my position."

"So you claim. But…what if I could redeem you to polite society?"

Scorn edged her laugh. "I told you before. Polite society will want nothing to do with me!"

"You would be accepted with no questions asked, if you were to return…as my wife."

Jill stared. She opened her lips. She counted slowly to five, then took a deep breath. "You counsel me to remain quiet, Doctor. Is this how you think to calm me?"

"The best possible treatment for you, Lady, is to leave this ship and begin a new life. An honorable life, as an honest woman. Yes, this *is* my counsel. I hope you will take it. I dare to hope you will take *me*."

"I challenge you to find a woman more honest than I! It is my honesty that most disturbs you."

"Perhaps you are right. I am only sure there is none to match you."

"And where exactly would we find this 'honorable' life, Sir?"

"Not in England, unfortunately. But in my homeland. Heidelberg, or Vienna."

"And live the rest of my days pretending—"

"Your truth does indeed wound me, Madam!"

"I don't mean pretending to care for you— that might come easily if I allowed it— but pretending to be other than I am. Is this how 'honest women' live? I suppose you will suggest next that I should wear gloves at all times, to hide the shameful stain of my experience?"

"You could hardly explain such a blemish."

"Yet you yourself bear your experience on your cheek."

His hand hurried to his jaw. "My mark is one of honor."

"And so is mine."

"Only in this depraved world of piracy. Surely to be accepted among society is worth some sacrifice?"

"You must have noticed," she said. "One sacrifice is never enough for society."

"But to live among decent people again—"

"Decent people have always disappointed me."

"But I shall not. If you'll only come away with me, I will prove it to you."

She smiled again. "Raising the question of your own decency. But even if I were so inclined, and for many reasons I cannot say I am, just how do you think to accomplish it? Do you expect Captain Hook to bend to the propriety of your suggestion? To bless our union and send us off in a skiff full of rice and flowers?"

"You must trust me. I believe a way off this ship has opened for us. I cannot yet be certain."

"Doctor Hanover. Please leave now. I can't listen to any more of this fantasy!"

His whole being inclined toward her, as if he longed to touch her. "Madam— Jill! I assure you, this is no fantasy."

"Don't speak to me again until you know what you are offering. I will hear no more— no more— until you have real means of deliverance. Until you can tell me everything, tell me nothing!"

"Yes. Yes, I understand. I will do as you ask."

"No, you don't understand, but you will. Until you can tell me not only of your plans, but also of yourself, I won't even consider marriage to you. Why, for example, Sir, can you not return to England?"

The surgeon stiffened and pulled back.

"As you see, I am many things, but I am not foolish— Johann."

Again, shock struck his face. "You know my name? But how?"

"In the same way, maybe, that you surmise I am the wife for you. But guessing about a husband isn't acceptable, Johann. The life I lead may be questionable to the world at large, yet I know who and what I am. I can guess your name, but I don't yet know who you are."

"I am the man who will save you. I will take you away from here and—"

"Here, I have some measure of control over my destiny. I am a queen. I won't trade my position and my identity for any mysterious 'maybe.' I will know your history. I will know your secrets. I will hold them in my red-handed grasp before I set foot on 'societal' soil again!" Angrily, she averted her eyes.

Hanover bristled, but as he regarded her loveliness, his face softened and his tension took a new course. When he spoke, his voice was low, intense, a thrilling mixture of control and passion.

"If you would allow it, if I were not a gentleman, I would take you tightly in my arms right now, and kiss the very life from your body."

Jill still didn't look at him. She cast her gaze down and sucked in her breath. Quite suddenly, she believed him. This time, she concealed the shiver.

"You ask me not to touch you. But I will. I touch you with words, today, now. I will touch you with my hands, one day. And then, what will I not do? When the law I obey determines that you belong to me, I will not leave any part of you untouched."

Like the gray-eyed girl she was just beginning to comprehend, Jill didn't speak. She listened.

Keeping his arms in check, he leaned closer. "You want to hold my secret, woman? Yes, I would lavish the same carnal love upon you as do any of these pirates. You make me admit the truth: I own the same passion. And I have the means to induce it…in *you*."

His eyes fired as they claimed her gaze. He held his graceful frame poised above her. His lips formed an ironic smile. "And like your pirates, I would even bring you jewels, if you wished."

Her gaze traveled downward, to his medicine bag.

"Diamonds," he said, as if he stole her thoughts.

He was too adept. Too close to her weakness. Now she understood why the captain had insisted Smee should guard her. Grateful to feel the bo'sun's protective presence on the other side of the door, she only hoped he couldn't see her. Neither Smee nor the doctor would need instruments to gauge her heartbeat now.

"Now you hold, Madam, the secret of what I will and will not do."

Except for her breathing, the lady lay still. Hanover remained some moments, leaning above her, then slowly corrected his posture and pulled his coat cuffs into place with a series of smart little tugs. He looked down on her, approving.

"She is an intelligent woman who knows when to remain silent." He considered her, and then he shook his head. "I cannot argue with what you have said this evening. You are altogether wiser than I perceived, and I admire you the more for it. I am confident that not only are you the woman I need— I am the man *you* need. But good fortune, perhaps, does not come to us so readily. Not today, at any rate." He squared his shoulders. "All right. I agree. We will discuss the subject only when I can assure you of my integrity, and of our good chance of escape."

Warily, Jill lifted her eyes to meet his. "You do not ask me, Sir, to tell you more of my history."

"No."

"And when will you do so?"

He angled his head in a gesture of dismissal, and as he opened his mouth, she interrupted.

"Do not say 'never.' I am not such a fool."

"Very well. Then my answer is…'Not today.' "

She smiled, surprised at how difficult it was to do. "And that is my answer, also." She steadied her voice and raised it, to warn Smee away. "Please, send Liza to me now, so that I may follow your sage medical advice."

"I will. Whether or not you truly required it."

"I can tell you honestly, I am very glad to have received it."

The doctor regained his professional tone. "Regarding my earlier question, which you were unable to answer. I will ask you when we speak again, and if you are seriously considering my proposal, I expect you to say truthfully that you have, indeed, slept. Soundly and," his surgeon's voice was insistent, *"undisturbed."*

Her eyes widened. "And I hope to answer, also, the question I didn't have a chance to answer, and tell you he does not strike me!"

"You are, truthfully, a persuasive woman. I have every faith in your abilities." Hanover opened his bag and drew out a small glass vial. Moving with deliberation, he placed it on her lap, laying it over her warmest point, and applying a gentle, rousing pressure. "But should you encounter difficulty in carrying out my orders, I prescribe this sleeping draught." He withdrew his hand.

She looked down at the amber liquid slithering within the glass. She didn't touch it. "If I should accept your…orders, how much would you recommend that I take?"

"None."

She turned toward him quickly, questioningly.

"One half teaspoon in a few ounces of water will allow you very easily to lay a strong man's temper to rest."

She had been wrong, before. He was most attractive when he was comfortable.

"I see," she said. "I see you are resourceful. But both the captain and I are passionate creatures. Such an arrangement couldn't possibly last many nights. It is my hope that you and I may answer all of one another's questions. Very soon."

Hanover's trace of a smile was smug. "I would never be so discourteous as to keep a lady waiting. For *anything* she might require." He reached out to her. "Madam."

Slowly, watching his gray eyes triumph, she slid her crimson fingers into the manicured cage of his hand. He seemed to have overcome his distaste for their coloring. He brought her fingers to his lips and kissed them leisurely, one at a time, as he regarded her, then turned her hand upward to gain access to the inside.

"If you will allow me?" His thumb stroked her palm.

Gradually, she pulled her hand away. His remained empty, in the air. Her other hand secured the vial in her lap, over her warmest point.

"I can answer one question now, Doctor. I *will* allow you to kiss me. But…'Not today.'"

By the time Liza reentered the master's quarters, her hands behind her back, Jill appeared to have recovered from her malady. Standing as abandoned as a boy, legs apart and head thrown back, she faced the sideboard, pouring herself a splash of something from a brown bottle. She strode to the window seat and flung herself down among the cushions. "Bring my dressing gown and come unlace me, Liza. I need to breathe!…Look, the moon is beautifully bright tonight."

Liza kept her eyes on the mistress looking at the moon and padded to the daybed. She bent and, without a sound, tucked her father's walking stick beneath it. Then she opened the wardrobe and took down Jill's robe. She held its slippery fabric close to her plain brown dress, remembering the muscular thighs that had pressed their nakedness against it. Smiling as easily as Jill now, she approached her mistress and determined that the glass contained the same spirits she had tasted on Tom. Liza recognized the smell.

"That moon must be shining everywhere tonight. Even over my old home, far away in London. Tell me, Liza. Do you miss Bristol? Friends or family there?" She sipped the rum.

The look of confusion on the girl's face was answer enough; Jill had guessed another of the doctor's secrets.

"Oh, I'm sorry, I've mixed it up. I thought I remembered your father say Bristol." Quickly, Jill's intuition filled one more gap in the story. "It was Bath, wasn't it?"

Liza studied the floor. Then she nodded.

"Yes. I thought so. What an interesting place to live! People travel there from all over the world, I believe, to take the waters. Your father must have attended many rich and exotic patients."

The girl plucked at the dressing gown in her arms. On her finger she felt the presence of the pearl ring. As she stood, she favored one leg.

"Well, I have good news for you, Liza. I've found you a tutor. You will soon begin your reading lessons. But, 'not today.' Perhaps tomorrow!"

Liza's face showed no change in expression. Jill's was delighted. "You shall receive your instruction right here in my cabin."

The girl's eyes reflected alarm, then interest. But her silly hopes were dashed immediately.

"Don't be afraid. I'll be pleased to stay with you. There aren't many rules to this game, but after all, it wouldn't be proper to be alone in my quarters— with a gentleman."

Baffled at first, Liza began to unpuzzle the mystery behind Jill's sphinxlike smile. The woman was still smiling a few minutes later as Liza hung her dress away. The girl continued to observe. Captain Hook had entered, and the cabin overflowed with his presence. Both females immersed themselves in him.

As promised, Hook was bidding his lady good-night, and sharing the rum in an extremely intimate manner. And for the second time that evening, Jill's breath really did come too rapidly, and she truly did feel weak.

But she had no intention of following the doctor's sage advice. Not tonight.

The ship's surgeon accepted the order to remain on the *Roger* while the captain caroused aboard *L'Ormonde*. The irony was maddening, but Hanover was well able to control his annoyance, and his demeanor was calm as he braced himself for the next challenge. Under the genteel guise of curiosity, he volunteered to entertain the visitor and to escort him topside once the two ships were realigned and preparations for boarding were in readiness. But he was in no mood to take any nonsense from the Frenchman. As he stepped into the galley, he made sure LeCorbeau was alone, then checked the deck behind himself before closing the door.

"Well, LeCorbeau. It is extremely fortunate that you have found me."

LeCorbeau sprang to his feet to confront him. "Yes, I have found you. Did you think I would not?"

"It is of no consequence. You are here."

"I am. But, *quelle surprise*, Doctor— eh— Hanover!" He approached in measured steps, his hands locked together behind his back. "Imagine my distress! I return from the rendezvous with my contact from Alexandria. I receive your message. I locate your ship, run her down, board her," the privateer frowned peevishly and leaned into the doctor's face, "only to discover that you have vanished from her."

Hanover stood erect to look down on the Frenchman. "Imagine my own distress, LeCorbeau, when I was abducted by pirates!"

"Well. Your little change of plan has inconvenienced me a great deal."

"I assure you, Captain, the change was no part of my plan. You may sulk, but I am far more inconvenienced than you." He threw his hands up. "I am a prisoner on this ship!"

LeCorbeau stalked to the table, sat down and leaned back, lacing his fingers together and fluttering them. His hard little eyes looked the doctor up and down. "*Oui.* A prisoner who dines at the captain's table and holds the hand of his mistress when she is fatigued from too much love-making!" His fingers stilled as he leveled a stare at the doctor. "I begin to wonder, *Monsieur*, if our heretofore profitable partnership has been dissolved. You now appear to receive everything you need from my friend Captain Hook."

"You doubt my integrity?"

The privateer raised one finger. "Not only I, but also those you left behind on the *Julianne*. She is a ship empty of cargo, and full of suspicion."

"How dare you suggest—"

"Interestingly, Doctor, it was not I who first raised these doubts. It was the captain of your former vessel. Captain Whyte. He seems to feel that your disappearance, alone, might have been happenstance. But that your daughter, also, was taken, and all of your belongings…" His hands supplicated. "Well. Who could believe a pirate crew would be so considerate in choosing which articles to confiscate? Certainly not I!"

"But it happened in just that way! I knew nothing of Hook's movements, and until your appearance I had no idea even that the *Julianne* survived his assault."

"Oh, yes. She survived. *Alors*, it would have been better for us if she had not. Hook, as usual, makes the complications. He fancies himself a civilized man. He never forces when he can persuade, it is part of his charm! And Hook preserves his own interest always. *Mon Dieu!* If he sank every ship he sacked, there would soon be no more prey to devour! But this way, the *Julianne* can procure more bounty to carry to him, and her sailors will live to spread his fame in every pub and port from here to his beloved England, where he himself can now live only in legend!"

"Spare me your jealous fits, Captain." Hanover sat down, shaking his head in irritation. "Hook is far more shrewd than I at first believed. He discovered both my occupation and my daughter, and appropriated us for his use. I am outraged still at the thought of it! I have had no choice but to feign acceptance of his terms. My daughter—"

LeCorbeau snorted through his overlarge nose. "Do not attempt to deceive *me*. Your daughter is the one item aboard this ship with which you do not concern yourself. Even I, who have little use for the so-called fairer sex, can see what you disregard. The girl is obsessed with Hook! And he knows too well how to handle her. He keeps her intrigued! Yes, he ignores her, while the rest of his crew can't wait to—"

"You have spoken sufficiently on the subject of my daughter. Tell me what else is said on the *Julianne*."

LeCorbeau cocked his head to observe the doctor. "Very well. As I have indicated, your responsibility to your daughter is the least of your worries. I sat a long time with Captain Whyte, discussing his woes and listening to his men report the damage. Since your abduction, the rumor is abroad that 'Hanover' may not be your real name, and that you hail from another city than you claim. That you fled England to serve on a merchant vessel only until such time as you formed an alliance with a shipping partner who could more readily assist you in, eh, some lucrative trade."

Hanover paled.

"In short, your secret is guessed. The only error lies in who your partner is presumed to be." LeCorbeau's glittering eyes narrowed. "Unless, of course, it is *I* who have erred...partner?"

The doctor dismissed the captain's suspicion with a gesture. Leaning on the table, he rubbed his clean-shaven chin and swore under his breath. "Damn that Hook!" With the fingers of his free hand, he felt for his watch.

The Frenchman raised his eyebrows. He blinked. "So. I am to believe you are a victim. We have both been brought to heel like dogs at my old friend's knee?"

"LeCorbeau. I am an honorable man. I do not break the law, and I make it a practice not to endanger myself by associating with those who operate outside it. I am first and foremost a physician. My work is dedicated to the good of mankind. Until the day the *Julianne* was sacked, my reputation was beyond reproach."

"*Your* reputation, or that of 'Doctor Hanover?' "

"It is immaterial now. But I see that 'Hanover' cannot live long. You must get me away from this ship—"

"Ha! Now that Hanover is exposed, you need me again, eh?"

"You insinuate that I deliberately broke my word to you."

LeCorbeau jerked himself up to stand. "I insinuate nothing. I accuse!"

"It is outrageous, after all I have been through, to be treated thus, as a lying cheat!"

"And how should I treat you? The fact is you are here," LeCorbeau rapped the table, "living the high life, becoming rich on pirates' plunder, and not where you promised to be!"

"I shall dismiss your insults as the petty petulance they display! Find a way to get me aboard *L'Ormonde*. Then we will reform our partnership."

"You? And what of your daughter?"

"Yes, yes, her too, of course." And one other. The doctor had already shrugged off the nagging Frenchman's implications and was thinking ahead, his thumb massaging the back of his watch. "But this time I'll send the girl away, to a convent. Switzerland. As I should have done at the start."

LeCorbeau began to laugh. Hanover eyed him with annoyance. "I find nothing amusing in the situation. I consider my pledge to you sacred. It is not me but that blackguard, Hook, who is to blame for our disagreement. He is using my daughter against me!"

Allowing his mirth to erupt, the privateer indulged it. Once his wheezing subsided, he drew a fresh handkerchief from his inner coat pocket and wiped his eyes. "Oh! Oh, *mon frère*, you are a model of honor! Heh, heh! You expound to me upon the sanctity of your pledge, while your daughter serves a pirate's whore, lives among as randy a pack of dogs as ever sailed the Seven Seas, and will no doubt very soon lose every shred of her precious maidenhead!"

"For God's sake, LeCorbeau! Show some decency! There is no need to insult the captain's lady. And surely Liza's degradation at the hands of these pirates proves I had no intention of betraying you."

LeCorbeau waved the doctor's interruption away. "No matter. Whether or no, the little girl has been compromised by her virtuous father's carelessness, and all you can think about is the honor of an expensive prostitute— and eh, may I tell you that you reek of her?— and also of the inconvenience to yourself!" Wheezing again, he tapped his chest. "And *I* am called immoral! You are too much, my friend!"

He sighed, dabbed his lips and shook out the handkerchief. "Only my knowledge of your upstanding character persuades me to believe you are— heh, heh!— innocent!— in this predicament. You might not think to secure your daughter's best interests, but you surely would not endanger your business!"

"I pride myself on keeping a clear head at all times. If you find that quality to be immoral, I am sorry for you."

"A clear head? Was that your condition when your wife lay dying from your own—"

"And speaking of business, Captain, did your contact supply my material?"

Like a bantam, LeCorbeau puffed up his feathers. "No need to worry. As always, I have upheld my end of the arrangements."

"Let me have it!"

Now firmly the ruler of the roost, LeCorbeau smiled wryly. "Ah, *Monsieur*. As I told you shortly after we were introduced in that so-charming little hot-spring resort— when the time is ripe, I will make for you all things possible."

"I see no need to delay my work while I am imprisoned on this infernal ship!"

"I, too, am anxious to receive your medicinal product, both for personal and for profitable application. But this resource is too rare to trust to pirates."

"But you can trust it to me! My quarters are private, strictly off-limits to the sailors."

LeCorbeau's glare pierced the doctor's mask. "To the sailors, maybe. But what about the mistress?"

Hanover blinked, but refused to dignify the comment with a response. It was, he suddenly realized, too true.

"You are not as impenetrable as you pretend, *Monsieur*. Not to me. Not to Hook."

"No one dares to enter my cabin. It is the one dignity Hook allows me."

"It is the one *illusion* he allows you! The wonder is that your foolishness has not exposed you before this, Hanover. You really are innocent if you believe there is any safe place to stow your secrets on this ship. No! No! I put my foot down. Only when you are safely aboard my own *L'Ormonde* will we complete the transaction!"

The man called Hanover set his shoulders squarely. "There is no need to fret, Sir. You are too nervous. No one on board the *Roger* suspects what I conceal."

"As ever, your confidence overwhelms. But I do not share it." Then, deciding to smile, LeCorbeau bobbed around the table and bent, the picture of amiability, to fling his arm around the proper doctor, gripping his shoulders before releasing him. "Well! We will talk again as soon as I have found a way to clean up this mess Hook has cooked for us." As he straightened, he looked down at the surgeon. His cocky face dropped its good humor. "You will not cross me again."

Hanover stiffened; his eyes flew wide. The watch fell from his fingers to dangle and twist at his waist. Beneath LeCorbeau's handkerchief, a bit of steel gleamed in the lanternlight.

"And you will be thankful that, unlike so many others, I know you well, Doctor. If I did not, my *petit ami* would by now have pierced your *petit* heart, and in spite of your medical miracles, you would be a very dead man."

DéDé LeCorbeau finished polishing the nasty little stiletto with his handkerchief, and returned them both to his inner coat pocket. He strutted to the door to salute his partner with a flourish.

"*Au revoir, mon ami.* Not goodbye." He smiled. "Not yet."

Visions and Voices

The servant girl heard only soft sounds. The sea swishing against the hull. Breathing from the bunk. The portside curtains hung open, and the moon poured like liquid into the captain's cabin, illuminating it so brightly that the mistress had extinguished the lanterns to bathe in its pool. He would find his way to her side without false light tonight. Jill had set a cup full of cool water on the bed shelf, and retired, instructing Liza to honor her father's orders and stay until her mistress slept. Unaware of intrusion, Jill lay on the bed now. Her servant listened, but the woman didn't stir.

Earlier in the evening, Liza turned down the covers for her mistress and replaced the opal necklace in its drawer. She helped the lady into a nightdress. As she hung the dressing gown, Liza had left the wardrobe door the least bit ajar. That morning she had polished the mirror inside it, and she had made sure the door swung noiselessly on its brass hinges. After she curtsied a good-night to her mistress, she prepared the curtain that enclosed the couch— it was of primary importance tonight. She slid it into a thick velvet bunch at the end of its rail. Fashioned for a life at sea, the curtain's folds didn't sway with the rise and fall of the swells. Its plush hem nestled in a satisfying heap against the carpet. Appreciating the usefulness of such a drapery, Liza sat down on the couch to wait.

She had believed Jill to be asleep when the woman's voice surprised her, dismissing her for the night. Liza walked to the door, opened it, and without passing through, shut it. The bookcase loomed over the dim wall by the door. Silent as the moon, she wedged herself against it. She waited again. Jill didn't rouse. Eventually, in the half darkness, Liza had stolen along the carpeting toward the daybed. Her skin prickled as she moved, and her insides felt sick with trepidation, but she crept around the curtain and stood straight within it, absorbed like a wood-nymph within the bark of a tree. She was positioned perfectly to accomplish her objective— a pace before the daybed, a few scant feet from the wardrobe. Her confidence returned as Jill's voice said no more.

Liza found reason to slip out of hiding only once. After several minutes of quiet, she stepped forward and bent down to retrieve the cane she had stowed away. But just as her fingers brushed the floor boards beneath the couch, she heard her mistress sit up. Liza froze, her eyes alarmed and her breathing ended. Straining her ears for movement from the lady's direction, she nearly jumped at the noise of scraping wood. Then she tingled with relief. The mistress had opened a window. Liza looked up hastily and saw Jill kneeling with her elbows on the sill, gazing out at the bobbing lights of the neighboring ship. The girl felt along the floor until she grasped the walking stick. She lifted it like finest crystal, then fast regained her shelter within the drapery, where she could neither see nor be seen.

She clutched the ram's-headed cane. With her elbows pressed to her sides, she held it close against her body, waiting for the moment to use it. Her father, apparently having no stomach for carousing with pirates and privateers this evening, had retired to their quarters. She was certain he would miss neither his cane nor his daughter tonight.

Liza was determined that she herself would miss nothing. It was this determination that granted her the courage to remain in the cabin.

Now— hours later?— Liza's ears attended new sounds. Men's voices through the open window. The party on board *L'Ormonde* was breaking up. Boards clapped and bounced as men secured planking to cross to the *Roger*. The bedclothes rustled again, and Liza's mouth felt suddenly dry. She tried to move her tongue and found it impossible. In the next minutes she would be discovered, or she would be safe. As terrible as the master's anger might be, it was a relief to find the moment at hand at last. And would it be so awful, really, to be noticed?

Even struck or beaten? Discovered or not, either way, she would win something from her time here.

Liza took stock of herself. She was hidden, she held her tool. Her legs were sore, but she ignored them. She was used to that, yet she found herself squeezing her father's cane hard, harder even than he did when he used it, and she forced her fingers to relent. She sucked one silent breath.

Audible now came a round of cheerful salutes from the deck, then footsteps moving toward silence. Quieter footsteps approached the door to the captain's quarters. Liza drew herself into her velvet shell.

He entered. The door closed. Tense, Liza listened for the click of the key turning the lock, but the bolt remained mute. She relaxed her shoulders; when the time came, she would be able to escape soundlessly. Now she could concentrate on the present.

She never heard enough of his wonderful voice. Only once had he directed words, just three words, to her. She longed to hear him speak again, whether in language addressed to Jill, or toward herself. Even words of rage. She wanted to see him, yes, but always for Liza, so long denied her own voice, the height of any experience was its sound. On edge, she waited, anticipating her pleasure.

But he remained silent. Even his boots made no noise as she felt him closing in on her hiding place. Keeping her head straight, she watched from the corner of her eye. Without warning, something heavy hit the couch, and Liza pulled back. It shot a draft of air at her, rippling her skirt and the curtain behind her. She blinked and beheld his tawny-brown coat sprawling on the satin fabric of the daybed. Before she could steady her knees, his waistcoat joined the coat, and Hook himself sat down on the armless end of the couch. Liza didn't need the mirror yet. She could look directly on him, only four feet away. He bent, pulling a dagger from what seemed like nowhere, and it flashed as he laid it beside him. Then he gave a grunt, starting to work off his boots. As he faced the moonlight, inky waves of hair hung down his back, in contrast with his white shirt. Liza could smell him— leather, salt air, and spirits. She smiled into the silence.

As if summoned by his scent, a phantom drifted from the direction of the bed, a white-gowned ghost with flowing silvery hair. Gliding over the carpet, she came to him and took his face in her two hands. She leaned down to kiss him. He lifted his face to her embrace, and they hung together for a space of time— as if floating. Two white-shrouded lovers, belonging to no particular world.

Then the ghost-lady in the nightdress knelt down before him. Slowly, she drew off his boots. He received them from her hands and, rising, the two wraiths drifted from Liza's view. The girl took the opportunity to breathe again. As her mind cleared, she listened to the boots settling by the bunk, and the soft shush of rich fabric sliding away from richer flesh.

Not until the bed accepted their weight did Liza venture to use her stick. She had to be sure they wouldn't notice. By the otherworldly sound of their breathing, she guessed, and gambled. Grasping the cane by its top, Liza slid it outward, as low to the floor as she could reach without bending. She pointed its tip at the crack of the wardrobe door and inserted it. Pausing to listen, she heard only the hushing of the sea. She inched the door open, stopped, and listened again. Her gaze darted around in the darkness, then fastened on the mirror within the wardrobe. It showed the blackness of the closet's interior. She nudged the door again and saw herself reflected, vaguely, all eyes and ears. And still no voices, just spirits whispering in their shrouds.

One more push and the mirror swung away. Liza glimpsed white moonlight before it settled— too far! Her mouth fell open and she stood perfectly still, thinking. She was growing warm within her velvet snare.

Liza drew the stick back. Running her finger over the ivory carving and around the curve of the horns, she allowed one of the tips to prick her finger. And then she reversed the cane and reached the ram's head out to the wardrobe door. The cane was heavier this way, and her arm shook as she extended it fully. But, hooking the edge with the tiniest tap, she pulled the mirror into place. She was rewarded with the sight of her master and her mistress lying together in the pool of the moon. Liza's whole body felt damp as she recovered the cane, as if the pool encompassed herself as well.

He still wore his hook. It shone where it rested above his woman, on a pillow. He seemed aware of it, too, because he sat up then, and, pulling his shirt over his head, he shed his ghost-skin. He shook his hair free of it, bunched the sleeve to smooth the hook's passage, and tossed it away. Liza inhaled a sharp breath as the shirt landed near his other garments, but on the floor— at Liza's feet. She lowered her eyes to see it. When she spied in the mirror again, Jill was reaching up to free him of his harness.

The woman rolled toward the wall to hang the leather strap on its hook, while the man flexed his shoulders and breathed deeply of his new freedom. Liza couldn't see his empty wrist. It moved on the side of him farthest from her, and he soon hid it within the folds of Jill's nightdress.

Jill helped him slip her garment off, then lay back on the bed. She reached to bring down the cup of water, offering it to her lover. He took it; he sipped, then tipped it up and drained it as he knelt over her, with his back straight and, Liza discovered with a sudden tightening of her throat, his beautiful body primed for its purpose. The girl nearly reeled.

The blood drained from her head. She felt faint, dizzy. Clutching the cane, she employed it for its proper purpose, leaning on it for support. She could no longer control her breathing— she made far too much noise. But she must breathe or swoon, and either way, she was sure he would hear her.

But she couldn't hear *him!* She heard the clap of the cup on the shelf as he replaced it, but she didn't hear his voice. He hadn't spoken the words Liza craved! He wouldn't speak them. Not now. As she gripped the stick, tighter every moment, her eyes feasted on the heady sights within the mirror. The magnificent man leaned down, and, without a word, commenced making love to his splendid mistress. And Liza watched.

She took it all in. She gorged herself on rich dishes, her eyes ate until replete, but still, her ears felt famished. Their white bodies moved in the moonlight, backs, breasts, limbs, lips. She stared, she perspired, but she was anxious, now, frantic for his voice, his smooth-as-honey voice, to feed her passion, to complete it. Yearning, she wanted to swallow his tones and stock her memory along with the images— like dessert, a sweet lingering taste, to savor later, and forever.

She wanted to scream at him as he rocked in the mirror, *speak words to me!* Forcing herself to breathe through her nose, she pressed her lips together, knowing her own voice would sour everything.

But the moon slid higher in the sky, up and away, to tuck itself into its bed of clouds, and the hand of night covered it over. The cloudy light misted blue now. The movements in the master's bunk slowed and ceased. Had the ghosts sunk into their graves? Liza's heart slowed, too, and sank with them, and she waited, wearily now, only for the moment of escape. In a weird limbo she barely existed, her presence meaning nothing to him, her absence meaning nothing to her father. Liza stood in the darkness, aching, neglected even by the moonlight.

Her shoulders slumped with fatigue, and with surfeit, and disappointment. In the time she had watched and waited, she hadn't heard him speak more than one syllable. Her face twisted in irony. With all her heart, she wished she had never heard him speak at all.

Because the word he had pronounced, the senseless syllable he'd repeated, provided no sustenance for her starving ears. He had uttered only that single sound, and he'd uttered it over and over again, until Liza was sick to death of his wonderful voice.

She never wanted to hear him say it again.

But she knew now what this man's body craved. She had witnessed how to touch him. She had felt herself ripening as she watched, bursting her skin and shedding the last of her ignorance. When she could share his bed, when she dared to touch him, she would give him what he wanted— more than he knew he wanted— and she would find a way to rip that noise from his throat. She would replace it with two syllables, override that hateful— one.

Her burning eyes fell closed at last as he released the sound, one final time.

He whispered it…

"Jill…"

The girl awoke in a cold sweat. She sat up in her bunk. Her fingers clutched the bedcovers; her stomach jumped. Was he here? In her cabin?

She saw nothing in the blackness. To rest her exhausted eyes, she had drawn the curtain across her bunk. The starboard windows hid themselves, covered.

Had she dreamed him? Had she imagined all of it? It had seemed so real! Her body felt damp and swollen. Her legs still ached. Her bare shoulders shivered, fondled by the cool night air.

The waves had risen, pitching the ship. Had she felt only the stirrings of the sea?

Her head swung toward the bed curtain as she heard it again.

"Jill."

In the bunk below, her father sighed in a brief burst of voice, and rolled over. This time, the sound of that syllable woke Liza's smile. She was happy to hear it, one more time.

She could help her father. He could help her, without ever knowing it. As far apart as they were, father and daughter wanted the same thing.

Sliding her fingers beneath the pillow, she felt for the cloth. She drew it out, barely able to discern its whiteness in the night. Ghostskin. She could feel it, though. It was fine-woven linen. Looser-woven lace edged the cuffs. Holding it to her face once more, she inhaled. It smelled just right. Leather, and salt air, and spirits. She smiled into the silence.

Arranging the sleeves, she bound her arms. The rest of his shirt flowed over her breasts and belly, and lower. Gently, it buffed her skin. She pulled up the covers, lay back in her bunk, and dreamed.

Just tonight, the woman had told Liza there were few rules to this game. A reading lesson was as good a place as any to begin.

Feinting Away

"Don't finish off the biscuits— you remember what happened last time he didn't get any." Nibs sent Tom a warning look. He was perched on a barrel in a foremost corner of the galley, his long legs folded. Tom sat with two others at a nearby table. Several more crewmen were dispersed at tables about the room, finishing breakfast.

"By 'he' you mean Mr.—" Tom glanced at the door and cleared his throat. "Mr. Yulunga. We can say his name now, but by the Powers, it's a job!" He ran his sleeve across his forehead.

Cecco let loose his easy gypsy laugh. Straddling his bench, he leaned back, taking care not to touch his wounds to the wall. "It was lucky I had enough biscuit left to share with our friend. You young sailors, you have seen him disappointed. You have never seen him angry. If you had, you would not yet use his name, even so carefully."

"Tell us the story, Mr. Cecco. We want to learn everything."

"Everything?" Cecco shook his head and scraped his bowl with the last of his hardtack. "Just keep your eyes open, seize your opportunities. I am no storyteller. I leave that to your very lovely mother." As always when speaking of the lady, his voice mellowed, and he smiled.

"Wish *my* mother'd looked like that. A right old hag she was! I couldn't get to sea fast enough." Jukes shoved his bread toward Tom. "Have mine, mate, I've got that toothache again." He rested his elbows on either side of his porridge bowl and watched the others eat. The inky designs on his arms swirled and snaked all the way up to the fingertips that tenderly prodded his jaw. "Beats me, though, how the lady knows what she knows. She can't have learned it all from the captain. When Red-Handed Jill spins her yarns, she tells things about us even we don't know."

Cecco set down his empty bowl. "Our Mr. Yulunga was much gratified to learn he has a son. It causes me to be somewhat cautious, however, about asking for my own story." The smile on Cecco's face waxed complacent.

Straining his yellow shirt, Tom's already broad chest swelled again. "There's a magic about Jill. We've always known it, haven't we, Nibs?"

Nibs nodded, chewing and about to speak, but he couldn't talk of Jill with his mouth full; she'd taught him manners. He could talk of other subjects, though. "You should see *L'Ormonde*, Mr. Jukes." He swallowed. "The food that Frenchman served us— 'cuisine,' Hook calls it. You'd have liked the fancy soup, 'bouillabaisse' or some such thing, easy on your teeth. And the wine!"

Jukes winked. "Don't let Mr. Starkey hear that French talk, lad. He'll say you're putting on airs, getting above your station."

"Sure, I'm turning into a *gentleman*, like my brother!" He leered at Tom.

Cecco cocked his head and his large earrings swung. "There is much to be said for acting a gentleman, if there are ladies to impress. Our Tom, I think, is learning this."

Sighing like a heartbroken swain, Tom only partly jested. "Much good it does me, when the girl won't talk to me and the captain won't let me touch her."

"Won't let *anyone* touch her," Nibs corrected.

The Italian sailor sympathized. "In such matters, one must make one's own luck, my friend. Your chance may present itself, if you watch for it."

"And if the rest of us don't beat you to it!" Jukes interjected. "Mr. Nibs is right— you're not the only one watching that girl. She's a saucy piece, even without a voice. Now tell us about the party, Mr. Tootles. It's plain you're bursting with it."

Tom stowed Cecco's advice for future use, and launched into the previous evening's events. "The first thing was a tour of the ship. Mr.

Starkey angled for us to be shown around, to get a proper look at another vessel. She's beautiful! Almost as yare as the *Roger*, just a bit smaller. Not a lot of goods in her hold, but she doesn't leak much. She has stout sails and plenty of cannon— a twenty-four gunner— and the galley's full of barrels of some foreign kind of fish. They made the soup of it."

Nibs wrinkled his nose. "I liked the real food better. The captain's quarters, where we ate, it's not nearly as rich as Hook and Jill's, but just as pretty."

Jukes prodded, "Well, lad, and what did the Frenchy offer Hook to let you go?"

Nibs gaped at Jukes. "How did you know?"

Jukes and Cecco laughed. Coddling his jaw, Jukes mumbled through his toothache. "LeCorbeau collects young sailors. Didn't you see his officers? You could sign on with him and 'rise' to 'mate' in short order!" He sniggered at his own joke.

"I did see! I broke into a sweat when he mentioned me. But I didn't worry too much. Hook would never release me before talking to Jill."

"Aye, you lads are as close to Hook having sons as he'll ever abide!" Jukes guffawed, then quit abruptly, clutching his cheek. "Oh! I'll have to be seeing Smee about this damned tooth."

The Italian raised his eyebrows. "No, mate. There is now the doctor for such problems. He may be much preferable to Mr. Smee for pulling teeth. I perceive that he has smaller hands. And as he has examined my back, I can say they are *slightly* gentler."

"I'll see him today. I won't be put off food much longer. I'm getting as skinny as Mr. Nibs. Next thing you know, the Frenchman will be courting *me*."

Cecco eyed the tattoos. "You are too marked by experience, I think." Then he shrugged. "It may not be a bad life for a French boy from the gutters of a poor port-town. But I notice we never see the same lads among the crew when we next encounter *L'Ormonde*. LeCorbeau must not keep them long. This Renaud and Guillaume, they are new, and where are their predecessors?"

Tom volunteered, "Captain Hook asked the *commandant* the

same thing, in a round-about sort of way, of course— you know how he can talk. And in his Frenchified way LeCorbeau said some took sick and some took off. He didn't say it too loud, though. Renaud and Guillaume got funny looks on their faces."

But Cecco was more interested in the running of the ship. "What about his crew? They seem like capable seamen."

Nibs said, "All in order, just less showy than us. Blue jackets and pigtails. A few of them speak English, but we didn't mix much."

Tom's pride shone through his grin. "You should have seen them stare at Hook! I only knew what was said of him on the Island before, but he really does have a reputation on the high seas. You could see it on their faces. Awe, I'd call it. Every eye on the claw, and all the sailors standing stiff at attention, wherever he went."

"Did you catch LeCorbeau looking over his big nose at him, Tom? The Frenchy's crewmen respect him, but Captain Hook commands more notice."

"Not surprising." Cecco said. "Our captain is a man worthy of our service. If his temper is uncertain, still he makes us wealthy. Well, *L'Ormonde* is a neat ship. Her captain is an opportunistic privateer and no better a man than can be expected, but it is fitting that she is sailed by a competent crew."

Tom had been saving the biggest news for last. "And here's the reason they hailed the *Roger.* LeCorbeau will be trailing us for a while. He wants to pick the bones of whatever prey we bring down."

Cecco and Jukes stared, then Cecco's expression grew suspicious. "An unusual arrangement. I wonder what the captain has in mind?"

"Profit. LeCorbeau's giving him a pretty percentage. A bonus for us, and with no extra work! I guess the Frenchman holds Hook in high esteem, too, if he wants to follow him."

Cecco's eyes narrowed. "The Frenchman has always hated Hook. There is bound to be more to it than that, but apparently our captain finds it useful to humor the man. Hook has never considered any kind of partnership before. Always he has worked alone! So…It will be interesting to watch what happens."

Jukes groaned. "I'd better be off to find the surgeon. I hope he's as good as he looks."

Cecco's suspicion remained firmly in place. He lowered his voice. "Is anyone as good as *that* gentleman appears? I believe I know where you will find him. I trust our captain is keeping a close eye on him."

His mate dropped his voice, too. "He's mighty attentive to the lady, if that's what you mean. He spent quite a bit of time in her quarters last night, and for all she's so delicate-looking, I've seen her with a sword. I don't believe she's ever been ill in her life."

Nibs bent to lean toward them. "No, Jill's up to something. She's never had a fainting fit except in play-acting. She's good at it when she wants to be."

"Aye, she fooled him." Jukes nodded. "But that Hanover's got a hungry look about him. I'll wager he's not so far above profiting from plunder as he seems. And where the lady's concerned, Cap'n's sure to have the surgeon under control. Any day now, he'll be one of us."

"Or dead." Cecco's dark eyes aimed at the surgeon. Doctor Hanover stood across the room, in the doorway of the galley.

Tom was suddenly standing, tucking in his shirt, and after hearing Cecco's prediction, he jerked his head up. He kept his voice low. "I hope for Miss' sake the doctor makes the right choice." He ran his fingers through his disorderly hair. "I'll tell him you need him, Mr. Jukes. I'm on my way out."

Jukes' decorated face lost its symmetry as he smirked. "I wouldn't bother trying to impress the man, lad. Whether he's one of us or not, no sailor's going to be good enough for *that* man's daughter."

Tom grinned. "She's the stubborn one! If I can get *her* to like me, I've no worries about him."

Nibs tightened his kerchief and hopped off the barrel. "Forget the girl, Tom. Catch a captain's eye like me and Jill, and your fortune's made!"

"I'll stick with girls, thanks. But it's probably just as well Hook laid down the law. I don't want Hanover to cut me one of those scars."

"It could only improve you, mate." Nibs clapped his brother on the back and followed him.

Jukes chuckled, but Cecco remained silent, watching Tom strut toward the ship's surgeon. Hanover had collected his meal and taken possession of the captain's own chair at the center table— with no hesitation. The watch dangled at the man's waist as he sat with perfect posture in his impeccable suit. Cecco angled his head as he observed. The matter on his mind required some reflection, maybe some action. Profiting from the captain's plunder was one thing. Plundering from the captain, quite another.

The gentleman didn't claim to be a pirate yet, but he was certainly seizing his opportunities. Yes, Mr. Cecco decided, it was time to seize a few opportunities of his own. When Jukes finally left the galley, the common Italian sailor rose from his humble bench, rolled his shoulders, and sauntered to the captain's table. He smiled his easy gypsy smile, and he sat down.

With no hesitation.

Both Hook and Jill had slept well, if not long. Hook observed that the parties involved in the new routine were becoming accustomed to it. Jill's girl entered early and tidied up the clothing that littered the cabin. Smee recovered the boot knife from her curious fingers, and although unusually quiet today, he shaved the captain and polished the hook as Jill dressed with her servant's assistance behind the curtain. Jill emerged with a waft of exquisite perfume, and she had such a light in her eye that Hook decided on the spot to gift her with the ruby necklace at the next opportunity. Perhaps she sensed the bent of his thoughts; she had foregone her opals today.

Only one event ruffled the peace of the morning. Hook's temper was riled when the shirt he wore the previous evening couldn't be found. The suit lay where he left it when he undressed in the moonlight, and the girl hung it away. But Mr. Smee's habit of looking after the captain's garments discovered the discrepancy. A subsequent hunt proved fruitless. Instinct always told Hook to attribute trouble to the newest member of the company, but, reading his thoughts again, Jill forestalled immediate action against her servant, not addressing the issue directly, but reminding Hook in a guarded fashion that the girl's father had yet to be won— which reference sent Smee into a deeper mood than before. In any case, it was clear the shirt wasn't on the girl's person, and as nothing could be proved immediately, the captain held his annoyance in check. Confident Jill would handle the problem, he allowed himself to be placated, vowing inwardly to exact punishment if called for, later on. A captain's belongings must be sacrosanct, and discipline must be maintained.

Equanimity was restored. Established behind his desk, Hook sat comfortably. The cabin was set to rights, the girl sent away, and the lady settled with her morning teacup in a chair at Hook's right. His charts were rolled up and the instruments set aside. With his claw, he tapped the desk.

"Not only did we enjoy a fine meal, but we entered into partnership. You will be happy to know that your sons, Madam, as predicted, were of service to me."

"Mr. Starkey is doing an admirable job of training them, Sir." She smiled on Starkey, who balanced on the edge of a chair before the desk, bumping his fingers over the ridges of his ruler. His scar-marked face went purple above the loose knot of his kerchief.

"Thank you Ma'am. They're good lads."

Smee had refused a seat and stood beside Starkey, his back straight and his hands clasped behind his waist. "LeCorbeau went after the bait, Ma'am, showing off his ship to the new hands."

The captain continued. "With some urging by Mr. Starkey, the *commandant* could not refuse to make good his offer. I would say the events of last evening were mutually satisfactory— LeCorbeau enjoyed the company of our young men, and we acquired information."

Jill said, "A tour of *L'Ormonde*, her arms and contents. I'm glad the boys were useful. And did the *commandant* behave himself?"

"He was a model of restraint. He merely inquired what price I would consider in exchange for Mr. Nibs' freedom."

"Reminiscent of our Doctor Hanover's offer in regard to me."

"Excepting that the gentleman wished to *rescue* you from debauchery, my love, whereas LeCorbeau…"

"*Chacun à son goût*, as his countrymen say. But you refused him?" She sipped her tea.

"Oh, no, Madam. The decision is entirely up to the young man, as I indicated to LeCorbeau. I am not in the mood to deny our new partner anything at the moment. But the day will come! Mr. Starkey, instruct Mr. Nibs to employ discretion when in sight of our sister ship. We may engage in frequent rendezvous in the next weeks, and I've no desire to disappoint LeCorbeau prematurely."

Jill frowned. "I don't understand why he wishes to play jackal to your lion."

Pride roused Smee from his solemnity. He said, "He's a sly little rooster, but he could barely keep a civil smile on his face— the idea of playing second fiddle to the grand Captain James Hook! He'd not be standing for it, I'm thinking, without some prize waiting for him at the end."

Hook turned to Jill. "You witnessed Doctor Hanover's reaction to the advent of *L'Ormonde*. After our gathering in the galley, I am convinced there is a link between Hanover and *L'Ormonde*'s captain. It does not prejudice me against his joining us, but I must know everything. Once again, Madam, your talents are required."

Jill was about to voice her suspicions, but Smee interrupted.

"Captain, Sir." Smee's forehead furrowed. "You're surely not wanting to allow that man near the lady again. Not after last night?"

"Although I appreciate your concern, Mr. Smee, I believe the lady is capable." Hook swiveled to face her. "But is she willing?"

"Aye, Captain," Jill replied, "The game's begun. It would be a shame to forfeit now." Her eyes glowed in anticipation. "As you say, the stakes are fabulous."

The Irishman shifted his stance. "Sir."

Hook regarded his bo'sun, then nodded to Starkey. "You may go, Mr. Starkey."

The sailor stood. "Aye, Captain. Lady." He bobbed his head toward the pair, and clomped from the captain's quarters, untying his kerchief to mop the back of his neck. He was glad to get well away. He never liked being close to the captain and his claw, and Smee had been brooding since before the party on *L'Ormonde*. It was clear the bo'sun had something on his mind that the captain wouldn't be pleased to hear.

The door snapped shut.

"Now, Mr. Smee. Tell me."

Smee's agitated gaze settled to rest on Jill. "Ma'am, since taking on young Miss, we're missing our morning chats. But I'm thinking I know the direction of your thoughts."

She set down her teacup. It rattled on its saucer.

"There's more to Hanover than he lets on. It seemed to me you were holding your own with the man, but only just. I don't advise you to go courting that kind of risk again."

"Mr. Smee, the captain forbids me to take part as yet in the kind of danger the rest of you must face. In the meantime, this gambit is a service I can easily perform, at little risk. Very little, compared to the battles you gentlemen fight."

"Jill has informed me of the gist of the interview, Mr. Smee. Name your concern."

"Well, Sir…the man had the gall to propose that the lady should go away with him!"

Jill adjusted the cup on her saucer. "Yes. As I told the captain, the doctor's display of confidence was quite enough to take my breath away. But knowing you were near was a great comfort to me."

"Begging your pardon, Lady, but when he got to tempting you with the diamonds, I fair had to rein myself in."

Hook raised one eyebrow. "Diamonds, Jill? So you led him right to the heart of the matter! How ever did you refuse him?"

She regarded her lover with her clear blue eyes, unabashed. "Sir. I didn't."

The captain returned her gaze, only half of a shrewd smile coming to his lips. His tone was thoughtful. "I see. So the game is advancing more swiftly than we anticipated.…Very good, my love. You are doing excellent work."

Smee reddened. "But Sir, the things the man said! How he'll get his hands on her, that as soon as he gets the chance, he'll near kill her with his love!"

"Sentiments shared by every man aboard, Mr. Smee."

The color on Smee's face deepened.

As he registered the sincerity behind the bo'sun's discomfort, Hook's features sharpened. His voice assumed an edge. "Did the man touch her, Mr. Smee?"

Reluctantly, Smee shook his head. He glanced at Jill. His broad shoulders rose as he drew a breath, then he addressed his captain again. "But to be honest, Sir, it's only a matter of time."

Jill held her head erect and remained silent. It seemed that Smee had removed himself promptly from the companionway at her signal. Too promptly to have learned the extent of the doctor's orders, or his final request. Or Jill's reply.

"Very well," Hook said. "I have instructed the lady to act according to her own judgment. Madam, if at any time you require Mr. Smee's protection, you will inform him," Hook directed his gaze to the bo'sun, "and he will oblige. Now Mr. Smee, you will please bring the surgeon to me. I will assign him his new duty, as my lady requests, and also break the news of my decision. Unless he surprises me, you will proceed as discussed. Wait for him to grant you access to his quarters, where you will attend to the necessary arrangements. No doubt he will wish to accompany you."

"Aye, Captain. He'll not be pleased!"

"As I still hope for his eventual capitulation, we shall have to find a way to appease him. The lady will attend to that."

The lady inclined her head. "Aye, Sir. I had intended to inspect Liza's quarters today in any case."

"Excellent. The timing is right for this move. We are nearing the islands, and I expect we'll sight a choice vessel any day now. Thank you, Mr. Smee."

"Sir. Madam." Smee nodded as usual, but as he turned to go, the eyes behind his spectacles lingered on the lady. That strand of hair was out of place again.…He balled his fingers together before he could obey the impulse to fix it. He thought how her perfume smelled like her skin— sweet and exotic. And she had that look about her, part heaven, part heathen. It was no wonder the doctor had fallen for her so quickly. She returned Smee's look without blinking, and he had to be satisfied. For the moment.

As he made his way out of the captain's quarters, he heard Hook speaking to her.

"Diamonds, Jill? Can you long resist such—" The china saucer clacked on the desktop, and abruptly, his words were stopped.

The Irish bo'sun grew a resigned smile. His hand slid into his breeches pocket, where he closed it over a square of fine white cloth. He didn't pull it out. He already knew that a little of her scent still lingered on it.

She was good for the captain, and Smee was grateful for her. James Hook wasn't alone any more.

Smee hoped that that great man would never be alone again.

Containing his mood, the surgeon assisted the mistress as they descended the stairs and strolled aft below decks, trailed by Liza. Lit by the morning sunlight that squeezed through its gunports, this deck, too, was bordered on both sides by cannon. Only one or two poked their snouts out to sniff the breeze. All up and down the hull, the iron monsters were held in place by tackle, taut or slack, depending on the pitch of the ship. Boxes of shot to feed them were stored against the forward bulkhead, which closed off the galley. In contrast to the silent menace of the guns, a crate of chickens clucked and clattered, awaiting the cook. In a streak of white fur, the cook's cat scampered away. Hanover ignored the surroundings, supporting Jill's arm as he guided her past the weaponry and the mizzenmast, toward the aft quarters. Inwardly, the doctor fumed over recent events.

Three doors opened off the stern section of this deck: Hanover's to starboard, Smee's to port, and in the center, a cabin for use as need determined, infirmary or storage. Just that morning, Mr. Cecco had informed the surgeon that in spite of its proximity to Smee, who had administered his punishment, he'd taken his rest on the bunk there those nights when the fire of his back had prevented him from sleeping in his hammock. A handy room for Hook, into which his victims might slink.

This ship, Hanover reflected, was full of people suffering from Hook's decrees, Hanover and this lady included. And now a new outrage! With Smee, Hook's favored lackey, as always the willing tool. Masking his fury, the doctor arrived at the door to his quarters with Jill on his arm. He stepped aside, indulging his aversion at this moment to touching any part of Hook's ship. He signaled Liza to push the door open for them.

The girl wore a mauve dress today. She had grown since it was made for her. Early this morning her father acquainted her with the fact that the brevity of its skirt displeased him. As her ankles chilled in the sea breezes, Liza hung back from the doorway, hesitating. Her father and the mistress entered the cabin, but Liza stood pushing the dress against her thighs.

"Well, you must come in, Liza. I trust you tidied the bunks since this morning's business." Liza heeded the brusque note of anger in his voice, but understood that this time it had nothing to do with her. And unlike this morning, the lady's presence would assure that he restrained his annoyance. Finding it enough for one morning to have provoked the ire of both her captain and her father, she hastened to obey, and ventured inside.

The curtains hung open, and starboard windows illuminated the room. Two bunks lay straight ahead along the stern, one on top of the other, each with its own canvas curtain for privacy. A sea chest reposed at the foot of the lower bunk. On the inside wall of the cabin, left of the entrance, a pigeon-holed desk was secured, with two chairs waiting before it. The surgeon's bag, books, and instruments were arranged in orderly fashion on the desk. A lantern stood sentinel on either side of its top shelf. The other side of the cabin contained another chair and a small table, a chest of drawers, and a mirrored shaving cabinet hanging on the wall. To the right of the door were pegs on which Liza's few dresses were draped alongside the doctor's tailored suits. A wooden bucket in the corner contained her blue dress, saturated and ballooning over the surface of the water. Except for her clothing, nothing suggested that a girl lived here.

Jill stood just within the doorway and cast her gaze around the room. "Everything looks to be in order, Liza. You keep it tidy. It appears you have settled in."

Liza resisted the impact of Jill's smile.

"I will tell you that I am satisfied with your service so far, and I hope you will take full advantage of the opportunity granted you—today, under your father's instruction, you will begin to read."

The doctor bowed, but his speech was clipped. "I was gratified, once I understood that the captain's order was prompted by *your* request."

"Yes. I think it high time for Liza to begin her scholarship. Doctor Hanover's daughter must grow into an accomplished woman."

"Like you. And so kind of you to make your quarters available. To us."

"This cabin is pleasant enough, but hardly conducive to study. And I will be pleased to enjoy your company each morning— both of you."

Jill had done it again; the doctor sloughed off his bad mood. His eyes warmed, and he now reclaimed his smug smile. "The benefits of the arrangement have not escaped me, Madam."

Jill smiled at his insinuation, then turned to Liza. "Is there anything more you need, Liza?"

Sliding her eyes sideways toward her father, the girl pinched her skirt and lifted the hem an inch.

"Ah. I see." Jill bent to inspect the dress. She raised it a fraction, and Liza, under scrutiny of her father, clapped a hand below her knee, preventing further exposure of her leg. Jill looked up to the girl's frightened face. Pausing, she stored this puzzle for future reflection, then went on, "There is plenty of fabric here to lengthen it. You'll need a needle and thread."

Liza shook her head and retreated to the chest of drawers. She knelt down to open the bottom drawer, and removed a small sewing basket. Needles and pins made a prickly bouquet of its pincushion. She set it down on the floor and looked at Jill, bunching the tips of her fingers together, then pulling her hands apart.

"Thread, then?"

Liza nodded, her lips sketching the outlines of a smile.

"Our sail maker has only coarse twine. But there is one man aboard to supply your sewing needs. Our very skilled tailor, who can fix anything that needs mending, from sails to stockings. You must see Mr. Smee."

The girl's eyes panicked and she stood up hastily, backing into the table. Mystified, Jill looked to the doctor. His lips twisted in an unpleasant manner.

"Doctor? What is it?"

"Your Mr. Smee, Madam. The 'exception to every rule.' "

"Why? What has he done?"

"Liza." Hanover jerked his head toward the bunks.

The girl cast a wide-eyed look at her mistress, then stepped forward. The little pearls on her ring glowed in the daylight as she grasped the curtain of the lower bunk. She swept it aside.

At first Jill saw nothing but the darkened interior of the bunk. Then she made out a white pillow, and then a coverlet. A long, thin shadow lay over the pillow, something that didn't belong. It coiled around the bedpost and snaked in heavy links, ending in an iron cuff. Jill allowed her mouth to fall open.

"Shackles?" Her voice achieved uncertainty.

"Again, Liza."

The girl obeyed, reaching up and yanking the upper curtain open as well. Jill stood on tiptoe to see another iron snake stretched over the higher bunk, eighteen inches of cold captivation. She stared.

"Yes," Hanover remarked. "Your Mr. Smee is the man to fix everything! He has fixed us quite nicely, as you can see."

"Doctor…"

"Captain Hook summoned me this morning, as you know. After you left, he offered me my first opportunity to sign on officially as a member of the *Jolly Roger*'s company."

"You refused him?"

"Of course I refused! And then the consequences were made clear to me."

"So you are still considered a prisoner."

"Until I swear an oath and sign the ship's articles, it seems I cannot be trusted to roam free— under certain circumstances."

"But you're not to be marooned, or confined to the brig?"

"The captain indicated that he is being uncharacteristically merciful in my case, still hoping I will change my mind. Then he ordered his Mr. Smee to set these irons in place, to be used whenever the *Roger* approaches a port or a vessel."

"So that you can't escape in the confusion. But Liza, as well?"

"Your captain is a shrewd man." Hanover laced his words with bitterness. "He won't give her the chance to choose between her father and her master."

Her master. The girl shrank back, smiling only inwardly at the knot of satisfaction tightening her chest. She sat down on the end of the lower bunk. Inconspicuous, she listened, without seeming to do so.

"Yes," Jill said, "he is shrewd indeed....Johann, I am sorry."

The doctor raised his head. The anger in his eyes lessened. "It is almost worth the humiliation, to hear you say my name."

"It is worth saying your name to comfort you. Johann. It isn't surprising, is it, that Captain Hook already knows what I know? You would leave us if you got the chance."

"No, it isn't surprising. You warned me of his methods." He paced as far as the narrow limits of his cabin would allow. "How I would like to see him caught in his own chains! But…" The doctor turned and focused on Jill, his taut face relaxing. "Perhaps you could help me. It could mean helping yourself as well."

Jill was cautious. "What would you have me do?"

"I would never place you in danger. I seek only the answer to a question."

She shot a glance at the girl on the bunk. "I told you, Sir, I am not prepared—"

"No, no! A new question. I held a conversation with Mr. Cecco this morning. He impresses me as a decent sort, and unlike most of Hook's crew, unintimidated by that Irishman. Mr. Cecco had the courtesy to inform me of Hook's arrangement with Captain LeCorbeau."

Watching the surgeon closely, Jill commented, "Yes. We were all surprised by the *commandant's* unusual proposal."

"Madam, can you learn whether Hook intends to have me shackled when we rendezvous with *L'Ormonde?* And if so, persuade him otherwise?"

"So your hope of deliverance does have something to do with *L'Ormonde.* It was my guess, after our conversation last evening."

"Out of respect for your situation, I won't answer, Madam. But I must have access to her captain."

"I can ask your question without putting myself at risk. It is one I would ask the captain in any case. But I won't argue with his decision, whatever it may be. If you are to be restrained, you must manage to change his mind on your own."

"I understand. Thank you. I am sorry to say, however, that in light of recent developments, I will be unable to make the necessary arrangements as quickly as I had hoped." Bitterness surfaced again. "I am, to say the least, disappointed."

Jill noticed that Liza kept her head down. Jill, too, remained silent. She sensed what was coming.

"I was unable to ask earlier, and it seems immaterial now. But… did you sleep well, Madam?" As entitled as he felt to ask it, he had the grace to accompany his very personal question with a blush.

She hesitated, managing a modest coloring of her own. "As it happens, Doctor, I slept quite well."

"That, at least, is something. But I will not be content until a plan—"

"I will hear nothing more. You should know, Doctor Hanover, that I have signed the ship's articles. I have sworn the oath of loyalty."

Her revelation gave the doctor pause. He looked her up and down, not with anger, but with eager relief. "So *that* is it? That is why you are reluctant to listen, or to make promises? You are honor-bound to Captain Hook! But," he relaxed his stance, "once I have removed you from his power, such an oath to such a man will count for nothing."

"It would seem that, like Captain Hook, you are concerned with my honor only until it no longer suits your purpose. The captain has chosen his physician well! As I observed once before, Mister Hanover, we are *all* pirates here aboard the *Roger*."

"Perhaps I deserve that. I admit I am becoming reckless where you are concerned."

"You deserve it, Doctor. But since you admit the truth, I won't hold it against you."

"Your own set of standards, again?"

"Yes. You see it works to your advantage, as well. And I will be honest with you once more. If Captain Hook allows you to visit *L'Ormonde*, it may be a concession to win you to his side. But I know he genuinely wishes to appease you. He has merely ordered shackles, where he might have condemned you to much worse. The fact that he shows you such leniency should convince you how sincerely he hopes you will join us…as do I."

"I will never join a pirate company!"

"Would it be so bad? To be free of your rules, the restrictions of your 'decent society?' Whatever it is you hide from me, you would no longer have to hide from anyone, as a buccaneer."

The girl on the bunk kept perfectly still. Jill proved as canny as she had supposed. The woman's instincts concerning the brilliant Doctor Hanover were accurate. Almost.

Hanover protested, "It is not in my nature to avoid moral restriction, or my responsibilities. I have important work to do—"

"Whatever that work is, you can do it as well or better aboard the *Jolly Roger* than you did on the *Julianne*. Think again, Johann. Consider our offer. You have seen today how clever Captain Hook is, how he is three steps ahead of you. I told you the first time we spoke— if you open your mind to him as you have opened to me, you will come, in time, to admire him."

Hanover closed in on her. "Do you think I could bring myself to serve the man— the criminal— who is three steps ahead of me in possessing you?" His scarred jaw tightened. "When I think of the arrogance of that man, how he takes what I want, how he owns you—" He seized his watch, as if he wanted to throttle it. "How he owns *me*."

Jill's tone turned to ice. "Look about you, Mister Hanover. What you'll see is not slavery, but loyalty. No one, including Hook, owns me. If you look for ownership, I am hardly the woman for you."

"No indeed. I seek instead to release you. I watched your face last night, when I told you of my desire—" Hanover stopped, tossing a glance toward his daughter. He stepped nearer to Jill and mastered his voice. "I am learning this about you. You are a strong woman. As such, your ardor will be all the more rewarding, in the end, to unleash. I will bring you to heights of sensation, ecstasies, which you have never imagined."

The lady arched her eyebrows. "You think to do more than Hook?"

"I think of it, and little else." Standing close, almost touching her, he gazed down into her eyes. "And so do you."

She pulled in her breath and stepped back, bumping into the door. She hadn't realized he'd backed her nearly against it. Catching her balance, she forced herself to speak evenly once more. "Sir, let us go back to the deck now. We can walk again, the exercise will calm you, clear your head. And then, I think, you will be in a better temper to begin Liza's lesson."

"Yes. It is unbearable here, with those iron reminders of my helplessness."

Conscious of the medicine bag on the desk, Jill said, "You are anything but helpless, Doctor." She turned to leave, then halted before the doorway. "As I can see by your weapons. But these are beautiful swords, Sir."

Hanging on hooks in the wood of the wall were a foil, a rapier, and the doctor's walking stick. Made of fine workmanship, they swayed with the ship's movement.

"My old friends." Hanover took down the foil and stepped into the gunnery. Jill followed, and shortly after, Liza emerged from the bunk.

The surgeon strode to the center of the deck, where no shackles and no walls restricted his movement. He stood erect, holding the sword up straight, then waved it in a circle and thrust it, his left arm poised, his right foot plunging suddenly forward to bear his weight. He stopped then, and his pose sagged. Alone in the midsection of the gun deck, he sighed and shook his head.

This attitude of defeat seemed so foreign to the surgeon that Jill was drawn to him. Standing before him, she searched his eyes. She reached out with her scarlet hand to tuck his watch into its pocket. Her fingers lingered on its golden chain, then she placed her hands on his arm. The doctor studied her, puzzled. With gentle insistence, she turned him, and taking hold of his collar, she slid his coat from his shoulders.

"Now." She backed away, his coat in her arms.

He turned to face her, and regaining his stiff smile, cut a bow. He corrected his grip on the foil. Free of his outer layer of dignity, the surgeon made another stab, and then another, and he began in earnest to exercise his anger. In fluid, practiced motions, he waltzed with his sword, up and down in the open space between the guns of his enemy. He feinted and parried, pushed himself forward and pulled himself back, turning, slashing elegantly, and whipping the glinting foil until it sang a song of satisfaction.

Jill followed the movements of his white sleeves. She listened to the shuffle of his shoe leather on the boards, and she understood now, without a doubt, that the surgeon with the sword would never reconcile to become one with this ship's company. She watched with every outward sign of fascination and her heart sinking like a stone as the gentleman's smile opened up, and his sand-colored hair fell loosely down at last, over his ears.

This, she believed, is how the gentleman would look after a bout of love-making. Handsome, slightly disheveled…and aggressive. She raised her fingers to stroke the scar at her throat.

The doctor fenced with his imaginary foe for some minutes, and then Jill leaned toward Liza. Her eyes never left the swordsman.

"Liza. You may hunt up your thread. Your father and I will meet you in my quarters."

The girl dodged away toward the narrow stairs to the deck. The fowl in their cage fluttered at her approach, stirring up their dry, sour smell, and eyeing her in suspicion. Hearing the fencing foil slicing the air, she didn't pause to look behind her until the sound stopped and she was nearly up the steps. Then she beheld the lady and the gentleman.

She saw that the coat was folded and hanging over a cannon. Her father stood still now, his face aglow from the release of his fury, his shoulders heaving with his breathing. The lady beckoned to him, and then her fingers were pushing his hair back over his temples. Liza saw that he didn't touch the woman. He stood with his sword lowered, arms at his sides. But she saw that the two of them saw nothing but each other.

Liza was gone then, in search of Mr. Smee, allowing the clipped voice the privacy to ask a question she didn't need to hear.

He was still breathing heavily.

"Is it today, Madam?"

Only the doctor— and the poultry— heard her reply.

Pains and Needles

Hook had gone about his business, allowing time for Jill to conduct her own. The gunnery was clear now, and his boots tapped down the stairs. Closely followed by his bo'sun, he headed toward the spare cabin, shrugging off his coat as he walked, and appreciating the light, exotic scent that lingered in the air. The captain shoved the door wide with his hook, threw his coat over a chair, and eased himself down to sit on the bunk, propping a pillow against the wall behind him. In the light of two aft windows he examined a smudge on the toe of his boot, then crossed it over the other and reclined. His hook came to rest on the blanket.

Smee took note of his captain's expression, then looked out at the gun deck and half closed the door. "It's a mite musty in here." He moved to a window and lifted it open, hooking it to a ring on the ceiling. "I'll speak to Starkey about that botched blacking. Tom Tootles is usually doing a better job. Polishing boots was the first thing he volunteered for when he joined up."

"No need, Mr. Smee. I believe our two young sailors are merely over-eager about their upcoming task." Hook untied his shirt and tucked his hand into his collar. "Let it go." He ran his fingers under the leather straps of his brace, massaging.

"Aye, Sir. It won't be long before they're showing us what they're made of."

"I also intend to discover what constitutes our doctor."

"How so?"

"I and my cutlass shall take our exercise with Starkey's charges."

"Do you say, now? A rare treat for the lads! Are they ready for you?"

"I shall employ caution, of course. I'll alert you beforehand. It will be your responsibility to see that Hanover is on deck then."

"And will the lady be joining you?"

"She will observe, so that I may obtain a true reading of Hanover's swordsmanship."

"Hanover's? What of the lads?"

Hook's fingers ceased massaging and loosely gestured Smee nearer. He lifted his chin to one side as the bo'sun tied his shirt closed again. "Mr. Nibs and Mr. Tootles are only the pretext. It is the surgeon whom I wish to test."

"And the lady's job?"

"Her presence is vital to ensure his best efforts, but she'll not participate until I have authorized another examination by the surgeon."

Smee snorted, but declined comment.

"Now, Mr. Smee. No need for concern. I intend to chaperone this time. As you are well aware, I can be a generous man. But I do have my limits."

"So I've heard the lady say, in regard to your swag. But I'm that glad you're taking my warning to heart, Sir."

"There was never any question of it. Your instincts have often proven invaluable. And while I have every confidence in Jill, I make it a habit not to gamble more than I can afford to lose."

"As my old mum used to advise before packing my brothers and me off to the horse fair."

"You are becoming sentimental before your time, Mr. Smee. It must be the presence of a woman on board. I observe that the entire crew is somewhat addled."

"It's the truth, Sir, but nothing we'll not learn to live with."

Unnoticed, a shadow flitted over the floor by the half open door.

"All is well, I assume, concerning my prohibitions on the girl?"

The shadow froze, then drew itself against the wall.

"Aye, Captain. There's looks, but no trouble. It helps that she's a haughty little thing and mostly keeps to herself."

Liza crept closer, pressing herself thin. Pulled unresisting toward the voice of her captain, she stopped just before the tip of her nose passed the door-jamb.

"Good. But be on guard. Such an attitude on her part can encourage rather than discourage the men's attention. Except for the episode regarding my shirt this morning— about which, incidentally, I have now satisfied myself— Jill is contented with the girl, and I shouldn't care to burden you with double duty again, serving both of us."

"Not that I'd mind it. But it's more fitting this way, of course."

"There is certainly more 'fitting' of her clothing! Jill wears more of it now, and it is a trend which I find disagreeable."

Neglecting the errand for which her mistress had interrupted her first reading lesson, the girl in the gunnery didn't absorb the details, nor Smee's heavy footfalls pacing between the walls. She was listening to the captain's silken speech.

The Irish lilt answered him, "All part of her play-acting for Hanover. It took a tight corset to make that fainty-feint look plausible."

"And the man considers himself civilized! It was most fortunate that you and your lacing talents were on the spot, Mr. Smee. That offensive garment was the linchpin of the evening's events. I suppose it also afforded some protection. Matronly armor you might call it. Wherever did you find the ghastly piece? I order you to burn it at the next opportunity." Hook closed his eyes. "Have the courtesy to sit down, Smee. You weary me."

"Sorry, Sir. Will you be resting for a spell?"

The girl heard a shushing of cloth, and imagined his long body shifting on the bunk.

"Not without my lady. There is no point."

"Aye. You'd not be able to sleep unless she did. And she'd best not be dreaming this morning! She's got to be sharp as long as Hanover's about."

"A brilliant scheme, is it not? Stolen moments, shared while guiding a young mind toward its potential. Only Jill would think of that."

Liza's ears feasted at last. *This* was what she craved, the bounty she had missed in the dark of the captain's quarters last night— a tryst with the *sound* of him.

Smee was agreeing with his captain. "You'd think she'd have had enough of guiding young minds, wouldn't you, what with all those boys she raised? But I think she likes the girl. Shocked, she was, to learn the little thing couldn't read."

"Barbarous..."

Liza heard his sneer, and eagerly snatched it up.

"...Unable to speak, unable to write. Whatever the 'little thing' knows of her father is safely locked inside. Not only is he clever. He is cold."

"Tell it to the lady, Sir. I can see it plain as day, but he managed to get her warm enough last night. You should have heard him!"

With no warning, the velvet turned to ice. "I have heard, and I have heard enough." The bunk creaked.

Smee cleared his throat. "Begging your pardon, Cap'n. I was meaning no disrespect."

Liza's ears endured the silence until at last, Hook breathed deeply.

"We will allow the lesson another half an hour. The doctor should have gotten from A to L by then."

She sensed a sly *soupçon* of a smile.

"We won't permit him to move all the way...to Z."

They laughed together, and underlying Smee's rollicking chortle was the deep, rich, black-gold laugh of which Liza had longed to partake. Closing her eyes, she indulged in it, memorizing the sound, already drunk with it. The potency of his laughter frightened her, but she liked to feel frightened, overpowered, as she had been overpowered earlier that morning. It made her feel alive.

After the laughter, postponing the moment when she must open her eyes, Liza felt her way dizzily along the wall to her cabin, pushed open the door, and stole inside. Forgetting why she had come there, she simply stood and waited. Her legs began to ache again, and then her senses sobered enough to inform her of her mistress' errand. She scooped up her sewing basket with its crop of needles and yarns. Still off balance, she spun back toward the door. In the corner of her eye she caught a glimpse of her father's black leather bag, upright and clamped tight shut. It couldn't look more proper, Liza thought, but it couldn't be more deceptive.

That bag held secrets— cold, hard, glittering secrets, and slippery liquid ones. Hidden deep inside the bag, deep inside of Liza, were the tools and rewards of her father's genius.

Again, she felt the ring around her finger. It had slid off her mother's hand so easily that night. That last night, after all the horrid noises died with her. And he had just lain there in the spitting candlelight, panting like a spent bull, his hair unkempt, his own arm dangling off the bed, alongside hers. Her mother's, white as a ghost.

Liza's lip curled. She might have stolen his signet ring, too, for all he noticed her. He never even knew Liza had seen. He'd paid her no attention. Not then.

But the diamonds, and the liquids, they would both fetch Jill's attention, if they hadn't already. Liza wondered. Would those gems capture— could they fail to capture— Captain Hook's? Her gray eyes, misty now, shifted toward the door. She had another moment or two to think, her father wouldn't be eager for her to return. He'd want all the time with the mistress he could squeeze out of his new role as schoolmaster. Jill had been right. The doctor's principles were stretching to fit his purpose, to press his advantage. And it was working out just as Liza anticipated. She and her father were helping each other, whether he realized it or not.

Liza began to shape her thoughts into workable implements. Any pirate would want what was in that bag! If he used the spare cabin again, it would be easy. She would have to watch and see. Why and when did he come here? And who would be with him, and how often? Liza's blood was already so thick with the ideas taking form in her head that she couldn't hear the talk in the next room any longer.

With her whole body numb, she crept to the doorway and leaned against it, unable to feel the rough wooden jamb jutting into her shoulder. She anchored her gaze to a square of sunshine on the gun deck. One hand clutched her sewing basket to her bodice. One hand trifled under her skirts.

It didn't matter that he never spoke to her. It didn't matter what he said about her. She had gotten more than she hoped for— the master *thought* about her. He had thought about her this morning, too, because she had made his shirt disappear. And now his voice had spoken, ever so silkily, of her! The blood in her skull moved quickly downward, and her ears attended him again, ecstatic under the strokes of his speech. Her hands moved along with it, until she was able to feel her fingers and she recognized the piercing pain to be a needle wedged into the flesh between her finger and thumb.

She drew a quiet breath, and then she smoothed her too-short skirt to saunter over the threshold and traverse the sunny squares, up the open aisle between the guns. As she mounted the steps, she relished her torment. She had listened to her nurse in the past, she had picked out segments of coarse sailor-talk. She knew without his telling her exactly what that Tom Tootles was after. It would hurt just like this, the first time. The first prick! She smiled. She knew men loved to be the first, it was a special thrill, one most sailors never experienced, to make a girl bleed.

She would bleed when she pulled the needle out, outside the master's door.

Nibs saw her first this time. Broadening his paces, he caught up to her just before she reached the stairs to the companionway. "Miss, did you enjoy the party last night?"

Liza slowed, then turned, disdainful as a duchess. Seeing Tom close behind his brother, she lifted her chin.

"Red-Handed Jill can sure tell a story, can't she?"

She condescended to nod, briefly. Sizing her up, Nibs tried to determine how best to approach her, and his gaze lit on the sewing basket. "Going to do some mending, Miss? Jill tells a good story of how she once stitched a shadow to— *what happened?*"

Liza hid her left hand behind her.

"What's up, Nibs?" Tom arrived, looking between them curiously. Liza's expression was guarded; Nibs' was repulsed.

"It's her hand, Tom! Miss Liza, let us see it."

But Liza's face was set. Clutching the sewing basket, she didn't move.

Nibs reasoned, "We can help you, Miss. Don't be afraid."

Liza wasn't afraid. She was hurting, and vibrant. She eyed each of the young men. Then, like a soldier showing off a medal, she pulled her hand from behind her back and held it out for them to see. She was just as brave as these pirates. Maybe braver.

Nibs' and Tom's eyes widened as they stared. Within a splotch of liquid red, the needle pierced the skin between her thumb and forefinger, its point and eye both visible. A trail of gray thread dangled down her palm.

"Nibs, take the basket. Now, Miss, don't worry." Tom moved closer, slowly, to avoid startling her. He kept his voice even. "Just give me your arm, and I'll set you down. Right here, see, right on the steps. There, now." Guiding Liza to sit, he exchanged a look with Nibs, who grasped the basket and made way, shaking his head in warning.

"Tom, think what you're doing."

But Tom wasn't thinking about his own skin. When Liza was settled, he didn't release her arm. Instead, he sat next to her and secured her elbow in one hand, encircling her wrist with the other. He surveyed the needle. "That's a nasty piece of work, that is, Miss. No wonder you didn't want to pull it out yourself."

Nibs cautioned, "Remember Mr. Cecco, Tom!"

Liza was watching Tom suspiciously. She despised his interference; the needle and the hurt were her own to deal with. Jealously, she guarded her privilege to pain. These trespassers had no right to intrude upon the intensity that brought her to life. Liza wanted to revel in the sensation, to determine its duration herself. But Tom Tootles was just a sailor boy, too simple to see that. Too meddling. And Liza lived under the *captain's* protection. Tom wasn't supposed to touch her, and he knew it! He should listen to his brother.

Tom looked in her eyes and didn't understand. But he knew what he should do.

"Nibs, fetch Doctor Hanover."

Relieved, Nibs nodded. "Aye, aye."

But the girl started up, just as Tom expected, and he held her fast and pulled her back to sit on the stair. She shook her head in genuine panic, and Nibs halted, unsure what to do.

If Tom was unsure, he didn't show it. "He really ought to see this, Miss."

In the distance, Liza glimpsed Mr. Starkey watching, his fists rising to settle on his hips. A glance at Tom and Nibs told her they hadn't seen him yet. They were positioned on either side of her, and Nibs' back was toward their tutor. To prevent the young men from sighting Starkey, she relented, relaxing her arm and laying it deliberately on Tom's thigh.

"All right, Miss, I'll take care of you."

"Tom, no!"

But Liza turned to Nibs and flickered her eyelashes toward him. When she was certain he wouldn't move to summon her father, she assured herself that Starkey was watching, then engaged Tom again.

He grinned. "What did you do, shoot for your ear and miss?"

His humor seemed only to offend her. Tom still held her wrist, and she made a sudden, violent show of struggling— for Starkey.

Afraid she might hurt herself, Tom persevered, gripping her middle and remaining calm. "I've been thinking of an earring for myself, Miss. A big gold one." Once she stilled, he stretched his earlobe out for her inspection. "What do you think?"

Her lip wavered, betraying the beginning of a sneer.

"And Nibs here, he says he'll pierce it for me. But I don't trust him. I intend to go right to an expert. Do you think maybe you'd do it for me?" He smiled coaxingly.

She looked down, unable to repress the smirk as he so willingly walked into her snare.

"This needle has proven it can do the job, but it's already busy. We'd best give it a rest now, don't you think?" And he seized the eye of the needle, and yanked.

The girl flinched in pain, and her shoulders shot up. Her mouth opened in a soundless shout, then she closed it, unhappily, as her shoulders fell. At the same time, Mr. Starkey's fists fell from his hips.

"There now. I'll just wipe it clean for you. I see you're not afraid of blood, but it seems the gentlemanly thing to do."

Gentlemanly. Liza knew firsthand what gentlemen were capable of doing.

Tom drew the rag from his pocket and wiped the needle, then found a clean spot and dabbed the swelling red bead from her skin. Judging by the glare on her face, she wasn't grateful, and the sly look that replaced it puzzled Tom. With a lurch of his stomach, he thought again how different this girl was from Jill.

"Here, Nibs." He passed the needle to his brother. "Put this in the basket, where it won't hurt anybody." He got up, offering Liza a hand that he wasn't surprised she spurned.

"That's all right, then. You can thank me later, Miss. When you're over the shock."

Thinking she looked well over the shock now, Nibs handed the basket back to her but kept his opinion to himself. He peered over his shoulder up the deck, then jerked upright. "Let's go, Tom! Mr. Starkey's seen us and he's taking off his coat. I think you're in trouble."

Tom was watching Liza. "You go on. I'll follow."

"Best hurry, mate!" Nibs touched his forehead to Liza. "I hope you're all right now, Miss Liza." He jogged away toward Starkey, to begin explaining why Tom had been touching Jill's girl against captain's orders— and he wasn't sure he *could* explain.

Tom bent down to level a questioning stare at her smirking, smiling face. "I don't understand you, Miss. You pretty yourself up, but then you act like you don't care about the men. I did you a kindness, and you seem glad to see me in trouble for it. And now you've managed to bloody your hand. Like Jill. You're as strong as she is, I can tell, and I see you watching her, like you want to *be* Jill. But what I want to know is, who *you* are."

The look she aimed at him was contemptuous with disbelief. No one wanted to know who Liza Hanover was!

"Well, I do know one thing. I hope you'll think about explaining it to me one day. I pulled that needle from your skin, but you're still hurting." Tom turned away to stride up the deck and take his punishment. Catching Starkey's scowl, he cursed himself for a fool. He'd been a damned idiot! The captain always knew best. He should have let the doctor handle her, no matter how she objected. Aboard Hook's ship, neither a soft heart nor a soft head was an excuse for disobeying orders. And Jill would say the same.

He deserved whatever he got.

Liza collected herself and climbed the steps toward the master's quarters. She crossed the companionway, and on reaching the door she heard a shout. She paused to observe Mr. Starkey aim a vicious blow with the back of his fist that sent Tom reeling. As Tom stumbled, Starkey caught him by the shoulders, shoved him roughly toward the forecastle, and kicked him into the armory. Starkey stormed into the armory after him, and the door slammed shut.

Nibs hung back and turned away, bowing his head.

Liza licked the blood off her hand and smiled. She guessed she wasn't the only one who was hurting now.

She was learning a lot more than how to read.

The first lesson began at the dining table, amid parchment, ink, quills, a bowl of fruit, two tiny glasses, and a bottle of sherry. Settling into her studies earlier that morning, Liza wasn't fooled by her father or her mistress. He was more patient with Liza than she ever remembered, no doubt because he wasn't really concentrating on her. And Jill was always Jill, honestly deceptive. An effective teacher, herself.

Privately, Liza had acquainted herself with all of her mistress' belongings and their hiding places, but when asked to fetch her sewing things, she didn't point out the fact that the lady's own sewing basket lodged in the drawer under the captain's bunk. Jill would only have laughed and admitted the truth— she needed Liza to go. But the girl gladly left the pair alone to fetch it, as commanded, from her quarters. It suited her purpose.

The fruit bowl and the sherry glasses were full then. When Liza returned, sucking on her hand, the glasses were empty, and she found her mistress and her father ensconced in the window seat with only the fruit bowl between them. The lady's dainty bare foot rested on his shoe, and he was wiping her fingers with a napkin, as if each one were made of fine crimson china, and he had just enjoyed a meal. The blood rushed to fill Liza's head again, throbbing.

For the next half hour, she listened partly to her father and completely for her master, watching the hand wearing the signet ring spread curlicues over the pages. Jill had thanked Liza for the sewing basket and set to work, enthroned on the window seat with silken pillows and a piece of ladies' lacy mending. The picture she presented was a delightful contrast of royal privilege and domestic necessity. The doctor taught Liza her letters, and pretended not to find the scene enchanting, but the lady's every stitch sewed him more securely into her design.

Everyone jumped as a knock beat the door. Liza's pen dropped an ink blot, and Jill pricked her finger. Smee entered without waiting for permission, his seafarer's eyes taking in every detail of the situation. Liza stretched her neck, searching behind him, then slouched, disappointed. Hanover rose to his feet.

"The captain requests that you join him for luncheon in the galley, Ma'am. And you, Doctor. He's in a social mood today."

"Thank you, Mr. Smee." Jill laid down her mending and turned a smile toward the girl. "You've made good progress, Liza." She rose and walked past the surgeon without looking at him, her arm extended and her skirts swishing. "There, Mr. Smee, see what you've done. You startled me so, I pricked myself."

Smee smiled sheepishly and took her hand in his. Inspecting the red drop through his spectacles, he whipped out a cloth to dab it. "My apologies, Ma'am."

"Why, Mr. Smee! I do believe you've mistakenly borrowed my handkerchief."

Smee's surprised expression changed as he shifted his gaze past Jill, to Hanover. "No, Ma'am. There was no mistake about it." He regarded the doctor as if defying the man to object. "Knowing your ways, I thought you'd not be minding."

Hanover's jaw clenched.

"Not unless you were anyone else, Mr. Smee. As I recently remarked to the doctor, you are always the exception." Turning then, Jill addressed the surgeon, her hand still cradled in Smee's. "So you see, Mister Hanover, if you, too, care for a token, you must steal it. I believe you will find another handkerchief under my pillow."

His jaw slackened, and fell open. Smee's eyebrows shot up. Sitting still, Liza stared at her own prick-wound, and felt the silence tumbling down all around her.

Jill turned from them all and adjusted the wardrobe door to

appraise her appearance in the mirror. As she slid open her jewel drawer, her reflection smiled conspiratorially at Mr. Smee.

"Liza, fasten my opals for me please, and you may come to the galley once you've cleared away."

Both Smee and Hanover recovered in time to contend silently for the honor of holding the cabin door for the lady, and then they all left Liza, and she did clear away.

She cleared away the glasses, throwing her head back and tipping each one high over her tongue to taste the last drops of nectar. Removing the fruit bowl, she plucked the napkin from the window seat, with its sweet, sticky smearing of juices. She cleared away the sherry bottle, right under her skirt, down the stairs and into her quarters, where she hid it far back in the lowest drawer of her dresser. Later she would bring two glasses. And fruit, when it was practical. Everything else she could find in the galley, when the time came.

Just like Jill, she wouldn't let a lover go hungry. Not in any sense of the word.

Sitting back on her heels, kneeling like a proper servant girl, it occurred to Liza that she no longer regretted her kidnapping, nor resented her captivity. As her mistress had foreseen, she was freer, and happier, really, than she'd ever been before.

Drawing her finger along the rough wood of the floor, she shaped the letters her father had taught her, wedged neatly in the alphabet between A and L, the three letters that formed her first written word.

J— i— l— l.

She didn't mind that word anymore, not at all. When she thought about it, Liza was grateful for Jill. She was learning a lot from her.

Bending over her hand, she squeezed a few drops of blood from the wound, and with her finger traced another letter on her palm, in pretty red ink. Then she spread her hand wide and smiled at it.

H.

Mr. Smee made his way slowly down the steps to the gun deck, stretching his brawny arms and looking forward to removing his boots. Since Red-Handed Jill joined up, the captain didn't need Smee to attend him most evenings, and the bo'sun had a few more minutes to himself at the end of each day. Solitary minutes, sometimes, but Smee had plenty to occupy his thoughts tonight.

The night was as silent as it ever got on board the *Roger*. The ship and the sea made their sounds, joining together as fans of spray jumped through the gunports. A luminance shone through the crack under the surgeon's door— and also under Smee's. Squinting at it, he walked lightly down the deck. He pushed his door open. Peering in, he tensed his muscles, ready for anything. Then he relaxed. He knew that orange kerchief; Nibs was standing by the bunk.

"Mr. Nibs! What brings you—?" He stopped.

At the groan of the door, Nibs had turned to face the bo'sun. Now he stepped away from the bed. He didn't bother to explain.

Smee shut the door, and his chin lowered. "So. Tom Tootles."

Tom looked up at Smee through one eye. The light of the lantern on Smee's table showed his other eye to be puffy and discolored, swollen nearly shut. A two-inch cut leaked blood from his right temple to his eyebrow. He hunched on the edge of Smee's bunk, his arms folded across his stomach.

Smee angled his head. "I wondered if you'd be crawling out to see me. Thought you might come sooner, though."

Gravely, Nibs said, "Sorry to bust in on your quarters, Mr. Smee. Tom didn't want anyone to see him yet. He got through duty in the galley, then stayed below 'til dark."

"By 'anyone' I expect you mean the lass."

Tom looked away.

"Can't say as I blame you. It's a right ugly face you've got, lad. That cut's sure to leave you your first mark. How's the rest of you?"

Answering, Tom moved his bruised jaw joint as little as possible. His posture belied his words. "I'm all right. No cuts except my head. Can you stitch me up, Sir?"

"Me? We've got a surgeon for such jobs now, haven't you heard?"

Tom's eye shifted toward Nibs.

"Tom would rather not bother the man, Sir, seeing as it was his daughter made the trouble." He hesitated, wanting to say more, but thinking better of it. "Jill talked him into coming to you, Mr. Smee."

"That's all right, lad." Smee unlocked a cabinet in the corner and pulled out a bottle. "First thing to do is to dose you. Take this, and then I'll give you some more." He uncorked it, took a cup from the cupboard, and poured out a generous measure of rum, which he handed to Tom. "We've got to deaden the senses."

Tom swallowed some, his senses far from dead as the heat of the liquid ran down his throat to his belly. He paused, then drank again, resisting the grimace because of the painful muscles it might require.

"Light that other lantern, Mr. Nibs." Pouring some of the liquor on a cloth, Smee smiled crookedly through his red beard.

Tom muttered into the cup. "Damned fool."

"What was that?"

He squinted blearily up at Smee as the man dabbed at the dried blood, then set his teeth and said it louder. "I was a damned fool, Sir. I never should have looked twice at her."

"Well, I'm glad you've learned something. A lesson like that can guide you all the rest of your life."

Nibs had hung the lantern and kept himself quiet, but he defended his brother now. "Tom wasn't trying to hurt her, Mr. Smee. He only meant to help!"

Smee gestured to Tom to hold out his cup. The bottle clinked on the rim as he poured again. "Keep drinking, lad." He tossed the reddened rag on his worktable and corked the rum, then pulled a box from his cabinet. Rummaging through it, he collected a needle, a spool of fine, sturdy twine, and a knife. "What do *you* say, Mr. Tootles?" Smee kept his back to the boys.

Tom's gullet was burning now, just like his cut, but he swallowed some more rum. "I'd be all right, if I'd followed orders."

"Aye. And why didn't you?"

"I wanted to be a hero. She needs one."

Smee turned around to look at Tom. As he studied the young sailor, a thoughtful expression crossed his face.

"A hero, lad?"

"I don't suppose you'd sympathize with that, Mr. Smee."

"Wouldn't I though? You might be surprised to learn that the captain kept me from a nasty knife fight over a woman. Years ago.

She was just a tavern girl, but I'd have gladly died for her that night. I never thought of her again 'til now. I can't even recall her name."

"But, Sir, you always have luck with the ladies. You don't have to disobey orders to get their attention."

"Well, it depends on the lady, now, doesn't it? Some respect a man's duty, some deliberately tempt a man away from it. Your mother, now, she tempts better than any, but she understands duty. She knows I'd never—" Abruptly, Smee turned to the box and began measuring the thread. Forcing his mind back to the lecture, he continued. "She knows she's honor-bound to follow our captain, no matter what. Just like you two."

"Aye, and that little Miss is one to use the rules against a man! I've learned my lesson. My first loyalty is to the captain."

"Tell Mr. Smee what Jill said, Tom. Go on."

Smee pulled the twine through the needle and cut it. "What did she say, lad?"

"She came to me when I was drudging for Cook in the galley, Mr. Smee. She gave me that look she gets when she's mad."

Smee grinned. "Aye, I know the one!"

"But she wasn't mad. She grabbed my jaw and looked me over, and then she says 'Don't tell me what you did, Mr. Tootles. Tell me what you're *going* to do.' And I says 'Ma'am, I'm sorry and ashamed.' And then her eyes fired up and she smacked me hard on the face, and she says, 'No son of mine has any business being ashamed. Get on with your punishment and then get on with your life,' she says… because shame brings a man down, but learning from a mistake makes you strong. That's what she said, and then she sent Nibs for my spare shirt, cleaned me up, and offered to send for the doctor."

"Which you declined."

"Aye, and she wouldn't leave until I promised to come to you."

The bo'sun took a deep breath. "She's a wise one, for all she's so young. Listen to her, and hold your head up tomorrow when you see that girl again."

The rum was beginning its work on Tom. He blinked with one eye and leaned against the wall. "Aye. Once I'm stitched together again, I'll get on with my duty, and not bother with her any more."

He took a last gulp and handed his cup to Nibs.

Smee's strong arm slipped behind Tom and hoisted him. He shifted the pillow and laid the young man down. "Take this and bite down, lad. It tastes bad, but it'll save your tongue." He stuck a strip of leather between Tom's teeth. "But if you think your worries are over, I'll be warning you now. If you ignore that girl, she'll only find another way to make trouble. Mark my words, and be on your guard."

Nibs stared at Smee, questioning. "But that's what she's wanted all along. To be left alone."

"Has she now? Then why am I about to sew up your brother for helping her? Hold this lantern steady, and let's get on with it. Take a firm grip of his wrists, now, and don't look, if it makes you queasy."

"No, Sir, I'll watch. It's sort of a punishment for me, too. I should have taken better care of him."

"Tom made his own decision. And remember what the lady said, Mr. Nibs. No shame."

Smee took note of the way these young men were looking at him, and hid the smile. It was good to be a hero sometimes. And tonight, these lads needed one far more than did the ladies aboard.

Tom mumbled incoherently around the leather strap.

Bending over his face, Smee got to work. "That's right, Mr. Tootles.…Whatever it was you said."

Dangerous Truths

Discussion of the incident involving Tom Tootles and the girl had all but died down. Once the worst was over, most of the men ribbed Tom, but he remembered Jill's admonition and shrugged their ridicule away. The exceptions were Nibs, of course, who had lost his light-heartedness; Mr. Starkey, who badgered Tom to work harder than ever; and Mr. Cecco, who insisted wryly that when he had advised Tom to make his own luck, he hadn't meant for him to produce it under Mr. Starkey's scarry nose.

Tom was stiff and sore and his favorite yellow shirt was torn beyond repair, but the welts had changed color and there was no question that under the jibes, his mates accepted him. He'd made a boy's mistake, but he'd taken the consequences like a man.

Miss was more watched, and more alone, than ever. She and her tea tray were seen early each day heading from the galley to the captain's quarters, where she spent most of the mornings. Later she would run her errands, and then she kept to her cabin. It was noted, quietly, that she had taken to going barefoot, and her ink-stained fingers crocheted an attractive net for her hair that didn't offend her father's sense of propriety. When consulting the surgeon, the crewmen chose to talk to him in the spare cabin next to his quarters rather than run the risks inherent in close proximity to her. Consistent with his policy, the captain seemed to ignore her. Only the lady tried to talk to her at all, and she, too, was guarded. Everyone else steered clear of Miss. It was apparent that she was, indeed, bad luck.

The sighting of the ship made a welcome diversion for everyone.

The knock sounded above the brass plate, and Capt. Jas. Hook was summoned from his quarters where he was taking supper with Red-Handed Jill. Now positioned by the port rail, he gave the word to sheer the *Roger* off course toward the vessel. It took some time and some reefing of sails to enter within proper range for the spyglass. In the light of the setting sun, Jill appeared in the captain's doorway, her fingers wrapped around a cup of wine, and her hair flowing over scarlet taffeta, brushed by an early evening breeze that promised a warm night.

One devoted sailor had been watching for her. He'd asked Yulunga to keep an eye on the surgeon. These three oddly-matched men were becoming friendly; they had just shared a meal in the galley below. Assured that the physician was occupied for the time being, the sailor slipped unnoticed past the deck hands, some in the rigging and some at the rail, all straining to look east, their backs to the sunset. He heard the deck buzz with murmurs of excitement as his bare feet climbed to the top step of the companionway.

"Good evening, Mr. Cecco. Have you come to show me more of your magic tricks?" She was satisfied; she smiled. Rubies glowed at her throat.

And golden chains glittered on his neck. "I will be most pleased to entertain whenever you wish, Madam. But I have come to ask if you have recovered your good health and spirits?"

"I am quite well, thank you."

"Unlike your son's well-being, yours is, no doubt, attributable to the good doctor's care." He smiled with his even teeth.

Jill couldn't tell. Was there a touch of sarcasm in his accent? "Mr. Smee took very good care of Tom, and we are both fortunate to enjoy the solicitude of the captain and our shipmates, and also healthy constitutions. In fact, I had planned to resume fencing tomorrow," her gaze lifted toward the sea, "but it looks as if we may all be otherwise occupied."

Hook turned just then to assure himself of her whereabouts, and over the distance that separated them, they exchanged a smile.

He registered the presence of his sailor, and then he faced the sea and raised the spyglass again.

Following Jill's attention, Mr. Cecco twisted to search out the unidentified vessel. Confronted by the ugly marks on the man's back, Jill drew away, but she kept looking. The two ends of the leather strap that bound his hair dangled against his scars, too reminiscent of the whip. As he turned back to her, she shifted quickly to meet his eyes, but not quickly enough.

Cecco said, "We will know soon whether she is a prize or a warship. I am ready for some action! But I see that you are still concerned with *my* condition."

She spoke lightly, but carefully. "It strikes me, Mr. Cecco, that you have now paid for your most famous act of bloodshed."

His easy smile became tempered, a little dangerous. "You refer to Gao, Madam?"

"Yes.... The prison governor's back, and letters of blood."

"The day I carved my name on him. My shipmates are not usually so courageous as to remind me of this incident. But then, you are an unusual shipmate."

"I can't prevent the images from coming to me. It's part of your story, just as my red hand is part of mine."

Now he nodded, his amiability restored. "Yes, your red hand. The mark that proves you are one of us. May I?" His bracelets chimed as he extended his own hand to her, and when she tilted her head, he explained, "I mean to read your palm."

Smiling, she lifted her left hand, palm up.

"No, the other hand, the stained one. Blood will not mask the truth."

She complied, slipping the goblet into her left hand. "What do you see? Please, not more boys to raise! Tom has given me quite enough to worry about." It was best, she had decided, not to take Mr. Cecco too seriously.

He scooped his hand under hers and barely touched it, applying just enough pressure to support it. "Ah! I see....No, Madam, no more boys. Only men from now on...and...yes."

"Yes, what?"

"Yes, you will be adored always. But that has never been a mystery! Let me look closer."

"By all means, now that you've begun your magic again."

Disregarding her flippancy, Cecco allowed himself to hold her hand more firmly. Still standing on the top step, he placed one foot on the landing to steady himself, and rested his elbow on his knee. He bent over her hand, and, only half listening, she admired the smooth skin of his broad, tanned shoulders.

"I read here that you have left behind your home. Two homes.... The seas you have loved and sailed are dwindling away— as is the ocean you are now sailing."

"What?" He held her full attention now.

"You will change course yet again. Your palm tells me so. I see other oceans."

With his finger he showed her, tracing the branches of three creases, and setting off a tingling in the flesh of her hand. Studying the familiar folds, Jill drew her eyebrows together. She knew enough of magic to believe in it. But did she believe this gypsy?

Like all his people, Cecco was accustomed to doubters. He shrugged. "I would not twist fortune to mislead you. Such an act would bring twisted fortune upon myself. But fate always has its way. What I have foretold will come to pass."

Looking again toward the foreign ship on the horizon, Jill was reminded of the *Julianne*, and she wondered....In her preoccupation, she forgot that Cecco still held her hand.

He had not forgotten. His magic was working again. He placed his other hand flat on top of hers, and gently rubbed in a circular motion. On his third stroke, she became aware of him. Absently, she focused on his face, and, again, her intuition took over her conscious mind.

"Giovanni..."

His big fist grasped the tips of her fingers. His eyes lit up, gratified, but he held the smile in check. "You are too informal, Madam! You will please humor me with the proper form of address. I do not wish to provoke the chastening of our master, nor to incite the envy of my mates."

"Aye, *Mr. Cecco*. I'm sorry. As I say, I can't stop the stories as they come to me. And your prediction has surprised me." She looked down at her hand, and with a jingle of jewelry, he released her.

"The future is always a surprise. Now you are prepared, and perhaps, more open to the possibilities? I hope, always, to make your voyage easier, and more enjoyable."

Realizing how tensely she held her body, she relaxed it.

"But I came to inquire after your health; this I have done. And also I thank you, Lady, for your interest. The doctor has ministered to my back as you ordered, and today has determined I am satisfactorily recovered from my…foolishness."

"Flattering foolishness, Mr. Cecco, and I'm pleased to hear of the doctor's opinion."

He nodded, and his voice became flamboyantly mocking. "Now, knowing my interesting story as you do, and of my ardent nature, you will expect me to say something outrageously complimentary to you, such as," he gestured broadly, comically, and he bowed, "'I would gladly suffer another whipping for the sake of such beauty!'" Still in a bow, he lifted his head and cocked it, smiling again. "But naturally, that would be a lie."

She laughed. "A beauty of a lie! Have you any others?"

"Yes, certainly, if you wish for lies." He placed his open hand on his chest. "There is nothing I would not do for you."

"As I suspected."

"You are the most desirable woman I have yet to experience."

"*Very* good. And?"

"My words are only the beginning of my wanting."

"Oh! Oh, more, please."

"I will not rest until you have measured the depth of my devotion…"

"Yes, go on."

"Until you have tasted the honey of my passion."

"I've never heard that one—"

"I will love you forever."

"I *have* heard that—"

"I would bind you to me…*with golden chains*."

"Ah— I…I've heard that, too—"

"I will share with you all my treasure."

She exhaled quickly, in a sort of sigh.

"You tear my heart, as you tore my body."

"…Mr. Cecco—"

"I wish to steal you from my captain, but I cannot break my oath."

Jill's smile vanished. She pulled back, regal, her eyes wide open and disbelieving. Cecco dropped his playful posture. He stared at her, unsmiling, his dusky eyes deadly.

"Any *other* man who thinks to touch you, I will kill."

"Enough!"

"After I carve your name on his back. Tell this to your doctor. He will have a hard time, I think, healing himself." Giving her no chance to respond, he said, *"Adio, Bellezza!"* He kissed his fingertips and opened them. The next moment, he had stolen back among the deckhands, watching for the captain's decision as eagerly as the rest.

Jill's pent-up breath escaped in a burst, her hand clenched the rail. Her eyes followed him.

He couldn't be lost in the crowd, the bloody-orange sunlight reflected in his earrings and his armbands. Pushing through the sea of stripes and bold-colored shirts, he stepped on a cannon and hauled himself up to straddle the rail, knees and heels clinging. His jovial mates made as if to shove him overboard, but he waved them off and kept his balance, his clean-shaven face smiling like a boy's.

But he wasn't a boy. Jill's eyes narrowed as she watched him. He knew exactly what he was doing. Considering his words and his appearance, she tried to think as reasonably as she would have done if he'd stopped after telling her fortune— before telling his feeling, cunningly, as if it were a jest. Unlike the surgeon he so mistrusted, Mr. Cecco didn't keep secrets. Jill, the storyteller, intuited his history. The first name he hadn't used in years, that even his captain didn't know, had rolled effortlessly from her lips, and he had confessed a dangerous truth. He wore the scars of his punishment for all the world to see, and his very visible skin had soaked up the sun's rays and tanned to olive brown. No, Mr. Cecco was a man. A man who never hid much of anything.

There was something, though, that he covered. Some hidden treasure. And he wanted Jill to discover it. To *want* to discover it. Glancing again at the lines on her palm, she shivered in the sudden wind that snapped at the half furled canvas above her.

She believed him.

She was sure a change awaited her, and one more, dangerous truth. What had he said? Be open to the possibilities. One thing she knew; she was no coward.

More pleased than angry now, Red-Handed Jill wrapped her prophetic palm around her wineglass, and lifted it to her lips. Always, she thirsted for adventure. She watched the ship on the horizon, as did all the other sailors, and when her captain next looked for her, she let him read her heart.

She was satisfied; she was smiling. Golden chains on olive-brown skin glittered in the corner of her eye. Rubies burned at her throat.

And other oceans burned in her palm.

A fearless woman is difficult to defend. Hook tore his gaze from his mistress and examined the ship in the spyglass.

"She is a Dutch merchantman, Smee. Coming out of the west as we are, she'll not have spotted us. Sink us back into the sun. We will take her at dawn."

"Aye, Captain! Haul back west, Mr. Noodler! Mark her direction, and follow it."

"Aye, aye, Mr. Smee!" Grinning, Noodler worked his backward hands to turn the ship again, eyeing the compass.

"Drop sails, lads!"

The men in the rigging spread out to unfurl the canvas, and the spare hands on deck milled loosely in the vicinity of the captain, agitating with anticipation. Like the others, Mr. Cecco, still perched on the rail, craned his neck to inspect the far-off vessel. Hook stowed the glass.

"We will carry out the plan as conceived, Mr. Smee. Has the carpenter completed the job?"

"Aye, Sir. He's turned out four stout pieces, made to order."

"Alert Mr. Starkey and inform the crew." Under black waves of hair, Hook's eyes looked sharply about the deck. "*Only* the crew. And when darkness falls, no lights tonight. As soon as we cannot be seen, close in."

"Shall you be going along tonight, Sir? Join in the fun?"

"I think not, Mr. Smee. My attention is required elsewhere, and I shall be more pleasantly engaged. But alert me near midnight, when all is in readiness. I will come to the deck to give the order, and tomorrow, we'll all enjoy the fun."

"Aye. Shall I have the guns readied, Sir?"

"As usual, but it is my hope to take her without a shot. Raise the proper colors."

Smee chortled. "Ha! What's the proper color for a piece of cake?"

Hook's trim whiskers spread with his smile. "Quite right, Mr. Smee. If piracy gets any easier than this, I shall have to consider retirement before I expire from *ennui*."

"Ah, Sir, you're talking like the Frenchman. I suppose he'll be invited to the party?"

"Of course. How better to battle our boredom?"

Jill's crimson skirts swirled in the stiffening breeze, catching Smee's attention again. He admired her as she stood on the top step, feet apart, one hand on the railing. His quick eye had glimpsed it right away— she was wearing the necklace.

"Begging your pardon, Sir, but I can think of one better way. She's waiting for you now, and I see a ruby smile."

Hook regarded her with satisfaction. "I expect I'll not be able to retire after all, Smee. She'd beggar me with her penchant for jewelry." And like the glow in the west, his voice softened. "My one weakness, Mr. Smee." He strode away, his coat flaring behind him as he bounded up the steps of the companionway. He drew the empty goblet from her hand, and setting sunlight flashed along the door's brass plate as it closed behind them.

Smee looked after the master and the mistress, then took stock of the deck. Mr. Cecco's avid gaze had abandoned the shrinking merchantman, and trailed in the direction Smee's had done.

The bo'sun muttered under his breath. "She's your weakness, Cap'n. And every-bloody-body else's!"

As if the wind sensed the excitement, it rolled the ship along, in darkness. Wave after wave struck up against the hull, and the distant flickers of lanterns grew larger, outlining the shape of the *Roger*'s prey, first to port, then to starboard, as the ship tacked her way forward. The deck hands were ordered to silence in the rigging. Noodler had given the wheel over to Mullins, and the hulking shape of Starkey shadowed his charges as he and Smee readied the canvas bags.

Nibs hunched on top of a cannon, pulling at his boots. Tom shed his shirt and flexed his sore shoulders. His welts didn't show in the weak, watery moonlight, but he felt them.

"I tell you, Nibs, I'm looking forward to the adventure, but not the sting of saltwater!"

Little levity accompanied Nib's answer. "All part of the job, Tom. And it won't trouble you long. The water will be cold enough to distract you from the sting."

"Aye, I hope Mr. Smee's ready with the hot toddy when it's over."

The young sailors were nearly floating already. It was long since they had stretched their wings, and, apprehensive as they were, they were eager.

Securing his dagger in his belt, Tom spoke more quietly. "I hope it all goes smoothly. I want to show the captain he can trust me again."

"I want to get at that ship tomorrow, and haul in her riches." Nibs' voice was barbed as he anticipated the business to come, and then he waxed grim. "And when we get to port, we'll spend it on some of those ladies Smee was talking about. The kind that understand a man's duty."

"There's a happy thought! I've got to say, Nibs, what with my troubles lately, I was a bit worried I wouldn't think of one. And we *have* to fly tonight. Captain's orders."

Nibs' eyes sought Tom's face in the night. "You know better, Tom. Between the two of us, we'll always pull through. No matter what— or who— we're up against." His bare arm stretched through the darkness to find his brother's. They clasped firmly, then the two sailors reported to Starkey for work.

Close to midnight, Mr. Smee rapped on the captain's door. He listened, and he rapped again, louder. Smee had learned patience over his years of service, and he didn't begrudge the captain his contentment. The man had earned his pleasures. On occasion, he'd even shared them. After a respectable pause, Smee clicked the handle under his fingers, and a sliver of light spilled on the bo'sun's face.

"Captain?…Sir?"

Smee stepped quickly over the threshold and closed the door to hide the light. "Ma'am?" Only the swishing of the sea answered as he cast his gaze around the comfortable cabin. Under its rich hangings, the bunk lay flat and empty, just as Miss made it up this morning. Stepping in further, Smee relaxed. The agreeable aroma of fine tobacco greeted him. One lantern was lit and hanging, and most of the curtains were closed to imprison its light. The captain's boots stood by the bed, his shirt lay on the couch. His coat and waistcoat reposed over its back. A tapping startled Smee, and he swiveled toward the bunk again. The hook hung there, moored to the wall by its leather strappings. It was the only thing in the room, Smee acknowledged with a nod, not softened by the soft light.

The night was pleasant, but only one window was uncurtained. An aft window over the cushioned seat. Striding along the carpets, Smee stopped by the dining table to survey its remnants. The candles with their warm tallow drippings had been extinguished. Nearby, on the harpsichord bench, Jill's dressing gown and the captain's breeches were strewn. Smee pushed the chairs up to the table and tidied the dishes, placing them on the sideboard to show he'd been there. With a smile, he pocketed the cigar the captain left for him, already pierced, he guessed, by the lady's hands. Then, picking up her new treasure, he cupped it in his palm and turned to search out the window. Lured by the pungent smell of the sea, Smee rested one knee on the window seat, bracing his elbow on the decorative ledge and leaning out to breathe. The newborn moon, not visible from here, was distant and dull.

It was a perfect night.

On the way out of the cabin, Smee dropped her ruby necklace into the drawer in the wardrobe. It sprawled next to the opals on the velvet lining, and he spent some minutes under the swaying lanternlight arranging them both into the delicate shape of her neck. Smee knew every inch of that throat, and the velvet under his fingers wasn't nearly as soft. He positioned the jewelry with the catches toward him, as if she stood before him and he were looking down on her beauty again, with her hair just catching his beard. He rubbed the back of his fingers to his whiskers as he stepped back to admire his handiwork. For a woman so precious, that drawer should overflow with baubles. But there was plenty of room for more loot. And plenty of time to win it.

If he were the captain, he'd give her a bracelet next. Solid gold, and soon.

No, if Smee were the captain, she'd be wearing it now. On that soft skin.

He slid the drawer closed.

Casting one last glance around the room, the bo'sun left. He'd just have to tell the lads to wait. They'd have to learn, as Smee had done. It wasn't easy for an Irishman, but he'd learned it, that first night he ever laid eyes on the captain— patience paid off. Patience, and loyalty.

To those he trusted, James Hook could be a generous man.

With their bags slung over their shoulders, two hearty pirates bent their knees and shoved off at last. Soaring upward, Nibs and Tom laughed quietly to feel the freedom of the air, even more heady than the freedom of the sea. Looping and spiraling, they held the bags close, and then they darted toward the lights of the ship bobbing ahead, all unsuspecting of their coming.

The night air rushed warm against their skins, and they rolled and flew higher— high enough to avoid watchful eyes in the merchantman's crow's nest. Circling the vessel, they spotted a tricolor flag flapping, and a spyglass beneath a foreign-shaped hat, scanning the waters. Glimpsed between her square sails, her night crew stood dim on the yardarms and deck. Nibs and Tom fell behind and let the ship outdistance them, then they dropped below the level of her taffrail and opened their bags.

The curved wooden wedges were heavy, sturdy enough to hold all night. Nibs shot starboard, Tom angled to port, and they met in the middle, below the lowest aft windows. They flattened their hands against the damp, slippery paint of the stern, and worked their way downwards, until they felt the big wing of the rudder spring up between them. Nibs dipped his feet, then his legs, into the water, careful not to let the current suck any part of him into the crack for which he searched. Tom did the same on the port side, and each took a wedge from his bag, fitted it into the crack, and pushed it tight between the stern and the rudder. As quickly as their cold, wet hands allowed, the young men pulled out another triangle each, and taking full breaths, sank under the waterline, hanging on, and feeling their way down the stern with one hand, clasping the wedges to their chests with the other.

Relieved of their loads, the canvas bags floated and swirled above the divers, and through frigid water, the two men already heard the moans of straining chain. Directed by the steering wheel at the helm, the merchantman's rudder was trying to turn. As the cables complained, Nibs and Tom inched their triangles into place, then threw their weight behind their elbows, shoving as forcefully as strength allowed. Bouncing up for air, they thrashed in the waves, kicking hard to rise and dangle their feet above the surface. Airborne again, they caught up with the stern, located the upper wedges, and struck with their heels this time, to ensure the wooden pieces were securely lodged.

Chilled and dripping, the two sailors drifted up and away from the ship. This was the worrisome part; the *Roger* burned no lights. They hung low, but kept close behind the illuminated merchantman until enough time passed for their captain to deem it safe to show himself. Within minutes, a torch flared on the *Roger's* deck, and Tom grasped Nibs' arm and pointed. The brothers sped home, worn, wet, and satisfied. In the distance, shouts of distress came from the quarterdeck of the prize as the man at the wheel sought to steer a rudder that refused to obey, and among foreign swear words and rising panic, the rich, laden ship under the tricolor flag nosed slowly, but absolutely, off her master's course.

The torch aboard the *Roger* hissed in a bucket, doused. And off to the east, the merchantman's sails were hauled up and furled, her anchors splashed into the sea. More men roused and lanterns were lit, but there was nowhere she could go, and nothing she could do.

She wouldn't know until dawn that she'd already been attacked by pirates. Two tired but hearty pirates, with stinging eyes and chattering teeth, who, under an approving nod from their tall, dark captain, were mantled in blankets by a smiling queen.

After the eerie quiet aboard the *Roger* last night, the surgeon was startled early by a knock at his door. He dropped his coat over the chair and, hoping perhaps to impress a lady, smoothed his hair before pulling the door open. Looking up into the business-like faces of Smee and Yulunga, Hanover instantly understood why they'd come. He stiffened and stepped back.

"Sorry, Doctor, but we've got to be putting your bracelets on." Smee tried not to gloat.

Hastening toward the window, Hanover snapped the curtains all the way open. "So, it is another victim. Dutch this time."

"Aye, and she's waiting for us. If you'll please sit down, we'll be getting on with it." Smee stepped into the cabin, his ring of keys jangling as he pulled it from his belt, where a pistol and a cutlass also lodged. Yulunga entered, too, on silent bare feet, his big arms dangling and the boarding ax stowed at his waist, close to hand. Blocking access to the surgeon's hanging swords, he stooped under the ceiling and watched— regretfully, Hanover believed. Behind the African, Liza slipped in. With her eyes properly downcast, she avoided the pirates' glances, and crept to the table to set a breakfast tray there.

Unable to bear the sight of Smee, Hanover focused on the nearing ship. "How is it she allows us within such proximity? Her sails are furled— she is not even firing at us!"

"Well, now, it may have something to do with the flag. It seems we joined the Dutch nation during the night. But you'll hear plenty of noise once we've raised the Jolly Roger."

Yulunga was diplomatic, but insistent. "That will be soon,

Doctor. We had better do our job." He didn't move, but the surgeon understood. Yulunga would use force if he had to. Hanover eyed Yulunga with dignity and regret, but the look he sent Smee was filled with resentment.

"Very well. I see I have no choice." He seized a large, leather-bound volume from the desk, and tossed it on his bunk. "You will have the courtesy to allow me to watch over my daughter's imprisonment first."

Yulunga nodded. "Certainly. Miss?"

Reluctantly, Liza came forward, then remembered the tray. She backtracked to pick it up, and set it on the foot of her father's bunk before scrambling into her own. No one offered to assist her; her father didn't appear to think it necessary, and the sailors were under strict orders. Tucking her legs under her skirt, she made herself inconspicuous while Smee stepped up and dragged the chain from under her pillow. He had soon clamped the band around her little wrist and locked it with his key. The iron was cool, Smee's hands were warm, and as he pulled the chain to check that it was secured to the bedpost, the tug on her wrist made her think of Mr. Cecco's golden bracelets. She closed her eyes, then, and listened to the soft stirring of cloth and the hard clink of metal as her father retreated into his bunk and, grudgingly, submitted to his shackling. He expelled an irritable breath.

Smee attempted to reassure them. "Not to worry, it won't be taking us long to work this vessel. We'll be off and away, and you'll be free again by lunchtime."

Yulunga grunted his agreement, and the two pirates ducked under the doorway and closed it. Smee's footfalls resounded on the gun deck as they strode away.

The surgeon was silent for some minutes, then Liza heard him stir on the blanket. With a rattle of chains, he punched his pillow and threw himself down on it. Liza settled herself, and found some amusement in bumping her fingers along the cold iron links.

"Liza."

She turned her head toward him.

"Has the sailor boy left you alone since the incident?"

Her silence indicated the affirmative.

"And all the others?"

Silence, again.

The scrape of wood on the tray told her he was examining his breakfast.

"You have neglected to bring me a spoon, Liza."

She studied the beams across the ceiling.

Very soon, the flick of pages in the bunk below was superseded by hailing shouts tossed back and forth between vessels, and then the sounds of many men congregating on the deck. The merchantman must be close enough, now. Surprised exclamations and moans of dread became audible next; the Dutch colors must have been struck, and the black flag raised. Liza heard the bite of grappling hooks, and the boarding plank slapped down. Intimidating, the hollers of the *Roger*'s crew swelled, unbearable, and then came the surge of many boots. After that, it was all a jumble as the hold began to fill, and later, more goods were stacked between the rows of cannon in the gun deck, just outside her door. Chickens squawked as they were carried to the galley, and there seemed to be plenty of them.

Liza curled up on her bunk and coiled the chain around her arm. When the links were as warm as her skin, she fell asleep.

Her father's curt command intruded into her dreams.

"Liza. You will practice your letters while we are detained. At our next lesson, I want you to impress the lady with your mastery of the alphabet."

Obediently, Liza roused herself, rising up on one elbow. She practiced. As she drew the alphabet on the bedclothes, at length she felt the little ring slip around the wrong way so that the pearls caught between her finger and the fleshy part below it. Trailing her fingertip on the blanket, she spelled the new words to herself.

F— a— t— h— e— r.

M— o— t— h— e— r.

She thought some more, and worked another word out in her head. When she was sure she had it right, she didn't entrust it even to the blank slate of the blanket. She rubbed her fingers idly, back and forth across the bed, and wrote it only in her head. A word to fit between 'Father' and 'Mother.' A word that rhymed with 'Jill.'

A deadly sentence, carried out on the terrible night Liza claimed her mother's ring.

Father— kill— Mother.

Knowing she would never, ever speak it, Liza imagined how her sentence would impress the lady, and with a smile on her lips, she drifted off to sleep.

Guilty Parties

"Ah, *mon ami*, you should have seen the faces when my valiant Guillaume rose bubbling to the surface! First, the amazement, and then the applause! In his two hands he is holding yet another wedge, pried away from the rudder. Now the mystery is solved, and my Guillaume is the hero of the day."

Night was falling, the *Roger's* lanterns brightly burned, and the sailors of *L'Ormonde* were scattered among her own, all across the deck. Chairs and benches had been hauled up from the galley, and the feasting and drinking had begun, courtesy of the stores of the Dutch merchantman, left long ago with a token blaze on her bowsprit, but otherwise unharmed in their dual wakes. The captains' circle included Mr. Smee, Nibs and Tom, Renaud and Guillaume in their smart red and blue uniforms, and the *Roger's* reluctant surgeon. Yulunga, Cecco, and Mullins assumed duty once again, participating moderately while vigilant of the visitors, whose abilities to revel were proving a match to those of their hosts. Song, laughter, and watered wine abounded.

Hook's carved chair was placed before the wheel, and Jill sat close at his left side. He stretched his legs out comfortably in front of him. After the day's successes, he found himself enjoying the company of his old rival.

He said, "And as I predicted, the Dutchmen themselves didn't think to look below the waterline."

"No, no! Who would believe it could be done, to secretly cripple the steering of a vessel the size of this prize? And a good thing, too.

L'Ormonde might not have come upon her in time, had you not so thoroughly bewildered her master with this clever scheme. As it was, we were able to come to the aid of the good captain. We quenched the little fire, and were much fêted. After, eh, a necessary 'inspection' to see that no other sabotage was worked within the ship. The captain felt himself lucky that DéDé LeCorbeau and his pirate-hunters came upon the scene! And then we scurried away to chase after the foul perpetrators of the crime."

Jill smiled. "And to stow your own prizes, before they were missed."

"Of course, *Madame*, but once I explained our mission of running down such rascals as yourselves, there were no suspicions. The Dutchmen are convinced you are to blame, and confident we were of excellent service to them."

"Their confidence in you is well attested by my percentage... partner." Inclining his head, Hook raised a handsome ebony baton with which LeCorbeau had presented him, previously the pride of the Dutch captain.

"Yes, well, eh, you might have left a little more to my men, one of whom after all has risked his life to secure it."

"Like the *two* of my own who risked theirs. But, as a matter of fact, we took time to locate only the obvious, knowing you would tidy up the hiding places. I find our arrangement to be most beneficial for all, LeCorbeau. I wonder I didn't think of it myself." He admired the baton once more, then laid it across his lap.

At this point Guillaume could no longer contain a sneeze, which erupted loudly. His slender face appeared more peaked than usual as he looked sheepishly about himself. *"Pardon."*

"Mon Dieu, my boy, can you not keep this sniveling to yourself?" His captain dropped a lace-edged handkerchief to flutter into his lap. "But where was I? Oh, yes...then yet another wedge was located and removed, and the merchantman was free again, to go on her way— much lighter than before! She should make good time getting to shore to attempt an explanation of her losses. I do not envy her captain! No cargo, and little damage to rationalize its disappearance. Only char on his bowsprit, and two clever wedges."

Jill's face became doubtful. "Two? But my sons used four."

Catching his mistake, LeCorbeau smiled wryly. "*Alors*, the boy would have his souvenirs! I believe he has earned them?"

Mr. Smee said, "I wouldn't wonder if the Dutch captain himself is charged with thievery."

"Eh, in my sentimentality, I have taken care to protect him from such a misfortune. It seems his pocket-book somehow came into my possession. A souvenir for myself as well! Perhaps he lost it while I was consoling him, who knows? But, eh, he can hardly be called a thief when he has not a coin of profit in his pocket."

Guillaume sneezed again.

"Liza," said Jill, "please bring the *commandant*'s man a blanket. I'm afraid he has taken a chill." Liza emerged from the shadows behind the wheel and picked her way through the maze of men, all of whom drew back to give her passage wide berth. Walking with her head high and her back straight, she sketched a perfect imitation of her mistress, who now sent a look of apprehension to her sons. "Are you sure your midnight adventure hasn't caused you to take ill, as well?"

Tom and Nibs were seated on a bench next to Hook. LeCorbeau occupied a chair opposite Jill, and he used the pretext of her concern to examine Nibs. "I believe your young men are quite— how do you English put it? Hale and hearty. They appear in excellent condition and none the worse for the experience."

"Yes, Ma'am," Tom reassured her. "We're fine. Fit for duty." Reluctant to retain the Frenchman's attention, Nibs only nodded. After their success in paralyzing the merchantman last night, both of Hook's young sailors were relieved to have once again landed, literally, in his good graces.

And not only in their own captain's good graces; LeCorbeau beamed upon them. "You must be very strong swimmers to have performed this feat." His eyes fastened again on Nibs. "Such a one would be most welcome among my crew."

Nibs had his reply ready, but threw a cautious glance toward his captain. Answering first, Hook tapped the baton on one knee.

"I told you before, LeCorbeau. I am not thinking of parting with any of my men—" Liza had returned with the blanket, and as she chose to walk in front of him, Hook was obliged to pull in the ebony stick and retract his legs to allow her to pass. He had noted the girl becoming bolder in the last few days, and with a look, he signaled his displeasure to Jill, who acted immediately.

"Thank you, Liza. Mr. Smee will escort you to my quarters— now— and you may keep yourself occupied until our company departs, by polishing the silver. *All* of it. And tomorrow Mr. Smee and I will both remind you of our very first chat."

"Ma'am." Smee got to his feet. Hanover, seated next to LeCorbeau, scowled at his daughter, and she avoided him as she presented the blanket to Guillaume. Tom was aware of her, too, and as his color deepened, he felt the burn of his new scar again. He didn't look at her.

Liza saw that, as usual, Captain Hook's attention appeared to be anywhere except upon herself— but she knew him better by now. With a certain satisfaction, she understood that the captain was the agent of her sudden banishment. He had noticed her! Was it too much to hope he would find a way to punish her, personally?

"Come along, Miss." Motioning to Liza to follow him, Smee made sure that, this time, the girl passed behind the captain's chair. In a moment he was back, having shut her in the master's quarters.

LeCorbeau noted these exchanges, but was not distracted by them. With his elegant hands, he gestured in supplication. "But, eh, Hook, you later indicated that the decision should be up to Mr. Nibs himself. I think maybe you are raising the price of his freedom! Still, I now officially invite him."

Nibs spoke up, firm but respectful. "Thank you, Sir, but," he looked at Smee, who nodded his encouragement. "I recently discovered I still have a lot to learn aboard the *Roger*. I'd best put off leaving her until I'm more experienced."

"Eh, well, if it is *experience* you are seeking…"

"After today's rewards," said Hook, to Nibs' relief, "I see a bright future for our partnership. There is plenty of time to weigh your options, Mr. Nibs, and I advise you to use it in order to give the matter serious consider—" He was interrupted again by a racking cough from Guillaume, whose face flushed as his shoulders heaved under the blanket.

Doctor Hanover took the opportunity to survey the French sailor.

"Captain LeCorbeau, I am concerned for this young man's health. Has he been ailing long?"

The little captain waved the concern away. "No, no, only since his immersion this afternoon— except for a certain weakness of the lungs. But he has always afflicted us with that. I am sure there is no cause for anxiety."

"Nevertheless, this cough bears watching, Sir." The Frenchman's nonchalance maddened the surgeon, who massaged his left wrist. Still offended by the grip of the shackle that Smee removed late that morning, he cast his gaze to the side, where *L'Ormonde* floated tantalizingly near. He must get LeCorbeau alone to discuss the situation. Somehow, he had to board that ship.

As if attuned to his thoughts, Jill said, "I envy my sons their visit to your ship, *Commandant*. I'm sorry to reveal that I have never set foot aboard any vessel other than the *Roger*."

"Ah, *Madame*, *L'Ormonde* is my pride and joy! Like yourself, a most beautiful vessel."

"Then you must allow me to see her. Would you be so kind as to conduct a tour for me?"

Hanover's spirits soared. Surely, the lady's desire to speak to LeCorbeau aboard *L'Ormonde* meant she had accepted his proposal! Controlling his features just in time, he tensed, waiting for her ploy to succeed or to fail. How like her it was to forge an arrangement herself with the Frenchman. But the next moment, Hanover frowned. He might have guessed Hook would interfere.

"My love, such a visit is superfluous. You would find the French ship much the same as our own. Perhaps a trifle less well-appointed."

LeCorbeau's beady black eyes glittered. "A trifle more 'tasteful,' is the way I would put it, *mon ami*…but to each his own."

"I would also remind you, Madam, that LeCorbeau and his sailors might not welcome a woman aboard. You know how superstitious seamen can be."

"But surely the *commandant* is above such nonsense. I'll wager he won't disappoint me. Indeed, I am certain he will even allow Liza— with her father, of course— to accompany me." Archly, she turned, daring LeCorbeau. "Are you not courageous, *mon cher Monsieur?*

Would you be so bold?"

Feeling Hanover's stare boring into him, the Frenchman opened his mouth, but delayed answering. The last thing with which he wanted to deal was a woman on his ship— Hook's woman! He ignored the besotted surgeon's attempt to catch his eye and, with relief, listened as Hook prevailed.

"Don't trouble to find an excuse, LeCorbeau. Jill is wielding her feminine wiles to have her way. And this time, I won't allow it."

"But Captain—"

"I have made my orders clear. You are not to board another vessel."

"Not even that of a friend, Sir?"

Hook fixed his steady stare upon her.

Looking down, she smiled. She slipped her hand under his, along his thigh. "Aye, Sir. I understand. I see the answer is…" She raised her gaze to the surgeon's. "'Not today.' "

"You do have my permission, however, to go right on wielding your wiles. As you are doing so adroitly even now."

General laughter followed, in which Hanover did not participate, but sat rubbing his wrist again. This time, the fist above it clenched. How ardently he hoped Jill would slip his sleeping draught down that arrogant throat tonight!

Peeking from behind the captain's door, Liza observed the signs of her father's frustration, and also Jill's delicate hand trapped beneath the stronger one, on the captain's thigh, next to his ebony baton.

Seeking to preserve the pleasantry, the Frenchman said, "*Je regrette, Madame.* But, now that you are recovered from your most unfortunate weakness, perhaps you might tell us the story for which we long?"

She answered readily, "An excellent suggestion, Sir."

Hanover sat straight, the scar tightening over his jaw as, with suspicion, he watched the French captain. His unease did not abate as Yulunga's liquid laughter poured forth.

"Yes, Lady," Yulunga said, "And it is only fair for me to pick the next subject." He turned his broad but ill-omened smile on the surgeon sitting so stonily. "What do you think, Doctor? Whose turn to share in the glory next?" The doctor shook his head, but Yulunga was undiscouraged. "An easy choice. Our good friend Mr. Cecco has yet to hear his legend."

Having recognized the lash marks on the Italian's back, LeCorbeau joined in, his eyes eager as he tapped his fingertips together. "Yes, what of the *ami?* Surely this very decorative sailor has a history as interesting as his shipmate's?"

Cecco turned to the Frenchman. "As my *'ami'* can confirm, Sir, my history becomes more interesting by the hour. Especially to me. I would like to hear what the lady has to say concerning myself." He smiled his gypsy smile. Only Jill felt the chill behind it. "That is, if it pleases her to do so— so publicly."

Jill hadn't divined Mr. Cecco's full story yet, but she had a feeling that, already, he had entangled her in it. In the telling of his tale, she might reveal more of herself than of him— more than would be wise. And, once begun, Jill's stories didn't always end. Somehow, again, his gypsy magic clouded her reasoning. She felt herself struggling against the power of those dark, brown eyes.

"As a matter of fact, Mr. Cecco, it does not please me. I— I haven't quite gathered the threads of your story as yet. Perhaps another evening?"

Cecco's wide shoulders relaxed. "As you see fit, Madam. One thing I think you *have* gathered about me. You know I will be ready. When you are."

Jill wondered that everyone hadn't heard his insinuation, this time. Judging by the sudden pressure around her hand, Hook certainly had. But Cecco didn't flinch under the steel of his captain's regard, Doctor Hanover seemed relieved that the attention had drawn away from himself, and Smee's eyes at the moment were on guard only against the foreigners. As Cecco and Yulunga swaggered up the deck to rejoin Mullins at their vigil, Jill sat still, feeling the force of Cecco's passion, feeling the pulse beating beneath her scarlet palm. Mr. Cecco was no longer committing 'foolish flattery.' He was courting death.

And then she became aware of the moments that had passed, alert to the surgeon kneeling in front of her— in front of Hook— his voice filled with tenderness, and his hands at a loss. "Madam? My lady.... Lady, are you well? You are suddenly pale!"

Focusing on his scar, she saw in it a likeness to red stripes on a broad back. She had no wish to be the occasion for another— a far worse— punishment. But Mr. Cecco's fate lay in his own hands. He was aware of the risks he took. Feeling the intensity of Hook's gaze upon her, Jill compelled herself to smile at the surgeon. "I am quite well. Thank you." Guillaume began another fit of hacking. "But…" she seized upon the diversion, "you must see to the young man."

"Yes, just what I was about to suggest." LeCorbeau aimed a knife-like look at the surgeon, so conspicuous in his attention to this female. It gave him a bad feeling. "If it is not too much trouble, *Monsieur*, would you be kind enough to examine Guillaume? I would not want him to sicken for lack of the most excellent medical care which is so close to hand."

Rising, Hanover addressed Captain Hook as if the words burned his mouth. "Have I your permission? Sir."

If Hook objected to the surgeon's gallantry toward his lady, he didn't yet reveal it. "Of course, Hanover. Show Mr. Guillaume to your quarters."

LeCorbeau sprang from his chair. "And I will, of course, accompany you. Guillaume is most dear to me. I would not leave him at such a moment." Fussing over his mate, he clucked, "Come, my boy, on your feet!"

Scrambling up, Guillaume clutched the blanket. Although not relishing the thought of an examination, he found it prudent to follow his captain's orders, and soon felt his shoulders supported by his suddenly solicitous master. They followed the surgeon toward the hatch. Guillaume cast a sideways look at Renaud before disappearing down the steps.

Acting on his captain's cue, Smee grinned. "Here, lad, let me fill your cup." He hoisted a jug of watered wine and poured for Renaud.

"Merci, Monsieur." Renaud took advantage of his master's departure and drained the drink quickly.

Smee refilled it with a generous portion. "We've much to be celebrating tonight. Tell me, how is it you managed to avoid diving after those wedges yourself?"

Renaud smiled weakly. "I cannot swim, Sir." He cast a doubtful look into his wine. "But then, neither can Guillaume."

Smee chuckled. "There's a lot to be saying for rank, lad! How long have you served aboard *L'Ormonde*, then?"

Conscious of his orders regarding Mr. Nibs, Renaud answered carefully. "I joined my captain twenty months ago, and am very glad to have done so. I have never eaten so well in my life! We found Guillaume stowed away a week later, half starved. He is my cousin and would not leave me. As it turned out, the *commandant* was glad to accept him, as his first mate had recently died. That is how I came by the job. But, I am afraid, *Monsieur*, it is Guillaume who is dying now."

Taken aback, Jill said, "Doctor Hanover is a fine surgeon, Renaud. I'm sure he will take good care of your cousin."

"Thank you, *Madame. Monsieur* Nibs," Renaud leaned forward. "It would be very fortunate for my cousin if you were to join us aboard *L'Ormonde*. I speak not for my captain, now, but for Guillaume."

Nibs' forehead wrinkled, and he exchanged a look with his brother. "How could my joining up help Guillaume?"

"We grew up together. Guillaume is like a brother to me. You understand. You and your brother are close, like we are." Looking over his shoulder, Renaud reassured himself of his master's absence. "Our captain has taken an interest in your advancement. If you were on *L'Ormonde* to occupy him, perhaps— perhaps Guillaume could have the rest he needs to recover his health. I am strong, I will perform most of the duties, but…"

Hook gathered his legs and rose. "An excellent attempt, Mr. Renaud. Your captain has schooled you both very well."

"Monsieur?" Renaud's eyes widened with surprise.

"Apparently my Jill isn't the only storyteller among us."

Surprise turned to pique. "But I am telling you the truth!"

"Have no fear. I won't betray your failure to your master."

"Sir, you insult me, and you insult my master!"

"You mustn't blame yourself. I'm sure you gave us your best performance. And if your 'cousin' is really ill," Hook's baton pointed at his two young sailors, "I shall send Mr. Nibs *and* Mr. Tootles to replace him. Come, my love, I would have a word with you before we join our other guests."

Jill accepted his arm, and they strolled away from the astonished expressions of their company.

Stealing onto the companionway, Liza huddled behind the rail to watch the party, unobserved. Renaud in his tidy uniform sat on his bench as if starched, until Mr. Smee replenished his wine.

Tom and Nibs emptied their cups, too, and feeling older and wiser than they'd been an hour ago, got some more and drank to their captain's health. And Guillaume's.

Hook guided Jill through the increasing animation of the crowd, and high up onto the forecastle, where, holding her tightly round the waist as his hook toyed with her throat, he questioned her.

"Your lovers, Madam, are flagrant in their indiscretions this evening. Do attempt an explanation, and satisfy me in this regard. As you satisfy me in so many others." He said it with a smile.

Employing a smile of her own, she engaged his affection and disengaged his hook. When she could breathe again she answered, demure, "Why, Captain. Have I ever given you reason to distrust me?"

"Reason. That is the crux of the argument, my love. Reason would be offended, were you to cause me any kind of misgiving."

"It is impossible, Sir. You would read it in my heart. Wouldn't you?" A challenge, but not only for her captain. She must not lose this game. She knew him…did she not?

He raised his hook, he snagged the shoulder of her gown. Yanking her close, he lifted her chin with the baton and bent his blue gaze upon her. "You know me, Jill. But not, as yet, as thoroughly as I know my Storyteller."

The iron of his hook burned cold on her shoulder.

Jill told him everything he wanted to hear.

After the couple concluded their tête-à-tête, both the *Jolly Roger's* company and their guests enjoyed the captain's very good humor far into the evening. His lady's gaze returned repeatedly toward the stairs. Disguising her agitation, she waited in vain for the attentive surgeon to rejoin the party.

Upon retiring and sending Liza to her bed below, Jill knelt down at the master's feet. She removed his boots and passed him his cup—and made sure that, if, on the morrow, anyone inquired how she rested, she could truthfully reply.

Hook and Jill slept well again, that night.

Her indiscreet lover, the surgeon, did not.

"But, my noble Doctor, really, am I asking more than you?"

"A good deal more, LeCorbeau, and if I may say so, your motives are not inspired by honorable desires."

"And yours are, of course!" The Frenchman's black eyes kindled in the light of dual lanterns as he leaned forward in a chair before the doctor's desk. Having discarded the blanket, Guillaume stood at attention behind his captain, miraculously cured of his sneezing. Drifting through the closed door came the sounds of music and revelry from the upper deck.

"Which honorable desire motivates you, *Monsieur?* Lust for the woman, or hatred for the man from whom you would steal her?"

"I have no need to justify my motives to you!"

"Nor I to you. But surely your overactive conscience can be assuaged. In fact, the young man will fare better in the hands of legitimate privateers than apprenticed to the pirates you so despise."

"The only point, so far, on which I agree with you."

"I do not require that you agree. I want what I want, and I find myself in a position to demand it."

Hanover's jaw tensed. "My position is not so fortunate, yet I must abide by my principles."

Easing back in his chair, the privateer rested his elbows on its arms and tapped his fingers together. "Very well. You can remain on this ship with your principles intact, and continue to strain against Hook's leash. Perhaps when he tires of his concubine, he will throw you a bone! Heh! heh! By that time, who knows? Your blossoming daughter may have succeeded at last in capturing his attention."

Livid, the surgeon pounded the desk with his fist. "For heaven's sake—"

"No!" LeCorbeau leapt from his seat. "For your own sake, drop your foolish pretensions! We have business to pursue. I, for one, am eager to return to it, and to its profits."

With his fists still clenched, the doctor sat back. "Well, what is your plan?"

"Very simple." LeCorbeau turned his back on his partner and, linking his hands behind him, strolled within the confines of the cabin. Guillaume retreated out of his way. "After my merciful beneficence to the *Julianne*, I am running short of water—"

"Yes," Hanover couldn't resist the barb, "I am amazed at your philanthropy. You must have wanted to find me very badly."

"Not to worry, Doctor. My Guillaume has learned well how to please his master. He made sure the casks I so generously shared with Captain Whyte were only one-quarter full! But Hook does not know this. He will believe I must make port to replenish my supplies, and since taking two prizes, he, too, will wish to go ashore to dispense with his goods. You will accompany his party…and find an opportunity to slip away. My ship will be moored well apart from the *Roger*, and once Hook has been assured I am not harboring the fugitive, the, eh, tumult will die down. I will then send a boat for you. Under cover of the night, you will board *L'Ormonde*, keeping out of sight— and working on your product— until our business with Hook is concluded."

"And what is your grand scheme for the others?" For the moment, the doctor controlled his skepticism.

"Ah! It will take time and patience, my friend, but, eh…on one prearranged dark night while all is calm, your daughter will require her mistress to tend to her sickbed, in this very room. And perhaps the son will also attend her? Very soon they will have lowered themselves out this window into a waiting dinghy. But understand. In order for it to be worth my while to bait the wrath of James Hook, you must make me a wealthy man! After this audacious theft, I may find it necessary to spend the rest of my career avoiding him. I prefer to do that with very much gold to limit whatever, eh— regrets— I may have."

"But why not take us all at once?"

"My dear Doctor, I have just told you. Hook knows I have no use for his woman. But if he believed you had taken her from him, he would pursue *L'Ormonde* to the far corners of the earth. There would be no end to his fury! But as you will be left in the town, and the ladies will vanish far out to sea, he cannot suspect you." Looking pleased with himself, LeCorbeau concluded, "And in addition, your disappearance supplies a motive for your daughter's so-unfortunate suicide."

"Suicide!"

"But yes. You will instruct these women on the roles they must play. Your daughter will exhibit the despondence when you abandon her, and so sadly, her kind mistress will perish also, drowning in the misguided rescue attempt. A few items of clothing will be found, but, I am afraid, this is all that will appear to be left of these females."

"And the young man?"

LeCorbeau opened his hands. "A mystery! Perhaps he died trying to play the hero."

"You presume, then, that Mr. Nibs will be persuaded to join you, and willing to perpetrate this deception."

"That, Doctor, is *your* concern. You shall persuade him."

"I? Act as your procurator!"

"You need not tell him everything. Once he is among my crew, I can break through his defenses— very easily, with your fine medicine to assist me." Sliding his eyes toward his mate, LeCorbeau spoke over his shoulder. "Is this not so, Guillaume?"

The sailor dropped his gaze to the floor, his slender cheeks pink. *"Oui, Commandant."*

Hanover exclaimed, "You know I never intended my formula to be used for such purposes!"

"Oh, yes, of course. It is merely to keep marital harmony, is it not? To discourage vice."

"Used properly, my philter will eliminate vice."

"You will make far more money by encouraging it! At least, I do."

"An unfortunate necessity until I gain wider recognition in the field of medicine. I have found no other way to secure the key ingredient. But I deplore your use of the philter under these circumstances! How if, this time, I refuse to be a party to your corruption?"

"Oh, very well. That option is open to you. If you wish to surrender your daughter…to the lust of your enemy."

"What?"

"Oui, Monsieur, her fate rests with you. If you cannot bring Mr. Nibs, I will be forced to leave the girl behind, as well." He shrugged. "With Captain Hook."

"You cannot mean—"

"But I can." Mock concern replaced the cruelty on the Frenchman's face. "Only think of the poor man's feelings! After you pluck his most precious flower, he will be wanting fresh female companionship."

"A disgusting suggestion! And Hook will be furious. He will rage over losing Jill. It is entirely possible, LeCorbeau, that he will pour his retribution on Liza. Once Jill is gone, there is no telling what he would do, or order done, to my daughter. That savage man would stop at nothing to defile what I hold pure!"

"Then, eh, the kindest course for you to follow is to enlist my young man. No?"

Hanover stared darkly. "This is a new low, even for you, LeCorbeau."

The privateer remained unruffled. "You think so? You have not known me so very long, Doctor. Why, in your dealings with me you have learned for certain only that I consort with fugitives and," his expression lost all congeniality, "murderers!"

"You go too far!" Hanover tugged his waistcoat smooth. "I am not about to argue the finer points of my conscience with you. And there is one serious flaw in your plan. When we arrive in port, I will not be at liberty to disembark."

"Really, Doctor, your chivalry goes beyond reason! Both your paramour and your daughter will live without your protection for a few days."

"It is not a matter of choice, Sir. Aboard this ship I suffer greater indignities than you imagine. The fact of the matter is—" Exasperated, Hanover shoved himself out of his chair and seized the bed curtain. Throwing it aside, he watched a look of incredulity dawn on the privateer's face as the man perceived the shackles.

"Mon Dieu! Hanover…but you are thorough in making your enemies!"

"You are not so very wrong when you say I am on Hook's leash."

To Hanover's chagrin, LeCorbeau began to smile. "My old friend Hook…Heh! heh! He is as shrewd a man as I have ever known, eh, excepting myself, of course! If he does not understand you as well as I do, he is certainly a man of intuition." LeCorbeau's derision grew in intensity, and soon brought on a bout of his wheezing laughter. Moving quickly to his side, Guillaume returned the lace handkerchief to his master. "Thank you, my boy. Heh, heh, heh! I can imagine your sputtering outrage, Hanover, when you were informed of this arrangement!" Wiping his eyes, the Frenchman sat down again, his mirth subsiding. "Well. I have had my little joke at your expense. But I am running out of time. Tell me, when does he order you restrained?"

"Whenever we approach port, or a vessel other than yours."

Squinting over his beaky nose, LeCorbeau said, "But you hide something from me. Hook has otherwise behaved as if you were one of his officers. You claim that you feign to be so. Why should he not trust in you?"

Looking down at his cuff, Hanover dashed a piece of lint from it. "Because I refuse to take an oath of loyalty."

LeCorbeau gaped at the surgeon as if the man were a lunatic. Turning an ear toward the doctor, he blinked. "*Pardon?* You refuse? When a simple swearing is all that stands between you and your freedom?"

"In binding myself with such an oath, I would not gain freedom. I am a man of honor. I cannot pledge to serve a pirate."

"I can understand that you might not serve a pirate. But— to balk at telling a lie? It is absurd! You have the power to walk off this ship, and you refuse it. Worse, you refuse me my very profitable commerce!"

"Nevertheless. I cannot falsely swear."

LeCorbeau cursed. "Always, Hook finds the weakness and uses it to his advantage. You and your honor! But this time I will not be outfoxed. No! Wily as he is, he will not win!" The captain stamped. "You shall defy him! Swear his oath, or your honor will be compromised as you break your pledge to *me*." The Frenchman's fingers slipped into his pocket to fondle his stiletto. "You remember that pledge. The last time we spoke, you declared it was so sacred to you."

Eyeing the Frenchman's pocket, Hanover flushed. "And I do honor it. There is no need to threaten me. You must simply find another way to get me off this ship. Frankly, I am shocked that you would suggest such a deception on my part. It places you on a lower level even than the pirates I have witnessed serving under oath to Hook."

"Fortunately, I do not depend upon your opinion. Only upon your talent to perform miracles." Seizing control of his temper, LeCorbeau breathed deeply, and as he collected his thoughts a sly smile stole across his lips. Taking a card from Hook's deck, the captain played on the doctor's other vulnerability. His beady eyes surveyed the surgeon. "And, as you may recall…I have authority to perform miracles of my own."

Encouraged by the sudden greedy look on Hanover's face, LeCorbeau waxed generous. "Yes. A man of principle such as yourself has need of my authority, in order to honorably engage in the liaison with the woman. A ship's captain has the power even to unite the happy couple— in matrimony."

"When?"

With a coy look, LeCorbeau answered, "Well, eh, certainly not until all desirable parties are safely aboard *L'Ormonde*."

Hanover sat silent.

"So, the sooner you can bring yourself to 'join' Hook's company, the sooner you will leave it." The Frenchman strutted to the bunk. Jingling the chain there, he trilled, "Ah, which of us does not love to see a wedding! I am sure the occasion will bring the tears of joy to my eyes. Come, Guillaume. It is time to begin sneezing again." The shackles thudded onto the mattress and LeCorbeau gathered up the blanket. The cocky little captain draped it over Guillaume, and linked the young man's arm in his own. At the door, he turned.

"But I should hate to see the so-innocent bridesmaid left behind, shrinking hopelessly into the distance. The only female on a ship full of pirates, never to be seen again." In a helpless gesture, he lifted his shoulders. "Abandoned by the father who saw fit to give her— body and soul— to the one man in this world he judges most immoral."

Hanover stared, unseeing, at his desktop, his right hand clutching and releasing his watch.

"Or, Doctor, shall we instead more pleasantly plan the honeymoon? A nice leisurely voyage, perhaps— to Alexandria? I understand that the lotus blooms there."

Liza discovered she had underestimated her mistress. It was a mistake she wouldn't make again.

Kneeling in front of her, despairing, the girl stared at the design of the carpet. Its colors swirled before her eyes, illuminated by morning sunshine. Liza smarted as if she'd just been whipped, but the punishment she was to receive was worse.

The lady stood cool and calm. "I warned you at the start to stay out of the captain's way. Until you learn your place, you will serve me only when I am alone."

A spasm ran down Liza's spine.

"Mr. Smee will come for you in the mornings, and after your duties here and your lessons, you will be confined to quarters."

In her relief, Liza almost relaxed. She could still slip away to the empty cabin, when he was there—

"In the shackles I so wisely advised the captain to install."

Liza didn't move. The shackles! And they had been Jill's idea?

"I trust I have made myself clear."

Smee prodded, but only with his voice. "Answer your mistress, girl."

Sulking, Liza nodded.

"No, Miss, you can do better than that."

She inhaled, and looked up at the pirate queen. The bloody drops on her throat, Liza reminded herself, were only rubies.

"One more lapse will land you in the brig. But of course, you won't have to stay there long." Jill tilted her head. "There are quite a few empty islands in these waters."

Panic mounting, the girl shook her head. Jill smiled.

"I am so glad you understand. It will make the rest of your service more pleasant for everyone. Mr. Smee, remove this creature to her quarters." Turning away, Jill headed toward her writing desk. But before she progressed more than a few steps, she heard a muffled thump. She halted and whirled.

Her eyes widened. Liza had collapsed on the rug. As the girl scrambled to her feet, she clutched at the hem of her dress, tugging it down to hide a ghastly discoloration of her flesh.

Indignant, Jill exchanged a glance with Smee. His jaw had fallen open, and now he gave a curt shake of his head. Liza lurched toward the door, limping, but in one stride Smee blocked her exit. Jill bridled her temper and closed in to confront the girl.

"Liza. How did this happen?"

Still forcing her skirt down, Liza shook her head.

"Never mind! I know how. No one but the captain and I hold the authority to touch you." Jill lifted her chin. "Who dared to beat you?"

The obvious answer begged to give itself, but something loyal in Liza refused to convey it— and Jill would never believe Captain Hook had done it. The girl's eyes darted wildly as she thought. Smee? No, the look of surprise on the man's face was too genuine. Everyone knew Yulunga was vicious enough, but why would he bother? Cecco had never so much as looked at her. Only one choice remained.

As Jill and Smee stared, Liza stood as straight as she was able. Slowly, her hands reached down to gather her skirts, and she raised the mauve material above her knees. Smee watched her frozen face. Jill's lip curled as she beheld the bruises— long, purple-black stripes on the thighs of both slender legs.

"Ma'am?"

"Yes, Mr. Smee. I want you to see this."

Smee's gaze shifted toward the girl's legs. His eyes narrowed behind his spectacles, and then he watched the mistress.

"Enough, Liza."

The girl dropped her skirts.

All the power of the pirate queen condensed into Jill's one word. "Who?"

Drawing the muscles of her face together, Liza expressed regret.

"I promised you the protection of the captain. You shall have it."

Liza's gray eyes opened wide, trusting. Then, resolutely, her little hand with its pearly ring rose. Her finger pointed. She rested it on her temple, and gradually traced a line—— to her eyebrow. The exact path of a new scar among the crewmen. A well-discussed scar. Her finger lingered there for a moment, then her hand dropped.

When the lady spoke at last, her tone was icy.

"Tom."

Liza bowed her head.

Smee restrained himself from wrapping his arms around the lady, to buoy her. She wouldn't want the girl to witness any sign of weakness. Sharply, he turned to Liza. "Get out!"

Only after the door closed behind her did Liza let loose the smile. It seemed she herself had been underestimated. Maybe the master wouldn't see her for a few days, but she had arranged it so he would have to think about her.

Fair enough. Liza had thought of him under every one of that 'gentleman's' excruciating strokes. And wouldn't the gentleman be grateful she'd had the intelligence to lie for him? Jill would never have to know— until it was far too late.

"She's lying, Sir. I swear it."

Hook regarded Tom Tootles with a chilly stare. Starkey sat uncomfortable before the desk, surveying the stick laid to rest upon its surface, the gift of ebony from the privateer. The tutor was loathe to call the captain's notice, but now he spoke up, running a finger around his collar.

"I don't know when the lad could have done it, Captain," Starkey said. "I've been working him hard, and as far as I can tell, he's not been near that girl since his thrashing."

"The fact remains," Hook stated. "The girl was beaten, and by someone aboard my ship."

Tom opened his mouth, but before he could think what to say in his defense, the hook cut a swath in the air, silencing him. The captain continued. "Now that this matter has come to light, we shall settle it logically, and unpleasant as it may be for some of the present company, all of you will understand the truth." His gaze fell upon Smee, who, with a grim determination, forged ahead.

"Captain, the marks have the look of a rod."

"A rod. Yes."

"And it's not the child's first set of bruises. Some older ones lie beneath."

With gathering distress, Jill nodded. "Yes…I've seen her limping before this. I didn't understand. And she made a point of hiding her legs from me the day she lengthened her skirt. That was the morning you were so displeased to find your shirt missing, Captain."

"Yet she has never made any reference to the subject?"

"Not to me."

"So. Unless Mr. Tootles is indeed guilty, the girl is protecting her assailant. One presumes, out of fear."

"Maybe not. Maybe he is someone for whom she cares." Jill's expression was doubtful. "But I know of no one, other than Tom, who has spent any time with her at all."

"Ma'am, she pulled a dirty trick on me, but I wouldn't—"

"Mr. Tootles," Hook interrupted, "Since you are determined to speak, tell me what you surmise about the girl's relations with other members of ship's company."

"Well, Sir…Mr. Yulunga used to tease her, but he's stopped that since— since I got in trouble. And Nibs and Bill Jukes and all the men, really, watched her, same as me. But as far as I know, Sir, no one but me was ever idiot enough to touch her."

Still cold, Hook's regard shifted from the scar on Tom's temple to Smee. "And when would you estimate this beating took place?"

"Recently, by the looks of it. Last night, Sir."

"Ah! Then our only hope to deflect culpability depends upon last night's boarding party. What of LeCorbeau's men?"

Considering, Smee slowly shook his head. "No, Sir, she was never alone with any of that lot."

"You are sure of this?"

"Aye. I shut her in your quarters myself immediately after she angered you, and shooed her in again when she slipped out later. After that I watched closer than ever, but she stayed put. You saw her here, yourself—" Smee stopped abruptly. His ruddy face paled as he realized exactly what he had been on the verge of saying. But already, it was too late.

Hook raised an eyebrow. Perversely, he prompted his bo'sun to continue. "You are performing admirably, Mr. Smee. Pray go on with your deduction. You were saying?"

Smee's stomach pitched in a sickly fashion as he finished his sentence, his voice fading to a murmur. "I was saying, Sir, that you saw her here, yourself. When you fetched the lady's cloak."

With an elegant formality, the captain inclined his head. "I did, indeed. She was all by herself, serving penance for drawing my attention to her. And, Mr. Smee, how long would you say I lingered here, alone with the 'child?' "

In an agony of discomfort, Smee cast his eyes down. "Not more than five minutes. Sir."

"Five minutes. Yes."

Jill scanned the company's faces, but the men avoided her eyes. As Hook addressed her, she returned his look with one of disbelief.

"Jill, my love. What was it you said when I offered to bring your wrap? Remind me."

"Captain, I don't recall—"

"Of course you do. You have a very sharp memory. Like my own."

"I believe I remarked that I would fetch the cloak myself rather than risk a further affront to you from Liza."

"Yet I did the gentlemanly thing. Well, then. Now we all know the facts surrounding the incident." Deliberately, he picked up his ebony baton, weighed it, and rolled it in his fingers. "And knowing my character as you do, there is only one possible answer. Isn't there?" Hook's face hardened to a wintry satisfaction. "The girl misbehaved, and she was punished. By the one man who has not been prohibited from touching her." He looked each sailor in the eye. "There will be no further discussion of this incident."

"Sir?"

"No, Madam. You will not mention it again, even to the girl."

"Captain…I promised her your protection!"

Answering, his velvet voice fell smooth. "From my men. And none of them has harmed her."

As she looked into his eyes, the full implication of his words struck her. Her mouth opened and her heart began to pound. She abandoned questioning. Just this one time, she didn't want to be told the truth.

Her words nearly choked her. "Aye, Sir."

"Leave us."

Smee, Starkey, and Tom rose quickly, disguising their surprise. Glancing at the captain, Tom felt considerable relief that Hook didn't blame him this time. But Tom wasn't quite sure who he did blame. Turning to leave, he saw Starkey exchanging a puzzled look with Smee who, still preoccupied with the ramifications of Hook's conclusion, hastily waved Tom and his tutor away.

Pausing by the door, Mr. Smee awaited further orders. There were none, just a lethal glint in the captain's eye. Still worried, Smee stepped out of the cabin and its tension, leaving the master and mistress to speak alone.

"Madam. Are you not aware that you have been flirting with danger?"

Unable to help himself, Smee loitered outside the door to hear just a bit more.

"Sir, I am not afraid."

"Jealousy can be a powerful monster."

"I trust that you would never allow *me* to come to harm."

A chair scraped on the boards, and the stick slammed onto the desk. She gasped then, and the bo'sun regretted his eavesdropping.

Mr. Smee would protect her as far as possible, but in the end, the lady made her own choices.

She'd just have to live with this one.

The End of the Game

Mr. Nibs rested his chin in his hand, oddly serious among the other off-duty men in the galley. The gunports gaped open, but he had an uncomfortable feeling that the walls were closing in on him. He'd never felt that way on the *Roger* before, but now he itched to kick off from her deck and soar over the waves. It was suddenly taxing to be confined, even in such a beautiful ship, and today, with a test of skill awaiting him, Nibs wished only for the companionship of his brother, and an open sky between them.

But Tom was below, polishing their cutlasses and busy avoiding doctor and daughter. Here in the galley, observed by a loose crowd of onlookers, Mr. Yulunga and several others hunkered near the floor, playing a dice game at which Yulunga was winning in spite of his losing tosses. The African king had a way with dice no one cared to dispute. In Tom's usual place by Nibs stood Mr. Cecco, relaxing against Nibs' barrel with a mug of grog in his hand. Leaning toward the younger sailor, Cecco spoke confidentially under the skittering of the dice and the exclamations of the sailors.

"You are wise to refuse the play, Mr. Nibs. Although my fearsome mate and I share much between us, in order to retain our friendship I long ago stopped engaging in all such games with him. It seems he cannot be beaten."

"I noticed that. But I'm not in a mood for games, anyway."

"So I see. Tell me, besides your challenge today, what is your ailment? You and your brother seem at odds these days."

Nibs shook his head. "We're not at odds. Tom's just not over what that girl did to him. I thought he was all right for a while, especially after we disabled the Dutch ship and earned the captain's approval again, but in the days since then he's refused to even talk about her."

"A wise precaution. That little girl is best left alone."

"She's done something else to him, I can tell. Mr. Smee warned us she'd make more trouble, even if we ignored her."

Lifting his gaze to the ceiling, Cecco intoned, "Mr. Smee! The ladies' man. But even he, it seems, cannot win the girl's civility. And you are right. I have been watching; something has happened to cause your lovely mother to distrust her, even after young Miss offended the captain."

"Tom knows what it is, but all I can get from him is joking."

"He was not joking when he left you here at breakfast."

Tossing his head, Nibs shifted on his barrel. "I know what that's about. The doctor."

"Since falling out of love with the daughter, Mr. Tootles seems no longer concerned with impressing the father."

"Aye. But Doctor Hanover's changed. He seemed so cold when he first came aboard, but now he's acting more friendly. At least to you and me and Mr. Yulunga. He's not so bad. I don't know why Tom avoids him."

"When a girl has disappointed you, her father is the last person you want to meet. Not that I have firsthand experience of this phenomenon, you understand. I have never been disappointed. Nor do I expect to be." Cecco's smile flashed and Nibs laughed, then the younger sailor's face returned to its set expression.

"I'm not likely to meet any girls' fathers, unless I decide to take up the doctor's offer."

With a shrewd look, the Italian paid closer attention to his shipmate, who had now touched on the matter he wished to clarify. "I have observed the man advising you. What offer has he made?"

Nibs smiled without levity. "You'll laugh, Mr. Cecco. Doctor Hanover thinks I'm too good for piracy. He's of the opinion that I should go to medical school."

Cecco's olive face darkened, and a dangerous light sparked in his eye. "You?" So the surgeon had begun to court the lady's sons, too! "Of course….Well, I admit you would make a fine job of any profession you chose, but…what is his purpose?"

"I asked Jill what she thought of the idea."

"And?"

"She reminded me of my oath."

"You were very young when you took it."

"So was Jill."

"Yes." Too young, Mr. Cecco hoped, to bind herself for long. Carefully, he probed for more. "Our captain might release you both, if she requested him to do so."

"I know that, from the discussion about joining LeCorbeau. Doctor Hanover asked me about that suggestion, too, and I told him I'd never sail under any captain but Hook."

"I agree with you there. If for some reason our worthy captain ends my service, I intend to be my own captain. But such ambition is a long way off for you, and so our doctor encourages you instead to become a gentleman, as we have so often poked fun at your brother for seeming?"

"Jill ordered me not to offend him, but just imagine me as a gentleman! But then, I can't think about much of anything today, I'm that nervous. So's Mr. Starkey. Tom and I saw him slipping a nip from his flask when he thought our backs were turned."

Falling silent, Nibs would have brooded again, but Cecco prompted, "Has the lady expressed any inclination to be released from her pledge to our captain?"

"Not to us. And Hook pays more attention to her than ever. He's stepped up her sailing instruction, and except when she's writing or when she's with Miss, he's always watching her. She can't make a move he doesn't approve. And she turns his vigilance to her profit. Have you seen her new ring?"

"I have seen everything." The gypsy eyes never missed anything about the lady, and never overlooked a trinket, not even a trinket of much lesser value than the mistress' new ring, or one displayed on less colorful hands. But the jewelry, for once, wasn't Cecco's concern. "So, as I have observed, the lady is guarded, and rewarded with jewels for her loyalty. Content to keep her promises." For now.

"Sure. But when Tom and I had supper in the captain's quarters last night, she seemed unsettled. She said she was anxious to start fencing again. Cooped up too long by the doctor's orders. Hook laughed at her for following them, but she said it was all part of the game."

The game. Raising his mug to drink, Cecco hid his expression as he stored his companion's information. He was forming a clearer picture of the lady's relations to the doctor. After the warning Cecco gave her, she must have a reason for her continuing attentions. A reason running deeper than mere attraction. Cecco had no question she took his threat seriously; she was careful, now, to remain aloof under the eyes of the sailors— and the captain. But still, she managed every day to spend time with Hanover. Listening closely to Nibs, Mr. Cecco watched the dice roll and skitter as the young sailor continued.

"And she was excited about what today means for Tom and me. We made a lot of toasts, but the two of us were careful not to drink too much. Have to be sharp this afternoon. The captain, too. Jill rationed the wine and even made Hook drink a cup of water before she sent us off to our beds."

"You two are settling. It is a good thing. This I know, because I have always been a wanderer. And what were your toasts on the propitious eve of your trial?"

"The captain proposed 'Success in every endeavor.' "

"Yes." Cecco lifted his grog. "I will drink to that."

"And Tom hoisted a glass to 'Disaster averted.' I thought of today and made mine 'Proving worthy.' "

"And the lady's?"

"I didn't understand her toast at all. She got a gleam in her eye, so I know it was special to her."

"She drank to her new ring of emeralds, perhaps?"

"No. I saw rainbows from the candles when she raised her crystal glass—"

"In her scarlet hand."

"Aye. And then she smiled the way she does when she's got a secret."

The Italian had abandoned his mug and begun watching the young man's face intently. Now he nodded. Giovanni Cecco knew in his soul what his red lady had said. His voice mellowed, and he spoke her words slowly.

"'To other oceans.'"

Amazed, Nibs blinked. "You knew? How?"

Crossing his arms, Mr. Cecco gripped his golden arm bands and leaned against the barrel. "Gypsy magic, my friend. Your lovely mother is a wanderer, too."

Considering, Nibs said, "I guess you're right. She's forever looking for adventure."

Always ready to seize his opportunity, Cecco was well prepared for this one. As in Yulunga's dice play, the outcome of the game was decided. Cecco had only one question, and it didn't really matter what the answer happened to be. He was merely curious.

When Red-Handed Jill renounced her oath, would she come immediately to her devoted sailor— or would he have to kill someone first?

Yulunga's rich laugh resounded through the galley over the groans of his opponents, and one string of his colorful necklace burst at last. Beads went flying, to bounce and roll crazily all over the wooden floor. Glad of something to do, Nibs slid off his barrel and helped to hunt them down.

Mr. Cecco leaned back and watched, thinking how easily beautiful things— and their promises— could be broken.

Doctor Johann Hanover sat brooding over his desk, staring at the leather-bound tome between his elbows, and not seeing a word on the page.

This morning, like each morning of the previous weeks, had been pleasant. He breakfasted in the genial company of Mr. Cecco, Mr. Nibs, and Mr. Yulunga. Then he enjoyed a stroll on deck with the lady, marred only by the fact that she now consistently declined to take his arm in front of the sailors. Their constitutional was followed by yet another reading lesson. Until yesterday, Liza's movements were restricted, and as she lay on her bunk in the afternoons, chained, Hanover had rebuked his daughter until her behavior met with Jill's satisfaction. Confined to only two cabins on the ship, yet she obliged her father each day by leaving her lesson to fetch something from his quarters— more parchment, a bottle of ink, anything, really— granting the physician a few minutes each session to inquire hopefully of the lady once again, *Is it today, Madam?*

Every day, with a flattering little obstinacy, the lady refused to answer until he told her something of himself. She now knew of his travels, his early experiments and his emigration to England, even his reasons for selecting his first wife and the fact of her tragic death from heart failure. When pressed to expound upon the diamonds with which he tempted Jill, Hanover was indulgent, remembering that, after all, she lived among buccaneers; but to date he had indicated only that his profession was a lucrative one. True to his word, he held himself in check, waiting until she granted permission to touch her. And each day, when she at last capitulated— just before Liza's knock— he was fascinated by her answers to his question, *Today?* and the brief but stimulating manner in which she delivered them, always leaving him aching for more— *tomorrow!*

In general, however, she was proving difficult, much more forward, more headstrong than other women, and the result was that he was further intrigued by the problem— and possibilities— she presented. To say the least, this Jill was an interesting study. The doctor's watch hung neglected as he considered her. An exotically scented piece of cloth had supplanted his timepiece, and he rubbed it between his finger and thumb. His pulse hammered as he remembered how she had rewarded his very first act of theft. The handkerchief wasn't the only prize her pillow harbored that morning, and he had stolen whatever he could take.

And on that pillow, Doctor Hanover had examined the lady once again— disappointingly, under the watchful eyes of the captain— and pronounced her fit. It hadn't been proper to ask, of course, but it was obvious that after her specious fainting episode, the lady ceased wearing a corset. Hanover was undecided as yet whether he would insist she adopt such a garment after their marriage. It was a question that had preoccupied him just now, while he was attempting to conduct some medical research. He couldn't concentrate. Employing empirical facts, the only hypothesis the surgeon set forward had rendered a simple, foregone conclusion: the sooner he could have her, the better.

Bitterly, Hanover regretted the conditions under which LeCorbeau would conduct their marriage, and an acid taste rose in his gullet. Hating himself, Hanover had begun courting Mr. Nibs— yes, courting was the word for it— befriending the young man, even attempting to interest him in a medical career. Jill had only laughed when, claiming to long for a son, Hanover suggested the possibility to her, even offering to sponsor the boy's education and wield his influence to enter him at Heidelberg. But Hanover was nothing if not persistent. She was listening, and soon he would find a way to persuade her to act in the boy's best interests— at this point the surgeon's conscience always brought him up short. Nibs' well-being had nothing to do with it. The story was only a fabrication, to deliver the young man into LeCorbeau's lascivious grasp— and to release Hanover himself, his future wife, and his daughter from Hook's.

To make matters worse, after today's reading lesson, Mr. Smee was sent to invite the surgeon and the lady to lunch again with the captain, commandeering the lady's arm and handing her to Hook. After the meal, Hanover retired to his quarters, nauseated by Hook's ostentatious possession of his mistress. *His* mistress! The entire situation, really, was what sickened Hanover. He acknowledged that the captain only behaved as he himself would do, if he had the right— *when* he had the right— but in the meantime, it was nothing short of infuriating to watch another man claim the intimacies only a husband should enjoy.

And at LeCorbeau's insistence, Hanover would forswear himself. In the next few days, he must pledge loyalty to Captain James Hook, the man he hated most in all the world, knowing himself to be perpetrating a falsehood. He would wait until the last moment to do it, hoping against hope that dishonor might be avoided. But, in the end, there would most likely be no other way to secure escape, for anyone.

Attempting to justify what he must do, the doctor admitted to himself he agreed with his amoral partner on one point: his distasteful assessment of Liza's position. She was a servant to a concubine, and in grave danger of losing her innocence herself. She should have been packed off to the cloister right away. Instead, Hanover dragged her along on his travels in a misguided attempt to erase the memory of her mother's demise. School was out of the question in any case. If she'd learned to write there was no telling what might have happened. Liza was a child, unable to grasp the nuances and implications of medical experimentation. Even now, she couldn't properly interpret whatever she had witnessed. Hanover was still unsure what she knew, but the little he did understand was unsettling enough. As soon as he got her off this ship, she would go to the convent in Switzerland, where vows of silence and a liberal dispensation would prohibit any prying sisters from asking questions. Then, free to assume his real name again, he would safely reestablish himself in Europe.

With his new wife. As long as her unsavory past was kept quiet— and Hanover was an expert at keeping secrets— Jill would be an asset to his work. It was already profitable. After a little more research and application, his labors would be recognized as a miracle. A formula to eliminate connubial inhibition. A blessing to the institution of marriage. Doctor Johann Heinrich's career was breaking ground in a bold field of endeavor— unbearably delayed by the insufferable arrogance of a self-serving pirate! A thief, a liar, a fugitive, murderer, and seducer. James Hook was everything Johann Heinrich hated.

And exactly what the good doctor had become.

"Damn that Hook!"

When Hanover heard footsteps in the gunnery, he slammed his book shut and stood, pocketing the handkerchief and shoving back his chair. Assuming Mr. Smee approached to insult him with some new outrage on behalf of that buccaneer, Hanover flung the door open. Mr. Cecco discovered the usually self-controlled surgeon in his shirtsleeves, eyes smoldering and one fist grasping his walking stick like a cudgel. When Hanover realized his mistake, he lowered the cane and collected himself.

"Mr. Cecco."

"Excuse me, Doctor. I have been sent to say, will you enjoy an exhibition on deck?" As he regarded the surgeon, Cecco agreed with Mr. Smee; Doctor Hanover would not take kindly to the bo'sun's presence here again. In recent conversations, Hanover made it clear to the sympathetic Italian that the Irishman offended him beyond endurance with the installation and application of the irons in his quarters. The observant Cecco saw also, although the surgeon didn't discuss the lady, that, like he himself, the doctor resented Smee's proximity to her. A strong and mutual antipathy had developed between Hanover and Smee, one on which Cecco had not been reluctant to play in order to gain the doctor's confidence. And although Jill heeded Cecco's threat, she had evidently not given her admirer the direct warning. It was just as well. Cecco gained greater advantage by employing the policy of keeping his enemy close. The gypsy found his gestures of friendship toward the doctor welcomed, and this afternoon Cecco volunteered when Smee went looking for someone to deliver the captain's invitation.

"An exhibition on deck, as opposed to that in the galley?" Hanover's stomach clenched again as he was reminded of Hook's complete and public possession of Jill. His fist still gripped his cane.

Cecco remained friendly. "You are still new to the ship, Doctor. The rest of us have become used to the state of affairs, if you will pardon the expression."

"I have never approved of open displays of— marital bliss." His dueling scar had turned angry red again.

"Take some wisdom from my gypsy philosophy, my friend. It is not ours to approve or disapprove of the captain. All of us, including his mistress, follow him because he has shown himself to be the strongest man. Until this changes, the only objection from his crew is that we ourselves are not committing the offense." He peered at the surgeon. "And I think, Sir, you are one of us in this matter. Yes?"

"Mr. Cecco, you have consistently shown me a deference I hadn't expected, so I will not be offended, nor will I offer further comment regarding the lady. What is this exhibition of which you speak?"

"A rare event. The captain will be testing the young sailors on their skill with swords. Will you join us?"

"To watch Captain Hook show off? I hardly think so!" As if the matter were settled, Hanover hung his walking stick on the wall, turned away from the door, and threw open his book.

Cecco's eyebrows rose. "Ah! But you may wish to seize the opportunity to show off yourself, Doctor."

The surgeon stilled. After a moment, he closed the book. He removed his waistcoat and was on his way out when, as an afterthought, he stepped toward the bureau. Pulling a black ribbon from the top drawer, he smoothed his hair and tied it back in a neat, short bunch. He tugged his shirt collar into place and adjusted his cravat. He turned back to Cecco, who nodded pleasantly now, but had regarded the surgeon's preparations with dark, narrowed eyes. Hanover snatched his foil from the wall. Thinking again, he also caught up his rapier.

"Very well, Mr. Cecco. As you say, Hook has shown himself to be the strongest man. Until that changes…"

"I see you are ambitious, Doctor Hanover. I am now interested in witnessing your swordsmanship." But soon his even white teeth no longer smiled. "Be warned, however. There are many, like myself, standing between you and Captain Hook."

Mr. Cecco led the way up to the deck, and Hanover followed, watching the muscles move beneath that hideously scarred back, unsure whether he had just been threatened— or accepted into some sort of buccaneer brotherhood.

Starkey had the deck cleared of all moveable obstacles. The sea lay reasonably calm today, and full sails cast a pattern of alternating light and shadow under the yards. The *Roger* sailed among the abundant trading islands where her prey berthed and loaded, and the air was spiced with promise. Swooping and circling around the topsails, seagulls uttered their cries.

Nibs the Knife and Tom Tootles took another look at the cannons and the ropey web of shrouds extending from masts to rails. They checked the positions of the grilles and hatches underfoot. The brothers knew they hadn't a chance to defeat the captain. They just wanted to avoid looking like fools, getting tangled up or tripping on some obvious stumbling block. Their fellow sailors surrounded the deck, some leaning over the quarterdeck and forecastle rails, still others clinging aloft for a better view. Everyone was watching. Even the ship creaked her attention.

Cecco and Hanover took up positions next to Yulunga on the perimeter of the action, aft of the mainmast, and the African smiled broadly to see the surgeon and his swords.

"So, Doctor. You have come prepared." His massive black hand rested on the ax in his belt.

Hanover looked askance at the weapon. "I see you, too, are armed. But not for sport."

"It depends how you look at it. This close to the islands, we may encounter another prize. Or the law. I like to be prepared."

Cecco laughed, looking at the young men. "I think perhaps these lads would rather face the weapons of the Royal Navy than a mock battle with the captain's cutlass. But they look in good spirits. Always those two have been ready for action."

"And except for beatings, get too little of it!" Yulunga had spied Liza, aloof and inconspicuous in her mauve gown. She was halfway down the steps of the companionway, bearing a tray of wine. But Yulunga didn't let the doctor see the direction of his comment.

Hanover was preoccupied in any case, his head high and his eyes scanning the crowded deck for the lady. Surely she wouldn't miss her sons' exhibition? But she was nowhere to be seen.

Cecco and Yulunga exchanged amused glances. She stood right behind him.

"Good afternoon, gentlemen."

Hanover spun around.

"Madam." Cecco beat him to her. "A moment of trial for your sons."

"Yes, we'll see how they have progressed under Mr. Starkey's instruction. They tell me you, too, have been generous with your advice, Mr. Cecco." She gave him a pointed look. "It seems you have counseled my sons— in addition to counseling me."

"Lady, I merely advise that there are more ways than one to use a blade."

The surgeon frowned as the lady and the two sailors laughed. Jill was prepared for Cecco's darker reference, had even invited it, and as she thought again of the bloody incident Cecco perpetrated at Gao, her laughter was tempered.

Gratified by her reserve, Cecco pushed further. "But I am happy to assist anyone who reaches out to me." Again, his brown eyes clung to her form, and his gaze slid down her arm to her hand. A larger hand closed over hers, with rings sparkling in the sunlight.

"Gentlemen." Hook's stabbing stare returned Cecco's.

"Sir." Cecco and Yulunga nodded. Looking up at Hook, Jill smiled, and laid her other hand, which bore the rich emerald ring, on his chest. Hanover stood stiffly as the captain's regard included him. Hook didn't miss the rare absence of coat and waistcoat, nor the swords at the surgeon's side. Appearing behind the captain, Smee carried a cutlass, a rapier, and a blunt foil.

Hook raised his head and called, "Mr. Starkey! Let us begin!" He reached out to command the cutlass from Smee. He bowed to his lady, then swept away to circle the mast, stretching his arms. He was dressed in simple breeches and a white shirt, his collar open. His filigreed earring glittered freely this afternoon, as his black hair was bound against his forehead, under a scarf of peacock blue. Watching him, Jill was grateful he scorned her further use of the corset. Had it trapped her breath, she would surely swoon in reality now.

The two youngest sailors looked the captain over, too. They hadn't seen his hook so gleaming and treacherous since it raked a crimson furrow on a boy on the Island, not so very long ago.

Tom and Nibs had flipped a coin. Tom lost; he had to go first. Now he planted his feet on the deck before the mainmast and waited, a sinking feeling within his barrel chest as his fellows backed to make room. He felt of the scar at his temple, then, pulling his rag from his pocket, he dried his palms and got a fresh grip on the handle of his sword, which shone from this morning's polishing. He forced his dry mouth into a grin of sorts, and shot a defiant glance toward the mauve dress and its contents. His defiance didn't hurt, but it didn't help, either. Starkey stood next to a cask as near as safety allowed, his old schoolroom ruler protruding from his pocket, and his kerchief dabbing at his neck. His nervous, scar-flecked face was hardly an encouraging image. Of more practical value was the look on Nibs— apprehensive, sober. And determined. Tom felt much better after that.

He had no time for further preparation. Without warning, Hook launched into the exercise. Confronted by his charging sword point, Tom jumped, raising his weapon and falling back just before falling to, with a will. Aloft and below, the seamen cheered.

Tom used every defense in his repertoire, three times at least. Keeping his eyes open and his boots light, he became aware that the captain wished to provoke and assess each different parry. Tom's instincts kept him going, and after the shock wore off, he discovered he was holding his own. As the sweat oozed from his skin, he also recognized that in a real battle, he himself would have to do the attacking. At the next opportunity, Tom broke through the urge to simply preserve himself from slaughter, and lashed out at Hook. The young sailor held himself back at first, to avoid causing injury, then, realizing the captain felt no concern for his own safety, Tom went after him in earnest. It was at that point he knew he was succeeding— Hook began to smile.

Tom scarcely heard the whistles and calls of his mates. His ears were full of the clashing of blades. His face glowed with effort and adventure. He saw the captain's sapphire eyes upon him, the hook looming nearby, behaving but menacing, and he felt the strike of each blow in his bones. Tom's arm ached from tension he hadn't felt since his earliest bouts with Starkey, and he only just had time to breathe. The only security he knew was the feel of the boards under his feet, and ultimately, the mast at his back. Tom's eyes opened wide, then clamped shut as he dove for the deck. Hook embedded his cutlass in the mainmast, exactly where Tom's neck had been a moment before. The sailors were wild, stomping and yelling, the deck trembled with the vibration, and they were shouting Tom's name. Clutching his head with one hand, he felt along the planks with the other. He grabbed his weapon and rolled— the wrong way— and Hook reached down between his boots, seized him by the scruff of the neck, and hoisted him to his feet as if Tootles hadn't been the beefiest boy on the Island. The hook stared the new sailor in the face.

"Well, Mr. Tootles," the claw seemed to say in a well-oiled voice. Tom blinked and realized Hook himself was speaking. "You've given a good account of yourself. Kindly lower your cutlass and send me your brother."

Becoming aware that he was holding the point of his sword poised under the captain's jaw, Tom Tootles grinned. He was released to the applause of his shipmates, who hooted some more and pounded his back. Mr. Starkey handed him a mug of ale, and Jill wiped his face with her own kerchief. "Well done, Sir!" Her eyes and her smile shone for him. Standing next to her mistress, Liza stared at Tom with those charcoal eyes. He didn't feel equal to comment. He drank.

Disengaging the captain's cutlass, Smee made a mental note to caulk the mast. Hook tidied his throat with a handkerchief as Jill offered a cup of wine from Liza's tray. After drinking and returning it, the captain moved close and looked down upon her.

"It seems, Madam, that our boy has grown up."

Jill's eyes reflected her surprise. "'Our' boy? Do you think of him that way?"

"It is not a matter of how I think of him." He bent to murmur into her ear. "It is how I think of *you*. All you hold dear belongs to me." Abruptly, he turned away and confronted Nibs. Forgetting to breathe, Jill pressed the cup to her bodice.

Nibs had the advantage of witnessing Hook's approach to Tom. He was determined not to be surprised, and therefore hurled himself at Hook as soon as the captain gripped his weapon. Hook allowed Nibs to show his attack strategies first. He then beat his young sailor back, evoking the defensive measures with which Tom had begun. This bout ranged up the deck toward the bow. Nibs nearly lost his footing as he backed toward the hatch to the hold, a good six inches off the floor, but he stepped up just in time, and kept fighting. The match ended when at length Hook's blade enveloped Nibs', yanking it from his grip. The sword sailed away and clanged onto the deck, skidding to the gunwale. Instead of diving from the captain's final cut like Tom, Nibs chose to jump away. He bounded so easily up and backward that he seemed for a second to fly. When his feet stood solidly on the deck once again, he looked defensively around himself, then lifted his chin and rubbed his wrist. Shouting, the men exclaimed their approval. The captain squinted at him.

"My compliments, Mr. Nibs. But have a care to keep your talents secret. The element of surprise is one's sharpest weapon."

Nibs' swarthy face became darker. "Aye, aye, Sir." As Hook dismissed him, Nibs scooped up his sword and dodged into the crowd to join his brother. Tom and Jill congratulated him. His orange kerchief was soaked with perspiration, and he tucked his cutlass into his belt, downed an ale from Starkey, and asked for more.

Hook strolled back from the bow. "Thank you, Mr. Smee." He handed the bo'sun his cutlass. "An excellent display, Mr. Tootles, Mr. Nibs. Next time, you may use knives, and we will exercise my hook as well. Mr. Starkey, you have done a fine job of instructing these young men. It is time, I believe, to put that ruler to rest."

Starkey looked as damp and happy as if he'd just jumped out of hell and into a cool bath. "Thank you, Sir." He stowed his kerchief and submerged his upper lip in a cup of ale.

Laughing with relief, Tom and Nibs toasted each other, clapping their mugs together. Then they ganged up on Starkey and toasted him, too, a generous portion of their drinks ending up on their tutor, who snarled, "Keep that up and you'll be swabbing the deck again!"

Jill left her sons to their celebration and resumed her place at Hook's side. "Captain, a wonderful exhibition." As she offered him wine, her gesture was halted by a firm grip. Jill turned a surprised look over her shoulder, to see that the surgeon's arm encircled her. He was holding the cup, too. He didn't touch her fingers, and he wasn't looking at her. His gaze encompassed the captain.

"May I join your sport, Sir?"

Chillingly, Hook returned the doctor's stare. As he did so, he removed the vessel from Hanover's grasp. He drank from it, then, with deliberation, replaced the cup in Jill's hand.

The men around and above them had fallen silent, watching warily. They breathed a collective gasp as the doctor seized the captain's cup from Jill's fingers— and drained it. Hanover passed it behind him. Liza, discreet now but never far from the captain, collected it. Earnestly, Jill shook her head at the surgeon, once.

Hook no longer smiled, even half-way. He said, "Your audacity implies more than sport."

"However you wish to view it."

"A gentlemen's match?"

"I fight for my freedom. No less."

"Am I to understand, Doctor, that you are challenging me?"

"Have I surprised you at last, Captain? Another surprise, then, to raise the stakes. If you best me, I will swear your oath of loyalty."

Jill stared at him, and then at her captain. Hook lifted an eyebrow. "You are confident, Hanover, but which is it? Do you consider me worthy of your service, or unworthy of your blade?"

"Try me and see."

"A duel, then."

"With foil or with sword. The choice, Sir, is yours."

"Your preference, Jill?"

"Captain! Foils, if you please!" Her face was shocked, but exhilarated. Hearing the tone of her voice, Nibs and Tom wiped their faces and shoved their way forward, to stand staunch on either side of her. They and the others watched in curiosity to see what the captain would do to this reckless man.

Hanover said, "Foils, then, to please the lady. It is the one goal we share, isn't it, Captain?" He backed toward the open space, toward the mainmast, and raised his foil. Its stubbed tip didn't waver.

Advancing on his opponent, Hook reached out to receive his sword from Smee. "The weapon of choice is foils, Hanover." He sauntered toward the surgeon, his face at a dangerous angle. "Belay the language, and have at it."

Since the morning of his capture, Hanover had been eager to fight this pirate. He sprang into action. The foils clashed, dully. Their blunt edges lacked the ring of finality the doctor craved, but he would have his satisfaction. Hanover thrust forward, determined in so doing to thrust back onto his captor the humiliation he had suffered. His feet worked gracefully to support the motion of his sword. With the taste of Hook's wine on his tongue, he pressed into Hook's space, aware of his lady's attention.

Hook fell back, subduing his temper to accomplish his purpose. Humoring the mood of his surgeon, he observed. He intuited. Following the attack with defensive action, Hook evaluated the man's strategy. He bided his time, learning. As Jill had informed him, this doctor proved an excellent swordsman. Hook felt her watching them both, and he smiled. The man was, indeed, a worthy opponent.

Smee viewed the pair with interest, revering his captain, but not forgetting his duty to keep an eye on the mistress. Casting a glance toward her now, he looked twice. He saw Jill gripping Nibs' arm and staring at the duelists with a mixture of admiration and apprehension. Surely, Smee wondered, she couldn't be fearing for the captain? She must know he'd not be beaten! Or was her concern— impossible as it was to imagine, was her concern for the *other* party? Smee eyed the surgeon, who wore a frigid but confident smile.

Standing behind her mistress, steadying her tray, Liza couldn't see the lady's expression, but she recalled the vision of Jill smoothing the surgeon's hair into place. The girl watched her captain, wishing to do the same for him when the battle was over, to untie the silken scarf and finger his long wavy hair. For now, she gloried in his mastery of the art. Surely, here was a man who could best her father!

As the match wore on, the sailors recovered their boisterousness, encouraging both contenders in the spirit of sportsmanship, and raising their voices in approval as each man demonstrated his expertise. Those aloft inched lower, as the seabirds screamed and the ship bore its company battling over the waves.

Hanover was no novice. It took some moments to adjust to the left-handed moves, but he had already gauged Hook's skills from the preceding demonstrations. He knew the captain was baiting him now, assessing him. On guard for advances from the hook that floated at the captain's side, far sharper than these dull practice implements, the surgeon balanced his movements. Hanover held himself in check, pushing Hook, goading his foil, waiting for the pirate to throw himself into the fray.

That moment came, just as Hanover anticipated, when it should have been least expected. Hook reversed himself, suddenly ceasing to deflect the doctor's charge, and whirling to attack him from the side.

Jumping away, Hanover parried as, serious now, Hook bore down without mercy, determined to force his foe backward toward the mast.

But Hanover had seen him pull this trick with Tom. He dodged, then he circled so that Hook spun and it was Hanover now who pressed his opponent back upon the mast. Hook wouldn't allow it. Feinting to the left, he distracted the doctor just long enough to leap to the right.

From then on, the duel was a dance. Hook threw himself forward, hurtling up the deck, driving the doctor before him, then pivoting and giving way as the doctor waltzed him backward. The adversaries engaged, turning round and around, charging fore and aft along the deck, first one, then the other holding sway. Both men smiled, the light of competition in their eyes, gray and blue fires, feet scuffling, their shirts roiling up and down the ship like whitecaps on a beach. Neither man tired, neither gave way, and Jill watched in an ecstasy of delight and concern, her breaths coming sharp in her lungs.

The crewmen fell back to make room as the duelists flew toward them, then the pair swiveled away to bounce off the gunwales. Thrusting at the same time, their foils locked together at the grips. They wrestled, and Hook braced his feet to give a tremendous heave, propelling Hanover to slam his back against the mast. Hanover exhaled and shook his head, and shoved away to beat Hook backward toward a cannon. Hook hit the muzzle and rolled along it, to spring out again with redoubled effort. Their lungs heaved with exertion, and still they kept on, hacking and clanging their swords together.

Always aware of the lady, Hanover stole a glance at Jill. His next move made her gasp. He plunged the point of his foil at Hook's belly, forcing the captain up on his toes to pull back, doubling over. In the next instant, Hanover swiped at Hook's jaw. Barely in time, Hook yanked his spine straight, flinging out his claw to steady himself. But Hanover's blade slashed again, at Hook's cheek. Hook jerked his head backward, his earring swinging, his flesh intact but his eyes wide with outrage. As he recovered, his eyes narrowed. Lowering his jaw, he drew a deep breath, then thrust with his whole body, launching an assault that drove his opponent back up the deck toward the bow.

Relentless, Hook's blade clashed with the doctor's, yet the doctor persevered— until Hook backed him into the raised grille of the hold. Caught at the heels, Hanover threw out his arms for balance. His blade swung wildly upward. Hook dropped the point of his foil, turned to the side and charged, ramming his shoulder against the doctor's chest.

Hanover tumbled backward, landing on his back with a crash of splitting wood. The lattice-work doors of the hold gave and groaned, but held. The wind was knocked from the doctor's lungs, and he lost his grip on his foil. Hook jumped to the grille and kicked the sword savagely, out of his enemy's reach. It went scuttling away. Hook stood staring down at the defeated man between his boots. Hanover struggled to suck in air, glaring back at him. The match was over.

No one was smiling now.

"A foul move, Sir!" The doctor panted, barely able to speak. "To bodily assault me!"

"As foul as the move that brought it on." Hook's shoulders rose and fell with his breathing. "If you'd had your way, I'd have been ripped open and scarred— by a blunt tip!" He paused for breath. "Hardly an honorable mark to carry from a gentlemen's match."

The men pressed in around the contenders, all talking at once. Hook didn't offer to help the surgeon up. Cecco set one foot on the hatch and reached down to him. Yulunga steadied him as he got to his feet. Smee removed the foil from his captain's hand, and Hook dragged the scarf from his head. Nibs hesitated, then fetched the doctor's foil, and when the man stood upright, held it toward him. Hanover snatched it from Nibs, his hair loose, the cheek under his dueling scar livid, and his stare still boring into Hook.

Jill grasped Liza's arm to pull her along. Clutching a cup from Liza's tray, she stepped between the men. "Captain. A drink, Sir." She made sure he accepted it, the scarf fluttering like a banner between his fingers, then she picked up another and looked meaningfully at Hanover. "And you, Doctor, I insist. To cool you." Tearing his gaze from Hook at last, the surgeon pushed his hair from his face, without Jill's assistance this time, and seized the drink. He swallowed it, but said nothing.

"Thank you, Madam." Hook lowered his empty cup and thrust it away, not caring that Liza took it, or that her fingers caressed his own.

He did, however, very definitely mark that Jill waited for Hanover's cup, to welcome it to her bosom as the man returned it to her. At the moment, Hook chose to tend to business.

"The oath can wait, Hanover. Or are you prepared to honor your word immediately, and pledge your loyalty to me now?"

"No. Fair means or foul, I am obligated to honor my promise. But…" In his dishonesty, Hanover couldn't bring himself to look at the lady. Stiffly, he shook his head. "Not today."

With the slightest movement, the surgeon's new master acknowledged his intention.

Handing the captain's swords to Tom, Smee waved the girl away and turned to the men. "All right, we've had our fun, lads. Clear the deck and get back to your stations!"

The sailors dispersed. Those not on duty climbed down from the higher decks and rigging and surged reluctantly off, swiveling their heads to catch a last glimpse of Captain Hook. He remained, immovable, where the fight had ended, his head erect and his legs wide. Hanover turned away. Cecco and Yulunga followed, bearing his weapons. The surgeon's posture sagged only slightly after his exertion; his head remained high as he made his way below decks, under the captain's victorious eyes.

Jill and Smee waited, standing next to Hook. The claw and the peacock scarf dangled at his sides. As a cooling breeze lifted his hair, he observed the doctor's retreat. When his words emerged, they revealed nothing of his emotion.

"A satisfactory bout."

Smee asked, "Sir?"

"I now have the measure of the man."

Jill watched his face, cool as a statue's, a cautious, curious look on her own. Smee watched them both as the captain continued.

"I haven't a doubt in my mind. Your assessment was correct, Jill. Doctor Hanover will never join us." Hook paused, his fine features impassive. "Unless he offends me again, I am finished with him."

Jill ventured, "He gave you his word he would join us."

"He lies." Still studying the hatch through which the doctor had descended, Hook said, "Madam, do what you have to do. And once you have discovered the secret source of his riches, we will discuss the means by which to dispatch him."

Smee absorbed the look on Red-Handed Jill's face. And then his big hands held her, because she swayed.

"The game is over," she breathed. And a sudden urge surged in Smee's loins as her scarlet fingers clung to his biceps in a manner he mightn't have resisted— if his captain hadn't been near.

Smee swore a promise to himself never to touch her any more, because he might not be able to stop. And then the wind laughed in his face, and that unruly strand of fair hair floated, stroking his neck and tangling in his beard. And next moment, he'd blessed the breeze and broken his promise.

She rewarded him with a smile. And as she spoke, Smee felt the shock, as if a bucket of ice water trickled its contents down his back. Jill released her hold on the bo'sun and spoke to Hook, coolly this time.

"I shall require your indulgence, Captain."

"When have I ever refused you?"

"Then you won't take it amiss, Sir…when I accept the doctor's diamonds?"

With a penetrating look, Hook studied her. "Madam. Now that you have prepared me, I shall take it all in stride. And then I will run him through."

"Yes. I know." She wore that dark smile that always incited him. "One way or another, I intend to become a very wealthy woman."

Mr. Smee wasn't sure, then, what he read on her beautiful face. But just now, if he were the captain—

He'd do exactly what James Hook did. The captain's lip twitched, and there and then, that powerful man gave his mistress something she wouldn't forget. Something violent.

And then, as he steadied her, "Shall we retire, Madam?"

For fear the tears would overflow, Jill couldn't speak, and although he'd given ample evidence he could read her thoughts, her captain expected an answer.

He was the victor. Only one answer could be given.

She nodded.

Hook seized her arm and propelled her to his quarters. Nothing stood in his way. The sea was calm, the air spiced with promise— and the deck cleared of obstacles.

Like the crest of a wave, the evening reached its peak and receded, leaving a residue of sea-blue sapphires encircling the lady's ankle.

Her night passed undisturbed.

Deep Waters

Discernible over the brine came the smell of vegetation— the tang of orange groves, and the balm of palm trees near the shore. With her Dutch flag flying in the breezes, the *Jolly Roger* rode at anchor in deep waters, just off the coast. Her hatches were thrown open and her men milled around the holds preparing to hoist the goods, securing block and tackle from the masts. Conferring in the master's quarters while the temptations of the island wafted through the windows, Smee and the captain completed their plans.

"Cecco and Yulunga are outside, Sir. They'll be standing guard when the lady and the surgeon come back from their morning constitutional."

"Before that, Mr. Smee, a small item to address." In his most subdued suit of chestnut brown, the captain stood behind his desk. "As Mr. Tootles and Mr. Nibs are as yet unknown, they may join the men rowing you to shore this morning. After you have established that the streets are clear of the law, you will see the young men to the appropriate taverns." Hook reached into his pocket and pulled out a golden coin. He clapped it on his desktop. "You know what to do."

A smile struck Smee's rugged face as he picked up the coin. "Aye, Captain! I'm knowing exactly what to do."

"They have passed their trials in weaponry of all sorts. Male *and* female. Spend it all."

"You're a generous man, Sir."

As a knock sounded on the door, Hook lowered his chin. "That remains to be seen, Mr. Smee."

The door opened, and Jill and her suitor stepped in. Keeping close behind the surgeon, Mr. Cecco also entered. Jill nearly flew to Hook's side and grasped the hand he held out to her. In preparation for strolling the streets of the port town, she had dressed in crocodile skin boots and a long Turkish tunic, black, over loose crimson trousers, embroidered in scarlet and gold about the neck and cuffs. "Captain, it's a lovely morning! So good to see hills and trees again. When shall we go ashore?"

"Madam, Mr. Smee will precede us and test the conditions. If the port is friendly, we shall disembark this afternoon. I have much to do before then."

"Aye, Sir, and so have I." Jill had a few discreet letters to write, to London. "I'm to tell you that Mason spotted *L'Ormonde* approaching. She's mooring a little way up the coast."

"Very good. I expect Captain LeCorbeau will dine with us this evening. I know of one or two establishments that are nearly fine enough for my lady."

His lady smiled.

In his modest gray suit, Doctor Hanover stood like a soldier before the desk. Feeling he had waited long enough, he announced, "Well, Captain. I am prepared to begin our arrangement."

Hook's mood remained gracious. He waved his iron claw in an expansive gesture. "A fine day for new beginnings. I look forward to accepting your service, Doctor."

"Now that I have made up my mind, I am eager to get on with it, Sir."

"As am I, Hanover. I am afraid, however, I must disappoint you this morning."

Hanover blinked. "I beg your pardon?"

"I find it isn't convenient today."

Unable to believe his ears, the surgeon paled under his scar. "But I don't understand, Sir."

"Going over the ship's articles is a serious matter, on which I judge it advisable to spend some time. Before signing them, you must fully understand the terms."

"I have discussed your articles in detail with Mr. Cecco. I believe

I already possess a clear understanding of them."

"Excellent. Thus you hold some concept of their complexity."

"Indeed. And I assure you, I will abide by the rules agreed upon by my shipmates."

"And then of course, we must consider the subject of remuneration."

"I am certain you will be fair, Captain." Only the edge of desperation sharpened the doctor's accent.

"I appreciate your confidence, but in the interests of all aboard, we shan't be hasty in determining what percentage you will take from the spoils."

"I will not object to any portion you deem proper. Please, do me the honor of accepting my service immediately!"

Jill avoided looking at her suitor during this exchange. She watched Mr. Cecco instead, knowing he pretended an amiability toward the surgeon that he did not feel. But the Italian's expression was unreadable, even to the lady. While the other men were occupied, he returned her gaze, and smiled. Her eyes fastened on his golden earrings, which swung a little as he moved his head to admire her exotic attire.

As instructed earlier, Mr. Smee cleared his throat and interrupted the conversation. "Sir, the boats are ready to launch. The lads will be waiting in the hold."

"Of course, Mr. Smee. Be at ease, Doctor Hanover. Given your present attitude, I find it unnecessary to keep you shackled during our entire anchorage. Mr. Cecco has volunteered to release you and stand guard whenever appropriate."

Hanover heard the fateful clink of keys as Mr. Smee handed them over to Cecco. The surgeon's face betrayed panic. His fist clenched on his walking stick, and only with difficulty did he conceal the full horror washing over him. "But, Sir. I— I have come to you this morning, fully prepared to submit to your command. I am ready to swear!"

Hook smiled half-way. "No doubt you *will* swear, Hanover…but not to me this morning. You may be prepared, but I am not. I find that with the business of unloading our cargo and replenishing supplies, I am much too pressed to deal with you. When, in a few days' time, we are back at sea, I will be at liberty to discuss our terms in depth, and then, in honor of your wise decision, we shall celebrate in grand style. Until that time, however…" He nodded to Cecco.

With a respectful manner, Cecco stepped forward. "I regret, Doctor, that I must now escort you to your quarters. But as I have found this particular port not to my taste, I will be pleased to keep you company while our shipmates go ashore."

"But— but…" Hanover sent a desperate look to Jill. "After all this time, when I have swallowed my pride and…realized that my professional skills can be put to best use aboard the *Roger*…" The lady's face remained clear, as if she didn't comprehend his dilemma. Turning to Hook once again, the surgeon glared, his anger surfacing. "Captain, you can't deny me—"

"Shore leave? But you are very much at home aboard the *Roger* by now." Hook's eyes glittered, like his claw. "I perceive that you have found all you desire right here. Anything else you require, any tinctures from an apothecary, for instance, Mr. Yulunga will obtain for you. Make a list; you'll have plenty of time. Now I must see to the doings in the hold. My love…" Taking Jill's chin in his hand, Hook kissed her, and then he strode from the cabin, followed by Smee.

Too surprised as yet for the outrage he would soon feel, the surgeon sank into a chair, his shoulders almost slumping. As he leaned forward on his walking stick, its ivory edges pressed into his hands. He ached to talk to Jill alone. But what could he tell her? Respecting the awkwardness of her position, he hadn't confided the details of their escape to her. Her fluid measure of right and wrong seemed easily to accommodate his need to swear allegiance to Hook. She had, in fact, been pleased by the depths to which her virtuous suitor would sink to free her— indeed, it was this flaw in his character, rather than his integrity, that finally won her!

For Hanover had lost the duel, but not the lady's love. Jill had yielded suddenly, during the usual break in one of Liza's lessons. After pledging to join her pirates, Hanover was astonished to feel Jill insinuate herself into his arms. Declining to hear the specifics of his design, she had promised that, if he found a way off the ship, she would follow him. Guided by LeCorbeau's plan, Hanover intended to slip out of sight in town. *L'Ormonde*'s boat would find him later. Then, in the dark of night, LeCorbeau would watch for a signal from the starboard quarters and pluck Mr. Nibs and the 'drowning' females from the pirate ship. Hanover had outlined his instructions and sealed them in a secret letter for Jill to open in private as the *Roger* next weighed anchor— *sans* her surgeon.

But, except for an unusually tender scene when Liza left the two lovers alone yesterday morning, Hanover hadn't indicated to Jill that he would soon be absent. Now, in an instant, LeCorbeau's grand scheme had gone up in smoke. Devastated, the usually self-possessed surgeon was at a loss as to what to do. And Jill had been quite correct. Hook was three steps ahead of him. Even in his current state of shock, Hanover realized her predictions had been accurate— and he almost admired the man!

Watching him struggle, Jill disguised the fact that she had guessed his plan of escape and prevented it. Accordingly, she wouldn't lift a finger to help him. The delicacy of her situation was eased by the fact that Hook had arranged for Mr. Cecco to stand guard. Cecco's presence curtailed discussion of the surgeon's dilemma. As ever, Jill had been strictly honest with Hanover. She fully intended he should belong to her. It was just that she had her own plans for the man. Now, she simply waited for her fiancé to recover, and trusted her instincts.

"And…exactly where are we?" Dazed, it was all the doctor could think to say.

Standing behind him, Cecco shrugged, and Jill became suddenly alert. She watched the gypsy closely. His casual speech didn't fool her.

"A dismal place, of little importance. A tropical settlement founded long ago by Venetian merchants. From my own country."

Despondent, Hanover shook his head. "I am not familiar with these islands." He had to gather information, pull himself together. Think of another way. "What…what is the name of the port?"

Mr. Cecco turned to the lady, his disquieting eyes daring her to speak. Showing no sign of her apprehension, she returned Cecco's stare and answered his challenge.

"You may have heard of it, Mister Hanover. This place is known for its interesting history. And it is notorious also…for its prison."

In silent warning to change the subject, Cecco fingered the knife in his belt and aimed a black look, first at Jill, then at the surgeon's back. Jill marked his motions, but refusing to be intimidated, she managed a smile for Hanover. "It is called…" Once again, her eyes met those of her dangerous, devoted sailor. She spoke softly. "Gao."

"Such courage." Cecco, too, spoke softly, struck to the heart. She was his ideal woman! "I never thought I would enjoy to be reminded of this place, but your voice, Lady, gives it music. One day I will command my own ship, and I hope very much that a brave storyteller like yourself will join me."

Holding sway but still wary, she smiled again. " 'Captain Cecco?' The name does have a pleasant ring."

"A ring, yes. A golden one! Waiting for the *right hand* to claim it." With reluctance, Cecco pulled his gaze from Jill. "Now if you please, Doctor, Mr. Yulunga is waiting, and we must follow our captain's orders." He bowed to his lady. Only she heard the music in his own voice.

"Bellezza."

Mr. Cecco's magic this morning was a dark magic, yet, once again, he succeeded in distracting Jill. Finding she had given her demoralized fiancé hardly a thought as he left, she gathered her wits. She drew a folded parchment from its hiding place within her sleeve, picked up the captain's dagger, and ripped open the seal, four days early. Settling into Hook's chair, she rested her feet in their crocodile boots on the edge of the desk, and began to read her affianced husband's itinerary for her 'death'— and subsequent departure.

And then her senses pricked as a bundle of gray velvet fell from a fold of the letter into her lap, and with a surge of pleasure, she smiled, and thought only of him as she unwrapped it. The heat of passion swept through her as the contents trickled like solid little raindrops into her crimson palm. A dozen perfect diamonds. Rich with sincerity, the surgeon's pledge to his betrothed.

Doctor Hanover *had* sworn his oath of loyalty this morning, after all.

The tantrum under the French flag that evening was ugly. As LeCorbeau stamped and railed at Renaud, Guillaume hid himself away under the canvas cover of *L'Ormonde*'s dinghy, to wait until the storm passed over. The skeleton crew of sailors not yet enjoying shore leave gave their captain a wide berth, looking forward to the morning, when their mates would return to duty and they could escape for a day.

The Frenchman's first impulse was to recall his men from port, up anchor and heave to, and blast the *Roger* until the surgeon was released. But, as usual, LeCorbeau's sense of self-interest prevailed. Even with sober gunners and the advantage of surprise, *L'Ormonde* commanded only twenty-four cannon. The *Roger* was a forty-gunner. And deep down inside, LeCorbeau suspected that Hook would not, in fact, be surprised at all.

And so he swore, and he sweated. Conducting his business on shore each day, LeCorbeau feasted with his enemy in a sumptuous tavern each night, and laid his plans again. On the final evening, he insisted that Hook and all his officers dine aboard *L'Ormonde*. Guillaume was privately attended by the physician and his condition found unimproved— in need of more frequent professional attention.

When DéDé LeCorbeau made his move this time, nothing would go wrong. James Hook would raise no objection as his surgeon, his servant, his step-son, and even his mistress paraded across to LeCorbeau's ship. Hook wouldn't be in a position to prevent them.

He would lie at the bottom of the sea.

As he fastened her bracelet, Mr. Cecco's hands were gentler that Smee's. His smile was gentler, too, and when he looked at her, she felt interesting. But he didn't look at her much. He talked to her father.

Lying on her bunk with her wrist in iron jewelry, Liza watched the big gypsy sailor. He wasn't as tall as Captain Hook. He was heavier, more compact, and his skin was darker. He smelled like an olive tree, or how Liza imagined such a tree might smell, growing in Italy, under the hot sun. When Mr. Cecco moved, his bracelets made melodious tones, similar to those of Liza's chain. She remembered hearing those tones when he kissed her fingers and stole her ring that first day in the brig. She would know him in the dark, by his melody.

Twisting the ring, she rolled over in her bed so that she wouldn't be diverted. She had to be ready, maybe as soon as tomorrow, when the gently bobbing ship would leave port and head out to sea, when the crew's regular routine would be reestablished. Ignoring the voices of the men— Cecco's low accent and her father's clipped responses— she went over her plans in detail, one more time.

From her father's improved temper during the days before mooring, Liza knew that the lady had at last accepted him. There was some setback here in port, but Liza didn't worry about that. In his chains or in the company of Mr. Cecco, her father and his moods didn't much affect her. And whether or not Jill's feelings for Hanover were genuine, the fact remained; after the doctor and his medicine established control of the lady, Hook would need Liza.

He didn't know it yet, but she'd make him understand. With or without words, he would hear her. He'd follow a trail of treasure and come to that special place— and Jill would never get Hook back.

Hook would never get Jill back. Hanover was determined. His sense of honor no longer troubled him. As he told Jill once before, an oath to such a man meant nothing. But the ship left the port of Gao this evening, with *L'Ormonde* a short distance behind, and Hanover was no longer eager to pledge his loyalty. Nor did Hook seem inclined to demand it.

The surgeon was only mildly surprised that his conscience didn't nag him as he and the Frenchman designed the newest plan of escape— and added an element of revenge. Hanover's only concern now was getting all parties off the ship before detection. It wouldn't be easy, and LeCorbeau insisted that every detail be nailed into place this time. Nothing must go wrong.

Mr. Cecco himself gave the doctor the idea in his remarks to Jill that first morning in port. It was a bold scheme. 'Captain' Cecco must have no reason to suspect the surgeon, and every reason to trust the privateer. For a short while, Jill would be distressed. How fortunate that her new husband would have just the right tonic to recover her spirits.

Mrs. Heinrich would, in fact, discover she had nearly inexhaustible energy— but none to spare for mourning her pirate captain.

Relieved at last from his guard duty, Mr. Cecco leaned his elbows on the rail, eyeing the flickering lights of Gao in the distance. The first time he'd left this town, he hadn't seen her lights. He'd been stowed away in the leaky hold of a broken-down tramp, an island-hopper, stinking of fish. An hour before, three of his brothers released him from his cage. They hadn't seen him in six months, but there was no time for reunion. They'd handed him a knife and some gold pieces, and at great risk to their own freedom, stood guard while he conducted his business with the prison governor. Then they'd bundled Cecco into a cart, headed for the docks, and paid the mate to look the other way as Cecco, in his bloody prison shirt, slid over the side to conceal himself below. The boat pushed away from shore and, over time, the nightmare of Gao receded.

It all happened so fast— gypsy, prisoner, pirate. With good fortune, he happened upon this ship off the next island. But Cecco had been lucky most of his life. The days of his youth were spent traveling the Italian countryside, tinkering, mending knives, watching his mother tuck coins in her sash as she read the white palms of ladies. His mother taught him to respect fine things. Her business proved profitable for her, and enlightening for her son. She understood these girls. When he was young, he watched how she flattered them, how she built suspense into their fortunes, milking the rich ones for a few more coins. And as he grew handsome, his mother got a glint in her eye, and always, after that, the boy of her predictions was dark, and persuasive, with a gold-colored ring on his finger and a shining smile. The girls emerging from her wagon had only to walk a few paces to meet him. For the sake of his pleasure, Cecco learned to put up with the giggling. But he never got used to the giddiness. Gypsy girls had much more sense. He had always intended to choose one. But fate intervened, and he hadn't had time for that to happen. Giovanni the gypsy tangled with the wrong girl, a mayor's daughter, and within hours of exchanging rings on a bed of pine needles, he lay bleeding on the cold stone floor of a cell. Cecco was never sure which had angered the mayor more, the exchange of passion, or the exchange of a brass ring for gold. In any case, the girl was shut in her room to see if she'd ripen, but the gypsy boy was shipped far away— to rot. Here, in Gao.

As the lights on shore receded, Cecco wondered if, there in Gao, the prison governor still lived. If so, the name of the hot-tempered young 'thief of a gypsy' he had so loved to bait would still be etched in scars on the man's back. He'd been robust for a bureaucrat, a man with not enough feeling and too much power. He'd made it his mission to beat the spirit from the dirty wanderer who'd had the gall to dally with decent girls. Duty demanded he teach the gypsy a lesson. The lessons Cecco learned, however, were of a more practical nature, and by the time he got his knife and his opportunity, the man's clothing was the only impediment to justice. Cecco shook his head as he remembered. He still regretted that, in his hurry, he'd had to tear that shirt away. It had been a fine material.

Thanks to his luck and his brothers, Cecco made his way aboard this ship. She wasn't as pretty then, but she, too, was in a hurry to sail out of these waters, and having lost some men in dealings with the Royal Navy, her bow-legged captain welcomed a new rogue to his ranks. With a notorious name and a bounty on his head, Cecco found himself respected by his fellows. Two years later, no richer except in experience, Cecco was the first to approach the newest man— a huge, unruly runaway slave— feeling that this one was a kindred spirit. And mere months after that, while berthed in a European port, their captain was surprised in the dead of night by a moody, black-haired gentleman and a brawny Irishman. Deliberately, the entire crew was roused by the intruders. Right there in front of his men, the captain, gripped at his scruffy neck by a hand bearing impressive rings, was offered his choice between giving up the ship or a knife in his throat. Two minutes later, his pockets were empty and he was floating face down, and no doubt the authorities buried him in an anonymous grave. No one else felt inclined to challenge the newcomer after that. True to his threat, the new captain made the men work. But true to his promise, he made them rich. That was when the gypsy became a pirate in earnest.

Appreciating his change in fortune, Cecco often wondered where his brothers were now. After their brave show of loyalty, did they find a way back home? Such courage. Courage and loyalty, and a healthy disregard for the law. Gypsy virtues. He had never thought to find that combination again, so far from his people. And then, in the hidden bay of a secret island, a lady flew from the darkness and into his hand, and her face in the lanternlight was perfect above the red seam on her throat. Never again would Giovanni Cecco look farther for his desires. He'd have waited far longer for her to turn to him, but now, waiting wouldn't be necessary. He had read her future in her blood-stained palm. He could feel it in the wind; the change was coming. Like Mr. Cecco, it was sailing out of Gao.

Under the stars of the open sea now, anything seemed possible aboard the *Roger*. After all, a drifting gypsy had become a shrewd buccaneer, and the moody newcomer was the famed sea captain of legend. With luck, the ship for Captain Cecco would fall into his hands as easily as she had fallen into Hook's. Already, he knew what he would rename her.

She would be his very own…*Red Lady*.

Behind Capt. Jas. Hook's brass-plated door, lessons resumed. Hanover hardly waited for it to shut behind Liza as the girl went off on another errand.

"My darling, how I have missed you!"

He seized Jill's shoulders and spun her around, eager to collect the kisses he'd lost over his four days' confinement. But as he leaned toward her, she backed away, wrenching her shoulders from his hands. Before he had time to blink, she drew back her hand and dealt a blow to his marked cheek that left it burning. Her eyes blazed.

"You dare to touch me!"

"My dear…I do. I have! Why should I not?" The surgeon held his hand over his face, and even in her anger she saw that he had removed his wedding ring.

"You claimed to respect me. I see you have lied, in that and in other things."

"Of course I respect you. I am going to marry you! I had thought that once you agreed to be my wife, you would hardly stand upon ceremony any longer, making me plead with you." Never had he seen her so magnificent as in this fury. He had to touch her. "But if it will make you happy, I *will* ask. Madam, may I kiss you?"

"No, Doctor. Most definitely, 'not today.' "

It was Hanover's turn to be angry. "What on earth has gotten into you, Jill? Why have you turned on me?"

"I, turned on you? Quite the opposite, Mister Hanover. You were about to leave me."

Hanover stood staring at her, his mouth slightly open, and then widening into a smile. "Ah!" Nearly laughing in his relief, he caught himself just in time. She would surely have taken such behavior as evidence he was trifling with her affections. Instead, he spread his hands. "My dear, I had no opportunity to ask you to return my letter. All my plans went awry. You should never have read it."

"You instructed me to read it; I promised that I would. Unlike you, I kept my promise."

His voice was affectionate, indulgent. "And you kept my diamonds?"

Her features softened. "Yes." As he moved closer, her temper flared again. "Until I could throw them back in your face!"

Now his gust of laughter was impossible to suppress. "My pirate queen! I know you far better than that. You have my diamonds tucked safely away in your jewel drawer. Or no…you have hidden them from Hook." At last, the surgeon's expression waxed grim. He stepped nearer, appraising her with a physician's eye. "How have you fared in my absence? Has he hurt you?"

Looking down, Jill allowed the moment to fester. She intended to draw and quarter every second of suspense.

"Jill?"

"I will never tell you what passes between him and me."

"Now you are being cruel."

"I hope I am."

"If he has abused you, you must tell me."

"I will tell you nothing."

"I hope there is nothing to tell."

She looked at him, her face just slightly averted.

"You were intimate with him!" He grasped her arms. "Did he force you— or did you turn to him, believing I had betrayed you?"

With a quick intake of breath, she prolonged his torture.

"I could kill him!"

"I told you not to touch me—"

"Enough of this nonsense. You are my fiancée. I have certain rights."

Twisting in his grip, she tried to shove his hands away. "You are not yet my husband."

"And neither is Hook. Tell me, what has happened in these four days?"

She stilled. Leveling a cold stare, she stung him again. "In these four days, you have become less than a gentleman."

He dropped his hands. Her chin rose, and she looked away.

"I apologize, my dear. Of course you are confused."

"Oh, no, I am thinking quite clearly. You thought a few diamonds would pay for the damage you caused when you misled me."

"No, Jill. The diamonds were meant to demonstrate my sincerity, to assure you of my return. I am sorry to have put you through this upsetting time, but, quite frankly…it warms my heart to see how strongly you feel about me."

"Really, Doctor. The diamonds were much more effective than this sweet talk. After attempting to desert me, you cannot pretend you intended to marry me. You paid me off, instead, like a common—"

"You know to what lengths I will go to marry you. I have even tarnished my honor for your dear sake."

"So you say, Sir, but I don't see you making good your promise to the captain, either. You have yet to swear *that* oath, as well."

"Only because the captain has not called for it. You witnessed my attempts to make the pledge before he confined me. As I wrote in my letter, I was only going to slip away for a little while. You must believe me. If Hook hadn't prevented us from following my plans, we would even now be man and wife."

"Of course I must take your word for it."

"You took my diamonds. Why not my word?"

Suddenly, she surprised him. As the sun breaks through after storm, her smile dawned upon him, and she rushed into his arms. "Johann!"

"Madam…now?"

But although she smiled, she pulled back once more. "Now, only…I was devastated to learn you would abandon me, even for just a few days. Of course I knew you would return to me."

"Sweet girl!"

"But I must have one more reassurance from you, dear. We will spend the rest of our lives together, if you will only tell me what our life will be. Johann. It is the last time I will ask you."

Now it was Hanover who pulled back, hesitation shading his happiness.

"Sir…where did you get so many diamonds…and will you be getting more?"

The doubt dissolved from his features. He coaxed her toward the couch; she went willingly. They sat together on the luxurious fabric, surrounded by the splendor provided by her pirate lover. Her bare foot abandoned the Oriental carpeting and settled on his shoe. The sapphires sparkled on her ankle, the emeralds ornamented her hand. Holding the pirate queen in his arms, the good doctor, at last, told her everything she needed to know.

"I have never broken the law. Except where freeing you is concerned, I have been an honest man. After many years of research, sacrifice, and experimentation, my labors have been rewarded with success. Basing my studies on ancient legend, I developed a formula to be used for the benefit of mankind. Only I know the secret of its concoction. This philter induces passion— yes, real, physical love— in those who believed themselves beyond it. Think, Jill, how much good it will do. Wives who for one reason or another withhold themselves from their husbands need no longer be afraid. Husbands who thought themselves…unable…are now capable of performing their marital duties. It is a miracle, Jill, a stabilizing influence on families. Fathers will feel no need to stray, wives need no longer feel reluctance. And a beneficial side effect is that the evil of such dens of iniquity as— please excuse me for being so frank— brothels, may in time simply fade away. If all men are happy in their homes, the unfortunate women of the streets will cease to be used and degraded. It is a bold vision, I admit, but I am a bold man. And I have now chosen a wife who will, I am sure, sustain me in this wholesome endeavor.

"But I see in your eyes that you are still wondering. The partner who has proved invaluable in this venture is Captain LeCorbeau. He has managed the distribution of my philter, and through his connections secured the unique ingredient— the beautiful lotus flower, which grows in far-off Egypt. The diamonds, my dear, I carry because the gold I have gleaned from selling my product would be far too cumbersome to transport. Jewels are much more convenient.

"Yes, my darling, I am a wealthy man. Far wealthier, I can guess, than anyone you have previously known. And I will only become more wealthy as my philter is recognized in the medical community and put to use throughout the civilized world." He smiled modestly, and blinked. "I have pleased you now, haven't I, my lady pirate? And I will make you even happier. We will take the ballrooms of Vienna by storm, and dressed in yards of whispering silk, you will waltz with me, and how all the dashing young officers will vie for your lovely gloved hand! How they will envy your husband! On many a misty morning, I shall have to call the gentlemen out and defend you with my sword. This is what our life will be, my darling. A rich, breathtaking dream. Ours for the taking, for as I told you before, I am confident that I am the man for you."

He stopped speaking then, realizing he should have told her the truth long before. Because with her scarlet fingers she had begun to stroke his scar, soothing the sting of her angry slap. And then her touch slid caressingly down his neck, over his shoulder, to draw him closer. Her eyelids lowered, and her gaze wandered lovingly all over his face. Her breathing accelerated to an alarming level. No philter was necessary to inspire her passion. Her lips spoke only one word before they granted him a husband's embrace.

"Today!"

Falling back on the silken cushions of the couch, she pulled him with her so that they both stretched out, and his weight pressed down upon her body. Her hips rose to meet his; his lips as he kissed her detected the pulsation of her own, and their hearts pounded together as she felt his manhood firm against her femininity, and then her fingers raked his hair.

Really, the couple was so happy that it was a shame Liza chose that particular moment to signal her return with a knock, on Capt. Jas. Hook's brass-plated door.

Hours later, as the ship headed away from the islands, the wind picked up, lashing spray against the hull. The *Roger* moaned in the night, rocking most of her company into uneasy sleep. Mr. Smee threw off his blanket and heaved himself up from his bunk. From his many seasons as the *Roger*'s bo'sun, he knew her sounds. She was complaining tonight, and it unsettled him. With an effort, he pulled on his boots and replaced his spectacles, then he trudged his way topside, holding his lantern aloft. There at the top step peered Nibs, with the tail ends of his kerchief whipping in the wind.

"Mr. Smee, I was just about to wake you. Mr. Noodler didn't know if the captain should be told. He says he's been watching *L'Ormonde*. She's tailing us closer than she usually does."

"She's burning lights, then?"

"Yes, Sir. She's still behind us, but off to starboard."

"You were right to come to me, lad. Tell Mr. Noodler not to worry. I'm thinking the captain knows what she's about. And for all it's an evil night for rowing, tell him to keep a look-out for her boats— with or without lights."

"Aye, aye!" Nibs bounded away and sprang up the ratlines to join Noodler in the crow's nest, under the flapping flags.

Smee shook his head and set off on his rounds, inspecting the ship. He couldn't sleep anyway. He might as well make sure all was in order. His lantern moved in the darkness, seeming to the gang in the rigging like a bead of light strung together with the ship's lanterns, sliding down the port side and up the starboard. He climbed to the forecastle and leaned over the rail where the wind battered his face, then he rattled down again to inspect the armory. Level by level, he descended to check the decks and holds. Because of the pitching waves, he had to take wider steps than usual, and above the crew deck the heavy hammocks swung. But so far as he could see, all was in place and as it should be.

Uneasy still, Mr. Smee retired to his cabin and stretched himself down to rest. He'd have to be sharp tomorrow, on guard for the captain's safety. And the lady's, whether she liked it or not. That Hanover didn't fight fair, and he was one hell of a swordsman. Almost as good as the captain.

When Smee finally closed his eyes, he took his mind off his troubles with thoughts of an island flower…his Lily, with her soft, fringed skirt and dark braid. *There* was a woman, now, who understood duty. She'd been cool at first when he'd shown her the captain's gift of golden bracelets. She'd done Hook the favor because it was the right thing to do, a fair return for another. Smee missed Lily all the more, since port call. The little blonde barmaid he'd charmed in Gao drew a neat pint, but she hadn't taken the edge off his thirst.

And in spite of her resemblance to the lady, he'd found that, after all, the girl in Gao hadn't satisfied him so very well. She didn't favor a corset either, but as it turned out, she preferred to work her own lacings. Smee rolled over on his bunk and exhaled, sighing like the ship.

That little barmaid didn't know what she was missing.

Still awake and listening to the *Roger's* keening, her captain drained his cup and set it on the bed shelf. Concluding with his mistress, he had wrapped his arm around her so that with her finger, she traced the swirling tail of the mermaid tattooed above his wrist.

"You will remember what I've taught you."

"Aye, Sir. You needn't worry."

"I never worry; I prepare. A habit you are acquiring from me, perhaps? You've come a long way since I found you on that island."

"You've given me much since then."

"Only an equitable exchange, my love." As the ship leaned to starboard, his hook swung away from the wall where it hung. Pitching back, it struck the wood again. "Sleep now. There is no point in putting it off. Tomorrow will come."

"I am hesitant to end it. With only a few exceptions, it has been a pleasant experience. Without exception, it has been stimulating."

Hook raised an eyebrow. "You have borne the unpleasant exceptions with spirit."

"It seemed to me there was no other choice, Sir."

"One always has choices, although perhaps not desirable ones."

"You taught me that things are not always what they seem." Pulling away a bit, she ventured, "A lesson I've seen proved again recently."

"You were a quick study."

"And you are very sure of yourself." Her blue eyes matched his as she looked earnestly into them. "Whatever else I have believed of you, I have always admired that."

A sentimental man, Hook thought, might drown in the deep waters of her eyes. "Yes. And I am sure of this: that we shall have no regrets, even after our affair is finished."

"And is this truly the way we should end it?"

"You are saddened, but that will pass. And if anything should go amiss— if for instance, LeCorbeau makes difficulties— follow my directives."

"Aye, Captain." She waited before saying, as a final gesture, "I hope I have done my duty."

He touched her cheek, and his gaze grew intense. "You have never disappointed me."

She smiled. Laying her head down at last, she closed her eyes. "Tomorrow…"

The sea was restless, and the claw continued its intermittent knocking. Watching her, Hook stroked her hair until she slumbered, and then he kissed her one last time before he slept, dreaming of his mermaid. Scales of emeralds bedecked her tail, and lotus blossoms twined into her hair— golden hair that swirled all about him, entangling his heart…even after she slipped from his arms and disappeared, smiling, into the depths.

A Change of Plan

"There's been a change of plan, Miss. The reading lesson's over. You're to stay in your quarters until you're called." Mr. Smee removed the book from Liza's fingers, and, with a decisive rap, replaced it on the doctor's desk. "Mister Hanover won't be needing this after all."

Squeezing her hands together, Liza backed from the big Irishman. Curiosity lit her eyes.

"No, I'll not be telling you what it's about, and if you don't stay put, I'll be clapping your bracelet back on. Mind, now." Jingling his keys for emphasis, he turned his back and shut the door.

A moment later it opened again, and the girl stood with her hand on the door handle, straining her ears for clues. As Smee strode toward the galley, the cook's pick of chickens, already unsettled by another passer-by, ruffled their feathers and beat their wings. Liza watched stray plumes fling themselves into the air, and by the time they floated down to settle on the deck, Smee's footfalls had faded. The cook's cat sat with its white tail curled about it, its eyes large with calculated innocence. Over the sloshing of the sea, Liza caught the sound of voices behind the galley door.

Creeping from her room, she stole closer, hugging the cannons, her bare feet cautious on the rough wooden boards. She began to distinguish the different voices of the sailors. As she listened for the one she sought, a smile bloomed on her lips, and she turned her gaze aft again. This time, she didn't linger. She hurried back to her door but didn't enter. Pressing herself against the wall instead, she edged toward the spare cabin in the middle of the stern, and with one wide, gray eye, peeked in. Liza turned back then, freeing her hair from its net and shaking it loose over her shoulders as she entered her quarters.

There had been no change in Liza's plan. She would do exactly as ordered. She'd stay put.

"No, Doctor." With a smile full of intrigue, Jill folded the parchment and tucked it into her bodice. "I have written something down to admire, but no one must read it." She had counted on the man responding to her advances this morning, and he was more abandoned than she anticipated, his old confidence returned in force. It couldn't last, and she was enjoying every second of his attention.

"You are charming when you try to deceive me. Show me." Hanover pulled her into his arms. "What have you been writing here at your desk, while Liza was studying her letters?"

Laughing, she tamped the paper more deeply into her bosom. "Now I know my secret is safe. Your refined sense of propriety will forbid you to delve any further into my…privacy."

There was no doubt about it, Hanover decided. She was tempting him. "Madam, you have wrought a change in me. I am prepared to break any rule necessary to make you happy." His generous lips smiled, more amorous every second. "And I know now how to please you." Holding her waist in one taut, swordsman's arm, he brushed the tips of his fingers over her scar.

Half closing her eyes, she tilted her head back and welcomed the warmth of his mouth as he kissed the red mark. His fingertips lingered on her throat, then slid beneath her ruby necklace, and lower. As he kissed her lips, his hand arrived at its destination and gently probed for the parchment. She almost forgot to wonder how long Liza had been away on her errand, but she heard nothing outside her door, and, too soon, the doctor drew the paper and his fingers from her bodice.

"Now I have it. In a moment I will know what you hide from me." Still holding her, he snapped the paper open and began to read. Jill inspected the door, then met his eyes as he smiled on her.

"So! You have been practicing your new name. How many times? It must be a hundred! And I thought you were busy writing another of your stories."

"It *is* a story. I have made it all up, and supplied a happy ending— 'Mrs. Johann Heinrich.' You see, we will have the same initials when we are married. Johann Heinrich, Jill Hein—" She stopped, turning pale.

"Jill? What is the matter, my darling?" Hanover began to release her, but even in her surprise she seized his arms and kept him close.

"I didn't notice before. It seemed so right." She stared at the inky lines on the parchment.

"Notice…" His gaze followed hers to the paper. "Ah. Yes. Yes, I see now."

She was gazing at him, perceiving an aspect she'd never taken in before. "Our initials will be the same…but the name is not what I expected. Heinrich. Your true name is Heinrich."

"Yes. Like you, I have temporarily taken what you might call a pirate name. 'Hanover' is a pseudonym I adopted to pursue my endeavors at sea. There is nothing sinister about it, I assure you. I simply didn't want to be traced on my travels from England. I intend to assume my proper name when we return to Europe. I am very proud of it."

"Of course you are. It isn't surprising, then, that I should write it. We have become so close."

He squeezed her waist. "Closer every day, now."

"Why did you wish to hide your whereabouts?"

"There was a slight misunderstanding about my experiments. Merely an unpleasantness as I sought to learn the proper dosage of my philter. I have since corrected the problem."

"I see." Making use of the natural pause, Jill listened for approaching footsteps. "Well…I am hardly the one to fault you for taking a new name. And when we are married, we will both take the old one."

Her smile was irresistible, and Doctor Heinrich didn't try to deny it. By now he had decided there were far more advantages to associating with pirates than he ever imagined. Neither he nor his fiancée paid the slightest heed as the parchment fluttered to the floor.

After some moments the surgeon relented, allowing the lady to catch her breath. "Tell me, Madam. Have you any other documents hidden away?" His fingers strayed once again to the edge of her neckline.

"We mustn't chance it. Liza is late. She may return at any moment." Jill pressed her hands flat against his chest, but her fiancé didn't release her.

"That never bothered you before, my darling."

"It doesn't bother me now. But after finding us so fervently— engaged— yesterday, your daughter must be wondering about the situation."

"It is of no consequence. Liza never asks questions, and I have always impressed upon her the importance of discretion."

"You are in a very cheerful mood today! Considering the complications in port, I'm glad to see you so confident of our future." Pushing herself from his arms at last, Jill began to pace the carpets, drawing closer to the entrance. "Still, I wonder where Liza has gone. She's never stayed away more than ten minutes or so." She shot a glance at the door.

Hanover caught up to her and appropriated her hand. "How I should like to be 'engaged' with you again." Raising her fingers to his lips, he kissed them tenderly. "I ought to be ashamed, being alone with you, behaving like such a rake. But I find I cannot regret it."

"Of course I find it pleasant, too…but the men will begin to take notice." The anxiety in her voice, she found, was genuine. The door should have been flung open by now.

Unworried, the surgeon detained her hand. "I know how to settle you. We will make plans. Tell me, what kind of ring shall I place upon this finger?"

"Ring?" Every little noise distracted her; this sound was only her scarlet skirt brushing against the couch. But she should be hearing other noises. Where were the footsteps?

The surgeon laughed. "Your wedding ring, of course. I propose a circle of diamonds, a sweet reminder of yesterday. Shall it be only diamonds, or shall we make it rich with other stones as well?"

Forcing herself to pay attention, Jill renewed her smile and fingered her necklace. "Oh! I should like rubies, too, I think." Deliberately, she moved herself back into his arms and took his handsome face between her hands. At last, she had heard steps on the stairs. She drew him toward her. Unhesitating, he wrapped his arms around her and accepted her embrace— a deep, passionate kiss, lent added ardor by her unrest.

They both startled as a fist beat the door. Hanover released her immediately; Jill held on to his shoulders. Her lips parted, but when she said nothing, Hanover's regard grew quizzical and the knock pounded again. Collecting herself, she backed away from her fiancé.

"Come!"

Mr. Smee opened the door. He cast a look around the cabin first, then stepped in and nodded. "Lady." He cleared his throat.

"Yes, Mr. Smee. Is it time for lunch already?" She turned her back to the doctor, her eyes urgent, questioning Smee.

"Aye, Madam. *Past* time." He raised his eyebrows. "I've come to ask if you've seen the captain?"

"No, of course not. He never disturbs Liza's lessons. No doubt we'll find him in the galley." Her face showed confusion as she surveyed Smee, but by the time she turned toward the surgeon, her expression was clear. "Shall we go?"

"Yes. I must locate Liza. I will speak to her about this lapse. She is making good progress." Smiling in his self-satisfied manner, Hanover tugged at his cuffs. "Such success shouldn't be interrupted."

Jill returned his look, but as he collected his walking stick, she seized the arm Smee held out to her. They stepped over the threshold, and then she stopped abruptly. "Oh— Doctor, would you be so kind as to collect my letter? I believe I left it near the escritoire."

"Certainly, Madam." Realizing their mistake, Hanover hurried to correct it, and Jill propelled Smee down the steps. She kept her voice low.

"Why didn't the captain come?"

"I'm wondering that, myself! I waited outside your door and sent Tom at last to fetch him from the galley. The lad said he wasn't there. I couldn't let you go on any longer."

As a soft tread signaled the doctor's approach, Jill straightened and spoke more clearly. "Very well, Mr. Smee. I'll see to Liza later. Thank you, Doctor Hanover." Absent-mindedly, she tucked the guilty parchment into the sash at her waist, where she usually kept her dagger. "Mr. Smee tells me he had a little task for your daughter to perform. Nothing to worry about after all. Next time, he won't take her away from her lesson."

Smee touched his forehead. "Aye, Ma'am. I'm sorry."

"Will you join us for lunch, Doctor?"

Everything was going splendidly for the surgeon. He was in too good a mood to spoil it by sharing his lady pirate with her shipmates. "I think not, Madam. I've some business to attend in my quarters." He bowed. "Until later."

Jill held the sigh of relief until the surgeon, tapping his walking stick, strolled away toward the hatch. Her eyes searched the deck for her captain, and then the rigging.

"It's no good, Ma'am. He's not topside, either."

She and Smee looked at one another. "Something has gone badly wrong."

"I have to be agreeing with you. It's not at all like the captain to leave you with that bounder."

"Nor to miss a good fight! Hook would never willingly fail to carry out this scheme."

"Aye, something's forced his hand. When I left him earlier this morning, he was more than ready to storm in and find you in the doctor's arms—"

"And challenge him! We went over the plan enough, it should have gone smoothly." Jill grasped Smee's elbow and towed him toward the hatch. "Mr. Smee. Check the spare quarters. He almost always works there when we're holding Liza's lessons. If you don't find him, round up some of the men and search the ship." She stopped and clutched at her stomach.

"Are you all right, Lady?"

She shuddered. "I've just had a terrible feeling. But don't worry about me, we must see to the captain."

She made to go with him, but Smee laid a hand on her arm. "No,

Lady. Until we know more, you'd best stay above so as not to call attention to the captain's absence."

Jill's first impulse was to rush to Hook's aid, but she awoke now to the signal her presence below decks would send to the crew. Seeing the lady inspecting holds and hammocks would serve only to alert the men to a problem. "Yes, Mr. Smee. But check everywhere. The boats, the holds."

"Aye, Lady." Smee set off, gesturing to a group of deckhands to follow.

Frustrated by the impracticality of seeking Hook herself, Jill turned, her fist clenched over her belly, and stared into the roiling waters of the sea. As she clung to the rail, she leaned against a cannon and, suddenly, the ocean around her lost its color. Iron gray, like the cannon, the once welcoming horizon seemed only a menace. She fought the feeling but it persisted, as sure as her love for her captain. Casting for a sensation potent enough to dispel it, she focused on a memory, one of Hook's violent embraces— the incendiary, savage kiss which, when provoked, left her reeling and in tears. Just such a kiss had set her off balance after Hook's fencing match with the doctor. But the recollection only left her longing for him, and, as the empty minutes passed, she fell further into gray despond. Her honesty wouldn't allow her to pretend, even to herself. Jill followed the truth, and it led her to paradise. And perdition.

Hook treasured her. Since the day of the battle that marked her throat, he undertook to ensure that no harm befell her— from any quarter. A forceful man from whom even the most tender passions might erupt, yet he never raised his hand against her. From the moment Jill joined Hook, she felt his protection constantly, surrounding her like his ship. And in recent days, while working toward the culmination of their ploy, Hook was adamant. He made it clear as he watched and guarded his Jill— her safety was the only point on which he would not bend. Hook would never fail her at the critical moment.

He was in trouble.

It seemed an eternity before Smee awakened her from her nightmare, laying a gentle arm around her shoulders. But the dregs of the dream lingered, because, like the sea around her, the bo'sun's face had lost color, too. He was pale with concern.

"I'm sorry to frighten you, Lady, but the lads and I have done the job. Twice. We found no sign of the captain, but..." Reluctantly, Smee showed her what he held. "We did find this."

Hook's sword, in its scabbard. Jill's hand flew to her mouth, and she stared. This was the weapon Hook intended to employ as he staged his challenge to the surgeon. Both eager and hesitant, she asked, "Where?"

"In the spare quarters, Ma'am. On the desk, lying there with his charts. But he's not about."

"Then look again! Smee, he has to be *somewhere.*"

"Aye, Ma'am. Of course we will. But it isn't good, the way things are looking. I want you to be bracing yourself." He pulled her gently, encouraging her toward the companionway. "Will you be in your quarters, then?"

Halting, she balked. "No! I'll have Mullins furl sails, and then I'll question the deck gang. They might have seen something from above."

"Stop sailing? I didn't want to suggest it." Only then, when he knew she understood the gravity of the situation, did Smee allow his apprehension to show. The color returned to his face in full. "You're thinking the same way I am, then. It's that serious."

As she pressed her hands over the ache in her abdomen, her voice came low, vibrant. "I know it is."

Smee considered for only a moment. "Then better have Mullins drop anchor, too."

"Aye, I will."

"I'm off, then, Madam. Watch yourself." Smee sped away and hurtled down the steps.

"Mr. Mullins!"

"Yes, Ma'am!" The call came from the wheel.

Commandingly, Jill shouted out her first order. "Furl sails!"

Mullins didn't question it. "Aye, aye. Away aloft, lads, furl sails!"

With a sense of relief, Jill watched the men above her scuttle to do her bidding. She strode to the helm and spoke more quietly. "We'll be dropping anchor next, Mr. Mullins. See to it." As calmly as she could manage, she snatched up the spyglass and crossed to port to scale the steps to the quarterdeck, balancing herself with a grip on the ornate banister. Fighting a wave of panic, she resisted ringing the ship's bell as she passed it, and when she reached the taffrail, she pulled the glass to its fullest extent and lifted it to her eye.

The wind beat her skirt against her legs. Her hair whipped around her face. Impatient, she set down the glass to tug at the knot of her scarlet sash. As it came loose, the parchment she had tucked into it was stolen by the breeze. It winged its way off the stern to freedom— and a watery grave. 'Mrs. Johann Heinrich' was now, and always had been, just another story. Without a thought for the tragedy of that lady's ending, Jill lifted her face to the wind and bound the sash around her head. Having tamed her hair, she raised the glass again.

L'Ormonde was there. As Smee informed the captain this morning, she had moved toward the *Roger* in the night and dropped back at sunrise, slightly to starboard. She was close, but no closer, still trailing within range of the spyglass. Jill didn't yet know if the presence of another ship this far at sea was a comfort or a calamity. Hook never trusted LeCorbeau, and upon learning the extent of the Frenchman's partnership with the surgeon, his suspicions were confirmed. Yet, as the worst offense of which Hook could accuse the *commandant* was an unwillingness to share the profits of the doctor's business, Hook shrugged it off, reasoning that any venturer would do as LeCorbeau had done. Similarly, Hook himself had no intention of dividing the doctor's diamonds with the privateer. Nor did he intend to share Jill with the doctor. Not after this morning.

The men combined their strength to work together. Lowering the glass, Jill heard their commotion at the capstan, and watched as the aft anchor splashed into the sea and the heavy cable paid out from deep in the hold. As if raked from the ocean floor by the flukes of the anchor, all her fears, submerged under Hook's protection, rose rippling to the surface.

How could she bear it if Hook never came back to her? Her whole life had been lived moving toward him. While waiting to know one another, she conjured stories about him, and he dreamed of her as his mermaid. Partners in every sense of the word, Hook and Jill completed each other. But the discovery of this truth was too recent.

Even as the pirate queen, Jill was as yet dependent upon her captain. She had mastered the basics of sailing, but there was much to learn that only experience could teach her— experience that almost all the pirates under her command owned in abundance.

Standing here among these buccaneers without Hook at her side, Jill felt alone, as Hook used to feel before she came to him— but far more vulnerable. She had been careful to maintain cordiality between herself and the men. Now, with the captain hurt or missing, that strategy would be put to the test. With another twist of her insides, Jill realized how precariously her position teetered without Hook's iron fist to steady it. In his absence, whether temporary or permanent, the more ambitious men would not easily be denied. They were sure to seek his power, by any available means— including the possession of his mistress— and one of them would take it. Only one.

The strongest man aboard.

But surely, Jill rationalized, shivering as the chill crept up her spine, surely all her worries were for nothing. Mr. Smee was on guard, and the captain would be found before *L'Ormonde* caught up to the *Roger*. There were only so many places he could be on this ship, and all of them friendly. Only an unfortunate circumstance would keep Hook from executing a scheme such as he planned for today, especially such a lucrative one, and he would never leave his Jill for long in the amorous arms of the surgeon. Some accident must have occurred. Something serious, but certainly not disastrous. Smee would find him, and then this ache inside would be allayed. Hook wasn't gone for good. She would sense it if…if he were dead.…Hook and Jill were too closely connected not to feel each other's heart beating. He must be feeling her heart struggling now.

No, Hook was alive.…But where?

Jill's thoughts were disturbed by the sound of boots. Mr. Smee, Nibs and Tom, and many others moved toward her. Emerging from the hatch, they scattered across the deck, and, Jill noticed, began to gravitate toward the gunwales. A sudden fear stabbed her, reversing the certainty she had labored to achieve. "No!"

The grim look on Smee's face afflicted her, and she backed to the balustrade. Casting a wild look about the decks, she saw that everywhere men were bending over the rails. Some climbed to the forecastle to peer down from the bow, some leaned out from the shrouds. All were searching the sea.

The sea!

Nibs, Tom, and Smee scaled the quarterdeck stairs. Their steps slowed as they approached her. Smee was shaking his head. "We've not found a sign of him, Ma'am. We looked everywhere."

"No, you couldn't have. He's here!"

Tom moved to her side and, bending down, looked into her eyes. "I'm sorry, Ma'am. He's vanished."

Assaulted by a rush of pain, Jill jerked around to clutch at the rail. Sickened, she leaned over it, nearly losing her balance. Tom and Nibs seized her arms to support her. It was just as well. If they hadn't held her, she'd have jumped. For below her, Jill spied a terrible sight— crimson cloth, flapping in the breeze. Under the ornamental windows of her own cabin, it protruded from the aft porthole, two decks below. A fine-tailored banner of red velvet, its sleeves groping at the sea, the wide, embroidered cuffs empty of hand or hook.

The captain's coat.

"Hook!"

"No, Ma'am! Don't you think of diving in! We'll do it. Nibs, hold her!"

But Nibs was already hopping on one foot, tugging his boot off. Smee's flesh had turned a mottled red, and he quickly shed his keys, knife, and boots. He whisked off his spectacles and threw them down, too, then vaulted over the rail, plunging feet first into the water. The splash as he entered the waves was followed immediately by Nibs'. Held securely by Tom, Jill leaned over and watched. As she gripped the balustrade, her fingers dug into its gilded wood.

"Hook!…Hook!"

Alerted by her shouts, the crewmen abandoned their look-outs and rallied to her. But as the mass of men behind her swelled, Jill's hopes diminished. Smee and Nibs dove again and again, coming up spluttering, each time with empty arms. Shaking water from their faces, they gulped for air and submerged again. With an awful fascination, Jill watched their efforts, and, as they tired, she called to them.

"It's no use. Come aboard! Hook isn't there— he's not there. Come aboard!"

At last, no more could be done. The two exhausted sailors took hold of ropes their mates flung down, breathed hard for a few moments, then braced their feet against the slippery hull. They climbed, dripping, to be hauled to the deck. As he slid from the rail, Smee lowered his head. His eyes met Jill's, but only just. His words fell soft.

"I'm sorry, Ma'am. I'm sorry....He's gone." From his sodden shoulder he dragged the captain's coat. "From the lower aft cabin, Lady. Snagged on a splinter just out the window, or we'd have seen it before, from inside."

Now that the first shock was over, Jill felt strangely composed. "This coat means nothing, Mr. Smee. The captain is not drowned." The men stared at her. Then they fidgeted, their gazes shifting from one to another. She ignored their doubts. "Thank you for your efforts."

"But Ma'am—"

"We'll have to seek him aboard the vessel. He can't have drowned." Fixing Smee with a meaningful stare, Jill persisted. "You know why. A man who has his...abilities...cannot drown."

Nibs and Tom understood immediately, then Smee's face lit up. "Yes, Ma'am....That's right!" But his face clouded again. "Unless someone saw to it he was unconscious."

"No, Mr. Smee." Turning to the men, Jill spoke with authority. "All of you. You understand that the captain and I share a rare bond. You must listen when I tell you: Hook is not dead. We will keep looking."

A low murmur spread among the men. Their gazes kept returning to the heap of red velvet drooping from Smee's hands.

Jill's tone was firm, displaying the edge of her temper. "I want the ship searched, one more time, stem to stern. Now!"

"Aye, aye!"

"Yes, Madam." If the lady's aspect hadn't held so regal, her sailors might have taken her optimism for hysteria. But they all knew Red-Handed Jill better than that, and wanting to believe her, they moved off, dividing into groups to do her bidding. She remained immobile until the men had gone their separate ways, and then she pivoted to face Smee, a sudden spark in her eye.

"The armory! Has anyone checked there?"

Smee sent a questioning look to Tom, who gaped, a glimmer of hope dawning on his face.

"No, Ma'am!"

Snatching up her skirts, Jill ran down the stairway and sped across the long deck toward the forecastle, the ends of her red scarf streaming in the wind. She flung open the armory door and surged inside. The door banged shut.

The light here was dim. She waited, winded, for her eyes to adjust to it. As she stood panting, still holding her dress above her ankles and willing her own heart to sense another, her vision cleared. Though gloomy, the room was light enough to show her what she didn't want to see.

Except for the usual lethal contents hanging from its walls, the armory was empty. Jill dropped her skirts and focused on the tall cabinet to portside. In a moment, she had grasped the knobs and opened it. It was filled, as always, with rags, shot, grease, and oil. Slowly, she dropped her hands and turned to face the last possible place of concealment. The coffin-like bench at the bow. Jill's feet steadied her against the motion of the waves, approaching the chest without her conscious guidance. Bending down, she placed her fingers under the lip of the lid. She listened to the hinges groan as she pulled it upward. Her heart banged against her ribs, and only when the bench was all the way open did she lower her gaze to absorb its contents.

Gently, she lowered the lid. She sank down on it and caught her breath. Filled to the brim with cannonballs, the chest held only round, deadly iron. As she pulled herself together, Jill tried to collect her thoughts. Surrounded by cold metal and punishing leather, she felt that ache again, nagging in her stomach. It was a profound emptiness, like nothing she had ever felt before. The half of her that was Hook was hollow. Rocking on the bench, Jill told herself she must get up, she must keep searching the ship.

But contrary to the feeling in her gut, common sense informed her there was no point. If her captain was aboard this ship, he would be standing at her side right now, victorious after a magnificent duel with the surgeon.

Hook was gone.

She didn't know how long she sat there, hurting. But the door wailed on its moorings at last, and a rectangle of sunlight fell across the floor. As she looked up, blinking, a shadow stretched from the boots standing in the doorway to her bare feet beneath the bench. She could see only his silhouette, black and muscular, but she knew who he was. One of the strongest men aboard.

He stepped into the room.

"Lady."

She knew why he had come. Her spirits sank, if possible, even lower. She bowed her head.

"The time has come." His presence brought Hook's absence home to her, in a wave of devastation. Unmoving, she resisted it.

He insisted. "The men are waiting."

She closed her eyes. But still she saw that huge, dark shadow, looming, coming closer. She smelled his familiar scent.

"You must trust in me."

She shook her head.

"I will protect you."

Her voice when it sounded was unnatural, strained. "It is far too late for that."

The shadow slid nearer. She watched it on the floor.

"I will preserve the ship, then." And as he held out his hand to her, she heard his customary sound. His bracelets chimed.

At last she faced him. In the dim light of the armory porthole, she could see, gleaming like the pistols and swords surrounding her, the golden chains adorning his neck.

"Aye...Mr. Cecco. Hook's ship."

The line of his mouth softened, and then, ever so gently, he smiled. As if it were a gift, Mr. Cecco accepted the red hand she extended to him.

When the pirate queen emerged on the arm of her devoted sailor, she stood straight and proud. All hands were on deck. The murmuring died down until everyone was quiet and their agitation ceased. Sunlight glinted here and there on the knives in their belts, and in the many eyes observing her so closely. The surgeon had joined the company. He stood stiff, his marked face mingling elation and alarm. Nibs and Smee, having combed the ship again in spite of their earlier exertions, stood weary, shedding drops of seawater around their feet. Smee still held the captain's coat, a limp, crimson sham of itself.

With a keen blue stare under her scarlet scarf, Red-Handed Jill dropped Cecco's arm to look each man in the eye. She kept them waiting before she spoke. Timing was a tool.

Her voice was clear, commanding.

"We will remain under the provisions of the ship's articles until a new regimen is established. I want this vessel in order within the hour. Mr. Smee, see to it. Mr. Nibs, Mr. Tootles. Wipe up this deck. Mr. Mullins, you will resume sailing on our previous course. If *L'Ormonde* comes alongside, put her off— and tell her nothing." She paused. "I will now retire to my quarters. When I order the bell rung, we will assemble again and I shall inform you of our course of action. Any questions you may have will be answered at that time." Looking straight ahead, she reached to the side and gestured. Reluctantly, Smee draped the captain's coat on her arm. A captain's burden.

She assumed its weight. She didn't look at it.

"You are all dismissed. Get back to your posts."

The knot of men broke away to allow her passage. Not many noticed as Mr. Smee laid a weighty hand on the surgeon's shoulder, restraining him, or the surgeon's scowl. The attention of most of her sailors was riveted on Jill, and from the corner of her eye she perceived a new look on the men's faces. A look of undisguised interest. Things were changing now, their eyes said. Possibilities had opened up. Jill returned their stares with a quelling look. She couldn't afford to be afraid.

Processing to her quarters, she heard Mr. Cecco's boots behind her. As she exhibited no need for assistance on the steps of the companionway, he stopped there to watch her ascend. Brashly, the shiny brass plate on the door boasted the name of its missing master. Upon entering the cabin, Jill chose not to look behind her before shutting the door. Silence had followed her thus far. She trusted that all her men were watching, and all were wondering.

She would have to move quickly to fill the void of the captain's absence.

The door clicked shut.

For Red-Handed Jill, first, last, and always, came the welfare of the ship. With many duties to perform, she had only a few minutes to spare for the tears. Sinking to her knees on the carpet, she clutched her captain's coat to her breast, and as if to accommodate her lack of time, the hot tears came all in a rush.

First, Last, and Always

L'Ormonde had gained on the *Roger*, but Mullins' skills got the
pirate vessel underway again, and he managed to keep the
privateer out of hailing distance. Having learned the disposition of her
ship, Jill ordered the bell rung and listened to its jangling. She struck
a pose on the companionway, framed within its splendid carving,
and looked down at the company assembling before her. With a nod,
she signaled Mr. Smee to join her. She would require more than Mr.
Mullins' skills to keep Hook's ship on course. She must employ all her
own abilities, and Mr. Smee's as well.

Although never far from the lady in the previous hour, Smee had
felt it wise to leave her alone. From the day Jill came aboard, the captain
charged his bo'sun with her welfare, cautioning him to guard her in all
contingencies. Knowing she must now rely upon him without seeming
to do so, Smee made sure the men would have no cause to claim he
influenced Jill's decisions. At her summons, he sprang up the stairs to
stand erect, two steps from the top. A knife blazed in his belt as he
clasped his hands behind his waist. His eyes scanned the crew.

Jill began. "The captain left instructions to be followed in the event
of his absence. As his partner, my first duty is to preserve order aboard
the *Jolly Roger*." She had used the little time she had wisely. After
deliberating upon the situation, she washed away all evidence of tears
and tended her appearance. Now her hair was bound again beneath
the scarlet scarf around her forehead. Below her red skirt she wore her
boots. Her pistol and Hook's jeweled dagger hung at her waist, tucked

within a golden sash. Her bare arms bore no bracelets. She wore no jewelry at all but her earrings, which swung in the breeze as she spoke, flashing in the late sunlight.

As they surveyed her appearance, the men took heart. This was Red-Handed Jill. Alongside or apart from her king, she was their pirate queen. After one look at her, any question whether she might prove, under distress, to be a weaker woman was extinguished, and only Doctor Hanover showed signs of dismay.

During her seclusion, he had hovered near the companionway, prevented from ascending to her by his shipmates— and by a consultation between those with whom he had formed a friendship. Observing his fiancée now, Hanover conceded with an unsettling honesty that she acted every inch a pirate. Yet, as he recalled the morning's intimacies, he anticipated the end of the day, when he would pull away that kerchief to discover again the fascination beneath the façade. A woman free of entanglements. Exactly the woman he wanted.

Now, like the surgeon, all the men listened, attentive to the confidence in her voice. "Once again I will assure you. Captain Hook is alive. Our ship's articles, signed by all but one of the present company, remain intact. I put to you the following arrangements, to be in effect until such time as the captain returns to resume his position.

"Mr. Smee. You will continue as ship's bo'sun, maintaining the *Roger*'s physical condition, including that of the captain's quarters. Mr. Mullins. I entrust to you the post of sailing master. You will chart our courses and keep our bearings. Mr. Yulunga, as my newly appointed duty officer, you will assign my sailors to their shifts, and maintain discipline.

"Mr. Cecco....You are promoted to first mate." The men's astonishment was audible, a ripple of inhalation. Jill disregarded it. "It will be your duty to make my orders known to my other officers and to my crew." Her gaze remained on Cecco. Her voice stayed steady. "I charge you with my personal safety."

Cecco stood unmoving, his expression pleasant but noncommittal. As the sailors absorbed Jill's words, they traded glances among themselves, but no one interrupted while she concluded.

"Mister Hanover, you will decide today. After I and my officers discuss our terms with you, you may sign the articles and serve as ship's surgeon— or you may buy your freedom."

Hanover's posture didn't compromise, but a brief, surprised smile crossed his face. Obviously the lady was angling for enough power to get them both off the ship. Still, he would take no chances. Her scheme *might* succeed. Without a doubt, his own design *would*.

"My officers will meet first thing each morning to advise me…as I act in the captain's place."

Murmurs broke out as the crewmen turned to one another to comment. Nibs and Tom shifted on their feet, bobbing their heads in support of Jill's proposal, encouraging the others to approve it. Mullins tucked his beefy thumbs in his belt, considering. Hanover and Cecco exchanged significant looks, and Yulunga, looming behind the Italian, digested the lady's words with a dark smile. Jill didn't weaken her stance by seeking Smee's support; she knew she had it. They both kept their eyes on the crew, unsmiling. She allowed only a moment to pass in indecision.

"We shall put it to the vote."

All gazes turned toward Jill. She was about to call for ayes when Yulunga stepped forward.

"Lady." He hardly had to lift his head to her as she rested her hands on the majestic rail. "I will be happy to take the job of duty master— if my shipmates agree. Yours is one suggestion. But there are other angles to consider." He swung around to face the crew. "All of us worked hard under Captain Hook's regime. We found success, turning our labors to gain. We're most of us seasoned sailors. Don't we want a leader who can hunt down the prizes and prod us like the captain's claw?" In answer, the men nodded. "The lady assures us of Hook's return. But is her assurance enough to profit us?"

Smee took one step down. "It is for me! Red-Handed Jill knows us. She's made a wise plan to be going on with, and I say, let's follow it. If we slack off, it'll be our own faults if we're not raking in the treasure."

Several of the men hollered, "Aye!" and Nibs and Tom were the loudest among them.

Yulunga shrugged his bulky shoulders. "Let us consider another proposal." He raised his gaze to Jill. "With all respect, Lady. We men have waited a long time for the privileges Captain Hook used to claim. Why shouldn't at least one of us benefit? I say that until our old master returns, a new man should serve as captain."

A gust of enthusiasm blew up from the crowd. As Jill had foreseen, plenty of her men had enough ambition to favor the election of a new captain. To preserve Hook's authority for him, she had tried to head those ambitions off before discussion. Her apprehension increased when Yulunga finished his thought.

"I only say what everyone's thinking. A new man in the captain's quarters would serve also to keep the lady from feeling lonely."

With sly exclamations, a number of men approved. Jill sought Mr. Cecco's expression. By appointing him her protector, she hoped to curtail such aspirations. Not surprisingly, like those of several others, Cecco's eyes smoldered at the opportunity to seize not only the captain's command, but the captain's lady. As she expected, these hearty men possessed more than ambition. They wielded a more dangerous combination— a mix of two sure ways to rent the company's unity. Lust, and a hunger for power. Already, Smee was bristling, and Nibs and Tom fingered their weapons. The surgeon, however, merely observed, unruffled, and toyed with his watch. His detachment made Jill more uneasy than Yulunga's proposition.

With undisguised desire, Yulunga turned to her, his tone calculated to sustain the eagerness of the men, and to instill panic in Jill. He gestured toward his mates. "You see, Lady. Choose or be chosen! We all want what the captain owned."

Smee balled his fists, barely holding himself back as he waited for Jill's response. Crossing her arms, Jill looked Yulunga up and down. She leered as he had done, assessing his physical assets as if he were back on the auction block. Then, as the crewmen smiled, she spoke again.

"Neither of us is for sale to the highest bidder. You came aboard the *Roger* to escape slavery. You know better than any of us," she shook her head, once. "No one on this ship is owned."

Smee and the others settled, their tension easing. Yulunga waited for the chance to stir the men up again.

"Yes, Lady. Point taken. But the fact remains. You are no longer only one man's woman."

Placing her hand on her dagger, Jill stood firm. "I am as I have always been. My own woman." She raised her face to the others and said brusquely, "I see no reason to delay my duty any longer. I'm ready to take charge of Hook's ship."

"But Lady, you aren't the only one who is ready to take charge."

The moment had come. As the men agitated, Jill proved equal to it. Her sapphire stare, so like the captain's, pierced the massive man. Unflinching under his intimidation, she waited for silence, and then she aimed her words with precision. "I am the only one the captain *commanded* to take charge. Don't forget who spoke your name…Mr. Yulunga."

Squinting, the African nodded. The murmur rumbled once more, and Jill allowed it to swell. With a grim smile, Smee approved the respect in the men's eyes. His fists relaxed as Jill seized the moment.

"All right then. No more discussion. There's a cask of ale in the galley, and our next prize may be waiting on the horizon." Again, her blue eyes blazed like Hook's. "Give me your agreement, and we'll get on with it!"

Vigorous cheers arose from the sailors, and they stamped the deck with their boots. Jill felt the tremors in the soles of her feet. She smiled with satisfaction. In another minute, she would have them. Hook's men would be her own, and the *Roger*'s security restored. As her own mistress, Jill would be free to employ her energies as she saw fit. She could carry out the captain's orders, anticipating Hook's return without fear for herself or his interests.…And then, amid the shouting, Doctor Hanover strolled to the foot of the steps. He raised his hand for attention.

"Madam. As you observed, I am not yet officially a member of this ship's company. I now remind you that I have every intention of becoming one. If certain conditions arise."

Smelling trouble, Smee interjected, "You've said it yourself, Doctor. You've no business meddling until you're sworn in. I'll cast the first vote. Aye! to the lady's regimen!"

Nibs, Tom, Mullins, and several others sang out, "Aye! Aye!"

Raising his voice over the din, the doctor broke in again. "I feel it incumbent upon me to point out a sad truth which cannot be ignored— despite the fact that it will increase the burden of responsibility Captain Hook left on our lady's…fragile shoulders."

Incensed, Jill summoned every ounce of her dignity while she sought words cool enough to refute Hanover's implication. His pretentious smile struck dread into her heart. Dread that doubled as, in one sentence, the surgeon upset the balance she had striven to establish.

"I am not convinced Captain Hook will return."

"We will discuss your reservations when we discuss your future, Doctor Hanover. This is not the time."

Hanover blinked. "I apologize if I upset you, my dear. I understand how distressing this tragedy must be to a young woman like you."

The young woman bit back an angry retort. Losing her temper would only prove his point— and he knew it.

He turned to the crew. "As much as it pains me to grieve the lady, as a man of science, I find it beyond logic to hope, against all indication, that the captain lives. Thorough searches of the ship have yielded nothing to prove his survival, and the one piece of evidence we did discover points toward his drowning."

Smee snapped, "If you don't mind my saying so, Doctor, you're hardly the man to be passing judgment on our ways. You've held a grudge against the captain since the start!"

Jill grasped control. "Well said, Mr. Smee. Gentlemen, it is up to Hook's loyal crew to—"

"I admit it!" The surgeon threw his hands up. "As all of you know, I objected to the manner in which Hook ordered my capture and detained me. But if a new captain is named, I will sign your book of articles without hesitation."

"All very interesting Doctor," Jill rejoined, "but again, you are interfering with decisions that concern only ship's company."

Nibs leapt to the starboard rail, gripping the shrouds to balance there, his legs spread wide. His gaze darted among the crowd as he addressed the men, respectful but forceful.

"I'm not saying the doctor is right. But if anyone else is feeling the same way, well, let's have a captain, then." Jill, Tom, and Smee stared at Nibs. Steadily, he returned Jill's regard. Then he lifted his head. "I say we make it official. Until Captain Hook returns, let's call Jill what she is. Captain Red-Hand!"

Enthusiasm erupted from the deck, and glad shouts burst from Tom. Smee pounded his hands together, grinning with pride, and it took some time for the noise to abate enough for further discussion. With victory in her sights, Jill surveyed her sailors. "My proposal has been amended. Who says 'Aye?' "

As the crowd of men gathered its breath, a simple gesture stopped Jill's momentum. One man stepped calmly forward, tapping his chest. "I."

All heads turned to see him.

"I have a comment, which I believe is critical to our decision." It was Mr. Cecco, watching Jill, as always, with admiration. "As you know, Lady, I have every confidence in you. You are a jewel among women. And I have no objection to your captaincy…" He shrugged, "Except for one thing."

Jill met yet another setback, steeling herself for a battle of wits. "Well?"

Cecco tilted his head. His earrings swung. "I prefer to serve a captain who has more experience of sailing than myself."

"If you recall, Mr. Cecco, I have selected experienced officers— including you— to advise me. I am the captain's choice to guide the *Roger*."

Over the years, Cecco, too, had observed Hook's methods. Now his timing was impeccable. Before he spoke again, everyone was listening, with rapt attention.

"Aye, Madam. You *were* the captain's choice. And a beautiful choice…for his mistress."

The silence split the sky. Jill inhaled, but stared without wavering. Cecco's remark was both an insult and a compliment. Although Jill was more than able to stand under Cecco's assault, he had cunningly designed it to play on the faith of her men. Compelled to observe their reactions, she pulled her gaze from Cecco and scrutinized the surrounding faces. In the stillness, everything changed.

Considering what argument to employ, Jill found that no words of her own could prove Hook regarded her as more than his paramour. In front of those he distrusted, like Hanover and LeCorbeau, Hook intentionally played down her importance in order to protect her. Her duties as Hook's partner were subtle, obvious only to those who studied the couple— such as Mr. Cecco. And now, speaking as a veteran crewman, Cecco indicated he regarded Jill not as an extension of Hook's power, but merely a symbol of it. Falling for his deception, the men who had rallied behind her hesitated, rethinking the confidence they placed in her.

A clipped voice addressed her, expressing solicitude. "Are you quite well, Madam? You look faint." Placing one foot on the stairway, the attentive physician held himself poised to rush to her aid. Smee planted himself in the middle of the stairs, blocking the doctor's path.

Jill narrowed her eyes. Her reply was stony. "You know, Mister Hanover, that I do not faint."

"Perhaps, under the stress of this catastrophe, you have forgotten the evening I first attended you for your unfortunate condition. I am afraid that, once again, you are overwrought."

Tom barged his way to the fore to confront the surgeon, the cut on his temple throbbing with outrage. "Jill was only shamming that night!"

Hanover smiled, condescending. "Indeed? And this is your professional opinion?"

"No, but I know Jill! She's never been delicate like you're implying! She was pretending just to get you to—" Tom halted and shot an uncertain look at Jill.

Her position was already precarious. Knowing the folly of revealing the truth to the surgeon, she finished for Tom. "To get you to speak privately with me. You are well aware, Doctor, that I feigned that spell. And why."

"I am aware that you are effective in manifesting your will. I understand your young men's desire to support your bid for the captaincy. Life on the *Roger* has been pleasant for your sons— with their mother in a position to influence their advancement and intervene in their interests. In point of fact, my daughter indicated that Mr. Tootles managed to avoid a severe punishment."

Catching Tom's eye, Smee gave a single shake of his head to restrain him, and, just in time, Tom remembered Hook's order of silence regarding Liza's beating. Knowing Jill must feel more frustrated than he, her son looked to his mother and watched her eyes burn as she answered.

"Hook never engages in favoritism."

Her fiancé gestured toward Smee, throwing Jill's own words back at her. "Come now, my lady. We both know of one exception to every rule."

"It seems your rules of integrity have found an exception, Mister Hanover. If Mr. Tootles avoided punishment, it was because he deserved none."

"In your opinion, I am certain he didn't. My daughter, however… Well, let us just say that she didn't get *her* way with a fit of fainting."

Jill clung to her dignity. "I remind you, Sir, that you purport to be a gentleman. As such, it would be to your credit to place culpability on the appropriate shoulders. And to show more respect to those you claim to revere."

Mr. Cecco intervened, serene in his composure. "Lady, we are none of us gentlemen, but we respect any female enough to let one fainting episode pass. If there is some question as to methods of discipline, that is now in the past. A mystery vanished with our master. It is sufficient to know that one of two things are true. Either you suffer from a delicate constitution…or you deceived our captain to contrive an assignation with the physician, with whom, as we have just witnessed, you enjoy to make the sparks fly."

Restlessness buzzed through the crowd as the men considered Cecco's insinuation. Not one of her sailors believed Jill was weak. Just now, they had seen her defy Yulunga. She was skilled with sword and pistol, and demonstrated her courage time and again. Those close enough to Cecco's lash-marked back were reminded that the lady first won their admiration the day he himself requested her mercy— and was denied. She had always insisted on strict adherence to Captain Hook's authority. But did she feel differently where her sons were concerned? Tom Tootles hadn't hidden his interest in the girl. He had taken one beating for it. Had his youthful urges earned him another, which Jill prevented? There was no doubt of the lady's influence on the captain. Would any of her men, even Cecco, deny her what she wanted? They were all besotted. Wasn't it possible that Hook's irresistible mistress had used his affections to manipulate him, had even cheated him?

The sailors' eyes shifted between Jill and the surgeon. Her aspect was tense, and his indulgent. Each man recalled, with envy, the numerous attentions Jill had awarded Doctor Hanover. The two made a handsome pair promenading the deck each morning, afterward withdrawing to her quarters. And with or without the servant girl in attendance, any of these men would find a way to take advantage of a situation like that. Gentleman or not, no doubt the good doctor did the same.

Thinking back on it now, it was apparent Jill had encouraged the physician, and, supreme in his confidence, Hook never openly objected. Bound by their oaths to the captain, the sailors had accepted Hook's right to her. But one and all drew the line at allowing her to favor any other man. Yulunga was right when he declared she was no longer only one man's woman. Since Captain Hook's disappearance, she belonged to all of them, or none. Whatever her motives, her dalliances from now on would be restricted. In the minds of her crewmen, Red-Handed Jill's role aboard the *Roger* quickly narrowed, and solidified. Still magnificent, she stood before them, their pirate queen— the emblem of a captain's privilege.

While the damage wormed its way through the company, Jill remained, steadfast, behind the gilded railing that separated her from her sailors, the companionway now seeming more like a prisoner's dock than a platform of power. Her mind raced, like her heart. She couldn't deny she had courted the doctor. Nor could she divulge before Hanover the reason behind her attentions. And even if she attempted to explain, who would believe she was acting on Hook's orders? Even Mr. Smee, who adored her, had once or twice betrayed twinges of suspicion. She had played the game too well.

Hiding a shudder, Jill remembered how fervently Mr. Cecco believed in her pretense the day he threatened to kill the doctor. And she recalled his words the afternoon he first dared approach her.

When something lovely becomes available to me, I take it. He was taking her now! Watching the ruthless Italian, Jill had no doubt who had counseled Hanover to thwart her bid for leadership.… *There is nothing I would not do for you.*…And Hanover, naturally, had agreed, wanting her to abandon the ship. How cleverly Cecco caged her! Gypsy magic…With a stab of pain, Jill was reminded of Hook. He, too, had used his wits to win her, trapping her in her own truth, cutting away all hindrances until she surrendered her heart to him. Now, the dashing Mr. Cecco stood smiling at her, subtly, with his arms folded, the golden bands gripping his powerful biceps, appreciating her beauty. And biding his time.

But she wouldn't give in to him. She would fight. Jill read the men's mood, gauging the effect of Cecco's attack, and she considered her options. The men admired her still, but doubt lingered in their eyes. Pleading her case would only weaken it. Guided by her instincts, Jill followed the only course left open to her.

"Very well, then. I bend to the wishes of the company. I propose that the captain we choose to act until Hook's return should be his most experienced seaman, the man who has served him longest. There can be no doubt of his ability. He already commands our respect, and he has proven his worth time and again." She played her ace:

"Mr. Smee!"

Again, hearty cries arose. Jill smiled her approbation, displaying no hint of the disappointment dragging at her spirit. Nibs jumped down from the rail, and following Jill's lead in championing the bo'sun, he and Tom, among many others, whistled their satisfaction. At last, the matter was resolved in a manner that reconciled Hook's interests and the majority's wishes.

Taken aback, Mr. Smee glanced at the lady for confirmation before he smiled. Then, rising to join her on the companionway, he acknowledged the tribute with a simple nod. His broad chest expanded as he opened his mouth to speak, but he was interrupted before he began.

"All very well, but the real issue has not been addressed."

Jill whipped around to confront the surgeon, incredulous at his temerity. Once again, he ventured his disastrous opinion before she could stop him, and the one man who as yet had no say in the matter splintered the accord.

"Voting to install a captain at this point is well and good. But shouldn't you appoint Mr. Smee, not as a temporary substitute, but as your permanent commander— as indeed, he most likely will be when, in time, Captain Hook does not return? After all, this is a serious decision. Power is not easily transferred once it is established."

Jill watched as Smee's expression changed to shock. "Mr. Smee…"

But Smee's blood was up. He glared at Hanover. "Now, don't be pushing your poison on us, Doctor! I'd never stand to replace the captain! My loyalty is sworn to James Hook, and if I can serve him by guiding his ship 'til he comes back, I'll do it. Unlike some here, I've no taste for taking advantage of a man's misfortune."

"Are you sure you are motivated by loyalty, Mr. Smee? I have often witnessed the liberties you take with his mistress. Perhaps you merely want official license to be the first to enjoy the captain's prerogatives?"

"Look who's taking liberties! If I'd had the captain's prerogative, I'd have given you what you deserve long ago, Hanover! You should be thanking your lucky stars for my loyalty. The captain's order is the only thing that's saved you from a thrashing!"

"And is this what we must look forward to under your command? Threats and thrashings when we disagree with you?"

"Thrashings, is it? You'd be knowing a thing or two about that, now, wouldn't you? Such a fine gentleman!"

"I've seen the damage you have done, if that is what you imply."

"*My* damage! I've been that worried for the females aboard ever since—"

"A handy excuse, no doubt, to hover over Red-Handed Jill."

"I followed my orders."

"And your inclination. And see how far it's advanced you— *Captain* Smee— little feminine favors to begin, and now, the full command!"

"You've stolen your own share of favors—"

"I'm sure we can all understand your craving for the captain's lady. Which of us would not jump at the— opportunity— she just offered you? But as far as governing men goes—"

"You lying bastard!"

Jill seized Smee's arm, but it was too late. His Irish temper was stirred to the boiling point.

"I'll never steal Hook's woman the way you've been angling to do, Hanover. And I'll never take his captaincy! Never!"

Closing her eyes, Jill listened, helpless, as the foundation of her plans crumbled to dust, blasted by Smee's fidelity. Every man aboard now knew what she had always known. Smee would serve and protect his captain to the death. But no matter how capable, Smee was unwilling to equal him. Still, she tried. He was her last hope.

"Smee—"

"No, Ma'am. Don't ask me."

Turning her back on the company, Jill begged him with her eyes. "It's what the captain commands!"

Becoming aware of her hand on his arm, Smee stared down at it. He looked up at her again, surprised, and then scanned the greedy faces of the crew. As if her hold seared his skin, he shook her off and backed away. "No! I won't take the ship from him. Not even if the rights to *you* come with it."

"I am counting on you, Mr. Smee. So is Hook. That is why you must accept this responsibility, no matter what comes with it! For the captain's sake."

He almost whispered. "How can you be saying such a thing? Tempting me from my place, in the captain's name!" He faced the men. "James Hook will be back, don't you be doubting it. And when he comes, you can be sure he'll be making an account of who worked *for* him in his absence, and who against. We've sworn our oaths to do our duty, lads, and it isn't fitting for any of us to shirk it." He aimed a hostile look at Jill. "Especially you, Ma'am. I'll die before I betray the captain, and I'm ashamed for you, for even thinking it."

Regal again, Jill pronounced, "Clearly, you have misunderstood me, Mr. Smee. In any case, you have said quite enough."

Yulunga's voice rumbled like thunder, alerting the company to a grim reality. "We are already fighting among ourselves! It is time for one of us to take a firm hand."

With her heart sinking, Jill's gaze slid slowly from Smee to

Yulunga. She knew what he would say next. She was powerless to prevent it. She had played her highest card, and lost.

"If Hook does return, it will be up to him to defend his position. We need a captain now. I propose…" Yulunga turned. Hoisting his powerful arm, he gestured to the man at his right. "Our Mr. Cecco."

The first thing Jill saw was the complacence on Cecco's face. Second, the gratification on the surgeon's. They, too, had been busy during her hour of agony.

Jill knew Cecco aimed to be captain. He had admitted as much that morning at the port of Gao. Backing up his friend, Yulunga had chipped away at Jill's autonomy. And Hanover— Jill watched, sickening, as the face under the dueling scar sneered at Smee— Hanover wanted to destroy the trappings of Hook's power. He had started with Jill, and progressed to Hook's right-hand man. In front of the entire company, Hanover had destroyed Smee's credibility as relentlessly as he destroyed Jill's, to avenge himself on Hook, and to get Jill well away. In disgrace, if need be. As the crewmen raved for Captain Cecco, Jill didn't have to count the votes. She heard the verdict. Three strong men had won what they wanted.

She thought the struggle was over then. But the complications were only beginning. Cecco hadn't yet secured everything he desired. He came forward from the crowd and mounted the stairs, exuding a sense of entitlement that swelled with every step. Nearing the top, he halted, diplomatic as he waited for Smee to make way. Begrudging the position, the bo'sun shifted, and the two men passed each other as one rose to the summit, and the other descended in proud defeat. Nibs and Tom thumped Smee's back and drew him to starboard. He wouldn't look at the lady. For him, the fight was done.

Cecco addressed Jill first. "Madam. I am proud to share this place of honor with you." In his pleasant accent, he spoke loudly enough for the entire company to hear. "Please be at ease. I assume this post at the insistence of our men. I do not consider it an affront to our former captain, but rather, a practical solution for our dilemma. And, a great show of confidence in myself."

The clamor of exultation burst forth again. A feeling of relief was palpable, sweeping through the company. Balance was restored, without the in-fighting and bloodshed that might have torn the crew asunder. They didn't object to bloodletting when necessary, but for the most part, these pirates had served years together. As Hook understood, a division of loyalty would destroy their fellowship, not to mention their productivity. No one could afford discord. Even those who still favored Smee welcomed Mr. Cecco's ascendancy. The lady herself had chosen him first officer, and with good reason. He was fearless of a fight but good-tempered with his mates. He was physically impressive, his intelligence proven. He knew the ship, he knew the sea. He would be a strong captain. He was the strongest man aboard.

Only one matter remained to be settled, and now the men watched with increasing interest. The opportunity was over for them, but their new captain faced one last trial in order to gain their complete allegiance. Nibs and Tom looked about themselves, wary of the new, sudden tension. They exchanged glances, concern etching the two faces that months ago held only innocence. Smee jerked around to study the crew, and then he shot a horrified look at Jill. Only now did he realize the full result of refusing the captaincy. But it wasn't he who would bear that burden.

Staring at Jill's face, Smee watched as understanding dawned there, too. His gut reacted before he could think. "No! Lady, you don't have to be doing this. You've said it yourself— the captain will be back!"

Unwilling to see the new accord broken, the men stirred uneasily. Jill noted their discontent. So too, she saw, did Cecco. But although his brown eyes glittered, the new captain demonstrated both his reserve and his self-assurance, granting the lady the courtesy of answering for herself.

Turning empty eyes upon Smee, she tried to smile. "It is because of all I have said, that I *will* do this."

Smee read the look on Cecco's face. He saw the notorious knife in the man's belt, like his jewelry, reflecting the last hopes of the sun's rays. But worse, Smee saw the light dying in the lady's eyes, and he gaped, unbelieving, as the lovely features of James Hook's mistress grew resigned. Gradually, as the crew of the *Jolly Roger* watched, she accepted the consequences of everyone else's decision. Red-Handed Jill was no coward. Bitterly, Mr. Smee remembered. She never disappointed her captain.

With a griping of nausea in his belly, Smee turned away. Torn between him and Jill, Nibs and Tom watched his face fall. Then the bo'sun pushed his way through the crowd and stalked to the hatch.

Jill saw him go, and the strength bled from her spirit. She closed her eyes to stop the flow. Struggling for command of only herself now, she felt the ache in the hollow of her soul. Golden chiming struck the air, and when she finally opened her eyes, Captain Cecco was offering his hand. With one important exception, all of Jill's men waited, eager to see what the captain and the pirate queen would do— together.

"Madam. I must now demand of you to declare in front of our company. Do I have your support?"

Feeling as if, like glass, she might shatter at any moment, she slowly inclined her head. "Of course…Captain Cecco." She raised her chin. "But only on condition that the welfare of our ship stands to you as it stands for me. First, last, and always."

"This time I don't pretend to tell you lies." He smiled as he pressed his open hand to his chest in a gesture reminiscent of his confession. "I pledge it. The *Jolly Roger*.…First, last, and always!"

The air filled with hats and kerchiefs as the men of the *Roger* hollered, whistled and stamped. Assured now of the ship's good fortune, they celebrated their chosen chief. As if painted by a master, the scene unfolded and fixed itself in their minds, framed by the gilt of the companionway. In her scarlet scarf and with her weapons at her waist, their magnificent queen prepared to confirm her consort. In slow, graceful motions, she reached out and opened her blood-stained hand. Then, with ceremony, she bestowed it on their captain. His sun-browned grip accepted her, and as Jill disciplined her features, the old regime and the new joined together.

Cecco kept her ice-cold hand in his own. "Mr. Mullins!"

"Aye, aye!"

"Sheer us off to the south. We will catch a wind and lose *L'Ormonde* for a while."

"Yes, Sir." Thrusting himself through the rowdy press of shipmates, Mullins made his way to the binnacle by the wheel.

"Mr. Yulunga!"

"Sir!"

"Have some supper sent in to me, then broach that cask in the galley. As my first mate, you will oversee the celebration while the lady and I…" his voice mellowed, "come to terms."

Yulunga's response was drowned in the uproar. He clapped the surgeon on his gray velvet back, knocking the breath from the man. As the crowd surged away to the galley, Yulunga gloated, "Well, Doctor. We have done it. As planned, our friend Cecco is now our captain. A promotion for all of us!"

Hanover nodded, recovering and reaching for his watch. "Indeed, Mr. Yulunga. At last the era of that arrogant criminal is ended. It is a lucky day for this ship, and just the beginning of my own happiness." Hanover watched Jill with pleasure. Sooner even than he contrived with LeCorbeau, he had executed the installation of a friendly captain on the *Roger*, and Jill would be speedily forced to give up her role as pirate queen and sail off with her fiancé aboard *L'Ormonde*. Hanover would leave all his troubles behind him, abandoned with the shackles in his bunk! He couldn't contain his burst of a laugh.

As Jill and Cecco entered the master's quarters, Yulunga chortled in his rich tone. "Those two are too much alike to guess. But we will know in the morning which of them comes out on top."

Hanover pulled up short. The door with the brass plate clicked shut. "What do you mean, in the morning?"

The bolt shot home.

Yulunga's broad, dark smile creased his face as he turned to the surgeon. "You mean you didn't know? I thought you fancied yourself a pirate, Doctor."

"Know? Know what?" Hanover clutched his watch. A sudden cold froze his confidence as he observed the African.

"What you just did to the lady."

"I? We have all three worked together, to free her."

"Just the opposite, Doctor. She is bound more firmly than ever. Now she serves not one, but two masters. The old captain, and the new." Yulunga leered. "Captain Cecco understands her. She will never leave. She is too loyal."

"Yes…Yes, he understands, and he will relieve her of responsibility and grant her release. Isn't that what he is doing right now?"

Enjoying the surgeon's confusion, Yulunga shook his head. "Oh, no. He is assigning her new duties."

"But he got what he wanted— to become the captain!"

"Mr. Cecco is a gypsy. He has not always desired the captaincy. His ambition is a recent acquisition, fired only after *she* came aboard."

The last puff of smugness vanished. "But he never gave any indication that— He never— She is promised to *me!*"

"I have been Captain Cecco's friend far longer than you, Doctor Hanover. You will just have to wait your turn." Yulunga's two remaining strings of beads bounced as he laughed. He slapped Hanover's back again and strolled away to keep order in the galley.

The surgeon stared, wild-eyed, at the big man's back, and then he gazed once more at the brass-plated door before he dropped his watch and rushed to the rail. His skin turned clammy. He shook with chills, and bracing one hand on the iron muzzle of a cannon, the proper doctor vomited his bile into the sea. When the seizure was over, he searched his pockets for a handkerchief and wiped his mouth. Standing straight again, the doctor noticed an exotic scent on the linen at his lips. He pulled it away and held it up to see. Stained with his sickness, it was the token he had stolen from Jill.

She had warned him. Hook was a master of manipulation. As she predicted in their first private encounter, by the time Hanover knew he was mastered, it was far too late. Through Jill, he had willingly given Hook all his secrets! And her elaborate play for power this afternoon. It hadn't been a ploy to gain freedom for Doctor and Mrs. Heinrich, after all. She was doing her duty to her captain— her first captain, trying to retain his one-handed grasp on authority.

Hanover, a man of science with a bitter taste under his tongue, considered the evidence. She claimed truth was a weapon. She had plied it expertly, deceiving him over and over again, even as she told him no lies. She promised they'd spend the rest of their lives together. Now he knew what she meant. Just like her lover, the woman was a murderous, thieving pirate, and content to be so. Perverted as it was, her only genuine virtue was her loyalty. What vile act wouldn't she perform for that man? Even amid the devastation wrought by the captain's absence, she was following his orders, doing anything and everything to hold the *Roger*— for Hook!

First, last, and always, Hook was three steps ahead of him.

Hanover crushed her handkerchief and flung it into the sea, and then his stomach heaved again. Because just as he'd determined the moment she first appeared to him, bewitching him, luring him toward destruction, like a sea siren— she was exactly the woman he wanted.

Coming to Terms

"Don't blame yourself, Mr. Smee. Duty or no, there was nothing more you could do."

"I could've kept my ruddy mouth shut." Restlessly, Smee leaned forward to drop his elbows on his knees, a mug of rum in his hands. His bunk creaked beneath his bulk. "I was right refusing to take the captain's place. But I didn't have to say so in front of the company."

"No," Tom insisted. "It's the doctor who should have kept his mouth shut. I fell right into his trap! He was only waiting for the chance I gave him. Then he made it look like Jill got Hook to grant me special favor."

Perched on the table, dark and silent, Nibs nursed a cup of ale and watched his brother and the bo'sun. Seizing the bottle, Smee poured himself another splash of rum. "Ah, no one will believe it come morning, lad. That Hanover's only shown himself to be the blackguard he is, insinuating such things of you and your mother. As if the cap'n would fall for any such trick! No, the men'll know better by tomorrow." He eased back against the wall, where he expelled an angry breath and muttered to himself, "But the damage is done."

"Damage." Tom shot a glance at Nibs. "To Jill?"

"Never mind, lad. What the lady does is no business of mine."

"You don't mean that, Mr. Smee. Jill relies on you."

A silence grew between the three men. It swelled like a thunderhead, to become oppressive. From the galley at the opposite end of the gun deck, the sounds of celebration rolled toward them. Every so often, the hubbub increased as a group of revelers emerged and clambered up the steps. Tom caught Nibs' eye at last, but Nibs looked away.

Tom cut the silence. "What's the matter with you two?"

Smee sealed his mouth with his mug, and drank deeply. Nibs pulled out his knife and ran its tip under his nails. As the lantern under the beams swayed with the waves, its light fell upon three brooding faces, and the planks of the *Roger* bemoaned the discord.

Tom stood his ground. "All right. I'll say it then. Jill's with Cecco."

Nibs spoke at last. "*Captain* Cecco."

"Aye. And what of it?"

"Well, Tom. Captain Hook's barely gone, and she's chosen another man."

"I'd hardly say *she* made the choice."

Bitterly, Nibs replied, "I did what I could to keep her in charge. We all three did."

Mr. Smee looked up then, and this time it was the young men whose eyes avoided a meeting.

"I know what you're thinking. That it was me that let her down. But you're not understanding. I couldn't break my oath."

"Jill did. After reminding us of ours so many times."

"Now, Nibs," Tom said, "What alternative did she have? We elected Cecco."

"We elected him to be our captain. Not Jill's mate."

Smee's red face flushed deeper. After a moment of hesitation, he blurted out, "*She* elected him mate. Right from the start, when she appointed officers."

"Mr. Smee!" Tom gazed at the man in astonishment, then turned on his brother. "Nibs? Is that what you think, too?"

Nibs drained his drink and stared at the bobbing lantern.

The galley door banged closed again. Footsteps prowled the gunnery, soft leather shoes. Tom made his voice as fervent as privacy allowed while Hanover entered his starboard quarters. "Start to finish, Jill did what she had to. When she couldn't take the helm, and Mr. Smee wouldn't take it, either, what else could she do?"

"Well, she didn't have to betray Hook, did she, Tom? I was all for her, until I realized how far she meant to take it."

"Nibs, Hook left the ship in Jill's care. She couldn't let his company divide itself."

"Any division was over when Cecco took command."

"No, it wasn't. Jill knows it wasn't. Think about this, Nibs: if Jill hadn't shown complete accord with Cecco, there'd be risk of a faction rising to bring him down, even now— in favor of Jill's captaincy, or somebody else's. No, it was crucial for the men to name a leader, with no possible challenger remaining. Jill figured that out quick. She's seen to it that Cecco's authority is seamless."

Nibs retorted, "She could have let Cecco lead the company, and left him alone."

But Tom was adamant. "How would it help Hook for Jill to give over the ship? Don't you see? She has to hold on to leadership any way she can. Not from below decks, but in the captain's quarters, as the captain's queen."

"As queen, she might have kept the quarters and sent *him* below!"

Tom said, "If she'd defied Cecco, he could have thrown her in the brig."

Smee spat out, "She *knows* he'd never do that." At the sting of his scorn, both brothers stared. Never before had they heard Smee disparage the lady. "She knows she's too ripe a plum to put by in storage."

Tom's reply was heated. "All right then. But if she'd refused him, it'd be the worse for all of us. Everyone would be wanting her. Just look at the trouble Yulunga stirred up! You left her high and dry, and Nibs and I are no match for the whole crew. Without Cecco's protection, Jill might as well jump ship. But she's loyal. She won't do that. Not while Hook's alive to come back to it."

"Back to his treasure. I'm guessing she's finally got her hands on all of it."

Nibs' jaw jutted. Tom gaped, incredulous, at the familiar face behind the spectacles. "Mr. Smee— you're drunk! Otherwise you'd never say such a thing about the lady! We all know she's devastated by Hook's disappearance. It's plain on her face."

"You think that slippery gypsy sees it too, then? Or cares?" Smee heaved himself up to sit straighter. "Ah! I'm sorry, lads. I'm forgetting my place. It's just I'm that afraid. What he'll do to her—and where could the captain be? For all the lady claims he's alive, I don't see why he'd leave in the first place if it was possible for him to return."

"But Jill is certain—"

The conversation broke off as the doctor's door clicked shut. They waited for Hanover to move away, but a moment later a rap sounded on Smee's door. Smee stared straight ahead and ignored it, finishing his drink. Nibs sprang from the table, his knife in his fist.

Realizing neither of his mates was fit to deal with the surgeon, Tom pushed himself up and tramped to the door. After assuring himself the others hadn't moved, he opened it and stepped out, propelling the doctor backward to the gun deck with no lingering pretense of respect. He shut the door behind him.

"Should we kill the man now, Mr. Smee?" Nibs' swarthy face was hard. A permanent crease marked the space between his eyebrows. Gripping his knife, he edged his lanky form toward the door.

Smee sat grim and motionless. "No, Mr. Nibs. Cap'n's orders."

"The old captain? Or Cecco?"

"The only captain."

"You mean Hook, then."

"Aye. When I call that gypsy 'Captain,' I'll have stopped believing in loyalty!"

Nibs' posture sagged. "Tom spoke reason, Mr. Smee. I know Jill's trying to be true to Hook, in her own way. I just want to understand what she's thinking."

Smee slumped forward, and he rested his forehead on his hand.

"What are *you* thinking, Mr. Smee?"

"I'm thinking of James Hook, of course. I don't know what's happened. But he's out there somewhere. All alone— again."

Tom opened the door, easing his shoulders in. "Mr. Smee. I think you'll want to hear what Doctor Hanover has to say."

Smee grunted his disgust and turned away.

"He's got an idea." Tom stepped back into the room. "Not a good one."

"Tell the man to go to hell."

Hanover's curt voice cut in. "It concerns Red-Handed Jill." With his shoulders square and his back taut, he entered the room, realizing and not caring that his presence was an insult to all its occupants. "Mr. Smee. I have been discussing the situation with Mr. Yulunga. I believe if we form a party, Captain Cecco will allow us to speak to the lady once more. Perhaps we can persuade her that she does have other options." As no one responded, Hanover stepped forward and looked between them, his gray eyes urging. "Before it's too late!"

Smee refused to look at him. "You mean the option of running off with you, Hanover?"

"A far preferable choice than giving herself to that— brute!" Regaining control of himself, the surgeon assumed a more reasonable tenor. "Mr. Nibs, you once told me you would never serve any captain but Hook. Perhaps you will now accept my offer and come with us. To Heidelberg."

Nibs the Knife surprised even himself with his restraint. "You're a fool if you think I'd model myself after you, Doctor, after what you did to Jill today. If it was up to me, you'd be lying dead with your throat slit." The shining blade in his hand pierced the gloom, but remained still.

"Of course I excuse your hostility, Mr. Nibs. Most unfortunately, in my zeal to free the lady I misunderstood Mr. Cecco's intentions. I now realize just how treacherous our new captain is. Naturally, I regret that I misplaced my confidence."

Eyeing the surgeon at last, Smee snorted. "A shame you didn't catch on before you shoved her into his arms, Hanover. I don't know what you thought you were doing, but you made a right mess of it!"

Hanover brushed off Smee's contempt. "If you care for the lady, I should think you would cease imbibing your vile spirits and come to her aid now, by striving to change her mind."

Seeing the bo'sun sit resolute, Tom puffed up his chest and said, "Nibs, Mr. Smee. You said yourselves that the situation isn't right. Here's your chance to try to fix it. But me? I want no part of it." He swung toward Hanover. "I trust Jill. She knows what she's doing." Tom strode from the cabin, leaving the three alone.

Ignoring his departure, the surgeon needled the others, stating, "And *I* trust she can be made to see reason, even if her sons and her stubborn 'protector' cannot." He glared at Smee.

Nibs sighed and, with reluctance, thrust his knife in his belt. "I'll come along with you, Hanover. To hear what Mr. Yulunga thinks. Whether we like it or not, he's the first mate, now. We'll have to get used to dealing with him." He headed for the door and stopped. "The doctor's right about one thing, Mr. Smee. You promised the captain you'd take care of her. Not long ago, you told me he stopped you playing the hero before a nasty fight." The crease between Nibs' brows deepened. "Maybe Hook saved you, then, so you can save Jill now."

Recognizing that the situation called for discretion, Hanover kept silent. As he had done earlier in the day, he used the bo'sun's conscience to do his work for him.

Nibs modeled himself after the doctor just this once, and did the same. While Smee poured himself another shot and downed it, Nibs judged that he'd found the only way around the Irishman's wounds.

"You have to be her hero, Mr. Smee. It's your duty."

In the familiar luxury of the master's quarters, everything was the same, and everything was changed. Candlelight filled the room, but the night pressed in. His dark eyes, as always, clung to her. Yet where before they had been hopeful, they now touched her with an air of possession. But, as in the past, Captain Cecco held himself in check. He pulled Jill's chair from the dining table, assisting her to rise, and then he ushered her toward the plush pillows of the window seat. Unlike their mistress, the cushions felt as comfortable as ever.

"And now, Lady, we must attend to our business." Cecco watched impassively as she settled, but he himself remained standing. "I am certain you know the questions on my mind. You will please answer them."

Before supper, Jill had removed her boots and her weapons, more in token of her fearlessness than her capitulation. The gesture had had its effect on Cecco; he had voiced his admiration— and he hadn't laid a finger on her. Rather, throughout the meal, of which she had partaken only to show that she could, he engaged in light conversation designed to set her at her ease. But supper was over now.

Jill's tone was flat. "Your first question is in regard to the surgeon."

Cecco watched her.

"As you have discovered, Doctor Hanover is a useful man. Not only is he a brilliant physician and a skilled swordsman. He also possesses great wealth which the captain—" She looked down and collected herself. "Which Hook determined to take. My task was to persuade Doctor Hanover to join us. Failing that, I was to find the source of his riches, and steal it."

"You seduced him?"

"Only in his imagination."

The suspicion in Cecco's eyes evaporated. "And so, the physician means nothing to you."

"On the contrary. He means a great deal to me."

With a grunt of amusement, Cecco laid his hand on his dagger. "So he has not enjoyed the full pleasure of you, yet I am to have the pleasure of carving him, after all."

"You swore it. He touched me, many times. I hold you to your word."

"You want his blood, then?"

"I want my name cut into his back." For the first time, her devoted sailor felt the full force of her sapphire eyes. "But I don't want you to kill him."

He tilted his head. "I am warned, Lady. Your passions run deep."

"As deep as your knife."

"Well. I will make no promises. No doubt the man himself will make the decision for us. Go on."

Shadows from the candlelight flickered across her face. "I don't know where Hook is. I only know he lives."

"Lovely storyteller, I have heard this tale before." Her eyes still affected him. "And I see you believe it to be true. And my next question?" He turned to walk a few paces, running his fingers over the sleek wood of the harpsichord, then lifting his gaze to assess the opulence of the captain's quarters. The long laces binding his hair swung across his back, and the marred flesh beneath the leather assaulted Jill's eyes— just as the gash of Hook's wrist had done at first— setting off a coiling in the pit of her stomach. It was she who was responsible for the damage to both of these men. Hook had taken his revenge. Now that Cecco had his chance, what price might he exact?

When she didn't answer his question, Cecco turned back to her, his eyes narrowed. Diverting her gaze, she rubbed her right wrist.

His face cleared. "Ah, I see. You are still fascinated with the scars you have caused. And is there another who deserves such stripes?"

"No! He made his feelings clear to everyone. It cost him the captaincy. Mr. Smee would never betray Hook." She had to wrench the bo'sun's name from her lips. It hurt to speak of him.

"He has never touched you?"

Holding silence, Jill stared into his smoky eyes.

"You have defied me before this, when I was not in a position to object. As on those occasions, I find your courage most provocative." Wryly, he smiled, "If sometimes painful. But I will let it go. After tonight, the Irishman will be no longer an issue. What of the letters you posted in Gao?"

He had succeeded in surprising her. "The letters? Only messages to my family, to assure them of my welfare."

"Nothing else? No hints of your whereabouts to be passed along to the authorities? I understand Hook's capture carries a heavy bounty in England. To say nothing of my own."

Jill rushed to her feet, her eyes blazing. "Never! I have been loyal to Hook, and to *all* my shipmates."

"So I have finally turned your ice to fire! Be reassured, Lady. I have always known the fuel that warms your heart. And as I once told you, I aspire to make your voyage— on whatever ocean— enjoyable."

Her chest heaved. "Other oceans—" The words tasted like chalk on her tongue.

"As I foretold. But I will prove to you that the situation in which you find yourself today is not so very different as you may imagine."

Turning away, she cast her gaze all round the room. Everything was in its place. The comfortable furnishings, the tasteful trappings remained. But even surrounded by her own belongings in her own quarters, Jill was keenly aware that the most important thing had, indeed, changed. His successor stood before her now, waiting patiently. The wave of anxiety washed over her, and then, composing herself, she renewed her determination to prevail. As her eyes settled on him again, Cecco bowed and reached out in the gesture that was becoming familiar. In time, Jill thought, her response might come more easily. Slowly, she placed her hand in his, expecting him to kiss it as he had done in the past. Surely that much hadn't changed.

But he held her fingers lightly, caressing them with his thumb, and the memory of his magic sent a shiver up her arm. Cecco was remembering, too. "The first time I touched your fingers, you had come to parley with Captain Hook." While his bracelets made music, he raised her hand and brushed her fingers with his lips. "Now we will discuss the terms of our own accord."

"Accord? But we are not enemies."

"Far from it. Still, agreement must be reached."

"Yes…" Outside the cabin, darkness had won over the twilight. Inside, the candles fought on.

"As you yourself have said, there is no reason to delay your duty." He retained possession of her fingers, tightening his hold. "Here are my demands. First, you will reserve yourself for me alone. We have seen today what ill feeling may arise if you favor certain of the men, and not all."

"Yes, of course, there is no question." As usual, Cecco indicated no reserve whatever, but now that the subject of their approaching intimacy was under discussion, Jill felt another surge of alarm. Until this moment, she had succeeded in conducting herself with composure, believing this liaison to be a rational act. An act with which she might regain a measure of control over the ship— but already, she was having difficulty keeping her pulse steady.

"Second," Cecco went on, "if you wish him to live, you will have no association with the surgeon."

The look in Cecco's eye was much colder than his hand. Quickly, she answered. "Agreed."

"Third, as you are a working member of ship's company, you will continue to receive your designated percentage of plunder. I will, however, grant you a share of my own in addition, as recompense for your support and favor."

With her cheeks burning, Jill retorted, "That is hardly necessary. I have made my choice. I seek no payment."

His smile, as he kissed her fingers again, was gratified. "I am pleased that our arrangement is mutually agreeable. But I insist that you profit by it." Jill pulled her hand away, speechless, now fully understanding why Mr. Smee's Lily had at first scorned that gift of golden bracelets. But Jill couldn't think of Smee anymore. It was too painful.

As if he read her thoughts, Cecco said, "Next, you will restrict your relations with Mr. Smee. He has already shown himself to be opposed to our union, and the history between you will naturally cause my crewmen to watch the two of you closely."

"*Your* crewmen?"

Cecco merely waited.

As the seconds passed, she looked down at Hook's costly carpets, and then up again at the new captain's face. "Your crewmen. Yes."

"Yes. And last, if I am to rule them, I must rule you first. You will show me every respect and attention you exhibited toward Hook. I have observed that you are shrewd, adept in the ways of leadership. You will understand this requirement."

"Yes, I understand." Instinct told her she must be firm now. "But my demands are these. I will be allowed full freedom of the ship and among its company." Cecco started to speak, but she went on. "I shall, of course, be discreet. Aloof, if you will."

He inclined his head.

"Second. You will show no favoritism toward my sons."

"Agreed."

"Nor will you demonstrate any prejudice against them."

"An unnecessary point, but also agreed."

Jill paused to gather the proper words. "You have pledged to me that the welfare of the ship will be your first priority. I must be allowed to make suggestions to that end, without threat of punishment."

"Granted. You should dread only a breach of our terms. And this, I will punish severely."

Jill pulled back a little, fighting the fear shooting through her heart.

She managed, for the moment, to tame it. "I respect your candor, and honor it with my own." She drew herself up. "Lastly, and most important. I have already told you I believe James Hook to be alive. I insist upon this article: when he returns, the alliance between you and me will be ended. I will harbor no ill will toward you, but you will no longer have any claim on me. Our prior bonds will preclude all we agree today."

"*Bellezza*…my poor little one! I admire your loyalty. I applaud it. You inspire me to win that loyalty for my own. But you must know how little chance exists that our brave captain will rise from the sea and take up his place between us."

With a cool stare, Jill said, "Are we agreed then? Have we an accord?"

He gave a curt nod. "We have an accord."

She felt relieved, but not for long. As before, her ice inflamed him.

"The bargain must be sealed." He stepped closer. Cecco wasn't as tall as her captain, but he stood so near she had to bend her neck to look into his eyes. Those clinging eyes.

"In regard to our personal relations, Madam, you have nothing to fear from me. In my country, it is a tradition that men strive to please their women. A point of pride, to bring pleasure where we take it."

"I mean no insult to you, Mr. Cecco, but from our arrangement I expect only a moderate degree of contentment. My heart is otherwise engaged."

"You think perhaps to compensate for your compliance? To deny yourself in honor of your late lover?"

Jill blinked. "I didn't realize you were so versed in the ways of women." He had guessed exactly what she planned— to give herself only so far, making up for her physical infidelity by withholding her passion, as if she could somehow shield herself and reserve her innermost recesses for Hook.

"A noble intention, to sacrifice your pleasure. But I tell you as a man. Such dishonesty can only dishonor him."

Considering his meaning, Jill realized she had deceived only herself. Cecco's words were true, and she swiftly understood. Cheating this man would not gain her absolution. She could acquit herself with honor only by accepting Cecco honestly, completely. In dissembling, she might in actuality earn the stipend he had granted. Better to be his partner— in every endeavor— than his prostitute.

And she was struck again by the thought she had had earlier on the companionway— How cleverly and how quickly he divested her of her armor!

Jill looked down. "Aye. You speak the truth."

Gently, his fingers applied pressure under her chin. "You will please humor me, with the proper form of address."

As she looked up at him, the ghost of a shadow passed over her face, but she acquiesced.

"Aye…Sir."

"So we are clear."

"We are." The hollow within her ached again as, under his vigilance, she awarded Cecco the title she longed to hold for Hook. "Captain."

"And now all that restrains me is my courtesy, which you will find I hold in abundance— if we continue to agree as we have done so delightfully this evening."

Jill controlled her expression, but at this velvet-gloved threat, doubt spilled inside her. "I will do my best to maintain harmony between us." Had she been wrong about Cecco after all? Had he merely been biding his time until he could take revenge for his whipping? She searched his eyes to determine how he might back up his warning, but found only warmth and confidence there. Captain Cecco was, apparently, very sure of himself.

"You look for reassurance. And you wonder, perhaps, how I know so much of your feeling?"

Again, he had intuited her thoughts. Although hesitant to confirm his supposition, she nodded.

"I am naturally understanding of women. And you I have watched closely every day. Sometimes to my cost." He threw off a shrug, indicative of his shredded back. "You took such pleasure in displaying your devotion to your former master. I remember every little touch and courtesy you lavished upon him. And your insistence that I be punished for his sake— a grand gesture!"

Jill drew back. Was Cecco expressing resentment, or adoration?

"It is my dream that I will move you to the same level of devotion."

"And if not? Sir?"

"Let us not dwell on the improbable. It is enough that I have learned much of your inclinations, and can easily guess at your… disinclinations." His even teeth showed in an indulgent smile. "You are far too intelligent to serve me other than satisfactorily."

Jill ignored the rising panic. "I am anxious to learn more of your inclinations, that we may stand on an equal footing. I hope you will be patient with me."

Cecco's posture relaxed now. His compact, muscular frame seemed to Jill to melt a bit. "Madam. I doubt that patience will be necessary. I am not a difficult master to please! And I will be honored to please *you*. Perhaps in ways you have not experienced before."

"Sir…" The panic would not be ignored, after all. It wrapped around her heart.

He stepped closer. "You never shared yourself with a man before our captain made you a woman. You have not yet partaken of the pleasure of two hands serving you." Cecco placed his hands on her shoulders. "I will improve your appreciation."

With tender force, he turned her around and began working the knot of her scarf. Under his ten supple fingers, it came loose. He pulled the scarf down to free her hair at last, and with it, a burden lifted from her shoulders. Jill was satisfied she had done her duty to Hook. From this point on, Hook's order to guard the ship required only that she retain Captain Cecco's trust and good will. Judging by his sigh of pleasure as he gathered her hair in both his hands, she thought doing so likely to prove easy— if only the emptiness didn't pain her so much.

Combing her hair with his fingers, Cecco took his time, appreciating it. He ran his hands through her hair, over and over, and breathed deeply. "So silky. And scented like the sunshine." The play of his fingers set her scalp to tingling. Obviously, Cecco's boast was accurate; he was a man who understood women, or, at any rate, how to please them. At least one. Jill had sensed his gaze following her many times, but she hadn't realized just how close, how flattering, his scrutiny had been. Tired of the heavy hurt within, she did as she had done when Mr. Smee attended her. Entranced, she closed her eyes and succumbed to her senses.

His fingers cleared a path on the back of her neck. Soon she felt his lips traveling along it, and his tongue just touching her. Now it was Jill who seemed to melt a bit. The sensation was inviting, a release from her tension. Sensing her pleasure, her new lover prolonged it. And she was sorry when he stopped at last, and sorry when he relinquished her hair, sweeping it over her shoulder. She stood still, waiting shakily, and listening to his adoring accents.

"Beautiful lady. No need for your little girl to come to you tonight. I will see to your needs, lovely one." Adroitly, he loosed the lacings Liza had tended that morning. In no time, the scarlet taffeta relaxed its hold. "And whatever service I cannot render, your Miss will have to perform. I will share such tasks with no other man." Cecco flattened his hands, such warm hands, on her back, then he slid them under her bodice and slowly pushed the gown over her arms. Jill twisted her shoulders to shrug it off. It was a natural impulse, but she would have followed it in any case. She was resigned. It would all happen, either way. The only issue left unresolved for Jill was exactly how much pleasure she and her new captain would take in their partnership.

Cecco smiled as he unhooked her petticoats. The symbolism of the act was not lost upon him. Jill thought of it, too, and felt increasingly vulnerable as, with every move, Cecco detached her further from Hook. Instinctively she glanced at the wall beyond the bunk. It was bare. No strings of jewels bobbed their enticement, no golden chains lay waiting to ensnare her. Most disappointing of all, the plain metal hook, which had held her captain's claw each evening, hung empty.

And then her gaze caught an object on the bed shelf that Liza had neglected to clear away. Jill's heart leapt. The empty water cup stood, placed there by Hook's hand last night, and it triggered her memory. The surgeon's sleeping draught! Should she use it? The unopened vial lay in the drawer beneath the bed. Would it really work as the doctor prescribed? Just one night might allow Hook the time he needed to return to her, wherever he was, and this exercise of fidelity through faithlessness could be avoided. Did she dare buy that time by turning the potion against Captain Cecco?

But Jill trusted the doctor less now than on the night he so seductively pressed the drug into her lap. The slippery amber liquid might prove to be poison, after all. And to harm Cecco now, when she depended on him for everything— her safety, the ship's disposition— would be a foolish mistake, indeed. A reckless violation of the terms of accord that would only serve to destabilize the company. And exactly what the surgeon needed to work his ends.

No, from such a betrayal Jill could only earn Captain Cecco's punishment. Or worse. She must follow what she could salvage of her original design. Calming her heartbeats, she submitted again to his amorous voice as he unhooked the last fastening.

"You see, although I am your captain now, I have not too much dignity to wait on you. And you will do the same for me?" It wasn't really a question. The mellow candlelight glowed upon her flesh, becoming warmer. Her petticoats fell to bunch in a circle around her feet. With soft scrapings, they brushed her skin as he turned her to face him. His eyes fired as they assumed their first possession of her loveliness. He didn't hurry.

After taking in the sight of her, he gestured to her hand. "I want you always to reach out to me. I will never touch you before you indicate that you wish me to." He waited.

He cocked his head. "Lady?"

Unashamed of her nakedness, she cast her eyes down only in grief. Her voice was dull. "You don't want to break your oath, even though you believe Captain Hook is— dead."

"It is always wise to be cautious. We gypsies are superstitious." He bent his head to capture her gaze. "But also, a very beautiful people, and full of the appreciation of life." The intensity of his regard confirmed his words.

"But what of *my* oath?"

"If Hook lives, Lady, you have already broken it with your scar-faced 'lover.' If not…" He held out his hand once more, expectant.

"You must know that if Hook lives, you will die."

"I acknowledge the possibility. But do not underestimate me, Madam. And of course, I would on no account allow him to punish *you*." His white teeth gleamed. "I see that you smile at my chivalry."

"I am amazed to hear anyone say they'll not allow James Hook to enforce his will." And defiantly, she raised her open hand, displaying its vivid color— the deep scarlet of Hook's blood, and her own. Her jewel blue eyes, so like Hook's, grew fierce. "If you are not good to me, I swear to you by his blood— *I* will kill you!"

Then she lowered her arm and turned her hand, offering it.

Cecco clasped her hand in triumph, and then he laughed. "Mutiny! But not, I think, until you have learned more of sailing, eh?" But his face lost all levity. "For now, you will learn more of men." He pulled her hands to his chest and pressed them there, and then he leaned forward as if to kiss her. But he stopped. "No. I want my first kiss to be one you will remember always."

He slipped his arm around her waist and drew her toward him. Her hands felt the tone of his thick chest muscles, the rise and fall of the breathing that caused his golden necklaces to glint in the candlelight.

"Here is where two hands can serve you."

She gasped as he cupped her breasts, then he caressed them with his thumbs. He bent his head, and placing his lips on one tinted tip, he kissed her, tenderly. She gazed upon his shoulders as his tongue circled, tasting the kiss. Lingering, he drank her in, and Jill's lips went dry. She opened them to breathe. When she looked down on his dark, feathery hair, she was tempted. But she couldn't bring herself to touch it yet. Her fingers moved, instead, on his chest.

Cecco kissed her, dissolving time. And the longer he kissed her breast, the more her mouth hungered for that kiss. She found herself longing for his same touch on her lips. How much cleverer he was, more winning, than she at first understood! She had, indeed, underestimated him, more than once. Truly, this kiss was one she would never, ever forget.

As the fire he had ignited burned below her belly, Jill's resolve to follow him faltered. Her fingers spread. Her hands pressed harder against his body. She tried to push him away but, effortlessly, the strongest man on the *Roger* overcame her resistance, and she learned how helpless she was. Her physical subjection stirred her doubts. Could she cross wits with him? And she became increasingly uncertain whether she would be able to carry through with this arrangement, or to keep any measure of control over the *Roger*, as Hook had commanded her to do.

But if Jill was a match for a man like Hook, she could match Cecco, too. What choice did she have? Her fingers stopped resisting. Instead, she followed the contour of his chest, moving her fingers up behind his neck and into his hair. She pressed him closer. And through the traitorous haze of her surrendering senses, she wondered again… where was Hook?

And where was Smee? What duty did the bo'sun owe her in this struggle? Her heart would feel so much lighter if this man taking charge of Hook's ship, the man commandeering Hook's woman, was her own Mr. Smee. Hook's Smee. Tears pricked at her eyelids.

And then Cecco banished thought, relinquishing his embrace and placing his hands on either side of her face. He lifted it. His dusky eyes contemplated the open lips that longed for his. He teased her lips with his thumbs, and then with his fingers, and then with his tongue. And when he finally granted her wish, that kiss was like a welcome consummation. Their lips pressed together. His tongue, impatiently awaited, thrust inside, and her own yielded to it.

Cecco's two hands now slid behind her hair, down her back, and lower, moving in circles and stroking her. He forced her toward him, massaging, insisting, against the eagerness manifest beneath his breeches. Taking hold of her red hand again, he placed it upon his manhood.

"As Hook's woman, you have consented to all my demands. Here is another demand. The first that I make upon *my* woman. Release me."

And until she did, she thought she might yet turn back. Even Cecco held his breath. He, too, must sense it wasn't too late. She could still choose the other course, reject Hook's admonition and abandon the ship to this man. But it was not for nothing that Jill had joined up with pirates. She had never been a coward. Unblinking, she watched now as Captain Cecco melted again, sighing.

She discovered a band of smooth, rolled metal encircling the base. "Ah." With hooded eyes, she looked at Cecco, inquiring.

"Yes. Your instincts are true. It is gold. As I intimated at Gao, a ring. For your pleasure, and mine." And he made her fingers to understand it, and her pulse beat against her skin.

"It is known, Madam, how you lust after precious treasure. You see that, like yourself, I adore jewelry. You will find me to be a more generous master than your first captain. I will delight to grant you any ornament you can remove from me. If you are successful, I will be most happy to replace my jewelry with new, so that you may win it again. In this way, all our desires will be fulfilled."

Her feet left the floor as Cecco, with his powerful arms, picked her up like an expensive doll and propped her in the captain's bunk where, of all places, she should have felt at home. But everything was changing now....He showed her again, gently, even lovingly, all over her body, what a man's two hands could do. Her breathing took on a rhythm of its own, and then slowed to match his movements as she warmed to this man's magic, in spite of all previous resolutions. It didn't help that he was adorned with gold. She ran her hands over its glossy texture, rich like his skin. She caressed the gold on his arms, the gold at his ears, his chest, his wrists. And...She fingered his ring. She couldn't help but want it.

Her touch, so intimate, spurred him on. "I told you no lies. You will share all my treasure with me, Lady. Starting now." His gilded chains swung from his neck as he leaned over her. His gold dangled over her breast. And she was surprised, mere moments later, how easily her thighs relented under the pressure of his knee and let him enter, in another welcome consummation.

But Cecco was in no hurry to seal this accord between the gypsy captain and the pirate queen. He had neglected to mention one last article, still unspoken, to include in their terms.

Surrender.

Despite her acquiescence, he controlled his passion, pushing forward only gradually, inch by inch as she clung to him, until, with her eager threshold, she just kissed his golden ring. Then he backed away.

She breathed, "Giovanni…"

She expected him to answer tenderly, as any lover might do. But as her captain, he corrected her instead, as he had done when he was only her devoted sailor.

"You are too informal. What am I, Madam?" He pressed inward

as he kissed her. Only after he withdrew did he permit her lips the freedom to answer.

She whispered. "You are the master— of this ship." He moved again so that she encompassed his golden ring. Then it slipped away. She pulled in her breath.

"Only of the ship?" He allowed it again, then…

He surged out, like the tide.

"No!"

"Who rules you?" He crested once more. And ebbed.

"My master."

With a motion, he rewarded her. "What am I to you?"

He abandoned her.

"The captain." Breathing was impossible.

As he advanced once more, his ring touched her again. Warm, smooth, and golden. "Whose captain…my Jill?"

It was gone. His bracelets jingled as he raised her hips to meet him.

And he delivered himself again.

"My captain." As she spoke it, some mysterious connection linked the lips of her mouth and the lips that embraced him. Even as her lover's insistence filled the void within her, she remembered the first man, she knew he still lived, and the movement of her mouth as she formed his word again, "Captain," sent her over the edge of sensation. No residue of resistance held her back. A golden ring, a golden earring, it was all the same to her now. She sighed, and retaining one shred of secrecy, denied her lips the utterance of her desire…Hook…and she gave herself over to the ecstasy. She found the shape for the word and called him again. "Captain." Here was her captain.

This man returned the favor, breathing huskily into her hair, "Lady…"

He was more than generous. He was lavish with his gifts. She found herself inviting them, accepting them, and ultimately, gathering in his bounty of liquid pearls. She held fast to his golden armbands, hot to her touch, and took all his offering as they coupled together there, on the captain's bunk. But when at length their two bodies stilled, he didn't allow them to lie long, satisfied. Coaxing more, Cecco sat upright, renewing his efforts. Never surrendering her fastness, he pulled her up by her wrists to kneel astride him. He drew her arms about his shoulders. She clasped her arms together, and still she filled her emptiness with his offering. Sometimes she kissed him, and sometimes she kissed Hook. She couldn't stop herself—

Someone else stopped her.

A tremendous blow hit the door and sent it smashing into the room. Jill jerked, clawing at Cecco as a tall figure stamped in and the door bounced back. At the sight of his familiar frame, Jill's hopes soared. Her eyes hungrily claimed him. He was lit from behind by the glare of torches, and from within by soft candlelight. His hair flamed in the flare of burning pitch as he braced his legs and slowed, his hand on his weapon, his boots stepping unsteadily.

Jill stared in confusion at him, the man she had needed an hour ago, in whose arms she should at this moment be sheltered. Come now, too late.

"Mr. Smee…" Pangs of disappointment stung her heart. Hook wasn't at his side.

Smee looked at her, and checked his forward motion. Jill's eyelids were heavy, she was panting, her arms around Cecco's neck, her beautiful flesh unmarked by violence. Clearly, the lady hadn't been forced. Her face was suffused with her passion. Cecco's sun-browned face, too, glowed with satisfaction. Intimately, their bodies intertwined. Their eyes burned too feverishly to mistake the truth. Even now, Jill and her consort were making love.

"Ma'am—" Smee's eyebrows drew together as he focused, then, haltingly, he backed away. "I thought you might be trusting me to take you out of here." Jill became aware of the doctor standing speechless in his suit coat, rigid behind the bo'sun. The gash of his dueling scar was gray against his open jaw as he blinked, utterly shocked. Nibs hung back behind the threshold, reluctant, with Starkey in his shadow. Mullins and Jukes crowded the companionway, and one of the torches was clenched in the black fist of Yulunga. His expression was unreadable.

Gathering wits enough to make his face blank, Smee finally said,

"I'd have done anything for you, Lady. But I see you won't be needing me, after all."

Yulunga stooped and strode in, elbowing the doctor from his path. His torch cast a glaring light, flickering amber on the naked bodies in the bed. Both lovers remained still, unabashed and exposed for all to see. But despite the exquisite vision before him, it was her eyes that sobered Smee.

He stood uncomfortably, Yulunga's flame reflecting in his spectacles. Then he squinted at the gypsy. "Begging your pardon…" His lip curled as he spat out the title of distinction, *"Captain."*

On hearing the word, Nibs looked hard at Smee, then sent a glance full of pain to Jill, as if he suffered a grievous wound. He turned and launched himself down the stairs. Starkey followed him.

Moving at last, Jill buried her face in Cecco's brawny arm. She felt the heat of his golden armband against her cheek. He stroked her hair, looking directly at Smee. "Fear nothing, Jill. You are under my protection now."

But the pirate queen's head snapped up. "Every man on this ship knows that I fear nothing!" She directed an icy stare at Smee. "I know where my duty lies. I embrace it without shame." The words escaped from between the two halves of her broken heart. "Take your accusing eyes, man, and get out of—" only she knew she faltered, "our quarters."

Smee's expression became set. He turned on his heel and stumbled toward the door.

"Wait!"

Halting, he swung around. In spite of his outrage, a ray of hope lighted the face above his red beard.

Jill said, "You will see to the door, personally, in the morning. We will leave it open tonight, so that there will be no doubt as to our disposition. Captain Cecco and I are agreed."

Smee's face hardened. He didn't wait to be dismissed again. He strode out and left the woman to her fate, without looking back.

She didn't blame him. He believed she had betrayed his master. Her master.

Perhaps he was right.

The silence was broken only by the spitting of the pitch. The doctor and the torchbearers gaped for another moment, then departed. Yulunga watched them go. As they clattered away, he addressed the captain.

"I'm sorry, Sir."

"You will show the proper respect to your mistress."

"Aye, Sir. I apologize for the disturbance, Lady. I would have stopped him from smashing the door, but I thought it best that they see for themselves."

The captain nodded. "You acted wisely, Mr. Yulunga. We will have no more trouble from that quarter." His fingers played with Jill's hair as it shone in the leaping torchlight. "Where is *L'Ormonde?*"

"To the northeast, Sir, off to port. She won't catch us tonight."

"See that she doesn't."

Yulunga grunted assent. The flame dragged behind his torch as he headed for the stairs. At the threshold, he turned. "And the door, Sir?"

"As the lady commands. Leave it open."

The first mate lifted his face in tribute to his mistress. "You display much courage, Lady!" Smiling sideways, he blended into the night.

Jill didn't hear his heavy footsteps descending the stairs; she believed she heard a tapping on the wall. But when she looked she saw that, as before, the captain's claw was not suspended from its hook. The panel was bare. She lay down, turned her face to the wall, and wept.

Cecco reveled in his good fortune. "You are magnificent, Madam! Such a woman! So full of fire. And you give yourself to me completely. You will find me more than worthy of your deference." Turning his ugly back to the ruined, gaping doorway, the new captain lay down beside her. He caressed her shoulder. "But now you weep. Ah, my lovely. I sympathize. I am a man who understands women. Such a shock....And you are grieving, of course." His expert hands stroked her, lending comfort and affection.

"After such passion and such loyalty, I do not expect you to give to me anything more tonight. You must shed the tears. I will take care of everything." So saying, he sat up and heaved his bulk above her, and his two good hands rolled her onto her back. Murmuring endearments, he gathered her wrists in his fist and held them firmly against the mattress, above her head. He positioned her legs, kissed her tears, and with a complacent smile, he mounted her.

"You must lie still, my Jill. Your captain will love you and demand nothing more." And Jill lay beneath him and followed her two captains' commands.

It was easy this time. Even with no chains or rubies to induce her obedience. Miserable in her grief, she finally followed Hook's own orders— and betrayed him again. She submitted to the captain's will. She wouldn't dare move her limbs until he was finished with her. In their make-believe play, Hook had warned her once, or maybe twice, before, and she understood the consequences otherwise. If she moved, she would lose everything.

But the ship moved. It pulled her forward, inexorably, into the night. Far away she heard the grateful kisses of waves on the hull. The salt on her lips must be kisses of the sea, too. She touched them with her tongue. She listened to the voice of the man above her, offering no choice but persuading just the same, speaking her name and claiming her for his own. She heard the golden chime of bracelets on two whole, well-formed wrists. The wrists of a man who urged her forward.

What, really, did she have left to lose? She had given up more than she intended, and taken pleasure in it, too. She had driven Smee away. Hook was gone. And Captain Cecco was here.

Strong, handsome Cecco, was here.

Everything was changed, and everything was the same. By the wreckage of the door, a phantom sea captain stood, his rapier upheld. *Identify the weapon…the weakness.* Still hearing his velvet voice, Jill closed her eyes. Her weary ears caught Cecco's cadence. Obediently, she listened to her captain.

And she surrendered. She gave all her self— heart, body, and mind— to Cecco. She knew where her duty lay.

She embraced it.

"Sir…"

"Bellezza." So tender.

"With your permission."

He studied her face, then released her wrists. Her hands raised up and ran through his hair. She traced the taut muscles of his neck, stroked them, then her fingers unfastened one golden chain. The heaviest one. She slid it off and held it under his eyes.

"Captain?"

He breathed heavily, and nodded. Lifting her head, she fastened the chain around her own neck. With her fingertips, she sampled its silky length from clasp to breast. His clinging eyes followed. When he bent to kiss it, she stopped him with a hand to his cheek.

"Madam?"

She stroked his face. "You are too formal. Say my name, Sir."

"…Jill."

"Sir. What are you?"

"The master of this ship."

"Only of the ship? Sir?" Her fingers played lightly over his arm.

"No."

"Who rules me?"

His voice roughened. "Your master."

"What are you to me, Master?" The mellow surface of his bracelet felt smooth under her touch.

"The captain."

"…Whose captain?" The shining band unhooked from his wrist.

"Your captain, Madam."

"Aye, Sir. You are my captain." Above her slender, well-formed wrist that bore his golden bracelet, her red hand, in the gesture that came easily now, reached out to him.

He admired her hand. He accepted her hand. He kissed her hand.

The faintest of smiles was born, and barely suggested itself at the corner of her mouth. Her dark blue eyes clung to him.

There were no sounds but those of the sea making love to a ship, and a master to his mistress. And a phantom-tapping on the wall.

Into all the sweet precincts and secret recesses in which she had harbored Hook, she now drew the scent and the seed of his sailor. As he possessed her completely, all of Mr. Cecco's dreams came true. And he learned, that night, that he could deny her nothing.

One or two of Jill's dreams lay dashed. Possessed by her captain, she learned, that night, that she would deny herself— nothing.

Captain Cecco was a man who understood women. He had observed that she was adept in the ways of leadership. He was not a difficult master to satisfy. Red-Handed Jill was his mistress.

And she had mastered him.

Ups and Downs

The ship went quiet after the uproar and confusion. Liza listened carefully to make it out but, in the end, she had to creep up the steep, clammy steps, barefoot in her nightdress, to learn what had happened. The men had subsided at last. Some, her father and Mr. Smee included, adjourned solemnly to confer in the galley. Some sat cross-legged on the forecastle with torches and bottles in their hands. In any case, the excitement was over for them. For Liza, it was only beginning.

To all appearances, Hook's discipline was over, too. Earlier in the evening, Liza heard Mr. Yulunga order another cask broached. The reek of rum reached her nostrils as she peered, half in and half out of the hatch. The smell reminded her of the taste on Tom's lips when he kissed her, so long ago now. Before he became the burly man with the scar on his temple. Liza considered the other men, too. Many of them bore scars, but, like his discipline, Hook's wasn't visible most of the time— yet one always sensed its existence.

The pirates were joking and shoving their elbows into one another's ribs. Every so often a burst of laughter erupted, then hushed as the men looked behind them across the long deck toward the master's quarters. Under cover of one such spasm, Liza hoisted herself to the deck and rolled away from the hole. Bending to keep her head lower than the rail, she scurried in the shadows from cannon to cannon, away from the gaiety, toward the companionway.

Mr. Jukes at the wheel appeared to be mapping the stars. The man's tattooed face fascinated Liza, as did his hands with inky swirls and spirals all up and down his fingers. She could see them in the lanternlight as he stretched to grasp the wheel, and she hesitated, wondering what the rest of him looked like. Never before had she found an opportunity to get a good, long look at Mr. Jukes. She had developed a new desire to compare him, and all men, to her captain. Crouching in the darkness of the stairway, she paused before climbing to the captain's quarters, determining which scene held more promise.

Then she heard the sounds, always more intriguing to Liza than the sights, and she slipped up the steps unseen by Jukes, drawn by sighs of spirits, the haunting breath of the dying. Liza knew what that sound was. She'd heard it before. It issued from the same place, too, only now there was an embarrassed hole instead of the stately door with its brass plate boasting 'Capt. Jas. Hook.' Candlelight flickered from within the cabin, to tempt her, offering for only the price of dignity to betray the sights there.

Liza's feet made no noise as she hastened upward, and her nightdress snagged on the ragged door frame as she lowered herself to kneel within it. She pulled it free with a tiny snap. Like a penance, her knees absorbed the discomfort of the splinters scattered within the entrance. Obviously, the crash she had heard through the crack of the doorway to her own quarters originated here.

The spirits were moaning now, their shrouds rustling under their feet. The clink of their chains littered the air. A candle sputtered, and Liza raised her eyes to verify the scene before the light might be extinguished in the windy breath of these phantoms. Her pulse quickened at what she witnessed.

She needn't have worried about losing the light. The candles shone in abundance. The scene played just as before, when she'd hidden behind the curtain to watch the master make love to the mistress. But tonight the semi-darkness was inspired by the flames instead of the moon, and punctuated by glitters of gold. Liza's eyes connected the flecks of light, deciphering their meaning. She had recognized the chiming as Cecco's bracelets, and it was his familiar cuffs that fettered the spirits who danced and whispered on the bunk. All illumined by the flickering eyes of tapers.

303

But other, invisible bonds connected the pair as well. The lovers were adorned, and adoring. They pressed together, rapturous, and only came away to rearrange themselves for further meeting. In the orange light of the candles, their bodies appeared very much intact, and their fully fleshed lips followed each other's contours, outlining the linking limbs for Liza's view. But where before a curtain of black hair had obscured her vision, Cecco's hair was bound, and now her mistress' face was clearly exposed and the girl could see their mouths pressing together and pulling away but not completely because their tongues were kissing too. Liza wrinkled her nose, then ran her own tongue over her lips. Caught up in this bonding, she could hear her heart beating again, too loudly.

And where, before, the master's body had been long and sculpted like a statue, this master was thick and heavy, bulging all along his arms and legs. But the mistress was the same as before. As with the other captain, her female frame somehow endured his weight, even gloried in it. Her arms made the motions they had made behind her first lover, pulling and pushing, her hands caressing everything. With Cecco tonight, she used new motions, too, rolling the ends of his leather strap in her fingers, and stroking the scars covering his back, working as if to heal them. Her legs wrapped around his, her hips rose and fell with the sighs she expelled. And when the path to it was clear, her crimson hand would travel up the man's thigh to touch the place where sometimes another glow of gold appeared, and her fingers would massage it, and she would close her eyes and sigh again.

The big man was smiling, always, and murmuring, and moving. At length he lifted the woman as lightly as if she were a toy, but precious. He sat up to position her on his lap, and then he stretched down on his back. Now it was the fair hair that drew the curtain on their upper bodies, and Liza felt herself become fluid as she watched their lower bodies coupling. Then she heard footsteps behind her, and a strangled gasp of outrage. She turned in time to see the signet on her father's finger flare in the candlelight before his hands seized her shoulders. He dragged her off the splinters and into the velvet that covered the cage of his arms. One look back showed her Jill's eyes, darkened to indigo now as she shook the hair from them, unashamed, even defiant as she identified the witness to her rites. But her body never stopped moving and her lips were parted and the man kept smiling and the spirits never ceased their airy utterances.

Liza pushed her face away from her father's neck. Yet after she made sure Jukes saw them pass, she let her hair cover her features to drape over her father's shoulder, as Jill's had done over Cecco's. Surely her father would punish her. Jill might punish her, too, and maybe even Captain Cecco would favor her with his attention, tomorrow. Liza's pulse beat brutally all over her body, and throbbed between her legs. What would her father do to her? He hadn't recognized her earlier transgression for what it was. *That* sin was still her secret. But surely he would react strongly now— and she would imagine that the black-haired captain with his velvet voice and his eyes like Jill's was watching.

The lady had moaned for him. The lady's glinting ghost moaned for Cecco, now. Would she one day moan for Liza's father, too, the way Liza remembered hearing as her mother died?

Liza smiled through her trepidation. When her father took his cane to her this time, she might surprise the good doctor again and moan for him— just like Jill.

He could still smell the sea. That was good. And the movement of the waves was good, unless it was only the continuing disorientation. He waited, and assessed....Yes. He was still aboard a ship.

The first time he'd come round, he learned not to open his eyes. He had jolted into awareness, staring with his eyes wide, striving to sit up. But he was immediately restrained, and gagged soon after by a foul-smelling rag in a firm hand, and that had been the end of it. Now, he listened instead. Steady breathing. The slap of the sea. Through his eyelids he perceived the light of coming dawn, through his nostrils, the scent of a warm female body, and the residue of the drug.

He flexed his fingers, but slowly. The band of iron still encompassed his wrist. He couldn't risk allowing the chain to jangle. He'd been stripped of boots and coat, but the soft linen of his shirt had been replaced since his last awakening. The hook, of course, was the first thing they'd taken. Moving his right foot ever so slightly, he affirmed the grasp of the metal cuff on his ankle.

The heavy ache of his head had not abated. Throughout his befuddled state of the past hours it throbbed, for he'd not been asleep. The drug had rendered him incapacitate, but had not delivered to him the blessing of unconsciousness. As always when his woman was wakeful, he was incapable of sleep. All through the dark time, something— most likely his absence— had prevented her rest. Now, though, he felt her to be drowsing, and sealing his eyes once again, he commended himself to the mercy of slumber, for however long he might enjoy it.

Floating at last, soothed in the waters of his dreams, he sought relief in the arms of his mermaid. Reaching for her, he discovered she was no longer at his side. He swam into the depths, stroking against the sea with all his strength, searching, spying out that emerald flash of scaling. But though he glimpsed the tip of her tail, the void in his soul told him she had gone too far to follow.

Hook's chains held him back, and Jill was sinking, away and down, into another ocean.

Yesterday, the fateful day of Hook's disappearance, Liza welcomed Smee's change of plan. Obedient to his order, she forsook the rest of her lesson and kept to her quarters. Her peek into the cabin next to her own confirmed her hopes, and she hastened to prepare herself, letting down her hair as she stole back to her room. It was there, at last, that she captured Captain Hook's attention.

As he rolled up his charts and prepared to quit the cabin, Hook must have heard the scrabbling of little stones, for with a rustling of papers, he scraped back his chair and rose. Liza listened to the tap of his hook on the door as he pushed it wider. She heard the cautious step of his boots as he emerged. With a swipe and a skittering, he nudged one of the gems with his toe. She thought he wouldn't resist picking them up, but as the sounds indicated, he forbore. Smiling to herself, Liza felt the swaying of the ship, and she appreciated her own cleverness. She had been wise to arrange a more immediate enticement as well.

From her hiding place behind her open door, Liza heard the shuffling noise continue. Hook followed her path, gathering the diamonds together with his foot, like so much refuse, and sweeping them toward her cabin. There was a silence during which Liza's heart careened, and in one final swish, he shoved them all to roll twinkling into her quarters. Then he paused.

Liza knew what had to be happening in that instant. Captain Hook was absorbing the sight of a dazzling diamond bracelet, positioned strategically on the sill of the open window and glistening in the midday sunlight. As the ship rocked with the waves, the visible end of the bracelet swung. Clearly, the precious ornament was worth a fortune. Just as clearly, it was in peril. At any point, the pitch of the *Roger* might send it sliding into the sea, to be lost forever. What pirate wouldn't act to save such a treasure? Liza held her breath as she watched its reflection glitter in the mirror over her bureau. This was the deciding moment. Success or failure hung on her master's next movement.

He didn't hesitate. Liza heard his boots stride boldly to starboard. Breathing again, she watched his red velvet image in the glass as he hastened to the window and snatched up the jewelry. At last, the great Captain Hook deigned to visit her quarters!

As she watched, his glance swept the room, noting a bowlful of fruit on the table, linen napkins, a sherry bottle and two familiar glasses. Lowering his eyes, he observed the loose diamonds on the floor. Then, choosing not to turn toward Liza, he cast his blue gaze to the mirror, where her reflection stood in the shadows behind the door. He weighed the bracelet in his one good hand.

"What game are you playing, little girl, and with your father's pieces?"

He had spoken to her! Her throat swelled with sounds fighting to escape. But she couldn't answer. Waiting for more of his words, her yearning compelled her to behold him directly. Her desire was so consuming that, as her face emerged, she forgot to push the door. He turned to squint at her, and she remembered. Taking a deep breath of courage, she pushed hard. The door swung silently to click shut.

He lifted one eyebrow. His eyes coursed down and up her

unclothed, ripened body. Without any indication of his thoughts, he turned toward the door. Liza flung herself between him and the exit. He halted with a jerk, his golden earring bobbing. When he advanced again, she fell back against the door, splaying her arms and shaking her head. The wood was rough and cool against the skin of her elbows, her back, and buttocks. She'd expected that. She hadn't known what else to expect. Anger, interest? Certainly not the containment with which he responded.

"Stand aside."

He was so commanding, so tall! His presence filled the room in the way she wished he would fill her body. Her wide eyes gazed up at his face. Her finger pointed at the gems shining on the floor, indicating that he should take them.

"None of this plunder is yours to give." Carelessly, as if it were a shuttlecock, he tossed the bracelet onto her father's desk.

She winced, and then she looked at the two pink pearls on her ring. Wrenched with clashing desires, she drew the ring off. With hope in her eyes, she offered it to him.

Like a long-suffering teacher, he said, "Little girl, I already have access to your jewels."

Her mouth opened as if she longed to speak. Her hands opened as well. With a leap of faith, she relinquished her precious ring, dropping it to rattle on the floorboards. Surely he would see that the ring, the diamonds— nothing— held meaning for her. Only *he* mattered. Gazing intently at the master, she ran her palms up her thighs and her hips and over her torso, drawing them under her breasts. Inviting, she held her bare arms out to him.

The patience in his wonderful voice wore thin. "Understand. Had you anything I wanted, I'd have taken you long ago. Move aside."

Liza lowered, slowly, to the floor. Her features grew stubborn as she blocked the doorway. Still watching his handsome face, she felt along the boards and scooped the diamonds into her hands. She caught the gleam of his hook, so lethal up close that she convulsed with shivers. Kneeling at his feet and in thrall to her urges, she obeyed the impulse to lay her cheek upon it. In the seconds she was allowed to touch it, it felt steely cold. Hook pressed it to her cheekbone as he forced her away. When he drew it back, she felt it still, like an ice-fire brand. She recovered her suppliant position, kneeling on the hard floor that punished her knees. Cupping her father's treasure in her two hands, she raised it in offering.

"Out of my way!"

Liza braved the anger in his eyes. She remained on her knees almost between his boots, breathing his leathery scent. Summoning the boldness that never failed her before, she leaned back to display her willingness, believing that in spite of his words, he was tempted. She saw him survey the womanly gifts of her body, confirming what she knew to be true— she, too, was lovely. Freed at last from her net, her hair was brushed to a sheen. It rippled over the tops of her shoulders. The strands fell loose toward her bosom, and she had cut her hair so that it stopped just short of her breasts. Their firm curves showed plainly, as did the dark points that crowned them. Her master must see she was no child! Liza was certain he was appreciating every detail, even the fading stripes on her thighs. He'd never seen those bruises before. But he would recognize them. Like her mistress' red hand, they were the marks she had won for provoking him.

"Enough of this. I have business elsewhere." He nudged Liza's naked thigh with his boot, ebony against ivory. But she let the diamonds slide through her fingers, to bounce off his boot and rattle all around. He shook them off, and in the second in which the gems distracted him, Liza seized his long coat, to climb up his body like a feral cat.

He drew away, but she clung. Before he could rid himself of her, she had wrapped her legs around him and she was pressing her breasts to his velvety chest, pulling his head down to meet her. Her lips pushed against his. She tasted him with her tongue and felt the prick of his mustache, and he overbalanced and staggered back to compensate, nearly colliding with the bunks. She had her fingers in his hair now, clinging like burrs. Trying to loosen them, he turned his head this way and that, angling his face to avoid her. He reached up to tug, but his single hand couldn't disentangle her. His claw threatened, flashing in the sun.

Liza didn't care.

She didn't care, and Hook knew it.

He understood from the beginning. This creature craved whatever form of attention he granted her. She would be his, as absolutely as his Jill.

And Jill was waiting for him. This little spitfire was costing him time. Jill must be wondering why he hadn't burst upon her to challenge the surgeon. The quickest victory would suit Hook now— he'd deal with the repercussions later. Relaxing, he lowered his hook to encircle the girl's waist, tightly. His hand abandoned the tangle of his hair to brush the strands of brown from her face.

"All right, little girl. I'll play with you."

Her eyes lit up. She set her feet back on the floor and stood on tip-toe to reach him. Her face as he touched her flushed with an eagerness that made her pretty. With the back of his fingers, Hook stroked her hot flesh, gratified to feel her releasing his hair and grasping his shoulders instead.

"We'll play a game of make-believe, shall we?" Her weapons in this fray were her hands. With calculated patience he collected them, one at a time, and pressed them to his chest. Then he gifted her with his beautiful smile. He watched her smile in return. He leaned as though to kiss her, and her eyes half closed and her body went limp with rapture. He tipped her far enough back to gain control, then scooped her up and off her feet. He pivoted, to fling her to the bunk on his way out the door.

The maneuver should have succeeded. His method was flawless— but so, too, were the diamonds studding the floor. As he turned to toss her, his boot skidded upon the gems. Instead of releasing her to the lowest bunk, he twisted and fell with her. They both tumbled onto the bedding. Hook felt a burn from the frame of the upper bunk where it had grazed his cheekbone. As he struggled to lift himself off the girl, the chains on the bedpost rattled warning. But his right arm was pinned beneath her. He'd had to let go of her hands to break the fall, and she seized his coat and dragged him toward her, longing for his kiss.

But Hook had, indeed, played make-believe. When the kiss wasn't delivered, she thrashed about, pushing against the bed, then lifting her face to meet his, and his arm slid free from her back. Circling the hook above her, he shoved his elbow down to pin her with his forearm, just under her throat, his claw barely avoiding a slash on her shoulder. And all the while his gut wrenched as he felt Jill needing him, and his precious time, like the doctor's diamonds, sliding away.

He'd have to pretend again. "I've no patience with this disobedience. Lie still and give yourself to me."

Hearing his voice directed only toward her— speaking the very words for which she craved— was too much for the girl. In a frenzy now, Liza redoubled her efforts, deliberately disobeying, knowing and desiring the punishment that could follow his pleasure— and displeasure. Her grip on his coat was desperate. As he straddled her, she thrust against the loins poised above her own and begged him for his passion, at any cost.

Time was running out.

"Be still, girl!" Again he collected her hands, plucking them like early fruit from a stubborn vine. He was just forcing her arms up over her head when the door slammed shut, and the fury in the gray velvet suit strode toward the bunk. The ivory-handled walking stick raised up and whistled through the air in a motion calculated to crush a rapist's skull. Bright lights whirled in the blackness then, and only after he collapsed, fading into oblivion in a heavy heap along her body, did the girl truly win Captain Hook's attention.

An inch from his ear, in a low, lovely voice, she moaned for him. *"Master!"*

Wide awake in the gray shadings of dawn, Hanover listened for a telltale clink in the bunk above. With a rag and the bottle of ether close to hand, he lay tensed, reliving the horrors of the previous day.

Ironically, the day began perfectly for the surgeon. Stimulated by his glorious session with the 'lady,' he retired to his quarters, still smiling and more hopeful of his future than ever— only to push open his door to behold the shocking sight of that crimson-coated criminal forcing himself on helpless, naked Liza! Hook's one hand was pinning her wrists to the bunk. His man's body moved in an obscene fashion, pressing down over the little girl's, and his claw threatened to slash her innocent throat.

But Liza hadn't screamed. A brave child, she had struggled valiantly for her honor. Dutiful toward her father even in her adversity, she obeyed his admonition to silence, uttering not so much as a single forbidden syllable. At once, Hanover perceived a losing battle for her virtue. He had arrived just in time. Another moment under that black-haired beast, and Liza would have been sullied for life. After such usage, no *good* man would ever have wanted her!

The facts had revealed themselves to Hanover as he stood clutching his walking stick, teetering in that one hideous second after the blow that laid Hook low. This despoilment was the 'task' Smee had arranged for Liza during her lesson, while his master counted on Jill's allure to keep Hanover away. The miracle was that Hook hadn't thought to clap the girl in her chains. Clearly, the man had planned this move, as evidenced by the bottle of spirits to combat her inhibitions, the fruit for flavorful distraction— the same method, no doubt, the pirate had used to seduce Jill. Hanover was pleased to find his daughter made of sterner stuff than anyone supposed. Obviously, she was more like her father than her mother, after all.

Further, Hook wasn't satisfied with stealing Liza's maidenhead. The pirate forced the girl to reveal her father's valuables first, pilfering Hanover's jewels into the bargain. His best piece, the bracelet, lay twinkling near the scene of the violence. Loose diamonds lay scattered on the floor— heaven knew how they got there! That 'aristocratic' pirate was the scum of the earth, and the Irishman no better. Their rapaciousness made Hanover's blood run cold. It wasn't enough for either of them to lay their filthy hands on Jill. They had to ruin Liza, too. No female, however young and inexperienced, was safe from their lasciviousness. The only wonder was that Liza had escaped Hook's depravity this long.

But, here, Hanover accepted his own responsibility. No doubt it was Jill's lack of attention that steered Hook's lust toward Liza. The idea made the doctor's heart swell with gratitude as the circumstances confirmed his hopes— Jill had been true to her fiancé all along. But then his spirit constricted. If Jill's neglect of the captain triggered Hook's action against the girl, some of the blame was his own. Hanover's presence had upset the balance, and Liza's virtue almost paid the price.

Hanover had saved her. This time. He had stared at his daughter trapped under the inert form of the villain, and vowed again to get both females off this ship and into civilized society, where he could properly extend his protection and authority over them. All these thoughts tumbled through his mind as he clenched the bloody walking stick, and the time it took to think them compressed to the size of a diamond.

But now, on his bunk at daybreak, Hanover had time to string his thoughts out. Like a whole chain of diamonds, the problems stretched, hard and insoluble.

Hook's downfall seemed such a fortunate event in the beginning. The solution to all the surgeon's troubles. Confident he was beyond Hook's control at last, Hanover cooperated with Cecco, maneuvering Jill out of her position of power and removing any obligation to her former master. Hanover was delighted to smooth Cecco's path to the captaincy. The plan had worked beautifully, and before even LeCorbeau could have expected, the *Roger* was released from Hook's domination.

Captain Hook's attempt at seduction had, in fact, saved Hanover a great deal of trouble. LeCorbeau's scheme would have been far more complicated to enact, and a clear violation of a physician's oath to preserve life. The administration of the sleeping draught and a staged tumble down the stairs would have been difficult, but the plot's most abhorrent aspect for an honorable man to carry out would have been the death of the captain, caused by a fall upon his own hook.

Now, of course, due to the obvious blow to Hook's head, this ruse was out of the question. Even to a layman, it was plain the man had been attacked, and the surgeon would be the first to be suspected of the captain's murder. But as events unfolded, Hanover seized his advantage without dishonor. In the immediate aftermath, Hook's disappearance was a blessing for all.

And then, thanks to the Italian's machinations, circumstances disintegrated into disaster. Not only did Hanover discover the duplicity of Captain Cecco; he learned the ugly truth about Jill. Dislodging her from her vices would be far more difficult than he at first believed, and Hanover had to steel himself for the task. Since recovering from his moment of weakness on deck, Hanover worked tirelessly to salvage the situation. He compelled himself to join forces with the Irishman— the lesser of two devils— to rescue Jill from the gypsy's clutches. But by the time the oddly-matched allies ceased their contention and prevailed upon Mr. Yulunga to allow parley with the captain, it was too late.

Hanover couldn't erase the vision of Jill in a state of undress— breathtaking— and degraded, indulging in fornication with that deceitful, opportunistic brute of a pirate. The woman desperately needed the corrective rod her future husband would apply, once he finally got her away from this ship of iniquity! Whenever he tried to banish the memory of her corruption, the other image haunted the blackness behind his eyelids— the derisive smile of Yulunga, ridiculing the good doctor's gullibility. And now, the situation that seemed so advantageous had become like a powder keg— too volatile; Hanover might never find a way to save himself this time, let alone his wayward Jill. His wicked, wanton Jill.

Immediately after the blow to Hook's head, Hanover had reeled back from the bunk, his breast churning. The first thing he did was lock the door. Then, as Liza lay whimpering, murmuring nonsense, he seized a hunk of gauze from his medical supplies and scrubbed his cane clean. When, a moment later, the cane hung innocently on its hook by the door, Hanover tackled the bigger problem. With the bloody gauze, he tamped the wound on the captain's head, then flung the rag out the porthole. Only when he felt pebbles slipping underfoot did he remember the diamonds. He plucked the bracelet from the desk and collected his jewels from the floor, scarcely noticing the pearl ring among them. Wondering if he should question Liza, he glanced at her as he worked. He decided against it. The poor girl was out of her head with shock, stroking the captain's long black hair and smoothing it with her fingers. In any case there was no time. Hanover spoke to her, urgently.

"Liza. Keep quiet now."

Rolling her eyes toward her father, Liza focused, surprised to see him. She panicked as she realized what he had witnessed. Glimpsing his cane in stoic stiffness on the wall, she crouched, waiting for his rage to erupt. But he was almost sympathetic as he hurried to replace the diamonds in his medicine bag.

"Do not upset yourself. I understand why you had to speak. I will not punish you; only keep quiet, as I told you." Moving efficiently, he dusted off his fingers and removed his coat. Liza nodded. In a dreamlike daze, she continued to stroke the silk of Hook's hair.

Sensing that, when his task was over, he must show not a wrinkle nor a hair out of place, Hanover hung his jacket on his chair. He went to work with a will, dragging the crimson velvet from Hook's shoulders. If he noticed the noise, he made no sign, but Liza startled at the rip of red lining as the hook tore its way from its sleeve. Hanover was about to cast the coat out the window when he stopped to think. Making a quick search of its recesses, he noted the contents. He paused over the ring of keys, blinking as he considered, and then he slid them into his own pocket. Now knowing exactly what he must do, he bundled the coat and stuffed it under the bunk.

Next, he rolled Hook to the edge of the bed so that Liza could escape. "Dress yourself, but only in your shift, then clear away the bottle and glassware." Relieved, the surgeon saw that the captain's breeches were still fastened. Liza may have been touched, but not damaged. Working with speed, Hanover began the business of removing Hook's waistcoat and shirt. Only half dressed herself, Liza crept behind her father to stare over his shoulder at the workings of the captain's hook. Without slowing his progress, Hanover, too, marveled at the ingenuity of the design that strapped the wooden form and anchored Hook's claw. Deducing that one clip at the man's breast secured the harness, he released it. Now the problem was not the removal of the hook, but the secreting of it. Hanover couldn't afford to toss anything significant out the window; it might be noticed by the gang in the rigging, or anyone stationed along the rail at the moment.

He'd deal with it later. "Liza, hide these things in the drawer, beneath your undergarments."

She seized the waistcoat and the hook, avoiding the barb but embracing her captain's belongings. Touching the chill metal to her cheek first, she laid it away in the chest of drawers. She smiled to see her shifts and petticoats snagged by his claw, then piled more clothing upon it. It was exciting to think of the powerful hook there, intimate with the clothing she wore so close to her skin.

"Tug his other boot off, Liza, hurry!" Hanover's confidence grew with each hurdle jumped, his plan sketched out clearer in his mind. "Throw them in my sea chest, the stockings, too." They both startled as a flash of silver fell from the boot in Liza's hands, darting to thump and spin on the floor. Liza crouched to pick up the boot knife, recognizing it as the one Hook removed as he undressed during her night of spying. Hanover snatched it, thrust it back in the boot and shoved his daughter toward his sea chest. "Away, girl, put these away!" He turned back to Hook.

The pirate lay naked, now, except for his breeches. Not stopping to examine his severed wrist, Hanover pulled the captain by one leg and one arm. Hook's head lolled, his hair fell forward over his face as the athletic surgeon knelt down by the bunk and hauled Hook's weight onto his shoulders. Staggering under the load, Hanover kept his back to the bed. He stood, hoisting the pirate to the higher bunk while Liza pushed his legs over the edge. Hanover released Hook to roll on his back. Stepping on his own bunk, he shoved Hook's body toward the wall, and climbed down.

Then, with pleasure, Hanover reaped his revenge. He drew Hook's ring of keys from his own pocket, and set to work on the manacles chained to his bunk. Unwinding the links from his bedpost, he dragged them clear. They jingled merrily as he tossed them into the upper bunk. He vaulted after them. A feeling of freedom washed over him as he secured the devil captain in his own cold chains, one at his wrist, one at his ankle, both firmly attached to the bedposts. And then the physician sat back and smiled.

But no time remained to gloat. Ordering Liza to tidy the bunks, he drew the covers over Hook and jumped down. "Liza. You are to take to your bed and remove your shift. I will put it about that you are not well." He reached under the bunk and dragged out Hook's shirt. "Stuff this under the bedclothes, by your feet." The coat he kept, turning his back on Liza and heading for the door. As she clambered up beside Hook, Hanover pressed his ear to the door to listen. He heard footsteps retreating up the stairs. When they faded, he slipped from the room and hastened to the spare cabin, closing its door softly behind him and shooting the bolt.

Hook's sword was there, lying across the desk. It presented another problem that the surgeon mulled as he eyed the wide open window. He soon realized the weapon was just what he needed. He threw down the coat and drew the rapier from its scabbard.

The sword was exquisite. The hiss of its blade as Hanover released it energized him. Its surface was satin, its keen edges ready for a duel. Hanover smiled, gratified to use it against its master. Leaning out the window, he worked the tip savagely in the wood of the hull, swiping stray hair from his eyes as he tore up a splinter below the sill. Before he left the cabin, the crimson coat was flying like a banner off the stern, and the sword resumed the place in which its master had abandoned it.

As his own door closed behind him, Hanover heard voices rising, and the trooping of boots surging down the steps. Men tore every direction, seeking their missing captain. Hanover shrugged on his coat and smoothed his hair just as a fist hit his door. Nibs entered with a crease deepening his dark brow, to discover the girl clutching a sheet over her bare bosom, wan and peeking from behind the upper bed curtain. In his habitual manner, the surgeon tugged at his coat cuffs.

"Doctor. I'm to search your cabin. On the lady's orders."

"The *lady's* orders? I will do as she commands, of course. But I trust you will not take advantage of your position to molest my daughter on her sickbed?"

Nibs shot one resentful look at the girl and said the same thing each subsequent searcher replied to the doctor's question.

"Sir, I want nothing to do with her."

"Captain Cecco…" Softly, her voice intruded into his dream. It matched his dream.

"Sir?"

He opened his eyes, and came immediately awake at the sight of a razor glinting inches above his throat. Seizing Jill's wrist, he launched himself to tumble her sideways, so that his body pinned her. He grappled for her other wrist and captured that, too. Her hand was empty, but her face was full of mischief as she smiled at his reflexes. Her four golden bracelets glimmered just below his fists. She laughed.

"Captain! Is this how your 'ideal woman' is to be greeted each day?"

He heaved a sigh, and the remaining chains around his neck mingled familiarly with her own as he kissed her. Her response was warm. It hadn't been a dream, after all. During the night, the captain and his lady had given each other everything they had to give, and on this bright new morning, the two were one.

The razor thumped onto the bed. Cecco released her hands to let her wind them, tinkling with gold, around the back of his neck. His own hands picked her up with no effort and set her on his knees, and the energy that had flowed so quickly to his defenses now poured itself somewhere else. Glancing at the ruined door, Cecco debated, then left the decision to Jill.

"Madam. The light is strong this morning, and our doorway is no barrier against the prying eyes of our crew."

Extricating herself from his arms, she stood, unveiling an intriguing smile. She was almost wearing her sky-blue dressing gown. With her back to the door, a great deal of her charms were revealed only to her captain. As she bent to retrieve the razor, she made sure his stubbly jaw grazed her cheek.

"Ah, Sir, the decision is easy. You are in need of a shave before we appear before the company, and…" She took him by the hand. "Everything is ready." She led him to the captain's shaving stool by the foot of the bed, set down the razor, and situated him with his back to the port windows, so that the gaping doorway lay behind her. She pushed him against the chair back and picked up the brush and bowl.

The chair was comfortable, Cecco noted, and it was covered in a thick towel. But he eyed the blade. "I suppose you are used to wielding that razor?"

"Oh, no, Sir. This is a service I can render to you that I have never performed for any man before."

His smile flashed before she might cover it with lather. "I appreciate the thought, but I will await the result before thanking you."

With caressing fingertips, she brushed the hairs from his forehead. "After your shave, I'll loosen your hair and comb it for you. I've never seen it down before. And then you can show me how you like it bound."

"You favor me with your attentions, Lady. As I demanded that you do."

Her smile disappeared. "As I *desire* to do."

He cocked his head, assessing her sincerity. "Yes. So I see. You do not disappoint me."

She drew breath at her captain's words, so loving and familiar, words Hook himself had used. Fighting off the ache for her missing master, she turned the conversation to business. "I sent Liza away while you were sleeping, Captain. She'll see that Mr. Yulunga brings your sea chest— but not too soon." She mixed the lather in its bowl, trying to ignore the other sea chest just behind her lover. She had been relieved this morning when the tapping she thought she heard all night resolved itself into Liza's knock.

"Ah, so you have seen to everything! I will need my finest breeches. And also, a few trinkets to replace some others I have lost."

Jill stopped stirring. As her new bracelets ceased to jingle, she looked in his dusky eyes. "Nothing you give to me is lost…Sir."

He grasped her hand below the shaving brush. "*Bellezza*. What would I not do for you?"

A dart of pain shot through her as she remembered Smee's words in the night. *I'd have done anything for you, Lady*…Steadily, she applied the shaving brush and buried the memory under the lather on Cecco's chin. "All I require you *not* to do at the moment is to move while I am occupied with this razor." She set down the bowl and held the blade poised above his beard.

"Then do not tempt me." With his hand, he restrained the razor.

"But we have much to do today, Madam. First, we will present ourselves to the company. The men will want to see us emerge from the master's quarters—" his eyes communicated his meaning, "Together."

Ship's matters came first, and pleased that Cecco felt the same, Jill delayed his grooming. "Aye, Sir. I'll wear the gold dress if it pleases you." Hook had taught her to think, and to strategize. She had determined exactly what issues must be addressed, but allowed the captain to take the lead.

"Certainly, the golden dress, to match your new jewelry."

"And next, Sir?"

"After the breakfast for which I am famished, I will make rounds of the ship. Then we will meet with our officers."

Jill smiled. *Our* officers.

"I will appoint Mr. Mullins second mate, and Mr. Starkey to quartermaster. I have a few more items to resolve regarding the ship's affairs, and then I will set a new course."

"You will speak with the surgeon, Sir?"

"Yes. But first you will tell me more of his story. And after I talk with him, he will clearly understand my expectations." Cecco's eyes were cold. "There will be no more of the reading lessons."

"I am relieved to hear it."

"I may grant him a new trial period, which will of course last only until I decide what to do with him. If he troubles you, his 'time' will be over."

"Thank you, Sir. But please guard yourself. I have learned that where I am concerned, the gentleman is untrustworthy."

"I am touched by your concern. But again, I assure you that you need not worry."

Both pleasant and painful, an echo of Hook's silken voice accompanied her answer— Hook's own answer, once upon a time: "I never worry. I prepare."

"You are too young to be so wise. There is an old gypsy woman in your soul."

"And a fine gypsy man in my bed! Surely, Sir, the best of all possible worlds." The best of a world that didn't harbor Hook.

"You flatter me very much, but I will not be distracted from our business. As for the surgeon's daughter, the men believe the girl to be unlucky. You will explain to me in detail the trouble she has caused, and if I deem it advisable afterward, she may continue to serve you."

"You will lend her your protection?"

"Until you tire of her."

"And then?"

"She is now of age to be useful in other ways." Watching Jill's eyes widen, Cecco shook his head. "No, I would not lower your standing among the company. Your Miss is not interesting to me, except as a bargaining chip."

"I am grateful for that. And…Mr. Smee?"

"As you commanded, his punishment is to mend the door. I anticipate no more problems from him. But Mr. Yulunga will be watching."

Jill hid her qualms; only time could teach her to trust Captain Cecco's officer one fraction of the way Hook trusted Smee. Time was required, also, for those who loved Jill to count on Captain Cecco. And try as she might, Jill couldn't foretell when, if ever, Captain Hook might be found. They must all cope, from one hour to the next. She said, "And with your agreement, I will speak to my sons. Nibs, at least, needs his mind set at ease. But perhaps the most important point— the hold is empty, Captain. The men will be watching to see how quickly you fill it."

"As I have said, you are a shrewd woman."

"And you, Sir, are a shrewd master. One who merits my respect."

"Lady, in spite of all I implied before the company yesterday, you would have made a fine captain."

"Captain Cecco….We vied for the position, and you out-maneuvered me. You deserve the post."

The captain smiled. "Together, we will run a tight ship." He gestured to his chin. "Finish this shave now, so that we may get on with our ventures."

"Sir, I will begin, and you may let me know if you change your mind about hurrying."

Captain Cecco must be taught to trust, too. Jill set down the razor and stood in front of him, swirling the shaving brush in its bowl, and as she applied it to his face, an abundance of warm, soapy lather dribbled down his neck and his chest. She dipped the brush again, and held it suspended over his thighs so that it dripped liberally there, too. As he reached for the towel she stopped him, set down the bowl, and drew his arms around her waist. He tried to kiss her again, lather and all, but she pulled away.

"No! Sir, you are all soapy. I refuse to kiss such a face."

He raised his eyebrows. "You dare to deny me?"

"I do, Sir." She moved closer and straddled his lap. The gown behind her draped from her shoulders to the floor, rubbing against his shins and shielding her lovely backside from sight while the pleasing aspect of her front delighted him. "But I am a passionate woman. I won't wait for this task to be done. You'll have to think of another way to touch me while I work, so that I can tend to *all* your personal needs."

Cecco required no more prompting, and the lather on his legs made it easy. Dropping his hands to her hips, he slid her closer.

His eyes grew dusky again. "With courage she defies me, and with grace she serves me. The perfect woman."

As she leaned forward and positioned him, he lifted her and set her down, gradually, keeping one eye cocked for the razor. She sucked in her breath. Seizing the blade, she leveled her gaze on his whiskers and steadied her hand.

It was a tricky business, but worth every nerve-wracking moment. The soap required fresh application every few strokes and, possibly because she had never performed this task before, it didn't always end on Cecco's beard. A good measure of lather transferred itself from his breast to hers. Exhibiting a worthy conscientiousness, he dealt with it until she relinquished the brush, and then both partners painted each other with sudsy fluid. When at last she wielded the razor again, she had to steady herself many times. Bracing her feet on the floor on either side of the stool, she raised up for a better view of his face…only to lower herself slowly, exquisitely, down again…to inspect under his chin. For two very good reasons, Cecco informed her that she had, indeed, changed his mind about hurrying, and the operation took quite a bit of time after all. But as Jill had ordered, no one disturbed their intimacy, and by the time his mistress allowed him to apply the towel, they were both dizzy, and the captain was clean-shaven, smiling, and slightly nicked.

He didn't care. As the blade in her crimson hand scraped his stubborn whiskers, he hadn't felt a thing. Except her love for him— liquid, warm…and soapy.

The sailors gave up any attempt at pretense. All the tasks on deck that could be done had been performed, three times. Even the flags were inspected and refolded. The black flag, Jolly Roger, was down as usual, waiting for the moment he'd be rattled up for action. The men were blatantly watching the portal where, months before, a lovely, disheveled girl had entered. That girl had emerged as a queen. Now, in spite of their confidence in their captain, the crewmen wondered not whether the woman would reappear, but whether her mate this time might prove to be a consort, or a king.

Those aloft hauled sails about in accordance with the helmsman's calls, but their heads bobbed like all the others', turning time and again to glimpse the doorway to the master's cabin. The empty bottles had been cleared away, the deck swabbed, and the spent torches pitched overboard to avoid displeasing the captain with any lack of discipline. No one wanted to be the first to try him, or test his intimidating first mate. Now they milled about, stacking and restacking cannonballs, cleaning weapons, eyeing the companionway and each other.

Tom polished the bell on the quarterdeck, taking pleasure in the pungent scent of the paste, and dawdling because his position afforded a fine view of the master's door. On Smee's instruction, Nibs had lowered himself off the stern to patch that part of the hull that snagged Captain Hook's coat yesterday. The task completed, he hauled himself up to hike over the rail and join his brother at his advantageous perch. Like Tom, Nibs' features were tense, but Nibs retained a brooding scowl.

Every so often, Liza's head popped up from the hatch, and she surveyed the scene before she disappeared again to inform her father of the activities. She was pale today, recovering from some ailment or other, and limping. But she'd reported to the mistress as both her duty and her curiosity demanded, following the lady's soft-spoken orders for hot water, the captain's sea chest, and time. The girl was disappointed not to get another look at the man in the captain's bunk, but seeing the steel in her mistress' eye, she didn't dare to cross her. Apparently Jill realized the girl had been punished for last night's spying, and reserved further castigation until routine aboard the *Roger* was reestablished.

Smiling ominously, Mr. Yulunga had amused himself by teasing the girl about the loss of her pearls. Then he took a perverse pleasure in making her repeat her mime until he admitted he understood the order to fetch the captain's sea chest. Having delivered it, the first mate loitered at the base of the companionway, leaning against the stair rail and picking his teeth with a splinter.

Today he found himself ogling the girl with fresh interest. The new regimen seemed to pique her old curiosity about the men, and she demonstrated more pluck than she'd shown since Jill confined her for calling attention to herself. Smirking, Yulunga recognized that Liza, too, liked to stir things up. By now, the entire ship's company knew of her spying, and speculation as to her impression of what she'd witnessed was rampant. Watching her movements, Yulunga also kept his eyes open for signs of the surgeon and the bo'sun, but neither had ascended to the deck as yet.

Those who rose early had watched Hanover curiously when he turned up at breakfast. Evidently his appetite had increased since last night's ordeal, for he dished up almost a double ration before ensconcing himself once again in his quarters. Mr. Smee, after issuing his orders to Nibs, disappeared into the carpenter's shop, where he was grimly gathering tools and materials for repairs to the captain's entryway. The last item he picked up caused the big man to hang his head and deal again with his heavy heart. It was the screwdriver he would need to execute the unspoken worst of the lady's order. In the bo'sun's fist, this simplest of implements would dismantle the last vestige of Captain James Hook's power— an august brass plaque on a meaningless door.

At last, just as Smee tramped up from the lower deck with his boards and carpenter's box, Yulunga uncrossed his arms, shifting to look up the stairs. The murmurs of the company fell quiet. Smee stopped where he stood and followed everyone else's gazes. Nibs nudged his brother, who looked up from his busywork. Tom draped the polishing cloth on the bell, Nibs tightened his kerchief, and they both bent over the quarterdeck rail, leaning forward to behold the new master as he appeared in his doorway. Everyone stared.

Captain Cecco wore a leather vest and boots, striped silk breeches, and a smug smile. With his rise in rank, he had donned his gypsy regalia. Circling his throat was a layered necklace, heavy with linking coins and dangling medallions. Around his head he had tied a fine crimson kerchief, and crowned it with a headdress of similar medallions. It was a crucial moment, and in his men's eyes he appeared as splendid as ever Captain Hook had appeared. While they gazed, the golden band on his biceps glinted in the morning light as he turned away and reached out his arm.

Another arm joined with his. A delicate arm wearing bracelets. The lady's bare feet stepped over the wreckage of the door, her golden taffeta rustled with a flash of petticoat, and then her glorious blue eyes raised up to greet the company. Captain and lady processed along the companionway, linked in unmistakable accord. She bore her usual weapons, her mother-of-pearl-handled pistol and a jeweled dagger, but on her arms that used to beg for bracelets, Red-Handed Jill now sported four thick and golden ovals. Two bright chains graced her neck, and embracing her upper arm, just below the puffed sleeve of her shoulder, gleamed the companion to Cecco's shining armband, molded by his own hand to fit her. The highest hopes of the crowd were satisfied; the suspense dissipated.

Of all the finery the lady wore, the most important, the one most lauded by whistles and calls from her approving crewmen, was her smile. Clearly, Captain Cecco had won the respect of their queen, and earned, in full, the confidence they placed in him. She inclined her head to the men and, with an affectionate stroke, relinquished Cecco's arm. Stepping back a pace, she turned her eyes toward their captain, waiting as expectantly as the rest for his first command.

He squared his shoulders, and his compact, muscular body seemed easily to accommodate the weight of a captain's burden. "Well, men. I trust we all enjoyed the revelry last night." The crowd assented with a hearty chorus of ayes. Captain Cecco's even teeth showed as he smiled. "Now the hold is empty, and treasure awaits us. It is time to get back to work— and make it ours!"

The sounds of approval issued from the throats of his men and from beneath their stamping feet. Jill's heart beat with them, in glad relief. Tom clapped and hollered as readily as the rest, and Nibs was stoic as, watching Jill's face closely, he brought his reluctant hands together, too. Only Mr. Smee remained silent, his arms full of tools, his eyes studying the lady.

But the rumbling of the boards under the sailors' feet disturbed the surgeon in his lair, who started up from his books and seized his medicine bottle on the way to the upper bunk. Chains rattled with a violence as a prisoner jolted to consciousness, too startled this time to control himself. And although his outraged shouts for assistance were drowned by the jubilation on the deck above him, from her perch within the hatch the gray-eyed girl heard his frustration before her father's ether cut it short.

The company's exuberance echoed off the waters and rolled away until, a league to northeast, the scout in *L'Ormonde's* nest swung his spyglass toward the *Roger*, where he could make out nothing clearly on the gilded pirate ship as she sailed except the black flag being hoisted aloft to fly proudly in the breezes.

Jolly Roger had been down, but now he was up and grinning above his crossed swords, ready for anything.

A Comparable Captain

"**M**r. Smee." Jill paused at the door to her quarters and stole a quick look behind her. She and the captain had enjoyed a late breakfast among their cheerful crewmen, and now Cecco was making the rounds of the ship. There wasn't much time.

Smee managed a curt nod, then continued with his work. "Lady." The place smelled pleasantly of newly shaved wood, and curling pieces lay around the bo'sun's feet. Smee had restored the door to usefulness, and now it rested once again on its hinges. Avoiding the lady's eyes, he checked for splinters, running his fingers over the fresh wood. He left the door open.

Jill's voice matched her urgency. "I can't talk with you long. Keeping some distance from you is part of my accord with…the captain."

"You needn't worry. I won't be staying."

She ignored the impulse to lay her hand on the bo'sun, to restrain him. "No, Mr. Smee, you misunderstand. I asked you to fix the door so that I could have a moment to explain—"

"Asked? I'd not be saying you asked me, Lady. Commanded, more like."

"Yes, I'm sorry. Anything less wouldn't do. I had to earn Cecco's confidence."

"As if you hadn't earned more than his confidence by then!"

Jill looked down. "Mr. Smee. I'm doing all I can to preserve the ship." She raised her gaze to his, pursuing him when he moved away. "For Hook."

"I'm glad you're remembering him, anyway."

"Remembering isn't the hard part. It's going on without him."

Smee's gaze wandered out the door, and his chest heaved with his sigh. "Aye. And wondering how he's getting on without us."

"Yes, exactly." Her shoulders relaxed as he seemed to sympathize, but when he eyed her jewelry, she stiffened.

"And *you're* getting on, finally collecting the treasure you wanted."

"I'd gladly give it back—"

"You don't have to be saying it." He gathered his tools.

"I understand, Mr. Smee. His disappearance has hit you as hard as it hit me. But we don't have time to disagree; because you and I have been so close, the men will be watching us. Listen to me, before you have to go."

"Is that a command, too?"

She paused, considering how best to answer, then drew herself up. "If it has to be."

At last he faced her squarely. "All right, Ma'am. What is it you're wanting to tell me?"

Now that she had the opportunity, Jill couldn't think what to say to the man. The speech she had rehearsed escaped her as she stared into the familiar eyes behind his spectacles, perceiving the residue of old distrust, and learning that it lacked his former affection. If she had hoped to find comfort here, she now realized it might be a long time coming. She took what solace she could in the fact that Smee was, at least, listening to her. "Please. You have to keep searching the ship. There must be somewhere we haven't looked. That's your job. Mine is to support Captain Cecco so that as little as possible will have changed when Hook returns to us."

His eyebrows shot upward. "Little? From what I witnessed last night, I'd say *everything's* changed!"

"What hasn't changed is that I am devoted to Hook, and following his orders."

"As unpleasant as they may be!"

"No matter what the circumstances. And as unpleasant as it may be, Mr. Smee, you have to respect the new captain. For Hook's sake, and for your own."

"Did the gypsy tell you to threaten me?"

"Of course not. But you'll do no one any good in the brig. You must retain your position as bo'sun. That's simply common sense, and I say it because you have to hear it."

"Well, I've heard it."

"Smee, you believe I've betrayed the captain. But did you feel betrayed when your Lily opened her home to my twins?"

"Lily was doing the right thing by everyone, and I'm that glad your sons are there to take care of her while I'm gone."

"Don't you think Hook feels the same about me?"

Smee's face flushed. "He might…if he thought it was *me* taking care of you."

"We both did what we thought was right."

"And I have to be wondering, Ma'am, exactly what you're thinking will be the right thing to do with your new consort…once James Hook comes back to claim the *Roger?*"

Her hand hurried to her necklaces. Smee could see in her frightened face that she didn't want to contemplate Cecco's chances. That gypsy had already wormed his way into her heart! Smee's anger made him brutal.

"Never mind, Lady. We both know what'll happen. Someone will end skewered on a sword. *If* Captain Hook comes back."

Her eyes flamed. "Don't ever doubt it!" Then her gaze fell to the tool in his hand. As she realized what he held in the other, anguish twisted her face. She backed away. Smee smiled ironically and held it up for her to see. It flashed, one last time, in the morning sun pouring through the doorway. He read it for her.

"'Capt. Jas. Hook.' "

Jill whirled to face the door. Even needing a coat of paint it was, as always, the majestic entrance to a master's quarters. But it was only that and nothing more; Hook was gone. The hollow inside her heart broke open. She faltered, and staggered back a step.

Seeing the sincerity of the lady's distress, Smee felt the bitterness in his soul budge just a little. He remembered how alone the captain was before he found this woman, and how determinedly Hook worked to win her. How the simple act of desiring her had called forth a mercy for her and her sons that the ruthless man hadn't shown in years. Except for the threatening tears, Jill's eyes still matched the captain's to perfection, and however the struggle ended, Smee had seen her fight with all her strength to hold on to Hook's power.

From the first night of his service to Hook, Smee rooted his faith in the captain's judgment. Hook had interested himself in the feisty Irishman, kept him out of trouble and given him a position of trust. Smee had never known James Hook to misplace his confidence. Hook had been right to trust that young sailor; he had to be right in trusting Jill, too.

Smee relented. And as he did, he felt the relief of sharing his pain. Pain that confirmed the fact that, even in the captain's absence, Hook's two closest companions were linked. As Smee's gaze gentled to really see Jill, her beauty hit him like a sledge. The old urge to hold her returned in force, along with his protective instincts. His thoughts turned again to the lady's needs. Comforting as it might be for her— for both of them— Smee wouldn't touch her. Cecco would tolerate no more interference from the bo'sun who had so publicly objected to Jill's choice. Smee knew the chain of trouble even being seen with her would set in motion. Instead of wrapping his arms around her, he spoke softly and nodded his understanding.

"I'll do what you ask, Lady. For the sake of James Hook, I'll serve the new captain as well as I may. And I'll keep away from you. But if you're ever needing me, how will I know it?"

In grateful relief, Jill sighed. It was good to feel Smee's support sustaining her once more. "I will always need you, Mr. Smee. Just as the captain does. But you will know I'm in trouble…when I wear Hook's ruby necklace."

"*Hook's* necklace?"

"Aye, Smee. If I can only have him back, he can keep his treasure. I'll never want to wear another jewel."

"He'd say that *you're* his treasure, Ma'am." The tears in her eyes made her harder to resist. Smee pressed his arms to his sides. "If I see the rubies, I'll find a way to talk with you. I'd best be going now."

His eyes touched her. Restraining the urge to reach out to him, she smiled in return. It was the best they could do.

While Smee packed up his tools, Liza, wearing a knowing smile, materialized from nowhere to sweep up after him. When Smee left a few moments later, the brass plate nestled in his box, the lady worked at her escritoire across the room, and Captain Cecco was striding toward his quarters. Cecco halted on the companionway to await the bo'sun's greeting. The men of the ship were on guard for this encounter, and many sailors watched from the deck and the rigging.

Smee stopped. With his box slung at his side, he raised his eyes to Cecco's. He awarded him a brief nod. "Cap'n." Aware of the watchers, Smee waited to be dismissed. It hurt his pride, but he'd done worse work for Hook.

As was his habit in earlier days, Cecco read the look on the Irishman's face as the man left the master's cabin. Cecco smiled to himself, confident that his new mistress had put his bo'sun in his place. From now on, business could be conducted in civility. Jill was adept in the ways of leadership; she had handled Mr. Smee. Cecco returned Smee's greeting, and the two men passed.

Cecco was adept, too. He had known Jill also needed that moment with Smee to settle herself. And now she needed Cecco. Her devoted captain would have recognized her need even if she hadn't risen immediately upon his entrance, or her arms decked in his gold hadn't stretched toward him, nor her beautiful eyes begged for his comfort.

He shunted Liza out, noting the absence of Hook's plaque as he did so. Shutting the door, he tried it to be sure the bo'sun had properly performed the job, and then he turned to his woman. His voice was tender.

"*Bellezza*. Your captain is here." He accepted her crimson hand and guided her to the window seat, and as they sat there, the sunshine of their first day together soaked into their backs.

When she was sure his arms wouldn't abandon her, she asked, "Sir, may I tell you a lie?"

"Certainly. As I myself know, if one wishes to tell the truth, nothing is so useful as a lie."

Hesitant, she smiled, then the words burst out with a sigh. "I wish with all my heart that you were still my sailor!"

Cecco laughed. "You, lovely storyteller, are too truthful to lie successfully. I will say it for you. You wish that you could remain faithful to each of the men you love."

As her lips parted in surprise, he kissed them, and he collected the fervent surge of her gratitude. As he had boasted, Captain Cecco was a man who understood women. His understanding served him well.

She returned his embrace. Sometimes she kissed him; sometimes she kissed Hook. And sometimes…

"Mr. Smee." Captain Cecco's medallions stirred as he cocked his head. "You have a concern to mention?"

Smee watched as the afternoon sunlight bounced off the sea to swirl on the ceiling. He stood before the desk, his hands clasped behind his waist. Next to him were Mr. Mullins and Mr. Starkey, who had accepted chairs. Mr. Yulunga stood at the side of the desk, at the captain's left. Jill sat enthroned on Cecco's right, opposite Mr. Smee.

The bo'sun pulled his gaze from the ceiling to focus on the captain. "I'm agreeing with all you've said, Sir. I only have one question— about the post of ship's surgeon."

"Ah, yes. Doctor Hanover. The lady has informed me of Captain Hook's plans regarding him. Like our former commander, I find the 'gentleman' to be untrustworthy. Be that as it may, the surgeon is of value to me. I intend to make him a member of ship's company this afternoon."

All the officers registered surprise. Only Smee voiced it. He cleared his throat first.

"You mean to be saying, Sir, that you *know* his intentions toward the lady, and you'll be letting him live?"

"I have found it rewarding to keep my enemies close. But it is the lady who asked me to spare him." Cecco turned to her. "Jill has my full permission to end his life at whatever time and in whatever manner she sees fit."

"Thank you, Captain." Jill's crimson hand fingered her dagger. Her smile was colder than any of these men had ever seen it. Even so, Smee had to fight the instinct to protest on the grounds of her safety. He knew he'd have to trust her judgment, and watch for the rubies.

But it seemed the new captain was ahead of him, and equally concerned for Jill's welfare. "On Captain Hook's orders, the lady led Hanover to believe she would leave the ship with him and become his wife. On *my* orders, Mr. Yulunga informed him otherwise. Ever since I assumed the captaincy, Hanover has known that the lady deceived him. If he signs the ship's articles, he will remain at liberty."

Smee stepped closer to the desk. "But Captain, we know from the lady's conversations with Hanover that his pledge means nothing!"

"This is the reason I want you all to be on guard for treachery. Until he shows himself to be dangerous, we will use him to our advantage."

Jill didn't question the wisdom of allowing Hanover to sign on. Instead, her prompting worked more subtly. "Sir, what of his partner, Captain LeCorbeau?"

"Another reason not to alienate our surgeon. As long as Hanover is nominally free and in good health, LeCorbeau is at my mercy. The Frenchman cannot reap enough plunder by simply following the *Roger*. No doubt he anxiously awaits the moment he can take Hanover aboard *L'Ormonde* to resume their very lucrative trade in the doctor's love potion."

"But how does this delay benefit us?" asked Jill. "If you intend for the surgeon to purchase his freedom, why not offer it now?"

"My lovely one, I have a larger prize in mind." Cecco turned to face his men. "It will be highly profitable for us when, in the end, LeCorbeau gives up and in desperation agrees to pay— not only the ransom I will demand for the surgeon's return, but a continuing tribute from their future earnings."

As Cecco cast his gaze from officer to officer, his sly smile spread. He watched the gratification grow in each set of eyes. Clearly, he had impressed them with his canny plan. Even Mr. Smee looked upon him with admiration.

"Captain!" Jill's face lit up with a reverent warmth that increased as she anticipated the riches Cecco would haul in at the conclusion of his scheme. "An admirable strategy."

"Aye!" said Mullins. But he speculated, "Still, it might have been easier to keep the man in check, Sir, had he not been advised of the lady's deception."

Cecco shrugged. "This is unimportant, Mr. Mullins. I have made a study of the man. His pride alone will keep him in check. The surgeon's obstinacy is such that he will continue to strive for the lady's favor, and his arrogance will find a reason to believe she wishes to escape with him. But this way, Jill is relieved of his attentions, and authorized to defend herself if need be."

"And what exactly will the gentleman be told?" Yulunga asked. "He has found access to the lady before."

"But only with the lady's encouragement." Cecco's dark eyes rolled toward Jill. His voice was smooth. "And of course, as agreed in our accord, there will be no more of this."

Jill looked down and, in a graceful motion, inclined her head.

"After I speak with him, the surgeon will be either a pirate or a prisoner. And he will understand that the lady is forbidden to communicate with him and he is forbidden to question her— with dire consequences if he dares. What better way to prolong a man's fascination than to keep him guessing? Yes, men, I expect the doctor's full cooperation."

Less coolly this time, Yulunga said, "But Sir, what of the girl?"

"Ah, Mr. Yulunga. I have spoken with the lady."

At the captain's nod, Jill answered his mate. "I am considering the wisdom of granting your request, Mr. Yulunga. I acknowledge that the presence of a girl aboard ship has proven unlucky. Captain Cecco feels it is too soon to ask her consent, and as I made clear to you yesterday…there will be no slaves upon the *Roger*."

The captain concurred. "Whatever the girl's wishes, offending the doctor at this point would be unluckier than keeping things as they are. I am afraid you must exercise patience, my friend." Cecco's gaze caressed his own woman. "I myself can tell you that waiting for such a prize makes the taking of it sweeter."

With obvious appreciation, Yulunga acknowledged his captain's treasure. "Aye, Sir, so I see."

Smee shifted his weight.

Cecco said, "Until then, the former prohibition applies. Any man who touches young Miss will find himself harshly punished. Mr. Yulunga, you will make this law known to the crew."

"I will, Sir. But you should understand that the girl is growing bolder. And all the men are talking about her intrusion on your privacy."

"Then the men must see to it that *she* exercises patience, as well. As for your request for quarters, Mr. Yulunga, I will put off that change for now. The surgeon enjoys to employ the spare cabin for consultations when his daughter is in his room, and I wish to use it as a balm to placate him when he learns of the restrictions I am imposing upon him. Those quarters will be yours once we have settled this business of Hanover and LeCorbeau. And we can afford to spend time on this scheme. If we play it out properly, Hanover will pay us a very high price…" he paused, "for the *lady's* freedom, as well."

Staring in surprise, Jill caught on immediately. "And once the price is paid and I am free, I will, of course, choose to stay aboard the *Roger*." Her expression grew guarded. "There are, however, many ways to communicate beyond words. Does this mean, Captain, that you wish me to use indirect methods to encourage the surgeon?"

"There is no need. The man's imagination will do this for us. I ask only that you try not to kill him before we can collect our reward." Captain and lady smiled at one another.

Mullins sat back and tucked his thumbs in his belt, a broad smile across his face. "Captain Cecco, you're as wily as Hook ever was, and that's as high a compliment as I can give!"

"Aye, Sir." Yulunga shook his head in wonderment, "I knew you were the man for the job! You always seize your opportunities. We will have more riches than we can spend, whether the hold is full or not."

Reluctantly, Smee grinned. "Aye, Captain. A plan worthy of Hook himself." As Smee's gaze slid to the lady, he saw through her elation. Ready for her next adventure, she gazed adoringly at Cecco, impressed and pleased for the company's good fortune. But now that Smee had forgiven her, he could plainly see that on the other side of her smile, she was grieving. Faced with the evidence of Cecco's skill, Smee was beginning to understand how Hook's Jill could feel two opposite things at once. Cecco was good for the *Roger*, and proving to be very like the man she loved. And the more Cecco resembled Hook, the more Jill must be tearing herself apart. In some ways, it might have been easier for her if the new captain was overbearing and incapable. Instead, intending only to wait for Hook, the lady sensed that circumstances were conspiring to replace him. Smee looked away from Jill before she might catch his eye and read the sympathy on his face. Knowing that Smee acknowledged the situation might make it too real for her to bear.

Captain Cecco made it real for Smee just then. "Mr. Smee. I regret that it will be necessary for you to give up your keys. As bo'sun, you must have your own set which can be made, along with a set for me, next time we are in port. But as first mate, Mr. Yulunga must carry these keys now."

"Aye, Sir." Smee reached into his pocket. "Here you are, Mr. Yulunga; the keys to the shackles, the armory, the brig…and to the master's quarters." His voice had lowered, but showing no other hint of his reluctance, he tossed the key ring.

It jingled as Yulunga caught it. "Thank you, Mr. Smee."

Watching Smee's face, Jill kept her own features neutral. For both of them, the missing set of keys was a painful reminder of Hook's disappearance. She felt another layer of security strip itself away as Hook's officer relinquished the key to her quarters to this disquieting sailor. Although Cecco trusted Mr. Yulunga, Jill couldn't help but shiver as she remembered the man's history and his suggestion yesterday that she make herself available to the men. On top of that, her own recommendation blocked his pursuit of Liza. Jill welcomed the distraction when Cecco clasped her hand, addressing his men once again.

"The last order of business concerns Red-Handed Jill. I want it to be understood by you, my officers, and you will make it clear to all aboard. Unless the lady's orders conflict with my own, she is to be obeyed immediately, and without question."

Cecco looked intently at each man in turn, receiving from every one an "Aye, Captain," before moving on. When he was satisfied, he prepared to dismiss them. "Good. As this ransom scheme is perhaps too subtle to satisfy the crew, I wish to take a prize at the first opportunity. Be ready.

"Mr. Yulunga, escort the lady from our quarters. You will then bring the surgeon to me and remain with us while we come to terms. And see that he brings his instruments." Cecco stood, assisting Jill to rise. After pressing a kiss into her hand, he smiled into her sparkling eyes. "I believe the surgeon's medicine bag holds the cure to all our ailments."

His body was perfect. Even asleep, he was the handsomest man she'd ever seen. The only man, except for Tom, she'd ever touched. As Liza lay beside Hook, she touched him now.

Listening for signs of impending interruption, she paused a moment, but she heard only the water on the hull and the crooning of the *Roger*'s beams. The hour was well past lunchtime, and no sailors hung about the galley. Her curious fingers continued their exploration, following the outline of her master's muscular arms, and then she pulled up his shirt and spread her fingers over his chest, feeling the coarse black hairs rough over his smooth skin. She ran her hands down to his waist, and then around to his back. It was smooth, too, and the least bit damp with perspiration. Pressing her lips to his stomach, she kissed him, and the warmth of his flesh made her mouth tingle. His salty, leathery scent filled her lungs as she breathed him in.

She sat up, grimacing because of the bruises on her thighs and, once again, drew his sleeve above his wrist. Beneath the fine lace of his cuff, his wound emerged, a repulsive gash of scarred, misshapen flesh. Liza had cringed and squinted the first time, but it was easier to look at now. One day she would touch it.

Having his hand cut off must have been excruciating. How had he endured it? And the tattoos— how much pain had they caused him? During the commotion yesterday, as the men elected a new captain, she'd had plenty of time to study the image of the grinning Jolly Roger on his upper arm before her father replaced his shirt, and now she used her opportunity to gaze on the mermaid above his severed wrist. She wondered if it was tattooed on his arm before the loss of his hand, or after.

The sea creature was enchanting. She looked like Jill. Like Liza! The girl had paid attention to her mirror. As Jill had predicted, Liza blossomed like an exotic bloom in the unconstrained environment of the pirate ship. She lacked only one experience to make her a woman. Her father hadn't remembered, but this was her birth month, and she was giving herself that experience as a present. She was unwrapping it now!

If only he were awake, they could pick up where they left off, before her father came bursting in. Shuddering, Liza recalled the sickening crack of the cane against her master's skull, worse to hear than the smack across her legs later in the night. It was her fault Hook had been struck. When he woke, he might be angry with her. But Liza *had* intended to lock the door. In the excitement of the moment she had forgotten. The locked door wouldn't have made much difference anyway, except that Hook would have killed her father if he'd heard him coming. Liza wasn't sure if she preferred it that way or this way, with the captain in her bed and all to herself. At least she didn't have to share him with the mistress anymore. Jill had her own man. Liza didn't really care if Jill's man was Captain Cecco or her father. Liza had Hook.

The doctor made sure the pirate was asleep before he left on Cecco's summons, and although she hoped otherwise, Liza believed Hook wouldn't come to consciousness for a long while. Taking his face in her hands as she had seen Jill do, she kissed him— because she could, because he was beautiful. Because he was hers. Maybe, as in a fairy tale, he would awaken to true love's kiss. She smirked at the idea, scorning its childishness. She was old enough to know such stories never came true. It wasn't her love, but her desire to serve that would earn this man's attention.

Sliding her hands lower, she stroked the unshaven whiskers on his jaw and on his neck. This throat was the source of the velvety voice that intoxicated her— silent now, to her sorrow. Had he heard her own voice calling to him as he slipped into unconsciousness? If her sound had pleased him, she must talk for him again, but she would wait until he commanded her to speak, for she had heard her father's admonition many times; an intelligent woman holds her tongue. Then, banishing the thought of her father, Liza brushed her fingers over the short black beard and mustache that shaped themselves neatly around Hook's mouth. Rubbing her cheek against him, she gloried in the way the bristles scraped her skin. Every touch of him informed her— he felt like a man should feel.

And Liza felt like a woman. Last night when her father had finally fallen asleep, she shucked off her nightdress and nestled against the captain. Careful not to rattle his chains, she had settled one aching leg on top of his and lain on his chest, listening to his heart beating, strong and slow, feeling his lungs rise and fall under her breasts. His long wavy hair sifted silkily through her fingers until, in the earliest light, she dressed herself again. When her father checked on her, she was lying on the edge of the bunk, as ordered, with a rolled up blanket between them, so that he wouldn't carry out his initial threat of making her sleep in the spare cabin. But Liza wasn't worried about that notion. She knew her father dreaded any change in routine that might draw questions from their shipmates. Everything had to seem normal; Captain Hook was their secret. And Liza would seize her chances. After her master had made love to her, it would be too late for her father to do anything about it, and Liza would belong to Hook forever. If only she could awaken him, he could take her now!

Liza drew his arm toward her. It was heavy, made more so by the chain that bound him. Pulling his hand close, she freed up the links, extending their reach. Their music amused her as she worked one of his rings off his fingers. She lay back and tried the ring on her own hand. The extravagant jewel bobbled loosely around her finger. Wondering what had become of her pearls, Liza decided it didn't really matter. The little ring used to bring her comfort, in memories of her mother. Now, having seen more of the world, Liza recognized how weak her mother had been. Long before she died, the woman had abandoned Liza; the life had left her delicate frame, dwindling as her husband developed his contacts and found rich investors in his product— and employed that product, increasingly, on his wife. Although Liza's mother paid the ultimate price for her husband's success, she and Liza had become secondary, mere pretexts for the great doctor's career.

Playfully, Liza twirled Hook's big ring. No, the little pearls didn't matter at all. After Liza's plans became reality, she would have plenty of chances to earn richer treasures, like this one. She admired the ring. Raising herself up on one elbow, she watched it sparkle as her fingers toyed with his earring, too. Appraising its golden filigree, she decided that she would pierce her own ears soon. As soon as Mr. Yulunga gave her the earrings he promised this morning. He'd started in provoking her when he noticed that her pearls were gone. Then, with his black eyes shining and his face one wide, menacing smile, he tormented her about delivering the lady's orders to him, pretending he didn't understand Liza's signals.

But it would be worth more of his teasing to show off a fine set of earrings. And his voice was so low and rich, quite pleasant to hear. Yulunga was good-looking in an unusual way, and much bigger than her captain. Like Hook, he had scars— Liza envied the slash-mark cut by the master's claw on his shoulder, showing plainly to whom he belonged— and he bore circles all around his ankles and wrists, scored into his mahogany skin by the shackles of his slave days. His chest was satiny, with no hair upon it at all. His flesh would feel different from Hook's. Maybe tomorrow, if she smiled at Yulunga, his fluid voice would grant her permission to touch him, and she could compare. The idea of touching him made her salivate. Her mind whirled to think of it.

And then Liza lost the train of her thoughts, because directly under her chin, a pair of blue eyes blazed into awareness, and the chain jangled as his hand snapped up to seize her by the throat and press her backward into the pillow.

Hook was awake. And angry.

The tip of the quill scratched over the paper. Hanover finished with a flourish. Jabbing the pen into its stand, he stood proudly. "There you have it, Captain Cecco. My signature in your book." He faced the Italian, tugging his waistcoat into place. "I hope there will be no more distrust between us."

Seated comfortably in his chair behind the desk, Cecco smiled. "None at all. I now have complete confidence in my ship's surgeon. I am certain you will serve me to the best of your abilities."

"And I am certain you will prove an admirable captain." Hanover had mastered his resentment; a cool head would best accomplish his purpose.

"Having witnessed your discomfort in the port of Gao, I am sure you are relieved that there will be no more need for the shackles in your quarters."

Hanover startled and blinked. "You…you intend to have them removed, then?"

The doctor was not as free as he imagined, and Cecco was pleased that the girl provided an excuse to preserve the means to restrain him. "I apologize, Doctor, but I intend to leave the manacles. My lady has had occasion to confine your daughter before, and the girl's behavior last night has caused us to doubt her obedience." He indicated a chair. "Please, sit down and have a drink with me while we discuss the situation."

With a brusque "Thank you," Hanover sat down. Yulunga offered a cup of wine, and the gentleman accepted it. Hanover cast a look around the master's quarters, lingering fondly on the window seat on which Jill had granted him little liberties. He remembered the taste of the red strawberries, and the sweeter taste of her matching fingertips. When summoned by Cecco, Hanover had hoped Jill would be present at this interview. He was soon disappointed. Only a trace of her perfume lingered in her quarters, but it was enough to keep hope alive that she might return at any moment, and as Yulunga had indicated a need for the medicine bag, Hanover believed the lady had contrived an excuse to speak with him again. Perhaps she was already changing her mind about Captain Cecco. Perhaps she required more of the sleeping draught. And whether this was the case or no, how pleased she would be that, at last, her lover had signed on with her pirates!

For Hanover had determined. He *would* be her lover— in every respect— as soon as he could find a way to get her alone. After much soul-searching, he had determined that no honor could be lost by consummating their alliance now. Already tarnished by her liaisons with two pirate captains, the woman was far from innocent, and her fiancé had every intention of marrying her in the end. If making love to her hastened that moment, Hanover would possess her at the very next opportunity, drawing her into his power and salvaging his pride at the same time. And, by now, he knew better than to ask her permission first. Just like two of the other pirates who had signed that book, he would simply take her.

Captain Cecco studied his ship's surgeon before the pleasant atmosphere dissolved. Although the man must be roiling inside, his generous lips were smiling, and he looked much the same as always. Today he wore the gray suit. Tomorrow he would find it necessary to wear the beige. Sealed primly shut, the medicine bag sat by the doctor's soft leather shoes. On the man's cheek the dueling scar stood prominent, and his sandy hair was pulled back, secured by the black ribbon, as if the physician was concerned with keeping every hair in place. Cecco's gypsy instincts alerted him to the removal of the wedding ring on the very day it happened, the first day in the port of Gao, when he had guarded Hanover in his quarters, watching as the doctor twisted his confusion into rage— and then repressed it.

But the cause of that rage, Captain Hook, was now gone. Hanover's most recent anger had been directed toward Jill and Cecco. To his credit, he seemed to have released his grudge. With Yulunga in attendance, Cecco began to test the man's limits.

"Doctor Hanover, returning to the subject of your daughter. Jill is distressed to discover that the girl may be more trouble than her service is worth. The men inform me of a boldness in her demeanor, and you are already aware of last night's indiscretion. I am certain you interpreted my lady's courageous command to leave our door open as a symbolic gesture. We did not intend for our intimacies to be observed."

"I offer you and the lady my sincere apologies for Liza's shocking lapse. I can only attribute it to youthful curiosity, and…well, the circumstances aboard a pirate ship are after all not ideal for bringing up a young girl." As the memory of Hook's assault on his daughter flashed through his mind, Hanover congratulated himself for delivering this understatement so successfully.

"Yes. I regret that as your captain, I must caution you to keep the girl in line from now on."

However unfair, this aspect of the conversation worked in the doctor's favor. He pursued it. Thanks to Liza's misadventures, the chains would not be disturbed, and to keep Hook's imprisonment secret, it would be necessary to guard him almost constantly. "In that case, you will be pleased that I have instructed my daughter to keep to our quarters as much as possible."

Cecco drained his wine and signaled to Yulunga to pour again. "You please me very much, Doctor. I see that we will be able to move beyond any bad feeling that yesterday's events occasioned."

"I would not have signed on as your officer if I believed otherwise."

"To demonstrate my goodwill, Doctor Hanover, I will allow you to voice your opinion before I make my next decision. Regarding the spare quarters next to your own."

The surgeon's attention focused. "Indeed?" Hanover disguised his anxiety behind a sip of wine. If that cabin was taken over, the risk of someone overhearing the missing captain would be too great.

"Yes. Now that Mr. Yulunga is promoted to first officer, he has requested those quarters. I am inclined to grant his wish, yet I observe that the room is useful to you in your professional duties."

"It certainly is! You know from your own experience that the men prefer to consult me in a place apart from my daughter. And as I have just promised, from today Liza will be confined to our quarters more frequently."

"Your point is well taken. Mr. Yulunga, your private quarters must wait— until other arrangements are made for Miss Hanover."

Standing by the desk, Yulunga simply said, "Aye, Sir. As you advised, some things are worth waiting for."

Trying to read his expression, the surgeon watched cautiously, puzzled by the satisfied smile that marked the black face instead of the belligerence he had often witnessed there. It seemed Captain Cecco exerted influence over the fearsome African, authority similar to that of Captain Hook's. "Thank you, Captain, and Mr. Yulunga, for your understanding. And…I'm afraid I must beg one more instance of your indulgence."

Cecco's hand waved with a tinkle of gold. "Please."

"As you are aware, the one concession Captain Hook made to me and my daughter was to place our quarters off limits to the rest of the company. It is my hope that you will continue this courtesy."

The Italian smiled his easy gypsy smile. "These simple arrangements are the least we can do, Doctor Hanover, when you exhibit such equanimity in the face of defeat."

"I have learned to be philosophical. In the course of my career, for instance, matters have not always arranged themselves to my satisfaction. Yet, over time, perseverance has always served me."

"You will do well to continue directing your perseverance in the arena of your profession. Red-Handed Jill will no longer be available to you."

Hanover felt his pockets for Jill's handkerchief. Sorry for its loss, he grasped his watch instead. "I did not intend to imply—"

"It is a powerful thing, the emotion a woman such as my Jill can inspire in men! And so unfortunate that because of our emotions, you and I were compelled to disregard our friendship and deceive one another."

"A regrettable truth."

"As we begin our mutually rewarding arrangement as members of the *Roger*'s brotherhood, I must lay down some rules. I am sure that as my lady's former suitor, you will understand as I impose some restrictions on you both."

Having prepared himself for this inevitability, Hanover remained calm. "Yes, Captain. I understand."

"You are, of course, at liberty to stroll the deck each morning, as has been your custom."

Delighted, Hanover smiled.

"But, of course, my lady will no longer join you."

The smile faded. "…Very well."

"If you wish to continue the reading lessons for your daughter, I have no objection. You will, however, conduct them in your own quarters."

Here Hanover raised his eyebrows.

"Without my lady."

The surgeon inhaled. "I see that Jill has been frank with you."

"You will not speak her name so casually."

Taken aback, Hanover conceded, "Again, Sir, I apologize."

"My lady has no other choice than to be frank with me." Taking another taste of wine, Cecco lingered, savoring the tension as the doctor sat rubbing his watch. "She urged me to remind you that she has been consistently honest with you, as well."

"Yes.…The lady may rest assured that I am aware of her candor." He himself would tell her the same thing, when—

"You will not speak to my lady again."

"Sir?" Hanover ceased to stroke his watch.

"I have forbidden Jill to communicate with you. I now forbid you to speak or write to her."

"But…we are shipmates.…How it will be possible to carry out such an order?"

"You are a clever man, Doctor. You will find a way."

"I feel I must ask.…Is this order prompted by the lady's request, or by your desire to control her?"

The layers of medallions that circled Cecco's neck glowed golden. "Can any man control that woman? It has been proven only that *you* could not."

Hanover glanced at Yulunga before replying. "Out of respect to the pledge I just made to you, Captain, I choose to disregard your insinuation."

"A wise decision, Doctor."

"But I must protest this severe penance for the sin of courting Red-Handed Jill. You can hardly blame me for feeling as I did!"

"I do not blame you; I simply inform you that your hopes are at an end."

"Regardless of my hopes, I fail to understand how, living in such close quarters, we can avoid speaking to one another."

Cecco set his cup on the glossy surface of his desk. He followed it with his dagger, which he clapped down smartly. "Any of my men can tell you. I have a reputation for my carving skills."

Hanover stared at the knife.

"I will not wait to ask the questions first. Any association between you and Red-Handed Jill will earn your disfigurement."

The surgeon's face paled, his scar darkened. He set down his cup. "You might have mentioned this before I—"

"You have been warned."

Hanover gripped the arms of his chair.

"The lady is mine now, and I will afford you no opportunity to steal her."

Hanover bit back an angry retort, choosing an even tenor. "I am no longer under the illusion that your mistress cares for me. The facts were…laid bare to me last night."

Yulunga snorted.

Cecco allowed an edge to enter his accent. "I find your humor to be in bad taste, Doctor. Further reference to my lady's charms will end my forbearance."

Hanover's scar twitched. "Very well. I am not so foolish as to try you." He reached for his cup and took a steadying swallow. This captain was proving to be nearly as clever as the first!

"And now that we are clear on that subject, one issue only remains to be settled between us."

Hanover experienced a sinking sensation in the vicinity of his stomach, informing him the worst was yet to come. Managing a heartier tone than he felt, he braced himself. "I am at your service, Sir."

"Yes. And to guarantee that service, I require some surety." He motioned to his mate. "Mr. Yulunga, please."

Yulunga strode forward. Under the astonished eyes of the surgeon, he grasped the medicine bag. He shoved the wine cups aside, placed the valise on the desk, and opened it. Stepping back, he positioned himself behind the doctor.

The captain closed the book of ship's articles, then moved the knife and the quill so that the desktop in front of him was clear. With a gesture, he directed the doctor. "Remove the contents, please."

"I don't understand!"

"Among other things, I wish to see this miracle love-potion you have devised."

Hanover drew a deep breath. "You know of my formula, as well. I see." His gray eyes sparked with anger, but he obeyed. He stood and seized the mouth of his bag to yank it wide. Then, gentling his motions, he began to transfer each of the vials to the pirate's desktop. Every click made its impression in the surgeon's soul. When a neat row of bottles stood before Cecco, Hanover said, "These are all of the medicines I carry with me. I keep replenishments in my quarters."

"The instruments, too, please."

"But—" From the determination on Cecco's face, Hanover knew protest would be useless. He bent to his task, and too soon all the tools and symbols of his profession lay displayed for the captain's examination. When the bag was empty, Hanover stood with his chin high, holding his breath and hoping against hope to escape the coming nightmare, praying that Jill had *not* told her captain everything. Perspiring, he strove for an air of calm.

Cecco's gaze moved over the instruments, his eyes narrowing as they contemplated the powders and liquids in their little glass bottles. "And which is the famous philter?"

Not without pride, Hanover indicated a purplish fluid in a plain vial. "This. This is all I have left of it."

"All? Then you will be concocting more?"

"I cannot do so without the key ingredient."

"Ah. The lotus, I believe?"

On the brink of the abyss, Hanover gave only a nod.

"And these others, for what do you prescribe them?"

The surgeon attempted a casual attitude. "There are too many to go into detail— one is a sleeping draught; another a cough remedy. This one is to relieve symptoms of ague, this, for cleansing wounds, this, to settle an upset stomach, and this, for weakness of the lungs and liver— I have dosed *L'Ormonde*'s mate with it. As you may recall, he is due for more treatment."

"You will see to him soon. And this one, of which you have an abundance?"

Hanover considered the large, tightly-corked bottle. "Ether. Very useful in performing painful procedures. I carry an abundance because life at sea requires treatment of many serious injuries."

"And, I believe, too much can be lethal?"

Hiding his urge to use it now, Hanover answered. "Yes."

Cecco looked to Yulunga and, with a ring of his many coins, jerked his head. The African established himself beside the desk, signifying that the doctor should resume his seat. Shifting his gaze between the two men, Hanover did so, balancing uneasily on the edge of his chair. Yulunga took hold of the medicine bag and reached into it.

"What are you doing?"

The captain's accents reassured while his words alarmed. "Please calm yourself, Doctor. Knowing your very interesting history, I find I cannot simply accept your pledge that you will be loyal to me. Mr. Yulunga is merely collecting the surety which I advised you I require." Cecco's gaze was distracted from the surgeon's panicked face as Yulunga yanked out the bag's false bottom.

"No!"

But Yulunga tipped the bag over the desk. A delicious peppering of gems sprinkled the surface. With his eyes shining, Cecco set his arms on either side of the jewels to stop them bouncing away.

The physician watched, in mounting horror, as the pile of treasure grew. Then, from the huge hand of the African slithered the best piece, the bracelet encrusted with diamonds. Next issued a necklace and a watch fob, each set with precious, clear stones, far beyond price. Last of all, as Yulunga gave the bag a final shake, out rolled a plain gold wedding band, and a dainty pearl ring. Yulunga grinned at the sight of the little girl's trinket— modest, indeed, compared with her father's affluence. All three men stared at the pile of brilliants between the captain's forearms.

"Well, Doctor! I understand why you wished to keep this cache a secret! I see that you are concerned it might be taken from you." Cecco shrugged. "Do not worry yourself. Now that you have signed our book, we are brothers in ship's company. As such, none of us may steal from you. All I demand at this moment is assurance that you will remain with the *Roger* and serve her men to your highest capability."

There was nothing to say, and Hanover said it.

Smiling at the opulence shining alongside his bracelets, Cecco spent a moment filling his eyes with the sight, then concluded his business with the physician. "I now grant you a trial period, at the successful end of which I will return your precious treasure. You and your daughter may, of course, keep your sentimental pieces— both of the rings. Mr. Yulunga, you may return the pearls to Miss Hanover. Perhaps they will bring to you the same luck I enjoyed."

Yulunga extracted the rings from the pile, and he smiled as he pocketed the pearls. "Thank you, Captain." He offered the wedding band to the surgeon.

Pale and sweaty, Hanover finally swallowed and reached out for it. He didn't want to ask what luck the pearls had brought to the gypsy, whose self-satisfied smile made his medical officer ill. When he was able to think about it, perhaps he would question Liza.

Cecco said, "You may return your supplies to your valise, Sir. But you are perspiring! Please, feel free to remove your coat. I will not stand on ceremony when one of my worthy officers has experienced such a shock."

It didn't occur to Hanover to slip the wedding ring on his finger. He deposited it in his watch pocket and clenched the arms of his chair. Having lost his athletic grace, he hauled himself to his feet and searched his coat for a handkerchief with which to tamp his dampness. Yulunga said, "Doctor, allow me." He grasped the gray velvet coat collar, sliding the garment from the surgeon's shoulders.

"Yes. Now we will not disturb you as you replace your belongings in your bag." Cecco tossed his dagger to Yulunga.

Catching the knife, the first mate grinned his darkest grin. He held the coat over the captain's desk, then proceeded to rip the satin lining. Within seconds, more diamond drops were raining on the glittering hill.

Hanover flinched at the sound of renting fabric. For one moment, he recalled Hook's claw tearing its way out of its sleeve. As he lowered himself into the chair, he wondered for the hundredth time how he would ever disentangle himself from this web of deceit. His bones turned brittle as he realized that in officially allying himself with these buccaneers, he had bound himself more firmly than he could have imagined. Even his signature was trapped now. His own pirate name was listed boldly in their book, right under the elegant script of the lady and the scrawly signatures of her sons, Nibs the Knife and Tom Tootles.

Hanover saw now, quite clearly, how mistaken he had been to believe his friend Captain Cecco would prove easier to escape than his enemy Captain Hook. And most important, Hanover no longer blamed Jill for anything. If the brilliant Doctor Johann Heinrich had to wage a struggle of epic proportions to outmaneuver these pirates, how could a woman— a woman with such a passion for riches— be expected to prevail? The surgeon's damaged heart warmed to her, a fellow sufferer. Like he, she was a victim of the vices these buccaneers embraced by the armful!

His earnings disappeared clattering into a leather pouch in Cecco's hand. Dragging his gaze away, Hanover pressed his handkerchief to his upper lip. Then, gathering his forces, he tucked it tidily away. When every last diamond was caught, Cecco drew the pouch strings tight and knotted them.

Hanover raised his eyes to meet the captain's. "Sir. In spite of this inconvenience, I want you to understand that I regret no part of our association. I intend to make my service as dedicated as every other man's."

"I admire your magnanimity, Doctor, and I thank you for it."

"I hope you will grant one favor in token of my— cooperation."

"What is it you would ask of me?" Casually, Cecco tossed the bag of jewels to his desktop. It landed with a satisfying chunk.

"Allow me to extend my apologies to the lady. Personally."

To his astonishment, Captain Cecco smiled. "Agreed!" Yulunga grunted in surprise. Both the surgeon and the mate stared as the captain said, "As I indicated to my Jill, I can be a generous master. Under trying circumstances, you have shown me deference this afternoon, Doctor, and this should be rewarded."

"You mean to say— you will grant my request?"

"Certainly! I will arrange for you to meet with my mistress and clear the air once and for all." Cecco stood, snatched his knife from the desktop, and stowed it in his belt. "I shall be delighted to see the two of you put the past into the proper perspective. And I give you my sacred word that I will see to it, Doctor Hanover….But…I am afraid…" He grinned, and, shaking his head slowly, pronounced the two words that, in any accent, Hanover most hated to hear.

"Not today!"

Surrender

Shocked by Hook's attack, Liza couldn't breathe. His grip forced her down. Under his sudden surge of attention, her heart pounded with excitement. The hand that encircled her throat so easily was warm, his chains stretched to their fullest extent. She stared into his brilliant blue eyes, waiting for him to kill her.

Afire with fury, he hissed, "Where is your father, girl?"

She blinked. His fingers tightened. Her eyes rolled upward, toward the captain's quarters.

"Where are my keys?"

Again, her eyes directed upward. Under his weight, the pain from last night's beating shot through her thighs.

His grip eased. "Get me some water. Now." His demand sounded parched, a shade of the voice that commanded her to lie still more than a day ago. Liza nodded, regretting the feel of his body rolling away from her. The flask her father had provided was tucked between the mattress and the board. She reached for it, feeling her master's ring bobble on her finger. Quickly, she slid the jewel off and stowed it under her pillow.

With his chains clinking behind her back, Hook felt of his head, and grunted. When Liza sat up to pass the flagon, he raised up on one elbow, reaching for it greedily. Seeing him pull the cork with his teeth, she realized her mistake— of course he couldn't use two hands. She should have opened it for him. She captured the cork and watched, disappointed but fascinated, as he gulped half the contents in one draught. She wouldn't have much time.

She thrilled as he shifted his gaze to her, catching his breath. His voice continued harsh. "Why am I still alive?" As she shook her head, he scowled in impatience. With his next sentence, he answered her question— he did remember her voice!

"I grant you permission to speak." His eyes narrowed. "Why hasn't he killed me?"

Liza smiled. Her sound had pleased him! She opened her lips and breathed deeply. Some precious moments passed before she could manage to say one word.

"Master…"

"Answer the question!" More striking than ever, his features sharpened with anger.

"Because of me."

"You?" Hook's face relaxed. "Ah…the good doctor cannot kill in front of his daughter." The surgeon's dilemma seemed to please him.

"He has sworn the physician's oath."

Hook sneered. "Yes, his sacred word. Yet his conscience allows for his daughter to administer his potions." He took another drink of it. "I've no time to waste. You will fetch me those keys. When I awaken tonight, you will have them ready."

He was hazarding everything on this creature's willingness. Feeling her touch his body as he returned to the world, he had known the surgeon wasn't near. The lack of noise indicated no one who might be of aid was close, either. Hook had assumed the keys to his chains were with his captor, wherever he was, and the girl had confirmed that assumption. But she showed herself to be besotted with her 'master.' Surely she would do whatever he asked. Again, the quickest victory would suit Hook's purpose. He didn't care how he secured it.

"But—"

"I've no time to parley. What do you want in exchange?"

She who had been silent so long didn't hesitate to express her desires. Her gray eyes burned like coals, and her low voice resonated. "Make me your mistress!"

Already, his eyelids felt heavy, yet he downed another draught of water. He'd imbibed not a drop since his capture. Hook had few choices, but he would choose the time to exercise those options he held. At this moment, his body needed fluid more than consciousness.

Liza itched to seize the flask, but by now it was too late. When he lowered it, his lips were wet. His hoarse voice whispered, "Keep me alive…"

Before she could stop him, he swallowed the last of the flagon's contents. His hand went limp, relinquishing it. He fell back heavily onto the bed, his long black hair spread all around him. She tossed the flask aside and heaved herself on top of him, one hand on either side of his face to claim a kiss before his lips became inert. Liza licked the moisture from them. Then she stroked his hair again, gazing on his handsome face.

Liza felt herself smile. He still wanted her. All she had to do was care for him, as she would have done in any case. When he woke again, she would have food ready for him, and untainted water. The cabin would be dark, the ship quiet. Her father hadn't slept much at all last night. He would be so exhausted by evening that he should sleep soundly. Liza would make sure of it.

She rose and felt for the cork. Clutching it and the flagon, she climbed down from her bunk, drew the bed curtain closed, and refilled the vessel from a jug of water she'd drawn in the galley. She left the flask on her father's desk to indicate the need for more sleeping draught, then padded to her bureau. She rummaged until she found a petticoat, one made of flannel, and her sewing scissors. She tossed them into her bunk. Glancing at the door as she climbed, she estimated the time before her father might return. She should have a good chance to tear the petticoat into strips. Only the ripping must be finished before her father walked in. Later on, she could take her time threading the strips of flannel through the links. Her agile fingers could easily weave the material into the iron. Then the clanking would be muffled. After he retired to his bed, her father wouldn't know Hook moved in the bunk above him, earning his freedom and enslaving a heart. Once her master had partaken of food and drink, he could take all night to do it, if he wanted. No one, not even her father, would be aware of what was happening as a bold little girl became this magnificent man's woman.

For once, Liza relished the quiet. She had spoken to her master now. Sounds weren't important anymore. She had looked her fill at him in this last night and day. Sight, like sound, would be secondary tonight. Only touch would be significant when he rallied— sensation. The feelings of thirsts being slaked and hungers satisfied. She knew what he wanted, and he knew of her desire. Both a man and a woman would awaken in the darkness of this evening. Liza's pulse throbbed in anticipation. It would be a long, soundless night.

Rousing herself, she tended to the matter at hand, clipping cuts in the fabric of her petticoat. Taking it between her fists, she tore away strip after strip.

As from a great distance, Hook heard the scream of rending cloth. It puzzled him, but the sound was not enough to call him from the shadows, nor did he stir as the cold band of the jewel slid onto his finger. Vaguely, he heard a door open and click closed, and then his mind retreated where his senses couldn't follow.

The medicine bag, much lighter than before, settled onto the desk with a thud.

"Liza," Hanover's clipped voice spoke in approval. He turned to blink at the girl sitting primly at the table with her sewing basket in front of her. "You persuaded him to drink it?"

Unable to restrain her smile, she nodded.

Flipping up the bed curtain, Hanover peered into the upper bunk to reassure himself. "That, at least, is a good thing. And I have made sure of our privacy. Now all we need is a miracle!" His coat lay folded over his arm. He held it out to Liza, and on the instant she hurried toward him to receive it.

"Stitch up the lining, Liza. I will prepare another draught, but next time he becomes conscious, I expect I will be forced to use the ether again. No matter. It will serve to keep him thirsty."

Wondering how the coat had torn, Liza worked it with her fingers. As she felt the absence of the little stones, her eyes questioned her father.

"Never mind. I have a question for *you*. How did your mother's pearl ring bring luck to Captain Cecco?"

Liza's eyes widened.

"Well?"

She hung the coat over her arm. Miming a grip on invisible bars, Liza indicated her imprisonment. She kissed one of her hands, and at the same time made the motion of drawing off her ring.

Her father nodded. "And?"

She thought for a moment while the truth became clear to her. Plainly, she remembered the mistress' indulgent tone as the woman realized Cecco had stolen Liza's ring. The theft was just an excuse for the sailor to approach the mistress. Cecco had guessed Liza would ask for her ring, and he used it like a key to unlock the lady's door!

Pleased to have driven the wedge between Hook and Jill before meeting either one of them, Liza managed to mask her smile. Instead, she spread her right hand flat and stroked it to signify Jill's red hand. Then, bunching the fingers of her other hand as if to hold a ring, she deposited it in her palm. Kissing her hand again, she watched her father's scar darken as comprehension dawned.

"So! The gypsy used us from the very beginning!" Angrily, Hanover stared past his daughter into the mirror. "That ring brought Captain Cecco very good fortune, indeed." He untied the black ribbon, allowing his hair to fall loose. "Mr. Yulunga now has the pearls."

Liza's head snapped up.

"As far as I am concerned, he can keep them. In spite of Mr. Yulunga's jibes, Captain Cecco is unlikely to share his luck with even his first mate."

Hanover didn't understand, but his daughter did. She stepped back, staring at the floor. Mr. Yulunga possessed her pearls…and he would use them, just as Cecco had! But her father needn't worry about the mistress; the African would pursue his luck in another quarter. Liza's knees went weak as she wondered. Did the prohibition against touching Jill's girl still apply? Did Cecco care if his men pursued her? Maybe a withdrawal of his guardianship was her punishment for intruding on the master's quarters last night. The only man who had ever protected Liza now lay unconscious in her bed, and not one of his sailors knew he lived. No wonder Mr. Yulunga engaged her this morning! He was Cecco's right-hand man. He would be first to act when Liza was fair game. Beyond a doubt, the offer of earrings was his initial advance. Again, the thought of the brutal African made her dizzy, and the room spun as she planted her feet more firmly on the boards. Hearing her father's voice, Liza looked up in time to see him standing with his hair loosened, handing her the ribbon.

"Put this away. I will ready the flask." He turned his back to open his valise.

Steadying herself, Liza obeyed, then crept behind her father to observe his movements. He removed the cork from the flagon and drew a vial of liquid from his bag. After measuring out a half teaspoon, he poured it deftly into the water, resealed the flask, and shook it. He didn't look at her as he passed it along. "Put this flask where you can reach it."

She nodded and, standing on the lower bunk to reach the upper, tucked it away. Liza turned as she stood, so that she could see where her father replaced the vial. Its amber fluid matched the one Jill secreted in the drawer under the master's bed. With these observations, a sense of power flowed through Liza's veins, as if she had drunk it from one of those bottles. New knowledge inspired it, and she smiled to herself. Like a dutiful daughter, she sat down in front of her work basket. As she rubbed the gray velvet against her cheek, she thought again how grateful she was to her mistress. Each of her father's medicines was labeled, their dosages marked in his neat hand.

And now, Liza could read them.

Even if Hook forgot his promise upon achieving freedom, even if Captain Cecco gave the woman up to him, by using her father's potions— and poisons— Liza would keep Jill from the master. And since the surgeon had been spurned, everyone would believe his jealousy was to blame. In one stroke, Liza would be rid of both her father and her mistress, and no one would suspect it the work of a clever 'little girl.' A daughter who, in matters of life and death, might emulate her sire. Watching her frowning father pace the room, Liza remembered to hide that smile she had stolen from Jill. The one that came to her lips so easily.

Right now, there was only one woman aboard the *Roger*. That was the way it would stay.

Near sunset, the two men clattered up the steps of the companionway. They wanted to give plenty of notice of their coming. After the interruptions of last night, none of the company wished to surprise the captain and his lady again. When they arrived before the door, Tom laid a hand on Nibs' shoulder to delay his knock. "Are you sure this is what you want, mate?"

"What I want has nothing to do with it. It's what I have to do."

"Then I'm in, too."

"We'll see what Jill has to say about that. We agreed."

Tom's usually cheery face was troubled, and he fingered his scar. "Aye, but it goes against the grain! We're brothers."

Nibs summoned the spirit of his old smile. "It's like I told you before. We'll always be that, no matter who we're up against." He and Tom clasped arms, then he faced the door, raised his fist, and struck.

After a moment's pause, the voice of the new captain answered. "Enter."

Nibs led the way in. "Sir; Lady." He nodded his respects as Tom's voice echoed his own.

"Tom, Nibs! Come in." Jill stood near Captain Cecco, her face flushed and her eyes sparkling. Cecco was placing a leather pouch in his sea chest, which had taken up residence at the foot of the bunk. As the captain secured the lock, Nibs cast his gaze around the room until he found the other chest, the one belonging to Hook. Still padlocked, it now reposed in the corner with the bookcase. At the sight of it, Nibs' face set in determination, the grim crease between his eyebrows deepening.

Tom was observing Jill. Although she smiled readily, he remembered her efforts earlier this afternoon, when she'd met with her sons to lay their concerns to rest. Jill had spoken encouragingly of the changes on the *Roger* and hopefully of Hook's return. When, at that point, her tears caught up with her, she tried to banish them by relating incidents revealing Captain Cecco's cleverness. Nibs and Tom were relieved he was kind to her, but the young men had exchanged glances as she continued to speak of her new lover. Jill's arms glowed with his gold; less obvious to the lady herself was the extent to which their friend the Italian sailor engaged her affection. Difficult as it was to contemplate, her sons found comfort in the fact that Jill would not be alone if Hook failed to return.

But, as Nibs and Tom discussed after she left them, that comfort was offset by the consequences facing both Jill and Cecco…if and when Hook materialized. From what they knew of both men, the one certainty was that neither would give up his winnings. And the longer Hook was away, the more difficult it would be to recapture his supremacy— on the *Roger*, and maybe, in Jill's heart.

Although Nibs doubted at the beginning, he agreed at last that Jill was following Hook's orders. Loyal, no matter what. He now had an idea of doing the same. Tom felt his innards lurch as he watched Jill, the way he had felt in his first storm at sea. She wouldn't be smiling by the time she'd heard Nibs' decision. The moment would be difficult. But Jill respected truth, painful or otherwise, and Tom was sure Cecco did, too. It was better not to delay. Puffing out his chest, Tom spoke up. "Captain, Nibs and I have a request to make."

"So you have come on business." Eyeing the two sailors, Cecco indicated his desk. "Please." As he settled into his chair, the captain took the initiative. "My lady informs me the three of you came to terms this afternoon. This pleases me."

Nibs tightened the knot of his kerchief. "Yes, Sir. I apologize for busting in on you last night. I understand now. You have Jill's confidence, and you're the men's choice for captain. I'm with you, Sir."

"Thank you, Mr. Nibs. I accept your apology, and I bear no ill will. Because I have known the two of you since you were boys, I have often witnessed as you questioned and sought answers. In spite of a captain's tendency to wish for instant obedience, I recognize these as traits that make good officers."

Nibs suddenly believed Jill's claim that Cecco was a wise leader. "Thank you, Sir."

Hearing the new esteem in Nibs' voice, the lady smiled. "I discussed your situation with Captain Cecco, Mr. Nibs. He is gracious enough to understand that you were motivated by duty."

Cecco turned to Tom, questioning.

Tom said, "I'm with you, too, Sir. Like the lady, I want what's best for the *Roger*."

"Then we are all agreed." The captain's pleasant expression hardened then, and he sat back in his seat. "But I see by the look on the faces…there are more questions."

Jill's face clouded. "You don't have bad news to report?" All at once she was afraid. She leaned forward, her hands clenching on the arms of her chair. This afternoon her sons promised to keep searching for Hook. Had they found evidence of an accident— or worse?

Nibs recognized the panic in her eyes. "No, Ma'am, it's not what you're thinking. But I'm afraid you won't like what I have to say." He shifted on his feet. "I've reconsidered LeCorbeau's offer."

"No!" Jill shot from her seat. "No, Nibs, you can't!"

Cecco rose to stand behind her. Laying his hands on her shoulders, he spoke softly to her. "Lady. Do not upset yourself. Listen to what your son has to say." With gentle pressure, he pushed her into her chair. As he seated himself, his expression was unreadable. "I had wondered if this would be the case, Mr. Nibs. Go on."

Finding the right words, respectful but final, was harder than Nibs anticipated. "Well, Sir, with Hook gone and all, I'm not bound to the *Roger* anymore. I got to thinking maybe I should try something new, see how things are done on another vessel…gather more experience." A long silence followed, during which Nibs returned the intense regard of the captain and avoided looking at Jill. She had recovered, but she was staring at Nibs with a mixture of pride and dread. At last Cecco broke the stillness.

"Well. And Mr. Tootles. What have you to say?"

"Sir…Ma'am. I can't stand to see Nibs go off alone. If you grant me leave and if LeCorbeau will take me on, I'll go with him."

Jill sat with perfect posture. "No. I won't allow it."

Cecco said, "Madam. I will make this judgment with your participation, and I will not decide in haste."

"Captain, you know what kind of man LeCorbeau is! Look what he's done to his officers. In front of everyone he shows them disrespect. They cringe at his displeasure, yet they lie for him, even procure for him. And if what we hear is true, he has a penchant for luring boys to his service. He gives them no choice, using them for his own amusement! He's already made overtures to Nibs—"

Tom broke in, frowning. "We're hardly boys anymore, Ma'am!"

"I am aware of that. But what chance will you have if that despicable man uses his stores of the surgeon's philter?"

Glancing at each other, Tom and Nibs fidgeted. Nibs said, "We hoped you wouldn't worry about that, Ma'am. We don't even know that LeCorbeau has any of that potion."

Cecco observed Nibs closely. "We have discussed the Frenchman in the past. You are aware of the reason he courted you."

· "Yes, Sir."

"And still you will serve him?"

"In any way but one, Sir." Nibs' face was dark.

Jill's voice shook. "And how will you defend yourself when you are accused of disobedience?"

"I'm hoping it won't come to that, Ma'am. He's still got his mates."

The captain said, "It is as we discussed, Mr. Nibs. LeCorbeau's mates do not appear to last so very long."

"No, Nibs! I won't have that happen to you. I forbid you to go!"

Cecco's voice was sharper than Jill had ever heard it. "Madam. You forget your place." Ignoring the shock on her face, he turned to Nibs. "Before I make this very serious decision, tell me what you are thinking."

Nibs looked at his boots to begin, then warmed to the subject. "I'm thinking I'd advance quickly under LeCorbeau. He favors me already, and it's a smaller ship, less crew. I'd soon be earning a good percent of the takings. And…well, I would be a legitimate seaman then, wouldn't I? Not as likely to be hanged by the Royal Navy."

The new captain spoke evenly, but his displeasure smoldered. "Never before have I heard you voice any such concern. If, as the lady fears, your chosen captain orders you to lie for him, you will now have had some practice."

Jill gasped, forgetting her place again. "Captain! Nibs has never been untruthful before! You must give him another chance—"

His bracelets jangled as he held up his hand to silence her. "Mr. Nibs. You are not afraid of LeCorbeau, and you are not afraid of the law. If ever a man was born to be a pirate, you are the one."

Nibs fell silent. Still staring at him, Jill shook her head. Frantically, she sought an avenue of retreat for him. She spoke quietly, dreading to incur Cecco's wrath on herself or her son, but determined. "Tell me this proposal is simply your reluctance to serve under Hook's successor, whoever was chosen. Then we can settle your doubts."

"No, Ma'am. I won't tell you that. Captain Cecco is a fine master."

"…Tom?" Her voice held a note of desperation.

"Lady, I don't want Nibs to go off without me, but we agreed that if you're needing me here, I'll stay."

Jill drew herself up. The pirate queen had never looked so regal. "I wouldn't dream of separating you. If you must perform this duty, you will find some other way to do so, and you will both remain on the *Roger*— where you have sworn your loyalty."

Tom said simply, "Begging your pardon, Ma'am, but we swore to serve Captain Hook. And he's gone."

Jill's face blanched. Nibs' words cut deeper still.

"Tom means to say, Ma'am, that Hook's just not *here*."

The tiny hope of finding Hook in LeCorbeau's grasp wasn't enough to risk her boys on it. Jill was ashen, now, with grief for Hook and anxiety for her sons. Surely, she believed, if this captain didn't punish them for dissembling, *L'Ormonde*'s captain would condemn them as spies.

Displaying no urge to comfort her, Cecco sat back and crossed his arms, one hand resting on the golden band that matched his gift to Jill. He leveled a stare at Nibs. "And you are determined to keep on serving Captain Hook. Are you not?"

Neither man answered.

"You will not say to me that you go to *L'Ormonde* to search for him. But this I know to be true." Cecco aimed an appraising look at Jill. "Most fortunately for your mother, it is also true that she does not encourage you in this folly." He studied Nibs, then Tom, and with a cold look he said, "You are both good men. I am sorry to dismiss you."

Jill's eyes opened wide. "Sir! Don't let them go on such a foolish errand."

"I have made my decision."

"Excuse them! They're in shock over losing Hook. He was the closest thing to a father my sons have known."

"Madam. You try my patience."

Reckless now, she faced him. "You've seen what manner of man LeCorbeau is. Please, Captain. Don't send my boys away in anger."

"Lady, I do not send them. They have asked to be released."

"And I ask you *not* to release them!"

Cecco said with dignity, "Of ship's company I hold no man, and no woman, against the will. As for anger, I harbor none. Only sorrow to lose two fine crewmen, who could not trust me to do right by our former master."

"But Captain—"

"Hush, Lady. It is clear that these men understand the situation into which they plunge." Jill had never seen his eyes so devoid of sympathy. "Like you, they are willing to take imprudent risks— in this case, for the sake of their…captain. That they are your sons is unfortunate."

Falling on her knees before him, she laid her hands on his legs, nearly sobbing. "Because they *are* my sons, Sir, you cannot let them go!"

"Lovely one." He looked down on her. Impersonally, as if she were an object of art, he ran his hand over her hair. "You yourself insisted I show no favor or prejudice. To do other than this would be a violation of our accord."

As all sense of balance deserted her, Jill closed her eyes and pulled her hands away. Feeling for her chair, she dragged herself into it. Tom saw her sinking.

"I know it makes it harder for you, Lady, to lose us, too. But Nibs is set on doing his duty, and I'm set on following him." Making sure his shirt was tucked first, he faced the captain straight on. "Sir. None of this is Jill's idea. She's devoted to you. Will you swear to us you'll take care of her?"

From far away, Jill heard Cecco's reply.

"You have my word."

"Lady. Don't worry too much. You taught us to watch out for ourselves."

The words tore themselves from her lips, "And to do your duty." She felt sick.

"Aye, Ma'am. And that." Tom leaned over the desk and bent his head to look into her downcast face, smiling. "There's no changing us now!"

Jill looked on her sons, and saw that they *had* changed. They were fully grown men, marked by their experiences, and honor-bound— soon to be bound to a man without honor. She pushed herself out of her chair and turned her back. "Captain. When shall we rendezvous with *L'Ormonde?*"

"It is my intention to allow her to catch us tomorrow."

Jill collected herself, then spoke over her shoulder to her sons, commanding. "Mr. Nibs, Mr. Tootles. You will say good-bye to me before you go."

"Aye, Madam. We will."

"Yes, men." Cecco remained firm. "You will have to cross your own names from the book. No one can do that for you." He dismissed them and they left, much more quietly than they'd entered. When Nibs looked back to close the door, Jill was wilting on the window seat, her head bowed and her hands spread over the pillows. Cecco still sat with his arms crossed, his dark eyes watching his sailors' departure.

They all noticed that Captain Cecco hadn't invited the men to return, after their search of *L'Ormonde* was over.

If you are brave enough to face it, change can be welcome. As her father accepted the teacup, Liza recalled her mistress' words from that very first day. The woman was right. Excitement and adventure waited to be found in the pirates' way of life, and for Liza it was only beginning. Her tale would be far different than anyone had imagined.

Hanover sighed. "You may go to bed now, Liza. The captain informed me that the lady won't need you tonight."

She lingered while he took the first sip, and squeezed her hands together.

Her father noticed her hesitation. "Don't be afraid. Our guest won't awaken for another hour or so. When he does, I will be ready with the ether." Hanover swallowed some tea, then set the cup next to the medicine bottle on his desk. "I will retire, as well. These last few days have been trying." He stood and removed his waistcoat. Liza took it from him and hung it neatly next to the coat, which she had stitched back to usefulness. Finding excuses to avoid her bunk, she sent furtive glances toward her father until he finished his tea. Wearily, he ambled to the door to check the lock, then turned toward his bed. Pausing only to slip off his shoes, he collapsed into it.

Liza crept near her father. His eyes were closed…he was asleep already! She collected his shoes to set them properly under the clothes hooks. Picking up his teacup, she inspected the contents, pleased to find no remainder. After wiping it clean, she replaced it on its tray. He would never suspect he had been drugged.

From her dresser drawer Liza removed a tall, corked bottle, and slices of bread and cheese wrapped in a linen napkin. She placed them in her bunk, following them with the small bowl of fruit from the table. In front of the mirror, she washed her face and brushed her hair, then shed her clothing and hung it. When Liza had turned up the flames of the desktop lanterns, she began to climb to her bunk. She paused. She dropped to the floor again and bent over the prone figure of her father. Slipping her hand into his breeches pocket, she removed a ring of brass keys, allowing them to tinkle, just for the pleasure of hearing them.

Not long after, feeling cool and refreshed, she locked the door again. A glance in the mirror indicated the necessity of smoothing her hair once more; her quick venture to the windy gun deck had mussed it. Satisfied then, she yanked her father's bed curtain closed and slithered into her bunk. Everything was ready for her master. Liza lay down by his side, breathlessly awaiting her next adventure— into womanhood. To pass the time until he awakened, she closed her eyes and imagined that Mr. Yulunga's big black hands had already wielded the needle to prick her ears, and she was flaunting those golden earrings.

The ship plowed on through the darkness, her moans lulling her off-duty voyagers to rest. All but one. For him, the song of the *Roger* was a stimulant.

When Hook came to awareness, he soon discovered that the chains at his hand and foot made no sound, and the girl was sleeping. The time had come to make his move.

It seemed long before Jill could face her duty again. When she did, her captain was cordial. He waited beside his desk, where she came to stand before him, looking up slowly. The lanternlight played on the linked medallions at his neck, and on his headdress.

"Captain."

"Lady." Honoring his promise to wait for her to reach first, Cecco didn't touch her. "You are not as alone as you imagine."

"So you would have me believe. In any case, we now have the answer to your question of this morning. We know what you would not do for me."

"Breaking my word would not be a service for you, but an injury against you."

"Do my sons offend you so deeply that you will allow them to go into danger?"

"They face danger every day on the *Roger*. But they offend me only by trusting me too little."

"I trusted you to look out for us. Sir."

"If they had confided in me, I might have understood their desire to seek their captain."

"Nibs and Tom were trying to be discreet, in order *not* to offend you."

"And they spoke for themselves. That discussion is over." He gazed on her, his regard intensifying. "But their mother displeased me— not once, but several times."

"Sir…I couldn't just let them go!"

"I know this is not your wish to see your sons leave our ship. Even under the best of circumstances."

"Is it your wish?"

"I have already told you. They asked to be released."

"And if I asked, would you let me go?"

"You, I must refuse. We are both bound by accord. And, I think, you are not asking such a thing. You belong on the *Roger*."

Gauging his displeasure, she ventured further. "Sir, what else do you know about me?"

"I know you believed you could not ask me, but you would have preferred that I find a way to inspect *L'Ormonde* myself."

"Then you have thought to search for Hook aboard her?"

"Ah, yes! But of course, LeCorbeau is not likely to show us anything he does not wish us to see."

"To do so would at least have saved my sons from that man."

"And saved you and me from a delicate situation. But as you have seen, they are not afraid. Nor do I shy from facing the sensitive circumstances between me and my lady."

"Aye, Sir, I do see. You show more courage than many men own. But is there no other way to ensure Hook isn't aboard *L'Ormonde?*"

"None that I can find."

"Then Tom and Nibs are right to go?"

He shook his head. "I have not said this."

"What else have you not said?"

"I have not said what you might not believe. That I honored my oath to Hook, and before taking his prize I, too, searched the *Roger* to find him, and considered he may have fallen victim to LeCorbeau. But, I have done everything that lies within my power. Tom was right, Lady. Hook is gone. We may never know where or how."

"But I can feel him!"

Cecco heaved a heavy sigh. "Lovely one, it is as I told you before. Gypsies are a superstitious people. With patience I have listened to your claim. Now I will hear no more. No more talk of the dead. I wish the man's soul to rest in peace." With his fingers, he sketched a gypsy banishing sign, down from his forehead and across his breast.

Recognizing that Cecco's indulgence was at an end, Jill bowed her head. "I spoke out of turn in front of your men. Please have patience one more time, Sir, and excuse me."

"You will not do so again. Always, you learn the lesson and move forward. It is one of the qualities I admire in you."

"Thank you, Captain. It is hard, losing so many people I love."

His dark gaze softened. "Many. But not all."

Jill read his face, then opened her palm to survey the color of her hand. It seemed to her that the stain should have paled in the last few days, but her hand was as crimson as the night she was marked.

Accepting Cecco hadn't changed that.

"Aye, Sir. Not all."

Just below her palm, one of her bracelets caught the golden gleam of the lanternlight. Unthinking, Jill rotated her hand to admire it, then realized that, as she did so, she was lowering her arm and reaching out to Cecco. Already, the gesture was so natural that it accomplished itself without her direction. Once over her surprise, Jill knew it felt right. She wanted Cecco's comfort. She wanted Cecco.

He didn't give her a chance to reconsider. He grasped her hand. *"Bellezza."* He lifted her hand to his lips and kissed it. "Always, you may count on me. As your palm predicted, you are adored." He straightened, and his grip on her fingers tightened. "But still, as I promised, the welfare of the *Roger* comes first. Now that we have settled ourselves, we must anticipate tomorrow and lay our plans."

"Of course." Even as she followed his lead, Jill admired his skill in inducing her cooperation. "We must show no sign of weakness to LeCorbeau."

He smiled. "Ah, my Jill! Now I see the spirit at work again."

"Aye, Sir, with your encouragement." When he smiled that way, she thought, he was so very dashing. Still bruised by her mingling emotions, she turned her mind to business. "The *commandant* should pay well to compensate us for Nibs. Do you believe he will accept Tom, too?"

"If it is the only way to obtain the services of one, he will take both. And pay for them."

"We must watch carefully to read his reaction to Hook's disappearance."

"Lady, we will stage a grand entrance, and I will make a show of my desire to be rid of your 'troublesome' sons. LeCorbeau will otherwise be suspicious. He is a canny man. He might easily guess their purpose, and I am sure you will wish to divert this. The Frenchman must believe I need your sons to go— in order to secure my claim on you."

Relief washed over her. Cecco *did* intend to watch over her sons, after all. Grateful for his concern, she pressed his hand. "Thank you for that. And the surgeon?"

"We will allow the business partners enough leeway to allay

suspicion. Hanover will attend the 'ailing' mate. Although our doctor has feigned to join us and his game is exposed, he still hopes to pass through his trial period, regain his jewels, and spirit you away on *L'Ormonde*. By the time it appears possible for him to buy your freedom, you must seem on the brink of running from your new captain."

His assumption that she would be faithful reminded Jill of Smee's old doubts, and she found she could think of Smee without pain, now. "You will trust me, in the end, to remain true to you? Even if I must string Doctor Hanover along until the very last moment?"

"'The very last moment.' An appropriate way to put it! For such it will be— if I am crossed." With a strong hand, Cecco encompassed her throat. As she tensed, he slid his hand to her shoulder. "But yes, of course I trust you to make the wise decision. I know of your loyalty. And as I have said, you are far too intelligent to betray me." He said it casually, but his eyes made their impression. Her heart skipped a beat. This captain was not a man to be trifled with. His hand remained, heavy, on her shoulder. He said, "Hanover is doing his part, as expected. Your 'lover' is already impatient to speak with you again."

Jill caught the note of mischief in his voice. Her eyes widened. "You don't mean to allow it?"

He shrugged. "As a token of good faith, I have already promised."

Shocked, Jill studied Cecco's confident face, and a gradual smile slid to her own. "Yes.…Of course."

"But you will not be alone. Mr. Yulunga will be watching. For that matter, so will the rest of the crew."

"Doctor Hanover will be pleased to learn of my son's change of allegiance. I was never sure, but now his sudden interest in Nibs is explained. He must have been following LeCorbeau's directive in luring Nibs away."

"Certainly. It seems our overly-moral surgeon is caught between pirates and privateers. He has surrendered more than a few of his principles to win you, and to win his freedom."

Jill shuddered. "To think I ever allowed that man to touch me!"

Cecco removed the knife from his belt. Setting it on his desk, he laid his hand firmly upon it. "You will have your satisfaction. And so will I."

Jill placed her hand on his, still resting on the dagger. With a thrill, she felt the power in that hand, and she understood that if she fulfilled her bargain, Cecco would honor his. He would protect Jill, and the *Roger*, and even Nibs and Tom, once they had learned their lesson. She was satisfied.

"You are a worthy master, Sir. And how will you manage LeCorbeau?"

"I will press for a new agreement with him. I and my officers will gather aboard *L'Ormonde* for parley tomorrow evening." He turned his hand upward to clasp hers. "You, my lovely one, will stay safely on board our own ship, behind the locked door of our quarters, with a sentry posted outside."

"Aye, Sir." Anxious as she was to examine the privateer ship and the circumstances under which her sons might be living, Jill felt bound by Hook's admonition not to set foot on another vessel. "I will stay behind, waiting for you."

"The thought of you here will make me wish to hurry. But if I am to continue the partnership, I must take whatever time is necessary to inspire the proper conviction in LeCorbeau. Also, I must collect his compensation for my sailors. I may return very late."

"I will demonstrate the same patience you have shown me— until you return."

"You must not wait up for me. Mr. Yulunga will unlock the door."

"He, too, has displayed patience. It seems his position of authority has settled him."

Cecco's even smile was knowing. "Yes. But still, he likes to stir the trouble! That is why the girl appeals to him, I think. She is much the same way. They may be good for one another."

"Perhaps under his supervision she will behave. Severe as they are, even her father's attempts to control her seem ineffective. I wouldn't be surprised if Mr. Yulunga proves to be the only man she will obey."

"I believe he will treat her no worse than her father does. But she is your girl. What are your thoughts about letting her go, once we have wrung ransom from the surgeon?"

"She is too unpredictable to remain under the terms I first outlined for her. But if she wishes to stay on in Mr. Yulunga's custody, I will give her that chance. With your permission, of course, Captain."

Cecco said, "I have no taste for defending innocents. She will stay only on the condition you state, and the two of them may occupy the spare quarters."

"And if the surgeon objects, Sir?"

"No doubt by the time he learns of it, it will be too late. But perhaps he will pay for *her* freedom, as well! With what, I do not know. By then he will have relinquished to us everything he owns— and a percentage of his future."

"And, Captain, just how do you intend to collect the tribute LeCorbeau will pledge?"

"Using the fact that our surgeon fled from England and changed his name. If *L'Ormonde* fails to meet us at our appointed rendezvous, the British authorities will be notified of LeCorbeau's involvement with the fugitive physician. After all, the Frenchman must report to his government regularly to pay its percentage and have his papers renewed. He will be easy for the English fleet to track down, unless he gives up his legitimacy and turns pirate. And then, he would be fair game for any navy to hang."

"Captain…" She smiled, slyly, and the enticement in her voice stirred him.

"Lady?"

"How did you become so clever?"

"Natural talent, of course! But also…" He tempered his smile. "I have learned from a master."

His forthright reply subdued her. "Yes. As have I."

Placing his hands on her shoulders, he shook his head. "*Amore.* So full of sadness."

"I'm sorry. And you are so good to me."

"When you are dispirited, you must remember the 'lies' I told you. When I was only your devoted sailor." Gently, Cecco guided her toward the bunk. He swept the shining hair from her back and murmured into her ear, so that his voice made her tingle. "I told you then— you are the most desirable woman I had yet to experience." Loosening her laces, he kissed her neck, just above his necklaces. "I bind you to me with golden chains."

As he turned her, she faced him and gazed, entranced, into his deep brown eyes. She stroked his golden armband. "You share with me all your treasure."

"You taste the honey of my passion." He kissed her throat.

Her gaze rose to the ceiling as she remembered; his hands dropped to her waist. She said, "I had never heard that one before."

As his fingers worked, her petticoats fluttered away. He kissed her, then drew back only far enough to whisper, "I will love you forever."

"I *had* heard that." She raised her hands to his face. "I wanted to hear it again."

"You will hear it again. And again." With his muscular arms, Cecco swept her up and set her in his bed. She pushed the vest from his shoulders, and quickly he cast off his breeches and embraced her. Running her hands over his scars, she felt their furrows; the leather laces with which she had secured his hair that morning dangled over her fingers. Overcome with emotion, she barely heeded his command.

"Show me first that you are mine."

When she understood, she kissed him. The way she used to kiss Hook.

"More than this."

"I know your name. Will you allow me to say it?"

"It is not enough. Find a new way, something no man has known, to bind yourself to me."

"I already wear your jewelry—"

"Yes. And you wore his, too." With his fingers he stroked the seam on her neck, then hunted for her scarlet palm. "The boy scarred your throat. And you are stained with another man's blood. What mark will you suffer for me?"

She stared at him. She felt her heart beating against her ribs. Thinking, she glanced around the room, and his leather lace brushed her fingers again. Pulling it forward over his shoulder, she gathered the second lace, too. She looked into his eyes and read his approval there. Then she bent to her task. Leaving the lace in his hair, she looped its end around her wrist. Her fingers twined it. With teeth and fingertips she grasped the ends and pulled to tighten the knot— once, twice, then three times. She repeated the motions with the second lace on her other wrist, tasting the dry leather, and as she knelt before her captain, she lifted her eyes and her hands to him.

"Sir. We are bound."

"We are bound." His own capable fingers gripped the strings and pulled until the six knots at her wrists became small, and smaller, and no one's fingers, not even all ten fingers on two good hands, would be able to work them loose. "We are one."

Then he made love to her, her hands hovering near his shoulders, straying only as far as her bonds allowed. As her hands strained to touch him, the leather rubbed her skin, but she could still caress the gold of his necklace, and his face, and the top of his scars. Although his hands were free, Cecco's movements, too, were restricted, yet he found ways enough to satisfy both lovers. Enthralled with the other sensations he brought her, she barely felt the chafing of his leather, and when he was done, she slept in his arms, her own arms behind his neck and her mind mingling the tinkling of his bracelets with the phantom tapping of the hook.

In the morning light, he woke her to draw the jeweled dagger from beneath the pillow. Solemnly, he held her fists in his as he severed the leather. The laces falling behind his back were shortened, and she, too, was left to go not quite free, wearing thin brown bracelets. Raw from their bindings, her wrists were now encircled with his mark and his gold.

Cecco examined her scorings, and kissed them tenderly. *"Amore."*

"Amore."

His scourges would leave no scars to match his own. But Cecco read her eyes, and he understood his woman. He was satisfied.

His mark encircled her heart.

Prisoners of Love

In the light seeping through the bed curtain, Hook inspected his chains. He found their silence to be caused by a web of flannel threaded through every link. The girl was resourceful, no doubt about that. Still, steady breathing indicated that her father occupied the bunk below. The need for stealth was paramount.

First, he must satisfy his craving for water. Looking askance at the flask tucked between the bed and the board, he reached instead for the bottle. A small linen bundle and a serving of fruit also reposed above the girl's pillow, but Hook's throat was too dry to swallow food. He moved slowly to avoid jarring the girl, and after pulling the cork, he sniffed the bottle's contents. They were odorless. Deciding it was water, he took several swallows and stopped. He would wait to test its effect before drinking more. He didn't trust the doctor or the daughter. Or, perhaps, he trusted them too well.

Next he searched for his keys. The obvious place was on the girl, or in her hand. Lifting the linen, Hook discovered without surprise that she wore no nightdress. She wore nothing at all. Nothing except the brutal bruises of the cane. Had her father punished her for her lewdness, or had he simply unleashed his frustrations on her? The root of her craving for a strong man's interest was plain, and Hook found that need both appealing and pathetic. Even as the shackles she had inflicted held him prisoner, Hook was struck by her vulnerability. Her naïveté.

She didn't know with whom she was playing.

The keys were not on her person. He surveyed her hands and found nothing there, not even the pearl ring she had offered him. Running his wrist under her pillow revealed nothing, and slipping his fingers between the board and the mattress, he felt as far as his fetters allowed, to no avail.

His search turned up one item, however, of great interest to him. His own shirt, secreted at the foot of the bed, where it must have resided for weeks. Hook's instincts were true on that morning of its disappearance. This little girl already owned a pirate's heart. Pilfering since the beginning of her service, she'd tried to steal the master from the mistress, beginning with his clothing. Hook assured himself she hadn't hidden the keys within its folds, noting as he did so that his garment had absorbed her scent— a musky femininity. He stuffed the shirt back into its hiding place.

Finding the napkin barely within reach, he pulled a corner until he could seize the bulk of the bundle. He backed to the wall and unrolled it on the bed before him, cautious in case it concealed his jingling keys. He found only bread and cheese. The food was not abundant, but welcome, and after another measure of drink, he consumed it as he continued his surveillance.

Further exploration of the bedclothes produced no result. He reached for the fruit, prodding the bowl with his empty wrist, his body poised to prevent brushing the girl. Helping himself to more water, he studied her face with narrowed eyes. As the strawberries took only the edge off his hunger, he formulated a plan. He measured the intrigue of her proposition, the boon she demanded in exchange for his freedom. If she didn't hold the keys, she knew where they were.

Hook pushed the remnants of the meal away and felt of his whiskers. They were rough and long, about three days' growth. The ship crooned her lullabies, and her company continued silent. Clearly, it was late in the night. The third night. He could open the bed curtain with his stump if he wished to view a window, but he wouldn't pull it aside for fear of a sound that might wake the surgeon.

The untrustworthy surgeon…who for long had tempted his Jill. Like the daughter, the father was compelling. Jill indulged the man's attentions, basked in them, but she was too clever for him. Even in

Hook's absence, the man slept alone. No, Jill was managing, most likely with Smee's assistance. Her nights were restless. Hook knew from his own lack of sleep— Jill was agitated. He'd set a burden on her shoulders, and it was no wonder she lacked for rest. No doubt Hanover hounded her. No doubt Smee had his hands full fending him off.

What story had the surgeon concocted? A tale, Hook was certain, worthy of Jill herself. Did she believe her lover dead? Soon he would return, and discover to what extent his bo'sun consoled her. Perhaps something else disturbed her nights. Something beyond anxiety for Hook himself. He would know with one look. He would read it in her eyes. And in Smee's.

Jill was a passionate woman. No doubt the two had drawn together in the circumstances. What sailor could resist those eyes when they were full of tears, wet and salty, and blue like the sea? Certainly not Smee, who had already been tested to his limits, even before his captain's 'demise.' Smee habitually displayed his jealousy of the surgeon. Jill had played on Smee's jealousy, to increase the doctor's passion. And Smee had balanced near the brink as he held Jill after the fencing match, when she'd worn that dark smile that annihilated reason. In that moment, even Hook nearly lost control. So besotted was her captain that night that, as if conjured by a sorceress, the chain of sapphires appeared in his hand to slide through his fingers. Hook's every wish was granted— but not Smee's. Shortly thereafter, Smee went so far as to seek out and conquer the lady's look-alike, a little blonde barmaid in the port of Gao. But Hook remained calm along this line of thought. He'd shared women with Smee before. And Jill was his soul. On occasion, he'd shared *that* with Smee, as well. To those who earned his trust, James Hook was a generous man.

Those who abused his trust died.

Roused by his thoughts, Hook turned his gaze on the girl again. He assessed her appearance, noting the changes that had taken place since she joined up with pirates. Like Jill, she had ripened before his eyes. Unlike Jill, she hadn't piqued his interest until she threw herself at him. This slip of a girl wove a kink into his master plan— and he had allowed it! Hook had recognized her passion for him, perversely nurtured it, had reaped gratification from denying her the least grain of satisfaction. As Jill's charade with the surgeon intensified, Hook played his own game with the girl, timing his movements to avoid her, and watching to see what ploy she would invent to cast herself in his path.

But he was not immune to idolatry. Baiting the surgeon through his daughter was only one aspect of Hook's amusement. Before long, her wiles earned her a beating at her father's hands, and Hook found himself both repulsed and fascinated by the depth of her submission. And by the force of her will. He had misjudged the girl, assuming she would tire of the disappointments and attach herself to one of his sailors. Yet her desire for her captain proved tenacious. It had pleased him to lead her a merry chase, and of late he'd grown overconfident in his dealings with her. Hook acknowledged the truth: his own arrogance delivered him into her trap. He, who for years battled for supremacy over a boy, allowed himself to be entangled by a girl. The irony was bitter, but the lesson useful.

And what lesson would this Miss take away from her adventure? For she would live to learn one. Hook needed her to fetch the key. He observed her nakedness, and beneath it the rise and fall of her breathing, of which he could so easily make an end. She outfoxed him once. She wouldn't be lucky a second time.

His gaze traveled to her sleeping face. Miss Hanover had turned pretty. She modeled herself after her mistress. With a bit of imagination, the task at hand shouldn't be difficult to accomplish. It might even be pleasurable. After all, Hook had tutored Jill in much the same manner.

Smoothing his mustache, Hook drew a breath, smiled, and began.

Smee woke from his dreams and, for the hundredth time, cursed his stubborn streak. If only he'd listened to her, listened to reason. *He'd* be the man shouldering Jill's burden. Alone in the depth of the night, he let loose his inclinations— to lie in the captain's bunk, his boots beneath her bed, his strength surrounding her. She didn't lack for anything with Cecco beside her, but there'd be hell to pay when the captain got back. Smee's trust in the lady had returned so fully that he no longer entertained doubt. In the darkness he could admit it. He should have stepped in for the captain. He should have cared for Jill as Hook had cared for Lily. And not just in his dreams.

Hook would return. He'd return with a vengeance. First thing, he'd look to the lady, and he'd see it all over her. The gypsy's love. A man couldn't mistake that. Not a man like Hook.

Smee sighed and heaved himself upright. Second, the captain would look to his bo'sun. He'd see the regret, and then he'd shift those blue fires to Cecco, and his sword would shriek from its scabbard. He'd be ready with his sword, because Smee would hand it over the moment the captain materialized. He owed his captain that much. And more. Smee bent to feel under his bunk, and his hand closed on it: the finest rapier money could buy, awaiting its master.

Smee turned up his lamp. With a slow hiss, he drew the weapon from its scabbard. Having resolved his course of action, he set to work immediately. He'd cleaned and sharpened this rapier three days ago, before the ill-fated duel, but the least he could do was to keep it pristine. Making up for his mistakes. Smee's mouth tightened as he remembered his words to Nibs and Tom. 'No shame.' Easier said than done. The 'hero' of the *Roger* had let everyone down, most especially the captain. But the lady had pardoned him. He'd best take the lesson and get on with his duty, as she advised her boys. He'd sleep better when he'd seen to the sword.

He dropped the scabbard on the bunk and slid a cloth down the blade. The rag eased along the steel, already so smooth from Smee's labors three days ago that it met no resistance. Pulling the cloth from the point, Smee was surprised to feel it snag. The fabric had caught on the tip. Smee cocked his head and reached for his spectacles. Examining the point, he found it flecked with wooden splinters. Damp, salty splinters. Picking them off, he saw that the finish underneath was beginning to corrode. The sword had returned to its scabbard uncleaned.

The captain never did such a thing. If he wasn't inclined to wipe the sword himself, he'd hand it off to Smee or to Tom to do the job. Hook took pride in his weapons. Always kept them ready, in prime condition.

Someone else had used this sword— and thrust it in its scabbard, soiled.

As his hands began to smooth away the damage, Smee's mind worked as well. He retraced the actions of that day, piecing the puzzle together. Hook accepted the rapier in the galley that morning, just polished by Smee. The bo'sun held an image of the rings on the captain's hand as he reached for it, and the subtle smile as he anticipated the victory ahead. Hook was about to apportion the surgeon's earnings, and clearly, he relished the thought.

He must have kept the rapier with him as he worked in the spare cabin, for that was where it was found. Right across the charts at the top of the desk. Smee's heart quailed as he recalled the rest…the coat languishing outside that cabin, snared by a splinter— a splinter… that had no cause to be where it was! A gouge inflicted by a sharp instrument, just such a tool as Smee now held in his hands. As bo'sun, it was Smee's job to husband the *Roger*. She'd have told him, if he'd taken the time to inspect her wound. Indulging his grief, Smee hadn't thought it through before. Now the vision of the coat came rushing home, the crimson cloth flailing from a gash in the stern. The wooden stern, coated with salty moisture. Like this sword!

Smee's stomach careened. He broke out in a cold sweat. The captain's coat had been hung there to be found. Hook's own weapon had pried up the splinter. Someone arranged the scene to look as if Hook had drowned.

And most likely it was true. Chances were, Captain Hook was dead.

Avoiding the thought, Smee's mind jumped ahead to sort the possibilities. Who would benefit from the captain's disappearance? The obvious answer was the doctor. He wanted Jill. He wanted his freedom. Hook, alive, would grant him neither.

But the lady kept the doctor occupied that morning. He was too entangled in her charms to leave her side. And, thank the Powers, the man was no better off now that the captain was gone.

Reluctantly, Smee considered more treacherous possibilities. Who, upon Hook's demise, in actuality reaped the benefits? Who seized Hook's power, Hook's place, Hook's woman? Established his friends as officers, had every man aboard, including the surgeon, calling him 'Captain?' He matched Hook in cunning, embellished Hook's schemes. He'd stowed a pouchful of diamonds in his sea chest, and due to his inheritance from Hook, enjoyed the companionship— no, the *adoration*— of the most desirable woman on the Seven Seas.

The gypsy.

But one man alone couldn't keep Jill from power. Two worked in tandem to thwart her. Perhaps they had conspired further, to take Hook down, as well. The doctor and the Italian had forged a friendship. Both were manipulators. Both experienced swordsmen. Each knew better than to sheath a soiled weapon.

One of them had been in a hurry.

Smee raised the rapier and let the lanternlight play up and down its length. No trace of blood smeared the blade. Hook hadn't been offered a fight. No. The sea had killed him. His beloved sea.

Through a wave of nausea, Smee finished the job and set the sword to hand. He would keep it close. It would never leave his side. Once Smee learned the truth, he would use it.

No matter how the lady begged for her lover's life, Smee would act. Those who abused Hook's trust would die. Like his master before him, Smee would show no mercy.

And then he'd plant his boots beneath her bed.

Liza awakened to a sweet taste. A strawberry. But it was soft and moist, and when her tongue reached for it, a set of firm lips pressed down on hers, and the taste invaded her mouth. She came fully awake.

It was a kiss! The kind of kiss she had witnessed and hungered for. Her eyes opened to take in the glorious sight of black brows and blue— the bluest eyes! The captain.

His flavor lingered, and when her hands tried to reach for him she discovered he had trapped them, one in his own, one under his body. The kiss died and Hook pulled away, but only an inch. He whispered without sound. "Be silent."

With her heart thumping in her chest, she nodded. He kissed her again, thoroughly, and raising his chest from hers, he leaned on his elbow. He released her hand so that his could caress her, exploring slowly at the edge of his bonds, up her side and coming to rest on her breast. His hand left a pleasant tickling sensation in his wake. Liza felt her flesh break out in goosebumps. She also felt the heavy links he dragged, cold even through their wrappings. He lowered himself down on her, and his chain bit into her skin.

"I cannot satisfy your wishes until I am free." His voice made barely a sound, but she heard him. Wincing from the harsh embrace of the metal, she shook her head.

He pressed himself onto her, and the links pained his ribs as well. "The key, love."

She opened her lips as if to speak, her eyes questioning. He covered her mouth again with his own. She endured the chain's discomfort, and only when she whimpered with pain did he end the kiss. "You will fetch it for me." His gaze roamed her face before he rolled to the side. As his eyes, impatient, appreciated her body, she sighed in relief and reached for his hand, to place it on her breast again. He permitted it. His fingers tingled on her nipple as, idly, he stroked her. Liza placed one open hand on her lips and gestured away from them, asking once more if she might use words.

He favored her with his beautiful smile. "Clever girl, to keep silence. You may speak, but take care not to wake your father."

"Sir. Make me your mistress…first."

"Ah. My mistress, yes. But a mistress must obey her master."

"I will obey, Sir. It is my wish to obey." The blood was pounding in her head now, and within her thighs. As if he knew it, he rewarded her with a touch there. With his handless wrist. She shivered.

"Good girl. Now, my little one, set your master free."

"Master, I will do everything in my power to please you. But I cannot find the key."

In an instant, the pleasure on his face turned to ice. His touch abandoned her. "Did I hear you aright? You deny my first demand?"

"Sir!"

"Search the cabin."

Too afraid of the fire of his eye to protest, Liza turned away and slithered from the bunk. Under his watchful gaze she hunted through her father's effects— within his medicine bag, through the drawers, the pockets of his empty clothing, his sea chest. Glancing at the dark man brooding behind her bed curtain, Liza warmed to know she was naked and under his scrutiny. She was sure her movements pleased him. Although her search was fruitless, his observation was fertile, and Liza herself was more than ready to harvest its rewards.

Continuing the deception that her father might wake at any moment, she moved in silence, and, as drugged as his prisoner had been, the surgeon never stirred. Liza's search went on. She startled when Hook tossed a bundle of white to the floor. Puzzled, she seized it and looked to him. With a shrewd expression, he gestured to her to don it. She blushed in the lanternlight. He had discovered her thievery! She slipped his stolen shirt on, shoved the sleeves above her elbows, and resumed her quest.

When at length she satisfied her captain that the key was unattainable, he summoned, and she bowed her head and pulled herself up to her bed. Sliding under the bedclothes, she pressed against him. If he was heated by anger, so much the better. His passion would be ignited, her rite of passage more intense than she had dreamed. Steeling herself, she reached for him. He allowed her touch, allowed her hands to roam his body, to slide within his shirt, to discover his desire, to provoke her own— then he stopped her fingers and squeezed her wrist through his own purloined cuff. His eyes smoldered with his fury.

"You aspire to be my mistress. Yet you displease me." His grip on her wrist seared through the fabric. "Here is your reward for disobedience. A punishment that will leave no marks." He flung her hand away, his silent chain swinging, and with a sneer, her lord and master turned his back and faced the wall.

Searching the darkness for his soul, Hook determined that Jill slept. With the taste of strawberry bitter in his throat, he closed his eyes to sleep likewise, his displeasure rekindling with a vision of his mermaid reclining in his bo'sun's embrace.

Time after time, Liza attempted to raise her arms to him. Remembering the flame of his eye, she felt her courage fail. Not daring to move, she counted the pulses of her blood where it beat between her legs. She felt the flush of her skin, the heat rising within her, like smoke off a branding iron— no, not an iron, but a hook, red-hot and glowing, its smoke sharp, too, swirling and surging. The smoke seemed trapped inside of her, suffocating. The night became a long dark space the shape of a casket, charred to black with his brand and filled with that smoke. It was a night in which thinking was impossible. If he questioned her now, even if he threatened her flesh with his flaming hook, she would not be able to recall that his keys lay wrapped in a bundle, stuffed in the muzzle of the third cannon just outside her door. Her mind, like her body, was void.

He hadn't taken her. He hadn't affirmed her. He had not so much as scorched her with his mark.

Disappointment was her master, and he was cruel.

"Doctor. The lady, as promised." Yulunga relinquished the lady's arm; she thanked him. He grinned his wide grin and backed halfway down the forecastle steps, to take up a lounging position while he observed the encounter. The morning was fine and bright, and Yulunga was liking his new job. Working for Captain Cecco proved both profitable and entertaining. The lady, too, appeared to appreciate it. In a gown of sapphire-blue and bedecked with Cecco's gold, she faced the surgeon with every sign of assurance. The doctor, tailored in his beige suit, looked slightly reduced without his diamond lining. But as his eyes slid from Yulunga to Jill, he recovered his aplomb.

"Madam. The captain granted this meeting so that I may apologize to you." Forbearing to touch the lady, he indicated the forward rail, and, assuring herself of Yulunga's vigilance first, she complied. Surely this man couldn't hurt her again. It seemed to Jill he had already done his damage. In any case, Cecco's protection held her safe now. Still, she held her tongue. She was mindful of the captain's commands, yet headstrong enough not to make this assignation easy for Hanover, whatever he had to say.

Hanover strolled to the bow, as far from Cecco's mate as the forecastle allowed, then kept his back to him. The breeze from behind beat against their legs and blew the sound of their voices away from the mate. "I understand your reluctance to speak to me. No doubt you are ashamed."

Jill raised her eyebrows.

"And of course you are afraid to cross the captain's will. While I am not afraid, I assure you I will do nothing to endanger you."

Jill lifted her eyes to the sky. Captain Cecco was correct. The surgeon's arrogance sustained him.

"And I do apologize. Sincerely. I admit I miscalculated when I threw my support behind the captain. He played on my trust, and used it against me."

"And you are surprised."

Hanover blinked. "If you venture to speak to me, kindly do so in a more respectful manner."

Too shocked to retort, Jill stared at him, her wide eyes narrowing. Hanover took her silence for acquiescence.

"I have offered my apology. Now I will tell you that in spite of your licentious behavior, my desire for you has not abated."

Jill replied, "As I told you from the beginning, Doctor Hanover, I make the best of the circumstances in which I find myself. Captain Cecco is a worthy partner. You must know I will answer every question he puts to me about our meeting. Beware of abusing his good will."

"Yes, he has impressed upon me the extremes of your honesty. As you yourself have done. But again, I fear nothing— except your suffering. I will alleviate that suffering in any way I can."

Implementing her strategy, Jill softened her gaze. "Thank you, Sir. Since you endeavor to make amends, I do have one favor to ask of you."

The surgeon seized upon the opening. "Please. You have only to ask."

Permitting herself a fraction of a smile, Jill cast her gaze down. "It seems I will soon require another vial of your sleeping draught."

The doctor sent a quick glance toward Yulunga, then turned his face from the mate to smile. Certain now of his success, his features showed themselves to best advantage; he was comfortable. "My darling! Of course. You shall have it before another night sets in."

"I am grateful. And now we'd best return to Mr. Yulunga—"

"Not yet. You will hear me out. Another such chance may prove rare."

"A chance for what, Doctor? Captain Cecco made his orders clear. The life you and I might have shared is now impossible."

"You know me better than to believe that. I have pledged to make an honest woman of you. I will keep my word."

"But how—"

"You will know nothing of the details. I will arrange everything. Only trust me."

"Trust you! It was you who 'arranged' my union with Captain Cecco."

"And it is I who will separate you."

"No."

"My dear, do not let your disappointment obstruct our future. I will carry through with my promise."

"I won't say I am disappointed with Captain Cecco. It's just that I can hardly bear the fact that Hook is—" Without effort, her eyes flooded with tears. She turned to the sea. The stair groaned as Yulunga stirred, raising himself up to observe. Hanover backed a pace, but his voice grew urgent.

"Jill." As she flinched at this familiarity, his fingers searched for his watch. "The captain forbids it, I know, but I *will* call you my Jill. You shall find it necessary to come with me."

"Why? You can't tempt me with your diamonds any longer."

"You speak out of bitterness. But I shall regain my fortune. You will obtain it for me."

"I?" she asked, incredulous.

"Listen. When I leave the ship, under whatever circumstances I create, you will choose to accompany me."

"Why should I not choose to remain with Captain Cecco? And your diamonds?"

"Because after LeCorbeau unites us in marriage, I will tell you where Hook has gone."

It was the one thing she hadn't expected. Backed against the rail, pressed tight against the braces, Jill faltered, assaulted by emotion— hope, alarm, despair.

Hanover had placed himself between Jill and Yulunga, blocking her shock from view. "I would hold you if I could. You know I cannot. Not yet."

"Where is he?" The panic surged from her closing throat. *"Where?"* Her fingers went white on the wood. She struggled to contain her breathing.

"Ah, now I stir your interest! I knew I would recapture you."

Yulunga angled his head, and Jill modulated her voice. "Don't toy with me. Tell me where Hook is!"

"All in good time. When we are aboard *L'Ormonde*— and wed."

"I'll tell the captain. He'll thrash it out of you."

"Do you think so? I don't believe he'll welcome tidings of his old master. Think what he'd lose in the bargain." Hanover had learned a thing or two from his partner. LeCorbeau couldn't have said it better. "One word to the wrong party, and I will lose my memory. No, Jill, you will tell no one. And you will come to me, with my treasure, when I bid you."

"He's alive, then?"

Hanover shook his head slowly, backing away. "You will know what I know when you are mine. Oh, yes— and see that you greet me appropriately when I come calling. You will welcome your future husband…with open arms." He bowed, turned toward Yulunga, and strode away.

Jill clung to the railing. Her heart threatened to batter its way out of her ribcage, but it couldn't escape. However agitated, Jill's heart was trapped, as surely as its lady.

She had believed the battle was over, that she was safe in Cecco's care. But the handsome doctor, the wealthy pirate surgeon, found her weakness as easily as her pulse, and in his practiced hands, she was a prisoner.

Dreams Come True

"Well, Mr. Yulunga! And where is my good friend Hook? The captain is engaged, no doubt, with his so-charming mistress." LeCorbeau tapped his foot, his beady eyes observing the company as he waited to be greeted by the *Roger*'s master. Mr. Smee and Mr. Mullins flanked Yulunga, and crewmen lined the deck. The surgeon stood in attendance, formal, as befitting the occasion. Nibs and Tom were nowhere in sight.

Yulunga towered over the Frenchman, beaming. "Of course. But he will attend you—" As the door to the captain's quarters swung open, Yulunga looked up. "Now." LeCorbeau and his mates turned expectant faces toward the companionway, ready to humor Captain Hook's flair for the dramatic.

Hook's lady emerged, smiling her greetings. She was escorted by a man. A dark man and handsome, but otherwise very unlike the captain his guests expected to greet. The *Roger*'s visitors dropped their jaws as they observed the pair.

Cecco's arm encircled Jill's waist. He descended the steps of the companionway with an air of entitlement, touching Hook's woman with every indication of possession. That this man was her lover, her master, and her captain, appeared indisputable. But where was Hook?

Taken aback, LeCorbeau watched in silence as the couple strolled toward him. Raising his eyebrows, he said at last, "*Alors*...I am amazed, *Monsieur!* But what have you done with the elegant Captain Hook, who for so long has dominated the *Roger?* Surely, you have not vanquished him in some duel over the fair one?" Yet both the admiration and the amusement in LeCorbeau's voice showed that he believed this circumstance to be exactly what had happened. He could read the triumph in Mr. Cecco's eyes, and the passion, as the Italian looked at the woman. The eyes of Hook's man, Mr. Smee, also smoldered, but with discontent. As LeCorbeau ascertained earlier, the woman's sons were conspicuous in their absence. With utmost restraint, the French captain refrained from turning a questioning gaze on the surgeon, who he was certain must have had a hand in this miracle. A hand! No, a hook! LeCorbeau stifled his humor. His hopes were on the rise as Cecco answered.

"Surely you cannot believe me guilty of mutiny, Captain LeCorbeau. Only an unfortunate event could gift me with the good fortune I now enjoy." Cecco directed Yulunga with a look, and his first mate took up his cue.

"Captain LeCorbeau, I present Captain Cecco. And his lady, Red-Handed Jill."

LeCorbeau cut a bow. "Captain. I congratulate you! But, eh, one cannot help but wonder how you came to this position, which a week ago one could not have predicted?"

"The circumstances remain a mystery. Our noble captain disappeared from our midst, and the indications lead us to believe that he is drowned."

As LeCorbeau listened, he stole quick glances at Jill, studying her without seeming to do so. He observed that although she maintained her composure, her lovely face seemed frozen. Quick to read any emotion he could use to his advantage, LeCorbeau determined Red-Handed Jill was mourning, but wise enough to submerge the fact. The Frenchman arranged his features to sympathize. "Ah, my condolences to all the company! But I see a new regime is now in place. One that, perhaps, will prove fortuitous for one and all."

"Yes. And as captain of the *Roger*, I wish to forge a new partnership with *L'Ormonde*'s master and crew. It is my hope that you will listen to my proposals this very evening, Captain LeCorbeau. Not only will we discuss our mutual profit, but there is another, more personal matter, with which I hope you will assist me."

Jill winced, but her expression remained pleasant. She and Cecco had prepared their roles for the Frenchman's benefit— Cecco to be the brutal conqueror, Jill, his helpless inheritance.

LeCorbeau's cuffs fluttered with his gestures. "But of course, Captain! I should be most honored to host such a meeting, and, eh, assist you in any way possible. And the personal matter? Am I to anticipate…?"

As Jill averted her face, Cecco tugged her closer. "Yes, LeCorbeau.· If you will hear me out, your wishes and mine will be fulfilled. As I establish command over the *Roger,* I must discard some cargo that has proven troublesome to me— but of interest to you." Jill attempted to pull away from Cecco, but he cinched her waist and gripped her chin. As her eyes rose to meet her captain's, LeCorbeau perceived two large tears on the brink of spilling. His questions were answered. Cecco smiled coldly at Jill, as if defying her to object. When she remained silent, he released her chin.

LeCorbeau leered. "*Vraiment, Monsieur,* you have your ship in order! I shall be most happy to discuss the situation with you. Bring your officers, and your cargo. I will now take my leave to make all things ready. Until tonight." The French captain turned on his heel and signaled to his men. Licking his lips, he paraded over the boards to his ship. Renaud and Guillaume exchanged smirks, then departed after their captain.

As LeCorbeau descended to his own deck, he spun to observe the woman once more. Cecco perused the French ship, admiring, while Jill stood unsmiling at his side, glowing with golden jewelry— and staring at the surgeon. Again, LeCorbeau read the emotions. The angle of her head and the hand at her breast informed him. He smiled.

From all appearances, the man fated to succeed Captain Hook was not, after all, the master of the *Roger.*

The day was ending. As the sun faded, the captain departed the cabin, his dusky gaze turning toward his Jill where she stood before her sons. She looked away and down, at the leather-bound book on his desk. Just below her signature, the surgeon's was inscribed, brash in its bold lines. Above her name, the ink glistened wet. As she listened for the click of the door, Jill's soul felt scored, as if the boys had dipped the quill in her heart's blood before striking out their names. She thought of the anguish she and her sons would soon endure, all for devotion to Hook. The boys at the hands of LeCorbeau, but Jill— sinking into despair, she felt the grasp of the manicured hands that had appropriated her. She pressed her fingers to her temples, her hope fading with the sunlight.

"Please, Ma'am. Don't take on so." Tom tried to engage her with a smile. "Nibs and I have always watched over each other. We'll be fine. And we'll learn French in the bargain."

Nibs' grim countenance cracked a smile. "Aye. Think of it. Mr. Starkey won't know where to have us when—" He couldn't finish.

Jill looked up at Nibs. "When you come back?"

Nibs tilted his head.

"The captain hasn't said anything, even to me, to indicate he would welcome you. You are on your own. When our business is finished and LeCorbeau sails off, we may never see each other again." Part of her even hoped this was true. Where Jill had to go, she didn't want her boys to follow.

Taking her hand, Nibs said, "No. He hasn't asked us back. That's to be expected. But there's no point worrying. We'll all be doing what we have to do, and there's comfort in that."

Jill felt the reassurance of his grip. "Aye. What we have to do. Even if it means leaving inclination behind."

Tom observed her face. "You've had a bit of time to get used to our leaving. It's not your way, Ma'am, to bemoan the unavoidable. Is something else awry?"

Nibs' gaze fell on Jill's leather bracelets, and the pinkish skin beneath. "Is it Cecco? Has he punished you for our decision?" The crease between his brows deepened, and his hand strayed to his knife.

"*Captain* Cecco, Nibs, and no. You mustn't think it. The captain has been firm, but understanding. He's not at all pleased with you, but he's true to his word."

"He promised to look after you. Otherwise, we'd never leave."

"Then I'm sorry I told you the truth."

Tom massaged his scar. "Tell us the truth again. What's on your mind, besides our going?"

"Concern for the ship. As always." And the ship's captains, both of them. How could she do her duty to one, and remain faithful to her accord with the other? Since this morning's talk with the surgeon, Jill felt smothered by that endless question. Until today, her accord with Cecco seemed the best way to serve Captain Hook. But now…Shaking herself from her apprehension, Jill returned her thoughts to her farewell to her sons, who, like she, were about to risk their safety for Hook's sake.

She said, "I'd rest easier if I was certain you could fly. But you'll have to hide that, and who knows if after sailing under LeCorbeau, you'll be able to summon the spirit? Pleasant thoughts may not be easy to find aboard *L'Ormonde*. But I've given you my counsel. I hope you'll remember what I've advised. And Nibs. Keep this in your pocket." From within her bodice, Jill pulled a small glass vial.

The young men examined its contents. An amber liquid. Glancing at each other first, they looked inquiringly to Jill.

"It is a sleeping draught. One half teaspoon in a few ounces of water, I've been told, will stop a man in his tracks. I hope you never need it, but if you do, you must handle it discreetly. If LeCorbeau understood you'd used it against him…"

Nibs accepted the vial. "I understand. But how do you know this? Do you mean to say you've used it?"

"No." And again, her thoughts turned to the nightmare ahead. "Not yet."

Tom's eyes narrowed. "Ma'am? Will we be staying after all?"

"The captain won't allow it. And he's promised you to LeCorbeau. No, you have to go. And perhaps it is better if you leave the *Roger*."

"What do you mean by that?"

"Only that I've got my duty to do, too, and it's best to just get on with it."

Tom said, "We regret to leave you. It's that much easier that you understand."

"Aye, Ma'am," added Nibs, "But take care of yourself. We'll send word to you, somehow, whatever we find." But for each of them, the hope of recovering Hook alive was ebbing.

Jill opened her arms, and first Tom, then Nibs, took comfort in their mother's embraces, one last time. Blinking back her tears, she didn't try to smile. "We may meet again. Sooner than we think." She didn't burden the boys with her knowledge. The certain knowledge, now, that the family *would* reunite, and soon. Too soon, Captain Cecco would seethe to find the ink still wet in a slash across his lady's name. One day in the not-so-distant future, Jill would join her sons aboard *L'Ormonde*. On a day they would all regret.

Her wedding day.

Yulunga had his instructions. Until Cecco's return, only the girl was to enter the master's quarters. Captain Cecco bade his lady farewell in full view of the surgeon, who watched with an air of satisfaction at which Yulunga squinted. Then Cecco and his other officers trouped in twilight across the boards to *L'Ormonde*, ready to feast, drink, and parley. The boots of Nibs the Knife and Tom Tootles tramped behind the doctor's softer tread. With their sea chests on their shoulders, the young men alighted and turned to salute the lady. Her eyes followed her son's orange kerchief as he disappeared down *L'Ormonde*'s hatch. In two lithe steps, Nibs was gone. Tom took one assessing look around the deck, readjusted his box, and plunged after. Yulunga supervised the stowing of the plank before presenting himself to the mistress. Without a word, she acknowledged the mate, turned, and mounted the darkening steps toward her cabin. As ordered by the captain, Yulunga followed.

"Good evening Ma'am. I will be on guard. Call if you need me." He closed the door behind her, and waited to try the door once she had locked it.

When Liza pattered up the steps, Yulunga was ready for her. His golden earrings were the first thing she noticed. As her eyes opened with interest, Yulunga grinned.

"Yes, Miss. These are the earrings I promised."

She reached for one.

He pulled his head back. "No, not until you've earned them. And the captain says no man's to touch you. Yet."

Liza's gaze darted along the deck. Most of the men were off duty, below decks or observing the doings aboard the sister ship, whence sounds of merriment were rising. Sliding closer to Yulunga, the girl stretched out a tentative finger. As her touch grazed his chest, Yulunga felt an immediate stirring. He backed a step.

"Captain says you're to be patient, too, little girl. I aim to see that you are." But his pleasure shone in his black eyes. "I will be watching. You'll keep your fingers off the other men, or I'll see to it those eager hands are clapped in irons again." As she drew back, scowling, his laugh swelled and his necklace strained against it. "Go in to your mistress, now. It's the safest place for you."

Digging for the keys, Yulunga didn't hide his anticipation. He assured himself of the pearl ring that nestled in his pocket, then strode to the door and knocked. The mistress' voice, fainter than usual, consented. He unlocked the bolt and waited to shoot it home again once the girl had disappeared behind it. As he watched her saucy backside, his breeches felt the strain of obeying the captain's order.

The key snapped the lock. Jill didn't look up.

"Take down my nightdress, Liza. I'm ready to retire."

The girl did as she was told. She helped the mistress out of her gown and into night attire. As she hung the sapphire taffeta, Liza appreciated its likeness to her captain's eyes. Her heart soared and sank at the same time. Thanks to a steady application of medicines, Hook was insensible all day. But tonight would be different. Liza had applied an inadequate dose this afternoon, both of water and of potion. For a few hours this evening her father would be occupied elsewhere, and Hook was hers. She wouldn't fail to stir his desire again, as she had so easily stirred Yulunga's. And just as she obeyed her mistress now, just as she seemed to obey her father, she would perform every duty her captain commanded.

The surgeon hadn't missed the keys this morning. Liza had recovered her wits at last, and as dawn etched the sky, she crept to the gun deck to retrieve the brass ring. When her father woke, the keys were in his pocket, just where they should be. Captain Hook had eased last night's temper in the sleep that proved all too rare for him, and upon his rousing, his surgeon and his thirst forced him to drink the tainted mixture, meager as it was. His chains clinked as he reached for it, for Liza had hidden the flannel strips. His jewel-blue gaze cut through Liza's soul as he communicated his orders, again. He ignored Hanover, who stood by with his cane at the ready. Parched as he was, Hook paused to concentrate all his will on the girl, silently commanding her obedience. She thrilled as she read his message— deliver the keys, and Hook would deliver his passion. His rising passion.

When Jill's needs were satisfied, she dismissed the girl. But Liza balked. Looking sly, she turned her back and raised her skirts.

Jill lowered herself to the bunk, puzzled. "Liza? What—" She startled as a thump hit the carpet. From its hiding place around her hips, Liza was uncoiling a rope.

The girl continued to smile as she remembered Yulunga's forbearance. She had known he wouldn't touch her. Her advances ensured it. Had the man followed his inclination instead of his orders, he'd have discovered her smuggling. But she would win those earrings— maybe next time, when she returned to retrieve the rope, the 'key' to the lady's chamber.

Watching with a swelling dread, Jill sat stiff. Liza gathered up the coil and bore it to the aft windows.

"No, Liza."

The girl paid no heed. She raised two windows wide, hooking each of them to the ceiling, then looped the rope around the panel between, and tied it. Her hands were practiced. It was obvious an experienced man had drilled her on the knot. When it was secure, she tested it with a tug, then hoisted the coil and tossed it out to sea. Jill watched it go taut as it stretched to its fullest extent. She imagined its end, dangling just outside the window of the lower middle cabin. Liza poked her head out to inspect her work, then turned to approach her mistress.

"Liza. Tell him— tell him…" But Jill could think of no words. The power to refuse the surgeon had deserted her. The time to thwart him was past. Beyond all things, Jill needed to learn Hook's fate. Unwilling to allow her servant to see her helplessness, the lady rose to stand, commanding. "Leave me alone."

Liza curtsied, then pulled a scrap of parchment from her pocket and offered it to her mistress. As Jill reached for it, the girl looked down, then slid her gaze up again to witness the lady's response. Jill maintained her composure, but her face went as colorless as the parchment she unfolded.

Liza knew what it said. She recited it to herself as she recalled his handsome script, in bold black ink. She had hung over him as he penned it, daring, for once, to rest her palms affectionately on his shoulders as she watched his hand, firm and unyielding. His face had been the same.

Jill's lips opened as she recognized the writing. Above the rising voices of the party aboard *L'Ormonde*, Liza heard the lady's breath catch, just before she stopped breathing altogether.

It was a brief message, a single declaration. One harmless word. The word the man had waited to hear Jill speak. Now the word belonged to him. It was the doctor's order, and a husband's command.

Sickening, Jill closed her eyes and crumpled the parchment. She heard his voice as if he stood before her, in place of his daughter. As, with the assistance of his rope, he *would* stand before her, ready for a bout of love-making— looking handsome, slightly disheveled…and aggressive.

'*Tonight.*'

Jill and Liza stared at one another. Both females knew. Nothing remained to stand in the doctor's way. Not the captain, nor his intimidating mate, nor loyal Mr. Smee. The only thing that could hinder the surgeon's triumph— tonight— would be a miracle.

Hook's return.

Nibs followed Renaud to the crew deck, Tom on his heels. The young mate was smiling. His master was pleased, and life would be easy for awhile.

"Mr. Nibs. We very much welcome you aboard *L'Ormonde*. And Mr. Tootles. Already, Guillaume has high hopes of recovery! Your good doctor will tend him this evening, and I am certain he will find my cousin much improved."

"We're glad of that, but we just signed up for the adventure. With Captain Hook gone, we wanted a change."

"Do not be modest, Mr. Nibs. You have earned the captain's regard. His interest in your career will advance you. He knows you have the necessary qualities to make an officer."

"As he knew you have."

Flattered, Renaud grinned. "I cannot deny it! This is the crew deck. Mr. Tootles, here is your hammock, toward the bow. Mr. Nibs, you are to bunk in a private cabin, right next to my own and Guillaume's." After assigning Tom a forward hammock, Renaud led Nibs aft, where the two entered a tiny cabin in which Nibs had to stoop to avoid the ceiling. But there were windows, two off the stern. Nibs was satisfied. He could fit through those windows. Tom might squeeze out, as well.

"This is fine, Mr. Renaud. I'm that glad to have my own quarters. I never would have done aboard the *Roger*." The only drawback as far as Nibs could see was his proximity to the first and second mates. Nibs knew he'd be watched. And he and Tom were separated. As Tom entered to inspect Nibs' quarters, the brothers exchanged nods. Each was thinking the same thing. Somehow, despite their distance, they would have to keep in touch.

But Renaud's next words indicated LeCorbeau's wishes to the contrary.

"Mr. Tootles, you are assigned to the first shift, starting tomorrow. Get an early night's sleep, for you'll be in the rigging at dawn. Mr. Nibs, you are to join the captain's guests this evening and report for duty at the wheel at second shift." He smiled. "You are to be granted an honor. The *commandant* intends personally to supervise you. Come, I will show you to the captain's quarters, and you will be fêted by the *commandant* himself!"

Apprehensive already, Tom sent a cheerful signal to Nibs and said good-night. Within half an hour he was playing cards with the rowdy night shift, who had no duties tonight because of the parley. Within an hour he'd learned the French terms for Ace, King, Queen and grog, and he'd added a few francs to his pouch. Tom determined that before long, he'd be ignored by LeCorbeau and well enough accepted by the crew to begin inspecting the holds.

When Tom left, Nibs stowed his sea chest against the bulkhead, there being no room for it at the foot of his bunk. Stuffing his fist in his pocket, he felt the reassuring presence of Jill's weapon. He wouldn't need the potion tonight, but he'd keep it with him. With a glance at his quarters, though, and a look at Renaud's friendly face, Nibs determined *L'Ormonde* and her crew had much to offer a rising young seaman. He'd make the best of it, until he could find a way back home.

And he'd keep his eyes and ears open for signs of his captain. If Hook was alive, he had to be here, aboard the *Roger*'s sister. Nibs tested the knot of his kerchief and followed Renaud to the party, where, under the approving eyes of Captain Cecco, LeCorbeau welcomed him, literally, with open arms.

Smiling over the wine, Cecco hid his uneasiness. Except for the brooding of his bo'sun, he found no good reason for the feeling, but he couldn't shake it. His concern for his lady's sons nagged beneath his merriment, yet he surmised that those seamen were capable of fending for themselves. He, Mr. Starkey, and the rest of the crew had seen to that as the young sailors trained.

The lingering resentment on the Irishman's features set Cecco to thinking. Aware as he was of the man's devotion to Jill, Cecco couldn't help but believe Smee's glower related to her well-being. Once or twice the captain tried to catch the bo'sun's eye to divine a clue to his thoughts, but Smee spared his new master only a glance, and delved into his cup.

Watching the surgeon now, Cecco wondered again. The man's appearance always contrasted with his surroundings, so stiff and formal among sailors, and even more so within the elegant decadence of the Frenchman's lair. Yet tonight the doctor smiled and feasted with the rest, seeming equally at ease in the smoky, crowded room. He even appeared to enjoy himself. Cecco noted that the bo'sun's observation, too, followed Hanover, and Cecco's concerns were allayed. Obviously, Smee still resented the surgeon, both for his pretensions to Jill and his collusion to elect the new captain.

Relaxing, Cecco drained his glass and smiled at LeCorbeau. The Frenchman in his triumph was an amusing sight. And Cecco had to admire Mr. Nibs, whose sense of duty balanced his distaste, and who bore his circumstances with a philosophy beyond his years.

Cecco nodded to himself. Nibs had learned this philosophy from his lovely mother. As always, the image of the lady aroused her lover, and he shifted in his chair and counted the minutes until he might return to her. Perhaps, as LeCorbeau was so happily engaged, Cecco could slip away earlier than planned. Jill's captain would wake her with the pleasant weight, not of duty this time, but of gold. He would shower her with it. Cecco hailed another glass of wine, smiled, and patted the pouch at his belt.

LeCorbeau's gold.

The ruse was too good. Mr. Smee balanced Hook's rapier on his knees and strung the evidence together. Cecco made a show of dispensing with the lady's lads. He'd somehow bargained with the Frenchman until the little bag of gold strained like a sail in a gale, but Smee got the feeling in his craw that every gain Cecco made in pretense, he enjoyed in actuality. Now nothing and no one, excepting his bo'sun, could expose his betrayal. He was no longer hampered even by the surgeon who had connived with him through the first ruse, and lost.

Renaud offered Smee another glass, and the bo'sun accepted. He took one gulp and then, clearing a space on the brocaded tablecloth, he set it down. He wouldn't touch another drop. The wine was strong.

Not strong enough.

Hanover blinked in the light of the tapers and excused himself from the littered table. In spite of his elation, his stomach churned at the sight of his partner draping himself over the young man. Even knowing LeCorbeau's peculiarities, the surgeon was shocked. The collaborators had held the briefest meeting after LeCorbeau arranged for Hanover to attend Guillaume. Hanover had time to explain only that Hook had assaulted his daughter, and then Cecco had stamped in, demanding that LeCorbeau join the company, and congratulating the mate on his obvious recovery. But the lack of detail was of no consequence; LeCorbeau understood that Hook was out of the way, Nibs was in his power, and Jill would soon follow her sons to *L'Ormonde*. Now the company appeared inebriated enough not to notice the surgeon's absence, and he shot his cuffs and secured his medical bag. As he weaved his way through the oppressive haze of spirits and tobacco toward the cabin door, Hanover imagined the more sublime sight in which soon he would be reveling. The bridal veil of her hair, shining in the golden light of tapers.

Sooner than Tom expected, the crew deck fell quiet, the hammocks suspending their heavy contents and the lanterns burning low. He hoisted his bulk from his bed and made his way aft. *L'Ormonde* squeezed three cabins into this section. Tom determined to check them all, tonight. The chance that a captive captain was hidden in such an obvious place was a long one, but Tom intended to leave no possibility untried, and the sooner the better.

Lifting a lantern from its peg, he cast a look about and listened to the revelry upstairs, then he crept toward the mates' cabin. Best to start there, before the boys left the party. He laid his hand on the brass knob. Its chill sent a shudder up his spine, but he turned it, held his breath against a squeak, and opened. Only at the last second did he think to rap before entering.

Monsieur Guillaume sat back on his bunk, supine, his arms crossed and his blue-stockinged feet extended before him. At odds with his posture, his snappy coat with its brass buttons hung at attention from a peg above him. He looked up at Tom's knock, then he smirked.

"*Bonsoir*, Mr. Tootles! Have you, too, come inquiring after my health?" The second mate studied Tom's discomfort, and his eyes lit with mischief. "Or are you, perhaps, seeking advice on what, in our captain's opinion, makes a good sailor?"

Tom swallowed and grinned. "Evening, Mr. Guillaume." He cleared his throat, shifting his stance along with his tactics. "Whatever

I came for, I'm guessing I came to the right place."

With a smile as acute as his eye, Guillaume reached behind his pillow. Producing a bottle of cognac with a very old label, he ordered, "Come, Mr. Tootles. No need for we of lesser rank to miss the festivities."

"Doesn't Captain LeCorbeau enforce rules about officers fraternizing with the sailors? Sir?"

"Oh, no. Quite the contrary. Our captain requires that his officers train his men— in whatever skills they may be lacking." With the bottle, he indicated the foot of his bunk. "Make yourself comfortable. I had not thought of working tonight, but since you present me with the opportunity, I may as well begin my duties."

"That looks to be a respectable bottle of brandy, Mr. Guillaume."

"*Oui.* One of the benefits of serving a man of taste."

"It puts me in mind of my former captain. James Hook was a gentleman, head to toe."

"A gentleman? Don't make me laugh! There is no such thing. I've seen the world. It holds only two kinds of men. Those who have what they want, and those who want what other men have."

"And which are you, Sir?"

Guillaume eyed Tom. Deciding the sailor was more curious than cheeky, he exhibited the cognac. "I have what I want. And you?"

Tom thought a moment, reflecting on his reason for boarding *L'Ormonde*. He reached for the bottle and seized it. "Maybe I want what you have."

Not displeased by the gesture, Guillaume laughed and sat up. "As you say, Mr. Tootles. You have come to the right place."

"At last you have pleased me, Liza." He awarded her a kiss, and softly shut the door. The air of the gun deck was refreshing; he lifted his face to clear his head. After confinement in that cramped cabin, the sea air invigorated him— nearly as much as his anticipated reunion with Jill. The sleeves of his shirt rippled in the breeze, and he breathed deeply in the darkness. Then, without a sound, he entered the unoccupied quarters and eased the door closed. Jill would welcome her lover's return. How ironic that his little one had made it possible. For the great good that, in the end, the girl had done him, she claimed a pittance in return. A little affection, easily bestowed.

It was there, just as she told him. The lantern she'd left burning by the window illuminated the knotted end of rope, which swung with the movement of the ship. He hefted the sash, hooked it to the ring on the ceiling, and vaulted to the sill. From portside floated the sounds of mirth and music. The company on *L'Ormonde* pursued their pleasures, and none aboard her could spy the stern of the *Roger*.

Grasping the line, he shoved away from the hull, indulging in the heady feel of freedom as the cable swung him over the sea. His bare feet grasped the knot, which scraped between them as he thrust his body upward. As he gravitated toward the ship, he pressed his feet flat against it. The wood's dampness lent him traction for the climb. Wrapping the rope around his forearms as he went, he strained to pull himself upward. But he hardly felt the struggle. The time of privation had served to strengthen him. And that misery was over now. Thanks to the girl, the woman was in reach, and really, the effort was as nothing. Nothing but the promise of pleasure.

For with every heave he ascended toward heaven, and the angel who awaited him.

His little one busied herself the instant the door closed. All was in readiness. After moving it into place, she shed her clothing and climbed into bed. As tired as she was, she knew that this night, the night of her transformation, she'd win no rest at all. In her sleeplessness she would have plenty of company. Hook wouldn't sleep, nor would Jill, nor Cecco. Nor even her father.

Satisfied, Liza didn't bother to close the bed curtain tonight. She was fearless. No need to hide anything anymore. She needn't obey her father any longer, and Jill least of all. At last the tables were turned. Cecco was carousing, Hook had spent his last night as a prisoner, and from now Liza rightfully assumed her role as his mistress.

In her happiness, she toyed with the chains. Their clink made a merry sound that matched her mood. When the moment seemed right she sat up, snatched the bottle— already uncorked— and tipping it up, imbibed a long draught. Then she smiled, poured a measure over her breasts, and waited.

Hook would be quick about his business. Tonight, he belonged to Liza. His little one.

To Have and To Hold

He expected her to be watching for him. As he hauled his shoulders through the window, he shook his hair from his face and glimpsed the flickering interior of the familiar cabin. No welcoming hands assisted him as he pulled himself over the gilded sill. He settled on the window seat. His arms and his fingers burned from the bite of the rope, and he rubbed them on his breeches as he searched the shadows.

Sliding his feet to the floor, he felt the luxury of the Oriental carpets against his skin. Two lanterns glowed, one above the daybed, and one above the bunk. A candle lit the dining table, calling his attention to a goblet and a pewter cup there. He headed toward them. The goblet was filled, waiting for him. The cup appeared empty. Near them lay a parchment. Liza had assured him the lady expected his visit, and he anticipated the paper's message, sweet and poignant, like the wine. He tilted the letter toward the candle's light and read.

> *My dear Sir~*
> *Do as you will with this offering. Only believe that I do not betray you.*
> *With all my heart, I am trusting you.*

Gratified, he raised the cup and drank from the vessel her hands had filled for him, drinking in her affection, as well. He savored the taste, then exhaled, and as he did so the agony of the previous days diminished. Turning toward the bunk, he set down the glass and moved to reclaim her. His Jill.

She lay still in the lanternlight, her hair like gold against the pillow, her nightdress pure white. Her face was turned slightly away from him, her eyes closed, her expression troubled. Her lover knelt down at her side, breathing a delicate scent, and then he took her hand in his own. Marked with her precious blood, it appeared as crimson as ever. He kissed it.

She didn't stir. Smiling, he leaned over her to graze her lips with his kiss. The beauty did not awaken. He squeezed her shoulder, jostling her with a tender touch, but still she slumbered. Sliding his arm behind her, he raised her to his embrace, and he frowned to find her head lolling to the side.

His brows drew together; he knew these signs. He had experienced the effect often enough. He turned toward the table. That cup had held water— and, he now realized, a trace of amber liquid.

Jill had drugged herself to sleep, with the doctor's medicine.

He allowed her body to slide through his arms and fall back on the bed. Her hair sprawled around her face, unruly as a mermaid's. Slowly, he stood, his rage rising with his frame. He stared down at her, clenching his fingers, not quite believing what his eyes witnessed. He shook his head, refusing the frustration that threatened to set its teeth in him.

Raising his gaze, he now took note of the bed shelf. It was transformed into a treasure trove. Under the lantern gleamed her many bracelets, her earrings, her emerald ring, her anklet, and her several necklaces— gold, opal, and ruby. The jeweled dagger lay there, and near it her pistol glistened.

In preparation for someone's arrival, she had divested herself of all men's gifts. Bearing only two leather straps around her wrists, she lay naked of fetters or finery, free of belonging to anyone— as if uncertain who would awaken her. Thinking back, he understood that even her note was penned without particulars, devoid of specifics. She might have written it to any of her admirers. Now, cleansed and unconscious, with no protector but oblivion, the woman, like her jewelry, lay as vulnerable as it was possible to be.

I am trusting you.

Truly.

He stalked his way across the cabin and hoisted the goblet for another draught. When the glass was empty, he crumpled the parchment and tossed it away. Then, swiftly, he snatched up the pewter cup. In a movement of pure fury, he heaved the cup, dregs and all, out the window. Stiffly, he knelt on the bench, where he untied the knot the girl had secured, leaving the rope to dangle.

And then he rose, reached to the candle, and vanquished its flame between his fingers. Still feeling the burn within them, he strode back to the bed. As he gazed down at his love, his breast roiled inside, but he managed to tame his emotion. Yet even as he loosened his breeches, he smelled the reek of the dead candle's smoke. His fingers tingled with its fire.

Believe that I have not betrayed you.

Yes. In spite of the evidence, he believed. No man held a stronger claim on her than he. She was his Jill.

He lowered himself to her bed. He pulled open the ribbon of her nightdress.

And after all, he knew she wouldn't disappoint him. She was a valiant woman. Intelligent. She understood the virtue of silence. His smile turned smug. As it did so, Hanover felt the badge of his honor— the gentleman's scar— tighten on his face. From cheek to jaw.

Hook was parched, not fully awakened from the drugging, desperate for liquid. He had to have it. Liza had drunk some herself. How harmful could it be? Reckless, he lunged for the drops upon her body. With his tongue, he gathered the moisture she had sprinkled over her flesh. The droplets rolled down her breasts and he caught them, licked at them, and tried to swallow. But his thirst was not nearly slaked, and he craved for more.

The girl obliged, laughing as she fondled the neck of the bottle. Keeping it outside his chain's reach, she doused herself again, watching the wine trickle into a pool at her navel. He dove for it, his tongue delving for the drops, and she threw back her head and exclaimed. He hardly noticed her noises. He was thirsty.

Next she splashed her thighs, and again, he traced the rivulets. The linen became stained with her wine, the bedding moist between her legs, but she paid no heed to housekeeping. Like an extravagant courtesan, she poured for him again. His frenzy was catching, his tongue made her wild, and she pawed at his shoulders while his hair slunk over her belly. This time, when every drop of moisture on her skin was taken, the girl filled her mouth. Smiling, she lay on her back and, submitting to his body, let him have his way between her lips.

She had never felt so powerful, never experienced such heady pleasure. Her body thrilled to his stroking, her mind in ecstasy, too. He needed her, yearned for what she offered, and for these moments, she ruled him. The great man was at her mercy, dependent on her for his survival, and she relished these sensations. She filled her mouth again, and this time he fell back, hooking his handless arm around her neck and pulling her with him, and he opened his lips to receive her gifts.

The girl was generous. She filled him, again, and again.

And then she gave him the bottle. Trusting her, thinking with his throat, he drained it. As he lay panting, her fingers strayed to his breeches. One button at a time, she opened them. His eyes rolled toward her, growing luminous in the lanternlight, concentrating for the first time since he regained consciousness. He raised himself up on his elbow. He spoke, but his breath never evened.

"Now you will free me." In a spasm, his lip twitched.

She only smiled. "I will, Sir. When our agreement is fulfilled."

His eyes squeezed shut, tightly, and he pushed the words from his mouth. "Filled… fulfilled…?"

"We have time."

He squinted at the girl. She made no sense. "Time." He shook his head, and his stubbly black beard itched against his throat. "Time to go."

Liza relished his confusion. She played on it. Another minute or so, and he would be beyond even this. "Yes, it's time. Let me help you with your shirt, Sir." She shoved it over his shoulders and, unthinking, he ducked his head through the collar. She pulled it so that his sleeve slid up the chain and his beautiful body lay unsheathed. The little liquid she'd swallowed was having its effect upon her, too. She reached for his waistline, tugging at his trousers.

Succumbing to sensation, he lifted his hips and allowed her ministrations. Within moments they lay close together, naked on the wine-soaked sheet, their bodies heating toward fever-pitch.

And then his focus sharpened. He knew what she had done. With his desire uncovered, he glared at her, and his chains rattled as he seized her by the hair.

"Give me water, girl!"

She thrilled to his anger. "Water won't help, Master. But I do have what you need."

As if he held a fistful of snakes, he shook his hand free. He forced her away, but he couldn't stop himself. The next moment he pressed her closer. He hissed in her ear, "What I need is the key."

"It's here." She clutched his hand and held it to her heart.

Compelled by contact with her flesh, he rolled on top of the girl. His eyes blazed fire. "I'll take it, and leave you with nothing!" Unwillingly, he kissed her, shoving his face into her own and pressing his manhood to her flesh. She felt him, his teeth cutting into her lips, his weapon jabbing at her belly— and she was foolish enough to ignore his warning.

He raised his head, and above the uncontrolled jerking of his lip, his eyes appeared purple. "The philter. You administered the philter—"

"I'm yours now."

"I don't wish to have you!"

"You will, and then the fever will leave you."

He thrust up against her, crushing her, braising the skin of her abdomen. She tried to slide upward, to allow him access into her body, but he held her firmly in place. His teeth clenched. "You disobey."

"No, Sir. I swear to set you free."

His eyes were changing, alarmingly. "I won't—"

"But you need me."

He pressed her down, his arms as he leaned on them shaking with tension, but he strained to resist. "No!"

"You gave me your word!" Seizing him, she pulled herself up, rubbing her breasts against his chest.

With effort, he lifted his torso, separating from her. A cool draft floated between them, and again she propelled herself toward him. His arm shot out to distance her. He knelt, then drove her down and strung his chain across her chest, ice-cold against her heat, pinning her to the bed. The gash of his wrist grazed her face as he hoisted his right, handless arm. He glared at her with the red of his eye.

"I won't give you the satisfaction!"

He struck out with his forearm, slamming it against her temple. Her head snapped to the side, and she sank, senseless, into stupor.

Above her, feeling little relief, Hook rolled his burning eyes. He flung his hair from his face, and breathed. For a long, determining moment, with his one hand clenched to a fist and his shaking knees supporting his weight, he struggled against the drug. He tried to remember who he wanted this girl to be. But his nostrils sucked a too-familiar musk. His body swayed, and his mind filled itself— but not with reason. No shred of rationality remained.

The dampness of the linen changed, from wine to warmth. The man was lost to the world, knowing no sight, no sound. Nothing but the urgings of his lust. Unheeded, the chains on his arm and the chains on his ankle strained and rattled with his motions, and the timbers of the bunk whined to beg his mercy. Oblivious to violation, her body, neither willing nor unwilling, served him.

Rocking in his rhythm, he never heard the chink of his own brass keys, shaken off a nail and falling to the floor. Hook moved, fearless of discovery, hopeless of help, and still a prisoner— intertwined with the female, and in thrall to his thirst.

It was thus entangled, a sweat-soaked vision from a nightmare, that her father came upon them.

"*L'Ormonde* sounded lively from here, Sir, but all is quiet aboard the *Roger*."

"Thank you, Mr. Yulunga. It won't be so quiet in the morning. I have a bag of gold to divide among the men." Cecco's white teeth flashed a smile. He stepped back as Yulunga unlocked his cabin, then he dismissed his mate and entered.

Jill was sleeping. Cecco undressed, washed, and turned toward his bunk. Grinning, he tossed the pouch on it. It thumped against his pillow, sinking into a hollow, but the lady didn't rouse. As the captain sauntered closer, flexing his shoulders, he was curious. His mistress usually responded to him immediately, whether sleeping or waking. But then, she'd had a trying day, seeing her sons join the privateer. He would be gentle.

"Lovely one."

He slid under the comforter, anticipating the warmth of her body. But she was chilled. She wasn't wearing her nightdress, perhaps thinking he would come to her earlier. It lay across the foot of the bed, its ribbons spread open, as if welcoming a lover. He gathered her in his embrace to press his own heat against her bare, icy skin, and he rubbed her arms. It was then he felt the absence of his jewelry.

He followed her arm to the wrist. There, too, she was naked. Almost. Lifting her hand, he examined it. The fading mark of his binding was just visible under the strap of his leather. Cecco rose up to set the pouch on the bed shelf, out of the way. And there they were, all her treasures. But why had she removed them? Why display her weapons, and another man's gifts?

As his brow darkened, Captain Cecco shook his lady, who never before failed to please him in this bed. A suspicion began to flower. His gypsy instinct led him. Without his conscious direction, his hand slipped beneath her pillow. When it reemerged, a ring rested between his finger and his thumb. A simple band of gold. Too big for a lady. It was a man's ring.

A wedding ring.

Cecco threw off the covers. He raised up on his knees, flung the surgeon's ring on the shelf, and he slapped the woman in his bed until, as she never failed to do before, she awakened beneath his touch.

Her cheeks stung, and her eyes were misted, but she smiled to see him. Her eyelids drooped again, and she murmured, "Giovanni…"

The back of his hand collided with her mouth.

When she was able, she curled her fingers and pulled her hands away from the throbbing at her lips. This time, she uttered the proper word.

"Captain."

She didn't fall asleep again.

With a clarity born of experience, Doctor Hanover comprehended Liza's situation. He rushed into the room, knowing too well the danger to his daughter. Urgently, he yanked open his medicine bag and seized a bottle. He dashed its contents in a cup of water and leapt to the bunk.

"Drink this. Drink it! It will ease the symptoms— Drink!"

Beneath a tangle of black hair, Hook's wild eyes stared. His grisly wrist batted at the cup. Hanover braced himself against the bed frame and grabbed Hook's arm. It shook beneath his grasp. The man was already weakening. How long had he been this way? A glance at his daughter informed Hanover. He couldn't make out her face, but her body was pale— and bloodstained.

"Captain. You must trust me. Drink."

Whether due to the need for liquid or to the perception of truth, Hook allowed the doctor to clutch his skull and hold the cup to his lips. Like an animal he guzzled the substance, some of the fluid dribbling into his beard. He swiped his arm across his mouth. His breathing heaved, but the hideous twitching around his lip lessened.

Hanover threw the cup aside and hauled himself to the bunk. Pushing Hook by the shoulders, he eased the man's glistening body toward the wall, rolling him off the girl. Hook slumped there, panting, his hair matted with wine and perspiration. The red of his eye grew vacant. Hanover wasn't aware of the moment Hook's eyes closed. He had jumped to the floor and gathered up the girl, laying her ghost of a body on the lower bunk.

As he ministered to her, he shook his head. He brushed her hair from her face and, observing the purple bruise rising on her temple, determined the cause of her unconsciousness. Thank goodness, it wasn't from the drink; the effects of that concoction could render even the most robust physique febrile. Her lips were cut and swollen, her skin rubbed raw in patches, by his chains. She breathed, but without vigor. Her heartbeat lagged. Hanover felt of her limbs and found no broken bones.

But Liza herself was broken. Ruined. She bled from her wound, and no physician, however skilled, could repair the damage.

Liza was lost.

Hanover bowed his head over his daughter. Lost. Doomed from the very first moment she was dragged aboard this vessel, just as her father had feared. He should have seen it happening. He should have stopped it. That pirate had stolen her heart, and now— now he'd robbed her of the only possession a woman could truly own. The one belonging a gentleman treasured…her virtue.

In an instant, in the moment he'd pushed open the door to witness her degradation, the surgeon had understood. Despite his prejudice, regardless of his hatred, Doctor Hanover realized what this little one had done. She had dosed the man— overdosed him— with the philter. Hanover knew it. He was familiar with this man's agony. He'd seen those red eyes before.

In his reflection, on the night he murdered his wife.

Satisfaction

Gypsy fire smoldered in Cecco's eyes. "He was here."

"I saw no one."

"Here. In my bed!"

"I never knew it!"

Kneeling on the bunk, Cecco towered above her. "You have had a taste of the dish I will serve, if you lie." Dark rage marked his face, his hand upheld as if to strike.

"No, Sir, you know me. I tell you the truth!" Urgent as the instinct to shy from him was, Jill remained where she lay, shivering with cold. Everything depended on her courage.

"How do I know this, when I see you have not been alone?"

"But I was! So very alone."

He gestured toward her jewelry, his own bracelets flaring in the lanternlight. "And why this display?"

She turned her eyes toward the bed shelf.

"Answer."

She lifted her hands, palms up, to indicate her leather bindings. "Because these are all I need, to show to whom I belong."

He seethed, silent, his muscles bunched.

"Captain Cecco, I wanted you."

He shook his head, once. "So much so, you accepted another man's ring?" But as her face revealed her confusion, his shoulders eased a fraction.

"A ring?" she asked. "But I accepted that long ago— before we came together. Like the other things."

"I am speaking of the ring beneath your pillow. The wedding ring. Of the Doctor Hanover." He snatched it from the shelf. "This ring, my Jill."

Now he was certain. The look of horror on her face mingled with a look of surprise that could not be mistaken. Her voice shook. "Where did you get that?"

"As I told you. It lay snug beneath your lovely head." He angled his jaw. "Now tell me, my fine lady. How did such a ring enter this room to seduce you?"

"I will tell you what I know. I knew I wouldn't rest without you. I swallowed a sleeping draught…and then you woke me." She sat up, her hands moving as if to cover her breasts, and failing beautifully. She aimed her blue eyes at his heart. "Captain. I'm sorry I displeased you."

"Do not try to distract me."

"Please— I want *you*. I want you to make love to me."

He would not be diverted. "How did the man get past Yulunga?"

"Sir, you must ask Mr. Yulunga."

"Be sure of it. And be sure of this." He threw the ring on the floor, and then the pillows. Seizing her bodily, he lifted her up, and then he flung her across the bed, so that her head hung over one side and her feet reached for the other. "There will be no more soft pillows to hide your secrets. In token of your 'honesty,' you will hold your head up— until I am finished with you."

But even in his rage, Captain Cecco kept his promise; he waited for her sign of consent. Quickly, Jill offered her red hand to him. "Captain— You know you will never finish with me. Nor I with you."

"More of your 'truths.' "

"Yes! Yes, exactly! My words come true! Love me, right away, and you will see." By the careful use of potion, the judicious use of words, she had managed not to betray their accord— and she had kept the surgeon's secrets. Hanover would find no cause to withhold his information from her. Her prevarication cost her something, but she read Cecco's brooding eyes; she had half won him back. As she struggled to keep her head level, her lover entered her arms, more roughly than he had ever done. Jill welcomed him, pulled his body close against hers, sealed her lips with embraces so that no telltale words might escape.

She believed his fury would make him quick. Her aching neck informed her otherwise. Hoping she had done the right thing, striving to forget the distress of that terrible day, she indulged her passion for the man. In spite of his outrage, Cecco, as she had gambled, responded to her tenderness. Gradually, the flame of his anger turned to ardor. The hand that had struck her, only once, granted mercy, sliding at last beneath her head, to support her. He kissed her stinging lips and murmured in her ear.

"*Bellezza*. I will be gentle— with *you*."

And as she loved him, she felt his straps girding her wrists, a comfort in their constancy, and thanked the Powers that after all, at the very last moment, she had not been able to bring herself to cut them away.

The surgeon would attend to that. If he lived.

Tom shook the cobwebs from his head. They were quality cobwebs, spun by very old cognac. The party upstairs was abating, and he judged it time to slip away to his hammock. But even in his cups he remembered his duty. First he checked on Guillaume. The second mate snored, his blue stockings propped on his pillow, and Tom saluted the uniform on the wall. Then, somewhat woozy, he turned up his lantern, slid the bottle in his boot, and tucked both boots under his arm.

Easing from the mates' quarters, he stole starboard to search the cabin beyond. He didn't have to venture further than the threshold. Like Mr. Smee's, this room was cluttered with cabinets, paint pails and implements. The bunk was tidy, but empty. No unwilling guests.

Not surprised, but not satisfied, Tom made his way forward, past the bags of sleepers. These men, capable seamen all, were amiable enough. For the most part, he'd enjoy serving with them. That Guillaume, though, he bore watching. Tom's spur-of-the-moment mix of curiosity and aggression had squelched the man's suspicion. It also won his interest. Too handily. For the first time, Tom gave over his fears for Nibs and considered his own situation. The *commandant*, after all, had for a while to account to Captain Cecco for Nibs' well-being. But nobody— not even LeCorbeau— cared what game his officers played. Tom's instincts warned him to get about his business, and get off this ship.

He hauled himself into his hammock, where, before dropping off to sleep, he tested the edge of his knife. Captain Hook had run a tight ship. He'd commanded Mr. Starkey to work the young sailors hard. The lessons were painful at times, but Hook had looked after Tom and Nibs, in his own way. Tom felt prepared. He owed his best effort to Hook. Tomorrow, as soon as he descended from the rigging, he'd descend even further, to the hold. He'd keep his knife at the ready, and no matter what Mr. Guillaume had in mind, that was as far as he would ever descend.

Liza emerged from the fog to an unfamiliar feeling. A pleasing feeling. Delightful, but foreign. Strong, warm arms surrounded her. A firm chest pressed against her back, his skin smooth, slightly moist. As she lay there, she kept her eyes closed, in order not to dispel the magic of the moment. Feeling him caress her hair, she understood what had awakened her. He was stroking her, moving the strands from her face as if he cared for her comfort.

As if he cared for *her*.

No, that would be too good to be true. But he wanted her. The evidence pressed against her backside. And as Liza knew from her observations, this touching was part of the dance. She breathed in deeply to let him know that he stirred her, and his hand in her hair stilled for a moment, then continued its work. Only just touching the soreness at her temple, the too good fingers soothed her face. The right side of her face.

Still refusing to open her eyes, Liza stopped breathing. Of a sudden, her whole being rebelled.

He was stroking her. With his right hand.

As her body went rigid, the wrong arm wrapped around her waist, pinning her against his loins.

"Liza. You will not speak."

The bright new world broke into shards, and came crashing down around her. Her eyes opened. By the harsh morning light, she beheld the wall of her cabin…and the bottom of the upper bunk. Liza lay in her father's bed. In her father's grasp.

"You will dress yourself and report to the mistress."

"I am the mistress!"

"Do not test my patience."

Employing her elbows, digging into the bed, Liza flung herself around to confront her father.

His face was stony. "I have saved you. From your own foolishness."

Trapped again in the old grip of silence, Liza sat up to shake her head until the bed frame jiggled.

"I found the keys you stole from me. Nothing has changed."

With a growing dread, the girl observed the steely glint in her father's gaze. Slowly, she turned her eyes upward to indicate the occupant of the upper bunk.

"Yes. Your tricks have made our situation untenable."

She lowered her chin, waiting. Afraid.

"At the earliest opportunity, I will dispose of him."

Her face wrinkled in disbelief. She hardly felt the throb of her bruising.

"You yourself have orchestrated his death. He is severely weakened by your drugging. His recovery would be uncertain, even were I to order fluids and nourishment."

Incredulous, she raised her hand as if swearing an oath, and she saw her father's expression harden.

"Yes. As a physician, I have sworn no harm. The harm will be far greater if I fail to act."

With both hands, she seized him, realizing only now, as she gripped his vigorous arm, that she was naked in front of him, and he was clad only in his breeches. He shook her off and scowled at her, and in his daughter's eyes, the scar upon his face revealed his soul.

"And I now understand," he said. "In the same shameful way you witnessed the bawdy rites of our captor, you have spied upon me. While I engaged in the very act that creates life, you watched me extinguish it."

Liza's eyes, the eyes that had witnessed his crime, widened as she heard him speak of it.

"Your mother suffered from a delicate constitution. Like our prisoner, she outlived her usefulness." While Liza shrank into the bedclothes, he continued. "I administered too much of the philter that night. To your mother and to myself. And now you have made the same mistake. Your blunder, too, will cost a life. Let us hope it is not yours or mine."

Hanover rolled off the bed and dragged his daughter from it. "Now dress. Attend to the lady. Not a sign to anyone about your wretched captain, or I will see to it no man desires to look upon you," his gaze dropped to pass judgment on her nakedness, then he met her eye. "Ever again."

This morning, like every other morning, Mr. Smee watched for the lady. He worked on deck first thing, to get an early glimpse of her and determine if he was needed. So far, the ruby necklace remained out of sight. As he went about his business, Captain Hook's rapier swung at his side, sending the bo'sun an unnecessary reminder of his duty.

Yulunga rang the bell on the quarterdeck as Jill and Cecco came forth from their quarters. Eagerly, the company assembled beneath its clanging. The rumor had spread already. The captain had collected his first booty, and was ready to share it.

The lady was dressed in emerald today, a gown as green as the rolling hills of Smee's homeland, and highlighted with Cecco's gold. Smee wasn't sure if he'd ever seen her look so beautiful, with the sun gilding her hair as it lay against the green, and eyes to match an Irish twilight. But no rubies today, except for the color of her lips. She was smiling, her mouth appearing especially vivid this morning, her lips a measure fuller.

Cecco posed on the companionway in his gypsy regalia, holding up the filled-to-bursting pouch and shaking it as the men of the *Roger* cheered him.

"It is a good morning, my friends, which brings the beginning of our bounty from the Frenchman!"

Jubilation resounded. Yulunga mounted guard on the steps to marshal the men into order, officers first, so that each could collect his percentage from the captain's hands. As he did so, Cecco counted out his own take, stowing the bulk of his earnings in his pocket. The remainder he held out to Jill.

"Your promised stipend, my lady." He kissed her hands as she accepted it, and then he doled out Jill's own percentage of gold.

Smee bristled. The lady maintained her composure, but surely she must be mortified. The idea of a captain paying her from his own takings— as if she sold her loyalty! The bo'sun stood to receive his earnings from the gypsy's pouch, then heaved himself away, clutching the coins. The hilt of Hook's rapier grew heated within his other fist. 'Captain' Cecco was sure to feel its point. One day soon.

As the business progressed, young Miss slunk from the master's quarters. The noisy crewmen celebrated their riches, and she went unnoticed by most. But not by Smee. She wore the mauve gown. A hank of hair had come loose from her net to fall over her face, and she kept her head cast down as if she wished to be invisible. She wasn't. Yulunga shoved the men aside. "Clear the steps! Let the girl pass." He smirked as she descended without acknowledging his gesture.

Watching Cecco and his mate exchange smiles, Smee guessed Miss Liza, too, was sure to feel a point one day soon. Mr. Yulunga's.

Nothing new there. But *something* was different. Smee angled his head, keeping his eye on the girl. She behaved the same as always. Still haughty, still aloof. What had changed?

Hanover.

The man watched for his daughter. *That* was different. Poised in his gray suit, he loitered at the base of the steps, leaning on his cane in the midst of the sailors, even after he'd collected his share of gold. He stared at the lady, as he always did. Cecco's gaze raked him more keenly than usual, and the surgeon appeared impervious to it— again, as always. But he waited for Liza. As soon as the girl arrived within reach, he grasped her arm and ushered her forward.

Smee turned to peer over his spectacles as the pair wasted no time in disappearing below decks. He looked to the lady once more. And then he followed them.

"Captain," Jill smiled as she backed along the gilding of the companionway toward the majestic door of the master's quarters. She felt a happiness today that, since joining up with her pirates, she'd never expected to feel. Common enough for other females, perhaps, but unexpected of a woman in Jill's position. She reached out her crimson hand. It only shook a little.

Cecco accepted her hand with satisfaction in his eye. He followed her, his pockets full, the empty pouch dangling from his fist.

"Come, Sir, let's stow our takings. And then I have a request to beg of you." With her two arms adorned in his gold, she pulled him over the threshold.

"What is it, lovely one? Have we not already agreed on this morning's course of action?" He headed for his sea chest, and she hurried to secrete her coins in a hidden drawer of her escritoire. She found her nervousness not as easy to hide.

"Yes. I've no wish to change our plans. But I have something to say to you, Sir, of an entirely personal nature, and you may consider it to be everything— or nothing at all."

"You intrigue me. As always." He joined her on the cushioned recess beneath his windows. Noting a quiver at the corner of her smile, he said benevolently, "Speak to me of whatever subject you desire."

He waved his hand in a generous gesture as he spoke, and the surgeon's wedding ring caught her eye. She would have to get used to seeing it there.

"Very well, Captain. But the subject is a delicate one. I confess, it flusters me." Merely mentioning it made the rhythm within her turn chaotic. Yet ever so pleasantly.

Cecco laughed. "Now I must be told! What subject could possibly reduce my magnificent queen to common female vapors?"

Weaving her arms about his neck, she kissed him first, and in spite of her efforts to calm herself, she found her heart fluttering like a hummingbird. "I'm afraid that, where this matter is concerned, I am as weak as any other woman. Maybe more so." She pulled back to place two scarlet fingers on his lips. "But please, Captain. I am nervous enough. Don't say any more, until I have explained as well as I may."

Cecco held her, the best half of his heart, amazed to see her turned suddenly shy. She confided in him, and as she spoke, as her hands opened in petition, his dearest dream quickened and sprang into life.

"*Sì,*" he said, emphatically, without an instant of hesitation. "Yes. I welcome it."

Smee didn't have long to listen. What little he could hear through the wall of the spare quarters was one-sided, the surgeon speaking in low tones to his daughter. Sporadic commands. From what the bo'sun could make out, the doctor remained just as frosty toward the girl as usual.

Smee heard a jingling, though, that for some reason set his innards to churning. The chains, of course. No doubt Miss had been ordered to tidy the bunks. A squeaking from the bed frame followed, seeming to confirm Smee's hunch. Although the surgeon had signed on with the company, Cecco saw fit to keep his fetters handy. One point on which Smee agreed with the gypsy captain. He listened for more, but within minutes, the doctor and his daughter vacated the cabin, clicked its door closed and moved toward the galley. Smee clearly heard two sets of footsteps, both light, both stepping forward up the gun deck.

Odd, Smee reflected. Come to think of it, the girl hadn't visited the galley at breakfast time. Since Hook's disappearance, she had collected the majority of the surgeon's meals and waited on him in his quarters. All of a sudden, the man who had almost completely ignored his daughter seemed unwilling to let the girl stray from his sight.

But Smee had work to do. Storing his findings for future consideration, he made ready to leave the cabin. Just as his hand grasped the door handle, he heard a sound that made the red hair on his arms stand right up on end. It chimed through the wooden wall, and chilled Mr. Smee to his very bones.

Chains rattling.

The surgeon had gone. So had his daughter. No one occupied that cabin. Only the bad air must remain, the fug that had hung between its inhabitants. And then another sound issued from the woodwork, and this time, Smee knew for certain. It was a ghost.

Because a long, low groan emanated from the doctor's quarters.

Like a dead man rising.

Nibs had refused everything last night, including the wine— politely. He'd stuck to grog, and damned little of it. As a result, he was wide awake and staring this morning. Staring at the sea, and wondering what he'd gotten himself into. And gotten Tom into, too. Nibs couldn't see the *Roger* from his stern window, but it was good to know she was out there, leading *L'Ormonde*. Despite Cecco's play-acting for LeCorbeau, Nibs believed the sailor who not so long ago had taken two green lads under his wing would never desert them. Cecco was a good man. He had to be.

Wondering how Tom's end of the intrigue was going, Nibs attempted to pace. His cabin was so cramped it wasn't easy, but if he kept his head bent he could get in three good steps before bumping his shins on his sea chest. Although Nibs' job was distasteful, Tom's assignment was more difficult, and held more risk. It was obvious from last night's party that LeCorbeau was in no hurry where Nibs was concerned. He had his two mates. The sea lay before him, his escapade could last a lifetime. Clearly he enjoyed the chase, and savored the time it took to capture his quarry.

But the *commandant*'s attitude toward Tom was far different. He harbored no affection for Tom. If Nibs' brother was caught searching the ship, LeCorbeau might punish him cruelly. One day, he might even sink to pressuring Nibs by threatening Tom's welfare. Still, Nibs would jump at the chance to change places with Tom, if it didn't mean condemning a brother to the hell he himself hot-footed.

As he steamed forward once again, Nibs' eye caught a scrap of parchment crammed beneath his door. He squatted to pry it loose, unfolding and reading it even before he straightened to stand. It was from Tom, who had borrowed a pencil and paper from Jill for just this purpose.

Mate,
The cabins on this craft are clearer than my head. See you from aloft. Then I'll be below, too.

Nibs wadded the parchment and threw it out the window. Then, regretting his delay, he pulled open his door, thrust his hands in his pockets and assumed the privileges of LeCorbeau's golden boy. Soon he'd be at the wheel, with the fancy Frenchman breathing down his neck. For now, he'd roam the ship with impunity, and keep an eye open for her secrets. Nibs figured if he worked it right, his opportunities would evaporate. Fast.

Begrudging the interruption, Smee hustled Mr. Noodler from his quarters, shoving the paint pot into Noodler's backward hands and sending the sailor on his way to perform his task. In spite of her bo'sun's ugly mood, the *Roger* had to be kept pretty. Mr. Noodler had reported for duty, as ordered, just as Smee approached the surgeon's door. For the first time ever, Smee cursed his crew's reliability.

The Hanovers' quarters were still off-limits to ship's company. Once Noodler had clattered below decks, Smee checked that the gun deck was clear of witnesses. He thought he heard someone speaking nearby, but he waited a moment and, seeing no one, emerged from his doorway. He turned his steps toward the starboard cabin.

The restless spirit seemed quiet now. Smee reached to open the surgeon's door. Then another kind of sound broke the silence, and Smee paused. Compelled as he felt to investigate the haunting, duty called, in the form of the ship's bell. It pealed into the air, permeating every deck of the ship.

Smee couldn't refuse to answer it. In any case, his shipmates poured from the galley now, and the opportunity to enter the doctor's cabin on the sly was over. Smee felt the familiar need to tap his store of patience. However the mystery prickled, it would have to wait.

The galley disgorged the surgeon and the girl as well, and from all over the ship the company surged topside. Smee charged up the stairs, feeling for his weapon. When he reached the deck, he heard Jukes shouting from the crow's nest. As Mullins muscled the wheel to starboard, Jukes' tattooed arm pointed toward the bow. A ship had been sighted. A prize.

All the ship's company marked it, then turned toward the captain to collect their orders. He balanced on a cannon, grasping the foremast shrouds. His face glowed with exhilaration. Jill leaned over the rail ahead of him, examining the ship through the spyglass. Then she, too, turned to hear the captain's words.

"All hands! She's a slow mover, weighted down with swag! No escort in sight. We'll catch the wind and run her down. Fetch your weapons, mates, and man the cannons!"

The men were ready. Eager shouts followed in the wake of their captain's words. They spun to obey, but halted as he broke into the clamor.

"Avast! I have one piece of business to set in order first." Jumping from the cannon, Cecco smiled his gypsy smile. The medallions on his headdress flashed, his knife gleamed at his waist as he strode through the crowd. It parted to let him pass. Like the other men, Doctor Hanover had stopped and turned to look back.

When the captain neared his surgeon, he said, "I have a promise to keep."

He shot out his arm and caught Hanover by the back of the collar. He yanked the gray coat from the surgeon's shoulders and twisted, so that from the elbows down, the man's arms were caught and tethered. Hanover cried out. The men gasped. Cecco shoved the struggling doctor flat to the deck, chest down. As Hanover hit the boards, the breath burst from his lungs. Cecco dropped down to kneel, one knee on the small of his prisoner's back, pinning him. Hanover's face filled with horror.

Cecco seized the knife from his belt. He secured the doctor's coat under his knee and, grasping the top of Hanover's waistcoat, he slit it. Then he clenched the knife between his teeth while his fists finished the job. The sound of rending velvet ripped the air.

The men exclaimed, staring, and Yulunga spread his arms to force the crowd back. His big black fist captured Liza's wrist, but he simply kept it, and as she stood frozen he paid the girl no more mind. Jill drew closer to her champion, toying with her necklaces. The wind on her emerald skirts swirled against her legs. The sailors formed a circle around their captain and his victim, watching with wide open eyes.

"I warned you, Doctor. Any association between you and Red-Handed Jill ends in your disfigurement."

"No!" Bobbing, the doctor tried to lift himself from the boards. "No, Captain! You are mistaken—"

"I am mistaken in trusting you."

"But—"

Cecco stuck his blade in the collar of Hanover's shirt, and the rest of the surgeon's words were lost in the shriek of its tearing. Hanover strained to lift his body, but his arms remained imprisoned in his sleeves. The dueling scar was exaggerated, a red gash on his face. The muscles of his upper body bulged as he writhed, his back bared beneath Captain Cecco. The chill sea air wafted over his skin. The gypsy still knelt, straddling Hanover. He leaned forward.

"You claim I am mistaken. Yet my mistress now owns a piece of gold which I did not give to her." Cecco held up his hand and splayed it, exhibiting the wedding band upon his finger. Murmurs arose as the men began to comprehend the surgeon's transgression.

"Jill, my lovely storyteller. Can you tell your shipmates the tale of how this ring wormed its way beneath our pillow?"

The crewmen listened, eyes goggling, all silent now. Only the breeze could be heard, snapping among the sails as the ship hurtled forward, hunting down her prey.

Mr. Smee stepped forward to lodge himself by the lady's side. He didn't touch her. She stood pale but proud as she answered her captain in her firm, clear voice.

"No, Sir. I can't tell how it got there. I swear to you." As Cecco turned to the men, her eyes left her captain's face to flicker a look toward the surgeon where he lay thrashing against the boards. As their eyes made contact, Hanover stilled, glowering, and she shook her head, just enough.

Even in his extremity, the doomed man understood. He now perceived the full meaning of the message she penned to him last night. *Believe that I do not betray you.* Hanover realized the truth. He had erred in leaving the ring. He'd meant it to symbolize the consummation of his passion, but it served also to condemn. His vanity, not his lady, had betrayed him.

Cecco's cold voice held no mercy. "Mr. Yulunga. Show the men."

At these words, Hanover's brow creased in perplexity. Liza's head shot up, and she stared at her captor. Still restraining her, Yulunga produced the evidence and raised it. "Here, Sir. Broken strands of rope, found caught between your aft windows. And here…a vial of medicine."

Amid the exclamations of his men, Cecco nodded. "While I was away last night, you climbed a rope to my lady's window. You arranged for her to drink your sleeping potion. I am certain that every man aboard can guess what *else* you did to her, when you found her, lying all alone and helpless…in my bed." His knee bored into the surgeon's back. "Now, once again, I will pay out your earnings, Doctor Hanover." Gripping his knife, he raised up his hand, and, without hesitation, lowered it to the flesh of Hanover's back.

Smee abandoned caution. His brawny arms encircled the lady's waist. But she didn't require his support. Her eyes, hard as sapphires, never looked away from the surgeon. To the letter, she had honored her accord with Captain Cecco. Now, Cecco honored his word to her. To the letter.

And when her captain finished his carving, four bright characters spelled out her name. In pretty red ink.

Findings and Takings

Dragged between Smee and Yulunga, the surgeon stumbled down the steps. His back ran warm with blood, the tatters of his shirt drooped on his arms. Trying to stem the groans, he clenched his teeth and closed his throat. He didn't consider where they were taking him until Smee's voice raised the question, and then Hanover's mind succumbed to the panic he had so far fended off.

"No need to be using the shackles today."

"That is sure. He'll keep to his bunk."

Hanover twisted within their grasps, feeling the fresh flow of blood as he struggled. Tightening his grip, Smee spoke sharply to Yulunga. "No, mate. We're not to enter his quarters. Let's be stowing him in his work room, and he can fend for himself."

Grateful for this stroke of luck, Hanover subsided as the men hauled him toward the spare cabin. His secret was safe— for the moment.

"With a prize about, I'll not be finding time to stitch him up." Smee kicked the door open, and neither he nor Yulunga felt a need to be gentle as they dumped Hanover on the bunk. "Not that I'm inclined to lift a finger, mind."

Yulunga snorted. "Who's to doctor the doctor?" But his black eyes found her, just outside the door.

Like a wraith, Liza had followed. Now she hovered on the threshold, her hands kneading a lump of gray velvet. Men gathered on the gun deck behind her, stripping off their shirts and hauling on the tackle. Voices raised and boxes of shot grated along the floor. A certain savagery animated the girl's eyes as she beheld her father, and even in her mauve dress with her hair tucked up in its net, Liza appeared not so very out of place among the pirates.

Smee eyed her. "You'll be needing some things, then." As he exited, she backed from him. "Come along, and be quick about it." He headed to his quarters to gather up his mending box. Liza launched a look at Yulunga, who squinted at her.

"You're to stay below." His gaze scoured the girl from head to toe, and his smirk, when it formed, was rank with privilege. "We don't want you damaged— until you're ready." He struck one of his earrings with a thumb. Liza saw it bob, but her gaze fastened on the manacle mark encircling his wrist. Yulunga grunted his amusement, then spared a glance for the surgeon.

Prostrate and clutching at the blankets, the man looked daggers at the mate, but he lay on his stomach, unable to summon breath to object. Yulunga ducked under the door to tramp to his captain's side.

Smee met the girl at his door. "You'll be finding what you're needing here— needles, twine, a knife. Rags. Rum's in the galley. Tell Cook I sent you for it." Thrusting the box in her arms, he turned again to collect his weapons, and then he elbowed his way through the rowdy gunners as they primed and fed the cannons.

Within minutes, the *Roger* was ready to attack. It took Liza a little longer to prepare herself to fix her father.

Under the emblem of the Union Jack, the resistance disorganized. With her rudder shot away and her foremast in splinters, the prize was nearly secure. Cecco raised his boot and shoved his opponent, a merchant officer. The man dropped his sword, staggering away. Striding to starboard, the pirate captain kicked a knife from a smallish white hand, then he hunkered down and hauled the cabin boy from beneath a cannon barrel. Cecco faced the combatants, gripping the boy's throat with one hand while flourishing his cutlass in the other. The clamor died down as the *Unity* surrendered, only to start up again with the clatter of swords hitting the deck, followed by hearty hurrahs from pirate throats. Over the shouting came a chopping sound. Then, fluttering downward, the colors of the Union Jack were struck.

"Now tell me, my noble young man. Which of these gentlemen is your captain?"

The youth trembled inside his uniform, but tried to hide it. "The cap—" His voice broke and he had to swallow first. "The captain's abed, Sir, in his quarters."

"Under the covers? Has he better company than us?" Cecco's men laughed with him. When the boy seemed unable to reply, the pirate shook him. The golden jewelry jangled.

"He's ill, Sir."

Cecco frowned. "Nothing catching, I hope?"

"No, Sir. No quarantine. Pneumonia, says our surgeon."

"Ah! And is he alone?"

"The surgeon wouldn't allow him to fight, Sir. He's tending to him."

"Good. You will take me to your captain."

The boy darted a look to his officers. To a man, they nodded at him, the most vigorous affirmative coming from the first mate, in the grip of a huge African wielding a boarding ax. Regret marked their defeated faces. The *Unity*'s officers found themselves in no position to protect the boy. He understood their dilemma. He was the captain's nephew. As if fortified by the reminder, the boy squared his shoulders and met the pirate's eyes. "This way, Captain."

Cecco smiled and released him. "Mr. Yulunga! Secure the prisoners and throw open the holds." He turned to starboard and raised his hand to his mouth to whistle at the *Roger*, and at his shrill command the crewmen there fell to hoisting block and tackle.

At the base of the *Roger*'s mainmast, a lady waited. Her fair hair blew in the breezes and her emerald skirt clung to her. A flush of excitement adorned her cheeks.

Cecco shouted across the chasm. "Permission to board."

Jill came forward and Mason handed her a pulley. He opened the gangway and steadied her as she stepped to the edge. Then, smiling, she shoved off to sail over the water with her green skirt rippling behind her.

427

The vanquished crew of the *Unity* gawked at the apparition. Even the most seasoned of her sailors had never witnessed such a sight. A flesh-and-blood angel soared toward them, almost flying, to be caught up in the swarthy brigand's embrace. Her laugh played like music as he circled her around, joy strange to hear at the gloomy end of a battle. Yet only as she opened her hand to release the pulley did they fully realize she wasn't the pirate's hostage, nor did she seek freedom aboard their vessel.

She must be his partner. After all, however elegant the lady appeared, only a lady pirate would sport such a dagger, or such a pistol. Or that blood-stained hand.

"Lovely one. At last you have the pleasure to board a prize."

"Sir, you grant my every wish." As Cecco released her waist, she turned to study the boy. "But who is this?"

"Our guide, Madam."

"And just a boy." She smiled at him. "About the age I was when I ventured to the Island. And now," she offered Cecco her scarlet hand, "a new adventure, Captain, into the future. Shall we?"

"You have heard the queen, young man. Lead the way."

The cabin boy sought his power of speech and found it, and as he stared at this goddess, he prayed his voice wouldn't crack this time. "Aye, aye, Sir!" He backed into a cannon, and then he took his eyes from her face and marched his brass-buckled shoes to the master's quarters.

Two minutes later, the *Unity*'s crew sat corralled on the forecastle; most of the pirates were descending into the holds. The master's door cracked open and the cabin boy scrambled up from the steps to stand at attention. His uncle's voice, weakened from his ailment, issued from the doorway. "David, you're to come in, lad, and—" he broke off, coughing. When the fit abated, he continued, his words muffled in a handkerchief. "You're to come in, David, and uncork a bottle for us."

The lady's laugh glittered over the gloom again, and David hopped to his duty.

Liza pulled the leather strap from her father's teeth. It had helped him conceal his agony. Now he opened his mouth to test his jaw before he spoke. His teeth ached, but his back bristled with sharp, shooting pains. His voice gathered strength as he used it. "You have done surprisingly well, Liza. Now get to our cabin and take care of the other business. The men will be returning soon, and I thought I could hear— it."

She rose, observing the first word her father had taught her to read, splayed across his back: 'JILL.' It was bloody, embroidered with Liza's own stitching— and inscribed by Captain Cecco's knife on the most deserving of parchments.

Liza shoved her sleeves up over her elbows again and collected Mr. Smee's belongings, replacing them in their box. A heap of red-stained scraps lay piled by the door. Liza had hoped her father would lapse into oblivion so she could slip a hand in his pocket for the keys, but he had not succumbed. On the contrary, he had refused his own medication and maintained a stoic awareness, even guiding her through the stitching process.

Yet Liza was unsure what she would do with the keys if she recovered them. Hook had rejected her, three times. He wasn't likely to open his arms to her again. Far from it. Liza doubted that Hook was able even to lift his arms; his breaths barely raised his chest. He was dying, and by Liza's own hand. To reveal Hook's whereabouts to ship's company at this point must condemn not only Liza's father, but Liza herself. And Captain Cecco held the power now. With Hook so very weakened, Cecco couldn't be expected to relinquish the captaincy to him. Nor was anything to be gained on that front by appealing to Yulunga. At least, not from a direct appeal. He was Cecco's man. And Liza knew Mr. Smee would be no help. These days the bo'sun strode about with Hook's rapier at his waist. If she trusted Smee with the secret, he'd probably take one look at his master and run Liza through. No. It was better if everyone believed her to be the surgeon's tool. The keys were best left in her father's charge.

Hanover sighed as he prepared his tormented body for rest, but he wasn't ready to surrender yet. He kept his voice low.

"You are to administer only enough liquid to maintain un-consciousness. I prefer you to use the ether. Every half hour."

Disconcerted, she turned an ear toward him to verify what she'd heard.

"This is my order. No food. No liquid."

Liza's gray eyes rebelled, but even from his prostrate posture, the surgeon's hand flared out to seize her arm.

"Do not dare to cross me, Liza. Sooner than you think, I will be walking. Even if I have to use my *cane*."

She shrank from his threat, and when he released her arm, his finger marks were clearly visible, first white, then red. Tomorrow they would be purple.

Liza shook her sleeve down over her forearm. And then she left, to conceal another of her father's secrets.

The wind rose during the afternoon. The *Roger* groaned under it. As the day progressed, her swaying had caused the men to brace their legs and reach to secure the swinging goods from the pulley hooks. Now the hooks were stowed, the hatches battened, and hungry sailors held fast to the banisters, descending to the galley. Having gotten the ship under sail, the men in the rigging cheered their captain as, disregarding the pitch of his ship, he carried his lady along the companionway. He conveyed her over the threshold and into his quarters, an exultant smile shining across his face.

"Now, my Jill, we have captured our first prize, and the hold is filled to bursting with swag."

"Aye, Captain. I feel I've captured a prize, too." She laughed as she held up a shiny silver charm in the shape of a shamrock. "And to add to it, young David was most generous to present me with his lucky piece. All in all, a good day's work! The men will be pleased with their choice— as I assure you, I am pleased with mine."

He kissed her before he set her down, and then he moved to the aft windows to spy out *L'Ormonde*. "I see the 'rescuers' approaching already. LeCorbeau, too, will be pleased. He will glean much, I think, from his encounter with the *Unity*."

Kneeling beside him on the window seat, Jill said, "More than he bargained for! No doubt we'll enjoy an interesting party tonight after he learns of our 'adventure' aboard the *Unity*. But may we host the celebration here, Sir? I've had quite enough of visiting other—" She stopped, and she looked alarmed.

"Jill? What is it, my—" But Cecco heard it, too, in the interval between the *Roger*'s moanings. He reached to support her as the ship pitched again.

Her blue eyes widened, questioning. "*You* can hear it?"

He shrugged. "It is just the wind, rising as the sun sets."

"No." Jill gazed at Cecco, and her eyes seemed suddenly not to see him. She listened. In a moment, she heard it again.

Cecco brushed the stray strand of hair from her face. "Hush, my lovely one. All is well."

But although her gaze didn't leave him, her face turned, ever so slowly, away. Toward the bunk. Unwilling to abandon the comforting sight of Cecco, she indicated the port wall.

Her lover turned to look himself. His eyes searched the cabin for a moment and then stopped, riveted on a sunlit patch where the light streamed in. By the bed. His brow contracted, his brown eyes filled with disbelief. He breathed the words.

"Madre de Dio…!"

Jill watched as he blanched in horror, and then with his fingers he worked his gypsy banishing gesture, down from his forehead and across his breast. Quickly, he reached for Jill's chin, to turn her face away. But it was too late. She had heard it; now she saw it. Like a slow poison, the cold of it crept its way through her veins. The *Roger* wailed.

Hanging loose against the wall, swinging with the ship's movement, it tapped. The phantom that haunted her each night, that she believed she heard as she slept, and which she always woke to find an illusion, had returned. This time, it shone in the sinking sunlight, reflecting a bloody orange flame in its curving surface. Swinging and tapping.

The hook.

Nibs and Tom were not allowed to attend the party. They didn't mind. Assigned to the watch manning the ship, they welcomed the chance to come together. They hung over the rail, shoulders hunched against the wind, but sure their words would be whipped away from those who shouldn't hear. Before them, the *Roger* bounded up and down at anchor, in tandem with *L'Ormonde*. Her lights were a reassuring sight.

"No luck in the holds, Nibs. All quiet except for the pumps."

"I had a good look round this morning. I found two of those wedges we used to cripple the Dutch merchantman, but nothing suspicious anywhere."

"Did you find that locked cabin, in the aft section, near the powder magazine?"

"Near the magazine? No. Might be officers' privy."

"No, I've seen that. And they don't keep it locked."

"I've noticed keys on both mates. Maybe we can slip in and pinch a set while they're asleep tonight."

"They won't sleep tonight. At least, not so's we'd want to get at them."

Reminded of his predicament, Nibs scowled. "We've got to get in that cabin, Tom. And if Hook isn't there, we've got to keep right on searching."

"I'm thinking this ship isn't all that big."

"She's big enough to hold a secret."

"Maybe." Tom rubbed the scar at his temple. "I've been watching the men, too, to see who goes where. One advantage of being aloft all morning."

"I'm longing for the rigging, Tom. Lucky we met that prize today. LeCorbeau was teaching me words I never wanted to know—in French or any other language." Nibs pulled his kerchief tighter against the wind.

"I'm with you, mate. That Guillaume's taken a fancy to me. He shadowed me today. Thought he caught me once, down in the bilges. I was glad to hear the bell calling us to board the *Unity*, too. But I'll think of a reason to make him open that last cabin."

"You be careful, Tom." Nibs frowned, and the crease between his eyebrows deepened. "I might not be able to protect you if LeCorbeau turns nasty."

"I've got my knife, and I'm double Guillaume's breadth. But let me tell you, Nibs. It makes me think. One day aboard, and you and I have been all over this vessel. Not only is there no place to hide anyone— there's no place for anyone to hide."

The young sailors looked at one another in the flickering light of their home ship's lanterns. A light that, at this distance, cast more doubt than it dispelled.

Smee had troubles, but with repairs to the *Roger* and wounds to wrap, a chance to relieve his mind took a long time coming. He felt bound to appear at the celebrations, if only for the lady's sake, but at last he forced his way aft through the crowded galley. The lads were loud tonight, exhilarated by a full hold from the new captain's prize, and the merriment had redoubled when *L'Ormonde*'s company boarded, toting the *Roger*'s share of their takings. The ensuing hubbub was just what Smee needed to cover his venture to the Hanover cabin. Smee knew it was vacant; the surgeon still stretched on the bunk in the spare quarters…and Miss was at the party.

Smee wasn't the only one seizing his chances. He'd heard Yulunga's oily voice promise the girl a present if she sat with him. She'd changed out of her blood-stained mauve into her blue dress, and not long after, her pearl ring found its way from Yulunga's pocket to her finger. Yulunga had stood with his head bent against the beams, pressing his big hands on the ceiling, and amid the raised eyebrows of their shipmates, ordered her to fetch it out herself. Smee surmised she hadn't minded, for although she slipped away a few minutes ago, she returned. And as she did, her gray eyes surveyed the company from the doorway. Yulunga jerked his head at her, and she picked her way through the noise to rejoin him, passing right in front of the Frenchman. Perhaps, Smee thought, with her father out of commission, she felt drawn to the next man who offered to command her. She didn't smile, but tonight, somehow, Yulunga had gotten permission to touch her. And— to all appearances— not only from his captain.

Before leaving the galley, Smee turned to check on the lady again. She sat caught between the captains. Smee was especially concerned for her tonight. She had to keep up the play-acting for LeCorbeau, pretending to struggle against Cecco's domination. But she looked genuinely tired tonight, almost wan. It was lucky she hadn't come to harm this afternoon aboard the *Unity*. Smee's angry gaze settled on the captain, who, under LeCorbeau's beady eye, sat enthroned on Hook's own chair and pulled Jill's hand through the crook of his elbow. Obediently, she leaned against Cecco, but she engaged the French captain with her furtive glances.

Smee couldn't imagine what possessed the gypsy to allow her to board a prize today, and so soon after surrender. Hook had expressly forbidden it. But Jill could handle herself, and although she seemed distracted now, Smee had seen that this afternoon's change of scene made her happy, if only for a little while. It put a bit of color in her cheeks after the carving she'd witnessed this morning. Smee's only regret concerning that incident was that he hadn't cut the bloody bastard personally. The surgeon had gotten his comeuppance, at the hands of the only man aboard more contemptible than himself. Hanover, at any rate, had yet to commit mutiny. The bo'sun felt the weight of Hook's sword at his side, and with another glare for Cecco, he patted it. Smee's opportunity would come.

He closed the galley door and made his way aft, grudgingly conceding that the gypsy was probably right to allow the lady's boarding. Any kind of adventure was good for Jill. She'd spent too many hours shut up in her quarters, writing. True to his promise to Hook, Smee watched her as attentively as ever, but from a distance. Nibs and Tom were banished, and Smee had a suspicion that, aside from Cecco's demands, her stories were the only thing that took her mind off Hook's demise. If only Smee could talk with her, he'd ask her to let him read one. Then he'd know the bent of her thoughts. The way he used to know, in the first days, when he'd cherished the pleasure of waiting on her. Alone together, behind the master's door.

Lost in his thinking, Smee startled to hear the sound again. It floated over the revelry of the galley. A haunting chink of metal, and a growl of a groan. Recalled to life, Smee's attention focused again on the surgeon's door, shadowy in the flicker of the lantern. He listened for movement in the middle cabin and heard nothing from there.

Hanover must be resting. Peering around the gun deck, Smee found himself alone. He adjusted his spectacles, laid a hand on the knob of the starboard quarters, and opened it.

The lanterns burned low, lending the place a stuffy warmth and a dim glow. The room seemed deserted. No one sat in its chairs. Its bed curtains were drawn. Yet, contrary to the chamber's vacant appearance, the moment Smee set foot within it, a presence filled him. Such a presence as he hadn't felt since he'd handed the rapier to its master. Smee's sturdy heart jumped, and he tensed with hope.

A familiar scent filled his nostrils. A masculine smell, but more concentrated than Smee had ever experienced it. It was a lusty, musty smell, and Smee understood immediately whence it originated. He also understood that the body from which it emanated was in trouble— had been in trouble— for days.

Alive or dead, Hook was here.

Escorted by Mr. Mullins to the surgeon's sickbed, LeCorbeau made himself at home. He closed the door, drew the chair to the bedside and perched, flipping the tails of his splendid embroidered coat out of the way. His buttons glittered like jewels.

"Well, Doctor."

Hanover raised his head. "Have you come to mock me, Captain, or to relieve my anxiety?"

"My dear Hanover, you grieve me! Would I mock a man so obviously in pain? No, no, I am not so heartless." LeCorbeau peered over his large nose at the surgeon's back. "Who cannot be touched by the extremes to which you go to procure the affections of your, eh, sweetheart?"

"I assure you, LeCorbeau, this extreme may be attributed to my 'sweetheart's' lover."

"Most men would stop at a simple tattoo, but you have always shown, perhaps, a tendency to overdo. Nevertheless, I perceive that you have executed your commission— *pardon,* a thoughtless expression, considering the fate of our friend Hook!— and I of course, am here to fulfill my own."

"Get me off this ship."

"Patience, Doctor. I savor the moment. It is so tasty a delight, to see the *Roger* captained by so worthy a man— most notably worthy in the respect that he is not Captain Hook. But also, I enjoy to see my partner winning the lady's heart!" Once again he eyed the surgeon's wounds, raising his handkerchief to his nose. Having satisfied his curiosity and refreshed his senses with scent, he lowered the cloth. "Yes, Hanover, I believe your unorthodox methods of courtship are vanquishing your rival. I observe that the woman resists this Cecco's— eh, shall I call them 'charms?' And," LeCorbeau reached in the outer pocket of his auburn coat. "I have received a letter from her even tonight, which you will excuse me as I examine now." With a flourish, he pulled out a folded parchment, smiling. "Let us see how your suit has fared."

"A letter? Read it!"

"It is addressed to me, but in the interest of saving the time, I shall read aloud." The Frenchman spread the letter, cocked his head, and cleared his throat.

" '*My dear Commandant—* '"

He stopped. "*Alors*, the woman has an excellent hand! I cannot fault her penmanship."

"Go on!" Grimacing, Hanover raised himself to his elbows.

"Such impatience…..

" '*I write to you, hoping you will find it in your interest to assist me.*'"

The captain smiled. "Ah, the female is shrewd! To appeal to my self-interest rather than my nobler instincts. One can see the woman was tutored by Hook himself."

"Spare the remarks, LeCorbeau."

"You would have me reduce my enjoyment? *Quel dommage*….But I continue.

" '*Already, you have been generous enough to remove my sons from difficulty. I hesitate to beg further favor of you, yet this is exactly what I am compelled to do. Doctor Hanover has confided to me the facts regarding your partnership. I am forbidden to communicate with him, and so entrust this letter to his daughter—*'

"Eh, you should have seen your little girl, Hanover! Brazen as Jezebel, pressing the parchment to my pocket as if she had been passing love-notes all of her life!" LeCorbeau watched the surgeon's teeth clench, then returned his inspection to the letter. "But where was I? Ah, yes.

" '…*entrust this letter to his daughter to deliver to the one man powerful enough to help us.*' "

With a suspicious smile, LeCorbeau paused. "How she flatters me." He breathed in, then continued.

" '*My situation is dramatically changed~ you must know by now how completely~ and I wish to avail myself of Mister Hanover's gallant offer of protection.*' "

LeCorbeau waved the letter. "*Mon Dieu*, Hanover! But why bother to marry this concubine? She is desperate!…All right, all right, I go on:

" '*However my heart leads, circumstances force me to accept whatever my captain proposes.*' "

LeCorbeau raised his handkerchief again and wheezed merrily into it. Hanover's stare bored into him. Upon regaining breath, LeCorbeau licked his lips and went on.

" '*But I conceive a situation which might content us all. Doctor Hanover's cache of riches intrigues my master. As our captain, he is bound by honor to return it. Yet if I continue to oppose him as I have done since Captain Hook's disappearance, it may come to pass that Captain Cecco will weary of me, and become agreeable to a distraction.*

" 'Monsieur, you must prevail upon the doctor to make a generous offer for my freedom. He must do this in the presence of our officers. Once his men hear of the riches to be had, Captain Cecco will not long be able to refuse.'*

"But, Hanover, the vixen is a veritable schemer! You will do well to keep a tight rein on this female, my friend."

The scar along the surgeon's cheek tightened. "You need not concern yourself, LeCorbeau. Read on."

LeCorbeau shrugged. "Very well.

" 'Then, if we act quickly, I shall have opportunity to carry through with Mister Hanover's original plan~ that is, to board your ship, undergo a marriage ceremony, and escape, thus restoring you and your partner to your profitable business, and me to my liberty.'*

"Ah, Hanover! Like the bride, you blush with pleasure!"

"By God, LeCorbeau! It is all transpiring as I hoped."

"With, perhaps, one uncomfortable setback?"

Dismissive, Hanover shook his head and, giving a grunt, shifted on the bunk. "One I should have foreseen. But if such a display of brutality inclines the lady to turn against Captain Cecco, it was worth it."

"Bravely spoken, Sir! And now, may I pass you the smelling salts?"

"You may jest, but our escape is certain now."

"So the captain's woman would have you believe."

"And of course, Liza will accompany her mistress. I see only one flaw in Jill's thinking, easily rectified. She is an intelligent woman, but naturally, she fails to take into account the power of her allure. As my own experience attests, the more she resists, the more desirable she becomes. Captain Cecco will need another reason to part with her. I will find it."

"In what form, if I may ask?"

The sting of Hanover's back began to fade as his mind sought salve for his pride. "Perhaps I can kill two birds with one stone. That Irishman needs to be taken down a peg. He may prove useful to me, at last…as might Captain Cecco's famous knife."

"As I have remarked before, Hanover, you are thorough with your enemies! My observations demonstrate to me that you have chosen a mate to match you. I wait with the bated breath to witness the outcome of your collective handiwork."

Hanover gestured to the letter. "Is there more?"

"Is this not enough? But, eh, yes, to continue." His beady black eyes scanned the missive. "Ah, always, there is the catch!

" '*I would warn the surgeon, however, to prepare to bid for his own liberty, as well as mine.*' "

The captain declared, "An expensive dish, this lady— as I perceived from the inception. To conclude.…

" '*I beg you to convey my message, and find a way to communicate your answer indirectly, to prevent placing my dear doctor's life at further risk. For I confess- his welfare is more precious to me than he may imagine.*' "

LeCorbeau raised his eyes from the parchment to behold the surgeon's expression. "I see the dart has hit its mark."

"Yes.…My aim is true."

"*Your* aim?" The Frenchman's eyebrows disappeared beneath his hair. "*Mon ami*, if you but knew—"

"Now we have only to complete the arrangements."

Dryly, the Frenchman said as he folded the letter, "I think, *Monsieur*, the arrangements have been completed for us." He stowed the parchment away. "But no matter. All is working in our favor. I give you a few days to regain your, eh, agility. Then I will make an offer— to be repaid from your own fortune, of course— to hire you away from this Captain Cecco. No?"

The smile Hanover bestowed upon his partner revealed a satisfaction unwitnessed since the early days of their alliance. "Yes." Energized by success, Hanover turned to lean on his side. "I give you leave to bargain the price as high as necessary." He delved in his pocket, and as his smile grew smug, he drew out Hook's brass ring of keys. Access to the captain's quarters, the shackles…and a sea chest. "I will recoup my losses."

The greedy light flared in LeCorbeau's eyes. "Hanover— my partner! What does this mean?"

"Very simply, it means Jill is not the only jewel I shall pluck from the *Roger*."

"Captain." Smee spoke softly after closing the door, conscious of the surgeon lying in the cabin beyond the wall. Pressing the rapier to his side, he leaned over the desk to turn up the lanterns. Then he set his feet in motion, each step as if it might be his last. He didn't bother with the lower bunk. Smee sensed where his master rested. But he listened to the silence, and he dreaded it. He might have come too late. Some hideous sight might lie in wait for him. Hoping against hope to set eyes on the beloved figure of his master, yet he feared a vision to haunt his dreams.

Upon reaching the bedside, he stood staring at the curtain, unsure whether its motion might be due to a wave— or a specter.

"Captain."

Smee reached out. He grasped the canvas. Pulling it aside, he searched the shadows, and as his eyes adjusted they were drawn toward a patch of white. A face. The chain rattled, and the face disappeared behind a ringed hand. A moment passed, then the hand lowered. Barely audible, an unfamiliar voice croaked.

"Smee."

"Aye, Captain. Aye.…I'm here." Hardly able to breathe, Smee stepped on the lower bunk. It creaked as he hiked himself up to settle beside his captain. He leaned forward and spoke again, tenderly, like a father to a little lost child. "I've found you, then." Smee's breast swelled with emotion. Relief, blessed relief— and more. Behind his spectacles, he blinked the moisture away.

Hook lolled to his side and labored to hitch himself up on an elbow. His head hung unsteadily. Smee's heart near burst to look upon him. His captain lay chained, hand and foot. He languished on a blue-striped mattress stripped of linens, stained and reeking. His sleek black waves were unrecognizable now, wild, tangled, his face gaunt, his fine features blurred with whiskers. His lips were dry and shriveled, but his eyes— his eyes remained the same. Deep blue, and sharp as jewels.

Burdened by his chain, Hook held out his hand. Smee grasped it. It was hot, and dry. The two men clung together, each assuring himself of the other's reality. Then, not letting go, Hook turned his wrist upward under his shackle and issued a command, rasped but firm.

"Free me."

In one horrid instant, Smee's elation plunged to despair. "Sir," he said. "…Sir."

His gaze forsook his captain and fell to the bed, and it was Smee, now, who was a lost child. As their hands sank to the mattress, Smee listened to the tinkle of the chain. He breathed hard in the filthy air. Then he dragged his gaze to the dying man's face, to confess.

"I have your rapier. Right here, Sir, at my side." He shook his head, slowly, as if pronouncing sentence upon a condemned man. "But Captain—" His voice failed him.

Under the black brow, Hook's piercing eyes stabbed him, silent. A vision to haunt his dreams.

"Begging your pardon, Sir. But I don't have the key."

At first Jill was afraid to touch it. Its gleaming edge appeared as sinister as the day she first beheld it. So long ago, it seemed, on the Island. But after all, it wasn't the hook— had never been the hook— that frightened her. It was the man who wielded it. The powerful pirate, in his dashing black velvet, with piercing eyes beneath his jeweled hat. He had commanded her attention, and then her obedience, and finally, her love. She had been afraid to touch him, too, in the beginning.

But she *had* touched him. Now she drew a deep breath and laid a finger on his metal hand. Cold. It lay on the floor of the captain's quarters where Cecco, his eyes ferocious with gypsy superstition, had thrown it, to land with a hollow thud on the carpet. The same sound it had made when Hook dropped it, the first time Jill released him from his brace. So long ago. Just yesterday.

Gingerly, she took the hook between her fingers and raised it up. She held it by the wooden form, the piece that seated his wrist. The leather harness dragged against her skirt, and she shivered with emotion. But the spasm pumped a flow of warmth into her muscles and, strengthened, she laid her cheek against the metal. She kept it there until the heat of her face seeped into the hook.

All evening she had struggled to play her role, not knowing if this part of her lover was a sign of hope that he lived— or an omen of his death. No doubt the scheming surgeon was infuriated to find her sleeping last night. Perhaps he, who claimed to have knowledge of Hook's whereabouts, ordained this haunting as a reminder of his power. A cruel reminder, and unnecessary. Jill was ready to fulfill any requirement to gather a single crumb of information, even tidings of Hook's death. His too-likely death. She didn't try to think it through any more. She knelt on the rug, head bowed over his relic, and wept. Pent up too long, her tears for her captain flowed freely.

Since his disappearance, Jill had felt Hook's heartbeat, sure he would return. But when she beheld the hook in the setting sunlight, returned to its place by his bed, her own heart had stopped. Too numb, she hadn't felt him since. In the last day something had changed. No— several things had changed. It was as if in imbibing the surgeon's sleeping draught, Jill had put Hook to sleep, too, and he hadn't awakened. Whatever the reason, Jill had lost touch with her love. She pressed her hand to her womb. The faint pulse she felt within, and which yesterday she would have attributed to Hook, no longer reassured her. Was he gone forever, or was Jill, caught up in her new adventure, past recognizing him?

There was one way to know. Jill had flown this afternoon. Although, obedient to Cecco's order, she had held fast to the pulley, she found herself skimming across the water to the *Unity*, so full of a secret happiness she hadn't summoned any particular thought to do it. Now she got to her feet, carried the hook to the window seat and set it down. She opened the casement, wide. With an uncertain step, she set her foot on the seat. The other followed. Lowering herself to the sill, she inhaled a breath of salty air and, gathering up the brace, closed her eyes. The smell of the sea and the scent of the leather between her fingers helped her to concentrate. She searched her soul, and then she found him.

She could see him. She heard him laughing. A wild music sprang from the stars, and she longed to dance with him again. In silky sibilance, her skirt whispered as she dropped his hook to the bench and slid from the sill, and when she opened her eyes, she was floating. The sea lay below her, the dollops of light on the waves sinking farther and farther from her feet. Her hair billowed in the breezes, and the lanterns of the *Roger* winked at her. Imitating the sails, she spread her wings, and soared.

The wind's breath laughed with her as she remembered the night, not so long ago, when she and Hook tried to touch a star. There it was. That one, the star that shone so sharply between strands of warm, black cloud, reminding her of his earring. She shook the hair from her face and looked again, and now it was two stars. Two earrings. Two, like Captain Cecco's pair. But where was Hook's solitary ornament? Jill blinked to clear her vision, and the sky filled with gold, shimmering like her bracelets.

Turning her head, swirling in her gown like a swimmer treading water and searching for the shore, she looked for that single star again. It eluded her. Instead, the wide sky opened like a treasure chest and spilled its jewels all about her. Everywhere she saw diamonds, and pearls, and necklaces. Even when she stretched to fly, the gold on her arms sparkled like the heavens, and their beloved burden weighted her down. Rising to float nearer, deepening, the sea reached up to catch her. And she heard his laugh again, and this time it was a gypsy laugh, and the sky turned dusky. Drifting on the very same current that upheld her that afternoon— Cecco's current— Jill turned toward the shore of her shipboard home. Her anchorage....Her captain.

When, much later, Captain Cecco's boots took possession of his companionway, the hook would lie buried in the window seat. Jill would lie waiting in his bed. He would undress and stretch down beside his woman, and then he would turn his mutilated back to the wall from which, hours before, he ripped the hook's mooring. Resting her head on his chest, Jill would close her eyes and listen. She would hear her captain's heart beat, alive and constant. She would feel his kiss upon her lips. But she wouldn't hear the phantom. It was gone, now. The *Roger* would croon her lullaby, and the starry night stay still.

The reminder of her first love lay at peace, in the seat beneath the captain's window. She wasn't afraid to touch it. It wasn't the hook that frightened her.

It was the man who had wielded it. And his wrath.

A Last Supper

Behind the open crack of his cabin door, Smee waited for the girl to leave her quarters. She'd found some excuse to get away from Yulunga at the party, but she hurried back to him. Almost before she disappeared into the galley, Smee was through her doorway, lugging a jug and a bag of hardtack biscuits. It was all he could snatch without raising questions. He tucked the jug under his arm to secure the door, and in hurried steps that betrayed his anxiety, he approached his captive master.

"Captain, I've brought you some water." A smell of medicine lingered, and Smee was relieved to see the blue eyes opening as he spoke. He set the things on the bunk and swung himself up. "You're parched, I can see. Drink up, Sir, and then we'll be talking." His burly arms moved gently as he reached for his captain and helped him to sit upright.

Hook seized the jug as it neared, but Smee refused to trust it to his shaking hand. "Let me be helping you, Sir. You've gone without too long."

Hook drank, and then he tilted his head back and leaned against the wall, closing his eyes. Smee whipped a kerchief from his pocket and dabbed his master's cracked lips, lightly, to prevent paining him. "That's right, Sir. Take it slow now."

Hook didn't open his eyes, but he roused enough to inhale, and he murmured, "It is Jill."

At a loss, Smee whirled to see the door. It was closed, and no one stood there. Turning back to his captain, Smee stared, wondering if Hook was delirious. And then he drew back, realizing what he'd done.

"Yes, Sir, it's the lady's." Now he thought of it, he, too, could smell her perfume on the handkerchief. The scent was a welcome distraction in the fetid air of Hook's prison. Smee could only guess at the emotion such a potent reminder of her evoked in his captain. And he realized the implications of carrying her belongings. He felt himself redden. He must have jerked, for weak as the man was, the captain's eyes blazed suddenly upon him.

"You have kept her safe." It wasn't a question.

Smee opened his mouth, then closed it again. He made a business of tucking the handkerchief into his pocket, but he knew he took too long to answer. "As safe as I've been able. Sir."

Hook registered the bo'sun's discomfort, then wearily shut his eyes. His voice was nearly a whisper. "Never mind, Smee. I expected as much."

"Sir?"

"She is Jill. What man can deny her?" Hook gestured with loose fingers, and Smee hastened to raise the jug for him. When Hook had downed some more, he ventured to speak again, and his speech came a trifle stronger.

"The *Roger?*"

Smee nodded, glad to report good news. "Sound, Sir."

Hook shivered, then looked pointedly at the biscuit in the bo'sun's fingers. Smee had been soaking it. Now he raised it from the jug and offered it. "Take some vittles, Sir." Hook's dry lips parted to accept it. "I figure we've got a half hour or so before Miss comes back."

Hook squinted as he swallowed. His throat worked as if it hurt him. With contempt, he uttered, "Miss."

"Here, Sir, have another swallow."

But Hook stopped the jug with his ringed hand. "Where is the surgeon?"

"Ah! Well you might ask, Sir. You'll be pleased to be knowing he's got a bit of his own back." But Hook's eyes glittered with impatience, and Smee said, "He's laid up in the next cabin, Sir."

Hook accepted the water. Searching for hopeful signs, Smee

nodded encouragement as his fingers pushed pieces of nourishment between Hook's lips. As tenderly as his big hands could manage, he brushed the crumbs from the black beard. Bit by bit, Smee fed his master the biscuit. He didn't lack for courage, but for compassion's sake, he balked at feeding his captain the truth.

The *Roger* rocked in the wind, keening, while strains of music drifted through the door, along with the sounds of revelry from the celebration. Hook listened, but made no comment. He listened, also, to the silence of his bo'sun. Unable to swallow any more, he shifted his body on the dirty mattress and lay down, his breath as he did so escaping in sighs.

Smee reached out and felt of the tangled hair. "I'll be cleaning you up, Sir, just as soon as I'm able." Lifting it off the captain's face, he remembered how many times he had performed this service for his lady. As if the gesture communicated Smee's thoughts, Hook spoke again, and much as Smee longed to hear his master's voice, he dreaded the words his master would say. Even more, he dreaded the words fate forced him to reply. Smee could easily minister to the body. But to the spirit—

"Smee. You have not brought her to me."

"No, Captain."

"Nor the keys."

"I can't be doing that, Sir."

Silence. Was it wrath— or exhaustion?

"Sir.… The captain wouldn't be allowing it."

Hook raised one eyebrow. "The captain?"

Looking away, Smee collected the jug and biscuits. Careful not to jar the invalid further, he set them aside.

"Jill is not in command?"

Smee felt the full force of his blunder weighing him down. "No, Sir. And I take the blame."

"Belay that. Tell me."

As Smee responded to the rasped command, he began slowly, then rolled the story off his tongue. It felt good to get it out, at last. "She was handling everything, Sir. More than ready to assume her duty, she was. You'd have been right proud of her, Captain. She stood there on the companionway, Red-Handed Jill, bold as brass. She was winning the men's confidence, they were that ready to follow her. And then the three of them— well, Sir, the three of them conspired together to work it their way. Forced her to give up the captaincy, they did. And I had to give up my keys. To the first mate."

"Three of them." Hook's eyes narrowed. "Hanover. And who else?"

"It's Yulunga, Sir. He's the mate. I don't dare let on to him you're found. No telling what he'd do at this point. He's liking things the way they are. Even young Miss is coming round to his way of thinking, tonight."

Hook's lip twitched in a spasm, then he controlled it. "But Jill has eluded the surgeon."

"Oh, aye, Sir. He tries to cover it, but the man's fit to be tied."

"I gather the outcome was not what he planned."

"No, Captain. Hanover made a deal with the devil. And he's paying for it now!"

Hook took in the bo'sun's vehemence, considering, and then he stated as coolly as if he sat secure behind his polished desk, "And this devil, Smee. He has taken Jill."

"I should have followed her lead, Sir. She knew what he was about."

"I've not been sleeping. Nor has she."

"It's only too plain to everyone, Sir."

In the wake of Hook's hand, his chain snaked along the bed. He closed his fingers on his bo'sun's arm, and borrowing Smee's strength, he pulled himself up on one elbow. Once stabilized, he retained his grip, and it was firmer than his deprivation might decree.

"Smee." At last the cadaverous face came to life, and his voice regained its velvet edge. "Whom do I have to kill?"

Smee steadied himself with a deep breath. "It's the gypsy, Sir."

"Cecco." Hook said it delicately, as if he were tasting the name.

"Aye. He outfoxed us all."

The scarry stump of Hook's arm jerked in a gesture both confirming and dismissive. "I would have guessed it, given time. Like Jill, the man is obsessed with jewelry."

The line of Smee's mouth was grim. "Not anymore, Sir."

Hook's focus sharpened on the eyes behind Smee's spectacles, and just as Smee had known would happen, he sounded the depth of the regret there. "I see. And my lady?"

"Covered in gold, Captain. With a heart to match."

"Speak plainly, or do not speak at all."

"Aye, Sir, begging your pardon. You'll not be wanting to hear it, but you're needing to." Straightening his spine, Smee forged ahead. "Captain, the lady followed your orders, right down the line. She did what she had to do to secure the ship. But Sir, you're knowing women's ways. When a powerful man is kind and generous, and she's missing the one she loves— well, Sir…you might say she's partial to him."

The pause was brief. "You say the man is powerful?"

"Aye, Captain. He's been watching you these many years. He's seeming more like yourself than I care to admit." Smee leaned forward to emphasize his words. "However that may be, Captain, I know the lady will be overjoyed when I tell her—"

"You will tell her nothing."

"…Sir?"

"The lady carries enough of a burden. You will not endanger her with the truth."

"She has to be told!"

"No, Smee. I forbid it."

"But—"

"No one must know. The doctor's daughter is inexperienced with his ether. I will feign to be drugged. You will provide me with sustenance, and hunt down my hook. Until I am strong enough to challenge this 'captain,' I shall remain hidden."

"Captain, that Hanover could murder you at any moment! He must know that if one of the crew should discover you here in his chains, he's a dead man. I'm boiling to kill him myself! And the gypsy, too, if he's linked to him."

"The men, Smee. They follow Mr. Cecco?" His breathing was unsteady now, his body weakening.

"Aye, Sir. He's taken over your own schemes— squeezed every diamond out of Hanover— and just today he captured us a prize. Your disappearance is the last loose end to knot up before he holds both the lady and the *Roger* for good and all. It's a wonder he hasn't ordered your death already."

"His oath must still mean something to him. You are certain Cecco conspires with the surgeon?"

"Too sure to be begging him for the key!"

"All the more reason to choose my time. I will lay my plans and rebuild my strength. You will say nothing." But his voice was faltering. "Go now, Smee."

"Captain, I hate to be leaving you like this!"

Through chattering teeth, Hook expelled his last words. "Hold my sword at the ready." Near the end of his strength, Hook couldn't utter any more. But the look of determination on his unshaven face commanded. Smee watched then, with his heart near to breaking, as his captain's eyes fell closed and the force of his will subsided with his vigor.

Hook's long body lay shivering. He fought the seizure, but after some moments, the stump of his arm reached out to his source of succor, swaying in the air like a starved snake angling for a bird.

Smee didn't hesitate. He shoved the fine sword from his side to stretch down on the filth of the mattress. He gathered Hook's shuddering shoulders in his arms. As the chained hand clutched at him, Smee pressed his red forehead to the master's black brow. For the last minutes remaining of their privacy, he wrapped himself around this great man, who nourished his servant's existence the way Smee had fed him a biscuit, and Smee forced his body's warmth against his master's chill, and willed his rugged love to save him.

The Making of a Mistress

The night was half worn away, and the planks and beams of the *Jolly Roger* rocked the better part of two ships' crews. At the appointed hour, her captain sent Miss Liza to assist his lady's retiring. Mr. Yulunga attended Liza, as promised, when she left the lady in the captain's quarters.

"Wait here, little girl." Yulunga knocked at the open door. Stooping under the doorframe, he entered, murmuring to the lady. A few moments later he returned to shut the door, twirling the key ring over his finger. "You have behaved tonight. Windows secured, and no rope ladders." Liza only stood, squeezing her hands together. Mocking, he said, "No protests of your innocence?"

She cast her eyes down. Yulunga's feet, set wide apart to balance his bulk against the ship's sway, were half again the size of her master's. Of Hook's.

"Good. I want no lies from you."

Yulunga paused to listen as the lady locked the door. He tried the knob, then deposited his keys in his pocket. His duty done, he stood beside Liza, his gaze slanted sideways at her.

Unsure what to do, she blinked at him, and he signified that she was to link her arm through his elbow. She did so, and stared at her white hand resting on his ebony. The light of lanterns blazed about the deck. In their luster, the pearls on her finger glowed more orange than pink. Mr. Yulunga had used those pearls, just as Liza predicted. She hadn't predicted the circumstances that led her to accept them.

Feeling awkward on the mate's arm, Liza stepped with him down the stairs. Having pictured herself so many times strutting along the companionway upon the velvet arm of Captain Hook, some adjustment was necessary tonight. She had done her best, taking special care with her appearance. But of course she wore no fine gown, only her blue dress trimmed with lace at the bodice. Yet it was becoming. She had brushed her hair and coiled it under a new, intricate net. Her father rested in the spare cabin tonight, and without fear of his disapproval, she had pinched her cheeks and bit her lips to add some color. Here, at least, if not with Hook, her design met with success. As she glanced around the deck to take note of the sailors who might witness her discomfiture, she felt Yulunga's grip tighten, as if to demonstrate his possession of her.

Finding the galley too close, a dozen or more revelers had braved the wind to scatter themselves about the boards, carousing under the watchful eyes of Mr. Mullins and Mr. Mason. A group lounged by the mainmast, observing a game of dice. The pieces rattled on the planks, the men cheered, and then a pair of china blue eyes looked up from the game. Wearing a Gallic smile and a pale blond pigtail, the owner of the eyes saluted Liza.

Earlier, under a smirk of amusement from Yulunga, that blond sailor had shed his blue jacket and cushioned Liza's bench with it. In charming, broken English, he'd given her to understand how he admired her beauty. Not possessing the proper words, he'd used his hands, as Frenchmen do, to express his admiration for her soft gray eyes and the fullness of her lips. His fingers were sturdy, and rough from hauling sail— but expressive. Liza allowed his fingers liberty enough for this discovery, but too aware of her dependence on her escort's good will, she hoped she had been discreet.

Now, under that sailor's scrutiny again, her cheeks needed no pinching. She colored naturally as the others' gazes followed the young Frenchman's. But she raised her head, allowing a stream of pride to trickle into her manner. After all, that young man was only a sailor. Liza sloped her shoulder toward Yulunga as she leaned upon his arm. She wasn't the captain's choice— but she was the mate's.

Still, after all her efforts to win Hook's favor and take shelter under his power, she had failed to escape her father's rule. In making the attempt, she only became more deeply mired in the mud of filial servitude. Brutal as Yulunga might prove, it was *his* interest, now, to which Liza clung, seeking release from the nightmare unfolding within her quarters— frightening enough for her, but deadly for her former master. Surely, the situation could not turn worse, for either of them.

Mr. Mullins had loitered near the companionway since the lady's arrival this evening. Seeing Yulunga and the surgeon's daughter descend, he stepped to one side of the stair. "Sir." With a crooked grin, Mullins dipped his head to Liza, too. "Miss." Her posture became straighter. Once the couple passed, Mullins mounted the steps to stand guard at the captain's quarters. As second officer, Mullins listened to the gaming below, but he tucked his thumbs in his belt and kept a weather eye on the hatches. Captain Cecco's orders were strict, and sailors, French or familiar, were the least of the master's concerns. No telling what that surgeon might get up to this night. Mullins didn't envy young Miss having to live with that man. None of the men did.

At the hatch, Yulunga descended first and turned to assist Liza down. But when they reached the gun deck, he swept a look around and, finding it deserted, dropped his pretense of chivalry to seize her arm. He dragged her past the cook's cat, and it scolded him for the disturbance, arching its back before settling again to watch with luminous, suspicious eyes as he pushed the girl up against the mizzenmast.

The light was dimmer on this deck, but Liza could read the inky features of his face. She lowered her gaze to the beads at his neck. They bobbed as he spoke in his deep, murky voice. As the outward manifestation of his sound, their play had begun to fascinate Liza. And his beads weren't the only fascination. The vest beneath them hung open to display his sable skin.

"I have allowed you your fun, little girl. You came to the party. You drank a glass of wine. Only one, and watered, because I like a woman whose wits are sharp. I let you dance with that French boy, because I like to watch you move. Now," he pressed up against her, and her neck arched to enable her eyes to meet his, liquid black, like his voice. "Now you tell me what *you* like."

Her heart was pounding against her ribs. She felt the ring on her finger. The pearls had slipped around to burrow into the flesh of her hand. She envisioned her father lying in the room behind her, and Hook, a hairsbreadth from death in the quarters to the side, and her eyes grew wild with confusion. This man's big body exuded an earthy smell, a smell of sweat and of power. His chest glistened, and she raised her hand with her fingers splayed, to hesitate, hanging in the heat of the space between them. The sound of laughter in the galley assaulted her senses, but not as harshly as the blood that banged against her ears.

Yulunga's jaw jutted. "Go on. You can touch. I give you permission." He smiled as he said it, derisive.

Slowly, she rested her hand on his chest. Smooth, and moist. Burning. To her surprise, Liza felt his heart beating, too. And as his lungs expanded to breathe, her hand rose and fell with them. She stared at her hand, so fair. How could two skins be so very different, when two hearts pumped, and two sets of lungs exhaled and seized the same air? This man appeared to be unlike the two men behind Liza, but to her, tonight, he was exactly the same. Her father and Hook, in turn, had been her protectors. Now she looked to this exile from Africa to take that place. Liza raised her stare from the contrast of their fleshes, and appealed to his eyes.

"Yes, little girl. I know what you want. Let's go." More gently this time, but just as insistent, he guided her by the arm. Toward her quarters.

Liza balked.

"What, Miss? Your father isn't at home. He won't be disturbing us." His teeth gleamed in the lanternlight.

Liza jockeyed around to face him, edging toward her door, and wondered. Would Yulunga really protect her? The truth would out, eventually. Maybe Hook didn't have to die before then. Maybe she should let Yulunga see the secret in her quarters. She should open her lips and tell him. Right now. But her father—

"No? You want to keep me waiting. Then you will wait for your earrings, too."

Liza shook her head. She backed from him, and yet her hands

found their way to his ribs. Against her door now, she tried to decide. Should she open, and trust in him? He might shield her from her father's rage— or he might as easily cast her off, reviling her for her perfidy. He held her hands in his fists, and he was drawing her into his kiss. She had another moment to try to think. As long as their hands were occupied, neither one of them could open the door.

Yulunga's face made the long descent, and his lips burrowed into her neck. She gasped at the flame there, and his mouth fired his way up under her jaw. She didn't think her lips could bear his heat, but she couldn't turn his kisses away. He released her hands now, and pulled her by the waist, and she felt for the panel of the door behind her. Her fingers bumped over its roughness, searching for the handle. It was cold in her grasp. His mouth sidled along her cheek to meet hers, and as her lips parted to speak the terrible truth before he could silence them with his own, Liza felt the door handle turn and slip away from her grasp.

"Mr. Yulunga. My daughter is not available to you."

"Doctor." Yulunga straightened.

A chill breeze wafted over Liza, bringing the sting of salt air from the open windows of her quarters. Drenched in cold perspiration, Liza froze, staring into Yulunga's face. With regret, she felt his arms withdraw from her body. Once again, she stood alone. Unprotected.

"Liza. Come in."

Her lips hung open.

"I think, Mister Hanover, your daughter wants to say something to me."

Hanover didn't move. "I very much doubt it, Mr. Yulunga."

Her jaw worked, and her breath came panting.

"Maybe she wants to tell me goodnight?" Yulunga smiled at her distress.

"I will say it for her. Good night, Sir."

The surgeon's hands fell heavily upon her shoulders, and he pulled her into their quarters. "Now, Liza." Disregarding Yulunga's leer, he shut and locked the door. Looming in front of her, Hanover's presence bore down upon his daughter. Behind him, the ivory-handled cane hung, waiting on its hook in the wall.

Her passions interrupted, Liza gazed upon the gentleman, her father, and with heightened awareness, her regard moved from his face to study him, head to toe. Her heart began to pound again. Or had it never stopped? The surgeon wore no coat, no waistcoat, no shirt. His wounds prevented that, and he stood holding the muscles of his shoulders stiff, his scar tight against his cheek, betraying his discomfort. His sandy hair was contained by the black ribbon. His body seemed pale in comparison to Yulunga's, but equally smooth, and damp with perspiration. Although he stood with effort, he did stand, and handsomely. He had shed his bloody breeches and donned his fencing trousers, tight against his hips, and his feet, like the mate's, were naked. He bore no scar, no mark of any kind beyond that on his cheek. If one never got past his front, one would not suspect the ravages of his back.

Resisting her reaction to him, Liza pressed her knuckles to her mouth. She backed from her father, shaking her head, and tears formed in her eyes. He was much too fine a man.

"Get to bed now."

She turned to obey before he might reach for the cane, and she stopped dead. She spun around, questioning.

He nodded. "Yes. The lower bunk."

Her head tilted, ever so slightly.

"I cannot trust you. You will lie with me."

As with Mr. Yulunga, Liza made no protestations of her innocence. She blinked, and then, shakily, made herself breathe again. She obeyed her father, as she obeyed him in all things. Slowly she turned, and, watching her feet inch along the boards, Liza made her way to her father's bed. It was strange to her, and yet all too familiar. Awakening there this morning, she had expected to find her skin stained and sticky— with the wine she had poured, if nothing else. Yet every bit of her flesh had been cleansed. Every mound, every hollow….As she recalled the feeling, goose bumps arose, and she felt the hairs of her arms stand on end.

But those arms lifted the bed linen, and she prepared to lie down. Her father's voice stopped her.

"And what will you wear to entice your lovers tomorrow, if you sleep in that gown?"

Liza dropped the sheet. Keeping her back to him, she hesitated. Then she loosened her garment, spread wide the bodice, and she shuddered it off to stand clad in her shift. He moved behind her as she bent to step out of the skirt. While she clutched the empty dress to her breast, his surgeon's hands appropriated her arm. Without comment, he examined the darkening purple of the mark his fingers left that morning. Relinquishing her arm, he eased her gown from her grip. She heard his feet pad toward the corner, where the pegs held their clothing. Dressed in her shift, she laid her body, already over-stimulated by Mr. Yulunga, on the bunk beneath the dying man. And she wondered if, in the morning, she would find her father's presence had left bloodstains on the linen.

He walked toward her. Moving gingerly, he settled into the bed, resting on an elbow. Drawing back a little, she raised up on her side, and with one of his dexterous hands, he pulled the net from her hair. Her careful coil came loose, and the brown tresses tumbled down over her shoulders, ending just above her breasts. As he had done that morning, he touched the hair above her bruised temple. As before, his hand felt too good.

"Liza. You have cut your hair. I want you to let it grow again. Long, like my lady's."

She barely moved. Only enough to nod.

"As much as it pains me to say so, in these last few days, you have behaved like a harlot. You belong to me. Legally and morally, you are my responsibility until such time as I establish a suitable situation for you. But the interest your flirtations have provoked force upon me the realization that you are now a young woman."

Liza kept still, her eyes fixed on her father. He settled his smarting body more comfortably in the bed. And slightly nearer.

"I admit that, as your father, I have been remiss. I seem to be a man who has little indulgence for children. But I assure you. I won't neglect you again. Liza, I must explain to you…some things. About men."

He had studied her appearance as closely as she studied his. He didn't have to reach far to take her hand. Filtering her fingers through his own, he pulled the ring from them. "This is the ring I chose for your mother upon our union. When we have come to an understanding, it will be yours." He tucked it under his pillow, and his signet shone in the lanternlight. Orange, like the pearls.

"In regard to your conduct, you must be made to comprehend what you are doing." His voice slowed, and he considered each of his words before he spoke them. "Liza. When a man is captivated by a woman— any woman— her allure may cause…certain things to happen to that man. Any of these ruffians who surround us will naturally succumb to his urges."

As her eyes indicated, the lecture held interest for Liza. It held interest, also, for the man lying directly above her, feigning insensibility. Both listened, intently.

"But even an educated man, a gentleman, when aroused, may lose control. His intellect may be overcome by his passion. This passion can bring on certain regrettable actions. Actions such as…murder…rape.…"

Their two sets of gray eyes locked together. His voice softened. "Seduction."

Liza waited, too bashful to breathe, as her father beheld her face.

"Your lips, Liza. They are so like mine. Full, lush. Any man would want to touch your lips— you need not shy from me, I am your father— A woman must be prepared for a man to want to touch her mouth. He may begin with his finger, gently. And he may wish to trace it round…or simply caress it, from side to side. Then he may desire you to open your lips— as you have just done— so that he may push past them, into the moisture of your mouth.…Yes, any man would wish for this. You must prepare for this. But know that, always, his lips will follow his touch, and he will kiss you. Any man would desire to kiss you, Liza."

Urged by his passions— like any man— Doctor Hanover leaned toward his daughter and gifted her with a rare prize. His attention.

Their hearer, though chained and wasting and weak, knew himself at this moment to be a powerful man. Vengeance, sweet and terrible, impended like a sword above his enemies' heads, poised in the lethargy of his famished hand. A thin smile etched his withered lips. One chink of a chain could stop the progress of young Miss' lesson.

It never sounded.

The lower bunk in the aft starboard cabin of the *Jolly Roger* cradled a man and his daughter. She was an intelligent woman. She understood the virtue of silence. As her pulse battered against every inch of her skin, she responded to her father's teachings. Without a word, she accepted him as the authority. She acquired the knowledge he imparted, and when the night wore itself out and the lesson was over, there was no part of her father she didn't understand.

As she lapsed into sleep, she felt his ring slide onto her finger— the same finger on which her mother had worn it— and his full, lush lips pressed her palm.

Genuine Insincerity

From his perch aloft, Tom spotted trouble coming. Guillaume's tight-fitting uniform issued from the captain's quarters, with Guillaume in it, and headed down the companionway. His brass buttons gleamed with an air of self-importance. Equally bright, the young officer's eyes scanned the rigging. His boots halted, seeming barely to resist the urge to click together, and he issued an order to the sailing master. His voice was low, but Tom knew what he was saying. The master's grizzled head snapped up, and he bellowed.

"You there, *Monsieur* Tootles! Avast, and hit the deck!"

"Oui, Monsieur." Automatically, Tom felt for his knife first. Then he shuffled his bare feet along the yard. His new mates stared as he climbed down the shrouds, but his own eyes never left Guillaume, who stood upright, with his hands primly behind his waist and his smirk secure.

"Bonjour, *Monsieur* Tootles. I regret to greet you so early with bad tidings." The smirk made a liar of him. "But the *commandant* has ordered you to his quarters."

"Oui, Monsieur."

"You do not look surprised."

"Non, Monsieur. Nor do you."

Guillaume shook his head. "Your insolence will one day get you in trouble."

"Aye, Sir, mayhap. But not with you."

"You think you know this? Put it to the test!"

"That's why we're on the way to see the captain— Sir."

Guillaume's shiny boots came to a standstill at the base of the steps. "Then you admit you took it?"

"Are you asking?"

The mate's slender face frowned, and his bright eyes studied Tom. "*Non.* I leave that to the *commandant.*"

"Good. I've found the perfect spot to share it with you." Tom pounded up the steps, but hearing no boots behind him, he turned to look back. LeCorbeau's second officer hadn't moved. "Well, come on, then, if you're coming."

Guillaume stood scrutinizing him, his head to one side. "What game do you play, *Monsieur* Tootles?"

"No game, mate. This is life or death." Tom pivoted and charged the rest of the way up the steps. The officer had to hustle to catch up with him, and he seized Tom's fist just before he could annoy the captain with a hearty knock.

"*Non!* I see I have much to teach you, *Monsieur* Tootles. One must never bang on the door of the *commandant!* Especially after a late night. One must tap, like so."

"All right, Mr. Guillaume. I see we have a lot to teach each other. We'll drink to it this evening, shall we?" And to the mate's surprise, Tom buttoned up his new blue jacket, opened the door for him, and dropped all trace of cockiness. Like a lamb, he followed Guillaume into the captain's presence. Touching his hand to his forehead, he looked neither left nor right, but stood straight as a soldier, waiting to be spoken to.

He held his position while Renaud fussed about with what Tom took to be a silver teapot. Tom had been a guest in this room on his very first visit, and he felt its oppressiveness again as the plush, ornamental hangings closed in on him. LeCorbeau himself slumped as if under some burden, his arms limp and his eyes masked by a damp towel. At last Guillaume announced Tom. On the proper cue, Tom addressed the paneled wall behind his captain's velvet-cushioned chair.

"*Bonjour, mon Commandant.* It is an honor to attend you."

Renaud was pouring his master's chocolate into a bone china cup resplendent with fleurs-de-lis. At Tom's entrance he had looked up. At Tom's words, he slopped a milky-brown stream onto the crisp napkin. Guillaume, apparently, had already gone to work on this English oaf. But the rich, sweet smell of chocolate made Tom's stomach growl, and although both officers remained silent, they sniggered.

"Good morning, *Monsieur* Tootles." LeCorbeau emerged, pulling the towel from his forehead to inspect his new sailor. His eyes were edged with a delicate shade of lilac. "At least, I hope it will become so." His fingers motioned toward his cocoa, gave up the cloth and received the drink from Renaud. The gathered cuffs of LeCorbeau's nightshirt surrounded his hands, nearly hiding the cup as he sipped. His hair was tousled, reminiscent of a cock's comb, and lace bunched like wattles under his neck, furthering the likeness. His dressing gown flowed from his shoulders to his ankles, one long swirl of paisley. Renaud relieved him of the cup and stepped back to stand beside him.

Tom gave a brisk nod. "I hope I can be of service to you, Sir."

Guillaume maneuvered around the table to position himself behind LeCorbeau. His captain, he knew, had little interest in Tom Tootles. The young man grinned too much, and his body was bulky. Nor did he possess the dark, brooding features of his brother. But Guillaume found this facile sailor to be intriguing— in body, robust, in character, a chameleon— and he gravitated to a spot from which his eager eyes could watch Tom, unobserved by either LeCorbeau or Renaud.

LeCorbeau accepted Tom's servility, barely raising his fingers from his lap, then roused himself to lift his head from the chair back. "Eh, *Monsieur* Tootles.…When I agreed to take you on, I had not thought I should have cause to speak to you personally, and so soon."

"*Monsieur*, I'm pleased to have earned the privilege."

"Well, eh, we shall see. An unfortunate incident has occurred, on which I hope you will be able to shed some light."

"I'll do my best, *Monsieur*. I aim to please."

LeCorbeau opened his heavy lids a bit wider. "*Mon Dieu*, my boy, are you always so cheerful in the mornings?"

"Well, Sir, you could ask my brother Nibs about that. There's been a morning or two I was a mite short with him, come time to show a leg. But I'm a fairly cheerful sort, yes. Nibs isn't the one to complain, mind. He's quiet most of the time, but I've seen him surly as a serpent on occasion. Once, when Mr. Cecco— I'm sorry! I mean *Captain* Cecco, of course— once Captain Cecco— leastways, he wasn't captain then, yet, but Captain Cecco as *was* Mr. Cecco, once he—"

Tom broke off, sensible that the men in front of him were staring. LeCorbeau appeared wide awake now, and his mates' mouths hung open. Tom's eyes rolled from one officer to another. "I'm sorry, *Monsieurs*. Am I talking too much?"

"I should say so, yes." LeCorbeau's manner was dry as a desert. He reached out a hand to Renaud for his chocolate.

Tom produced a crooked grin. "It's a failing of mine, Sir. Mr. Cecco's said as much, time and again. I mean *Captain* Cecco, *Captain*—"

"Enough of this absurdity! *Monsieur* Tootles, you will kindly curb your tongue—"

"Aye, aye, Sir."

At Tom's interruption, LeCorbeau cleared his throat to signify displeasure, then proceeded, "…so that I may get on with the business at hand." He glared at Tom, as if daring him to open his mouth again. When silence reigned, he settled back. "Now, eh, where was I? *Ah, oui*. It has come to my attention that an item of value is missing from my quarters." LeCorbeau watched Tom for a reaction. Tom waited, then interpreted LeCorbeau's pause as an opening to answer. He kept it short.

"I'm sorry, Sir."

"It would seem that my finest bottle of cognac has been purloined. What might you know of this?"

"Sir, I might know all about it."

All three of the men facing Tom registered surprise.

"But as it happens— I don't."

LeCorbeau snapped, "It is too early in the morning, *Monsieur*, for riddles. The bottle disappeared while I and my officers attended the festivities aboard the *Jolly Roger*. You were seen on deck last evening, according to the night watch."

"I *was* the night watch, Sir."

LeCorbeau tossed his head. His head regretted the motion. He sighed. "Yes, yes, I know it. The other men report that when your shift expired, your brother went below."

"The lads are dead-on, Sir. That's just how it happened."

"And you were remarked loitering in the vicinity of my door."

"I don't doubt it, Sir. I *was* in the vicinity."

"And?"

"And if I was of a mind to pinch a bottle, I could easily have done it, Sir."

LeCorbeau raised his eyes to the heavens. "Of course. But, eh," his cuff agitated impatiently, "did you?"

"No, Sir."

"And you have no inkling what might have become of this bottle?"

"None at all, Sir."

"Ah."

"Unless you mean the bottle behind *Monsieur* Guillaume's pillow, Sir."

For a frozen moment, stillness ruled. Then Guillaume blushed, stuttered, and sputtered a protest. "*Mon Commandant!* I— I—"

LeCorbeau threw up his arm, lace and all, to silence him. He leaned toward Tom. "Young man, what do you indicate?"

"Oh, nothing Sir. It's just that you asked me, and—"

"*Mon Dieu, quel imbécile!* Tell me what you mean by this insinuation!"

"I surely don't mean to insinuate anything, *Monsieur*."

"Do you accuse your superior? Or do you not?"

"No, Sir! I'd never accuse an officer."

"Very well, then—"

"Any more than I'd expect an officer to accuse me."

The look emanating from above the captain's beaky nose waxed shrewd. LeCorbeau studied Tom, memorizing every line of his face. Lazily, he raised his finger to point at Tom's head. When he spoke, his words were not those Tom expected.

"From whom did you receive that nasty scar, my boy?"

Involuntarily, Tom raised his fingers to touch it. "From Mr. Starkey, Sir. Aboard the *Roger*."

"Yes, Mr. Starkey. Such a man.…No subtlety of any kind."

"Yes, Sir. Very different from your own officers."

LeCorbeau narrowed his beady eyes. "If it meets with your approval, *Monsieur*, I will be the judge of my officers."

"Oh, aye, Sir."

"And for what reason did Mr. Starkey administer this blow?"

"Begging your pardon, Sir— *pardonnez-moi*, I mean— he gave me plenty more than one blow. I was black and blue for a month! Nibs can testify to that. Mr. Smee had to piece me together. I came crawling to him, and let me tell you, he was generous with the rum that night! I was wishing for one of those wet towels next morning. Between the stitching and the headache, I still don't know which hurt worse. As you say, *Monsieur*, Mr. Starkey is anything but subtle."

By the end of Tom's speech, the captain's expression was glacial. "Young man, answer my question."

"Willingly, *Monsieur*." He stood blinking, his open face obedient.

Rage never suited LeCorbeau. He motioned Renaud to vent it.

Renaud raised his voice, but not enough to offend his captain's sensibilities. "Well, *Monsieur* Tootles? What is your answer?"

Tom stood hesitating. His features struggled to strike the proper expression as the three men leaned closer. "Sorry, Sirs.…Seems I've forgot the question."

"Idiot!" The first mate had to search his own memory first. "Why were you beaten?"

"Oh." Tom shrugged. "It was a punishment."

LeCorbeau's eyebrows rose. "A punishment? But your Mister— eh, you foul boy!— your *Captain* Cecco never mentioned this."

"Well, Sir. You've seen Captain Cecco's back." Tom angled his head. "I guess my little scar doesn't impress him very much."

The black eyes shone. "Yes, well, eh, one day I hope to hear *that* story.…" Tom opened his mouth, but LeCorbeau flung up a hand to shut him up before the raconteur might erupt again. "No! *Vraiment!* You are as full of tales as your mother! We are speaking of *you* this morning. So, am I now to discover you have been known as a troublemaker among Hook's crew?"

"No, Sir! I disobeyed orders once, is all."

"Once?"

"Once was enough. Sir."

"Exactly. And once is all I will tolerate from you. You will guard yourself from now on. Your belongings will be searched. You will be watched. If I find reason to implicate you in this or any other offense, you will find yourself breakfasting in my brig."

"Aye, Sir. Better make it a double ration, though."

LeCorbeau's eyes closed and he wilted against his chair, signaling to Renaud, who hastily replaced the damp towel on his brow. "And why, I am afraid to ask, do you make such a statement? Be quick! I am fading."

"Because, with all due respect, Sir, when I'm hauled into the brig, I'll be bringing company." Tom didn't look at Guillaume. He didn't have to. He had LeCorbeau's second mate in his pocket. It would be fun to see how soon his tight-fitting uniform streaked toward his quarters.

They'd drink to that. Tonight, in that last locked cabin— with a fine, aged bottle of cognac.

Breakfast began later than usual. The *Roger's* galley was scarcely tidied from last evening's merrymaking when the crewmen started to trickle in. Mr. Smee was there when the first shift departed to up anchor and drop sails. He ate his porridge. He was there when the ship got underway and the next round of breakfasters came and went. Smee filled his bowl again. He was there, still, when the surgeon and his daughter appeared, and then he was gone— with his porridge.

Mr. Yulunga waited there also. He straddled a bench and lounged against the wall not far from the porridge pot, his arms folded and a splinter of wood between his teeth. His obsidian eyes watched every move Liza made. She wore her blue dress, entering the galley as her father held the door for her. Devoid of formal attire today, Doctor Hanover looked younger, sporting soft velvet breeches and a shirt that hung loose around his body, no doubt to avoid chafing his back. He moved stiffly, but with a grace surprising to those who had witnessed his punishment.

Yulunga wasn't the only man keeping an eye on the surgeon. All the hands were curious, and the several sailors dotting the galley loitered a little longer than necessary. The rumor had spread that Yulunga's pleasures were interrupted last night, by the object of his pleasure's sire, and they, too, waited, to see what either man might do next.

As Liza entered, her gaze had flown immediately to Yulunga, then she looked away. Her lowered eyes shifted toward her father, who led her to the captain's table. Hanover chose her seat, positioning her at an angle to Yulunga, and held the chair for her. The doctor went so far as to fetch Liza's porridge from the pot himself, due perhaps, to its proximity to the mate. In his brusque manner, Hanover nodded to Yulunga. He chose the seat next to Liza and, as he ate, he watched the man who watched his daughter.

She appeared smaller and paler than she'd looked the previous evening. Yulunga noted that Liza took only a few tastes of her food, but upon encouragement by her father, she was persuaded to finish the serving. The surgeon spoke to her in low tones. Not moving his back, he bent his head toward her, and once, he smiled into her eyes. Rarer still, she smiled in return. But it was a tentative thing, as fleeting as the woman she had been last night.

Throughout the meal, Liza looked to Yulunga only one time, when Hanover left her to refill his cup. Her eyes were wary, as if she feared to face him, but it was enough for Yulunga. He hauled his body from the bench, stepped past her father, and stood before her, his bulging arms dangling and the splinter of wood rolling between his fingers. The men who ranged around the room perked up their ears and sat up straighter.

"Miss."

With swift, silent footsteps, Hanover returned. "Mr. Yulunga."

"Doctor."

"Is there something I can do for you?"

"I am still waiting to see if Miss Liza wants to tell me something. She didn't say good night. Perhaps she'd like to try good morning?"

But today, Liza's lips remained closed.

Yulunga smiled and raised a questioning eyebrow. "No?"

She lifted her shoulders a fraction, giving the merest shrug, and then her father's hand settled on her shoulder. She turned her head to see it. Hanover squeezed her shoulder once, then he sat down. Yulunga didn't budge. Looking up, Hanover acknowledged his presence again, with less courtesy than before.

"Well. I see no reason to keep you, Sir."

"The mistress wants me to bring you, Miss, as soon as you've finished your breakfast. I'll wait." Yulunga turned toward his bench again, but stopped as the surgeon called after him.

"There is no need for you to trouble yourself. I will escort her."

"Lady's orders, Mister Hanover. And I don't think you want to get too near the captain's woman again." Yulunga smirked and returned to hunker down in his place by the porridge pot. Watching.

Hanover ignored him. Upon finishing his breakfast, he folded his handkerchief, studied Liza, and leaned forward. With unsuspected gentleness, he dabbed his daughter's lips. Immediately, her cheeks were suffused with color, exactly as they appeared last night when Yulunga's hands had finally taken hold of her. Her father touched the handkerchief to his own mouth and prepared his damaged body to stand.

Shoving off from the bench, Yulunga manifested his considerable presence by the captain's table. Liza's gaze slid between the two men, and for a moment she sat undecided. Then she rose on her father's arm, pressed it, and before either man could speak, she turned her back on both of them. Darting away, she slipped out the door to run to her duty, leaving her would-be escorts staring after her. Neither man was happy. And both men smiled.

"Well, Doctor. What do you think?"

Hanover's wisp of a smile dissipated. "I think you have done enough damage, Sir. Further than this, I have no intention of discussing my daughter with you."

"Then there is no problem. Discussion is the last thing on my mind." Yulunga grinned his ominous grin and rumbled from the galley, slamming the door behind him. But once away, he relaxed his shoulders. The splinter of wood bobbed up and down between his teeth as he strolled toward the stairs to take up his post— not too far from the master's quarters.

He liked her when she defied him. Even more when she defied her father. After months of silence, Yulunga was sure she'd almost spoken to him last night— at the exact moment he didn't want to talk at all. He'd give the girl that dress he'd found for her. And he'd give her a bit of time. Most likely, she had some new bruises she was ashamed to show. But that swan-white skin would hide no secrets. Not from Yulunga. Not for long.

As Yulunga's feet disappeared up the hatch, Smee emerged, in a hurry, from the surgeon's quarters. He clutched a bowl in one hand. Hook's rapier banged against his leg as he staggered toward his cabin. Once within its privacy, he shut his door, flung the bowl on the table and listened to the crash of it. He yanked off the rapier and his spectacles, too, and threw them after. His soul gaped with a near-mortal wound. He knew only one way to deal with it.

Instinctively, he lurched toward his cabinet, where he scrabbled through his mending box until his fist closed on a hunk of leather scrap. Smee hurled himself on his bunk, on his back, and jammed the strap between his teeth. With his face red and his knuckles white, Mr. Smee lay writhing, grinding at the leather, blocking the curses from his mouth, but screaming them in his mind.

Bloody bastard! Bloody stinking bastard! Foulest scum of the earth— and your dear, dainty daughter's a fit companion for you. Devil's spawn! You've no business breathing, either of you! Bloody hell— I'll be murdering you both!

Mr. Smee still lay there when the crewmen began trickling into the galley for lunch.

"Have you forgotten my tea, Liza?"

Still reckoning how to manage the two strong men she'd just eluded, Liza stood before Jill, her face flushed with her hurry, and squeezing her hands together. Only half aware of the fact, she found the pearls on her finger staying put. On this hand, the one on which her father had chosen to place it, the ring fit properly.

Jill herself wore several new rings on her fingers this morning, and a silver shamrock dangled from a chain about her neck. "Help me to dress— the blue gown today— then you can fetch a cup of tea and bring me some breakfast. Or perhaps I'll visit the galley myself."

Cecco turned from his shaving mirror, wiping his neck with a towel. Jill had already tended his other needs, and after a late rising this morning, Cecco found it expedient to take charge of the shaving himself. "I am pleased to find your appetite returned, lovely one. And what will you be doing today?"

"I have a story I must set down. But first I'll take the air. With you, Captain, if you'll have me."

"As I have demonstrated, I will never refuse your propositions." Smiling, Cecco drew on his vest. "But I insist you dress first. You will find me on deck. I must speak to Mullins about our course."

"Aye, Sir. I won't be long."

The captain turned to Liza, surprising her with his notice. "I hear you have doctored the surgeon. Tell me, Miss. How is your father bearing his wounds?" His tone was anything but solicitous. "Well enough, I understand, to defend your honor last evening?"

Looking down, Liza nodded. She felt suddenly queasy.

"You may tell your foolish father what I say. Red-Handed Jill is the only reason he still breathes."

Liza met Cecco's gaze, and came alive under its force. The dark depths of his eyes displayed the same ruthlessness now that she witnessed when her father lay pinned under his knee.

"My lady begged me, on her knees, to show him mercy. He will do well to repay her consideration by keeping his distance." Illustrating his point, Cecco snatched up his knife and thrust it in his belt. He strode to face Jill, taking her chin in his fingers. Jill quickly grasped his wrist, as if to protect herself. Then, seeming to think better of her action, she relaxed her body and stroked his arm. Cecco exhaled an amused breath, then he released her and strolled to the door, where he halted to face the women. "Now get moving, both of you. The surgeon's punishment is over, and the men expect to see you going about your business." Pressing his fingertips to his lips, he gazed intently at Jill and released them, and then he left.

Liza turned to watch Jill, her father's promised wife. The lady's eyes remained on the door, as if she could still see Cecco through it. Liza wondered if Jill was thinking the same thoughts she was thinking— remembering the night Hanover risked everything to climb to the lady's chamber, and the secret letter the mistress had pressed on Liza to deliver to the Frenchman. Captain Cecco was a handsome man, a man who exuded raw power. But Liza understood, now, as she had never understood before, how very persuasive a gentleman her father could be.

Studying Jill this morning, Liza saw a reflection of herself. She almost pitied the woman. Hook, the pirate king whose features and refinement had commanded both women's hearts, was gone. Other men had come forward to advance their claims. Which master would Jill serve in the end? The choice she faced was a difficult one. Liza knew. She herself faced the very same choice. But when the moment came, Liza had little doubt the decision would be made for both women, and skillfully— by her forceful father.

Jill's face showed only a hint of her dilemma now, in a wrinkling of her brow. But her words betrayed her heart. "Liza." Jill smiled and ran her fingers through her hair, as if not considering her words at all. "Doesn't your father favor blue? And see, we shall both be wearing blue today." She turned, becoming brisk, and her new rings flashed as she indicated the wardrobe. "Hurry, now. We must follow the captain's orders."

Liza obeyed. But as she did so, she held her head a little more erect than she used to do. In a few more days, she wouldn't have to wait on a lady again. She would be concerned only with pleasing one person. The cost was dear, but somehow Liza had achieved her goal after all. She had, at last, secured the interest of a very strong man.

"Well, Mr. Yulunga, I see that for your sake I should have made a deeper impression on the surgeon."

Gauging Yulunga's mood first, Mr. Mullins grinned. "Aye, Captain! And for the girl's sake. She looked near as royal as the lady last night, prancing down the companionway on our mate's arm. Not so sure of herself this morning, though. I wonder what that man did to her after he caught her with Mr. Yulunga?"

Yulunga shrugged. "Nothing she cannot handle."

Cecco said, "She is still swayed by her father, of this I am sure. Jill and I put on a fine pretense for her just now."

"Once I have the charge of her, Sir, Miss will be mending her ways."

"You are speaking of a woman, my friend. The one thing of which a man can never be certain. Even my Jill remains a mystery to me. I cannot doubt her affection, but trust will come only with time."

"You hold the lady's heart, Sir. I'm not so sure young Miss has one. On that score, we will make a good match."

"I have yet to meet a woman who has no heart, Mr. Yulunga."

The mate grinned. "Maybe so. But I find the heart will follow wherever the body leads."

"And speaking of this, where is our faithful Mr. Smee? He is usually on deck every morning, watching for my lady."

Mullins shifted his weight. "I saw him late last night, Captain. On deck."

"Yes?"

"He made as if to pay a call to your quarters. But when he saw me standing guard, he stopped in his tracks and went back below. I haven't seen him since, Sir."

Yulunga observed his captain's expression as it darkened. "Sir, Smee was in the galley for breakfast. He stayed a long time. I thought he might be waiting for someone."

"Mr. Yulunga, you will keep an eye on him today."

"Aye, Sir. I'll hunt him up."

Yulunga turned to go but waited as the lady emerged from her quarters. Liza held the door for her. Jill scanned the deck, then descended to join the captain.

"Good morning, gentlemen."

"Ma'am."

But the lady remained distracted, her gaze roving the ship.

"You have not breakfasted, Madam."

"No, Sir. I find I am not hungry after all."

"For whom do you search, lovely one? Our surgeon, perhaps, to see how he fares?"

"No, no. I was rather wondering where our Mr. Smee has got to today. It isn't like him to sleep in, even after a party."

Mullins cleared his throat and excused himself. "Ma'am. Sir, I'll be getting to the charts then."

Yulunga, too, backed away. "And I will see to your order, Captain." He glanced at Liza where she stood peeking through the captain's doorway. Then he nodded to the lady, magnificent in her royal blue gown, with the shamrock twinkling at her bosom along with Cecco's gold. Yulunga didn't meet his captain's eyes as he departed to slip below decks.

Jill extended her arm to Cecco. "Shall we walk, then, Sir?"

He accepted her hand, but his eyes were cool. "We shall walk. We shall walk as long as we need to walk, until you have explained to me why you allowed 'our' Mr. Smee to place his hands around your waist yesterday, even as I punished the doctor for a similar offense."

As Jill's mouth opened in astonishment, Cecco ushered her up the deck, his own hands making their impression on his lady's waist.

Silently, the door of the captain's quarters closed, and having garnered more information, the surgeon's daughter executed his latest order.

Hanover didn't have to wait long. "Show me what you have found, Liza." He drew her into his cabin and pulled her close.

She hung her head. Her cheeks were burning, but her hands felt cold.

"Come, now. You are not stealing. It is a simple exchange, one jewel for another." He coaxed, "Now let me have it." Placing his hands on either side of her jaw, he raised her head and bent to kiss her. As he did so, she opened her mouth, and he reaped her harvest. One at a time with his kisses, three rich rings made their way between his teeth. He spit each of them out to jostle in his hand, smiling his approval. "You have done well, Liza. What else?"

She loosened her hair net. As her hair cascaded, her father sifted it with his fingers, enjoying its luxurance and gathering a handful of golden circlets, just the size of a lady's wrist— extracted from Hook's own coffer. "Ah! And so."

Under his interested regard, Liza led his hand to her pocket. When he withdrew it, his fingers were full of sparkling treasure. Bracelets, necklaces and a golden watch fob, all plundered from Captain Hook. Hanover's eyes glowed as she emptied the other pocket and heaped another share into his grasp.

"Yes! Yes, this is just as I had hoped. I will have it all— Hook's fortune, Hook's queen," Hanover gazed into his daughter's eyes. "Even Hook's paramour. Liza. You are proving most satisfactory. I thank you."

Her smile looked unsure.

"Do not be anxious about anything, my darling. Your father will arrange it all. A few more days of plundering Hook's treasure chest, and we will have enough to get clear of this ship and everything we have suffered here. You may keep his key. Use it at every opportunity. Soon I will have another task for you. No, no, don't be concerned. A simple undertaking. Now open my sea chest. I have fashioned a false bottom that should hide our secrets long enough for our escape."

Liza nodded, then moved to the chest at the foot of their bed. Hanover had piled its contents beside it, Hook's boots among the other items. They stood stiff and still, but empty, like a phantom sentry. When Liza opened the lid, she saw the clever hiding place her father had devised, padded with remnants of his gray suit. And in it, already, two pieces of treasure lay twinkling up at her from the velvet. Liza squeezed her eyes shut, and then she opened them to look to her father.

He wore his arrogant smile. "Yes, Liza. I, too, have gone gleaning. Like the spoils in his coffer, those are baubles he won't be needing anymore."

She rested her hands on the wooden rim of the chest. How many times, as she lay with her captain, had she done the same thing her father had done? But always, she had given them back. With the greatest difficulty, she restrained her hands from snatching the bounty her father had stolen from Hook— stolen right off his body. The two great rings, empty now of fingers. Tears filled her eyes, so that as he buried Hook's rings under his swag, the pile in the chest wavered and shone like the mirage of some cave of wonders.

"Come, Liza. You mustn't take on so." Her father knelt on the floor beside her. "Look, this one is a pretty piece. Let me put it on you. You may wear it for an hour."

She tried to blink away her tears.

"I will like to see you in it. And after all…I promised not to neglect you." His hands, so warm and competent, served his daughter. Then his regard, equally warm, attended her. "Yes, Liza. You look quite lovely."

At first the chain lay cold against her neck.

"You look breathtaking, in fact."

Before the end of the hour, the chain was burning.

Guillaume carried the lantern and followed Tom deep into *L'Ormonde*'s stern. The two men made their way to the most lethal location in the ship. The powder magazine, paneled in copper, where measured bags of gunpowder lay in wait for the next battle. Tom laid a hand on the door knob and turned to his companion, who, realizing his destination, backed off with the lantern.

Tom cocked his head toward the door. "In here, mate. I gambled it'd be quiet today. Would have been a nasty shock if we'd had cause to fire off the cannon."

"*Monsieur* Tootles— are you mad?" Seeing the undaunted look on Tom's face, Guillaume drew away to slip toward the window between the magazine and the aft compartments. "I will light you." Hanging the lantern on a peg, he directed its rays through the glass into the magazine. Tom stood inside now. Flashing a smile at Guillaume first, he squinted into the shelves full of deadly contents. Guillaume watched Tom's dagger gleam in the light as the sailor moved to reach a high shelf. He lifted a half empty bag and withdrew a brown bottle. Victorious, he held it up for Guillaume to see. The mate was not smiling.

As Tom secured the door and strode around the outside of the room, he grinned. "Nothing to it, Mr. Guillaume. I learned a thing or two growing up with a bunch of greedy boys. If you want to hide something, only two places will do. In plain sight, or in the most threatening location you can find."

Guillaume was pale, but recovering. "*Monsieur* Tootles— Mr. Tootles. You speak as if you had lived in an interesting story."

Tom shrugged. "I was just a boy. But I learned a lot."

"Perhaps you are right. Perhaps you have a good deal to teach me. Now, where is this perfect place you found to hide us? Inside a cannon, maybe?" Guillaume unbent enough to smile.

"Have you brought your keys?"

"Of course. But the brig is hardly a festive location. I hope always to avoid its hospitality."

"Very wise. But I don't intend to take up residence in the brig. Not until it becomes absolutely necessary."

"You are very strange, Mr. Tootles. Why should it become necessary?"

"It shouldn't. Unless you push me too far."

"As the *commandant* has indicated, you are full of riddles. Show me this mysterious place."

"Aye, aye. This way." Tom snatched up the lantern and led Guillaume to starboard, where the shadows lurking near a dark door leapt away from the light. "Here we are. I'll bet there's a comfortable little space in there, nice and quiet, with no witnesses to the destiny of this cognac."

Guillaume's brow furrowed. "This room? But this is nothing. Let us go to my quarters."

"And have Renaud spoil our fun? No, Sir!"

"*Monsieur* Renaud is attending the *commandant* tonight. Your brother is dining with them."

"All the more reason to avoid your cabin. The captain wants to get Nibs alone." Tom's eyes bored into his companion's. "Doesn't he?"

"Still, this is not a fit place—"

"Fit for what? We have a good bottle to enjoy. And good reason to keep it quiet."

Reluctant still, Guillaume frowned. "This compartment is strictly off limits."

"And so is this cognac."

"If the *commandant* were to discover I had allowed you to see…"

Tom's pulse quickened. He tried to keep the eagerness from escaping. "What's to see? It's just storage, isn't it? Or, maybe…quarters for prisoners?"

"Yes. But the cargo within is most precious. I am not certain what it is. The *commandant* discusses it only with Renaud."

"A mystery, then."

"All I know is it has taken months for the *commandant* to secure it."

"I'll just bet it has."

"The crewmen, too, know nothing of this cargo. It is very important they remain in ignorance." Guillaume shuddered. "I believe the contents of that room are as volatile as those of the magazine."

"So LeCorbeau's hiding something too. Not in plain sight, but in a scary place. He's a wily man."

"Wily, yes. And unpleasant when crossed. I do not wish to risk his displeasure."

"Mr. Guillaume, believe me. I won't tell a soul. And aren't you just the least bit curious?"

"Other men are curious. I am cautious."

"Then we'll balance each other out. Hand over the keys." Tom offered Guillaume the bottle. Guillaume stared at it, looked at Tom, and then accepted it. Tom helped himself to the key ring that dangled from the man's waist.

"*Monsieur*, I—"

Tom had already turned his back on the mate, and he inserted the key in the lock. "Keep quiet, Guillaume."

Guillaume pulled back, but at that moment his mind didn't dwell on enforcing discipline. He found Tom's off-hand insolence to be provocative. It made the officer's blood rise and his scalp prickle. And somewhere beyond his caution, Guillaume realized the two of them were conspirators, entering into an adventure. "*Monsieur* Tom—"

The lock clicked open. Without bothering to look at him, Tom tossed the keys to Guillaume. He gripped the door's handle and raised up his lantern. Before his heart jumped into his throat, he inhaled a deep breath. The door squawked as if angry to be disturbed, opening only with reluctance. It was a bad sign, Tom thought. No one had entered this room in quite some time.

A sweet, sickly smell leaked into Tom's nostrils, setting off his imagination. Horrified by what that odor might indicate, he hesitated, but, as in any crisis, his boldness took over. He plunged into the room. The light of the lantern swung into it, and the shadows fled once more to reveal a small space nearly filled with three wooden crates— and nothing else. Not a window. No bunk tossed with rumpled blankets. No refuse from a meager meal. No chains restraining a withered arm.

No Captain Hook.

Caught up in his thoughts, Tom forgot his companion. Disappointment choked him, and he stood staring. His stomach clenched with the cloying fragrance, and he remembered his lady mother's warning. She had been right. This was a fool's errand. He and Nibs had marched blithely into the fire, and in an instant Tom was certain they wouldn't retreat without scorch marks.

Guillaume followed Tom in and stood looking about. "Well, it is not much of a place, but we will have plenty of privacy here. What is that smell?"

Recalled to the present, Tom lowered the lantern to examine the nearest crate. Black paint marks snaked across it in some kind of oriental script. It looked like the notes in one of Hook's sheets of harpsichord music. Tom blinked, but couldn't bring himself to comment.

"Mr. Tom?" Guillaume moved closer. He studied the writing, and he studied Tom's face. "These are the crates we picked up when we met the ship from Alexandria."

Tom hung the lantern and ripped off his jacket. "Give me a hand." Tugging at the lid, he wrenched at it. The splinters dug under his fingernails until Guillaume set down the bottle and hastened to lay his hands on Tom's arm.

"No! You will do more damage to yourself than to that crate."

"I told you to help me."

Guillaume gaped at Tom, who still tore at the wood, then he slipped away. Intent on his task, Tom didn't realize Guillaume was gone until the man returned with a handspike. Silently he presented it to Tom, and together the two men pried the lid loose. It raised up with a ferocious groan. The sweet smell intensified. Tom dropped the spike, and Guillaume caught it before it could batter the floor. Snatching the lantern, Tom lifted the wood high enough to peer in. He shook his head, dropping the lid. It crashed, and he jerked his jaw to indicate the next crate. Guillaume obeyed him, and, in succession, the remaining crates were wrenched open, inspected, and abandoned.

Guillaume clutched the spike, resting against the last crate. "You look disappointed, *Monsieur*. Tell me this story."

Tom tossed his head. "There's nothing to tell."

The mate raised a lid and, reaching in, extracted a white piece of the contents from its nest between sheets of papyrus. He fingered its fragile texture. "Earlier today you said you were concerned with a matter of life and death."

"You should know by now. I don't mean half of what I say."

Guillaume moved forward a step, determined to manage this unpredictable sailor, and sensing he must do so carefully. "Mr. Tom. These boxes hold only the remains of flowers packed in Egyptian paper. What did you think to find here?"

Tom straightened up. "Something a bit more worthy of a fine old bottle of cognac." He seized it and pulled the cork. His voice was bitter. "Let's get to it. I'm ready."

A light kindled in the mate's eye. He tossed the petal. "Certainly. And how shall we decide who begins the teaching first?"

"I've had enough lessons tonight. Let's just drink."

Guillaume vaulted onto a crate and settled himself. His tight-fitting jacket relaxed as he unbuttoned it. "Yes. We must be rid of the evidence against us." Guillaume reached for the bottle. *"Salut!"* Catching up with Tom's intake, he took the first of many sips. "But this bottle is already half gone!"

"Don't get worked up." Tom yanked a flask from his back pocket. "I poured some out for safe-keeping, in case it was found." He gulped some down.

"Truly, you are an ingenious man." This facile sailor fascinated Guillaume. First ebullient, then absorbed. Now, within the close confines of the private compartment, he watched Tom lean against the crate and slide down to settle on the floor by the lantern, just plain moody. Like the captain. That was no problem for Guillaume. He had learned very well how to handle his captain, and good cognac never failed to assist in the effort. Guillaume leaned over the edge of his crate. Smiling, he touched the bottle to Tom's flask.

"Let us drink to the captain's health, *mon ami*."

"Aye." Tom yanked the bottle from his companion and brought it to his lips. "Here's health— to a dead man." He drank.

"Ah, I see you are riddling again." Guillaume studied Tom's face to find it suddenly resembling his brother's, dark and brooding. The scar on Tom's temple puckered as he scowled. With his heart in his boots, Guillaume dared to finger it. "Will you at least finish this story for me?"

Tom brushed Guillaume's hand away. "When I know the ending, I'll tell it to you, mate." His fingers fell to stroking his knife.

Attempting to dispel his companion's gloom, Guillaume joked as they shared the cognac. The warm, lingering taste of aged oak on the tongue was delightful. "Tom Tootles, when you begin to make sense to me, you may use that knife."

"Don't think I won't, Guillaume."

Guillaume disregarded the warning. He shed his jacket and oiled his way to the floor. The scent of the flowers remained strong, mixing with the quality of the drink. But Guillaume felt himself overpowered by something else. Something stronger.

"No, Mr. Tom. Now I know your secret."

Tom smirked. "My secret?" He drank again, deeply. Guillaume waited for his companion to satisfy his thirst.

"You told me yourself." Judging his time, Guillaume scooted closer. "You don't mean half of what you say."

"Don't let the stink of those flowers befuddle you, mate. I'm not like you."

Again, Guillaume ignored Tom's implication. "All men like the same thing, Mr. Tom."

"Do you like a knife in your gut?"

Guillaume laughed. "Come, Mr. Tom. It is your brother who is known as 'Nibs the Knife.' But where did you get such an appellation as 'Tootles?' "

"From a pushy boy who didn't know when to stop. You remind me of him."

Guillaume's eyebrows rose with interest. He offered the bottle to Tom. "A boy?"

"I wrestled his dagger away and I haven't seen him since. He's lucky."

Leaning one hand on the dusty floor, Guillaume pressed closer. "My captain tells me wrestling is a fine, ancient sport." Lured by this robust young man to a secret assignation near the most lethal location in the ship, Guillaume's new sense of adventure was stimulated beyond his control. He couldn't resist. His other hand came to rest on the inside of Tom's thigh. "I am not skilled in the art of wrestling. You won't find it necessary to employ it with me."

Setting down the bottle, Tom turned to his companion and aimed the full force of his drunken attention at him. "You're right. I won't." Quickly, Tom closed the gap between their bodies.

Thrilled by the sailor's aggression, Guillaume didn't see the flash of Tom's knife— until it was too late.

A Communion of Men

Tom had learned Mr. Starkey's lessons. He knew when to let go, and he knew when to hold on. Leaning into Guillaume, he smiled without humor, gripping the hilt of his knife with a firm hand. The man's mouth moved in agony, but he had the sense to keep quiet.

"Good boy, Guillaume." Tom released the knife, and Guillaume rolled his eyes downward to see it.

"Monsieur—" He gasped. The knife pinned his hand, neatly, to the deck.

"Don't try to talk. I'll keep it simple."

"Please!"

"Stow that. Now, I can leave you here and fetch the *commandant* if you like. He'd help you out, I'm sure. He'd be glad to have that bottle back, too."

Jerking, Guillaume shook his head.

"No? I suppose you're right. He won't want his dinner with Nibs interrupted, even for his cognac."

Guillaume panted, pleading with his eyes.

"I suppose you want me to fix you up, then?"

"Oui!"

"You can show me how grateful you are later. Just listen." Guillaume swallowed, and Tom grew more cheerful. "That's better. Now, for starters, have you got a kerchief somewhere?"

Guillaume whispered, "In my pocket."

"Any other day, I bet you'd like me to fish for it. But maybe you'll just say which one."

"The left, the left!"

Tom dug in Guillaume's pocket and produced a handkerchief. "Fine quality, this."

"Oui, Monsieur." Guillaume's voice was tight, strained with pain.

"A gift from your captain?"

"In a manner of speaking, *Monsieur.*"

"I like the respect you pay me, Guillaume. You'll keep that up."

"Oui, Monsieur."

Tom bent toward his officer and, with capable hands, proceeded to untie the man's cravat. Unwinding it from Guillaume's neck, Tom said, "Nice and easy, now. Bet that knife hurts a lot."

Guillaume barely nodded. He closed his eyes as Tom opened his collar. His neck flushed where Tom's fingers brushed it.

"Now, I'm going to pull the knife away, and then we'll bind that hand. Ready?" Tom didn't wait for an answer. He closed his fingers around the familiar hilt of his dagger and yanked it from the floor in which it was embedded. Guillaume gritted his teeth as the blade withdrew from his flesh. A red well gushed from the slit between the bones leading to his little finger and his ring finger.

Tom seized Guillaume's hand and held it up, pressing the handkerchief to both sides of the wound. "Keep it high, Guillaume, less blood that way. Hold this, and I'll wrap it." He bound the long cravat tightly around the kerchief, knotted it off, and set it on Guillaume's shoulder. "Now pinch your wrist. That's it. Cut off the flow." He nodded as Guillaume obeyed. "Just keep it there, and we'll have a nice chat." He snatched up the bottle. "Drink, mate?"

"Yes. Please."

Tom held the cognac for Guillaume, who gulped several long drinks. Then, looking pale, the French sailor slumped back against the crate, still clutching his wrist and holding it against his shoulder. Tom swilled a drink of his own. He corked the empty bottle and set it aside.

"There now. I had hoped it wouldn't come to this, but I did warn you."

"A simple 'no' would have been sufficient."

"Ah, there's where you're wrong, mate. Now I've got your attention— and you know how strongly I feel about you."

Perversely, Guillaume's doubtful face flirted with hope. *"Monsieur?"*

"You want to be my girl, don't you?"

The mate's mouth opened, but he remained silent. Tom saw his pulse beating, vulnerable, where the cravat used to hide it.

"To tell you the truth, the last girl I found disappointed me. But you won't disappoint me. Will you, Guillaume?"

"No, *Monsieur* Tom. I surely won't."

"I like what you called me before. 'Mr. Tom.' Has a nice English ring to it."

"Very well…Mr. Tom."

"Now I have a couple of jobs need doing. Not too difficult, and you're in just the right position to do them."

"Do these jobs involve more deceiving of my captain?"

"Pretty much the opposite. First, I want you to show the captain your cut. Tell him you don't want the sail maker sewing you up. You want that nice Doctor Hanover, with the gentle hands."

"But why—"

"Do you want the sail maker to stitch you?"

"No, but—"

"I want only the best for you, mate. I care, you know."

With a faint smile, Guillaume said, "I do not entirely believe you, but…it will be as you say."

"Good boy. Next, I want you to keep watch on my brother. Anytime LeCorbeau starts getting close to him, you jump in the middle. Understand?"

"*Oui*, Mr. Tom."

"You'll find a way to make yourself interesting. I learned a few tricks from some Indian women. I'll tell you about them. That should keep you two occupied for a few nights, anyway."

"I hope these tricks do not involve the hands."

"Don't worry. I didn't damage anything important."

As Guillaume was seized with a trembling fit, Tom slung his arm around him and patted his thigh. "You'll have to trust me, Guillaume. Same as I'm trusting you."

Guillaume breathed hard, and the convulsions abated. Tom released him.

"It's not so bad a deal for you. Once you've followed my orders, you can become the hero and find that missing bottle of cognac. LeCorbeau will love you for that."

"The bottle? But Mr. Tom, we have just imbibed it. Have we not?"

"I told you, Guillaume. I'm not like you. I'd never steal from my captain."

"But…" Maintaining his grip on his wrist, Guillaume gestured toward the flask.

"That? Oh, that's just grog." Tom tucked it back into his pocket.

"And where is the rest of the cognac?"

"Right where it ought to be. Don't you recognize this?" Tom held up the empty bottle.

Dazed, Guillaume shook his head.

"This is the stuff we didn't finish that first night I came aboard. After you nodded off, I thought it a shame to pitch it in the sea. Saved it for you. Glad I did, too."

"Then, the cognac for which the *commandant* is searching…?"

"Is still hidden away. Just in case you decide not to carry through with my requests. It might be tucked behind your pillow even now."

"Mr. Tom, I understand what you want— I think. I will perform these tasks for you, but why were you so insistent on getting into these crates?"

"I'll tell you why, mate." Tom leaned forward. "I was looking for a man."

"A man? Packed up and locked away?"

"Guess I've found him, haven't I?" Grinning, Tom reached to Guillaume's waist and, once again, took possession of his key ring. Removing the key to the compartment, he shoved it into his own pocket. Then he tucked the rest of the bunch into Guillaume's uniform. "Now that I've stumbled on this place, it'll make a good spot for keeping our secrets. Won't it?" Tom scooped up the cognac, lifted the top of the crate, and pitched the bottle in. It landed with a crackle of papyrus.

"Mr. Tom, I will ask for the surgeon. I will distract the *commandant*. And I will meet you here again whenever you say. But— I hope this will be soon."

"No promises. Now, keep that hand elevated. I'll lock up and see you to the crew deck." Tom heaved himself up. As Guillaume's eyes followed him, he located the handspike and pounded the lid of each crate into place. Brushing off his hands, he turned to Guillaume and, like a gentleman, offered to assist the mate to rise. He dusted Guillaume's uniform and helped him into his jacket, buttoning it up and neatening the collar.

"Be sure you tell the captain you stuck yourself with your own knife. Here." Tom picked up the knife and wiped it on Guillaume's wrappings. Then he pulled Guillaume's dagger from his belt and smeared it before returning it. Moving to the back of the crate against which they had leaned, Tom shoved. It grated along the floor to cover the small pool of blood. Holding up the flower petal, he said, "Next time you see this, you meet me here." He stowed it in his pocket, then tucked the handspike in his boot.

"All this, Mr. Tom, to keep your brother from the captain's favor?"

"Funny thing. My brother doesn't fancy him."

"I did not incline that way at the first, either. But I was hungry. I learned."

"Nibs is more likely to kill him. I don't want to see my brother hang."

"But if you showed the *commandant* the cleverness I have seen, he'd find you most interesting. Why do you not distract him yourself?"

"I'm just a sailor, Guillaume. As you say, my insolence would get me into trouble. And as fascinating as more scars might make me, I'm content with just the one." Tom cocked his head. "Besides, Guillaume. I don't like LeCorbeau nearly as much as I like you."

Guillaume gave a timid smile. His slender cheeks pinked, then blanched as Tom squeezed his bandaged hand.

"Now give us a kiss, love, and show me that you mean what you promise."

Between the pain and the ecstasy, *Monsieur* Guillaume nearly swooned.

Tom had learned when to hold firm. The cognac helped. He rolled his eyes and thanked his lucky stars that Mr. Starkey wasn't watching.

Cecco had watched Jill, and— not without pleasure— she studied him in turn. Jill convinced herself that Cecco wasn't concerned about Mr. Smee. Not now, when the rulers of the *Roger* enjoyed more intimacy than ever. Without doubt, Cecco sensed the sincerity of her commitment to him. Surely when he took her to task about Mr. Smee a dozen days ago, he had been continuing the show for Liza, to report back to her father.

Still, Jill was cautious. When Smee had appeared at last that afternoon, trailed by Yulunga, Jill hid herself away in her quarters. But now, as she scanned the pages she'd covered with writing in the aftermath of Cecco's questioning, she realized how very absorbed she was with the Irishman after all. And through him, in every drop of ink, seeped her feelings for Hook. Only three people could truly cherish this story. This work must be handled discretely. When Liza rapped at her door, Jill gathered the pages and slid them under her blotter.

"Come, Liza." Smoothing her features with her fingers, Jill rose to accept the cup of tea. "Thank you."

Liza set the tray on the window seat and remained standing, her eyes inquiring as she indicated her mouth with her hand.

"No, I can't eat this morning. I've no appetite at all. Even this tea tastes different to me today. But I want you to loosen my laces." Jill turned her back and shook her hair from it, smiling. "The captain doesn't know his own strength. It feels as if he's pulled them a bit tight these last few mornings." When she was comfortable, she breathed more easily. "Just make the bed, then, Liza. Nothing else."

Again Liza lingered, and this time she drew her open hand across her throat. Her pretty pearls shone, and Jill brightened. "Yes. I believe I'd like to wear my opals today. It's been some time." Some time… since Smee's big hands had strung them in front of her eyes, on orders from their captain. The first morning ever. Absently, Jill drank her tea. Her emerald gown glimmered around her.

Liza moved to the wardrobe, her skirts rustling. Hearing them, her mistress looked up. "Liza, let me have a good look at your new dress. It's quite becoming."

Liza didn't stop her progress. Only after pulling out the opal necklace and securing the jewel drawer did she turn to display her gown. Jill concluded that the girl must still be accustoming herself to it, for as Liza's back was turned, she had adjusted the neckline. It swooped in a graceful curve above a tapering triangle of cream-colored fabric that pointed toward her narrow waist. The skirt was wide, necessitating petticoats, which, Jill clearly observed, Liza also wore. A deep maroon, the gown set off her brown hair perfectly. Like Liza herself, the dress was tasteful, but unobtrusive. Under Jill's direction, she spun once to show it off, then subsided.

"Yes, it's quite nice. But I see it laces in back. Now you face the same problem I have. I hope that, like my captain, your father is not too proud to help you dress."

Liza's breathing grew rapid. The pride she displayed a moment ago vanished, and she clutched her abdomen. The opals dangling through her fingers swung against the maroon, glinting ostentatiously in contrast.

Something about Hook's jewels in the girl's hands made Jill feel nauseated. She reconsidered her decision. The day Cecco interrogated her, Jill had laid away the boy David's silver shamrock. She knew that, today, she mustn't remove even one of Cecco's adornments to make room for Hook's.

"Never mind the opals, Liza. Please, put them back." Turning away, Jill heard Liza's skirts swish and the working of the drawer. She busied her hands with her teacup. Settling to rest on the window seat, she stared out at the sea, not really relishing the drink today, but feeling its warmth within the hollow of her stomach. Usually, that warmth sustained her.

"Is the captain preparing to board *L'Ormonde*, Liza?"

Liza nodded.

"Your father, too?"

As Liza indicated the affirmative, Jill remembered her duty. She filled her eyes with eagerness.

"Tell me. How is he?"

Liza smiled. Not the pretense of a smile she so often used for her mistress, but a genuine smile of pleasure. Jill read its meaning as best she might.

"Then all is well, and we may look forward to a change. Remember that first day, Liza, when I told you? Change can be welcome."

The girl watched, but Jill's face showed nothing of the irony under which she must be suffering. Nor— yet— did Jill display the effects of the potion she was imbibing. She would do so, in time. To make sure of it, Liza picked up the pot and refilled the lady's teacup.

"Thank you, Liza. But how did you finally persuade your father to allow you to accept the gown? I understand it is a gift from Mr. Yulunga. A gift he offered many times."

Liza replaced the teapot on its tray. Then, looking concerned, she raised her hand to wave once, and her face cleared.

"A parting gift! Yes, that would make our dear doctor happy. You made him feel he has won an extra point against his captors. You're a clever young woman, Liza."

Liza's next gesture caught her mistress by surprise. She tapped her chest to indicate herself, raised her finger to her eye, and then, with a steadfast gaze, pointed at Jill.

The lady stared at her, her smile slowly deepening. "Watching me…and following my example?" She returned Liza's gaze, and her manner was satisfied. "It seems between the two of us, we will manage your father very well." Jill rose to stand. The lack of nourishment must be taking its toll, she thought; a spell of lightheadedness caused her to falter and catch herself. The weakness passed. She was pleased that Liza didn't appear to have marked it.

"Go now, Liza. Don't fuss with the bed. As it happens, on this particular morning I choose *not* to be watched."

Liza curtsied and bustled away, feeling the pleasant tickling of Jill's ruby necklace where it hid between her breasts. Captain Cecco had exhibited some interesting objections to Mr. Smee. With the assistance of the lady's teacup, Liza was about to put the captain to the test.

Jill's solitude was short-lived, and as matters unfurled, she was grateful for the fact. The master's door opened and closed, and she looked up, expecting to see Cecco. Only the captain would enter unannounced. But instead, Jill saw another face, a beloved face, unkempt, full of concern, but most welcome. She sat staring at him, and then she smiled. Standing, she shoved the hook from her lap to roll gleaming to the cushioned seat. Like a girl, she picked up her emerald skirts and ran into his arms, her bare feet skimming the carpets.

He set down his burden and without question, bent to welcome her into his embrace. Flinging her arms around him, she pressed her cheek to his rough beard. She hadn't imagined him. Smee was real.

"You're here," she sighed.

"Where I belong." He saw no reason to let her go. On the contrary, he held her tighter. "I came soon as ever I could."

Only now did Jill become cautious. She pulled back an inch, holding Smee's strong red arms. But she didn't allow him to drop his hands from her waist. In the back of her mind, she acknowledged she had been longing for just this feeling, this touching. More than that. She had craved it. But she didn't stop to wonder why; time was of the essence. "Is Captain Cecco away then?"

"Aye, and all the lads are busy with the Frenchmen. No one saw me come in. I judge we have a wee bit of time to talk."

"What of Mr. Yulunga?"

"Seems the lass is giving him her gratitude for the dress. She's got him up on the quarterdeck. But Lady, what's the matter? Why were you sending for me? Is it—" Smee glanced across the room to the cushions where she'd been sitting. Shock struck his face. "Where did you find that?"

Jill turned and followed his gaze to the hook. "Oh! Smee, thank goodness you've seen it. I'm not allowed to mention it."

Suspicion darkened Smee's features. "Not allowed? So it's Cecco's doing?"

"The captain's? No. But he won't permit me to discuss it with anyone. Please, you must take it. I'm afraid if he sees it again he'll throw it into the sea."

Smee disentangled himself from her arms and with a resolute

hand, set her aside. Striding to the windows, he studied the hook. "Aye, it's true right enough. I hardly dared to believe it." He picked it up, reverently, as if it were the very bones of his captain. "And this is why you were sending for me, then?"

"But— I thought you had news for me."

Smee turned to hold out a fist. Unclenching it, he displayed a pile of glowing red stones. "Here they are. Your signal."

Jill's hand flew to her throat, where she had so often worn those rubies, just below her scar.

Smee said, "I was surprised to be finding them on my door handle. I've looked for you first thing every morning, thinking if you needed me you'd be wearing them."

Grateful to be alone with Smee, whatever the reason, Jill was tempted to ignore the pricking sense of danger. She didn't want to think about it. When she tried, the puzzle of the necklace made her mind spin. She shook her head to try to clear it, but suddenly the opportunity to speak with Smee alone seemed the sole matter of importance. Drawn to the comfort of Smee's presence, she declined to confess she'd never sent the rubies. Instead, she moved closer. "I'm only glad you came to me."

The intensity of her blue eyes made Smee's heart skip a beat, so he smiled, pressed the rubies into her hands, and turned away with the hook. "I'll be keeping this safe, Ma'am. You were right to entrust it to me." Smee retrieved his tool box and knelt to conceal the hook within it. "I thought I might be needing an excuse for coming, so I brought my tools. It's a good thing. I'd best not be seen with the captain's claw in tow." He replaced the box by the door.

Smee noted how lonely Jill looked, standing by herself where the hook had lain. It would be painful for her, Smee guessed how very painful, when, in the end, she understood exactly how Cecco came into possession of the hook. Once her lover's guilt was proven, the lady was sure to be overcome with regret.

But Smee would be there for her, just as he was here for her now. He reached out to her, taking the necklace from her hands and fastening it on. Aware of how near to him she insisted on standing, he inhaled her exotic scent again. After long absence, her proximity tended to make him dizzy— but he couldn't avoid those eyes. Not even if he wanted to.

She surprised him, seizing his arms as if she sensed how much she'd soon be needing him. Knowing the shock in store for her, wishing he could spare her the coming sorrow, he gazed with tenderness on her lovely face. Something was different about her this morning. Something that made Smee hold her tight, even after the necklace was secure. "Ma'am, if it's not wrong to be saying so, I'm missing the early days, when I had the charge of your mornings."

"So am I, Mr. Smee. And I've been thinking of you. I've a story set down, and no one to show it to. Would you—"

"It's what I've been wanting." Just as he had done with Hook, Smee gentled his voice. "Let me see it."

Slowly, Jill released him. She turned to her desk. Drawing the papers from under the blotter, she presented them to him. "It's not long, but it will be a relief to share it."

"Aye, Ma'am. I've been that worried about your being alone, and grieving." He adjusted his spectacles and glanced at her elegant script. Looking up again, he turned a shade redder. "Ma'am— I know this story."

"Yes, Mr. Smee. Read on, and tell me what you think. I'll have another cup of tea and keep an eye on *L'Ormonde*."

Ignoring the noises drifting in from two ships' decks, Smee addressed the pages. As he read, he began to pace. Jill poured her cup, spilling a little on the saucer, and moved within range of the portside windows. She stepped carefully, for although the wind was low, the ship beneath her feet seemed to pitch more than usual. Steadying herself against a bedpost, she felt its satiny texture beneath her fingers. Stopping there, she stroked the wood to feel its luxuriance. Then, settling against a pillow on the unmade bed, she sipped and stared.

The fine china lip of her teacup felt smooth and firm, seductive in the way it induced her to drink. She searched for a thought she'd been chasing a moment ago, but soon wearied of the effort and let it go. An unfamiliar taste hung on her tongue. Sweet, almost like a flower. She forgot it as she caught the brilliance of Nibs' orange kerchief and glimpsed Tom's unruly head beside it. For now, it seemed, her boys were safe. The French vessel dipped in the brine, her sailors exchanging yarns and bursts of laughter with the *Roger*'s seamen. Jill smiled to think that, however the captains crossed purposes, the men of the sister ships were now comrades. Pleasantly, persuasive sips of tea slid down her throat.

Every so often, Jill glanced at Smee, each time her gaze lingering a little longer. For too many days, she had been unable to really look at him. She indulged herself now. Immersed in the story, Smee ceased his pacing. Gradually, he stilled to seat himself beside Jill. His absorption in her work was gratifying, and she watched his strong, irregular features with affection. It occurred to her that, as many times as Smee had touched her, she had never really touched him. Restraining her fingers, she took another swallow of tea. It was warm. Jill felt her cheeks flush. She'd had no breakfast, and hunger began to gnaw within her— a yearning, within her belly, and below. The hankering assailed her, the desire to be enfolded in a man's arms. She set the cup down on the bed shelf and allowed herself a harmless liberty, going only so far as to rest a hand on Smee's knee. Yet that insignificant contact sent a raw, urgent thrill through her senses.

The rings on her fingers glittered hypnotically as she moved them on his knee. Her eyes beheld the jewels, unfocused. She knew what he must be feeling as he read. The immediate surroundings faded for Jill, blurring as she retreated with him, into her story. She didn't have to follow along on the page. In her mind, she read the words along with Smee, from memory.

It was the story of the first meeting. A communion of men. Two men, who chose to share a destiny. The words had flowed through Jill's fingers that difficult day, to pour onto the parchment....

The place smelled of sawdust, sweat and sea. Wedged into a torch-lit cobbled street just off the wharves, the port-town tavern was not so crowded that it couldn't yield one table to a solitary occupant. It was an inconspicuous table, scored, like all the rest, by knives and years. Its only virtue was a clear view of the door, the bar, and the stairs.

He sat there, a pack of playing cards for company, and his sharp blue eyes at work. Tall and dark, fine-featured, with an indigo kerchief round his head and the curls of his thick black hair just brushing his shoulders, he wore a pistol in his belt, good rings, and a loose white shirt with lace fine enough to boast of success, whatever his business might be.

His business today was watching. He watched as the sailor lads bobbed in, with their striped shirts and pigtails and their buckled shoes. But his gaze shifted as the more colorful tars swaggered in, unshaven, with glints of gold in their eyes. These were the men he observed carefully.

He noted the girls of the house. They approached him as often as propriety allowed, and he'd learned their names. But he'd show them a card trick and he'd send them away with a smile, and sometimes with a shilling. If they lingered longer, they found no more success, and soon became bored with the intricacies of the game he dealt to amuse himself while he watched. He watched every day for a week.

The day Nancy got his shilling, she got his attention, too. Nancy was a pretty girl, round and blonde beneath her cap, and more than one admired her charms that afternoon. But once her brawny, red-haired tar threw open the door, she had eyes only for him.

He was glad to see her. He stamped in along with a mob of jostling sailors, just shipped from warmer climes, and called for his Nancy before he called for his ale. His thick arms surrounded her and his head nearly touched the beams as he threw it back, ordering a pint. When he took her in his arms to cross the room and set her on the bar, he lifted her as easily as a feather pillow, pushing the crowd aside like the prow of a ship in smooth waters— and just as effortlessly. The dark stranger watched, and was aware he wasn't the only man who noticed. He dealt his cards.

The landlord smiled as he pulled the tap. This crew was a scruffy lot, but silver lined those vests, and it would find its way to the till. These men would drink and pay. They'd be quick with the girls, and then they'd drink and pay some more. Not like that Nate, the tatty freeloader in the corner. Or that solitary stranger who sat and watched all week, attracting too much of the girls' interest and drinking little enough. Not that he hadn't paid fair rent for the table. Seven silver pieces, and no questions asked.

The tavern grew darker and noisier with evening, and with songs and laughter and stumbling boots. Nancy brought her Irishman another drink, and she had to shout to be heard. "Smee! Pat says will you roll up a keg with him? You and your mates has gone and drunk this last one dry!"

"I'll help him, aye, but I'll be picking the next keg myself. That last was bitter, and never worth tapping." He vaulted over the bar to land on his feet and turn for the cellar, as nimbly as if he'd tasted none of that bitter keg at all. Nancy's smile followed him until from the corner, the lanky man in a worn-out coat snapped his fingers. She waded through the company to his side, collecting glasses as she went, her tray balanced over her shoulder.

"Well, then, what now, Nate?"

He pulled her down by the sleeve, and her tray dipped as he whispered in her ear. She smiled, but shook her head. She picked up his cup. "No, but I'll bring you another glass if Pat's not looking. Then it's off you go." She turned to leave him and his face turned sour.

"Too busy for me tonight?"

"Too busy for them as can't pay!"

The stranger's ringed hands paused over his cards. His blue eyes observed.

Nate got up, shoved his chair back, and swayed on his feet. As Nancy pushed her way to the counter, the look beneath his stringy hair bored against her back.

Smee had got to work behind the bar now, looking at home there, drawing drinks and cheerily serving the ale. The landlord, Pat, made no objection. He liked him. So did they all. Smee raised a glass and handed it out. "Here you go, lads. Drink up! First night in port I'll be pulling the pints if you'll all drink a toast to me old mum, who's doing the same for the boys on her god-forsaken island!"

Nancy's tray of cups clattered as she set it down. She laughed at him. "For shame, Smee! Your mother's working hard in Ireland, and you be sailing the world. You should get yourself home. Settle down, and help the dear old thing."

Smee's lips formed a line. "No, Nancy, nevermore. Though the climate on that island's damp and chill, I loved it there. But the law's done what mother nature couldn't. It's far too warm now for the eldest son to linger." He shook his head. "I'll be taking my comfort where I find it, and not go home any more."

"Poor sailor!" Nancy's eyes went soft, and she reached out to pull him into a kiss over the bar. Clearly, he liked the taste of it. He wouldn't wait any longer. He urged her toward the room upstairs, and she went eagerly, amid hoots from his mates, who'd heard his story before.

"Aye, Smee! No need to go home— your dear old mum is catching the girls for you here!"

Smee tossed his hand good-naturedly and took the first two steps in one stride. He turned to hold his arm out to his Nancy.

His arm froze.

The hand Nancy meant to reach to Smee was arrested. She stood strangely still. Her eyes had gone wide and her pink face drained of color. Nate stood behind her, one hand around her wrist, the other around his dagger. He pricked her ribs, and the air left her lungs. The sailors' heads jerked up, the hush rolled in like a fog as the tavern stilled.

"Nancy," Nate hissed into the silence. "I asked you first."

Nancy uttered a whimper, her eyes appealing to her Irishman. No one seemed to move but Smee. His eyes narrowed and his fingers formed into fists. One of those fists gripped a knife. "Steady, mate. Let Nancy go, and we'll be settling the trouble between us."

Nate's hungry frame leaned inward. "You get out, and I'll settle with Nancy myself."

"No need to be risking your life, man." Smee was more than ready. Nancy was in his way.

Nate brayed, an edge of hysteria in his laugh, like a man who had nothing to lose. With his body protected by Nancy's, he pointed his dagger at Smee now, inches from his belly. "Look who's risk—"

A pistol clicked below his ear. A silky, arrogant voice issued orders. "Unhand the lady, and allow *me* to deal with the Irishman."

The gun was cold as it dug under Nate's jaw. Cold as death. Nate's knife dropped to rattle on the floor, spinning until it was captured under a smooth black boot.

"Now you will leave this place. Rest assured that Nancy will be protected, and the offender removed."

Nate slunk backward, his gaze brushing over the stranger before aiming for the exit. The huddle parted to let him through. Quick hands opened the door.

As the door slammed shut behind Nate, the stranger lowered his pistol. Smee exhaled his tension, realizing only now how narrowly he'd escaped a skewering. Nate's crazy laugh still rang in the air. That madman hadn't wanted a fight. He'd wanted a killing. Maybe two. Smee descended the steps to see to his Nancy. He glanced at the man who'd come to her aid.

Smee's focus sharpened, and he stared. Never before had he seen this kind of man in this kind of place. Even when pretty Nancy tugged at his sleeve to draw him upstairs, Smee couldn't take his eyes off him.

Lithe, strong, and tall as Smee himself, the bearing of an aristocrat, and startlingly blue eyes. He had the air of a buyer who'd found what he'd been looking for— the account was settled, the goods would be wrapped and sent on.

Smee's rugged face creased. Absently, he tucked his knife away and applied his arm to Nancy's waist. He nodded to the man. "Thank you, Sir."

"Not at all. Now I am afraid Nancy will have to excuse us. We'll use the back door. I would rather avoid your rival, and we have business to discuss."

Smee let Nancy go. Her mouth hung open as, without a glance, her Irishman abandoned her. Smee stepped toward the stranger, his eyes never leaving the chiseled face. This was quite the handsomest man Smee had ever laid eyes on.

Pat, feeling that the stranger had caused enough trade to lag, clapped his hands and whistled, and all the girls collected themselves to get on with the serving of drinks. Nancy shuffled away, reluctant, eyeing Smee over her shoulder and tucking the stranger's shilling into her bodice. Smee's companions resisted the urge to clap the dark man's back in congratulation, as they would have done for anyone else, resettling themselves to gossip around the bar instead. The murmurs of the crowd swelled again, so that Smee's self-consciousness left him.

"What kind of business would a gentleman like yourself be having with the likes of me?"

"You are a sailor, are you not?"

"Aye. I am that."

"Then, naturally, we will speak of sailing." Without another word, he tucked his gun in his belt, left his cards on the table, and strode out the rear door of the establishment.

Smee watched him disappear, then he looked down at the knife lying in the sawdust on the floor. He picked it up, and he followed the gentleman.

It never occurred to him not to.

The two oddly-matched men sat on cushioned chairs in a quiet, hospitable inn, finishing their supper. It was a reputable place, such as Smee couldn't afford to frequent. China lined the sideboard, paintings graced the walls, and the dark wood of the paneling was barely illuminated by firelight and the many candles that left smoky signatures on the ceiling.

It would be a cozy room when well-heeled travelers filled it with cloaks and crumpled skirts. Tonight the room was devoid of company, yet Smee found it full of intrigue. The dark stranger had a word with the landlord, then treated Smee to a meal as he outlined his proposition. The sailor was fascinated by his two jeweled hands that wielded a pistol as elegantly as they now handled knife and fork. The wine was good and the meat superior, the slender, well-dressed young woman who served it respectful even as she seasoned it with her smiles. Smee had helped her carve the roast. Now she stood by the steps, candle in hand, and waited as the gentleman concluded.

"You'll get your hands dirty. But your pockets will be rich, and your existence never dull."

Smee was mesmerized by his refined speech, the voice smooth as honey. He hesitated to use his own rough pipes. He cleared his throat. "My hands have been dirty before. But why me, if you don't mind my asking?"

"Is there a better man?"

Smee paused, then slowly shook his head. "No, Sir. There isn't." His gaze wandered the room as he considered, then returned to the gentleman. "But the ship, Sir?"

"Is waiting for me to take her." His eyes held sparks.

More familiar with his face now, Smee studied him still. "Do you know— I believe you'll do it."

"I'll do it. But not alone."

It was the first time Smee heard that word from this man's lips. This great man *was* alone. Conor Smee, common as he might be, was needed.

He decided. "And what would you be having me call you, Sir? You must have a name."

The man drained his cup and rose with the grace of a seabird. Hastily, Smee got up, scraping his chair on the flagstones.

"I am known as James. Within the week, you will call me… Captain." He signaled to the young woman. She came forward, the candle's flame leaning backward and black smoke trailing.

The flame righted itself as she dropped a curtsy. "Shall I light your way up, Sir?"

"Yes." He still watched Smee. "The landlord will lend you a place by the fire. Our first task is to buy your freedom. Rise early, and we will begin." He pulled a gold coin from his pocket and clapped it on the table. The woman turned and, holding up the candle, rustled toward the stairs. Smee waited, then moved to the bottom of the steps to watch from below as her petticoats ascended and Mr. James' fine boots followed. He was left by himself to the comforts of the common room.

That was all right with Smee. He knew his place.

It wasn't in Ireland. Wherever it took him, his place was just to the right of that great man.

An hour later, as Smee lay wrapped in a blanket and wakeful by the fire, he listened to the ashes resettling in the grate. He was satisfied. He had a job to do. Somehow he'd find a way to say goodbye to his Nancy. A new sound stole his notice. The murmur of petticoats slipping back down the stairs.

The young woman came to him. She set down the candle. Her petticoats rustled to the floor. She opened the blanket, Smee opened his arms, and she laid her slender body within them. Mr. James was generous, and Smee was grateful for her. Kindness deserved kindness in turn. Gently, he rolled above her and took her chin in his rough, sailor fingers. She raised her hands and drew him down, like a priestess summoning the moon.

When he kissed her, her mouth was full of another man's kisses. The thought made this strong man suddenly weak. But he didn't stop. When he nuzzled her neck, he scented beyond the fragrance of her skin a darker, richer aroma. Smee inhaled it.

When he filled her, she was already full of another man's passion. Smee made that passion his own. And when he loved her, his heart filled to bursting with love.

So complete did he feel that night, Smee found no need to stir up the flames within the grating. He was grateful to the stranger, who had found it useful to save his Nancy. And after that moment, Smee never once thought of his Nancy again.

It wasn't just a story. Smee remembered it all. As if still linked to that woman at the inn, he felt Jill now, slender, refined, pressing urgently against him. He looked into her eyes, so like the captain's. Tears pooled in them. He'd never seen tears in the captain's eyes, not even as—

Smee dropped the papers, letting them sail away, each to a separate place on the carpet. He tore off his spectacles to toss them next to her teacup, and he searched her face. He'd been entrusted with her care. When he spurned her that first time, she fell square into the gypsy's arms. Now, once more, she was pleading for deliverance. Counting on Smee to wrench her away. Counting on his devotion.

He'd sworn not to fail her again.

Jill tilted up her head, inviting, and with his thumb he touched her lips. Why hadn't he seen it before? Like the tavern lass, no matter how many embraces she'd accepted from another, her mouth was full of those kisses. Hook's kisses.

Smee placed his hands on her face, and made those kisses his own.

What happened next was exactly what he'd feared would happen. He held her in his arms, he pressed against the softness in the green-as-Ireland gown, and he kissed her, and he kissed her, and he was unable to stop. Lovingly, as she wrapped her arms around him, he bore her down against the pillows. Her golden hair was silk between his fingers, her body in his arms felt feverish. And she welcomed him. More, she strained against him, as if wishing to mingle her very flesh with his own. Smee knew what should happen next.

He mustn't deny her. And he shared her desire. He whispered it against her lips.

"You're mine now. By god, I'll make you mine."

With her pen, she'd written it in his story, and now she said it for him to hear. Nothing else she might say could encourage him more.

"Conor."

"Jill. You know us. Better than we know ourselves."

She raised her hands to draw him down, like a priestess summoning the moon. Implicitly, Smee trusted her. She had done— always would do— right by James. And the story, after all, had begun in her hands.

The captain's hand, the iron one, rested in Smee's toolbox. But whose hand had delivered it? Allowing Jill to fill his mind, to lead him to her heaven, Smee thrust the question away. She was just like Hook; she knew better than Smee what twisting paths would take her where she had to go. Her breathing was erratic, and his own hand worked behind her, to free her of her stays.

But as their motions agitated the bed frame, the teacup rattled on its saucer above them. Smee looked up. He focused on the cup, and his forehead furrowed— and then his dream fell shattering into shards that lodged in the wound of his heart. He felt Jill's body beneath him, uncharacteristically careless, flouting the discretion she employed so well, struggling instead like a wild thing to engulf him, and suddenly, the most intoxicating taste ever to bless his tongue bittered, and Conor Smee, that strong man, was afraid.

The storyteller was not the power devising this ending. She was not leading him where she chose to go. Someone else had chosen for her.

The captain's words echoed in Smee's head. *Is there a better man?*

No. There wasn't. Smee shook his head.

Not a better man. But another. A gypsy. And surely, even Cecco wouldn't sink so low.

Captain Cecco had to be told. His Jill had been dosed…with the lotus.

Nibs and Tom had a fine time catching up with their mates from the *Roger*. They called across the narrow channel between the ships, and sometime during the jocularity, a letter winged its way over the brine, weighted with a flask, to be caught by Mr. Starkey. It was addressed to Jill, in care of the captain. Starkey rolled his eyes and tucked the letter in his pocket, then he flung the flask back, empty now. Grinning, Tom saluted him. Nibs nodded at Starkey, the crease between his eyebrows deepening as he searched for another face. Then both brothers ignored the couple on the quarterdeck.

As the sailors conducted their banter, Mr. Yulunga enjoyed his dalliance with the girl. She was attentive while her father was gone, and looked fetching in the gown he himself had given her. But he kept one eye on the French ship while the captain was away, and the quarterdeck was no place to get serious. Now Yulunga had business to look after.

"Get along, little girl. I'll catch up to you later." But his progress was delayed as Liza held fast to his arm. His wide smile shone down on her. "Don't worry. When I want you, your father won't get in my way. Not for long."

Coloring, she released him and stepped back. He tweaked her earlobe, then adjusted his belt and sprang down the steps to make his way to the master's quarters. Liza pressed her body against the rail and watched him go. She'd satisfied her father's wishes with her attentions to Mr. Yulunga, but her own desires were only piqued. Now she kept to herself on the quarterdeck, waiting.

She didn't wait long. Within seconds, the door to the master's quarters swung open. Yulunga halted on the companionway, his face disbelieving, his shoulders drawing back from what he witnessed. For a moment he hesitated, as if in doubt whether to launch himself forward or turn and head for *L'Ormonde*. Holding tight to the rail, Liza stole down the steps to obtain a better view. Mr. Smee's command surprised her.

"Mr. Yulunga! Fetch the captain— now!" Emerging from the captain's quarters, Smee strode through the doorway.

Liza gaped at the sight. It was different from the scene she expected. Very different. Smee stood braced on the gilded companionway, a bundle of emerald satin in his arms. It was the lady, moving, twisting. Golden hair streamed all over Smee's shoulders. Like cobwebs, some of it stuck to his beard. Jill's arms worked as she clutched him, plucking at his striped shirt. Her golden jewelry blazed in the sun.

"Well, go on, man! The lady's in trouble!" Smee wheeled with his precious cargo, heading back to the sanctuary of the captain's quarters.

Yulunga ran. He didn't need to do so; Nibs and Tom saw it all from the deck of *L'Ormonde*. Tom ignored Mr. Guillaume's early admonition to tap, pounding instead on Captain LeCorbeau's door. He shoved it open. Two seconds later, Cecco burst through it to stamp down the steps. Nibs swung him a rope and, mirroring Yulunga on the *Roger*, herded his shipmates aside. Cecco caught the cable and bounded to the rail. In an instant, he sailed over the channel between the ships.

Cecco strode toward the bunk, unaware of the papers that harbored Smee's memories, even as they crackled under his boots. One hand rested on his dagger, and he glared. His mate followed him into his quarters. His bo'sun sat bending over his bed. His disheveled bed— and his woman.

At Cecco's advance, Mr. Smee straightened to face him. Jill clung to Smee, her breath catching in her throat and her blue eyes unseeing. In one awful moment, Cecco's heart froze. He saw drops of blood where, in a line of crimson, horribly like a slash, the rubies quivered against her neck. Instantly, Cecco's dagger steeled his hand, and he plunged it at Smee's heart.

Turning Tides

Inches from Smee's heart, the dagger dragged to a stop. Yulunga clutched Cecco's wrist, struggling to check his captain's wrath.

Smee leaned backward. His eyes went wide, lowering to focus on the blade. Cecco bore down upon him, but too entangled in Jill's fingers, Smee was trapped.

"Captain! It's not what you are thinking." Yulunga restrained Cecco by the waist now, and with a grunt, he heaved Cecco away from the bed, nearly lifting him off his feet. The two men stumbled backward, and Cecco swore.

"He dares!" His dark eyes never left the bo'sun. Surging forward again, he burst from Yulunga's grip.

"He's been helping her, Sir." In one swift stride, Yulunga shoved himself in front of Cecco, blocking his path to the bed. Wary of the blade, he braced his arms against Cecco's shoulders. "It was Smee who called for you. The lady isn't well, Captain. See for yourself."

Cecco halted. Quickly he turned to stare at Jill. Realizing now that the drops of blood were only Jill's necklace, Cecco breathed again. Her complexion was rosy— too rosy— and she moved, raising herself on the pillows, her hair tumbling all around her. She seemed unaware of the battle that had just taken place. Her face turned from Smee and slowly, she recognized Cecco. Her eyelids were heavy.

"Captain."

All three men gazed at her, disbelief upon their features. She was smiling. Like she'd done so many times, Jill reached out her hand to

504

Cecco. Unlike any other time, her left hand remained fastened on Smee. Her arms sagged, seeming unable to support the weight of Cecco's gold.

"Please, Sir…let him stay."

Yulunga moved aside, and Cecco strode forward. Infuriated as he was, he accepted her hand, the red one, as always. He would never refuse her hand. But he shook his head, fighting to suppress his rage. He accused the bo'sun.

"What have you done to her?"

"Sir, it wasn't me."

Cecco snorted. "You expect me to believe this?"

"Look at her, Sir. And take a taste of that tea."

Cecco's gaze darted to the teacup on the bed shelf. He tucked his knife in his belt. Waving Smee away, Cecco attempted to take his place at Jill's side. But it wasn't easy; like cat's claws, Jill's fingernails snagged Smee's striped shirt as he pulled from her, and only when her fingers came free did she grope for Cecco. As he sat on the bed, she scratched at his skin.

"Sir—" Her words came haltingly. "I— need you." Her tears had dried now, and stained her face, and her eyes were glassy. The air entered her lungs in bursts. The captain worked to contain her agitation, pinning her wrists to his chest. He wrapped an arm around her.

"Lovely one, I am here."

Jill's head rolled. She arched her back. Cecco supported her and confronted Mr. Smee. "How long ago?"

"Not half an hour, Sir."

"The girl?"

"It had to be, Captain. The doctor was with you. But I'm doubting she acted on her own."

Cecco smoldered while he weighed Smee's words. His arms confined Jill, who fought to free her hands even as her body, like a caress, curled around him.

"And how do you come to be here, against orders?"

"The lady sent for me, Sir. She must have known she was in trouble."

Cecco turned to Jill and shook her. "Lady—"

"Please—" She could manage no more.

"Jill."

She blinked, but never stopped her tortuous movement.

"You must trust me. I will care for you."

Jill stared at Cecco and then her eyes opened wide, as if seeing him for the first time. Her face drained of color and the ash of shock replaced it. She tugged away, but weakly, and immediately flung herself back upon him.

Cecco murmured into her ear. "*Bellezza*, do not fear. You have not broken your word. I excuse you."

Jill didn't seem to comprehend, but Smee listened, and a river of relief washed over him. Cecco twisted to face him.

"Leave now, quietly. Keep to your quarters. I will deal with you later." Cecco summoned Yulunga, who grasped Jill by the shoulders. Cecco released her to remove his knife and unbuckle his belt.

Smee looked to the lady to determine her wishes. With her breathing still ragged, she pressed against Yulunga now. Her eyes closed; she rubbed her cheek on his ebony arm. Smee remembered his promise and, uneasy, shook his head. "I can't be leaving her. Not like this!"

"It is I who cannot leave her." Cecco's command came sharp. "Do your duty, Mr. Smee, before you forget to whom you owe it."

Yulunga freed a hand from Jill's grasp, and planted it on Smee's shoulder to push him toward the door. Smee found he had no choice. Realizing the truth of Cecco's words, he exhaled, and at last, the tension left him.

"Aye, Sir."

Cecco pulled off his boots, throwing them aside to thump on the floor. One of Jill's pages flew up in their breeze, as if startled. While Cecco was distracted, Smee collected the papers. The danger for Jill wasn't over yet. Not until this tale was hidden. He squeezed the parchment small and held it against his side, heading for the door.

Cecco enfolded Jill in his arms again. "Mr. Yulunga. Get Hanover off *L'Ormonde* and sheer away. You will keep watch on him. Tell him nothing, and take nothing from him." Anger emphasized Cecco's words. "Or from his daughter."

Yulunga nodded. "I will see to it, Sir."

"Tell me every move they make." Cecco looked pointedly at his mate. "Tell me, this evening."

Smee snatched up his toolbox and with a last glance at Jill, left the cabin. He still felt her grip ensnaring him, still felt the cold threat of Cecco's blade. It should have daunted him. But Smee was made of stouter stuff. In spite of everything, he'd do it all again, given half a chance. He'd held her in his arms, now, she'd shared her precious kisses, and for Smee, there was no going back. He was part of her story. Hook's story.

Yulunga's long stride caught up to Smee, and he shut the door. On the companionway, the two men regarded one another.

"Well, Mr. Smee."

The crewmen milled about on the deck below, waiting for news, but Smee didn't budge. He kept his voice low.

"Mr. Yulunga, the sooner you're having the charge of young Miss, the better off we'll all be."

"I agree with you. Clearly, it is her father's object to separate the captain and his lady."

"Who knows what all he intended? I'd not be breathing if it weren't for you. That Hanover's a slimy bastard. Never to be trusted—except on one point."

Yulunga raised his eyebrows.

"That love potion really works."

"Aye, but it's working against him now! And if I know the captain, he won't allow Hanover to pull such another trick. The man will lie in chains again, a prisoner in his bunk."

Smee's head jerked up. "Aye." His grip on the toolbox tightened. "That he will." Smee collected himself and nodded to the mate. "I'll be glad to take the job of chaining him, Mr. Yulunga, if you care to be passing it along." And without further comment, Smee descended the companionway, to shoulder his way through the sailors and hurry below decks. He had orders to follow.

After that, he had an old memory to revive. And, in spite of its interruption, a new one to treasure.

From the crow's nest of the *Roger*, Bill Jukes observed as the rest of the day's events unfolded below. He kept his tattooed eyelids open, but the doings on deck proved more informative than the leagues of empty sea. He watched to see if his suspicions were correct.

He saw Mr. Yulunga eyeing Mr. Smee as the bo'sun headed toward his quarters. Then, reassuring the waiting sailors, Yulunga shooed them back to work. Hustling to portside, the mate called to *L'Ormonde*, ordering the surgeon home. A few minutes later, Doctor Hanover emerged from below decks with his bag in tow and made a dignified crossing to the *Roger*. He kept his carved back stiff, as if the feel of his coat prickled against it. Once on deck, he looked around and questioned Mr. Yulunga, who answered briefly and sent him on his way before bellowing out the order to sail. The men scrambled to unfurl the canvas, and Mullins grasped the wheel. The doctor then strolled toward the hatch, taking his time to stare at the door to the captain's quarters before descending.

At this point, Miss Liza materialized on the steps of the quarterdeck. Apparently she'd been hiding behind the ship's bell, watching, no doubt, as keenly as Jukes in the crow's nest. Then the sails dropped and Jukes lost sight of her behind the canvas.

Shortly afterward he saw her again. Her new skirt trailed behind her as she dashed for the hatch, but it stopped to swirl around her ankles as Mr. Yulunga turned just in time to catch her wrist. He issued a command, terse, and released her. She stood for a moment as if undecided, then scurried down the steps. Yulunga strode to the base of the companionway and took up his station, lounging against the stair rail.

Jukes picked up the spyglass and scanned the sea. Nothing of note marked the horizon. He inspected *L'Ormonde*, bobbing at an increasing distance. Her captain's shiny coat was visible as he paced his deck, flourishing his arms and indicating the *Roger*. Her sailing master took the wheel and she, too, got underway, her men climbing like blue-backed spiders into the rigging. LeCorbeau gestured in his flamboyant manner, and soon Nibs in his orange kerchief joined him at the rail. Jukes caught the gleam of Nibs' knife, near to hand in his belt. LeCorbeau stepped close to him, talking all the time he watched

Cecco's ship hauling ahead. One of his skinny mates sidled up to him, slipping between Nibs and the *commandant*. LeCorbeau turned, threw an arm around the mate, and inspected the bandaged hand the young man held out to him. Jukes smirked and counted the seconds. It didn't take Nibs long to melt away below decks.

Jukes checked the horizon again before looking down to see Mr. Starkey steaming his way over the boards. He met up with Mr. Yulunga and lowered his head, seeming to confide some news. Jukes saw Starkey's hand slide from his coat pocket to produce what appeared to be a letter. Yulunga held it up and examined it. But when he lowered it again, he was smiling. He dismissed Starkey, who departed, then he sent a look up the companionway. Tucking the letter in his breeches pocket, he settled back again to stare upon Miss Liza, who inched her way toward him with a pewter cup.

She offered it to him. Yulunga shook his head and pointed at her. Lowering the cup, she took a half step back. But Yulunga moved to tower over her and she obeyed, raising the tankard to her lips. He nodded and she drank. Gesturing with his fingers, he urged her to drink more deeply. She paused to breathe— Jukes grinned to see the curve of her breasts rising and falling above her neckline— and then she lifted the flagon again. Yulunga's smile was broad enough to show his teeth even at this distance. He snatched the cup from her lips. While she was still off balance, he caught her hips and squeezed her against his body, then he spoke into her ear and shoved her away.

When she turned, she was chalky pale. She raised her hands suddenly to cover her mouth, and rushed to the hatch. Yulunga laughed, moved to starboard, and tossed the rest of the drink in the sea. Jukes didn't see Miss Liza again that afternoon, but he saw Yulunga make short, repeated forays down the stairs.

The sea continued clear and the sailors went about their business, but the door to the captain's quarters remained shut tight until suppertime. Mr. Noodler surfaced from the galley with a covered tray that he delivered to Mr. Yulunga. The mate pulled the letter from his pocket and tucked it under a dish. Stepping up to the captain's door, he bent his head and put his ear to it. After listening a few moments, he rapped and entered. Jukes was waiting to watch Yulunga reemerge when Mason's head appeared over the rail of the crow's nest. "Shift's up, mate. Get some supper."

"I will. Any idea where we're headed?"

"The order was to sheer off from the Frenchies."

"Did you get a look at the lady?"

"Who didn't? Mr. Smee's confined to quarters."

Jukes' tattoos crinkled as he sniggered. "Aye, that Irishman. He's a way with the women, and no mistake."

"I'd say it was a *big* mistake. He'd no business being in there with her."

"Ah, Alf, he was only following orders. Who can blame her for calling on Smee instead of the doctor?"

"Aye. It's as much as Hanover's life's worth to look at her. And anyone can see the lady's not well."

"And about time, too."

"What?"

"Come on man, you know the way of it. I'll lay you a wager—she's breeding."

Mason opened his mouth and blew a breath. "Well. I guess we'll be spending some time on the Island, then."

"Aye, I've a hankering to get back there. And you can be sure the captain will prefer that those Indian women tend to her needs when her time comes. Meantime, we'll tend to theirs!"

"Trust you to mention those women, Bill, when they're not in reach. Now keep your mouth shut and don't remind me about females again until we're sailing into the bay."

"I'll do that." Jukes grabbed the shrouds and hopped over the rail. "Keep an eye on the Frenchman, Alf. My money's on Mr. Nibs."

"Captain, you needn't worry any longer. I am very hungry, but I feel fine." Jill did feel fine, wrapped in Cecco's concern as he draped her dressing gown around her. He had demonstrated his love for her all afternoon, easing her cravings, gratifying her demands until at last, she was able to lie at peace in his arms. They had risen as the sun set, to prepare for the evening.

"When I saw the rubies at your throat, I went mad with worry. I thought I saw blood."

"Oh. Yes." Jill touched the jewels, then raised her hands to remove the necklace. "I remember how I came to wear them. But not much else."

"Our fine physician ordered his daughter to serve his famous drug. With your tea."

"And you found me?" Listening closely for Cecco's answer, she slid the rubies into her pocket. His eyes followed them.

"Yes. I found you. In the arms of Mr. Smee."

Her fears confirmed, Jill tensed.

"I know that you sent for him. Because you were unwell."

"Sir, I apologize—"

"Mr. Yulunga saved his life. He assured me Mr. Smee acted properly. It was Smee who insisted I be called back from *L'Ormonde*."

"Then you won't punish him?"

"He is confined to his quarters. This way, the doctor will believe his ploy was successful. I am certain Hanover wished to stir the trouble between you and me. Most likely he desired to make an end of Smee as well."

"And he nearly succeeded."

"Yes. In several schemes. Had Mr. Yulunga watched me act on my impulse, the entire ship would have been in uproar."

"A clever attempt to eliminate Smee— and weaken your authority."

"The doctor remembers how close the men came to electing Smee captain. He knows my crew respect him."

"How fortunate that Mr. Yulunga intervened. And that you are wise enough to see beyond your passions."

"Nor are you foolish. I realize you would not seduce a man in my own bed."

Jill looked down. "No. Never." She had seduced the man, in her story. On paper.

Cecco touched her chin and raised it. "Lovely one. We have to trust one another now. We are bound."

"Yes, Captain. In more ways than one."

"It would appear that even 'our' Mr. Smee understands this."

"And so, at last, you will rid the *Roger* of Hanover?"

"If he was not a member of ship's company, he would now be a corpse."

Jill's heart filled with relief, for the lives of one man she cherished, and one man she couldn't afford to lose. Laying her hand on Cecco's arm, she raised up on tiptoe to kiss him, another man she prized. Yulunga's knock sounded, and the captain broke away to answer.

"Enter."

"Cook sent up your dinner, Sir." Yulunga closed the door behind him and moved to the dining table. He set down the tray and removed the cloth, releasing the aroma of a savory stew. He presented the parchment to the captain. "And Mr. Starkey has delivered a letter from *L'Ormonde*."

Cecco took it. "It is addressed to my lady. Sit down, lovely one." He assisted Jill to her place at the table and seated himself next to her. The parchment lay where he tossed it, on the polished wood between them. Jill stared at it, reluctant to unsettle the serenity she had only just achieved. Cecco pushed it toward her. "Read it, my Jill. I know you are eager for news of your sons."

"Thank you, Sir." She picked it up and unfolded it. Scanning the contents, she didn't know whether to laugh or to cry. She managed to do neither. Cecco read over her shoulder.

"So our spies are settling in to their duties. But they have found nothing. No evidence of our missing master." Cecco's hand stroked Jill's knee, comforting. "*Bellezza*, I am sorry. It is even as I predicted."

Jill set the letter on the table, carefully, as if it might shatter at the least jarring, and nudged it as far away as she could reach. "Yes. It is unfortunate. But not unexpected." Hungry as she was, she sat staring at her plate. Another faint, irrational hope was dying. Hope of Hook.

"Eat now. You must regain your strength."

"As you say. Sir."

"And Mr. Yulunga, how did the afternoon pass?"

"All in order, Sir. The Frenchman sails behind us. Neither the Hanovers nor Mr. Smee have left their quarters. But the men are talking."

Cecco looked up from his meal. "Yes?"

"They are concerned for the lady, Sir. They all saw her. They all know Smee tended to her."

"Then they know the truth."

"Aye, Sir."

Yulunga's look questioned the lady, but she held her head high as she said, "I see I must make a point of appearing on deck this evening. I am quite well, thanks to your attention, Captain."

"If this is what it means to minister to patients, I should have become a physician myself."

Jill smiled, and Yulunga's laugh rumbled. Cecco's mood was light. He had been crossed this morning, and nearly tricked into murder. But he'd enjoyed a long afternoon of vigorous love-making, thanks to the doctor's medicine, and to sweeten even that, his retribution was near. "Tomorrow I will convene my officers to discuss LeCorbeau's proposal. We will soon be searching for a new surgeon. One who, I am hopeful, will prescribe more conventional treatments."

Jill brightened, anticipating. "And the exchange, Sir? Tomorrow?"

"We will come to terms tomorrow. But no doubt our doctor will keep hold of his treasure until the very last moment." Jill's eyes met Cecco's. Clearly, they both remembered his threat. *The very last moment.* But Jill read only assurance in Cecco's gaze. She wondered what he read in her own.

"Jill, my lovely. I see you anticipate his diamonds already. I will settle a high price on the doctor's freedom. And a higher price on yours." He smiled, and then he circled his hand around her neck. With his thumb, he massaged her scar. "Do not forget. In the eyes of the surgeon, I must be angry at your supposed betrayal. Ready to be harsh with you."

"Yes, Sir. And I will do—" Jill heard her voice catch, "my duty."

Cecco observed her pale features. "You are certain that after the marriage ceremony, you will be able to escape?"

"Yes. I will fly as soon as I have everything I want from the surgeon."

"Everything. Including your revenge. But I do not like you to wait until *L'Ormonde* is under sail."

Jill said, "Doctor Hanover will feel at ease by then. He must be completely unprepared when I make my move."

"I wish I could be there. Not only to protect you, but to witness his devastation. But are you sure you can fly?"

"Yes, Sir. I know I can." She smiled, and her heart warmed again at his care for her. "I have only to think of you, and of the life we have created together."

Cecco caught her confidence. "It is good. A surprise Doctor Hanover will never forget! His wife, his angel, winging away."

"Captain Cecco….Is it too much to ask…?"

His earrings swung as he tilted his head.

"Sir, may I encourage my sons to return to the *Roger?*"

Cecco's gaze cooled.

She said, "They have accomplished what they set out to do."

"But have they learned their lesson?"

Jill looked away, toward the letter.

"If they approach me, I will listen. Further than this, I will make no promise."

Yulunga asked, "And what is the plan, Sir, after the lady rejoins us?"

"The lady's scheme is a wise one. If she delays her departure, we, too, will be well underway, in the opposite direction from LeCorbeau. By the time *L'Ormonde* can come about to chase us, we will be beyond his reach."

"And well rid of the doctor." Jill's voice was both bitter and triumphant.

Yulunga shifted his bulk. "And Sir. The girl?"

"She will be given her choice—"

"No." Jill's face set. Her expression turned savage.

"Jill?"

"No, Captain. Liza will do as *you* decide."

"But you yourself have declared there will be no slaves aboard—"

"If you see fit to give her to Mr. Yulunga, or to any of the men, I will not object."

Cecco and Yulunga exchanged glances. Cecco leaned toward Jill. "You are certain?"

"Neither Doctor Hanover nor his daughter is worthy of my mercy." Jill set down her fork and straightened, regal. "Liza is my captive. I give her to you."

"Well, then. Mr. Yulunga, after I have induced the surgeon to pay her ransom, Miss Hanover is yours."

Jill leveled a stare at Yulunga. "Be sure, if you value her health, to keep her well away from me."

Yulunga bowed, his malevolent grin spreading. "Yes, Mistress. I can do that."

Cecco's eyes fired. "My Lady! As I have observed, your passions run deep."

Jill's dark smile formed. The rubies in her pocket burned against her thigh. These jewels had nearly cost Conor Smee— Hook's Smee— his life. But as it turned out, Liza hadn't really stolen the necklace after all. On the contrary. She and her father would pay for it— and pay for it dearly.

Yulunga's liquid laugh rolled from his throat to fill the room. Jill wrapped herself in the sound. She no longer felt hungry. Captain Cecco and his mate satisfied every craving Doctor Hanover stirred within her.

Jill felt fine.

"I wish to end this unfortunate business without delay." As if in physical discomfort, Captain Cecco settled behind his desk the next morning, his shoulders tense and his swarthy face stern. For the ruse he was about to perform, his gypsy upbringing was indispensable.

In her usual place beside him sat Jill, resplendent in golden taffeta. On Cecco's other side stood Yulunga. Mullins and Starkey had taken seats in front of the desk, and Smee planted himself behind them. Cecco's officers had been instructed. Like Jill, each was ready to play his role in this lucrative charade.

The surgeon sat gingerly before the captain, careful not to touch his back to his chair, just as Cecco himself had been cautious in the early days of their acquaintance. The love of the lady, Hanover reflected, had a way of inflicting pain. And soothing it. He listened to the festering voice of the captain.

"Mister Hanover. From the moment your daughter set foot on board, the *Jolly Roger* has been plagued by bad luck."

Hanover bristled. "You are blaming a child for the actions of your crewmen? Really, Captain. It is preposterous."

"Even your science cannot dispute the circumstances. I never approved of taking a girl on board. In his foolishness, our former captain cursed even himself into oblivion. It is clear the time has come to eliminate her presence."

Jill made her voice sound tired. "But Captain—"

"Madam. I heard your protests yesterday. You will now hold your tongue, unless you wish to leave us."

"To leave?" Lowering her chin, Jill studied the rings upon her fingers. "No, Sir. I beg your pardon."

Cecco returned his frown to the surgeon. "Captain LeCorbeau must now depart for France to declare his prizes to his government. He has made me an offer for your services, Doctor."

Hanover brightened up, as if LeCorbeau's proposal were news to him.

"At first I refused. We cannot afford to sail without our surgeon."

"But…now?"

"I assume if you accept his service, you will take your daughter and her bad luck with you. And, as it happens, LeCorbeau is willing to pay handsomely for your release."

At these words, the officers exchanged interested glances. But Yulunga leered. "It had better be a significant amount, Sir. I know the men were eager to watch Miss Liza grow up." He smiled crookedly at the surgeon. "Your pardon, Doctor. But I'm sure even you admit the truth of it."

"Captain. Are you to allow this crude kind of talk?"

"All the more reason to get the girl off my ship, Doctor. She has caused enough trouble, starting with the young sailors like Tom Tootles— and ending with those who should know better. Like Mr. Yulunga."

Although Yulunga acknowledged Cecco's dark look, his lewd expression didn't change. "I'm sorry, Captain."

"Mister Hanover," Cecco said, "It is impossible to assess your daughter's degree of complicity in your own violations. I take into consideration that she may have been commanded by her father to overstep her boundaries. For the incidents I can prove, I have exacted my punishments. But today…"

Hanover's eyes lit with anticipation.

"Today I have had enough of bad luck."

"Your gypsy superstition?"

"Call it what you will. What do you offer for your daughter's freedom?"

The doctor angled his head, calculating. "Well, Captain. I cannot possibly bargain with you until you return the goods you are holding for me."

"Mr. Yulunga." Digging in his pocket, Cecco produced a key. He tossed it to his mate. "Fetch the diamonds."

"Aye, Sir. Gladly." While the other men stirred, Yulunga strode to the sea chest at the foot of the captain's bed. The lock turned with a click, and Yulunga lifted the lid to seize the leather bundle. He smiled and snapped the lock shut once more. When he tossed the bag to Cecco's desk, all the company listened with delight to its rattle. Cecco's officers didn't have to pretend for the doctor's benefit; they licked their lips and shifted in their chairs. Her spuriously low spirits restored, Jill's eyes glowed as she beheld the promising pouch.

Hanover, too, stirred in his chair. He resisted reaching for his diamonds. Instead, he thanked the captain. "I am now prepared to come to an agreement favorable to both of us."

"You intend to join LeCorbeau, then?"

"Yes." At last he laid hands on the bag. A surge of pleasure rode up his arms. Unknotting the laces, he smiled. The dueling scar seemed to soften on his cheek. With pride, Hanover listened to the men's exclamations as he poured a fistful of glittering gems into his palm. He counted them, then with a flourish of his manicured hand, spread them on the captain's desk. The pirates' gazes riveted on the surgeon's treasure. "I believe this will compensate my lady for the loss of her attendant."

Cecco looked at Jill. "You may answer."

"Yes, Mister Hanover. I now formally accept your offer."

Relishing the lady's double meaning, Hanover smiled at the welcome in her sapphire eyes. After the long setback, he had won her at last. She had consented to his proposal. His gaze lingered on her face until Cecco's voice prodded him.

"And what do you offer my men, for the loss of a promising companion?"

Although affronted, Hanover reserved his retort, deliberating instead. "As barbaric as the concept is, I will concede the point." He weighed the profit he'd earned in his attempts to eradicate vice. Choosing to ignore the irony, he measured another handful. "This should buy your men any number of low female companions." Magnanimous, he laid it on the desk.

"Indeed." Cecco's grin began to emerge. A greedy gleam was growing in his eye, and in that of his officers. In spite of herself, Jill's heart was hammering. The jewels winked at her in the morning light. They stirred a memory of a morning, months ago, when she lay with her lover in a bed lined with riches, never conceiving the trials she would soon endure.

Smee peered over his spectacles at the captain. "Begging your pardon, Sir, but does this mean I'll be doing the doctoring again?"

"In the absence of a surgeon, yes."

"I haven't the time to be mending every cut and ill. The *Roger* is a fine ship, but she isn't getting any younger. I'll be needing a mate, now, to be doing my job properly."

Resting his elbows on his chair, Cecco laced his fingers together. The wedding band that used to be Hanover's shone there. "Mr. Smee makes a good point. He cannot be expected to do the work of two men. How shall we pay for the hire of a bo'sun's mate, Doctor, to tend to the ship while Smee tends to the men you leave behind?"

Hanover's smirk decreased. He opened his bag again.

"And, Sir," Starkey joined in, "since I lost the lady's boys to the Frenchman, I've a hard time keeping the weapons cleaned and oiled. And then there's the brass to polish."

Firmly, Cecco shook his head. "I refuse to take those rebels back. Let LeCorbeau deal with their independent tendencies. It is enough that I have to deal with their mother's."

Jill shot an offended look at Cecco, then stared at the diamonds.

Starkey persisted, "We'll be needing at least three cabin boys to take their places. And I'll have to spend some time training them up."

All the men looked expectantly at the surgeon.

"And why should I be responsible for this particular expense?"

"You should not." Cecco shrugged. "For the sake of fairness, I might make one exception. I will accept Mr. Nibs if he wishes to return to my service."

Hanover's gaze wandered the far corners of the room. LeCorbeau had made his conditions clear: he wouldn't weigh anchor with Liza on board unless Nibs was in his grasp. Hanover cleared his throat. "No. No, that won't be necessary, Captain. Out of respect for your consideration, I shall see to it you don't require Mr. Nibs." Onto the desktop, he sprinkled some more solid drops.

Mullins hitched his thumbs in his belt. "I don't like to mention it, Captain."

"Well, Mr. Mullins?"

"There's been some talk, is all. Among the men."

"Please, tell us."

"When we took the *Unity*, Sir. It's no bother to me, mind, but I've heard grumbling among the others. Mister Hanover was laid up that day, if you recall. After your, uh, discipline."

Cecco nodded and smiled. "Yes. I remember. With very great pleasure."

"It's just that, well, he didn't rightly earn his share that day. And I saw Mr. Smee patching up the injuries. Seems to me Smee should receive a surgeon's share of the *Unity* takings."

"An excellent point, Mr. Mullins. You are quite right." Cecco's gaze bored into the doctor.

Another cluster of gems joined the pile. Mullins smiled and sat back, grunting his approval.

Hanover tied up the bag. "And now, Captain. I trust you are satisfied."

"Yes. Certainly."

"And what is the next step?"

"I intend to negotiate the terms of your transfer with Captain LeCorbeau this afternoon. As you are aware, he must pay the company of the *Roger* for your release."

"Yes, of course. I am sure the *commandant* will be generous. When will Liza and I be leaving the *Roger*, then?" Hanover tasted victory already.

"Tomorrow. After you have compensated me for your freedom."

Hanover's eyebrows lifted. "My freedom?" He darted a glance at Jill. She had warned him, in her smuggled letter to LeCorbeau, to prepare to bid for his own liberty as well as hers. "I see."

Avoiding any disturbance of the diamonds, Cecco slid the *Roger*'s book of articles across his desk. It lay open to Doctor Hanover's handsome signature, just below Jill's. "When you signed our book, you became as valuable as any other crew member."

"Yes. Yes, I understand. Let us dispense with the issue now." Untying his pouch strings, Hanover managed to maintain his equanimity. He measured another cascade of jewels and held it up for Cecco's inspection. Cecco snorted. Hanover braced his back and poured a few more. Not bothering to utter his contempt, Cecco turned to gaze out the window. Smee coughed.

Hanover looked at Jill again. She lifted her several necklaces from her breast, rubbing them between her fingers. Hanover stared at the pouch in his lap. He poured another helping. Casting her eyes down, Jill smiled. But she shook her head.

Intruding on the surgeon's inner debate, Yulunga said, "Perhaps, Doctor, you are having second thoughts about leaving us? You are welcome to remain aboard. Miss Liza can sail to France on *L'Ormonde*. I am sure she will fare just as well on LeCorbeau's ship as she has done here. I know for a fact that two or three of the French sailors have expressed interest in her. She will not be alone."

"There is no question of that. As her father, I will continue to care for her." Recklessly, the surgeon plunked down another heap.

"And of course," Yulunga couldn't help smirking, "there is the matter of the dress I gave her. If I can't have the pleasure of watching her wear it, I want to be repaid."

"She will return it immediately."

"So that I can wear it?" Yulunga laughed, and his mirth was infectious. The room resounded with guffaws. "I think not, Doctor!"

Hanover knew he was beaten. He gave again.

In good temper once more, Cecco came to his relief. "On behalf of your shipmates, I thank you, Doctor."

Again Hanover tied up the bag, feeling at last that, whatever the cost, he was well rid of the long, insufferable imprisonment Captain Hook had imposed. He cherished the extra pleasure of knowing that his sea chest secreted just compensation, snatched from the very man who had begun his bondage. He sighed in satisfaction, then said, "And now, Captain. I will make another offer."

The men perked up. This proposition was what they wanted to hear.

"I cannot help but overhear the gossip. I understand that a sensitive situation arose yesterday. It is that incident, to which you allude as the latest stroke of bad luck, that has pushed you to this point."

Cecco frowned.

"I don't wish to be indelicate, Captain, but I believe I can relieve you of your anxiety."

"To what 'anxiety' do you refer?"

"I will be blunt. Much as you desire her, Red-Handed Jill has become a liability."

Jill's head jerked up. Cecco drew back, and his face hardened into a mask. The officers surrounding him sucked in their breaths. Cecco let the silence blister before he answered.

"You dare to say this?"

"I dare to speak the truth. Your exclusive possession of the lady has become a bone of contention between you and your officers."

"It is a lie."

"You nearly murdered a man over her."

Mr. Smee startled, and then he charged at the surgeon. He had no difficulty in acting this role. "You bloody—"

"Silence!" Cecco pounded his desk. The diamonds danced. "I will not have a brawl within my quarters!"

Yulunga had stepped forward to make a show of restraining Mr. Smee. The bo'sun shoved him away, but continued his attack with words. "We never had trouble on the *Roger* until you came aboard, Hanover!"

"Yes. I believe the lady was quite content. Until she met me."

"You're an arrogant one, and no doubt about it. Captain Cecco did us an ill turn when he let you sign on. Now all hell's broken loose."

Cecco sprang up, his fingers in fists. "Mr. Smee, do you insinuate that I do not maintain the discipline? Or are you disappointed that I don't allow you the favors our former captain—" Cecco glared at Jill, "and his courtesan— once awarded you?"

Jill pushed herself from her chair, protesting, "Captain Cecco, I—"

"I have warned you. Be silent."

Feigned rage spurred Smee on. "The only wise move you've made in your captaincy is to rid us of this bastard! Begging your pardon, Ma'am."

Hanover leapt to his feet. "My point is made! Sir, you can end this argument now. Accept my offer to purchase liberty for Red-Handed Jill."

Jill sat down hard. Her mouth hung open as, seemingly astonished, she viewed the chaos erupting around her.

"No!" Cecco shouted. "From the very first, Hanover, you have wormed your way into my lady's affections. I won't give her to you. Not for *any* amount of treasure."

The officers all shammed restlessness now, shuffling their feet and shaking their heads. Yulunga looked around, gesturing to the men. "Sir? You can see how we feel. We don't want this opportunity to slip through our fingers."

Accusingly, Cecco said, "Opportunity, Mr. Yulunga? The only opportunity for which you angle is to slip yourself— between the lady and her lover!"

Yulunga's face turned ominous. "You command her to be quiet. Let us hear what the 'courtesan' has to say for herself. After all, she'll soon be the only female left on board."

"Mr. Yulunga. Let me be clear. Losing the girl does not bring you closer to taking my Jill. I will *never* give her up."

"That decision is not up to you, Captain. We men have a say, too."

Mullins was standing now. "Aye, Captain. Just look at that bag of diamonds!"

Starkey shoved back his chair, his scar-covered face obligingly turned purple. "You can't rightly keep us from treasure, Sir, not if the doctor's willing to part with it!"

The gypsy fire flared. "Not even a mountain of gold—"

"If it's gold you want, by god, I'll be buying her myself!" Smee's angry red face loomed over Cecco's desk.

Cecco's hands shot out and he snatched Smee by the neck of his shirt, dragging him until he bent over the desktop. Smee's fists rushed to grip Cecco's. The captain's brown eyes smoldered. "Do not test me, Irishman. I should have sliced you up yesterday when—"

"Stop!" Jill rose, her eyes blazing. At the sound of her anger, Cecco released Smee and swung around to face her. All the men fell silent, staring.

"I see that my usefulness aboard the *Roger* is at an end." With her scarlet hand, Jill hoisted the leather-bound book from Cecco's desk. She thumped it down before her. As the men gaped in disbelief, she seized a quill and dipped it in the inkwell.

Cecco closed his powerful hand over hers. "No, lovely one. You will not leave me."

Jill looked him straight in the eye. She thrust his hand away. "I'm already gone." She bent, pressed the pen to the paper, and slashed a black line through her name. The pirates gasped.

Cecco stared down at her mark. A look of genuine horror grew upon his features. This gesture, this act of finality, was no part of their plan. He had never intended for Jill to take the charade as far as this. Slowly, his eyes traveled upward to search her face. The sting of his own declaration pricked his soul. *With courage she defies me…* His magnificent queen. He barely comprehended her next words.

"Mr. Yulunga, I will send Liza to fetch my things. You will kindly assist her to move them to the spare cabin."

Hanover smiled. His satisfaction swelled as Jill moved to his side. Laying her stained hand on his shoulder, she held his gaze with her own— and eased the bag of diamonds from his fingers. Upending it over the desk, she released the bulk of its remaining contents to skitter over the surface. Leaving a healthy fistful in reserve, she snapped the strings tight, rolled up the bag, and thrust it in her bosom.

She crossed to the wardrobe to fling its door wide. From the interior she withdrew a single kid glove. The men watched, amazed, while her distinctive red hand disappeared within its confines. As the silence ached, Jill strode to the door. Standing there in her golden gown, her gloved hand on the handle, she was the picture of defiance. She turned to face her captain, one last time.

"My dear Sir. I give you the *Roger*. First, last, and always."

Casting her gaze to each of the men, she smiled, stroking the diamonds beneath her bodice. "Gentlemen. It has been a pleasure."

The pirate queen turned on her heel and vanished. She left behind her a pair of manicured hands emptied of their treasures, an imploding gypsy heart, and a set of smiling eyes behind gold-rimmed spectacles, full of the sight of Red-Handed Jill. The master's mate.

Deal with the Devil

Jill sat on the bunk of the spare quarters, watching darkness dim the water behind her beloved *Roger*. Moored a short distance off, the sister ship was fading to a shadowy shape in the sea. The room in which Jill would sleep tonight was comfortably furnished, but to her, it felt empty. Echoing.

A heavy knock sounded, intruding on her thoughts. She rose and, holding her head erect, opened the door to face the dark figure of Yulunga. He threw a pallet and a blanket to the floor of the gun deck. A gust of air blew up from them, ruffling the skirt of Jill's black Turkish tunic. She smoothed it down with one gloved hand.

"Good evening, Ma'am. Captain's orders I should look after you tonight."

"I see."

"And a good thing, too. Already, the jackals are prowling. I just shooed off both of your neighbors."

"Mister Hanover and Mr. Smee. The best protection I could require."

"Yes, Ma'am. They seem to have been watching each other." Yulunga smiled. "But no longer." He glanced at the quarters his captain had promised him, occupied now with the fragrance of Jill's perfume, her weapons, and the few feminine trappings she had requested Liza to gather. "You didn't ask for many of your things."

"I won't be needing much." She touched her bodice, where the diamonds dwelled. She would have to find a safer place for them.

"You put on quite a performance for us this morning."

"Yes.…Tell me, Mr. Yulunga. How is the captain?"

"How do you think?"

Jill looked away. "I hope his meeting with Captain LeCorbeau went smoothly."

"There was not much work for him to do. The Frenchman was agreeable to our terms."

"Even a share of future profits?"

"He didn't like it. But a rendezvous was established. One year from now."

"So we may proceed as planned."

"No. You can proceed with *your* plans. Captain Cecco is finished."

"Of course." Jill remembered the look on Cecco's face when she deserted him. His agony arrested her. Still aching, she brought herself back to the present. "Thank you, Mr. Yulunga, for the use of both your quarters and your girl."

"Lady, it is my pleasure." But instead of saying good night, Yulunga lingered. His body filled the doorway, and his fluid voice grew insistent. "And now, I want something in return."

In spite of her tension, Jill remained steady. "Yes. I thought you might."

"Something that is sure to satisfy the both of us." With his warm black eyes, Yulunga watched her, waiting.

Jill considered. She searched the gun deck, what she could see of it behind the massive form of the mate. And then she took one step back.

"You may come in, Mr. Yulunga."

The man bent his head to stride through the doorway of his new quarters. He cast a look around as he shut the door. Then he locked it. He smiled. The place felt like home already.

On the gun deck, another dark figure broke away from the shadows. He raised his dusky hand to his lips, bunching his fingertips to send a kiss flying toward the just-closed door.

Inside, Jill observed Yulunga's smile. She said, "You'll need one more thing to make the comfort of these quarters complete."

His look was shrewd. "And you can give it to me."

"Mister Hanover has Liza." Jill settled herself on the bunk. "And you have the captain's ear."

"That's so." He lowered his bulk to the chair and leaned back, stretching his legs out before him. "Exactly what do you suggest I tell him, Lady?"

"The truth, Mr. Yulunga. He gave you the girl in good faith. He will listen to the truth."

"He would rather hear it from you. Shall I open the door?"

"No. No, I can't take a chance that my fiancé will overhear. The truth must come to Mister Hanover only gradually."

"All right then, Lady." Yulunga bent forward. "Let's see what we can do for one another."

In the gloom of the gun deck, Cecco ended his vigil, divining now that the door would not reopen to him. He turned and made his way slowly up the steps, toward the captain's quarters. The room in which he would not sleep at all was comfortably furnished. But to Cecco, this long night, it seemed empty. Echoing.

On his last night aboard the *Roger*, the night before his nuptials, Doctor Hanover celebrated. Pouring the wine, he shared it with his daughter. As she sipped, he watched a rosy tint flush her face. Enjoying her fresh young beauty, he relaxed the muscles of his ruined back. He had turned the lanterns down when she'd finished dressing his wounds, but he was moved to turn the flames up again to see her better. The wine bottle stood open on the desk. Mindful of tomorrow's events, he corked it.

"Only this last glass, Liza. You must be sharp as your needle there, in the morning. You will assist your father's bride to dress, and then— then we will quit this ship at last." He cast a glance at the closed curtain of the upper bunk. "And leave what little remains of our troubles."

Liza laid her sewing aside. Many more of Hook's jewels were stitched securely within the folds of her new gown. She had learned to smother thoughts of what might have been, and now her eyes avoided the captain's bunk. Accepting the glass, she regarded her handsome father instead. Now that she could love him, could touch him, she understood that Hook must be forsaken. His death was heartbreaking, but inevitable. Her father, on the other hand, remained vigorous, and very much alive. As

Liza predicted, the surgeon had handled everything to his satisfaction. The decision was made. Sewn up, like her dress, by her father's capable hands.

"You seem pleased, my darling. As you should be."

The warm, mellow liquid heated her insides, along with her memories. Liza had captured all she sought here aboard this pirate vessel. She had gone adventuring. She'd become a woman, finding herself desired by powerful men. She and her father had enriched themselves with treasure, and a family, of sorts, would soon be restored to her. A proper home, a grand house in Vienna, where a young person could dwell in decency, in security. And, in Vienna, Doctor Heinrich's position in both science and society would preclude his daughter's servitude, including her subjugation to his wife. Liza and the lady had found a mutually agreeable balance—two moons orbiting the sun of the surgeon. Except for one tiny worry, Liza was content with her situation. She and Jill would never be friends, but, combining their abilities, they proved excellent allies. Jill's marriage to the doctor might be the answer even to Liza's last nagging little anxiety.

Her father's hand on her knee recalled her from her reverie.

"Liza. I'm sure I have no cause for concern. You will be discreet about our arrangement."

Her gray eyes were serious, and she nodded.

"Your prudent behavior will ensure that I will always care for you."

Liza set down her glass. She laid her fingers on her father's. Her master's. She drew his hand to her cheek. He smiled as he touched her face.

"I will be a fortunate man when I return to Vienna. Perhaps the only man who can, without offending propriety, house his wife and his mistress under one roof."

His mistress rose. Taking his hands, she coaxed him from his chair. Their bed lay waiting.

"Yes, Liza. We must retire. After all, I am to be married tomorrow. My last evening as a single gentleman must be memorable."

Liza thought so, too. She shed her shift, and left her sewing basket open.

Smee soothed his worries this evening. The *Roger* bobbed at anchor on the brine, crooning her night song. Still, his inability to act tonight nettled him. But he'd done all he could to prepare. Jill seemed safe enough in the cabin next door. He knew she'd tap on his wall if she needed him. Tomorrow would come, and not soon enough.

That Hanover wouldn't bother her now, not with Yulunga nearby. The insufferable surgeon had strutted from the fracas in the captain's quarters this morning, a smirk across his face as long as his dueling scar. A body would never know the man had just spent away his fortune. Smee understood that extravagance. The cocky doctor believed he'd bought a bride from the *Roger* at last. But when the dust settled, the victory would be the lady's, after all. Her own share of his diamonds, her freedom, and soon, a better man established as her captain. Hanover would have his wife, all right. He just wouldn't have her *with* him.

And the gypsy got his warning. In spite of all his conniving, Jill had surprised him. Everyone could see the shock on his face when she turned the tables on him. She'd done half Smee's job in one stroke of her quill. Smee, too, felt the power of her pen. He'd kept her story and read it over and again. Its message was clear. He knew what she wanted. *Who* she wanted. Of all the men aboard the *Roger*, only her own Mr. Smee could come close to giving her what she longed for.

He had just one more task to accomplish tonight. It would have to wait. He stepped to his cabin door to snap open the lock and secure the key in his pocket. He stood listening again. The low voice of Yulunga seeped like water through the wall, too softly for Smee to make out. Staying alert in case Jill felt the need to summon him, Smee finished sharpening the rapier and set it on his bed, where he laid his red head down to rest. The lady's head would rest again, tomorrow night, on a captain's pillow.

The gypsy's would be bobbing on the brine.

In the deep of the night, Yulunga took his ease on the pallet before the lady's door. When a hand touched his chest, he startled awake. His instinct kept him quiet as, gripping the little wrist, he stared into Liza's eyes. The lantern that hung in the corner of the gun deck touched her with a muted light, staining her white skin amber. She was unclothed. Ready. He heaved a breath, and then he yanked her off balance. She tumbled onto his chest. A moment later, he crushed her beneath him. In another moment, he, too, was naked.

Liza couldn't breathe. She didn't care. She reached for his neck and, feeling his beads pressing into her palms, pulled his face to her own. But Yulunga didn't return her kiss. He opened his mouth and encompassed her lips, her tongue, her teeth. Far from kissing Liza, Yulunga devoured her. Shifting his weight to his knees, he lunged. His hot skin rubbed against her, inside and out. She couldn't scream; he still covered her mouth. After a time she didn't need to scream. She didn't need even to breathe.

Yulunga breathed for her. He pushed his air into her lungs, and somewhere beyond her shock, Liza felt her ribs rise with it. The feminine parts of her body had been opened before— but never her lungs. With the force of his breathing, Yulunga dominated her passages until the overdose of oxygen made her dizzy. She had come to him to be loved, violently. Now he ravished her very airway, shoving his breath in her and forcing it out again. Both purged and plundered, she lay dazed beneath this African king, filled physically, mystically— and absolutely entered.

Used beyond her comprehension, Liza surrendered to his black oblivion. Yulunga exercised his rights, taking his ease on the pallet before the lady's door. Deep into the night.

Guillaume clutched the flower petal and pushed the dark door. He hoped he wasn't too late. But light escaped through the opening crack, and he sighed in relief. Stepping quietly inside, he closed the door again. The cloying fragrance of lotus surrounded him. In spite of Guillaume's ordeal at Tom's hands, the smell of the flowers evoked a more pleasant memory as well, and all in all, entering this compartment again gave him a good feeling.

Tom lounged against one of the crates, his jacket open and his shirt loose. "You're late, Guillaume."

"Mr. Tom. I came away as soon as I was free."

"Been on a job, have you?" Tom eyed his new comrade.

"*Oui*, Mr. Tom. Captain's business."

"Soggy business, I'd say. You're hair's wet."

Guillaume's uninjured hand snapped up and worked to smooth his hair. "Wet, yes, and cold. I was hoping you had decided to open that bottle of cognac after all. I am chilled to the bone."

"Sorry Guillaume. Not tonight. But have some of this." Tom pulled out his flask.

Nodding his gratitude, Guillaume reached for it. *"Merci."* His hands shook as he tried to open the drink. Tom commandeered it.

"I'll do it." He uncorked it and watched, his head to one side, as Guillaume pried his chattering teeth open to swallow the grog. "Drink it all. Looks as if you could use it."

When Guillaume lowered the flask, his face had regained some color. He passed the grog to Tom, then turned away to cough.

"Don't tell me you've got that weakness of the lungs again. I thought our doctor cured you of that."

"Yes, Mr. Tom. Doctor Hanover is an excellent surgeon." Guillaume held up his bandaged hand. "As you can see, I am able to use my fingers again."

"That's not Hanover's work. You tied that wrapping yourself. Didn't you?"

"Oui." Guillaume's face was wary and his lips closed tight, as if he judged it best not to say any more.

"I wonder what kind of 'captain's business' you were about just now?"

"You may wonder. But I may not say."

"Took the bandage off to go for a swim, did you?"

Guillaume shivered, but his resolve remained firm.

Tom tossed his head. "Oh, all right. Whatever it was is between you and LeCorbeau. I respect any man's loyalty to a captain. Even him. Now let me see that." Taking Guillaume's damaged hand in his own, he unwrapped it. He turned up the lantern. "Looks to be healing properly. Good thing I keep my knife nice and sharp. It's a clean wound." He shook out the bandaging and began to apply it more neatly. "This is the last time I'll have to do this. Looks as if *L'Ormonde* will keep Doctor Hanover after tonight."

"Yes. The men are pleased at the prospect of sailing with a surgeon. And also—"

Tom grinned as he tied up the wrapping. "You can say it, Guillaume. They can't wait to welcome a lady on board. Two ladies, actually."

"Well, yes, from what I have overheard. I intend no disrespect to your mother, of course."

"Not at all. Jill's used to sailors' attentions. It's the other one they should look out for."

"You refer to your…your sister, Mr. Tom?"

Tom's grin grew ironic. "You know, I never thought of it that way. Miss Liza *will* be my sister, won't she?" He laughed. "Wait until I tell Nibs! I can just picture the look on his face. We have six other brothers, but I have to say, none of us ever imagined a sister— leastways, not a sister like Miss Liza."

"Six more brothers, Mr. Tom? You must have been hungry!"

"Not a bit. There was plenty for all of us, there at home."

"In France, I had too many sisters and not enough to eat."

"And stowing away to join LeCorbeau got you fed."

"And educated. It was he who taught me English. Among many other things. You may think it strange, yet in his way, our *commandant* has earned my loyalty. But your other brothers, they do not sail with the *Roger*. Where are they?"

"Three live in London. Learning to be what you don't think exists— gentlemen. The others…" Tom's smile faded. "I may never see the others again. They're on our Island."

"Island, Mr. Tom? But of course. The same on which your Captain Hook claimed he found your mother."

"That's my home. Paradise. One place LeCorbeau is sure never to make port."

"Why so?"

"There's only one way to find it. The Island has to be looking out for you." Tom's eyebrows lowered. "Even I won't land there if the Island doesn't want me."

Observing the rare regret on Tom's face, Guillaume was cautious. "You hope to return one day."

"The best port in the world. Lots of adventure. I already told you about the Indian women. Waterfalls, woods. And the Lagoon— you'd never believe what you'd find there."

"I would like very much to see your home."

Tom returned from his visions to study Guillaume. "Come to think of it, it might do you good, Guillaume." He roused himself. "Now let's get to business. It's late, and I have another job for you tomorrow."

Disappointed, Guillaume let his gaze fall. He shivered again.

Tom sighed and shed his jacket. "All right, Guillaume. Come on over." He hiked himself up to settle on the crate. He silently commanded and, obeying, Guillaume followed. The sturdy sailor draped his jacket over the mate's slender shoulders and wrapped his arms around him, rubbing to bring on some heat. "You're chilled through and through. Sit closer, then."

Guillaume laid his damp head on Tom's shoulder and soaked up his camaraderie. He didn't know how long this attention might last, but he decided to simply enjoy it. This sailor brought him a good feeling. What was the proper word for it? He could find it in French. In English? Warming, Guillaume smiled. Mr. Tom had six other brothers. They had grown up in comfort, with plenty to eat. He and his brothers would all understand the word. Guillaume's lips moved before he realized it.

"Companionable."

"What was that?"

"Nothing, Mr. Tom. Please, tell of this task you would have me perform."

"I will, Guillaume. And then I'll return your key for this compartment and tell you where you can find that missing bottle of cognac. That will set you up fine with the *commandant*."

"You are ready to trust me?"

"*Mais oui*, Guillaume. You've made Nibs' life a lot easier here on *L'Ormonde*. I consider you a friend."

"A friend?" Guillaume felt warmer already.

"Like you said, Guillaume." Tom rested his head on Guillaume's. "Companionable."

"Like brothers?"

Firmly, Tom nodded. "Just like that. *Mon ami.*"

The heavy scent of lotus blossom lay upon them like a blanket. Riding at anchor, the ship rose with every wave, only to settle into the sea again. The grog lent its heat to their bellies.

It gave them a good feeling.

The piercing pain in Liza's ear awakened her, but she couldn't jerk away. Yulunga lay on her still. He had found the needle she'd set by the pallet, thrust in a white patch of gauze. Now he was pulling it from her earlobe. He clenched a golden ring between his teeth, glimmering in the lanternlight, and he spit it into his hand. She had thought he'd use the gauze to tamp the blood, but his lips sucked Liza's wound, and she felt the moist balm of his tongue. He pulled away from her ear to press her mouth, not a suffocation this time, nor an overabundance of air, but a kiss. Liza tasted the sharp, rusty flavor of her blood. When he finished kissing her, her lips tingled with it.

Yulunga drew her by the wrists to sit up on his thighs. His fingers stretched her earlobe and the golden ring made love to her flesh. The discomfort was sweet to her. She closed her eyes to feel it better. With his thumb, he toyed with her earring, and his low laughter rolled. The gold was heavy, dangling in an agreeable way. Its partner still hung from Yulunga's ear.

Now Liza felt the other feelings, the damp and the hurt between her legs. She knew she was bleeding there, too. She had gotten what she came for. Liza was utterly, completely satisfied. She fell back on the pallet, fell back into sleep.

Yulunga set the needle between his teeth, jogging it up and down like a toothpick. He laughed silently as he pushed her body aside to make room for his own. She would do. She would do very nicely. She had responded fittingly to the purification rite, the renewal of her air. This night had been worth the waiting. Now he'd never have to wait for her again.

But next time, he'd make her wash first. Ordinarily he didn't mind using a girl other men enjoyed. But even after the cleansing ritual, the smell of the surgeon disgusted him.

The dawn light cast its rays upon the *Roger*. It filtered through her gunports and cabin windows, driving demons of the nighttime away. Soft sounds of water surrounded her. Within her, on the portside, lay a swarthy man with weary brown eyes, craving a shave. To starboard, a bridegroom tied and retied his cravat. His mistress slept for a few more minutes, until he was satisfied with the knot and bent tenderly to awaken her. At rest in the bunk above lay a sea rogue's remains. Next door, a lady slept to save herself from waking, while in the cabin beyond, her loyal sailor strapped on a deadly rapier. Before her door, a brutal man born to royalty sat cross-legged on his pallet, squinting in puzzlement at the golden earring between his fingers— the bloody mate of the ring upon his ear.

The day was come. Scenting battle, the *Roger* roused to life.

535

The Last Moment

32

The French sailors smiled, full of good humor. Today, a wedding was to take place. Soon they would be celebrating, not only the English marriage, but also their new course— sailing for port, wherever that might be. Ambling up the steps, they balanced the last of the boxes on their blue-tailored shoulders.

Doctor Hanover, dressed formally in his beige suit, dropped his watch in his pocket and followed to ensure that his belongings, and those of his fiancée, were stowed safely aboard *L'Ormonde*. If his sea chest weighed more than it had the day he was forced aboard, these privateers wouldn't know it. The box of medical books was heavy, too, but he would trust the medicine bag to Liza. It, unfortunately, was much too light.

Ignoring the gypsy stare from the quarterdeck, Hanover acknowledged LeCorbeau's signal. He then descended, one last time, below decks. Once in his quarters, he tied back his hair and armed himself with his sword. It would please his lady to see him wearing it, he knew. More to the point, it would lend the both of them protection should the captain, at the last moment, prove belligerent. The surgeon's rapier, after all, had a longer reach than Cecco's famous knife.

Smirking, Hanover scanned his cabin again. He didn't bother to glance behind the curtain enclosing the upper bunk. He'd taken his last golden prize this morning, while Liza was attending Jill. A pair of empty black boots stood at the foot of the bed. Liza had polished them until they shone, but Hanover had no use for such apparel.

With a light heart he left, securing the door. Calling to collect his bride from the next room, he rapped softly, anticipating the sight of her lovely face.

Liza opened the door, wearing the maroon gown her father's diamonds had purchased from Mr. Yulunga. Smiling shyly, she looked peaked but pretty. She had balked over breakfast, indicating her weariness of Cook's porridge and an eagerness to sample the cuisine of LeCorbeau's chef. She, too, was elated. Hanover had sensed her excitement last night. It had kept her awake and somehow, in her giddiness, moved her to pierce her ears. She understood, however, when her father cautioned that she shouldn't wear Hook's jewels for a few more days. Not until Jill was firmly established as his own. He had cleansed and tended her piercings, and allowed Liza to wear her hair down today, to disguise the damage. Even so, he took pride in her appearance as she accepted the medicine bag and made way for her father to behold his bride.

"My lady. I have come for you at last."

As enchanting as Liza looked, the sight of Jill stopped the bridegroom in his footsteps. She stood at the back of the cabin, her chin high, gazing out the window at the sea. As he entered the room, she turned her head. Hanover held his breath, believing he was in danger of drowning in the blue of her eyes.

On this, her wedding day, Jill wore her finest gown. No, Hanover corrected himself— any woman might wear a gown. Jill *enhanced* the black silk, the same in which she had danced with him far into the night, that very first evening. The silver slippers peeped from beneath her skirts, a concession to propriety. So, also, were the long black gloves that, in elegantly covering her arms and elbows, masked the leather bands at her wrists and the stain of her hand. The only mark of piracy she retained was the jeweled dagger, gleaming at her waist. The lady still bore the gold she'd won from her gypsy lover, and the opal necklace that sparkled a spectrum of colors. Although, like Jill, these treasures came to him from other men, Hanover smiled to see such riches. Soon enough, he would consider them remuneration for the price he had paid for her. For now, still staring, he forgot his haste to be gone.

Jill's fair hair had been captured. Twisted into an elegant knot, it was pinned up, one golden lock left to straggle, curling down her shoulder and over her breast. In her superlative black gown, she appeared both widow and bride— an appropriate balance, Hanover reflected. He was only too aware of the wretched remains he had abandoned in his shackles. But he would be patient. He would ease Jill's time of mourning. Soon the couple would sail into France, then post to Paris, where he would order trunkfuls of the most fashionable raiment. Doctor Johann Heinrich intended to arrive in Vienna in grand style— a handsome coach, more wealth in the bank, and two beautiful women on his arms. He had endured his trials. Nothing could hold success from him now.

Feeling vigorous with victory, he crossed the room. "Madam." He kissed her hand, suddenly regretting the glove that covered it. "You are exquisite."

"Thank you." She squeezed his hand. "Johann, I am ready." She smiled, and her eyes lit up to match his own. "Today."

"Today!" He couldn't wait any longer. With gentle pressure, he pulled her hand under his elbow and urged her toward the door. "Today, my darling."

Arm in arm, the couple promenaded over the gun deck. The silent cannons brooded, the cat squalled. The *Roger* creaked as they crossed her, to no avail. The pirate queen had abdicated her throne. This ship would have to carry on without her.

Refusing to look back, Hanover led the way up the stairs. His daughter kept pace, only slowing to send a last regretful glance toward her cabin, the site of her misadventures. The room full of secrets which, with both bitter memories and sweet, she would always harbor in her heart.

Turning to emerge from the hatch, Liza blinked in the sunlight to distinguish a calloused hand reaching to assist her. She looked up into a pair of china blue eyes. As she slid her fingers into the French sailor's grip, his Gallic smile spread across his face. It was her admirer, and his delight in her move to *L'Ormonde* shone upon his countenance.

"Bonjour, Mademoiselle." He bowed and removed the bag from her grasp. Keeping a steady hold on her hand, he led her toward his

captain's ship. He seemed unaware of the glower aimed at his long blond pigtail, but Liza felt it. Averting her gaze from the rail from which Yulunga's scowl emanated, she never dared to look away from the young Frenchman's face. Of last night's trysting, all that remained was the sting of her earlobes. She knew who she was now: *Mademoiselle*.

Jill kept her eyes on *L'Ormonde*. Only after gaining footing aboard the French ship did she look back. She didn't have to search. Her gaze lit immediately on Cecco's face. He was sallow, angry. His hand rested on the dagger in his belt. The medallions of his headdress shimmered in the wind as he stood, legs wide, high upon the quarterdeck. He made no sign to her. She made no sign to him. The matched pair of golden armbands, each aboard a different ship and separated by the sea, glittered in the sun.

Jill turned away to place her black-gloved hands into those proffered by the bowing *commandant*. The planking scraped over the deck and clattered against the gunwale. Cecco's voice pealed out. "Ship's company! Cast off!"

A rich, deeper voice took up the call as Yulunga shouted, "Make ready to come about!"

Liza heard that voice as she followed the French sailor to stow her father's bag in his new quarters. Hanover listened from the deck, his face full of the satisfaction the finality of those words brought to him.

Jill, too, listened. She saw that greetings issued from LeCorbeau's mouth. *L'Ormonde*'s sails dropped and caught the wind. Jill glimpsed Renaud standing nearby in full dress uniform, heels together, a small black book tucked under his arm. She felt the *commandant*'s lips brush the fabric over her hands. She smelled the tang of victory that hung about her fiancé. But her ears heard only the sounds of the *Roger*, preparing to sail away, without her. The loose curling hair on her neck tickled in the breeze. The pitch of *L'Ormonde* as she sheered away felt identical to the pitch of the *Roger*. To settle her stomach, Jill inhaled a deep breath of sea air. Automatically, she acknowledged LeCorbeau's courtesies.

Within minutes, she might penetrate the mystery of Hook's disappearance. Her final duty to her captain. Much too late, but too compelling to refuse. All this time, she'd never managed to subdue the illogical stirrings of hope. They kicked at her now as she struggled to stand firm on this foreign vessel. A vessel Hook himself had forbidden her to board. Yet no matter what she learned, with luck, her husband would soon be soothing these fears, making her safe. She had chosen to trust him. Before long, she would lie in his arms, reassured by his embraces— and sailing for home.

Wherever that might be.

Captain Cecco strode to the quarterdeck rail. In silence, Yulunga joined him, handing over the spyglass. The two men, master and mate, ignored the activity around and above them, endeavoring to make out the movements on the deck of *L'Ormonde*.

"I should never have let her go."

"You had little choice, Sir."

"I have a choice now."

"Captain, it won't be necessary to—"

"We shall soon discover what becomes necessary." Cecco observed through the glass. "Ah, I see the lady's sons. She is happy to be reunited with them. Hanover has even taken his hands off her long enough to allow her to embrace them." Cecco's voice turned bitter as he spied. "How victory is changing him! He condescends to shake their hands."

His queen held court in the center of *L'Ormonde*'s deck, before the mainmast. A table covered in a white cloth stood nearby, laden with drink and delicacies, a wedding feast. Cecco saw Jill smiling. She rested a hand on each of her sons as Hanover greeted them. Liza returned to the deck to inch her way through the blue coats of the sailors. Beckoning to Liza, Jill directed her to approach the young men. Liza curtsied. Tom bowed, and then he laughed and shook Liza's hand. Nibs neared her, too, solemnly offering his handshake. Soon Hanover gripped Liza's shoulders, guiding her to a position facing LeCorbeau while Nibs and Tom snapped to attention. Hanover stood up straight and took Jill's hand in both his own. Through the glass, Cecco watched the bride and groom exchange a glance, then, sober, address their full attention to the *commandant*.

"They waste no time."

"No, Sir. Nor did you."

Cecco snorted, never lowering the spyglass.

The Frenchman stood erect before the couple, dressed in his finest coat and an abundance of lace at his throat. His ornamental sword hung at his side, shining like his buttons. He flourished a hand, into which Renaud deposited the little black book. Guillaume stood near his captain, bearing a tray containing parchment, ink and quill. Those men not occupied with the sailing of the ship gathered at a respectful distance, grinning. Each gripped a pewter cup; one or two held fiddles and a concertina. Obviously a party was brewing. Yulunga interrupted Cecco's speculations.

"Captain. You wanted to put as much distance as possible between ships."

"So I led the lady to believe."

"Shall we make sail, then?"

"No. Not yet."

"But the plan was to be beyond *L'Ormonde*'s reach when the lady rejoins us."

"You should know me better, my friend. I have no intention of fleeing from a fight with LeCorbeau."

"Sir?"

"Tell the men to prepare for battle. Quietly."

"And…when shall we attack?"

"Mr. Yulunga. We will wait." Cecco lowered the glass. He remembered the feel of Jill's throat, warm within his grasp, the pulsing of her blood against his touch. His heartbeat quickened, and his swarthy face set. "We will wait. Until the very last moment."

LeCorbeau's smile was sleek. He was enjoying himself. Sailing free at last with his wayward surgeon secure and their prospects restored, he prepared to preside over the ceremony. He grasped the book, inhaling a breath of satisfaction through his overlarge nose.

"And now, before we may begin."

Hanover shifted, restless to commence, and felt the sword at his side brush his trousers. He tightened the grip of his elbow where Jill's hand nestled within it. "I assure you, Captain. My bride and I are more than ready."

"Do not fear, my brave Doctor Hanover. I have only one question. For the lady."

Attentive, the lady raised her eyebrows.

"Are you quite certain, *Madame*, that you wish to enter into this, eh," he tossed his head, "situation?"

"*Commandant?* But of course."

"That is, eh, you are aware, are you not, of the consequences of your…decision? The strictures of the law?"

"I assure you, Sir. I know exactly what my decision means. But I thank you for your consideration. Please." Gazing adoringly at her impatient fiancé, she leaned on his arm. "Begin at once."

"Very well, then." LeCorbeau cleared his throat. His men bent forward to listen. The sun shone down upon the celebrants this glorious morning, a good omen for a marriage. *L'Ormonde's* white sails swelled full of the freshening air, as if she held her breath to hear the vows.

Tom, standing next to Liza, turned to grin at her. His mood was so infectious she felt herself smiling back. Even Nibs nodded at her, his lips turning upward.

"Join hands, if you please, and repeat the *consentements*. I, eh— But *Monsieur*, by what name shall you call yourself?"

Startled, Hanover blinked. As he beheld his Jill, his smile returned in force. "Heinrich. Let there be no doubt about it."

"*Alors*, so it shall be. I, Johann Heinrich, receive you, Jill, as wife."

The surgeon gazed into his fiancée's eyes and made his assertion certain. "I, Johann Heinrich, receive you, Jill…as wife." The long awaited moment had arrived, and Hanover's pulse beat strong and quick. The vows rolled from his lips.

"And I promise to remain faithful to you, in happy times and in times of trial…in health and in sickness, in order to love you all the days of my life." His smile was tight with happiness, his grip on her fingers firm.

When LeCorbeau turned to her, Jill felt the pressure of the surgeon's hands pressing hers, as if they might meld into one flesh.

From the corner of her eye, she caught a glare of gold across the sea. Did she hear or did she remember the jangle of those bracelets?

Halfway up the *Roger*'s mizzen shrouds, Captain Cecco leaned against the ratlines. He watched through the spyglass as LeCorbeau offered words to his woman. He witnessed her declaration. She nodded once as she spoke— showing no hesitation.

The Frenchman motioned with his lace-bedecked arm, and the blond sailor brought a salver full of cups from the table. LeCorbeau received a silver goblet from his hand. Bestowing it on the groom, he bowed. Hanover turned to face Jill, raised the cup to her, and drank. He placed the cup in Jill's black gloves. Cecco caught the glint of his own gold at her wrists as she lifted the drink to her new husband, smiled, and sipped. Hanover removed the cup from her hands and returned it to the sailor.

At LeCorbeau's signal, Guillaume came forward and offered the pen to Hanover. Guillaume held the tray with its parchment steady. The surgeon dipped the quill and dashed off his signature. Cecco couldn't see the pompous smile as Hanover presented the pen to Jill, but he didn't have to see it. It was the look on Jill's face that interested him. It was difficult to make out, but he could imagine it. Her engaging eyes, her smile, and the subsequent movement of the quill in her fingers as she signed yet another oath of loyalty. What were her feelings at this moment?

The surgeon's feelings were too clear. Jill turned to him, and he held her face between his hands. He bent to kiss her. Cecco gritted his teeth. Even at the lengthening distance, he could tell. It was a lingering kiss, and tender. The company surrounding the couple cheered and stamped, waving their tankards. LeCorbeau, too, snatched a glass from the salver and raised it. The ruckus of the revelry grew louder, drifting over the water so that Cecco could hear as he watched. Cecco's grip on his spyglass tightened. Jill had flung her arms around the surgeon's neck to press her body against him. Too clearly.

Cecco heard strains of music drifting across the sea now, as the French sailors applied themselves to their instruments. *L'Ormonde* was making headway, the particulars of the scene shrinking even within the spyglass. But Cecco could see the couple clasped together, swaying, their side to side movement broadening, lengthening, to break at last into a waltz. He made out Jill's billowing black silk, swirling as Hanover swept her around and around. Lilting back and forth across the deck, they seemed absorbed only in one another, not looking about but trusting the sailors to make way. The couple's movements were elegant, perfectly attuned. They fused together as if, after long separation, they might never let go of one another again. Captain Cecco narrowed his staring eye.

The men's hands and feet kept time to the music. After long minutes, Jill broke away from Hanover, her arms going around Tom. They danced a few steps, halting near Liza, where Jill drew the girl into Tom's arms and pushed the two of them into the waltz. Hanover gestured his approval to his daughter, after which Liza picked up her skirt and danced.

LeCorbeau took the opportunity to present a roll of parchment to the groom. As Hanover tucked it within his coat, the blond sailor emerged from the crowd again to hover near Liza. Guillaume appeared then, to tap the young man on the shoulder and thrust the tray of writing utensils into his hands. In his dapper uniform, Guillaume became officious, shooing the sailor toward the master's quarters. He did the same to several others, herding them away from Liza and Tom, steering the men toward the cask before the table.

Nibs stepped up to take his place with Jill. After a few turns he surrendered her to her new husband, who swirled her away once again. Tom kept Liza dancing, guiding her all around the deck, eventually pausing at an unpopulated spot behind the helmsman's back, to port, where Nibs, toting drinks, strolled aft to join them.

Cecco's vigilance sharpened now. The party on deck had reached full pitch. Jill and Hanover waltzed on as if surrounded not by the planks of a privateer, but by the marble halls of a palace. They ascended to the quarterdeck, and as the musicians turned the tune to a folk dance, *L'Ormonde*'s men's attention wandered from the bride and groom. Jill and Hanover gravitated to stern. Cecco ceased to track their movements. The time had come for action.

"Mr. Yulunga," he bellowed from his vantage point, "make sail!"

"Aye, Sir!" Yulunga pivoted to relay the order. The men were ready.

Red-Handed Jill was waiting for them. With a will, they set to work. Mullins grasped the wheel.

Cecco slid down the mizzen backstay, to land upon the deck. "Mr. Mullins, catch the Frenchman. Make all speed."

"Aye, Captain!" As the sails unfurled, Mullins eyed the compass. He looked up again, feeling a good, strong breeze. "We'll take her in no time, Sir." The sails caught the wind. The ship began to turn. Mullins planted his feet wide apart and, putting his back into it, he hauled on the *Roger*'s wheel. Then, from deep within her hull rose an ominous note. She wailed.

Mullins listened. His brow furrowed and he rolled his eyes upward to squint at the sails. They stretched with the wind. Mullins pulled once more. The *Roger* was moving, but she wasn't responding to the helm.

The sounds aboard *L'Ormonde* had faded, inaudible now. Cecco whirled to stare at Mullins.

"Mr. Mullins. Why are we not on course?"

"Sir…She's not coming about."

"What—" Cecco's eyes flared, and then he dashed for the stern.

Yulunga exchanged looks with Mullins. "The rudder?"

"Yes, Sir. The rudder must be jammed. I can't steer her at all."

Grasping the taffrail, Cecco peered down into the depths of the sea. The big wing of the rudder stood at attention, stock-still. His ship was moving, unalterably, away from *L'Ormonde*. Away from Jill. Looking out over the water, Cecco could distinguish only a blur of black silk, receding into the distance. The vast sea loomed between them. Cursing, he yanked the spyglass open again. Within its brief round space, Jill's dark dress faded to blend with beige.

Cecco stared, his wild eyes aching, until the very last moment… when she was gone.

Flights of Fancy

Tom was watching. Jill laughed and he caught her signal; her black gloves slipped the doctor's coat from his shoulders. Tom turned to Liza and surprised her, taking the cup from her hands.

"That's enough for now, Miss. Let's set the drinks down." Exchanging a significant glance with Nibs, Tom leaned an elbow on the portside rail. He unbuttoned his blue jacket. "You know, Miss, Nibs and me, we're your brothers now."

"Aye, Miss Liza. And your father's ours." Nibs adjusted his kerchief, making ready.

Liza's wide-eyed look showed astonishment. Clearly she hadn't thought of this. As if seeking reassurance, she looked over her shoulder toward the surgeon. Unfettered by his coat, he held Jill tightly in his arms. The newlyweds swayed together still. Their dance had slowed when they moved toward the stern. Alone on the quarterdeck, they seemed to have abandoned their every concern with the *Roger*. Tom allowed Liza a moment to collect herself, then recalled her attention.

"I think it's fine. A fresh start for the two of us. Don't you think so?"

Liza's uncertain expression remained. Her gray gaze wandered toward the dwindling pirate ship, where the unpleasantness between her and Tom had taken place.

Tom's gaze followed. Already the *Roger* was more distant than he liked. "She's a fine vessel, the *Jolly Roger*. I'm sorry to be parting company with her."

Behind Liza's back, Nibs craned his neck to monitor the progress of the party. Having rigged the sails, the men on duty had descended for a cup of cheer, and ship's company made merry around the cask. Cheeky music from the fiddles joined with the wheeze of a concertina. Like his men, LeCorbeau was relaxed, enjoying himself. With one fluid arm, he kept time to the music. His other arm linked through Guillaume's. The second mate was keeping his promise, ensuring that his captain's back remained turned to the stern. Guillaume had engaged Renaud, too, in a conversation. As also arranged, Tom was keeping Liza occupied. With a final glance at the crow's nest, Nibs swung a long leg over the port rail, balanced for one moment, then slid seaward. His departure made not a sound.

Tom hiked himself up to perch on the rail. "Might as well get comfortable, Miss. This party looks as if it has a mind to go on all day." He inspected the decks. All clear. Jill was managing just fine, luring Hanover's attention well away from his daughter. When the man on watch pointed his spyglass over the bow, Tom aimed a stare behind Liza. "Well, look at that!"

She turned. Moving quickly, Tom slapped his hand over Liza's lips. Yanking her against his chest, he leaned back and rolled over the rail, dragging her with him. He let gravity tug them down, then he directed his thoughts to the sky.

Liza stiffened, and as her fingers tore in panic at the hand over her mouth, Nibs' hold secured Tom. The two men hung over the water, rearranging their grasps so that each brother gripped one of Liza's arms. Nibs supported her hips. Tom made sure to keep her mouth covered. She'd never made a peep before, but he wasn't about to gamble today— she'd never flown before, either. She wouldn't get a chance to holler.

Keeping low to the brine, the brothers and their terrified captive made straight for the *Roger*. The rest of the raid on *L'Ormonde* was up to Jill. Even with her weighty message for Cecco in Nibs' pocket, the young men weren't sure of the welcome with which the captain would greet his prodigals. But they knew, without a doubt, Mr. Yulunga would be eager to see them. Jill had told them all about the scheme she and Yulunga concocted alone in his quarters. She'd appeared at

Nibs' cabin window last night, looking as blown and wild as she'd ever done upon the Island. Once she slid inside, she outlined her instructions. She had negotiated a shrewd bargain with Cecco's mate. One girl— for two boys.

Her sons only hoped she could negotiate as successfully with the surgeon. But by the looks of the man as he married her, if he ever once got her alone below decks, she'd be lucky to see topside again this voyage.

And, unfortunately, Jill seemed just as ardent. Last night, insisting Mr. Yulunga was waiting with a lantern, she'd flown off into the darkness, leaving no explanation for her desire to carry through with the wedding. Their last glimpse of her aboard *L'Ormonde* was a worrisome image that lingered in their minds— her black gloves loosening the knot of Hanover's white cravat. They had to trust that his good looks and his riches wouldn't tempt her to get herself trapped in his cabin. Her sons knew of her weakness for pirate treasure.

The trouble was, so did the dashing doctor.

The sails were reefed and Mullins secured his cable, preparing to inspect the *Roger*'s rudder. From his post at the stern, Cecco eyed the increasing sea between his ship and LeCorbeau's.

"If my suspicions are correct, Mr. Mullins—"

"Ahoy, Captain!" Mr. Noodler called down from the crow's nest. "Something approaching, Sir, to portside!"

Cecco had already seen it. As its movement became distinct from that of the waves, he leapt to the port rail, snatching a shroud for balance. Raising the spyglass, he waited for the image to clear. He felt his heart constrict. A wide skirt whipped in the wind. Two figures supported the female. Her dress was dark…but it wasn't Jill's.

It was Liza. With Nibs and Tom.

Scanning the sea behind them, Cecco found no sign of Jill. He hurtled down and threw the spyglass to Yulunga.

"Your girl."

"Yes, Captain."

The two men locked stares. Cecco drew out the moment, then, scathingly, he said, "Jill has kept her word to one of us, anyway."

"You must give her time, Captain. As she requested."

"I am finished with giving. Now I take something."

"Sir?"

"If LeCorbeau wants Mr. Nibs, he will have to fight for him."

Yulunga didn't risk a smile. "The lady hoped you'd feel that way, Sir."

"The lady presumes too much."

Cheers from Cecco's men interrupted, greeting Nibs and Tom. Cecco turned to glare at Jill's boys.

Out of breath, the young sailors alighted on the rail. The girl swayed between them, weak-kneed and windblown.

Nibs panted, "Permission to board, Captain?" He lowered his chin, anticipating Cecco's wrath. Tom's shoulders heaved, too, but he couldn't hold back a grin.

Cecco scowled at them. "Mr. Yulunga."

Yulunga strode forward to pluck Liza from the rail. In shock, she collapsed into his arms. As Yulunga carried her down the steps, her frenzied gaze roved the deck of the ship she'd thought never to see again. Her captor settled her on the wooden deck to huddle before the mainmast. His huge hand swept the hair from her face, and he caught sight of her ears.

He grunted as he examined them. Two piercings, one on each lobe. But no earrings; Yulunga wore those. "You will stay here where I can watch you." He gripped her wrists. "You should know. Before she left with your father, Red-Handed Jill gave you to me."

In her panic, Liza clenched her hands. She looked everywhere, in case her father had appeared on the *Roger* as magically as she did, but she already knew the truth. He wasn't here.

"You gave yourself to me, too, last night. You'll do it again later."

Liza gaped with widening eyes. That wasn't what had happened. It was just the once. She'd only meant—

"I have work to do." Yulunga released her wrists. "I think you know better than to make more trouble?" He leveled a stare at her.

Liza blinked. She nodded.

"I didn't hear you." Yulunga angled his head to bring an ear closer to her lips.

She was still bound to her father. He forbade her to speak, about anything. He trusted her to hold his secrets. And Liza trusted him; she trusted he would find her here and snatch her back. Wouldn't he? Liza searched behind her but she couldn't see *L'Ormonde*. She had no need to see it. She knew she couldn't anger her father now. The two of them had come to an accord. Duty and pleasure had at last combined.

"You may speak. I'll say it one more time."

She wished Yulunga would order her to do something else—anything else.

"You know better than to make trouble."

Liza knew better than to cross Yulunga. He squatted right in front of her, inches away. She could feel the heat of his body. Her father was far over the sea.

But Liza's voice was imprisoned. It couldn't escape, not even in a whisper. Slowly, Yulunga shook his head, a malevolent gleam in his eye. Liza shuddered.

"As I said. Later." He touched her earlobe, the one he himself hadn't pierced. Looking down on her, he rose to his full, terrifying height, blocking out the sky.

He was a mountain of a man. Liza felt herself go weak. She could smell his power. She felt dizzier now than when Nibs and Tom had somehow spirited her across the water. At last Yulunga turned away and charged up the steps to his captain's side, leaving Liza to sit stunned, in continuing silence, wondering what would happen to her next.

As Yulunga had borne his captive from the rail, Cecco signaled to Nibs and Tom. They'd jumped down to stand penitent before their captain.

"I have no time to deal with you young rebels. Your mother sails farther every moment, and our rudder is jammed." He strode away to the stern.

Nibs and Tom gawked at one another. At the same instant, the answer dawned on each of them. They bent down and hauled at their boots. When their feet were free, they scrambled for the stern, peeling off their French blue jackets as they ran. Nibs sent his orange kerchief fluttering to the deck, then dug in his pocket to toss the pouch holding Jill's message on top of it. Bounding over the rail, the brothers dove.

Cecco, Mullins, and an increasing crowd of pirates hung over the stern, peering into the water where the lady's sons had splashed and vanished. The white water churned, then settled. A few bubbles broke the surface. The *Roger* rode up and down on the waves.

After a minute Nibs' head emerged from the brine, sleek as a seal. "Captain," he gasped. He drew breath to shout. "It's those wedges! The ones we used on the Dutchman." Tom's wet head bounced up beside him, spitting.

Cecco leaned over the rail. "As I suspected. You know what to do— if you wish to make yourselves indispensable."

Nibs dark face lit with determination. "Aye, aye, Sir!"

Tom grinned. "Right away, Captain!" Drawing deep gulps of air, Cecco's sailors bobbed up, then sank into the depths.

As the salty water swallowed them up, they hardly noticed the chill. Their captain wasn't satisfied with his rebels yet. But it sure felt good to be home.

Jill had observed her sons over Hanover's shoulder, while she loosened his cravat. At the prearranged time, Nibs disappeared from the deck. Tom and Liza followed, more clumsily. Soon Jill spied them speeding away, an awkward flock heading out to sea, aiming for the pearl on the horizon that was the *Roger*. All according to plan, the tightness around her heart relaxed. She felt almost faint with relief, as light as a water bird, nearly soaring herself. Her boys had escaped.

Jill had only to pry herself from the surgeon now, along with his information. She retied his cravat.

"My dear Doctor. You have had your wedding. Now I must have my answers."

Hanover clasped her hands and raised them to his lips. Kissing each, he looked sorrowfully into Jill's blue eyes. "My darling. How I regret to be the bearer of sad tidings."

"If the news is sad, it matters little who brings it. Where is Captain Hook?"

"I am afraid the man you loved no longer exists. Perhaps he never lived."

"I ask for truth. You give me riddles."

Hanover bowed his head. "I am sorry. Quite simply, then. On the day he disappeared, I learned that your captain had defiled my daughter— ravished her…more than once."

Jill was stabbed by an ache in her gut. She resisted the impulse to double up. Hanover clung to her hands.

"Yes, I understand how difficult it is for you to hear the truth." He waited for her eyes to meet his again. "Liza was afraid to come to me. Ashamed. It was only when I came upon them, in my quarters, that I comprehended." The scar upon his face tightened at the memory, and his voice grew bitter with disgust. "Hook had torn her clothing away. He was covering her, like some kind of beast. Of course I had to stop him. I acted immediately. I struck him, with my cane…" Hanover's voice softened. "A blow to the head."

Jill's hand, masked in black, rushed to cover her eyes. She had tried to prepare herself for news of Hook's death. She had expected it. But this news was worse.

"Only long after I dealt with him did Liza indicate the extent of the captain's violations."

Jill shook her head. She had prepared, also, to discard untruth.

"I am sorry, my darling. I would spare you if I could."

She lowered her hand from her eyes. Her fingers curled. "You are telling me— that you killed him."

"I confess it. I had to defend my daughter."

Carefully, she blinked. The hilt of Hanover's sword came into focus. "And…what then?"

"I sought out my closest ally at that time."

"An…ally."

"With the captain dead and my daughter despondent, I needed another man's aid."

For a long moment, Jill closed her eyes.

"Again, my dearest, I apologize."

She stood dreading, expectant.

"I turned to Mr. Cecco."

"Cecco." Her jaw rose with her voice. "No. No, you couldn't have."

"I had no recourse but to enlist his assistance. He sympathized. He agreed that if the men discovered that Captain Hook had died at my hands, I would stand very little chance of explaining. I would be murdered." The surgeon's manner grew gentle again. "Cecco helped me to…to consign Hook's remains. To the sea."

"This cannot be true. I would know it."

"My darling." He gathered her into his arms. "I believe you *do* know."

A cold breeze lifted the ringlet on her neck. "His hook—"

"Has disappeared. I set it aside to prove to you— but it is gone. I believe that Liza, in her torment, disposed of it." Hanover reached within his waistcoat. "But I do have proof. It will be painful for you, yet I know you will wish to see it. Give me your hand."

But Jill stood staring at nothing, her eyes searching for a place to settle. Hanover cupped her hand in his. Something golden dropped into her palm, bright against the black of her glove. Jill refused to look at it.

"His earring, my dear. I wouldn't allow the gypsy to claim it."

Her fingers closed over it. Her heart threatened to close, as well. "The gypsy."

"I should have suspected then, when he demanded Captain Hook's jewels. I only knew he had acted to help me. I owed him a great deal— my life, even. I followed his instructions, tipping the balance to win him the captaincy. He promised to protect me, and to protect Liza. I didn't understand, then, to what depths he would sink to steal you."

"Almost as deep as those into which *you* have sunk."

"Jill. You are beside yourself, grieving. You will understand, in time."

"I understand now."

"Then you see, now, that your Captain Cecco has deceived you. He knew of Hook's fate all along."

"As did you."

"Captain Cecco held the power. He held my diamonds. And he held you. I was in no position to reveal the truth. You will remember that he forbade me even to speak with you. Cecco might have turned on me at any moment. My darling, I am not proud of what I had to do, but surely you will forgive me. I acted for the best. I used my knowledge of Hook's fate to draw you away from your new master. His own barbaric behavior helped. I was lucky to have escaped with my scars. Your pirate captain is a brutal man. Given time, I am certain he would have hurt you, too."

"You wish me to believe that my first love assaulted your daughter, that my next withheld the truth. And now my husband—"

"Loves you beyond the capabilities of either." He squeezed her hand. "We have both suffered damage. Yet the cruelest blow of all has descended upon the most innocent: our daughter. Our daughter needs you."

Jill's forehead creased with question.

"Liza requires a mother more than ever now. It is a matter of some delicacy. You see…I examined her, of course. She is as healthy as can be expected, under the circumstances. I have every reason to believe our daughter will carry Captain Hook's child to term."

For Jill, the brilliance of the mid-day sky went black. She reeled, pushing the back of her hand to her mouth. Hanover reached to support her, but she jerked up her elbows and tugged free. If she was ever going to escape this man, the time was now. She felt his lies weighing upon her. She couldn't afford to become bogged down in his tales. The ship seemed to pitch as she backed away. Groping for the stern, Jill blinked to clear her vision. She sensed the ship's rail at her back. She gripped it. Hanover caught up to her and took her in his grasp. As his body pressed against hers, his rapier prodded her hip.

"My Jill. My precious wife. You see why I wished you never to know. And why I am forced to inform you."

Jill looked to the sky. It seemed clear now. Not a puff of cloud… just black.

She shook his hands from her shoulders. She felt the necklaces encircling her throat, choking her. Her arms ached, heavy with jewelry, but his grip had gone. Jill twisted to face the sea. She raised up on her toes. She felt the deck beneath them. She waited for the waves to rise, to nudge the ship upward and give her a boost.

Hanover kept his distance, watching her. "Please, tell me how I can make your affliction lighter."

She kicked off her slippers. "Let me breathe!"

"Of course."

Something solid in her hand distracted her. She discovered she still grasped Hook's earring. Visualizing it in his ear, she stared at the horizon. She had to fly.

"Yes. Drop it in the sea. You will never have to look at it again."

She held it fast. The gold seemed to drag her hand down. That familiar, faint pulse within her soul started up, fighting back. She wanted to believe. Hook's heart was beating. It *had* to be beating.

"Jill. Let me help you."

"Yes, Johann. Help me." She spoke over her shoulder. "Tell me that you are as fine a storyteller as I."

"My dear—"

"You lie!" Pushing her toes against the boards, she concentrated. Captain Hook was alive. He never touched the girl. Never—

"You are distressed."

The *Roger*. Jill could see it. Hook wasn't aboard *L'Ormonde*. He might be on the *Roger*…

Jill became aware of a sensation. It was pain. Her toes hurt. She was digging them into the deck, trying to shove off from it. But the rough boards were stubborn; they wouldn't let her go.

The *Roger* lay just a few leagues away. Cecco was aboard her. If only she could touch him. Then she would know without a doubt. The surgeon's account had to be a fabrication. Hanover would say anything to break her. She knew it. She would swear Cecco never suspected what happened to Hook! Jill marshaled her faculties and sent all her thoughts flying toward the *Roger*. All her thoughts— but not herself.

Liza was aboard there, instead. Jill remembered now. Liza didn't look well. Jill recalled the sight of her opals, these stones she felt at her neck, now, bearing down upon her. Hook's opals, dangling against Liza's new dress…as the girl clutched her belly.

No.

Not Hook. The man who took liberties with Liza might be anyone. Yulunga. Not Hook. Not Cecco. Jill shoved Hook's earring inside her glove. She laid her hands on the balustrade. Her feet rose at last, to swing up to it. Her skirt swirled with them, sighing, and she settled to straddle the taffrail. She felt Hanover seize her waist. She swayed there, fighting off his hands. "Let go. Let me go!"

"My dear, you are hysterical."

She drew her dagger. "You're free to believe it. And I'm free to fly." Her knife flashed as she slashed at him.

He yanked himself back. "Jill!"

She ignored him. Gripping the rail with her heels, Jill leaned into the wind. She closed her eyes, envisioning the *Roger*'s figurehead— the Beauty…*Bellezza*. Her own face was carved upon it. The figurehead was she, and she was flying at the fore of her ship. She held the dagger aloft the way the Beauty upheld her hook.

When she opened her eyes again, she wasn't airborne yet, but another miracle had occurred. The *Roger* was coming about. Cecco must sense she was in trouble. He was coming! Jill stretched out her arms to him. The sun shone on them, shone in his bracelets. She would see their mates shining on his own arms, soon. He was sailing toward her. Jill's red hand reached for him. He never refused her hand. Cecco's love for her was true.

Jill was floating now, an inch above the rail. Straining for Cecco, she could see him in her mind. She heard his bangles. She felt his arms surrounding her, embracing her, just as the breeze was doing now. The same breeze that bore the *Roger* toward her. Induced by that breeze, the *Roger*'s sails bellied out full…like a woman with child.

Captain Hook's child…

Jill sank. Concentrating again, she managed to buoy herself. The dagger in her hand belonged to Hook. He'd stowed it under her pillow, to keep her safe. Hook's protection pulled her, even now. She squeezed the hilt, like a lever, to lift herself up. She rose to float a little higher over the railing. The jewels of his dagger dug into her scarlet palm. Jewels, with which Hook loved to tempt her. The jewels were real, they were solid, like Hook. She could feel him. She felt his lips in the kiss of the wind. She could feel the gems…through her glove. The glove that smothered the stain of Hook's lifeblood.

A black glove…the color of mourning.

The wood of the rail felt hard beneath her. Jill dropped her longing arms. The wind, not a kiss, whipped her lips.

Jill turned her face away.

Surrendering the dagger to her sash, she looked to the sea below. It was gray again, as on the day Hook disappeared. Gray, as her new husband's eyes.

Jill didn't look at the *Roger* again.

She turned to *L'Ormonde.*

Hanover settled his hands upon her. Gently, with his strong arms, he pulled her from her perch and set her on the deck. "Madam. You are in shock." He took her face in his fingers. "Let me tend to you."

She gazed into those eyes. Gray. The color of nothing.

He smiled and kissed her cold, cold lips.

At the prearranged time, all according to plan, Jill's charade had ended. But Jill wasn't home. The wrong man embraced her. On the wrong ship, bearing the wrong direction.

And then Jill recalled Cecco's fingers around her throat. She remembered the ruthlessness in his eyes…the threat in his voice, the chill of his knife.

Like a bird of prey, the *Roger* swooped toward her. Deep in the pit of her stomach, Jill churned.

"My own. My Jill. You belong to me now. You must leave everything to your husband."

"Yes, Johann." He was the wrong man…but he was right. "I will," she murmured. "I will trust in my husband."

She couldn't fly, but she still possessed her weapons.

And then she *did* fly— into the loving arms of the surgeon.

A Parting Word

"*Commandant! Mon Commandant! Le Joli Rouge! Il approche! Il approche!*"

Hanover stiffened. He jerked up his head to behold the black flag behind *L'Ormonde*, just like Jill's skirts, flapping in the breeze.

Feet pounded the deck as men rushed to the rail. Hanover's gaze shot back to Jill, his eyes accusing. "You knew he would come for you."

"No. But I should have known."

Hanover remained angry, but shed his hostility. "Yes, I can read the fright in your face. You must get below. Liza, too." He looked around. "Where is she?"

Liza was nowhere in sight. LeCorbeau was shouting. The ship's bell burst into frantic hammering. Renaud and Guillaume chimed in, urging the men to their stations. Sailors scrambled aloft, gun crews ran to their cannons.

"We must find her immediately. Then you will both keep to our quarters. Lock yourselves in."

"I will settle Liza in. But you married a pirate, Johann. I won't leave my husband's side."

He squeezed her shoulders. "My brave Jill. You must learn to listen to reason."

"What will you do?"

His hand fell to grip the hilt of his sword. "I will fight, of course. But surely we can outrun them. We have a head start, and *L'Ormonde* is a lighter vessel."

"Lighter, because she has fewer guns. And fewer men." Jill's pride fought with her fear. "If she grapples us, we haven't a chance."

Every man aboard knew it. All worked at top speed to let out every inch of sail and ready the weapons. The crew of *L'Ormonde* had witnessed the aftermath of the *Roger's* battles. After months of sailing as allies, they knew her men too well to stand at the wrong end of their blades.

LeCorbeau strutted to the stern, his spyglass in hand. "So, *mon ami*, now we are to be treated to treachery! *Alors*, one can never trust a pirate." Sharply, he said to Jill, "It would seem, *Madame*, that I guessed correctly. Your, eh…captain…is unable to make himself part with you." He raised the spyglass. "*Quel dommage.* I am not feeling generous today."

"Nor am I." The surgeon stared at the rival ship. "The only wonder is that he allowed us to get this far."

LeCorbeau smirked. "It is no wonder, my dear Doctor. My Guillaume saw to that. With his souvenirs— the clever wedges he pried from the Dutch merchantman."

Smug now, Hanover said, "So. A taste of her own medicine for the *Roger?*"

"Yes, certainly. I have only been awaiting the opportunity to administer it."

"Well done, LeCorbeau. You anticipated a chase, then?"

"I am, after all, one of those seamen who believe in the bad luck of lady passengers." LeCorbeau eyed Jill again. "Especially those who have allied themselves with pirates."

Jill drew her dignity around her, like a cloak. "Yet you, *Commandant*, also partner pirates. Do you not?"

Glowering, the Frenchman gave a warning shake of his head, then darted a glance at Hanover.

The surgeon's face set in determined lines. "No, Jill," he said, "That unpleasantness is ended. As soon as the wind carries us out of sight, we are forever free."

Jill looked back at the *Roger*, magnificent under full white sails, her gilded accoutrements gleaming. She caught the sparkle of water on the oars as the sweeps raised and dipped in the sea. Clearly, Captain

Cecco had ordered his men to make all speed. Jill's heart lagged behind *L'Ormonde*, dragging like an anchor. She wouldn't escape Cecco's wrath. He had sworn it, sealed with their accord.

Hanover said, "And now, LeCorbeau, where have you directed my daughter?"

"I? I remind you, Hanover, all the females aboard my ship are your responsibility. I last saw her dancing with *Monsieur* Tootles. Clumsy oaf that he is— no doubt you will soon be bandaging the damaged toes."

"Then you will excuse me." With grim resolve, Hanover swept Jill along the port side, searching for Liza the while. "I know I saw them toward the stern. I trust that your sons—" He stopped, and a flicker of doubt crossed his face. "Madam. Surely your sons would not hold a grudge?"

"Oh, no, Johann. They were eager for a fresh start, happy to be part of a family again. You saw them. They behaved like perfect gentlemen." The couple hurried forward once more.

"Then where have they—"

A distant thunder interrupted him. He and Jill halted, staring at one another. Turning aft, they saw white smoke rising in a cloud. The *Roger* still sailed well behind, out of range. But she had fired her first, warning shot. The blast of it struck terror in Jill's heart. The same terror any other quarry would feel.

With increasing urgency, Hanover guided Jill around the deck again, keeping well behind the guns and their crews, peering into every open space between. Cannonballs clanged as they rolled down the iron muzzles. Jill raised her voice to be heard among the mounting shouts of the sailors.

"Perhaps the boys escorted her below, Johann."

"But they were just here." Men were running with bags of powder. Pulling Jill from their path, Hanover drew her aft. The couple ascended again to the quarterdeck, where LeCorbeau swiveled his head about, as if he, too, had lost something.

"Renaud!"

His first mate hustled to his side, out of breath.

"Well?"

"I am sorry, *Commandant*," said Renaud, "I cannot locate him. He is not at his post."

"Look in his quarters. Look in his brother's hammock!"

With a dispirited countenance, Guillaume scurried toward them up the steps, his key ring jingling in his hand. "*Commandant*, I have already searched there. Mr. Nibs is not to be found." He looked down at his fingers, at the key to a certain compartment, rubbing it before stashing it away. "Nor is Mr. Tootles."

Another blast erupted from the *Roger*. This shot was no warning. It rushed whistling toward *L'Ormonde*, falling to plunk in the sea not far away. LeCorbeau raised his spyglass. "What is that madman meaning? He must know he cannot catch—" The captain went rigid. He stared through the glass.

"Commandant?"

His words came hissing, softly. *"Mon Dieu."*

"What is it, LeCorbeau?" asked Hanover. "You look as if you've seen a ghost." He released Jill and moved to his partner's side. Renaud and Guillaume turned to stare across the water. Their captain simply stood there, unmoving except for the rippling of the wind in his cuffs.

Jill caught sight of the *Roger*'s bow. Something had appeared where it didn't belong, blooming on the bowsprit, above the figurehead. She couldn't make it out. Silently, LeCorbeau lowered the glass. Hanover intercepted it. In another moment, he, too, exclaimed.

"How? How can this be?"

Jill knew what they saw, now. She laid a gentle hand on her new husband's shoulder. "Johann. Let me look."

He turned to her. Disbelief etched his features, the dueling scar a deep red line against his jaw. "It is impossible. And yet I see it."

Inhaling a steadying breath first, Jill hoisted the glass and examined the *Roger*. The lens revealed a tri-cornered hat in the crow's nest: Mr. Noodler. A full complement of men clung to the rigging. As they plunged their weapons in the air, the flash of them stabbed Jill's eye. She couldn't hear their jeering over the hubbub of *L'Ormonde*, but she well remembered it. Below the sails, a large black man leaned into the wind of the prow. A boarding ax waited in his belt. Next to him stood a sturdy man in a blue jacket. It was the unmistakable figure of Tom, his hands behind him as if tied there. Balanced astride the bowsprit rode the muscular form of Cecco. He held a cutlass, and the gleam of its point shone just inches from a huddle of maroon material. A patch of orange hovered above the dress, and a slash of French blue belted its waist: Liza, perched on Nibs' lap. She dangled above the water, on the beam of the bowsprit, secured there by Nibs' arms— and little else. To all appearances, the *Roger* held three hostages.

LeCorbeau's voice waxed thin. "Renaud."

His first officer leaned closer to hear his orders. Guillaume supported his captain's arm. Disbelieving, Hanover listened as the Frenchman delivered a brief command.

"Reef sails."

"Oui, Commandant."

Renaud moved to execute the order, but halted as LeCorbeau clutched his coat. "And…" LeCorbeau rotated, slowly, to level a vicious glare at Jill. "Strike the colors."

Renaud turned his head, as if he hadn't heard right. *"Monsieur?"*

"You heard me! Surrender!"

"The ship, *Monsieur?"*

Hanover strode forward. "LeCorbeau. You cannot do this!"

"Don't be a fool. Of course I shall not surrender my ship."

"Then— what is your strategy?"

Jill inched backward. From under her lashes, she watched LeCorbeau. His glittering stare pierced her.

"It is not my ship that Captain Cecco desires." With increasing malevolence, he rolled his black eyes toward Hanover. "He wants your wife."

Hanover staggered. "LeCorbeau…"

"It is even as I feared. The pirate makes the exchange, only to steal the goods later. Well. He shall have them!"

"No! Not after all I've endured to win her. My wife stays with me."

"Je regrette, mon ami. But I can afford to part with only one of you."

"We will negotiate. I will give him the remainder of my diamonds—" Hanover faced his wife. "Jill, you must give them up. Where have you stored the rest of our riches?"

Jill's complexion was white. "Johann—"

The captain swore. "Had the man desired your diamonds, *Monsieur*, he would already possess them! *Mon Dieu*, he is as stubborn as you! He will not relent until he holds Red-Handed Jill." He shoved his mate forward. "Renaud, carry out my order!"

"No, LeCorbeau," persisted Hanover, "You are a fighting man. You must resist these pirates."

"A fighting man, yes. My ship and my men are prepared for battle. But it is one thing to attack a merchant vessel of limited crew. Quite another to rescue hostages and fend off a pack of pirates!" He frowned at the *Roger*. "Hook's pirates."

Hanover dropped his gaze. "Hostages…"

LeCorbeau hissed, "If we are to remove your daughter and my Mr. Nibs from Captain Cecco's grasp, your woman must be the price."

"Too high a price."

"Johann." Jill stood rooted to the spot, barely able to breathe. The men turned to her. "Captain Cecco has no wish to recapture me."

Hanover lowered his brows. "I don't understand."

"If he wanted to keep me, he would have challenged you before we left his ship."

"He is challenging me now!"

"No, Johann. Captain Cecco wishes to preserve your well-being. After all, he has an interest in your survival."

"But this makes no sense."

"It makes perfect sense. He has demanded a piece of your future. Has he not, *Commandant?*"

"*Oui*. It is true."

Hanover spun to glare at the Frenchman. "You never promised him—"

"But of course I promised. You instructed me to bargain as high as necessary. In any case, I had no recourse but to agree. The greedy man would not release you without such an arrangement." LeCorbeau shrugged. "There was little to be gained by denying him."

"Exactly what have you done?"

"I have agreed to deliver a percentage of our profits. The first rendezvous shall take place in one year's time. Like it or not, you now find yourself in partnership with your adversary. He and I both have reason to keep you healthy."

"Then I will have the advantage." Hanover squared his shoulders. "I will fight him— for Jill, for Liza. For Mr. Nibs, even."

As he gripped his sword, Jill touched his sleeve with her black glove. "No, Johann. It will not be necessary to fight."

"Jill…What do you know of this situation?"

"I know that Captain LeCorbeau must allow the men of the *Roger* to board *L'Ormonde*. I know they will not harm you. Captain Cecco will release Nibs and Liza, and maybe even Tom."

"And carry you away?"

"No. Cecco will not take me back. It is too late for that."

"Then—"

"He made me a promise."

"A promise! More gold, I suppose. Or my diamonds?"

"No, Johann." Jill's gaze held steady. "Captain Cecco promised to kill me."

Hanover's horrified silence was shattered— by another blast from Cecco's cannons.

The moment the grappling hooks dug in, the officers of the *Roger* swung across. Mr. Yulunga and his ax, Mr. Smee, Mr. Mullins and Mr. Starkey, all armed with blazing cutlasses, pistols at the ready, and daggers in their teeth. The mass of the *Roger* loomed behind them, her sails furled and her black flag streaming, her masts tall as the pines from which they were cut. Jill watched her warriors, fearful and fascinated by the force Captain Hook had constructed. Their calls echoed in crescendo, a cacophony of threats fierce enough to eliminate resistance before it began. A practiced chant from merciless men, led now by Hook's successor— a man just as dangerous as he, every bit as ruthless, and, perhaps, more passionate.

He stood on the rail of the *Roger*, staring at Jill. With his hair bound back under his gypsy crown, with his weighty necklace, and his vest barely covering his upper body, Cecco looked as savage as his notoriety claimed. Jill felt Hanover tightening his grip on her shoulders.

Scanning the faces of Cecco's officers, she found herself leaning toward the shelter of the surgeon. To a man, the pirates' weathered features showed no lenience. Even Smee's eyes reproached her behind his spectacles. She was Mrs. Heinrich now. A traitor to the *Roger*.

Mullins turned to toss his cable back. Cecco caught it. He leapt from the ship and soared to *L'Ormonde*, his dark eyes colder than Jill had ever seen them— no flicker of love left to warm her. Even the glint of his jewelry struck chill.

On the portside, two planks bounced into position, and the bulk of the *Roger's* pirates stamped across, bellowing, swarming over *L'Ormonde*. Within seconds LeCorbeau's crew stood surrounded. As ordered by their captain, the Frenchmen stowed their swords. Starkey directed the victors as they herded the privateers toward the bow. Only LeCorbeau and his mates were left to stand before the mast, Hanover and Jill beside them. Dainty remains of the wedding feast lay spread on the table close by, the festive cask of wine near its head. The cries of the pirates died down, their weaponry lowered, and all hands turned to watch the captains.

LeCorbeau donned a sardonic smile. "Well, my partner. I had not thought to meet up with you again so soon."

"You did your best to prevent it." Cecco's broad shoulders were relaxed, but ready. His cutlass, too.

The Frenchman flung up his hands. "Merely a precaution against foul play. But, eh, you are welcome aboard. I trust you will inflict no damage, now that I have so grandly made this gesture."

"No damage that will distress *you*, my friend." Cecco's bangles played their familiar music as he set his hands on his weapons. Jill's heart sped at the sound. Once upon a time, she had welcomed it. Now it filled her with dread.

"*Madame* assures me, Captain Cecco, that your business is with her alone?"

Cecco's glacial gaze burned into her. "Yes. I have come for Red-Handed Jill." Like a living thing, anxiety rose within her, railing against her ribs.

Hanover stepped in front of Jill. "The lady is now my wife. Mrs. Heinrich."

"Ah, Doctor. My newest partner. Yes, I witnessed the festivities. This is the reason I am here."

"Captain, I must protest! You released the lady this morning. To go back on your word now is beneath you."

Cecco came forward to stand before the doctor. "But I do not go back on my word. I come now to keep it."

"You'll keep it over my corpse."

LeCorbeau hastened closer to reason with Cecco, attempting to draw him off. "Eh, you must excuse our doctor, Captain. He has not yet come to terms with our arrangement. Perhaps it will help him to see his daughter again?"

"Yes." Cecco turned to Yulunga. "Send for the prisoners."

Glancing across the water, LeCorbeau identified Nibs and sighed in satisfaction.

Yulunga gestured to the *Roger*, calling, "Permission to board!"

Nibs jumped on the plank and reached for Liza. Supporting her with a firm grasp, he assisted her across. Her eyes were frightened, her face pale as parchment. Tom followed, with his hand on her shoulder. Except for their blue jackets and Nibs' orange kerchief, the two men's clothing looked damp. When the prisoners descended to the deck, neither man released the girl, but instead stood protectively around her.

Moving to the portside rail, Mullins and Yulunga took up stations behind them, like jailers. Aware of Yulunga's proximity, Liza stood as if frozen, staring into her father's eyes. He nodded encouragement to his daughter, and she breathed more easily.

Jill looked Liza over. Her empty insides hurt as she became aware that the young woman held one hand on her belly, as if to protect her precious burden. Jill had raised several sons, not of her flesh, but, unlike herself, Liza bore a child in her womb. Jill didn't know that feeling. Did Liza, too, sense a lover's pulse beating within her? Jill stood staring, her new knowledge smarting like a fresh, raw wound. Her jewelry glimmered on her arms, her ankles, her neck, fingers, and ears. Her red hand in its black disguise rested on her abdomen— the one part of her body devoid of treasure. How much had Liza stolen?

Hanover put an end to her reflections, nudging his wife backward.

He turned to Cecco. "I am pleased to see my daughter's return, and my stepsons' also. I cannot, however, stand by and watch you wreak your vengeance on my wife." He drew his rapier singing from its sheath. "I can do no less than to challenge you."

"Very clever, Doctor. By now you know I have no wish to harm you. Which, assuredly, were I to accept your challenge, I would do." Cecco gazed past Hanover, to Jill. "Let us leave it to the lady to propose the conditions of her surrender."

As he stood before her, unrelenting and ominous in the strong sun, Jill blinked at the glare of his regalia. At the same time, Mullins raised his cutlass. Yulunga hoisted his ax. Flanking Liza, Nibs and Tom stood between these weapons. Cecco didn't have to turn to watch his orders to threaten Jill's sons carried out. He could see the alarm in her eyes. Hanover exclaimed, and LeCorbeau backed off, swearing.

Cecco smiled. "Jill. Lovely one. You are a brilliant strategist. How do you suggest we come to terms?"

Jill made to step out from behind Hanover, but he blocked her. "No, Jill. This is a fight between men."

"My dear Doctor," Jill said, "Will you never understand?" She slipped around him. "If it weren't for a woman, no one I love would be in peril." She turned to face Cecco. Her black silks surrounded her. Her fair hair shone. "I have done my duty, and I stand by my actions. Captain Cecco, I leave it to you to judge."

At last, Cecco laid his hands upon her. He drew her away from Hanover, who stood scowling at them, his sword poised to strike. But Smee had sidled up behind Hanover. The instant the surgeon moved, Smee gripped his wrist. Smee's cutlass rose swiftly to caress the man's cheek. "Let's not be hasty, now, Mister Hanover."

Restraining his partner's other arm, LeCorbeau reasoned, "Calm yourself, Hanover. Let us hear what the woman proposes." He turned a look of suspicion upon the female who had caused him so much inconvenience.

Standing before Cecco, Jill glanced again at her sons' predicament, then raised her chin. "Sir. I am trusting you."

"As I trusted you." Cecco wrapped his hand around her throat. Jill felt the heat of it.

Nibs and Tom shifted. Mullins and Yulunga moved malignantly closer to the prisoners, narrowing their circle.

Cecco's grip on Jill's neck tightened. She felt the opals, beneath his palm, digging into her flesh. Cecco looked into her eyes. His gaze was warm, now, affectionate, as if he meant to stroke instead of strangle her. To ease her gagging, Jill raised up on her tiptoes. She clutched Cecco's forearms. Her body tautened as she waited for the pressure of his fingers to increase.

Hanover struggled against Smee, but Smee held firm as his cutlass guaranteed to carve another scar. LeCorbeau's grip, too, confined the surgeon, and Hanover held his tongue, sensible that the sound of his voice might spur Cecco to the murder he promised.

As he restrained Hanover, Smee stood tensed, ready for anything. He'd seen Jill charm her way out of worse situations. As Mrs. Heinrich, she was still a match for a captain. Smee wouldn't have to allow the surgeon to intervene. The gypsy couldn't live without Jill— and he wouldn't have to. Hook's own sword would see to that.

But now, teetering on her toes, Jill could draw barely enough breath to speak. Her voice was reedy. "The terms of our accord—"

"Are intact." Cecco relaxed. He smiled his gypsy smile. "Mr. Nibs delivered your message." With his free hand, Cecco pulled a leather pouch from his vest. It was nicely weighted with a fistful of diamonds. As he dangled the pouch before Jill's eyes, it swung in a satisfying manner. His voice softened. "My Jill would never leave her jewels behind. Your heart is as loyal as my own." He lowered the bag into her black-gloved hand. "You would have returned to me, if you were able."

Recognizing the pouch, Hanover gasped. By the port rail, Mullins and Yulunga dropped their threatening stances. Nibs and Tom loosened up, laughing out loud, and between the brothers, Liza gaped, bewildered, as Cecco employed his grip on Jill's throat again— this time to draw his queen toward him, just as the *Roger* had grappled *L'Ormonde*.

Breathing freely again, Jill broke out a beautiful smile. She knew her captain; his love for her was true. As all doubt disappeared, she clasped her plunder and pressed against him. Cecco crushed his lady in his embrace, and to the hoots and hollers of two ships' crews, the lovers kissed with all their accustomed ardor, and more.

"Unhand my wife!"

Hanover's face was livid, his scar an ugly gash. As he struggled with Smee, he heard the Irishman murmur at his ear, "Wait your chance, mate." At the same moment, Hanover felt Smee's grip slacken. Confused, Hanover turned toward his captor. Could Smee be taking his side?

The bo'sun nodded, then his grasp on Hanover dwindled to a mere pretense of restraint. The men around them were cheering their captain and tucking their weapons away. Surprised but ready, Hanover watched his wife, waiting for his opportunity.

Smee leaned toward LeCorbeau and nudged him. The Frenchman immediately perceived Smee's shift of allegiance. Subtly, while seeming to watch Captain Cecco, he turned an ear in Smee's direction.

Smee's Irish lilt fell softly. "If you'll be backing my captaincy, I'll be sparing you this partnership. Your profits will be your own." Hanover heard it, too. LeCorbeau aimed a questioning look toward Nibs, and Smee answered, "Aye. I'll throw two young shipmates into the bargain." LeCorbeau's nod of agreement was swift.

Always at his captain's side, Renaud was ready for LeCorbeau's order. It came so low amid the pirates' hilarity that he hardly heard it. "Secure Nibs and the girl. We follow the Irishman." With a jerk of his head, LeCorbeau ordered the message relayed. A few moments later, Guillaume slipped away toward the bow to spread the word among his shipmates.

Cecco released his Jill at last and, smiling, raised her hand in his own. Their matching armbands gleamed. "Well, men. We have recovered our queen. Shall we stay for the wedding feast, or cast off for the honeymoon?"

His men laughed and slapped each other on the back. Those among *L'Ormonde*'s crew did the same with the French sailors, their friendships restored. Everyone grew easy, eager to enjoy the old accord.

Even Smee smiled broadly as he seemed to grapple with Hanover. All affability, he called, "Begging your pardon, Captain. I'm guessing the doctor here has a parting word to say to his wife."

"Yes," Cecco turned to the surgeon. "The word is…'farewell.' " He waved an arm and, preparing to lead Jill to the *Roger*, turned his back.

"Sorry, Captain." Smee was still grinning. "I'm thinking of a different word."

Cecco froze. The smile fell from his face. He turned slowly to stare at his bo'sun.

"Lady," Smee said. "I'm giving you the word. From himself."

Jill nearly dropped her diamonds.

Smee's voice was kindly, but authoritative. "It's time to be giving up your gypsy, Jill."

The *Roger*'s men turned astonished faces toward their captain. LeCorbeau stepped aside, slyly loosing his rapier. Renaud followed suit as the blue-coated sailors at the bow observed, and imitated.

Hanover stood up straight, a superior smile on his lips. "You are correct, Captain. 'Farewell' is the precise word." He yanked his sword arm free. "Jill—"

"Must be choosing one of us, for good and all." Smee strode forward, his cutlass raised, "And that's an order."

"Fight, men!" LeCorbeau hoisted his sword high, "For *L'Ormonde!*" He launched into action, his cuff fluttering as his rapier flew to engage Yulunga. Unprepared, the African jerked back. He drew his cutlass and slapped it at LeCorbeau's rapier, as if attacked by an angry bee. The little captain persevered in a series of stings, driving the massive man aft, away from the group of hostages.

Hanover rushed at Cecco. The pirate dropped Jill's hand and seized his sword, drawing it just in time to stop a deadly thrust. Hanover's eyes lit up. At liberty at last, he wielded his weapon against his rival. He had determined that when he finished, Jill's choice would be final; a dead man couldn't keep her. Cecco resolved much the same, and with a taste for battle, the gentleman and the gypsy fell to.

Smee cleared their way, commandeering Jill's arm and whisking her forward along the deck. Shocked by Smee's revolt, Jill looked around, expecting to discover the reason for it. All she saw was chaos as LeCorbeau's men unleashed their weapons to defend their ship. Taken by surprise, the pirates of the *Roger* fell back to regroup. The battle spread over the boards.

Upon his captain's command, Renaud had charged, swinging his sword at Tom. Tom didn't wait. He vaulted to the plank and retreated to the *Roger*. Renaud sneered, redirecting his threat to Nibs. "Come along, *Monsieur* Nibs, and bring the girl. If you make no trouble, I will let your coward of a brother go free."

"Come and get her!" Nibs dragged Liza backward and shoved her down in the lee of the nearest cannon. Shielding her, he seized the dagger hidden in his boot, and dodged Renaud's blade. Then he put the dagger to use, up and down, stopping Renaud's rapier with clanging jolts until the sound of Tom's feet pounded the plank.

"Nibs!"

Glancing up, Nibs caught the cutlass as it sailed through the air. He turned to Renaud again, and smiled. In short order, the sneer dropped from Renaud's face.

Tom held two more swords, fresh from the *Roger*. Gripping one in each fist, he looked to see where he was needed most. To Tom's right, LeCorbeau had been joined by Guillaume. The slender mate fought bravely, baiting the swinging ax in one of Yulunga's hands as his captain's sword battered the cutlass in the other. To Tom's left, Smee was ushering Jill to safety. Nibs had Renaud at bay. Mullins' beefy hands were full fending off the blond sailor who, spouting French and leading a bunch from the bow, had broken away and headed to portside to reclaim Liza. Tom jumped into the fray to fight side by side with Mullins.

Smee kept Jill moving to the fore until he pushed her into the shelter of the gunwale. She pulled her gaze from the mayhem to give him a desperate, questioning stare. "Conor! What can you be meaning?"

Casting a look around for peril first, Smee gazed down upon her. His eyes sparkled behind his spectacles. "Only this," with one hand clutching his cutlass, Smee snatched her into his arms. He lifted her chin and held it. Then, leaning close, he murmured a dear, familiar phrase.

" '…my love.' "

He kissed her.

Without thinking, Jill responded to those words: Hook's words. She let her arms accept him. With the noise of battle all around, the lost captain's companions— one man and one woman— joined together.

Jill's heart leapt up inside her, as if convinced this kiss came from

Hook himself. Like a tidal wave, the current of his embrace carried her above the conflict. She was floating. Just for a moment, a flash of time, her toes deserted the deck. Then the clash and clamor surrounded her again, the boards were rough beneath her feet— and Smee was gone.

Jill caught herself and steadied. There was a battle to be won. She had no intention of hiding in the gunwales. The blue of her eyes turned steely as she tucked away her diamonds. Pulling Hook's dagger from her sash, she looked first for her sons. Hook had seen to their training; Nibs and Tom were manfully handling the fray.

Jill searched the deck of *L'Ormonde*. Swords rang, blazing in the sunlight. By the mainmast, the white cloth on the table was stained scarlet, goblets lay scattered. The Frenchmen's blue coats mingled with the colors of the pirates. This fight was unanticipated, and Jill perceived that, reluctant to massacre men they considered companions, both crews were marking time, straining to make out the intentions of their captains. Jill looked up to find the rigging bereft of men. No menace there— nor a savior. Dreading the scene that most affected her, Jill braced herself and looked to her lovers.

Cecco and Hanover fought at each others' throats. Their sword hilts crossed, their faces hung inches apart. Cecco's eye held a murderous glint as he set his jaw and shoved. Hanover, his sandy hair disheveled, leaned into the struggle, his teeth gritted and his feet braced against the boards. Jill took in the sight of them, and, in her mind, she heard the voice of authority resonate again.

He had commanded her to choose.

She felt the leather pouch within her bosom. She remembered the feel of that bag in her fingers, when it was full…heavy and bulging. And she recalled the looks on the men's faces as they beheld the fruits of Cecco's schemes. She had vowed not to leave her husband's side. The thought of all those diamonds determined her. Wishing for her sword, Jill gripped her knife, and plunged into the mêlée.

Whatever else happened today, she *wouldn't* be a widow.

"Johann! Captain!" As Jill reached Cecco, he managed a smile but didn't take his gaze from his foe.

"Jill, my lovely. Shall I kill him after all?"

"No, Captain— the agreement."

"Run away from him, Jill." Locked in the struggle, Hanover urged, "Take Liza. Get below!"

"Johann, you married a pirate." Jill focused on the rivals' faces, only a hand span apart. She aimed the dagger at one of them, and thrust it forward.

And then a blast erupted from *L'Ormonde's* bow. As the concussion thundered through their chests, two ships' companies pulled away to gape. Their swords hung in mid-air.

The kick of the cannon rolled it to strain against its tackle, and the scream of the cannonball arched away over the waves. The echo rumbled, and then came silence. All eyes stared at the cloud that covered the privateer's prow.

The white haze billowed to obscure the foredeck. Vague within it, an image began to form. Then a glint of sunlight. As the stench of gunpowder drifted aft, the tread of footsteps hit the boards. Two boots took shape, striding forward from the mist. The men gasped, their faces upturned and staring. The weapons sank in their slackening hands.

LeCorbeau whipped around to find the offender. Guillaume yanked his captain from the reach of Yulunga's sword. The gesture proved unnecessary. Yulunga, like every other man, stood frozen.

Cecco and Hanover had ceased their contention. The gypsy jerked around to see. His eyes widened. His hand flew to sketch his banishing gesture. The surgeon staggered backward, a new cut on his face bright red against his pallor.

Jill's heart had stopped with the explosion, to start up hammering as she witnessed a wonder. By the smoking cannon stood her own Mr. Smee. A torch flared in his hand, and victory glowed upon his face. As Jill's black glove clutched her dagger, her smile began, and brightened. The cloud of smoke dissipated. Gradually, Jill's face grew radiant as the sun.

From oblivion, Hook emerged, to plant his feet and stand, commanding, at the fore of *L'Ormonde*.

Lies and Loyalty

Like his legend, Hook lived. His single hand held his shining rapier ready. Sleek and black, his hair cascaded over his shoulders. On his face spread a dark growth of beard, unshaven and untamed. He was lean, the muscles of his tall frame pronounced, and the bones of his face stood prominently over the shadowed hollows of his cheeks. Sunlight edged the crescent of his hook, which he held poised at his side. Not an ornament graced his person. He wore a flowing white shirt trimmed in lace, perfectly polished boots, and breeches the color of coal. He wore, also, a look of determination. No man mistook his purpose. Hook had risen from the grave, with a vengeance.

In a sweeping glance, he surveyed the scene. As striking as jewels, his sapphire eyes drew Jill's own, and held her. She stood in her black silk gown, a smear of blood on her dagger, rapturous. The force of Hook's gaze prized her heart open and spilled life inside her. The grateful tears gathered, but refused to fall. She didn't dare to blink them away, fearing if she closed her eyes for only one instant, her captain might vanish again.

But Hook was in no danger of disappearing. He was absolutely evident, his reality a palpable thing, arresting every soul aboard. Feared or revered, Hook's presence made captives of them all.

The company stood transfixed, awaiting the sound of his velvet voice. When it fell, it carried no hint of humor.

"Widow's black, Jill. An appropriate costume for this…marriage."

She answered softly, all her feeling concentrated into the word Smee had given her.

"Hook."

Slowly, Jill tucked her dagger in her sash. Concealed in her glove, her crimson fingers rose to touch her lips. Noting their disguise, Hook marked her movement, then transferred his gaze to the groom.

"Congratulations, Hanover. I have come to kiss the bride."

Hanover stumbled back. He didn't feel the trickle of blood on his cheek. His gray gaze traveled up and down, taking in the existence of Captain Hook— the wretch whose remains the good doctor could have sworn must give up the ghost. How on earth had he escaped? By what infernal power was he standing? Hanover felt the wave of shock engulf him, a surge of cold that left his skin clammy but his mind, to his horror, chillingly clear.

Hook had duped him. Somehow, some way, that wily pirate had manipulated the circumstances, again. Despite his chains, despite his deprivation, the man held even his own death hostage.

And then another revelation raised its hideous head. Hanover's every muscle tautened as the thought snaked its way, poisonous as a serpent, into his consciousness. Jill had warned him at the very beginning. Not only did Hook live— Hook held the surgeon's secrets. Every damned and damning indiscretion. Blanching, Hanover shot a look to his daughter. His stomach twisted. Unless he acted to silence the man immediately, it wasn't Hook, now, whose fortunes were endangered.

Hook's gaze followed Hanover's to Liza. Disdaining her as always, Hook spared the girl only a glance. The lovely dress she wore, he knew, proved a heavier burden than it should be. Supported by Nibs and Tom, the doctor's daughter stood wilting against them, her eyes wild. But Hook's stolen jewels were not the encumbrance that dragged her down; it was the weight of her secrets. Confident of those secrets' impending exposure, Hook was done with her. He found the Frenchman.

"LeCorbeau. Tell your men to put up their weapons."

LeCorbeau stammered, "Hook— Hook, my old friend…*Mais… Quelle surprise!* From where have you, eh, blossomed?"

"From the filth of a soil I shall soon sweep away. But I see no need for slaughter. I shall slay only one of your company today." His hook winked in the sunlight.

A sickly pallor spread over the Frenchman's face. "*Alors*, my comrade…of course I had no idea.…But, surely we can find a more civilized way to remedy this situation." He swiveled to address the sailors scattered over the ship. His hands sketched frantic gestures. "At ease, men! At ease!"

Smee strode forth to flank his captain. With the blazing torch in the bo'sun's right hand and the rapier in the captain's left, the two formed a formidable force, reminiscent of the first time Hook and his Irishman commandeered a ship— the *Roger*. His men recalled that fateful night. They conjured the vision of their long-ago leader, floating face down, and looked with doubtful eyes upon the little French captain who ventured to stand in James Hook's way.

Like a thunderhead, Hook's infamous courtesy hung over the company. His sailors recognized the chivalry that preceded his wrath. "I am relieved, for our friendship's sake, DéDé, that you choose to be reasonable. Any other response should prove so unpleasant." Lowering his chin, he aimed his eyes at the surgeon. "Doctor Hanover. I challenge you, for the hand of the lady." His rapier rose, gleaming.

LeCorbeau supplicated, "But Hook! I have never known you to act in the heat of the moment— against your own interests. You must now be practical, for the welfare of your profits. Of course you cannot be aware— how could you know?— the doctor has entered into a partnership with the *Roger*."

"With the *Roger*, yes." At last, Hook's gaze rolled to Cecco. "But not with me."

Assured that this haunting was no ghost, Cecco had overcome his shock. His dark eyes watched Hook, and when he was convinced of the honesty of his own senses, Cecco dragged his gaze to Jill. For the first time, her lover was hesitant to look upon her.

Her cheeks were rosy with emotion, her eyes bright— as bright as Hook's. Never taking those eyes from her first captain, she stood between Cecco and Hanover, as still as the wooden Beauty that graced the *Roger*'s prow. Cecco lowered his weapon. To ensure she was still the warm-blooded woman of his heart, he laid his dusky hand upon her. He drew Jill to his other side, making his body a barrier to the surgeon.

As Hook and the gypsy studied one another, a realization unfolded for Cecco— moment by moment— and he gathered the implications of his commander's return. With his heart sinking in his breast, Captain Cecco steeled himself and faced Captain Hook— the one man who possessed the power to end his happiness. The power to end his life. With his sword in his hand and his woman in his arm, Cecco strode forward. "Captain."

"Mr. Cecco."

"I must make the truth known to you. If you desire the hand of this woman, it is I with whom you must contend."

"I shall take you up on your offer, Mr. Cecco. After I have dispatched her husband." Hook's tone grew icy as he turned to Hanover. "Doctor. Let the terms be clear. We fight to the death."

"Agreed!"

Jill breathed at last, in a gasp. She turned to see the surgeon. She felt Cecco's hold tighten on her waist.

Hanover smoothed back his hair. Sending one long look to his wife, he adjusted his grip on his weapon. "Madam." With formal elegance, he bowed to Jill. Upon rising, the fire of hatred flamed in his eye, and he answered Hook's challenge. "To the death, Sir. Indeed, you are behind your time." Hanover hoisted his rapier and took up his stance.

"Ah. Time." Hook raised one eyebrow. "Thanks to your ministrations, I've enjoyed an abundance of that."

Using time again, Hook strolled forward to meet his opponent, assessing the surroundings. Smee stood sentry behind him. More lovely than ever, Jill looked back over Cecco's shoulder as he guided her reluctant footsteps to the shelter of the stern stairway. LeCorbeau and his mates gathered amidships, across from the table and its wine-stained cloth. Nibs and Tom restrained Liza, who struggled in a panic to free herself until Yulunga secured a grip on her, dragging her to the foremast. Granting the deck to the duelists, Cecco's other officers ranged along the portside. The rest of the *Roger*'s men settled on the periphery of the scene as LeCorbeau's sailors shinned up the rigging, seeking viewpoints along the shrouds.

Hook smiled. The layout of *L'Ormonde* appeared exactly as he envisioned it, over and again while he lay shackled, preparing himself for this fray. Hook recalled every cannon, every hatch and hurdle. Thanks to his captor, he'd had plenty of time— to make ready.

Although astonished by the turn of events, the surgeon disciplined his energies toward his task. He considered his tactics. He'd crossed swords with Hook before. He knew the man's approach, his unscrupulous methods. Hanover would bar no maneuver. He had learned a lesson in his affiliation with pirates. No trick was too low, even for a gentleman. He launched his attack, driving his rapier at Hook's throat.

With a powerful swing, Hook repulsed it. Unprepared for the strength in his prisoner's arm, Hanover was jarred, and he nearly lost his grip.

"Have a care, Doctor. Things are not always as they seem. Those who call themselves gentlemen, for instance."

"Yet you, I find, remain exactly as I first believed you." Striking again, Hanover put the force of his shock to work.

"On the contrary, Hanover." Hook had parried. Now, with a smile, he said, "I am stronger." He charged.

Released at last, Hook followed his strategy. Breathing the scent of sea air, with the warmth of sunshine on his shoulders, he felt the pent-up energy flow through his arm. He enacted strokes he'd had days to dream, pressing the surgeon without mercy. Hook didn't try to hide his gratification. He was in his element— his feet on the deck of a ship, a sword in hand, and an enemy at its point. He'd imagined this scene many times, rebuilding his strength there on the foul mattress of the surgeon's keeping. Using his chains and his own body weight, he had employed his hours of isolation, toning his muscles in every conceivable way. The new freedom of his limbs thrilled him. He moved them now, lashing out, slashing at his foe.

Hanover felt the captain's ferocity. He countered with a fury of his own. On the outcome of this contest balanced not only his life, but his reputation, the legacy he had striven to build, the brilliant career. His wife. His daughter and her— progeny. All squeezed in the one-handed grip of a devious sea dog. Unless he killed this man, immediately, irredeemable disgrace awaited the doctor. His sword spoke his torment for him, in words shrill and sharp.

Watching beside the aft stairway, Jill felt Cecco pull her into the protection of his hold. With her back against his chest, she gripped his arms, bolstered by his concern and hardly knowing how to justify it. Hook was home. Hanover was as good as dead. Soon enough, Cecco's own trial would commence.

But she wouldn't— she couldn't think about that trouble now. The men's blood was up. Just as she had done when Hook disappeared, she must do on his resurrection. She must remain calm, to determine what action to take. Unwilling to tear her gaze from her captain, she forced herself to do so, casting about the deck. A moment later, she caught Nibs' eye and gestured. His gaze darted after hers, and he nodded.

Hanover was in a hurry, but Hook was not. He conserved his strength. As the surgeon delivered a barrage of blows, Hook stood each one, giving way a step here and there, only to swing with his hook and force his adversary back again. Hanover redoubled his effort. Hook whirled, swiping again. This time the doctor's blade crashed into the iron curve, sending shudders through Hook's arm. As pain shot to his shoulder, Hook wrenched his claw and sent Hanover's sword flying. It clanged to the deck, and Hanover backed away. Lifting his empty hand, he turned a shocked face to *L'Ormonde*'s captain. LeCorbeau shoved his mate forward and, within seconds, the hilt of Renaud's rapier filled those manicured fingers.

Tom advanced just far enough to retrieve the fallen blade. Smirking now, Hanover tested Renaud's sword, swishing it in a crisscross flair.

Hook flexed his shoulders, attempting to shake the damage the doctor's blow had caused. It left a nagging ache in his biceps, but he knew the remedy for that: victory. Hook thrust his weight full forward. With his iron hand threatening, he drove his enemy down the deck.

Hanover gave ground under the power of Hook's assault. In a sudden movement he sidestepped, swerving into the protection of a cannon. Hook's blade slashed across it, rasping along the barrel.

Hanover ducked. Hook's momentum carried him aft past the cannon, then he spun, stopping just short of Jill, with his back toward her.

Behind her, she felt Cecco stir as Hook neared. She noted the knife sheathed in Cecco's belt as he held her, bearing against her back. A treacherous possibility occurred to Jill. She remembered his words, that first evening when she warned him of Hook's wrath. *Do not underestimate me.* Pushing against Cecco, she backed him deeper into the stairwell, willing him away from Hook. She gripped his arms more firmly, knowing even as she did so that, if Cecco chose to act, no one could restrain him.

Jill saw Smee at the fore of the ship, watching Cecco. On guard for danger to his captain, he took swift steps closer. Alerted, Hook himself glanced around. Jill felt the force of his gaze again, and Cecco's hands strengthening his hold on her. As if Hook could see her leather bracelets, Jill became aware of those straps that bound her to her gypsy lover. Hook faced the surgeon again, but under her gloves, the bindings pressed into Jill's flesh. Once more, she had no choice but to place her trust in Cecco. Captain Cecco.

Hanover knew the haven he'd found would soon become a trap. Quickly, he slid along the big gun's barrel and readied his sword. Jill read the confidence in his face, the loathing for his foe. His savage passion chilled her and fired her all at once. She knew that the same look animated Hook's face. No shame; no fear; no compunction. And Jill understood, now, what grasp the surgeon held on her. Why, for all her scheming, she had never broken free of him....

Like all her lovers, he was every inch a pirate.

Hook set his teeth and heaved forward, his hook glittering in the sun, his sword harassing Hanover's. The electric air carried the sound of metal smashing metal.

Amidships again, abreast of Cecco's officers, Hanover stood his ground, dodging the claw. As opportunity presented, he darted glances at Jill. The light in her eye emboldened him. Thinking like her pirates, he wheeled to pluck the dagger from Mullins' belt. Mullins grunted, his hefty hand rushing to clasp his sheath, too late.

Beckoning with his stolen blade, Hanover urged Hook to attack. "Come, Captain. Your fate awaits you."

"Yes." Hook's eyes glowed as he stood, legs apart. "A glorious victory. Unlike the ignoble ending you designed."

"Hell wouldn't have you. But I'll send you down again, to knock on the devil's door."

"I'll down a drink with him, and offer him your daughter." Hook tilted his head. "Or, no, that's been done. You saw to it personally."

Hanover's smirk dropped from his face. "You vile defiler!"

"Your mirror image."

"No more discussion. Your reprieve is at an end." With a weapon in each hand, Hanover tossed his hair from his forehead and rushed him.

As Hook evaded the assault, Hanover overshot his opponent, pulling up to turn and charge again. Hook bent, his sword tip swaying like a snake before a charmer. He backed toward the bow. "Miss Hanover, your father is a compelling man, is he not?"

Liza lurched, her maroon skirt wrinkling in her fists. Her bare feet peeked beneath a froth of petticoats. She looked frantically from her captain to her father. With her heart divided, she strained against Yulunga's grip.

Hanover lunged. Hook swung his blade like an ax, catching the surgeon's sword square. The force of the blow knocked Hanover off balance, and he stumbled. Hook took up his stance again, seizing his chance. "Come, now, Miss. You possess a lovely voice. Let everyone hear it." The company exclaimed, and all eyes turned to Liza.

Her father regained his foothold. "Hook— you have stolen quite enough from my daughter. Leave her some dignity."

"Fair is fair, Hanover. You and your concubine have stolen my treasure. Mr. Yulunga, weigh that gown you gave her."

The sailors looked puzzled, but at Hook's choice of words, Hanover's soul filled with dread. He hadn't been certain before. Now it was clear. Hook knew— everything. As foreboding cinched Hanover's heart, he thought fast.

Yulunga hunkered down to grasp Liza's hem. Finding a fistful of something, he looked up at Hook. "Sir! It's jewelry."

Hook advanced on Liza. Perspiring, Hanover attempted to divert the blame before the dam burst.

"Don't dare touch my daughter…again!"

With his rapier, Hook whisked off a hank of Liza's hair. She shied as her earlobe was exposed. "Pierced. Yet you won't allow her to wear my earrings. What a shame, when the false bottom of your sea chest conceals some superlative pieces. Not to mention those stowed in your crate of medical books." Hook leered. "I had intended to bestow them upon my *own* mistress."

Liza's hands flew to her ears.

"You are barbaric, Hook, to humiliate a girl. For shame!"

"Exactly, Doctor. For shame. And how will you conceal her shame— once she begins to show it?"

The observers began to gossip. Hissing like a flock of geese, the Frenchmen whispered the translation to one another. LeCorbeau rolled his eyes heavenward. Yulunga pulled Liza back, casting his gaze down to study her. Her white face blushed now, as her secrets broke open to color it.

Hook pressed his advantage. "My guess is you intended your new wife to pose as mother. A convenient cover. Jill couldn't refuse, could she?" He sent a solemn look to Jill. "She believed the child might be mine."

Hook held Jill's gaze, then continued.

"Nor could your daughter refuse you. Under your 'protection,' she could hide what you'd done to her…however ardently she accepted your advances." Whispers rustled again, in wonder at first, then in condemnation. Liza's head sank, as if her neck were too slender a stem to hold such a flower.

Livid, Liza's father defended her, and his honor. "I will silence you, Sir, if it is the last thing I do." He slashed his knife at Hook's gullet. Hook caught it in his claw, with a chink of metal.

"Not to worry," answered Hook. "When I've finished with you, your deeds will live on— in your ill-gotten child." Arm against arm, it was a battle of strength now. As their limbs shook with effort, Hook forced Hanover's dagger lower. "Or would it be, grandchild?" Clicking his tongue, Hook frowned in mock reproof. "So terribly complicated, isn't it?"

"Your corruption knows no bounds. You raped her!" Locked

together, knife and claw grappled.

Hook managed a laugh. "My dear doctor. I have never found it necessary to force a female." With a twist of his hook, he released the surgeon's blade. "But I bow to you. You *are* accomplished. A subtle seducer."

Hanover sputtered, "What depravity will you not plumb to discredit me in my wife's eyes?"

"What depravity have you not shown me?"

In answer, Hanover sliced his knife at Hook's cheek. The captain glided away.

"All those nights, as I lay chained in your daughter's bed. You both found it preferable that she should sleep in yours." Hook stepped backward, his rapier dancing, repelling Hanover's advance. But, blocked by the table, Hook was forced to a halt. Hedging at the point of Hanover's blade, he leaned backward, teetering over the wine-stained surface.

Smee held up the torch, ready to throw it, and Jill clutched at Cecco. Hook swiveled to look at her, and for one instant, they locked eyes. Hanover drove again, this time wielding his dagger.

Hook snagged the mainmast with his claw. Hanover's knifepoint gouged his shirt. The fabric moaned as Hook vaulted over the table, wedding feast and all. He moved so lightly that he seemed to float. The next moment, he stood on the other side.

"But all this talk makes one so thirsty." Setting his rapier on the table, he took up a silver goblet. "Drink, Doctor?" Hook raised the cup in a toast and enjoyed a draught.

Murmurs of admiration rose from the sailors. Hanover scowled. "I shall drink when you are dead." With his sword, he struck the goblet from Hook's hand. It sprayed red drops as it clattered on the deck. Hanover stabbed his dagger down, plunging it through the handle of Hook's rapier. The dagger sank into the table top, pinning Hook's weapon there. Hanover jeered, "My wife and I will drink together. To your memory."

"Do you refer to the wife you took today? Or to the wife you murdered?"

Jill went rigid. She knew from Hook's expression— he wasn't

bluffing. The men agitated, eyeing the surgeon with fresh mistrust. Liza kept her half-shorn head down.

Hanover's knuckles went white on the knife. "You foul liar."

"Is it I or you who lie? Did I not hear you confess to your daughter? Allow me to refresh your memory. It was the same morning you determined to starve me to death…and threatened to disfigure the girl if she spoke another word."

Liza turned away, burying the face she had preserved by perfidy in Yulunga's chest. He didn't have to restrain her anymore. She clung to him. His arm settled on her shoulders. He freed his ax from his belt.

Jill covered her open mouth, but her horror couldn't be concealed. Cecco voiced an untranslatable oath.

Weapons jingled as the pirates shifted, indignant. A scheme to murder their captain was heinous enough. Starvation struck them as cowardly. And for any man to mar a girl's beauty, a man's own daughter, made even these ruthless pirates feel sick. But the thought that the girl they'd been compelled to respect had been used after all, and used most vilely— by her sire— was past bearing. LeCorbeau's crew, too, cried out in disapproval. In French, Italian, and English, Hanover heard himself reviled.

The French captain fanned himself with a handkerchief, his mouth set as if tasting bad wine. In the rigging above him, the blond sailor thrust his knife in his teeth. His scuttling descent was soon discouraged by the hands of his shipmates, but their voices rose, urging Hook to battle. This fight was fated for two men alone.

Hook needed no encouragement. Armed with only his claw now, he called, "Mr. Yulunga. I believe this cask must be broached." Veering to starboard, Hook turned to watch.

The African obliged. Lifting his ax, he steadied his aim, then let it fly. The cask cracked open in a splintering of wood. Wine burst from the wreckage to flood over the deck. The heady scent of it escaped, and scarlet drops speckled the doctor's sleeve. As the men watched the flow, Hook's boots trod in the pool. He seized the ax. A moment later, its blade stood embedded in the table. In two shards, the knife bounced along the surface, tinkling against the goblets, and Hook held his rapier in his hand.

Faced with the ax, Hanover had retreated. Now he rounded the mast to confront his nemesis. Flecks of wine, like innocent blood, stained his shirtsleeve. He said, "In direst circumstances, I have striven to remain a gentleman. The dishonor rests upon you, who brought all this to pass." One last time, the surgeon took up his stance. "And it is you from whom I demand satisfaction, in blood."

"Granted."

Hook drove the doctor aft, leaving a trail of wine-colored footprints. The enemies bent to thrust and pulled back to parry, their eyes exultant, their white sleeves surging high and low, their feet scuffling to the rhythm of their blades.

This time, Hook's efforts to trip Hanover came to nothing. The doctor stepped carefully in his soft shoes, feeling for the rise of the hatches and treading with grace upon them. Sensing the column of the capstan looming, Hanover maneuvered so that Hook backed toward it. Leaping aside, Hook narrowly avoided it. Then subtly, surely, seeming to be drawn, he drew the doctor sternward. Hook had two birds to kill. One stone should do it.

Watching from the bow, Nibs spied his chance. He snatched the last standing cup from the table, then sidled down portside to join Jill.

Cecco spotted him. As the duelists neared, he urged Jill toward her son. At Cecco's signals, the other men cleared the stern, and Nibs set his arm around his mother. She allowed him to pull her to the side. Turning back to Cecco, Jill saw him kiss his fingertips and release them toward her. Clearly, he felt his own trouble approaching. Cecco wanted his love well away from it.

Hanover pressed Hook toward the quarterdeck. Hook's heel thumped against the lowest stair. Ascending backward, he fought on, moving within the confines of the banisters. With a grim smile, Hanover battled his way up the steps. At last, he held the pirate at a disadvantage.

But only for a moment. Hook swung his hook down and dug it into the rail. Supported now, he leaned out over the surgeon to rain blows upon him. Hanover's arm was tiring. Hook's too. Their grips were damp with perspiration, and each man's breath labored. In a sudden move, Hanover flung back his rapier to circle it high, and then he heaved it down to the left.

Hook's eyes flared. Buried in the wood of the railing, his hook trapped his arm. Hanover's blade came whistling. Hook tugged, but couldn't free himself. With a sickening thud, Hanover's sword split the captain's cuff, embedding itself in Hook's arm.

Hanover watched, victorious. But the bloom of blood he expected never appeared. He had struck not flesh, but the wooden form of Hook's harness.

Jarred by the blow, Hook's wrist throbbed, the bone ached. Yet now it was Hanover whose weapon was caught; Hook's rapier remained free. With one arm anchored to the rail, Hook made a vicious swipe— two, three. Hanover had to let go of his hilt and jump five steps backward, to land on the deck with a thump.

Hook stabbed his rapier into the stair. The weapon stood swaying as it waited by his side. His hand was free now to struggle with Hanover's sword, wedged in his wooden wrist. The surgeon moved to snatch Hook's rapier, but Hook aimed a kick, and Hanover backed away.

Searching for a weapon, Hanover quickly considered, then raced to portside. Although Jill's blood pounded, she stood regal. She reached for the silver goblet in Nibs' hand. Cecco watched from his post beside the stair, and drew his cutlass. Setting one foot forward, he braced, ready to come to Jill's aid.

Hanover grasped her shoulders. He tossed a glance at Hook, who still strove to free himself from the stairway. Hanover pulled Jill close.

"My darling. When this nightmare is over, you will— you must— see the truth."

"Johann, I have told you. You married a pirate." Jill's gaze was earnest. "And so did I."

Cecco snorted at her words. Amused in spite of the circumstances, he flashed his gypsy smile. But it faded as he continued to observe.

"Yes. You are exactly the woman I want." Hanover's smile turned ironic. "My finest prize." Jill offered him the wedding cup, and with his fingers covering hers, Hanover drank. "Thank you, Madam. Just what I needed." He slid Hook's jeweled dagger from her sash. "And I need *this* to finish it."

Cecco stepped closer. Jill gasped at the loss of her knife, but

Hanover was in a hurry. He placed a kiss on her lips, then snatched a belaying pin from the rail, a slender but sturdy club. Wielding it and Hook's own weapon, he left his wife, to slay her stubborn lover. Jill watched, raising one black glove to press her mouth. Cecco's smoky gaze followed the surgeon. Silently, he tucked his cutlass back in his belt. He might not need it after all.

Left alone, Hook had loosed Hanover's sword from his brace. He glanced about him. Seeing no danger to himself or to Jill, he strained to yank his claw from the banister, driven deeper by the force of the surgeon's hit. With a grunt, he pried it free. Through the railing of the stair, he glimpsed brown, brooding eyes surveying him. As promised, Hook would test Mr. Cecco later. Or rather, his sword would do so.

Now, Hanover posed at the foot of the steps. Hook straightened to focus on his foe. Loose strands of hair escaped Hanover's ribbon. His scar jagged crimson to his jaw, dwarfing the fresh horizontal cut on his other cheek. Above the beige waistcoat and once-white sleeves, those two dashes of violence on Hanover's face, old and new, lent him color— along with the jewels held fast in his grip, glowing in a familiar hilt: Hook's own dagger.

Fire kindled in Hook's eyes. He advanced, one step downward. The surgeon's rapier shone in Hook's one good hand. The moment he had awaited approached.

Hook brandished his enemy's weapon. Hanover tensed, ready to evade it. But instead of lashing out, the captain flung Hanover's rapier backward, sending it soaring over the quarterdeck. It landed with a crash and rattled to the rail.

Hanover exclaimed, but before Hook could regain his stance, the surgeon rushed for the stairs, leading with his dagger. Hook freed his own rapier from the step. Hanover slashed his knife sideways, swiping at Hook's ankles. Hook leapt up and backward, and his sword swooped to stop the knife. Hanover hoisted the belaying pin. As wood chips flew, the pin halted Hook's blade.

Cruelly, Hanover sliced again, one step higher and aiming for Hook's knees. Hook jerked backward, upward. Again his steel carved wood from the belaying pin. On the next step, Hanover swung the knife a third time. Hook backed higher to dodge it. More fragments scattered. The next pass sliced within a fraction of Hook's thigh. The blow Hook delivered exploded the remains of the belaying pin. A chip struck sharp on Hanover's forehead. He shook himself. Hook loomed at the top of the stairs.

Hanover dove, flinging himself under Hook's arm. Stretched out on the quarterdeck, he rolled, leapt up, and with all his strength, hurled Hook's dagger at its master's heart.

Hook threw himself to the side, smashing on the quarterdeck, and heard the knife cut the air. The next instant, it thunked in the mizzenmast. As Hook bounded up, Hanover dashed to the taffrail to snatch up his rapier.

The air rang with the sound of their swords. But evenly matched, they were evenly tiring. Mindful of the damage wrought by his captivity, Hook had paced himself. It was time to end the game. This was the point he'd left off on that fateful day, the day of his capture. His rapier, so lovingly tended by Smee, felt perfect in his hand. Hook anticipated its next move with pleasure. Polished and primed, its tip was honed to the finest point, eager for just this moment.

Hook thrust out and downward. A long, slender gash opened on the doctor's face. Crimson liquid leaked, then began to stream from the wound.

Too surprised to feel anything, Hanover slapped a hand over the cut. Blood oozed between his fingers, trickling down to stain his cuff, his cravat, his waistcoat. Incredulous, he pulled his hand away and stared at it. When the pain set in, he clasped his face again, gritting his teeth.

"Damn you, Hook!"

A slow smile spread upon Hook's face. It grew wide to express his satisfaction. The score was settled, Hook's vengeance complete.

"Well, Doctor. We have had our duel."

"It isn't finished." Hanover's palm muffled his voice.

Hook spoke loudly enough for captains, crewmen, and officers to hear, across the decks and up in the rigging. "But it *is* finished. We have dueled to the death— of your fine reputation."

Hanover's breath escaped in a hiss. His face bled, stinging with pain. He clutched his cheek, his eyes wandering among the men as he attended their restiveness.

Hook said, "You've less claim to the title of 'gentleman' than the lowest swab aboard. And now you bear the mark I have awarded you." Hook savored his words. "A complete victory." He raised his sapphire eyes and surveyed the company.

The silence burst like a wave, the ship suddenly awash in celebration. Huzzas arose from every quarter. The men shook their weapons and thrust their fists in the air. Smee's red face beamed. Jill's eyes flamed as she beheld her lover, and then she lowered them. As the deck vibrated with jubilation, Liza leaned against Yulunga, her loyalties torn.

Even *L'Ormonde*'s men exulted, for the famed Captain Hook lived. With his final stroke, his legend enlarged. Yet, as he'd warned the doctor, Hook wasn't the same. The sailors could see it in his stance, in his glittering eye, the unkempt blur of his beard. Hook's ordeal had changed him.

He was stronger.

As the cacophony swelled around him, Hanover seethed. "Your 'victory' isn't quite complete." His grimace turned to a one-sided sneer. He still tasted the bridal wine. "I have won the woman." He dropped his bloody hand and thrust again.

Again, the two blades crossed. Hook backed to the stairway, then he lowered his shoulders and barreled into the surgeon. Slammed backward, Hanover tumbled to the deck.

Hook turned away to stride to the railing. Leaning over it, he saw Cecco gazing up at him, one hand on the hilt of his knife. Hook poised his sword, tip down, and dropped it. The gypsy's jewelry rang as he jerked backward. The sword delved into the deck. Next moment, Hook hurdled the rail. The men leaned forward, exclaiming, but the heavy thump they expected never came. Seeming to slow as he fell, Hook landed lightly, on his feet.

Hanover, on his legs again, rushed to clutch the rail and peer down. Hook pried the sword from the floor. He flourished it, smiling, and saluted the surgeon.

Watching the rivals fight for her, Jill found that her fingers had nearly indented the silver cup. Now, as the hostilities ceased, she drew a deep breath of relief.

And then she froze as she heard Hook's final words.

"Come join me, Hanover, and we'll determine who will win the woman."

Hanover dashed down the steps. He spun around the post, to corner Hook at last. With the stairway on one side and the wooden wall behind him, Hook waited. On his other side, Cecco backed to make room, his eager eyes darting between the antagonists. From the surgeon's sword, Hook had no escape.

Hanover sprang.

But Hook's next move shocked him, and every other soul who saw it. Hook struck the doctor's blade, whirled— and tossed his sword away. Coming full circle, he planted his legs and presented himself to Hanover, flinging his arms wide.

With a look of disbelief, Cecco caught the rapier. He stared at Hook. The captain stood smiling, unarmed— a willing target.

Hanover didn't hesitate. He aimed his weapon at Hook's heart, and he lunged.

Jill screamed, Smee hollered, "No, Captain!" As the company watched, appalled, time slowed to an agonized eternity.

Then another sound broke through. A musical sound. A tinkling of bracelets. Bearing Hook's own sword, Captain Cecco strode toward him. As always, he had been watching for his moment. With a dangerous glint in his eye, he seized his opportunity.

In one mighty stroke, Cecco beat down the doctor's blade. He plunged between Hook and Hanover, establishing himself. A solid, menacing mass— shielding his captain.

Cecco waited only long enough for Hanover to register his outrage. Then he struck. Clenched in Cecco's fist, the hilt of Hook's rapier rose up and descended to deal a blow to the surgeon's temple. In a bloody huddle, Hanover crumpled to his knees.

Captain Cecco looked down on the doctor, and felt his own fortunes fading with him. In one instinctive stroke, Cecco's dream had ended. When it came, the iron ice of the hook on his flesh made the situation plain: Captain Hook had returned.

With a vengeance.

Treasures Returned

At the cold touch of the hook, Cecco lowered the rapier. He relinquished it. With a clink, the handle caught to dangle in the curve of Hook's claw.

"Thank you, Mr. Cecco." Hook draped his words in his treacherous courtesy. Cecco stepped back. Already Smee stood guard beside him. He'd handed the torch to Tom and drawn his cutlass.

Hook's gaze pierced Cecco. The gypsy stood solemn, unapologetic. Finally, Hook turned to look down upon his conquest.

Hanover knelt at Hook's boots, his head hanging. One hand clutched his rapier, one pressed his temple. Hook tapped the tip of his sword beneath the surgeon's chin, forcing his head high. Hanover's eyes smoldered as he stared up at the victor. On the left side of his face, the old scar ran in its crimson line. On the right, the new mark matched the first in near perfect symmetry. The nick from Jill's knife joined the new cut at the top, to form the shape of a seven. Even in defeat, the surgeon sketched a formidable figure.

"You have caused enough havoc, Hanover. I am finished with you."

"But *I* am not."

Hook looked up. With a swirl of silk, Jill emerged from the crowd. Nibs followed bearing the silver cup.

In Hook's eyes, the sight of his lady was more welcome than ever before. She hadn't ventured near enough earlier, but at this moment, with a surge of emotion, he caught the exotic scent of her perfume. He had never desired anything more urgently than to touch her, right now.

Jill looked at Hook as if her eyes couldn't drink her fill. But she moved toward the surgeon. She knelt beside him and, at last, her gaze left her lover to behold her new husband.

Her forehead creased. She reached out to him. With tender fingers, she smoothed his loose hair, pushing it back. She found her handkerchief and gently pressed his wounds. As he drew breath to speak, she shook her head. "No, my dear. I know what you'll say." She dabbed at the blood. "But if you get yourself killed, you will be of no use to me." He twitched the rapier in his hand, as if eager to fight again. Signaling to Nibs, Jill received the goblet. "A drink, now, Johann. To cool you." She held the wine to his lips. Looking up at her, he swallowed gratefully. His hand enveloped her fingers, and even through her glove, Jill felt his fervor.

Hook's face darkened.

Jill helped Hanover drink all he needed, and then she set the cup down. "Johann, I know it is your wish to keep fighting for me."

Hanover basked in her care, on his tongue the taste of her wine, in his gaze the fullness of his passion. His marred face grew smug as he looked at Hook. "How well you know me, my Jill."

Hook tensed, his weapon rising.

Jill turned in dignified appeal. "Captain. If you please."

Every man on the ship watched Captain Hook, keen with anticipation. He held himself in check for the moment, but his voice carried its velvet edge. "Who has won the woman, Jill?"

Her blue gaze fixed on him, then she turned to Cecco. She closed her eyes, and when she opened them again, her gaze shone upon Hanover. "Who else, Captain, but the strongest man aboard?" And she smiled. "Johann, you have proven to me just who that gentleman is."

"My darling." Hanover gripped her hand and kissed her palm. He strove to smile through his disfigurement. "If Captain LeCorbeau is ready, we shall leave immediately."

"Yes, Johann." Jill wrapped her arms around him. "You knew it from the very beginning. Long before I did." She gazed adoringly upon him. "You knew I must be yours, that I would one day be your wife." Jill's fingers slipped within her bodice. "And, with the strength of your heart, you determined that I *will* come away with you. But…"

She withdrew a small, empty vial and held it before his eyes. "…not today."

Hanover blinked at the bottle. His mouth gaped open. He turned to Jill, his eyes filling with horror— and then they closed. His head fell sideways and he slumped upon her breast, deep in sleep.

Hook's shoulders began to shake. A smile slid to his lips. His mirth grew until soon, he threw back his head and laughed aloud. The hearty chorus of his men's laughter joined him, and even Cecco grunted in amusement.

LeCorbeau, looking pale, alternated his gaze between his fellow captains and forced an unhealthy chuckle. Venturing closer on Yulunga's arm, Liza looked on in disbelief. She stood twisting the ring on her finger, not trusting her eyes.

Jill tucked the vial away. Caressing the surgeon's sandy hair one last time, she memorized the marks upon his face. Her two fingers moved downward, stroking his chest, to settle on the chain dangling from his waistcoat. Robbing him of his watch first, she tucked her bloody handkerchief in its place.

A chant started up among the men, bouncing from stem to stern, "Red-Handed Jill! Red-Handed Jill!" She smiled again and, with Nibs' help, she lowered the surgeon to the deck. Offering his arm, Nibs assisted her to rise. Jill transferred her bracelets from her right wrist to her left, loosened the fingertips of her black glove, and dramatically, she peeled it from her arm. The sailors' chanting reached its peak as she raised her red palm and splayed her scarlet fingers. Her twist of hair shone golden in the sunlight, her gown billowed black as raven's wings and the opals sparkled at her throat, just below her scar. The men's hearts swelled to see her.

But they were eager to see the situation settled. Full of good humor now, Hook waved his claw expansively and the sounds of jubilation dwindled. "Well, DéDé. What say you to an amicable cup of wine, and then we'll put the wind to our backs."

"Yes, certainly. I am eager to, eh, clear the decks and make sail for France."

"And, I understand, we are to meet again. One year from now."

LeCorbeau's smile had been weak. Now it died. "But Hook, surely— Surely you do not intend to pursue a further partnership! It will be all I can manage to persuade the good doctor to get back to work!"

"A distasteful but necessary part of your task, LeCorbeau."

"The man will never agree to manufacture his product knowing his profit will line your coffers! And when he wakes without the woman— *Mon Dieu!* I shudder to think!" LeCorbeau rummaged his pocket and pulled out his handkerchief.

Renaud noted LeCorbeau's motion. He gave a subtle signal, and *L'Ormonde*'s sailors began to crawl down the rigging.

Hook replied, "As stubborn as Hanover is, DéDé, I have confidence in your powers of persuasion. He will be anxious to replace the fortune he so recklessly threw our way."

"Yes! Yes, he will be anxious— to turn around and pursue the paramour, until he pursues himself to his grave!" The Frenchman tamped his perspiring face. "No, Hook, you must content yourself with the prizes you have taken, and never seek more from that quarter."

Blue-coated sailors lined the deck now. Watching, Nibs tightened the knot of his kerchief. Hook had taught him to use his eyes and ears. In his time aboard *L'Ormonde*, Nibs had listened to LeCorbeau's discourse. He knew the Frenchman's methods. Uneasy, Nibs stepped in front of Jill.

Hook remained unruffled. "My dear LeCorbeau. Why do you think I spared him? Why did Mrs. Heinrich not poison her husband instead of drugging him to slumber? No, no. If I am to forgo the pleasure of destroying the man, I must have my recompense."

LeCorbeau glowered, moving closer. "And, I suppose, you will not stop there. You intend to rob me of my seamen. My Mr. Tootles…and Mr. Nibs?"

"Mr. Nibs, I advised you to weigh that decision. Have you had time enough to consider?"

"Aye, Sir." Nibs raised a hand in salute to Cecco before answering. "My brother and I have been told we're indispensable to the *Roger*. With your permission, there is no captain we'd like better to serve."

"Permission granted. You are both welcome back." Hook shrugged, "As you see, LeCorbeau, your protégé has made his choice."

By now, *L'Ormonde*'s full ship's complement stood by. "*Alors.* I should have known. One can never trust a pirate." LeCorbeau gritted his teeth. "Perhaps, after all, what the *Roger* needs is a change of captains." Yanking his stiletto from his handkerchief, he thrust for Hook's throat.

Nibs seized LeCorbeau's wrist. He dug his dagger under the Frenchman's chin. Hook followed immediately, pinning LeCorbeau's gullet with his claw.

Renaud snatched his sword from Hanover's open hand. But Tom wielded the torch, and a second later, flames singed Renaud's eyebrows. He threw his arms up to shield his face. Tom forced Renaud backward with the fire, calling, "Guillaume! To me!" The *Roger*'s crew rallied; the men in blue jackets drew their weapons, advancing on the incited pirates. But, at a sign from Guillaume, they halted.

Guillaume shouted, "Mr. Nibs, Mr. Tom! There is no benefit in further struggle." Spreading his arms to hold off his men, Guillaume reasoned, "Please, Captain Hook. My *commandant* has suffered a severe disappointment. If you will release him, we will part company and get under way."

Rubbing his singed brow, Renaud goggled at his cousin. The *Roger*'s captain lowered his hook from LeCorbeau's collar. Excepting Nibs, Hook's sailors followed suit. *L'Ormonde*'s crew drew sighs of relief, but soon shared disgruntled glances. For the second time that day, their faith in their quirky captain was shaken; LeCorbeau had allowed personal rancor to endanger his men.

Hook inclined his head to Guillaume. "Thank you, *Monsieur*. I shall heed your advice and release your captain. Mr. Nibs, Mr. Cecco, kindly escort Captain LeCorbeau and his mate to a boat. Mr. Smee and Mr. Tootles, see to it that the dregs of Doctor Hanover disembark, likewise."

With Nibs' blade forcing his head up, LeCorbeau rolled his eyes toward Hook. A note of panic entered his voice as, careful not to move his jaw, he echoed, "A boat?"

"Possibly two. Let us discover how many of your sailors intend to accompany you."

LeCorbeau's face drained of color. "*Comment?* Accompany *me?* It is you who shall sail away!"

"Yes, LeCorbeau. With your own fine vessel. I hadn't thought to take her, but, as you have demonstrated such hostility…"

In the spate of French profanity, LeCorbeau came near to spearing his throat on Nibs' knife. The *Roger's* men hustled to the bow to ready a boat.

Hook raised his claw and it flared in the sun as he addressed the company. "I now cordially invite the worthy crew of *L'Ormonde* to remain aboard. Any who are hearty enough to swear loyalty and sail under my command are welcome to test their mettle."

L'Ormonde's crew stood motionless with shock. They watched their captain guided at knifepoint to the boat, he still peering down his overlarge nose and cursing. They hadn't much time. Considering quickly, the French sailors murmured among themselves, shooting glances between Hook at the stern and LeCorbeau near the bow. Their imaginations dwelt on the drama, full of Captain Hook's resurrection, his magnificent duel. They might sail to adventure with a legend— on the wrong side of the law— or trust their eccentric captain to find a new ship and recover his sense of business. One by one, those too honest or too timid to take to piracy bade farewell to their mates, and gathered by the boat that now swung from its davits off the bow of *L'Ormonde*.

LeCorbeau's chef was called up from the galley. Bearing a bag of victuals, he stood blinking in the sunlight, his blue coat faded with flour. His galley mate followed with a cask of water. The grizzled sailing master trudged up last, lugging his gear and shaking his head. "I am too old a dog to learn new tricks."

The chef dumped his bag in the boat. "I agree with you." With his belly preceding him, he trundled toward the pirate captain. "*Monsieur le Commandant*— if I may make so bold as to ask. What manner of wages do you offer a skilled mariner such as myself?"

"I pay no wages."

"No wages?" The French sailors buzzed with sudden indignation. "You would make us slaves, *Monsieur?*"

Hook looked down on the round little man. "Slaves to your own avarice. For the men of *L'Ormonde*, like the men of the *Roger*, I grant a fair percentage. The more prizes we take, the richer we all become."

The chef's plump face wrinkled. "A most mercenary outlook, *Monsieur*....How early shall I serve your morning chocolate?"

Under Nibs' knife, LeCorbeau spat. In silent fury, he glowered as his chef attended a new master.

"Chocolate?" Hook replied. "We will begin each day with my lady's tea." Hook sent Jill a commanding look that threatened her balance, leaving no doubt of his intentions. Then he turned to Smee. "We shall have our hands full, Mr. Smee, civilizing these savages." With his boot, he nudged Hanover's insensible form. "Now get *this* barbarian off my ship."

Smee's grin was wide as the sea. "Aye, Captain!" He bent to rifle the surgeon's pockets. With a triumphant gesture, he exhibited Hook's own keys. "Right where you said they'd be, Sir." He handed them over, then he and Tom hoisted Hanover by the arms and legs to haul him up the deck.

Jill, too, made her way forward, after a visit to the quarterdeck. Folded over her arm lay the doctor's beige coat, in her hand a rolled piece of parchment. At a nod from Hook, she held the parchment for LeCorbeau to behold.

"Captain LeCorbeau, I leave the matter to your good judgment. Is it in our best interests to destroy the certificate of marriage?"

LeCorbeau sat straight in the fore of his longboat, his auburn coat iridescent in the sun, his brass buttons shining. With a flutter of cuff, he sneered. "It is your own choice, *Madame*. I am sure that paper means nothing to me— except as a piece of evidence with which to have you hanged."

"It might prove a useful tool to spur our surgeon back to work. After all, each of you has suffered a setback. Within a short time the doctor must prepare his potions for your contacts. You must fit out another ship and deliver the product."

His eyes narrowed. "You foul female." The *Roger*'s men bridled, and LeCorbeau did likewise to his tongue. Having learned again the cost of allowing temper to interfere with commerce, he subdued his resentment long enough to consider. Grudgingly, he answered, "I judge it may be useful."

"Very well, then. I return this certificate to Doctor Hanover's pocket— and trust you will not enlighten him. *Bonne chance, Monsieur*, until we meet again." She smiled. Then she tossed the coat over the surgeon where he lay, limp and disheveled in the bottom of the boat. Her golden bracelets chimed as she threw him a kiss. "My dear Doctor. *Adieu.*"

With a sudden realization, LeCorbeau seized the boat's side. "But we can do nothing without the cargo from Alexandria!"

Tom said, "Don't worry, *Monsieur*. I know right where it is." He grinned at Guillaume. The two scurried below to return minutes later, burdened by a crate. The smell of lotus permeated the air all around it. "You'll have a fragrant voyage, anyway. But one's all you can carry." They loaded the crate in the longboat. "We'll keep the other two safe and dry until our rendezvous."

Smee opened his hand. "If you'll just be handing over your keys, Captain."

LeCorbeau's lip curled as he and Renaud surrendered their key rings to Mr. Smee. "Come along, Guillaume. We shall leave these *cretins*."

Guillaume went pale. *"Monsieur…"*

"Well? Why do you hesitate?"

"I— I hardly know, *Monsieur*." Guillaume's face clouded. "Mr. Tom, I had a hope that your Island might be looking out for me."

"You mean you want to join us, Guillaume?"

"*Oui*. With all respect to my captain— I do."

Tom looked to Jill, asking, "What do you think, Ma'am? Will the Island want us?"

"There is only one way to know. What is your opinion, Mr. Nibs?"

Nibs still stood guard over LeCorbeau. "Ma'am. *Monsieur* Guillaume has been a friend to us. He helped us out of a tight situation." Nibs turned his brooding countenance toward the *commandant*. "And he managed it without ever betraying his captain. He's proved his valor."

Jill said, "If this is so, we must allow him to choose his path. Captain Hook?"

"Agreed. You are welcome to join us, *Monsieur* Guillaume." Hook awarded Jill's boys a significant look— a look of fatherly pride. These worthy young men had risked their comfort, their futures, their very lives for him, and Hook felt a paternal pull of which he had never before conceived. The force of new emotion underscored his meaning. "My *sons* have vouched for you."

At these astonishing words, Nibs nearly dropped his knife; Tom snapped ramrod straight. Jill's pleased expression transformed to one of pure joy. Hook had never desired offspring. She hadn't dared to dream he might adopt her sons as his very own.

"*Merci*— Thank you, Sir," said Guillaume. "I am honored." He pivoted to bow to his former captain. "*Commandant*, I am honored, also, by your interest and affection. I thank you for it, and I hope you will one day find it in your heart to excuse me."

Renaud stood swiftly. The boat swayed on its davits. "Guillaume, you fool! Get your gear and get in this boat!"

"I am sorry to leave you, cousin. I wish you well. And, I hope, we will meet next year."

"*Non!*" LeCorbeau pulled Renaud down. As the boat's hull banged against the ship, he rebuked Guillaume. "It is too much! First my ship, then my companions! How much must I bear?"

Hook's silken voice poured balm on the wound. "*Mon vieux*, I admit you must exert yourself to replace this lovely vessel, but a man with your gifts will have no difficulty recruiting another waif. Or two."

"You think to flatter me."

"I think to rob you and be rid of you. Until I may rob you again."

"You are as arrogant as the surgeon— if more honest." LeCorbeau's features slid to a sly expression. "But, eh, what makes you confident that upon our reunion, I will not betray you to the authorities?"

"DéDé. I now possess two fragrant crates of the lotus flower. Will you be sailing back to Egypt to replace them?"

LeCorbeau looked away.

"In any case, *mon ami*," Hook continued, "you may rest assured that once at our rendezvous point, I will see *you*, before you see me."

Mustering his pluck, LeCorbeau aimed a stare over Hook's shoulder. "*Alors*, there is one I expect never to see again. Captain Cecco, I regret that our partnership must end so radically— in your demise, no doubt. I did have high hopes of you."

With Smee on his heels, Cecco approached. "I thank you for the sentiment, Captain, but I advise you to concern yourself with your own fate. You and your dozen men have a long row to France."

"Eh! You should have let the woman go."

"That, I can never do." Cecco's smoky eyes settled on Jill. She returned his gaze, melting, until the tap of advancing boots drew their attention. Cecco said, "But here is a chance to follow your own counsel, Captain."

With one hand behind him, Guillaume approached the boat. LeCorbeau gazed fondly on him, blinking a tear from his eye. "Guillaume, you have been dear to me."

"*Oui, Monsieur*. I have felt it. But take this, please. To ease your voyage." Guillaume smiled shyly as he extended his arm. Amazed, LeCorbeau beheld his fine, aged bottle of cognac. Taking it in his arms, he felt of its fullness. He cradled it like an infant. "Guillaume! My boy! But where did you find this?"

"Just where it should have been, *Monsieur*." Guillaume sent a glance to Tom. "We must have overlooked it."

LeCorbeau's rapture was silenced at the sight of Yulunga, looming suddenly by the boat. In one hand he gripped the girl. In the other, his knife.

Captain Hook didn't bother to look at Liza. "Mr. Yulunga, I understand you've acquired some property."

"Yes, Captain. And I will now restore your own." Yulunga squatted to spread his kerchief on the deck, then took hold of Liza's hem. Severing the stitches, he let Hook's jewels tumble free to sparkle in the sunlight.

Liza's gaze rose to study her father. He lay under his coat, bleeding and unkempt. To the others, accustomed to his dignified demeanor, he looked strange, unfamiliar. But to Liza, Doctor Hanover appeared as she often saw him since the night of her mother's murder: bloody, savage, and scarred. Half her heart took pride in him. The other half quailed.

Yulunga gathered the corners of his kerchief. Under Jill's interested eyes, he handed the bundle of jewels to Smee. Towering over his captive, he said, "Well, Miss. As I told you, Red-Handed Jill gave you to me. I have the right to keep you." Yulunga squinted. "And the sense to let you go." He squeezed her earlobe under the hewn hair. "Tell me if you will wear my earrings. Tell me with your voice."

Alarmed, she gaped at the massive form of Yulunga, then her gaze dropped to her father. She backed from both.

"No, Miss. You can choose to remain silent for the rest of your life. But you will speak to me, now."

Liza felt the stares of the company pressing upon her. A pair of china blue eyes stared, too. Her admirer, the young French sailor, held his bag slung over his shoulder, waiting for her words.

But only Yulunga spoke. "What master will you serve?"

As the breeze brought his masculine scent to her, Liza stared at the manacle marks on Yulunga's wrists. Standing next to him, Hook followed her gaze. He hooked the cuff of his own left sleeve and dragged it back to reveal his arm. With his eyes blazing, he displayed his new-made mark. The stain of chains, bitten into his flesh.

Liza covered her face. She didn't have to see the reproach in Captain Hook's eyes. She felt it within herself. Her complicity with her father had destroyed any possibility of winning the better master's favor. And even now, she was drawn to the man who demanded her devotion. Raising her bedraggled skirt, she made to climb into the boat beside him.

"No." Yulunga set his ebony hand on her arm. "I have to hear you."

Concern furrowed her brow as she gestured toward her father.

"There is no doubt he needs you. What do *you* need?"

In answer, she rested her fingers on her abdomen. Her pearls shone lustrous in the sunlight.

"So you think he'll allow your baby to be born?"

And Liza realized the unthinkable; her child, like she herself, lived in danger from its sire. A tiny sound escaped her, an exclamation, in half a syllable. Yulunga anticipated her thoughts, ripping them open like the hem of her skirt.

"And what of the next child he seeds in you?"

Her jaw dropped. Racing ahead, her mind envisioned the future. A fine house in Vienna, a hall full of servants. The opera, the theatre, dresses and dinner parties. But with all the privileges before her, Liza's spirit plummeted. She had no prospects…none of her own. In her father's opinion, she was sullied, unfit to be anyone's wife. Or mother.

And the lady had left him. He would need Liza more than before. As her father, as a respected physician, he would easily imprison her there, in his own country. And now he was a married man. He wouldn't have his wife— but he would have his needs. His 'honor' would prevent him from looking elsewhere. However willingly or unwillingly she partnered the brilliant surgeon, Liza would never be her own woman. Too successful in her aims, she had, indeed, secured the patronage of a very strong man.

Turning to Yulunga, she recognized another. With her father, her future was assured. With Yulunga, on a pirate ship, anything might happen. He was a brutal man. Selfish, like Liza. He might tire of her. He might murder her. He might—

Anything might happen.

"Well, Miss. What is your answer?"

Liza twisted her mother's ring. She twisted it off. In a twinkling arc, it sailed over the edge of the boat to beach on the velvet of her father's coat. Set in their golden band, the two pink pearls glowed there. They looked so chaste, so harmless in the bald light of day. But Liza knew better.

She faced Yulunga. He stood like an oak tree, tall and domineering. Only time could teach her to manipulate *this* master. Liza began immediately. In a low, unpracticed voice, she begged him. "Please."

The grin spread over Yulunga's lips. "Yes, Miss—"

"No."

Abruptly, Yulunga turned toward his commander. Captain Hook's unshaven face looked stern.

"Miss Hanover has shown unrelenting malignance. She saw to it that my son Tom was beaten. She facilitated her father's injuries to my lady. As for me, Miss Hanover engineered my abduction, and worse. When her lover demanded I should die— I, the 'master' to whom she pledged her devotion— she raised not a finger to preserve me. No. If Miss Hanover now desires to join my company, she must abide by my conditions." Hook's gaze scored her. "And I warn you, girl— I will be harsh."

Liza's eyes accepted the challenge. Yulunga recognized that look. This little woman thrived on adversity; Yulunga could provide all the adversity she craved. "Aye, Sir," he said, "What are your conditions?"

"Your girl will keep to *L'Ormonde*, never setting foot aboard the *Roger*. She will remain in your custody, subservient to your every word. And she will be referred to, from this day, by no other designation than the title she has so deservedly earned."

"Sir?"

Hook's stare bored into Liza. "Do you accept the terms? Shall you decline to espouse your…" he sneered, "affectionate father?"

Liza nodded. The blond sailor slid his belongings from his shoulder. With Liza's allegiance now decided, he dropped his bundle on the deck of the ship she had chosen.

Hook turned one ear toward the girl. "What was that?"

Liza shrank back, wondering if serving under Hook's command might prove more slavish than Hanover's. She took one last look at her father, and then she tried again. She managed two words. "Accept. Sir."

"Very well. You will consider yourself Mr. Yulunga's possession," Captain Hook's chest swelled; he took deep gratification in his concluding words, her permanent punishment…"Mrs. Hanover."

Liza's knees buckled.

Yulunga caught her. "You have no time for weakness— 'Mrs. Hanover.' You'll soon be studying again." At her puzzled look, Yulunga tightened his grip. "No more miming."

She swallowed. "Study?"

"Captain, with your permission, I propose Mrs. Hanover should prepare to take her father's place. His medical books are below. It will take some time, but we'll be needing a surgeon."

"An admirable idea, Mr. Yulunga. Mrs. Hanover is intelligent enough. And, to my cost, I have discovered she is not squeamish." Swinging around to salute LeCorbeau, Hook smiled. "It seems your crew is complete. Do give Doctor Hanover my regards. I wish him every prosperity. *Au revoir!*"

LeCorbeau's eyes tightened. "This one time, I shall prefer the English custom. *Good bye.*"

As the cables paid out with the boat, LeCorbeau and his crew sank from sight. Within moments, the cocky little captain could be heard issuing orders. Renaud sat stiffly, peering into a sextant as LeCorbeau flailed his arms, haranguing the oarsmen. His sailors' blue-coated shoulders leaned forward and pulled back. As they emerged from the shelter of the two great ships, their pigtails blew in the wind. Bouncing in the wide green expanse, the little French boat struck out bravely to try her luck on the brine. DéDé LeCorbeau and his pirate hunters, the saviors of the sea, ventured forth hunting succor for themselves.

Hook's increased crew waited, observing him as he stood watching the boat, his torn shirt rippling in the breeze. Jill moved to his side. "Captain." He looked down on her, unsmiling now. She didn't presume to touch him, but her eyes asked for answers.

His gaze shifted to Cecco and his gypsy regalia. Knowing the hour of reckoning was upon him, Cecco came forward to take his place at Jill's side. Hook studied him, his black hair stirring, his face impassive so that none could fathom his feelings. Guardedly, Cecco returned his stare, and the two powerful men confronted one another. Only the ship's sounds could be heard over the swishing of the sea. Lying next to her mate, *L'Ormonde* rode the waves, waiting for her new master's orders.

"Mr. Cecco. You took upon yourself the charge of the *Roger*."

"Aye, Captain. For this I cannot apologize."

Cecco's daring met with stony silence.

"Of all I have done in your absence, I regret nothing."

The *Roger*'s men exhaled. As on the day they chose him, this captain proved a brave man, worthy of their service.

"Sir," Cecco said, "under the terms of ship's articles, I know the penalty I must pay."

"Yes. You shall receive the full measure of your merit."

Cecco's dark eyes never wavered. "Captain Hook, I return to you what is yours. Your ship, your crew. My service. These things, I have the power to give." Cecco shrugged, and the many medallions glittered around his throat. "But one priceless thing I cannot return. She herself must decide."

Hook eyed the jewelry that blazed on Jill's arm. With his hook, he toyed with it, listening as it softly chinked. Under her last black glove, Jill's flesh tingled at his touch.

"Appearances speak in your favor, Mr. Cecco."

Jill's heart tore to witness discord between these men. Bound to both, she braced herself, and watched. She knew Captain Hook must secure his supremacy. She was aware, also, that Cecco's courage knew no boundaries. Her cheeks warmed as, disdaining to plead for himself, Jill's gypsy proved true to his promise.

"Although the lady bears my gifts, Captain, she never betrayed you in any way. Always, she remained faithful to her oath."

The crewmen shuffled, exchanging glances. When Jill beheld Hook again, his icy eyes were locked upon her lover.

"A gallant gesture. But unnecessary."

Cecco's broad shoulders relaxed. Hook faced the company and raised his voice. "I want it understood by every man aboard: in all she has done, Red-Handed Jill obeyed my orders. I instructed her, as my partner, to fight to preserve our ship— at *all* costs. She has done so, using every weapon available. No man will fault her for her actions."

Relieved, the men's tension eased. But as his regard lowered to Cecco again, Captain Hook's aspect threatened.

"As you see, Mr. Cecco, I am aware of the exact degree of my lady's loyalty. And yours. You have used my absence to advance your interests. You usurped my position, undertook my schemes. You commandeered my crew, my ship, my rank— and my queen. Most ambitious." He raised his hook, rotating it to find the most efficient angle. "What fate do you deserve for such devotion to your captain?"

Mr. Smee positioned himself behind the gypsy's back, making ready for orders. The *Roger*'s men remembered the stripes that Smee had paid out, the scars that lingered beneath Cecco's vest. Captain

Hook hadn't forgotten. He glanced at his bo'sun. "More than the cat-o'-nine-tails this time, I think. A far more fitting reward awaits you today, Mr. Cecco."

"Long ago I swore to serve you, Sir. My intercession with the surgeon might be my last act, but with it, I served you still."

"As you say, Mr. Cecco, judgment rests in my rapier." Hook stepped back, and raised it. With its tip, he pricked Cecco's throat. "My sword informs me you will never be my sailor again."

Cecco's fists tightened, but he resisted reaching for his weapons.

"Let all assembled bear witness: I now reclaim what belongs to me. The *Jolly Roger* is my ship, her crew are my men. But you, Mr. Cecco, will no longer sail her." With his hook agleam, he cut a flourish. "If you would serve me still, I grant you *L'Ormonde*. She is yours…Captain Cecco."

Cecco cocked his head, as if he couldn't comprehend what he was hearing. " 'Captain?' "

Hook sheathed his sword and extended his hand. "I thank you for your service."

Cecco stared at Hook's hand. Then, as if in trance, he gripped it. Searching his rival's face, he said, "Captain Hook…"

Jill seized Hook's arm. Her eyes glowed as she looked into his. "No. Not Captain Hook." With loving affection, she pronounced the heady title, "Commodore."

"Quite right. We sail as a fleet. The *Roger* has taken a lady."

Cecco almost whispered it, the name of his dream. "My own— *Red Lady*."

"Hardly an even exchange. But the best I shall offer."

"Commodore…" Cecco said, "I once claimed to be a more generous man than you. I know now— I was wrong."

"I have my limits, Captain Cecco. Pray do not test them. Mr. Smee, get the *Roger*'s men aboard her."

"Aye, aye, Commodore!" Beaming, Smee turned to give the order. "Look alive, now, mates! All hands to the *Roger!*" The deck soon resounded with eager footsteps as Hook's sailors headed toward the planks. His bo'sun stood by, waiting to escort the commodore and his lady to their vessel, while Hook issued his command.

"Captain Cecco, you may set your ship in order."

Guillaume signaled and *L'Ormonde*'s men jumped to attention. Regaining his composure, Cecco studied LeCorbeau's former mate.

"Mr. Guillaume."

"Oui, Commandant."

"I appoint you my second officer. Mr. Yulunga, Mr. Guillaume will assist you to order the crew. In one hour, I want ship's company on deck."

"Aye, Sir." Yulunga looked down on the dapper second mate. "Mr. Guillaume, assemble the men below for inspection. And you will escort Mrs. Hanover to my quarters." Yulunga slid her a sideways look. "We must unbury the rest of the commodore's treasure."

Guillaume clicked his heels together. "Yes, Sir. *Madame*, if you please."

But Yulunga stopped him. "No, Mr. Guillaume. You heard the commodore's order."

"My apologies, *Monsieurs*. If you please— Mrs. Hanover."

Blushing with mortification, Liza looked down and hastily gathered her unhemmed skirts. When Guillaume offered his arm, she clutched it. Guillaume employed his ready discretion, hustling her away and shouting commands— both French and English. Stealing one last glimpse at the man who outfoxed her father, Liza looked back over her shoulder.

Yulunga stood staring after her. Moving a step to the side, he crossed his arms and straddled the deck, blocking her view of the commodore. As she descended from sunlight to the softer atmosphere of the crew deck, Liza saw only Yulunga and his intimidating smile. Already, his features were imprinted on her senses. His imposing height, the arms too thick to hang at his sides. His glistening skin, lush voice, his overwhelming presence— Liza licked her lips and leaned more heavily on Guillaume. From toes to fingertips, she felt a nascent sense of power. Liza had learned from her father; power was the ultimate pleasure. When her devotee, the blond sailor, bowed to her, she acknowledged him with barely a nod. She was the first mate's mistress. And once she mastered a physician's arts, she might become an officer. She might even concoct a potion of her own. A philter, perhaps, to soothe men's tempers. For now, she must tidy her dress and her cabin, and then she'd count the minutes until Mr. Yulunga came to her. He would be pleased to find her studying…on his bed.

The two crews parted with hearty farewells, returning to their respective duties. Like seconds at a duel, Yulunga attended his captain and Smee took his place by the commodore, hands clasped behind his waist.

Hook stood near the foremast, watching the sailors disperse. At last he turned to Jill, and, finally, he touched her. With a gentle stroke that thrilled her, his hand settled on her cheek. "And now, LeCorbeau's boat fades from the horizon. It appears to be up to me to console you, Madam, as your husband has deserted you."

The gypsy accent interrupted. "With all respect, I must disillusion you on this point, Commodore."

It was Hook, now, who was surprised. "Captain?"

"The lady's husband has *not* deserted her. Nor has he any intention of doing so."

Hook's face grew suspicious as he contemplated the canny officer before him. Gradually, his features evened and he drew himself up to his tallest. Smooth as usual, his voice cooled. "I believe, Madam, that 'best wishes' are in order."

"Thank you, Commodore."

He raised an eyebrow. "You are, indeed, a crafty woman."

"I hope I have done my duty, Sir."

"You bound yourself, not to that loose cannon of a surgeon, but to my own sailor." Hook's shrewd look fell away, to be replaced with a satisfied smile. "You never disappoint me."

"I knew you would wish me to avoid entanglement with Doctor Hanover, Sir. I discussed the situation with Captain Cecco, of course, counting on his loyalty. He agreed that Doctor Hanover must believe himself to be my husband— and that I must remain free of any legal tie to that man. Thanks to Captain Cecco, we own the doctor's diamonds, we are assured a share of his profits. And best of all, I am unshackled— like you."

Cecco nestled Jill's hand in his own, regarding her with warmth. His feelings were plain to see. "I could not refuse my lady when she proposed marriage. I welcomed it, and, most happily, I took her to be my wife." On Cecco's hand glimmered the wedding ring that once was the surgeon's. "Under this glove, *Signora* Cecco bears the ring I exchanged for hers."

Smee's color deepened behind his spectacles. He blinked in surprise. Yulunga simply nodded, his face creasing in a knowing smile. He could see there was no danger of things becoming too quiet in this fleet. The truth was out, now, and already his good friend Captain Cecco was stirring up trouble with it. If Cecco survived this affair, he would need his first mate to steady his Italian temperament.

Still hoping for happiness, Cecco continued. "Commodore, the captain of the *Unity* obliged us the day we captured his ship. He was persuaded even to order his cabin boy to open a bottle for a toast. Our marriage is entered in the *Unity*'s log. Her ship's surgeon signed as witness."

"Ah. Indeed." The commodore maintained an even keel. "You see now why I forbade you to set foot upon any other ship, Jill. It seems each time you do so, you collect another husband."

"I apologize, Sir. In pursuing the *Roger*'s interests, I disobeyed that particular directive. I believed it the most efficient way to win the diamonds. And Sir—" She sparkled like the surgeon's gems. "We have secured them."

"Excellent work, Jill. When I hold them again, I will deal with your defiance."

The promise in his eyes made Jill dizzy.

Increasing the strength of his grip, Cecco brought her back to earth. Knowing his Jill, he gave her time to collect herself while he explained, "The lady and I saw justice in foiling Hanover with his own principles. She is a lawful wife, now. Just…not his own. His other treasure lies in my sea chest, Sir, waiting to be divided among us."

"I shall attend to that— Tomorrow." Hook knew his Jill, too. Half-smiling, he waited for her sense of duty to overcome the effect of his insinuation. Her pulse was pounding, and he knew it.

She subdued her plunder-lust, and steadied herself. "Captain LeCorbeau learned of our marriage immediately afterward, when he himself boarded the *Unity*. Before he performed today's ceremony, LeCorbeau made sure I understood the consequences. But, as I anticipated, he dreaded another delay. He didn't dare inform the doctor a legal wedding could not take place. As you heard, Commodore, LeCorbeau agreed that Doctor Hanover is more likely to produce our profits if he remains unenlightened."

"And so you declined to destroy his marriage lines." Hook laughed. "Two husbands, Jill! The gypsy and the gentleman."

"I'm afraid I am a bigamist. My signature could, indeed, get me hanged— as LeCorbeau is hoping."

Hook caught her in his embrace. "He'll have to capture you first." The power of his grip, the familiarity of his arms around her, made her weak with joy. "But you shall be safe with me, aboard the *Roger*."

"No, Commodore." The gypsy's hand on Jill's shoulder was equally warm, every bit as possessive. Once again, Captain Cecco was unapologetic. "She will be safe aboard the vessel her husband named for her. My *Red Lady*." Cecco drew her from her lover's arms into his own. With bewitching words, he murmured in her ear, "Lovely one. I know your gypsy heart. Wander with me."

"Captain—"

"The ship is ours. We will sail her together."

"But we agreed."

"Our accord is dissolved, but not our affection. *Bellezza*, you will not forget my first kiss." With no hesitation, Captain Cecco leaned down to embrace his lady.

But he didn't lean for long. She floated up to meet him, her feet dangling loose in the air, her arms rising of their own accord to wrap themselves about him. With Cecco's kiss burning on her lips, Jill remembered every night, every day of their union. She recalled her gaiety in the captain's quarters of the *Unity*, the pleasure of her fluttering heart the day she bestowed her hand upon her lover. Her red hand, stained with her blood— and another's.

"With grace she flies to my embrace." Cecco kissed her again, ardently, then lowered her so that her feet brushed the deck. "The perfect woman."

Hook strode forward. "I warned you, Captain Cecco, not to test my generosity." Jill released her husband, turning to look up into the heavenly blue of Hook's eyes— her own eyes.

"Madam Red-Hand." Hook inclined his head. His kiss hung, waiting, inches from her own. He didn't touch her. He didn't bend to her. He bided his time. Hook had mastered the art of patience, there in the surgeon's chains.

"Hook." Drawn by his magic, Jill took to the air. She was light as a butterfly. She was nearly level with him. She moved toward him, but he drifted upward. Just off balance, she felt nervous as a fledgling. His hand enfolded hers to steady her. Longing for his kiss, Jill left the ship below, ascending but never coming closer because Hook was rising, too.

Like a magician, he kept his Jill suspended. As they almost touched, they felt the winds encompass them. He waited, delaying until the moment she could bear his restraint no longer. Then, in a sudden movement, Hook pressed his kiss upon her. Her black silk swirled around his legs, his arms enveloped her while, like their first flight, they forsook the world beneath them.

Cecco stared up at them. He stepped back. Smee and Yulunga exchanged glances, then watched him warily. His eyes fired, his chest rose and fell with his emotion. The gypsy smile dimmed, this time, perhaps, forever.

His gaze fell slowly to the base of the mast. The wound Jill inflicted today cut deeper than those of his whipping. Like those marks, this was a scar he would bear for all time. Yet, on his face, a determined look manifested. Captain Cecco was a patient man. He had waited for Jill before— and won her. With an aching heart, Cecco looked up at his angel, and kissed his fingertips. Squaring his shoulders, he began his vigil. One day, his opportunity would come again. And he would seize her.

A little at a time, Hook and Jill descended. When she felt the deck supporting her, its solidity brought her back to the present. At the foot of the mast, Jill released her lover to speak to her husband. Her voice fell gently. "Captain."

Cecco's dusky eyes clung to her. He said, softly, "You are my heart."

"She is my soul." Standing beside Jill, Hook encircled her shoulders.

Jill looked down to her golden bracelets. One by one, she removed them. "Captain, I return your belongings."

"An insignificant portion. But you won this treasure. It is yours to keep, to remember me." He slipped the bracelets on her wrist, then he settled his hand on the golden band on her upper arm, the one that matched his own. "But this I will wear, to keep it warm for you." He pried it open and replaced it on his biceps. Then he took hold of the leather lace at her wrist. "I release you, until you wish to be bound once again."

"It cannot be untied." Jill felt the chill as the shining hook slid under the leather.

"Whatever this represents," Hook said, "it can easily be severed."

"No." Cecco grasped the band in both his hands. "The sacred binding cannot be untied. It must not be severed. But, like our union, it can be stretched." With the strength of his two hands, Cecco pulled. The leather lace grew longer, thinner, until Jill's wrist slid easily from its hold. She drew her last glove off, and Cecco did the same to the binding of her other arm. Then, catching her hand, he bent to lay a kiss on her crimson palm. But when he opened it, another glint of gold appeared. Surprised, he raised his gaze. "Madam?"

"You're familiar with this earring. It is the commodore's. The surgeon gave it to me, to persuade me that you were his accomplice." As Cecco's face clouded, she laid her hand on his arm. "I didn't believe him. I have learned to trust in you, always."

"Bellezza."

"Captain Cecco." Jill's heart seared as her joy and sorrow fused.

"I think, Madam, I am no longer your captain. You will please humor me with the proper form of address."

"Yes. You are my—" She smiled, uninhibited this time by his rank, high or humble, "Giovanni."

"Lovely one. So full of courage, so true to your word. A woman worth waiting for." He glanced at Hook before resting his eyes again upon his lady. "And now, I am restrained only by my courtesy, which you have found I hold in abundance. You will care for yourself, and send for me if you are in need."

"I will." She touched his handsome face with her fingertips. "You must care for yourself."

"As you command. *Adio, Bellezza.*" He laid a kiss on her fingers, and she slipped from his grasp.

Hook beckoned to Mr. Smee. "Kindly present the *commandant*'s keys to Captain Cecco. Now, Captain, let us prepare our vessels. We sail at sunset."

"Aye, Commodore. The *Red Lady* will be ready. Our destination?"

"Where else, Captain? We sail for home."

Delighted, Jill said, "Home, Sir? To the Island!"

"The men will be pleased." Cecco surveyed his ship. "A fine port in which to refit the *Lady*."

"And to share the tales of our adventures." Jill, the storyteller, was impatient to begin.

"We have all earned some shore leave." Hook's voice mellowed, "And, I believe, we will find diversion from our respective wounds. Captain." Hook nodded. "I wish you fair winds." Followed by Mr. Smee, he swept Jill toward the *Roger*. Their splendid vessel awaited, her gilt trimmings brilliant. As the couple crossed to her, their feet barely touched the planking.

Glad cries arose as the commodore resumed command, leaping lightly aboard his ship. Raising his hook in salute, he acknowledged his men, then turned to Jill. To whistles and shouts, Hook kissed the crimson hand of his queen. She smiled upon him, and harmony was assured. The men voiced their relief in avid approval.

"Ship's company!" Hook called, "I shall take this opportunity to effect some changes. Mr. Mullins, Mr. Starkey, you will remain in the offices to which Captain Cecco appointed you." Hook observed his men, noting the satisfaction in their faces. Mullins leaned back smiling with his thumbs in his belt, but Starkey whipped out his handkerchief to mop his neck.

"To my sons, Mr. Nibs and Mr. Tootles, I entrust the duties of bo'sun's mates."

Tom's face lit up like a lantern. His brother smiled, rolling his shoulders to ease off the French blue jacket. Like a proud parent himself, Smee grinned upon them.

"Thus freeing Mr. Smee to more efficiently administer his responsibilities. But, Mr. Smee, I find the position of bo'sun no longer suited to you."

Smee peered over his spectacles, nonplussed.

"I therefore assign to you the additional rank of commodore's steward, and…first mate."

Smee's face flushed with pride. He barely gathered words to respond. "Commodore…I'm that honored."

In the ensuing tumult, Nibs and Tom rushed to Smee's side. "Congratulations, Mr. Smee!"

Smee shook their hands, accepting their greetings and returning them, but his gaze was fastened on his commander's. Hook's deep blue stare conveyed meaning a commodore must not articulate, and Smee perceived every nuance— gratitude, respect, affection. Hook raised his hand in a graceful flourish, saluting Mr. Smee. Then, at last, his first mate freed his gaze to lift his brawny arm and acknowledge the hails of the crewmen. Eventually the uproar died down, only to erupt again at the commodore's next words.

"The Island awaits us. We cast off at sunset!"

Smee found his voice and then some, bellowing over the mayhem, "Get on with you, lads! We've much to do before we sail." He, Mullins, and Starkey stamped about, urging the rowdy men to their duties.

"Permission to board, Commodore." Bearing a heavy canvas bag, Yulunga stood balanced on the plank.

"Granted."

Yulunga jumped to the deck. "The captain sent me for his things, Sir." He raised the bag, "And I am returning your stolen treasure. I am also instructed to hand over a certain pouch."

"My first mate will assist you."

Never far from the commodore's side, Mr. Smee sent the African a sharp look. "And I'll be needing my keys, if you please, Mr. Yulunga."

"My congratulations, Mr. Smee." Grinning, Yulunga pulled the key ring from his pocket and tossed it, jingling, to Smee.

"It's good to be having the key to my quarters back. Thank you."

"Your quarters?"

"Aye, Mr. Yulunga. I had to substitute it for the key to the shackles, so you'd not be finding one missing. To free the commodore from his bonds, of course."

"But…"

"You were a mite too busy last night to be asking you for it. I judged it best to slip the key ring from your breeches."

Yulunga angled his head.

"They were lying there, after all. On the floor of the gun deck, next to the girl. Like yourself."

The smile grew on Yulunga's face, then he leaned back and laughed. Hearing his deep, rich cadence, the men of the *Roger* looked up from their tasks. Smee's rollicking laugh joined in, and the remaining strings of beads at Yulunga's throat threatened to burst like the first. But on catching the commodore's eye, Yulunga sobered. "I must beg your pardon, Sir. I would have used that key to free you myself, had I known."

"I've no doubt of it, Mr. Yulunga. Carry on."

"Thank you, Sir."

Smee jerked his head at Nibs and Tom, and the four men hastened to set the commodore's quarters to rights.

Jill stepped nearer and, with gentle touches, brushed her lover's hair aside. She polished his earring, then, tenderly, hung it in its rightful place. The filigree seemed solid between her fingers, but, not daring to believe, she couldn't take her eyes from him. "Hook, you must tell me what you've been through."

He held her. "We have much to relate. And a wealth of time in which to do so. As I calculate it, our Island is a week away."

"Our sailing master will chart the course."

"And our other officers will see to the ship's needs. I shall, personally, see to yours."

"Hook."

"All those diamonds, Jill."

"And one another."

"My love."

The sound of his endearment set her heart to singing. With hungry fingertips, Jill caressed his jaw. But she couldn't speak. The words would come to her, once they were alone. As she anticipated that moment, her feet were in danger of deserting the deck again. Anchored in his arms, she felt her dark smile curving her lips.

With increasing restlessness, Hook observed that smile, feeling its full effect as she stroked his whiskers. His lip twitched. "Madam?"

"I do believe, Sir, you are in need of a shave.…'Today.' "

He raised one eyebrow.

From the corner of his eye he saw Smee and the others descending the companionway. And then her widow's black billowed behind her as she ran, and her pirate king followed her, swiftly, to their quarters.

Red-Handed Jill was a captain's treasure. And a commodore's soul.

Other Islands

"**A**nyone can see you're proud to be his son and officer, Mr. Tootles." Hefting the tea tray, Mr. Smee halted on the top step of the companionway. "That plaque's as bright as ever I kept it."

Tom grinned and tucked the polishing rag in his pocket. "Aye, Mr. Smee. It's good to see it in its proper place again. And the commodore, too."

"The lady did a fine job with the lettering." Smee's chest puffed with pride at the gleaming sight of the name— *Commo. Jas. Hook.* "Well, and what's the wager today?"

"Most of the men say another necklace. Nibs bet on a ring."

"Ah, you're all daft. I've advised the commodore myself. It's a new bracelet she'll be sporting, and no mistake. Now see to the paint for the mastheads and take your brother with you. It'll give you both a job to do while you're spying for the Island."

"Aye, aye, Mr. Smee. We'll be that glad to get home!"

"Won't we all, lad?" Smee himself couldn't hide his happiness. The thought of his Lily shone on his rugged face. He'd trimmed his hair and beard in honor of his promotion, polished his boots and stitched himself a shirt. But Lily wouldn't mind all that. She'd love her redheaded sailor any way she found him. "Sing out when you see the Island, Mr. Tootles. The gunner's got orders to fire off a barrage."

"That'll bring the Twins, all right. Paddling their canoe alongside the *Roger,* with Lily and the ladies aboard."

Smee chuckled. "And I'll be shucking off my boots and diving in to join them! Off you go, now."

Tom shuttled down the stairs while Smee tapped on the majestic door, just above the brass plaque. Not waiting for a response, he entered the commodore's quarters. "Good morning, Sir, Lady." Smee closed the door behind him. His boots made no noise as he headed over the carpets.

The luxuriance of the room was already illuminated with daylight from the bedside windows. Endowed with crowns of sunshine, the pirate king and his queen leaned back against the pillows of their four-posted bed.

"Time to be rousing, Sir."

"You are too late, Mr. Smee." The commodore sent his steward a humorous glance. His black hair was disheveled, and Jill caressed his beard. The thick band of jewels on her wrist shone as sharp and blue as his eyes. "You are, however, just in time to save my neck."

Jill turned her tousled head to Smee. "I was proposing to perform your duties again, Mr. Smee. But I shall bow to your expertise with the razor."

"Aye, Ma'am. The commodore's cuts from your last barbering are nearly healed. We'd best not be inflicting any more." Smee smiled to see that the commodore had taken his advice about the bracelet. He threw open the rest of the curtains and took down the brocaded dressing gown. Inhaling a hint of her scent on it, he held it ready for the lady. Like every morning of the past eight days, he waited patiently for the master to relinquish his mistress. Hook had confided in him: possessing only one hand caused intriguing delays. But the couple had compensated where the jewelry was concerned. Between the two of them, new baubles were somehow secured upon the lady. Every night, now.

Jill fetched Hook's dusty-blue velvet from the wardrobe, then settled on the window seat, enjoying her tea while Smee tended the commodore. The men strapped the brace on Hook's shoulders and saw to the shaving. With pleasure, Jill watched her perfect pirate and his burly Irishman. Every mundane task reassured her— she was sailing on her own familiar ocean. Toward her Island, and, no doubt, adventure.

A fresh breeze wafted through the aft windows, and Jill turned for a glimpse of the sea. Instead she found herself gazing at the lovely lines of *Red Lady*. With a sudden pang, she was reminded of the unsettled segment of her heart. This particular contention, she hoped for everyone's sake, might never find an end. The men she loved would be thrown together now— and often. Their positions forced them to work in tandem. As ranking officers, responsible for two companies of men, they must consult and scheme together, find value in each other's skills. And each would seek his pleasure soon, on the shores of the Neverland…if she could keep them from killing each other.

Hook studied her reflection in his shaving mirror. "Your concern would be more profitably employed in regard to the boy, Jill. I wonder to what pass he has brought our Island by now."

"Aye, Sir. I look forward to speaking with Lily and my Twins."

Smee's hand joggled and Hook recoiled, scowling. "Perhaps, Mr. Smee, you had better surrender that razor to Jill after all."

"Begging your pardon, Commodore. But, Sir—"

"Yes, Mr. Smee. You may be dismissed at first sight of land." He gestured to summon the razor. "Not before."

"Thank you, Sir. I've waited this long to hold my Lily. Seems I just can't be waiting any more." Smee's features grew cautious, then. "And Sir. Shall I be asking the Indian ladies if they know of a young woman to wait on the lady?"

Jill watched Hook's face, relieved as it darkened.

"No, Mr. Smee. I have learned my lesson. I'll not be trusting anyone else. As the commodore's mate and steward, you alone are to care for my personal belongings." Hook shot a look at Jill. "All of them."

She smiled.

When Hook was combed and shaven, the two men perfected the fit of his suit. Jill herself buckled on her lover's sword. Hook cupped her chin and kissed her, thoroughly, then swept up his hat and her heart all at once. "See to my lady, Mr. Smee. I expect her to be perfectly happy. No less."

Grinning, Smee nodded. "Aye, Commodore. I'm the man for the job."

"You were created for it." Hook sent Jill an incendiary smile that set her insides ablaze, then surged from the cabin in a storm of blue velvet.

Smee closed the door behind him. As the master's footsteps faded, he reached for the hair brush. "Here we are, Lady." Observing the lovely tint of Jill's cheeks, Smee waited for her to recover her composure. "Shall we be putting your hair up in that pretty twist today?"

"Yes, Mr. Smee. And I'll want the sapphire necklace. To match my new bracelet."

"And to match your gown…and your eyes." Smee's husky hands forgot they were holding the brush. He simply stood staring.

Jill smiled and turned her back. "Sit down, Mr. Smee. I want you to take your time."

"Aye, Lady." As he had done for the black hair, Smee untangled the golden. Then, using the brush, using his fingers, he set out to comply with his orders. He knew how the lady loved his hands in her hair. Smee kept his eyes on her, avoiding the sight of the other *Lady* gliding behind them— with a handsome gypsy captain astride her bowsprit. Smee found a way to keep Jill's gaze from straying there.

But her eyes opened as she felt Smee's lips touch her neck. "Mr. Smee. You won't forget the commodore's command?"

"No, Ma'am," Smee murmured against her skin, making her senses prickle with pleasure, "You know I'd never be disobeying him."

Jill closed her eyes again.

"I'm ordered to be giving you his love. Whenever he's not handy."

She turned her head toward him in acknowledgment, relishing the warmth of his hands on her shoulders. Strong hands. Like Captain Cecco's.

"Aye, Conor. I feel his love."

As with the *Julianne*, as with all his prizes, Hook had arranged to leave her burning.

Acknowledgements

My appreciation to the officers of the fleet…

Jolene Barjasteh, Gary M. Burton, Stacy DeCoster, Victoria Everitt,
Greg Gressle, Catherine Leah Condon-Guillemette, Erik Hollander,
Maureen Holtz, Scott Jones, Kim, Mary Lawrence, Krista Menzel,
Deena Sherman, Ginny Thompson, Peter Von Brown,
Admiral Morgan Ramirez,
and my fellow captains of Under the Black Flag.

Respect and honor to

Marie Gillette and Ruth Brauch
of Rock Island High School,
who taught us to read, to write, and to think;

and to

Sir James Barrie,

the blackest pirate of them all.
And the brightest.

About the Author

A ndrea Jones is the author of *Hook & Jill*, a serious parody of Sir James Barrie's timeless tale, *Peter & Wendy*. Her debut novel, *Hook & Jill* won five literary awards, among them the Gold Award for Adult Fiction and Literature in the 2010 Mom's Choice Awards®, and Best New Fiction in the 2010 International Book Awards.

Jones graduated from the University of Illinois at Urbana-Champaign, where she studied Oral Interpretation of Literature, with a Literature Minor. In her career in television production, she worked for CBS, PBS, and corporate studios, also performing as on-camera and voice-over talent.

Jones' work is informed by a broad range of thinkers and writers, among them Alexandre Dumas, Jane Austen, Charles Dickens, Carl Jung, P.G. Wodehouse, Robert Graves, Patrick O'Brian, Dorothy Dunnett, and, of course, Sir James Barrie, who created the modern mythology of the Neverland and its endearing, enduring characters.

Andrea Jones is known around the world as Capitana Red-Hand of the web-based pirate brotherhood, Under the Black Flag. She is also a proud member of the Brethren of the Great Lakes.

Jones' home port is near Chicago.

O ther Oceans* is Book Two of the *Hook & Jill* Saga. Keep a weather eye for Book Three, *Other Islands*.